DUE DATE

After the War

AFTER *the* WAR

Richard Marius

Alfred A. Knopf   New York   1992

THIS IS A BORZOI BOOK
PUBLISHED BY ALFRED A. KNOPF, INC.

Copyright © 1992 by Richard Marius
All rights reserved under International and Pan-American
Copyright Conventions. Published in the United States
by Alfred A. Knopf, Inc., New York, and simultaneously
in Canada by Random House of Canada Limited, Toronto.
Distributed by Random House, Inc., New York.

Library of Congress Cataloging-in-Publication Data
Marius, Richard.
After the war/Richard Marius.—1st ed.
p.   cm.
ISBN 0-394-58322-1
I. Title.
PS3563.A66A68 1992
813'.54—dc20   91-23212   CIP

Manufactured in the United States of America
First Edition

For my editor,
Ann Close,
in love and gratitude,
and
in memory of my father,
Henri Marius Panayotis Kephalopoulos,
foundryman, farmer, Tennessean
1893–1988

And I, too, lived once in Arcadia

Part One

1

I AM NOT MAD; I never was. Wounded in body and soul, yes. Melancholy, yes. Suicidal, perhaps. Selfish? Deceitful? Disloyal? A liar, even to myself? Yes, all those things. But I never went crazy, no matter how it may seem in the story I sit here to tell.

I write late at night in a still house, waiting for sleep as a man waits alone for a train, not knowing when it will come, not sure that it will come at all. I have been an insomniac since the Great War. For years I read books at night—a lonely business, for people in Bourbon County have no taste for any book but the Bible.

Tonight I sit at my kitchen table and look over the darkened hillside pasture towards my lower field, where lespedeza hay grows lush in the summer dark. I can smell the heat—a baked, hard smell. We need rain. At my open windows insects beat against the screens, frantic for my small lamp with its green glass shade. I hear the infinitesimal thumping of tiny bodies against the wire.

Beyond the lower field in our shallow valley runs the two-lane highway to Nashville. The lights of passing cars blaze at intervals. Sometimes a truck rumbles by, and the sound carries up to me at this mysterious hour when a rural world is fast asleep. My solitary light must seem mysterious to them, too. More strange if they knew the memories that crowd around it and me.

I will tell my story. Brian Ledbetter said that if a man could not tell stories, he had not lived. Father Droos said we had to write things to know them. "Know thyself!" he said, standing over me at the Institute St. Valéry in Ghent—a world of cobblestones and yellow trams and orderly houses pressed wall to wall and orderly people in medieval streets and cafes and taverns, a lost Arcadian world—while I tried to master the art of writing essays in French. "You must know those words, Mr. Kephalopoulos."

That is my real name, Kephalopoulos, not Paul Alexander, the name I have lived by in these long years in America.

Father Droos lifted an ironic eyebrow.

"The Delphic oracle," I replied.

Father Droos wagged his cigarette in the prophetic mode. "Excellent! To know yourself you must write about yourself. I have always kept a journal." I wonder what happened to it; what happened to him? He used to sit and drink wine with Madame Boschnagel at the tavern she owned called the Vieux Gand. It seemed strange to see a plump priest in a cassock talking with her in his constrained and serious way, his face red with wine. He smoked cigarettes one after the other and waved them around his head as he talked about books. Sometimes Madame Boschnagel leaned forward on her elbows, her ruddy Germanic face in her hands, listening rapt to his words. He had read and remembered everything. Mention a character in a play or a novel, no matter how obscure, and Father Droos was off on a lecture. Madame Boschnagel adored him. We wondered if they were lovers.

On the August morning in 1914 when we marched to the railroad station to go to war, Belgian patriots were throwing chairs and tables out of her tavern, breaking them up on the street, and she was in their midst weeping, imploring them to stop. Father Droos was trying to defend her. He was fat and out of breath and helpless, his face blood red, his white hair whipping with his futile flailing, and people were jeering him. The Socialists swore not to fight the war; when the war came, they fought a fat old priest and a woman. I do not know what happened after that.

My story includes many stories—some without endings. A story should move from a beginning to a middle and to a climax just before the end. At the end everything is accounted for. I cannot account for everything. Parts of my story vanish in the dark. I once yearned to know how they ended. No more. I am resigned to some things—resigned to my destiny, the fragmented story I tell here.

I will write about Guy and Bernal. I will say that they lived and died and that I lived with them in life and in death. They have been gone for years. Long after they went away for the last time, I kept expecting them to return. I would be standing in the doorway to the barn at twilight when the men had finished throwing hay into the loft, the thick summer air heavy with the smell of mowing, fireflies drifting in the thin mist rising from the field, a summer torpor upon the earth. Observing with quiet pride my harvest, I would listen for Guy's soft laughter behind me and Bernal's murmur of friendly reproach. Bernal thought Guy patronized me. Guy did patronize me. I loved him anyway.

I thought that I would turn and look back into the gloom of the barn's interior and see Guy standing there with a smile on his face and his hands outstretched in his casual welcoming gesture, almost a shrug. "I am here. Of course you are glad to see me."

I supposed that if Guy and Bernal came to me anywhere, it would be in the barn. It was a fine and private place in the twilight. They were there when I built it, the two of them lounging in the shade. Guy smirked at my pleasure in manual labor. Jim Ed and I sweated and grunted and lifted beams and planks and held them while Clyde did the real work, the art. I write to keep something of them here, in the world of the living. That was why I talked to them after they were dead.

I never believed in the ghosts. In the part of my mind where I am most truly myself I always knew that they were like the imaginary companions children make up in a lonely world—or the God to whom the religious speak, imagining that they hear him speak in return.

It happened this way. I knew they were dead. I was alive. Barely alive. I lay still, bandaged and drugged against pain in the Royal Hospital in Chelsea in a long ward where the critically wounded lay in narrow beds beneath the high windows designed by Sir Christopher Wren. Despite the drugs, the pain throbbed in my head, my chest, and my legs.

I could not remember how they had died. I remembered them alive, and I could recall—can still recall—a thousand or perhaps ten thousand details about them. I remembered waking in the hospital train on its slow way up to London, feeling the rocking of the carriages, the crushing headache. I had never felt such pain. Guy and Bernal were dead. I could not remember how they died. I lay in my cot in London, wrapped in bandages that covered the wounds left by the German shell before Antwerp in September 1914. I was alive; they were dead.

The nights were worse than the days. My right eye was left outside the bandages. I could see the tiny electric light gleaming at the nurses' station at the end of the long ward. I smelled iodine, stale urine, fresh feces, gangrenous flesh. I heard the wounded groaning, whimpering, crying, snoring, breathing in the deep, pained, stuttering way that injured and dying men gasp for breath. From the distance came the horns of boats on the Thames and the rumble of trains, whistles shrieking—sounds of a city at night working at war.

At some moment when the air was crisp with autumn, I began talking to my dead friends.

Bernal was devout. His piety made me uncomfortable. It amused Guy. Bernal prayed in the Cathedral of St. Bavon in Ghent, kneeling in a chapel before the van Eycks's painting of the Adoration of the Mystic Lamb. He moved his lips, and the tears poured down his cheeks. I came on him there once by accident. I was embarrassed. We never spoke of it.

Guy claimed to be an atheist. "Prove the existence of God, and I will pray," he said. He knew the arguments for belief and could refute them all. Bernal smiled, untroubled, and said, "You do not prove that God *is* before you pray. You pray, and there you find God."

That is why I spoke to them after they were dead. If I spoke, they seemed to be present. It was fantasy—a harmless comfort. I knew every intonation of their voices, their minds, how they would respond to anything I said. What was wrong with talking to them?

When he was alive, Bernal feared such things. Necromancy was blasphemy, he said. During the retreat of 1914 we came on a fortune-teller in a village where every house had been leveled by shell fire, and she was sitting amid the ruins at a wooden table as though she were a daemonic functionary; and in the same madness that afflicted her and our ruined world, Guy and I had our palms read and our futures told.

"Please God, do not do this thing!" Bernal cried. "You cannot know the secrets of God; you cannot practice necromancy. Remember the Witch of En-dor." Guy and I laughed at him. Bernal thought that poor, mad woman could tell us the future because she communed with the spirits of the dead. She read our palms while Bernal slung his rifle off his shoulder and walked away, weeping. I could hear a Maxim gun in the middle distance while she spoke in the languid tones of the eternally undisturbed oracle. She told Guy that he would die in the war. She told me that I would cross the seas and marry a blond woman. Bernal said there was no hope for us after that.

I talked to them between waves of agony behind my eyes in the deep night hours. The leather shoes of the nurses swished along the smooth floors between the beds where the wounded lay groaning or comatose or dying. I could shut my unbandaged eye and whisper and imagine that they whispered back so that their voices were part of the wind that sighed around the eaves of the hospital's tall roof in the autumn dark.

It rained often in London. One night I was whispering to them, and I pretended I could hear their voices in the rain falling on the roof high above and running into the guttering. An auditory illusion, changing, first one thing, then another. Sometimes the sound was their voices; sometimes it was the distant running of water in the copper gutters. Their voices, then water; their voices, then water again; first one, then the other. I amused myself talking to them when it was as though they were far away, perhaps calling to me from some deep and forested valley cleft in granite. I imagined clear water running through the valley, and we sat in the grass and whispered to each other in the charmed solitude, and their voices were a singing of strange melodies that brought this physical world to the edge of a brightness where none of the things we think we know are quite as we think we know them.

When the sound became water again, I waited, knowing the voices would return and that the sound of water would go away. Suddenly I heard voices and water at the same time—the distinct sound of words, and the equally distinct sound of water running behind.

Slowly I understood. Voices and water together. Far off I heard clocks striking two in the morning. Solemn, heavy ringing, tolling the night away. I whispered tentatively. "Guy? Bernal? Are you there? Are you really there?" I heard Guy's laughter, low and distinct, and behind it, far up in the dark, I heard the water running.

"Of course we are here," Guy said.

I dared not open my unbandaged eye. Maybe even then I was afraid of them, as I feared them later on.

"It is true," Bernal said, his French accented by his delicate Argentine voice. "We are here."

"You are alive," Guy said reproachfully.

"It was not my fault," I said.

"All for one and one for all," Bernal said.

"We swore we would never be parted," Guy said.

"We reckoned without the war," I said.

"A promise is a promise," Guy said.

I opened my eye. There they were—standing by my bed in the deep gloom of the ward. Bernal wore his dark blue uniform, the black cloth cap pulled tight on his head. His uniform fitted him badly. He had ordered another from his tailor; there was no time. I looked at his feet. His heavy military shoes were caked with mud.

Guy's uniform was filthy. Even so, he looked debonair. He bowed gallantly from the waist. They smiled, Bernal slow and tentative, as he always smiled, Guy pleased as a child with his little surprise. I could see them as clearly as I see the white wooden frame of the row of windows where I sit, the table with the red checked oilcloth where I write, my lamp, the occasional lights passing on the highway across the expanse of my farm. I saw them. I heard them. I did not touch them. We were together, reunited beyond death.

I want to affirm here and now that I did not believe that they were real. I never truly believed it. I saw them. But something always stood behind the apparitions to tell me that I was not mad. Still, I saw them, and I wanted more than anything else in the world for them to stay with me and never to leave me again.

2

THIS MUST BE Pinkerton's story, too—Pinkerton the great and the terrible.

I came to him on a train, rolling through the night from the capital of the United States. There a Mr. Davis of the Dixie Railroad gave me a job as chemist in the railroad's car works in Bourbonville, Tennessee. "Nothing ever happens there, I'm afraid. But it's where we need a chemist." He shoved papers and a train ticket across the desk and dismissed me by rising half out of his chair, a jerk of his knees, and he sat down again and forgot me. Mr. Davis was busy. There was a war on.

In my last year in the hospital, I took walks in a small group led by a nurse in white. We wore blue convalescent uniforms. In a Lyons Tea Room in Piccadilly, an American at a nearby table dropped a coin. It rolled across the floor and fell at my feet. I returned it to him. He invited me to sit, and we talked. Later we had lunch. His name was Walter Babb, and he worked for the railroad. He offered me a letter of recommendation. "America's the place," he said in a big voice, a flat American accent. "There won't be anything left in Europe when this war's over. Mark my words, young man; it's curtains for the old country."

People at nearby tables scowled at him. Mr. Babb paid no attention. He wanted them to hear him.

My father was in America. I did not know where.

The voyage through the North Atlantic from Glasgow was gray and cold. We stood on the deck in the wind and watched out for German U-boats. The ocean ran in oily swells. October 1917.

I sat up all night on the train, looking at my thin reflection in the glass of the carriage window. Mr. Davis had apologized. All southbound Pullmans were booked. "It's wartime, you know. It'd take a week to get you a Pullman. Pinkerton says he needs somebody now."

I sat next to a man who wore a cheap suit and stank of whiskey and tobacco. Sometimes he fell against me in his sleep. I paid no attention. I stared through my reflection at a ghostly land gliding by. Little towns, bubbles of scattered lights in the vast darkness. I had an impression of forests and hills, an occasional yellow lantern glowing from a solitary house, the moan of the locomotive whistle far in front.

At first light I stepped down in Bourbonville amid the flurry that the train brought a country town—mail sacks taken off, boxes and crates loaded, a few people hurrying about. A traveling salesman with a black case tipped his hat as if he would gladly sell me something if he only had the time. There was no time. He climbed into the carriage. A shout. A conductor waving a metal lantern with colored lights. Five short blasts from the locomotive whistle. The engine gave a mighty heave. The carriages rattled their couplings and the train lurched forward, gathering speed, and then it was gone, and the sound died away towards Chattanooga and the world lying beyond. My father was there somewhere.

October in Bourbonville, Tennessee—the eastern mountains visible as a darker black against the dawning sky, dawn itself a bar of watery gray across the horizon, the stars fading, the autumn colors of the leaves dull in the gray light. It was an unpromising place—streets unpaved, air thick with the smell of coal dust and damp earth, the brick courthouse squatting amid the tree-filled square, a stubby tower rising through the trees and on its side, the white disk of a clock, dim in the early morning like a cyclopean eye searching balefully over the town, black hands stopped at a Gothic seven minutes after two o'clock. Around the square stood flimsy wooden houses.

"Nothing ever happens there," Mr. Davis had said.

Behind the square to the west rose a low ridge, covered with trees. Most of the town lay there in a tilted crosspatching of streets. A dog barked, a thin, staccato iteration. From a greater distance, another answered, hollow sounds in a lonely place. A cock crowed; then another and another. A breath of wind. It was chilly, and I shivered in my hard English suit.

I felt nauseated. I started to count. "One, two, three, four; one, two, three, four; one, two, three, four." Counting took my mind off things. Sometimes I could put off a headache by counting to four again and again. An aura of light seemed to glow around the courthouse. That was a bad sign.

"Hey there!" a voice shouted. An old man's voice. "Hey, Mister." I looked blankly around. It was the telegrapher, stumbling down the steps of the platform, a man tall and thin, with steel-rimmed glasses and an alcoholic stare. He walked stiffly. Arthritis, perhaps.

"You all right? What do you say?" He spoke with an irresolute loudness, a strange accent, the accent of East Tennessee, unlike anything else I had ever heard.

"Yes, I am all right. Everything in order."

"You look sick."

"What?"

"Sick! Are you sick? You look as sick as a pup."

"No, no. I am tired. I had to . . . I am . . ."

"Lordy, way you talk, you must be Pinkerton's foreigner. What's your name?" His face was like a blinding sun, blazing at my strangeness, my foreignness revealed in my uncommon speech.

"My name is—"

"Kephalopoulos," I heard Guy whisper.

"Alexander. Paul Alexander."

"Alexander. That's what it was, sure enough. Alexander. Pinkerton got the telegram yesterday. He told me to watch out for you. So here you are. I knowed you was a foreigner by the way you look and the way you talk. I can always tell a Jew or a foreigner."

He swayed on his feet. His eyes were unfocused. He was drunk.

"Moreland J. Pinkerton," I said. "You know him?"

"Hell yes. Everbody knows Pinkerton. Now you ask me what I think of him. That's what everbody asks me. What do I think of Moreland J. Pinkerton. Well, I'll tell you. Personally I don't hold nothing against Pinkerton myself," he said. "You'll hear this, and you'll hear that. But you won't hear me saying nothing bad about him. He made his mistakes. Sure he did. Just like you and me. Ain't that right?" His mouth went slack.

I thought I might vomit, and the pain beat in the back of my head, and I was dizzy. I wanted to lie down.

"The folks that went with him down to Cuba, most of them ain't never forgot it. I reckon you know all about Pinkerton in Cuba? God, it's cold today. Cold enough to freeze a witch's tit. It wasn't cold in Cuba."

He came closer and gaped at me with his red eyes. "Just don't let Pinkerton kill you," he whispered.

I backed away. "Could I wash my face in the station?" I said.

He stared at me.

"Could I wash my face?"

"Sure. In the washroom there. Cold-water tap. Want me to heat some water?"

"No," I said. "The cold water will be better."

I went in and scrubbed my face. The cold water felt good. The washroom was filthy.

I came out. The telegrapher pointed me the way to the car works, down Broadway (as the muddy street was called) at the city limits. I left my bag at the depot and set out to meet Moreland J. Pinkerton, manager of the Bourbonville Car Works of the Dixie Railroad.

3

I AM HERE because of Moreland Pinkerton.

At this remove of years, I cannot sort out what he told me himself and what others told me about him. He used to come into the laboratory where I worked with my bottles, my crucibles, my kilns, my scales. He talked. He required no response from me. He assumed my silence meant consent. Now I will put his story together as a mosaic of all his stories and of all the stories people told me about him.

Moreland J. Pinkerton served the Dixie Railroad as general manager for the Bourbonville Car Works. "One of the colonial officers," he said with affable bitterness towards his superiors on the line, the urbane men who lived in Washington City or in the Virginia suburbs and rolled down to Bourbonville in mahogany-paneled palace cars fitted with gleaming brass and pliant leather, the efficient and inquiring men who inspected the operation of the car works so they could write reports on creamy paper and file them on high, the moguls of steam who ruled the empire of speed from their headquarters in Washington City.

They descended from their rolling hotel, freshly shaved, perfumed, and dusted with talcum. They walked to the main office, a nondescript frame building painted bright yellow and located in a great open oval between the wheel foundry and the brass foundry. They consulted ledgers and papers with the officious care of sorcerers checking on enchantments practiced by their apprentices. They received flattery poured out on them by Dale Farmer, chief accountant and bookkeeper of the car works, who sweated much and bowed and explained his neat, precise, and invariably accurate-to-the-penny figures. They smiled with cold sunniness on Moreland Pinkerton, commander of their outpost in the wilderness.

They murmured to one another and nodded their heads. They marched in lockstep like Marines sent to keep order in Nicaragua or to shell Mexico. Amid the roar and the din of the wheel foundry, watched by every eye, they drew conspicuously apart and consulted with one another. Sometimes they removed black leather notebooks, expensively small and stamped in gold, from inside coat pockets, and they wrote. On occasion they stood in a row to watch some process, giving to uneasy workmen the impression of buzzards lined on a fence and studying something appetizingly dead.

They marched through the wheel foundry and put on blue goggles to watch the tapping of the tall cupola furnace and the gush of the incandescent iron into the great bull ladle and the stately progress of the ladle from mold frame to mold frame where the iron poured into the damp sand molds prepared for it and cooled into wheels that would eventually ride the steel rails of the line. They stood in the steel foundry before the open hearth furnace, and they visited the pattern shop, the machine shop, and the brass foundry, and they stood savoring the wood-sweet smell of the long shed where carpenters built fifty boxcars a day of oak and pine.

The carpenters were a caste. They looked much alike—long, narrow faces, high cheekbones, hard hands, sharp eyes almost invariably blue. They smelled of tobacco and sweat and clean wood dust. Carpenters taught their sons to be carpenters. They were diffident because they felt superior to other men.

Some had been there since the long summer when the car works rose out of what had been a swamp. A very young Moreland Pinkerton had coaxed them out of the country, out of doing first one job and then another, out of penurious independence, and he put them to work for cash paid every other Saturday morning in small brown envelopes stamped with the bent DR of the Dixie Railroad.

"Look at them!" he said more than once to me when they lined up at the pay windows. "If it wasn't for me they'd have them a dime ever other Tuesday, and they'd be making soap with lye and fat in a black kettle in their backyard. I brought progress to this shithole, by God. When I'm dead, they'll understand. Nobody appreciated Abe Lincoln till that actor son of a bitch shot him. That's the way the world is. Don't expect nothing from it, Alexander. Don't expect nothing, and you won't be disappointed."

The inspectors made their tours in a haze of cigar smoke and condescension. On Broadway when they walked for exercise, they tipped their hats with excessive gallantry to the ladies. They admired with too much zest the bucolic tranquility of Bourbonville, and they spoke too warmly of the salubrious air of a country town.

"They don't mean a fucking word of it," Pinkerton said. "Sons of bitches. Damn their souls."

Among themselves they laughed loudly. They smoked expensive cigars. At night in their palace car, attended by a silent black man in starched white, they drank bonded whiskey and ignored Tennessee's prohibition laws. They invited Moreland Pinkerton to share these evenings. He came with his face set in good cheer, but his cheer seemed carved out of wood. They flung off their coats. They exposed their suspenders, and they played poker.

"Poker's a waste of time," Pinkerton said. "Show me a poker player, and I'll show you a fool."

The inspectors treated Pinkerton as they treated Bourbonville: they flattered him. They pretended to treat him as one of themselves. But at the end, they pumped his hand, clapped him on the back, laughed loud, and abandoned him as they abandoned the town itself. As the train pulled out, hauling their palace car at the back, Pinkerton stood rigid like a Roman sentry guarding Pompeii. "God damn their bones," he said.

Moreland Pinkerton built the car works. He had been young and strong then, so handsome that he was almost beautiful. When he was only seventeen, in Virginia, one of his teachers said, "Moreland, I hope I live to see you famous. I want the world to know I was your teacher."

He looked like a man born to be famous. He was large and muscular, even when I knew him. He had a square face, and he gave off a heat of restless energy. Women adored him. Even his enemies thought his mind was filled with plans. "He's always thinking," Virgil Weaver said. "Look at that face, and you see a storm."

I believe his most profound thought, one that stayed with him until his violent death, was his conviction that he was more able than anyone else he knew.

"I watched the trains when I was a boy," he told me. "I knowed they was going places, and I wanted to go there, too, by God. They was going where there was something to life, and I wanted it. I wanted it all. I wanted to drink it up like whiskey. Hell no, not like whiskey—like manna. The stuff the Israelites ate in the wilderness. I wanted it. I had a terrible thirst."

He went to work for the railroad. "I never thought of doing nothing else," he said, his grammar slipping on the hard surface of his lost hopes. "They was boys, they wanted to go to sea or be lawyers or bankers or what the hell. I wanted to work on the railroad."

He did well, and he came down on orders to Bourbonville when he was only twenty-five years old, and he found a swamp southwest of town, a swamp that had been acquired by the secret peculations of the railroad, the ever-thrifty railroad, which bought the land through the covert agency of a hired, blond traveling evangelist named Thomas Sims—a man still remembered by some. Sims was thin and pulsating, and he had a large voice. He told people he wanted to buy the swamp to prove the power of God, that when he prayed, God would drive the water out of the swamp as he had parted the Red Sea to show his might to Israel and Egypt. When God had cleared the swamp, Sims vowed, he would build a tabernacle there, and he promised to bring Pentecostal holiness down and to have all Bourbon County speaking in tongues, and to heal the sick by the laying on of hands, and to open the eyes of the blind and to make the lame walk.

"The damn fools thought Sims was crazy," Pinkerton said. "They sold him their swamp for five bucks an acre. If they'd have known it was the *railroad* wanting that swamp, they'd have charged a *hundred* dollars an acre. They *believed* in the railroad. But they sold their swamp to Almighty God for a piss-poor five bucks an acre."

Sims had a cocaine habit. He did what the railroad paid him to do, turned over the titles, received ten dollars for every acre he bought, and hit the road, sniffing cocaine before preaching hellfire sermons in tents under the inspiration of the inspiriting powder.

"He decided to prove his faith to a mob of his crack-brained disciples," Pinkerton said, his voice breaking with laughter. "You know what the Bible says—'By faith you can move mountains' or some damned thing like that. Sims, he said a train wasn't near as big as a mountain. The son of a bitch tried to stop a train with his bare hands. By faith, you see. By faith!" Pinkerton laughed until his eyes filled with tears.

Mr. Sims committed himself by faith to the tracks, saying God would vindicate him by giving him the miraculous power of Samson. Alas, God nodded, and the followers of the Reverend Mr. Sims as well as onlookers who had gathered at a grade crossing in the countryside north of Knoxville were treated to a daunting and silencing demonstration of the authority of the physical over the spiritual. Pinkerton kept the clippings from the Knoxville newspapers that had reported the event. He spread them on his desk to let me look at them, and he laughed until he could scarcely breathe.

By the time Sims died, winter was breaking up, and Pinkerton had been in Bourbonville six months, drawing his grand design. "I brought this town progress. Progress! This place is my tabernacle, by God. My tabernacle." I can hear his voice across the years—the frenzy of it, his longing to be believed.

Now I hear the eerie howl of a wildcat freight whistle shrieking over the night and the rumble of a train rolling towards Chattanooga on the line four miles across the woods and fields at Martel. It is a ghostly sound, like a spirit crying for a body.

4

PINKERTON LUNGED out into the somnolent countryside to find men waiting out the winter by their stoves while the rain fell and the world was mud and there was nothing to do but wait. They did not know they were waiting for him. He found men who had never worked for wages in their lives. He paid them two dollars a day to bend their backs with picks and spades and shovels, with mule-drawn dredges, with wheelbarrows, with axes, with logging chains, with cross-cut saws. Men in Bourbon County had never heard of such wages. Still he could not coax enough of them from plows and fields, from fence rows and barns, from plodding through early spring planting in the wet, sweet soil, from the familiar worship of the land and its liturgies. Brian Ledbetter made things harder. "If it hadn't been for that crazy old man, I'd have hired enough white men to do the job," Pinkerton said, mulling over the scene again and again years and years afterwards. Brian Ledbetter fired a ten-gauge shotgun over his head and ordered him off the Ledbetter land, and after that it was hard to get white men to sign on. People respected Brian Ledbetter.

"I don't hold it against the old fool. I tell you what it is, Alexander! Habits make cowards. People don't want progress because it's different from what they know. That's the thing that wears you down. Damned if it don't wear you down! That's why I had to bring the niggers here: because chickenshit white folks didn't want progress. I've been good to the niggers. They love me, by God. You ask them."

"He come out here and made like I was some piece of white trash that would eat shit for wages," Brian Ledbetter said. "I told him I didn't want his wages and didn't want his car works and didn't want him on my land. He couldn't believe it. Moreland Pinkerton's the kind of man that gets his word direct from God, carved out on stone tablets. When he gets a revelation, he thinks it's clear as the sun in summer to the whole wide world. That's why I taken the shotgun to him."

Pinkerton hardly paused. He looked south to Sweetwater in its broad, rich valley eighteen miles away, and he found black people left over from slavery and enduring life with patient dread, existing in paintless clapboard shacks that reeked of hog fat and collard greens. The blacks toiled as sharecroppers on rich land they had no dream of owning. He went down there and sat in their shanties and walked into the fields after them in the mild March sun as they prepared the earth for planting, and he cajoled them with promises.

Finally he brought back three boxcars of healthy black men, picking them out like a man buying cattle at auction. He paid them a dollar a day, and they bent their backs alongside the whites, and when the swamp mud covered them all, God himself might have paused in telling them apart.

Darcy Coolidge always spoke up for Pinkerton. "The town misjudges him," she said, speaking a difficult truth that she expected none of us to contradict. "I must admit that Mr. Pinkerton does things I find distasteful as a Methodist. He imbibes alcoholic beverages. I never have known a man that didn't take a nip now and then. I don't permit it in my boardinghouse. But you have to be charitable. Men don't have the strength of women. Mr. Pinkerton has had a hard life. I think it's Eula's fault more than anybody else knows. I believe in religion. But I don't think the good Lord meant for us to be fanatics about it. Of course, she's had her troubles. But she could have done better. We all have troubles."

When he built the car works, he was Apollo, driving his chariot across a fiery sky. Old Bourbonville—stretched out for decades asleep in the torpor of its riverbank amid its enormous forests and its ragged fields—stirred uneasily as Moreland Pinkerton flung spears of light clanging into their drowsy world.

There they were, white men and black and young Moreland Pinkerton an amazing tertium quid, working harder than any of them—tireless, laughing, hollering, clapping men white and black on the shoulders, cracking obscene jokes, howling at the jokes of others, finding a jug of clear whiskey at just the right moment late in the day when the heavy twilight crept out from the western ridge, wiping his flat, dirty hand over the spout, taking the first fiery swallow and passing it on, mingling his spit with theirs, jumping here, jumping there, pointing, beckoning, commanding, mud in his thick blond hair, caked on his eager face, cursing, pulling, pushing, lifting, singing, cheering, as ubiquitous, tireless, and omnipotent as God.

They dug ditches five feet deep. White men and black men toiled with long-handled spades in muck to their knees, and they hacked the ditches crisscrossing through the swamp, sometimes uncovering a terrified water snake that fled for its life through the muddy water, the men roaring in pursuit and triumph, joyfully cutting the accursed thing in two for the glory of God. The ditches advanced relentlessly to the riverbank until at last the brown water poured down into the brown river, and the river swirled it away, and land that had been swamp for a thousand years dried slowly in the summer sun.

They chopped down the oaks and the pines, the hickories, the black gums, the cedars, the hackberries, and enormous chestnuts, and they piled the felled wood in heaps three times the size of a barn, and they had burnings—great celebratory burnings in the night, moved by some primitive thing that came on them as they worked to destroy the primitive bog, some awful piety akin to the powers of darkness, a kinship to the underworld stirred in them by flames in the night. "You could see the glow of them fires from ten mile away," Bessie May Hancock said. "I tell you what's the gospel truth. They was some, and who's to say they was wrong, they was some that said Mr. Pinkerton built them fires at night because he had sold his soul to the devil, and they was his offering to Satan. Them folks said you could look up in the dark and see two big red eyes looking down on them fires. Now, I ain't saying hit was true. But why would anybody tell something like that lessen hit *was* true?"

Filthy men, sweat-soaked and weary and jubilant, looking in their mud like the original of their father scooped from the clay of Eden, circled the pyres and watched the burning with the voracious glee of vandals burning a town. There was a demon leaping in the fire, dancing to strange music, and they could see the dance although their eyes could not quite make out the demon, and the dance cast a spell on them and made them forget what they were and remember things their ancestors had forgotten.

The blacks danced with the fire, moving faster and faster in the stamping rhythms of Africa, clapping their hands in a slow, steady crash of power, making hypnotic reverberations over their dancing feet. The white men slowly began one by one to dance after them, and the whiskey jugs passed from hand to hand while the great dance went on and on, and they howled at the night, howled with the release of some terrible and glorious thing.

Bourbonville was awake now, aroused forever from its ancient slumber, and for miles around, men came in bare feet and nightshirts to dark windows and stood sniffing at the smoke from the great fires, and they saw the red burning high against the night, and they saw fountains of sparks rushing up to die against the cold stars, and they saw the arrival of progress in their land. In the faint, wild cries of triumphant men carried on the night air and made inhuman by distance, they heard also something remote and savage from an age before progress began.

5

I WRITE NOW of Moreland Pinkerton's great work. The buildings went up as the long summer swelled and burst and declined into a brisk autumn and fell away to winter. It was 1890, and Pinkerton was everywhere, seeing if lines were plumb and corners square and foundations solid. He inspected cast-iron beams and rivets. He peered at levels and perused blueprints; and sometimes, out of simple, exuberant delight, he plucked the hammer out of the hand of some astonished and speechless carpenter and drove a nail expertly home and handed the hammer back with a flourish and strode on grinning, swaggering, his head cocked back like the hammer of a revolver ready to fire, leaving the carpenter slowly smiling and looking after him and thinking that Moreland Pinkerton was a star fallen to earth. "We loved him," Henry Morgan told me years and years after, as the big tears came into an old man's eyes. "That's the fact of it. We loved the goddamned mean son of a bitch."

The blacks loved him, too. At first they camped in tents on the low hills south of town, squatting on eroded red land overgrown with brambles and piny woods, land that the Reverend Mr. Sims had bought for the railroad, exceeding his commission, the railroad not caring. The black men brought their women and their children up from Sweetwater, and they sat at night in the steaming dark of summer in eastern Tennessee, and they smoked their pipes and talked in their murmuring and deliberately inoffensive way, as if they feared to have careless speech drift into the white town where it could cause trouble.

Sometimes Moreland Pinkerton came walking up among them like a spirit of the dark, squatted by them on the ground or else sprawled cheer-fully on one of the rough benches they had hammered together from scrap. He leaned back and smoked cigars and told stories, and he listened to their stories, and they laughed. They all laughed.

He looked in on their children when they had fever, and he complimented the women on dresses sewn from feed sacks printed with flowers. The women bent their heads and looked at the ground and giggled with pleasure when he told them how nice they looked. He ate cake baked in clay ovens and made with molasses, and he pronounced it the best cake he had ever eaten, and he wrote the recipe down on the back of a brown paper bag to send to his mother in Virginia. More than once he slipped a quarter to a black man with a bad tooth and directed him to a reliable white farmer who would, for that silver quarter, yank a bad tooth out of a black head.

I heard again and again the tale of the hot afternoon under a scalding sun when a white man named Reed, a hostile, squint-eyed imbecile with a round bald head and a belly that fell over his thick leather belt, slapped a black water boy whose bucket was empty when Reed snatched it out of his hand to drink from it. Somebody had drained the last drop, and the boy was starting back to the well for more when Reed wanted a drink, and not finding water, slapped the child so hard you could hear the crack all the way across the swamp, and when the child cried, Reed, wanting to make a show, jerked a little blue pistol out of his pocket and threatened to shoot his head off so there would be, Reed said, "one less nigger in the world to rape white women."

Everything got still. The white men leaned on their spades and watched.

The black men stood there, ready to see the boy die because they had seen that sort of thing before, and there was nothing they could do about it. Moreland Pinkerton appeared on the scene out of some instinct for danger threatening his great work, and he jumped on Reed like a tiger out of a tree. He slapped the pistol into the muck, and almost with the same smooth, hard motion, he slapped Reed flat across the mouth with an open hand, brought the hand back again across Reed's eyes, forward again across the mouth, repeating the motion so fast and so hard that it sounded like somebody hammering nails into Reed's head. When Reed finally had the presence of mind to bring his hands up to cover his face, Pinkerton took a step back and delivered a swinging, booted kick into Reed's testicles.

People said that Reed's hands came down with an electric jerk, and his face looked like a muskrat's head pulled wrongside out, bloody and amazed and shriveled up and gray, and he pitched forward into the mud, holding his crotch with his hands, and rolled over onto his side, breathless, stupefied, terrified, and incredulous.

Pinkerton grabbed Reed's head in both hands and lifted it up, the body following, and he put his face next to that broken, amazed thing, and he said that if he—Moreland J. Pinkerton of the Dixie Railroad—should see Mr. Reed five minutes hence, he would personally twist a penknife up Mr. Reed's prick just to see how far he could go before he found a brain. With that he hollered for a knife, and maybe two dozen knives came out of pockets, and you could hear the little clicks of the blades snapping open, and you could see the sun shining on elegantly stropped steel, and it was said that Mr. Reed thereupon discovered an energy and a purpose he had only momentarily before supposed vanished from him forever, and that he removed himself with such celerity that he left a wake in the swamp. Pinkerton turned fiercely around to the water boy and to the water boy's father, and he shouted, "You may be niggers, but by God you're my niggers, and this is my job."

I heard the story many times from both blacks and whites years afterward as if it had been engraved in steel forever. At the time word spread like a hurricane through the summer heat while Bourbon County boiled in unbearable uncertainty. White Bourbonvillians had one sure article of social faith: that was that blacks should be kept in their place. Now Pinkerton, a stranger, was changing things. Some people muttered about the mythical days when the Klan would have settled Moreland Pinkerton fast and for good.

The leader of the muttering was Mr. Oswald Mahoney, keeper of a hardware store still here when I came to town, still presided over by Mr. Mahoney, although he was steadily losing business to Douglas Kinlaw. Mr. Mahoney was paunchy and prim, carrying himself with the ceremonial stiffness of an elderly nun, a long, Irish face as white as milk because he could not go into the sun without raising blisters on his skin. He ventured out only at twilight and in the dark—like a vampire bat, Virgil Weaver said.

At the time Mr. Mahoney represented an opinion. Some people nodded when he spoke. The town fathers of Bourbonville passed without discussion a law forbidding any black person—man, woman, or child—to be on the streets after six in the evening. Rumors flew that a band of whites was preparing to ride into the black settlement one night and burn the tents and maybe kill somebody for an example. Under the fiery heat of summer another fire burned, and men sat around in Mr. Mahoney's hardware store and, it was said, made plans.

Mr. Mahoney put out the tale that Pinkerton meddled with black women. "Why else does he go down there at night? Why'd he bring them here? He ain't the first; I don't reckon he'll be the last." Mr. Mahoney laughed in his spitty way in the dark of his hardware store where he was king of steel plows and prince of pocket knives and lord of barrels and nails and saws and leather harnesses, where he was safe, he supposed, in his gloomy kingdom.

Pinkerton got wind of the slander. "I thought it was damn funny, you know. But hell, it was dangerous. I heard what those lazy bastards were fixing to do. I knew if I didn't do something, the car works might not get built. By God, I never was somebody to do nothing."

He chewed tobacco then, as most men did who worked with their hands; and with his cheek packed full, he marched into the hardware store on a sweltering Saturday afternoon when he could be sure men were idling there in the cool dimness. Mr. Mahoney stood behind his counter, grinning his prissy grin, wearing his boiled white shirt, his black suspenders, his black necktie. Suddenly Pinkerton's hard boots pounded across the porch planking. The men looked up and saw him moving with smooth, resolute inhesitancy, saw Mr. Mahoney's grin get bigger and bigger and suddenly die as Pinkerton swept to the counter, leaned over, plucked him up by the lapels, yanked him over the counter, and began slowly, methodically, and with maximum liquidity to spit brown tobacco juice into Mr. Mahoney's milk-white face. Mr. Mahoney struggled, and he could not free himself, and he yelled for help. Nobody in the store moved. Pinkerton went on chewing and spitting, chewing and spitting, and in the end Mr. Mahoney began to cry.

When Mr. Mahoney began to cry, Pinkerton laughed in a roar of satisfaction. He spat the cud of tobacco onto Mr. Mahoney's face and tossed him back with a crash onto the shelves behind the counter as if Mr. Mahoney had been no more substantial than a sack of straw.

Pinkerton reached over and wiped his hands on Mr. Mahoney's boiled and starched white shirt and then dusted them together as if Mr. Mahoney had been something filthy that had to be cleaned off. He glared happily around at the silent men. "Good day, gentlemen. . . . Nice to see *you*, Mr. Reed," he said.

Mr. Mahoney sent for the sheriff when Pinkerton had disappeared in the hot sunshine. Hub Delaney was still the sheriff then, a man in his fifties, his right shoulder stiff from a bullet he had taken from an insane preacher a few years before, a man still in charge of things, though he was no longer swift. He detested Mr. Mahoney, and despite his friendship with Brian Ledbetter and others who hated the coming of the car works, he admired Moreland Pinkerton.

"If I was you, I'd forget about it," Hub told Mr. Mahoney. "You ain't really hurt none. I mean, you look like you've had a spittoon poured on top of your head, but you can take a bath, I reckon, and they can do wonders with wool suits now. I could haul him off to jail, but then I reckon he could get hisself a lawyer, and maybe then he'd sue you for slander or some such, and maybe he'd take your store away and go into the hardware business on the side. I wouldn't fool around with *him* if I was in your shoes. If I *was* in your shoes, I'd get 'em off real quick, and the rest of my clothes, too, and then I'd take me a bath, and I believe I'd use hot water and lye soap, Mr. Mahoney. I mean, if I was you."

Hub's slow ruminations were enough. Mr. Mahoney kept silent afterwards whenever Moreland Pinkerton's name came up, and men who might have burned the black settlement drifted away because they were ashamed of Mr. Mahoney, and they were afraid of Moreland Pinkerton. Pinkerton represented progress and money. What he did to Reed and what he did to Mr. Mahoney proved that he was not bound by ordinary constraints. The blacks stayed out of the way. They did not want any trouble. They worked all day and walked home along the railroad tracks, keeping their eyes averted from white people, keeping their heads bowed, showing by every gesture and every word that they intended to stay in their place.

They thought Pinkerton was Jesus Christ and Abraham Lincoln and Ulysses S. Grant. They built a Mount Zion Baptist Church on one of their low hills, and on Sundays in this, the first church in what Bourbonville called Bucktown or Niggertown, although the blacks called it Huntsville after one of their preachers, the first roof of wood shingles and the first walls of pine planking that embraced their collective religious passions and shook with the thumping and shoutings of their devotions, their preachers prayed every Sunday for God's blessings to fall on the United States of America and on Moreland J. Pinkerton, and men and women in the throbbing congregation swayed and shouted, "Do it, Lord! Do it!"

They named sons after him, and at least one girl child was named Morelanda. They took off their hats when they talked with him. He slapped them on the back and called them all "Uncle" or "Aunt," and they grinned shyly back at him and laughed with true humor when he said something funny. They were the first people in Bourbonville to call him the name he loved best—Captain.

6

THE FOUNDRIES for brass and iron and steel rose where the swamp had been. The trains heaved in with the great metal parts of the furnaces in pieces on flatcars, and with the yellow fire brick on gondolas. Black men and white toiled and groaned and cursed and put the furnaces together, and they built a tall brick chimney that pointed to the sky like a spire, and a bricklayer named Smallen died when he leaned back too far, too high, and admired his mighty creation and lost his balance on the thin oak scaffold and fell tumbling and flapping his arms like a great, unsuccessful bird until he struck the unyielding earth with such force that people said his body burst like a watermelon.

Moreland Pinkerton wept. Black men and white men came to the funeral and stood around the open grave and the closed oak coffin, and they sang sad songs. "He died for progress," Moreland Pinkerton said, asked to say a few words by the preacher, who said "Amen" when Pinkerton spoke. "Progress has a price, and our dear brother Jack Smallen has paid part of that price for all of us. We must remember when we enjoy the fruits of his sacrifice and taste the goodness of progress that Jack Smallen did not die in vain. We will remember Jack Smallen forever."

The carpenters who had put up the buildings now became builders of boxcars. The steel foundry made trucks as mounts for the iron wheels rolling under the boxcars, and it made parts for locomotives, but it was an open hearth furnace, and something was always going wrong with the steel. "I swear to God," Pinkerton said, "the steel we make here ain't worth a nun's shit." The brass foundry made journal bearings for the great steam locomotives and for the boxcars, but the glory was the iron, the wheel foundry.

Men who had never known anything more complicated than seed time and harvest, rain and snow and drought, learned to prepare the damp sand for the molds and to press the oak wheel patterns into the sand and to tap the great furnace and to pirouette away from the great gush of the molten iron into the bull ladle, and how the colors—incandescent to cherry red—told them what the iron was and what it would become; and some of the religious among them long afterwards told me that the liquid iron squirting out of the furnace made them think of Tubal Cain.

The black men learned to be molders' helpers and to haul coke in wheelbarrows to stoke the furnace that melted the pig iron and the scrap, and they learned to take the eight-hundred-fifty-pound gray-iron wheels that the crane hauled out of the annealing pits, wheels so perfectly round that a nickel would not lie flat on the curved surface that rode the rails, and they could balance them on the flange and roll them into the long shed where Moreland Pinkerton's carpenters—he always called them *his* carpenters— sawed and hammered and fitted wooden boxcars together. They could, these black wheel dancers, working in couples, swing the wheels onto the axles and fasten them in place, and they knew what they could do, and they were proud.

Moreland Pinkerton looked at all of it, saw the foundry turning like a giant machine, and that he was the engine that made it run, and he believed that nothing was impossible. "I knew the goddamn railroad would call me up to Washington City in no time," he told me. "I didn't have the education a lot of those people had, and I didn't know manners, and I didn't know how to talk snob talk. But hell, talk's cheap. Anybody can talk. I was a go-getter, the kind that made America great. I could lead men. I could see myself in a black tie and tails. You know those things real gents wear when they get their pictures made? I could see myself in one of them outfits, shaking hands with important people, smoking a cigar with the President of the United States. I was sure I'd be president of the goddamned railroad one of these days, and if things had turned out just a little different, you might of talked about Moreland J. Pinkerton, President of the United States."

The man who spoke those words to me was soaked with whiskey, red-eyed, and seething with a bitterness like wormwood. He spoke them years after the Spanish War caused him to make the mistake that he knew made his dreams collapse and trapped him in Bourbonville for life.

7

HIS LAST CHEMIST had hanged himself. Under the rules of the railroad and the Interstate Commerce Commission, Pinkerton could not run the foundry without a chemist to analyze its metal products for impurities.

"Some people say he's in hell because he killed himself," Pinkerton said of the suicide, a man named Millard Sanders. "I say if the damn fool's in hell, he deserves to be there for stupidity. Now I ask you: if a chemist is going to kill himself, and if he's as smart as a chemist is supposed to be, don't you think he'd take a pill? Breathe some kind of gas? Not Sanders! Hell no! He had to go hang himself. Had to stay in the goddamn laboratory till after everybody went home, and he sits up all night in the dark and hangs himself so I'll find him in the morning when I'm making my rounds. Hell! His body's still warm when I touch him. I come in, and he's nowhere to be seen, and I look up, and I see him at the end of that yellow rope, hung up against the ceiling on a beam. Right there—that one? You see the one I'm pointing at? At first, I couldn't realize what the poor dumb bastard had gone and done. I couldn't make myself believe that he had hanged himself till I saw that stepladder he'd kicked away from under his feet, and it was lying on its side where he'd knocked it, and I knew then he was dead."

Death amazed Pinkerton. It seemed unreal to him, something that happened to others, a wonder always incomprehensible.

"I put my hand up to touch him, and he started bleeding. Bled all over me, the son of a bitch. Ruined my suit. Out of his mouth. His nose, too. Poured out of his nose. I never saw nothing like it—not even in Cuba.

"Funny thing about Sanders. Man told stories all the time. You'd see him out on the steps here at lunch, eating out of a poke and the men gathered around him laughing. He had a story for every damned thing in the world. And he hung hisself. Don't make sense, does it? Don't make a damn bit of sense." He shook his head, bewildered at the notion of a happy man who killed himself.

Sanders's demise meant that Pinkerton needed a chemist. First he hired a teacher at the high school, Juliet Fisher. "I didn't want a woman doing chemistry. What the hell are people going to think about me having a lady do that sort of work? She come down after school and worked late, and it made me nervous as hell, her here in the evening by herself. If I had my way, you'd never let a woman take chemistry in college. Hell, if I had my way, you wouldn't let women *go* to college."

I have said he was a big man, tall and once muscular, but when I met him he was chunky as men are before they go to fat. He held himself straight and tried to look military. When his secretary showed me into his office that first time, he assumed a formal pose and walked stiffly around the desk to shake hands.

"Moreland J. Pinkerton," he said. "Put her there. Welcome to Bourbonville. Stinking little shithole, but you'll get along. Have a chair."

"I am Paul Alexander," I said. "May I smoke?" My head felt dangerously uneasy. Smoking helped.

"Hell, you can *burn* for all I care," he said, uttering a loud laugh, swaggering around to sit in his swivel chair. "I smoke cigars myself. Tell you the truth, cigarettes always seemed sissy to me. But all the soldiers smoke them. Isn't that right?"

I recalled that Bernal had not smoked—he was an unusual soldier—and I said yes, all the soldiers were smoking cigarettes now. We looked at each other. Pinkerton waited for me to speak. I waited for him.

He lit a cigar and sat puffing at it, a good cigar, and the smoke swirled up and in a heavy fragrance, and it reminded me of my father's cigars and how prosperous he had seemed when he sat on the terrace and drew in the rich and fragrant smoke and looked out across the Bay of Faliron towards the faint lights of Athens glowing across the water. Pinkerton's cigar brought my father back to me in one of those powerful surges of memory that make the present seem fragile, even unreal, theatening to dissolve the progression of time that keeps life in order and makes such sense as there is to being alive. My father came back to me at that moment in a blinding whirl, so that he seemed almost to be in the room with me, with Guy and Bernal, young men he had never met, would never meet now no matter what happened in all the future, and it was as though I had been caught up in an enchantment or a dream. I could smell whiskey on Pinkerton's breath. The pain in my head was coming up behind my right eye. I smoked carefully, trying to keep the world in focus.

"I'm the boss here," Pinkerton said. "You can call me Captain if you want; that's what everybody calls me. I hire people, and I fire people. No appeal from me. When I say jump, folks better say 'How high?' You went to college, I reckon. You got the look of a college man."

"I attended the university," I said carefully in my too-perfect English. "I did not receive my diploma. The war came before I could be graduated."

Pinkerton nodded with respect. "Well, you're better off for it. College snobs make me sick. You don't need college in America. You just need ability."

The cigar smoke swirled around me. I breathed with difficulty. I wondered if my father was dead.

"You're Belgian," Pinkerton said.

"Yes, I am Belgian." I heard Guy snicker. My head began to throb, far down inside. Pinkerton asked questions: Where was I wounded? How long had I been in the hospital? What did I think of America? "Way you talk, you're going to have one hell of a time making folks understand what you're talking about. But hell, I didn't hire you to make speeches."

Beyond the plank walls of this flimsy building the great ventilator fan in the cupola furnace went on with a roar. The room vibrated slightly with the noise. The vibration seemed to catch hold of a tremor deep in my brain. I felt pain rising, and nausea. I smoked deliberately. *One, two, three, four.*

He talked on, fascinated with my war experience, wanting to know everything. I could not tell him everything; I could barely make myself coherent. The sound of the foundry pounded deeper and deeper into my head. *One, two, three, four; one, two, three, four.*

I told him about Antwerp, about lying behind the railway embankment, about the German attack, the fiery burst of the shell.

I began to feel dizzy again. The chair seemed to revolve, the room. I told him that I had been struck on the head and the chest and the legs with shrapnel, and I almost unconsciously lifted my hand to the place on my forehead above my left eye where flying steel made a hole that never did knit together in the bone, although the skin had grown over it. We did not wear steel helmets as soldiers did later; we wore soft cloth hats.

Pinkerton leaned forward, squinted, and followed the motion of my fingers with rapt attention. "I can see the scar," he said thoughtfully. "Don't look like much. But then I reckon it don't take much to kill a man, does it?"

He laughed in his loud, unnatural way. I silently counted. *One, two, three, four; one, two, three, four.* Sometimes counting could stave off a headache. His cigar smoke engulfed me; I thought I could see my father's face in it, coming and going as faces may appear in clouds.

Pinkerton looked at me. I looked at him. His face was beginning to blur. I tried to focus on it, and the dizziness got worse. The room was revolving slowly. He talked on; the questions fell like a barrage.

I could taste bile in the back of my mouth. Pinkerton leaned forward, smoking. I lit another cigarette and quickly put it out. The cigar smoke made me want to vomit.

"I woke up. I was in great pain," I said. "I could not see. I thought I was blind. I heard English voices. I called for help. I heard one of them say, 'Here's a Belgian. Let's pick him up.' They were litter bearers."

Pinkerton expelled a sigh of admiration and, I realized vaguely, envy. "I'll be damned. I'll be damned. They took you to England."

"Yes, they put me on a boat, you see. And took me across the Channel and to England. To London." Now I could scarcely see anything. The world was shutting me in, and I could not breathe. Pinkerton's voice came from a long way off. I was dizzy and sick—very sick. I stood up and started for the side door that opened onto the outside. I thought that if I could get there, I might breathe. I heard Pinkerton say something in surprise, a startled recognition.

I was vomiting. I had not eaten anything; I was vomiting bile. My stomach heaved violently. I was aware that Pinkerton was rushing to my aid. He was standing over me, shouting at someone, and I smelled his cigar so close that I vomited again. Everything faded into pain and then to blackness, and I lost consciousness entirely.

8

WHEN I CAME to my senses, I was lying in a large bed between clean sheets. It was afternoon. The pale blue wallpaper of the room was decorated with bright yellow flowers. A varnished chest of drawers stood against the wall, and on top of it reposed a purple crockery basin. In the basin sat a pitcher of the same garish color.

My battered gladstone bag was on the floor next to the chest of drawers. It was the property of an English soldier who had died in the bed next to me in Chelsea. His parents had brought it down with his civilian clothes when they thought they would take him home. They had expected him to be demobbed. They would dress him in his old clothes and take him home, and everything would be as it had been before the war. When he died, they abandoned the bag, and the nurses gave it to me, and here it was, lying against the wall in this room in a strange land.

My headache and my nausea were gone. I was exhausted, serene and drowsy. I realized that I was under the influence of a narcotic, probably morphine. I became aware of a man who sat in a chair at the foot of my bed, sedately smoking a pipe.

"You've been unconscious for several hours," he said affably. "Are you all right?"

I told him that I was. He laughed with a gravelly chuckle. "I'd say you've had one hell of a day."

"Who are you?" I said.

"Curtis Youngblood," he said. "I am the only M.D. in Bourbonville. Hell, I'm the only M.D. in the whole damned county."

"M.D.?" I said.

"Medical doctor," he said.

"Where am I now?"

"In your new home. Darcy Coolidge's boardinghouse. You'll like it. She cooks good food. She keeps a clean place. Some of the foundry men stay here. And Ted Devlin. He edits the newspaper. He stays here too."

I felt blissfully comfortable, at the doorway to deep sleep, a long cave descending to a pleasant coolness, and I thought—as I had thought on other occasions—that the cave was death and that at last I was about to step down into it and be safe. Guy and Bernal stood at the entrance. Far within, like Orpheus in the Greek underworld, Stephanos played the bouzouki. The plucked notes fell one by one through the tranquil dark. Guy beckoned.

Dr. Youngblood spoke again. "I gave you a shot."

He smoked methodically and said nothing for a while. "Do you have these spells often?" he said at last.

"I have headaches," I said. "This is the first time that I have fainted in public. I am very sorry!"

"Ummmmmm," Dr. Youngblood said.

"You have a strong heart," he said. "I've seen people with strong hearts die." There was another silence. He wore a shabby gray suit and a thin bow tie. "You sat up on the train all night?" he asked.

"Yes."

"You did not sleep?"

"I think not."

"When was the last time you had a good night's sleep?"

"I do not recall," I said.

"Ummmmmm," he said. He shook his head as if wakening from his own contemplation. "I suppose you can go to work tomorrow morning. Pinkerton's got to use his woman chemist one more day. He doesn't like that. He lost one chemist unexpectedly, you know."

"Yes," I said.

Dr. Youngblood's broad face turned somber. "Poor Sanders. This was his room. None of us expected it. He loved to tell stories."

"His room."

"Yes."

"The man who killed himself."

"It's not catching," Dr. Youngblood said.

"Have I offended Mr. Pinkerton?"

"Offended Pinkerton? No. He was very concerned."

"I am grateful," I said.

"He's an odd one," Dr. Youngblood said. "He was afraid you might die and leave him to the woman chemist."

There was a soft but insistent knock at the door. It was my first meeting with Darcy Coolidge. She was in her late fifties, tall, slender, and gray, carrying herself with great dignity, though obviously she had never been beautiful.

"Good afternoon, young man," she said stiffly.

"How do you do," I said. "What time is it?"

"It's almost three o'clock," she said. "How is he, Curtis?"

"Oh, he'll make it, Darcy. He's going to be fine."

"I have your solemn word of honor that he was not under the influence of alcoholic beverages when he was carried into my house this morning?"

"Sure you do, Darcy," Dr. Youngblood said, showing a hint of impatience. "Good Lord! There aren't many people under the influence before eight in the morning!"

"It has been known to happen, Curtis," she said sadly. "I have seen it happen. In my day I have seen many examples of the ruination demon rum can work on the finest of men—even before eight in the morning."

"Well, if you're talking about rum, I agree with you, Darcy," Dr. Youngblood said. "I never touch the stuff. Makes me sick as a hog. If you're going to drink, Darcy, leave rum alone. Stick to whiskey." Dr. Youngblood laughed again. Darcy Coolidge did not laugh.

"I shall let that remark pass, Curtis. I realize that you graduated from Harvard and are therefore smarter than the rest of us, but even Harvard graduates can utter statements unworthy of a response. I must say that I see nothing wrong with a mild little toddy now and then, but only for medicinal purposes. The drunkard is an offense to God and society and to his own family."

"I'm a doctor, Darcy. That's all I do with whiskey—take it for medicinal purposes. Everything I do is for a medicinal purpose." He laughed, and I thought she smiled.

Somehow, in the intervals of conversation about drink, we were introduced. "I would not have done this for anyone else on earth but Moreland J. Pinkerton," she said with considerable fervor. "To think of taking in a foreigner, sight unseen! I amaze myself, Curtis. Sometimes I truly amaze myself."

"You are an amazing woman," Dr. Youngblood said.

"That is what the Colonel always said," Darcy Coolidge exclaimed, dabbing at her eyes with a tiny handkerchief with sudden and genuine grief. "The late Colonel was my husband, Mr. Alexander. A truly noble man. You would have loved him, Mr. Alexander. Everybody loved the Colonel." I gathered that the Colonel had died some years before.

She looked at me and shook her head. "I wonder if chemists are just a naturally unhealthy lot," she said. "All those fumes. Poor Mr. Sanders, and now you."

"Sanders wasn't sick," Dr. Youngblood said.

"Of course he was sick," Darcy Coolidge said. "Healthy people are not in the habit of killing themselves, Curtis. You should know that."

"It's not what you'd call a habit for most folks," Dr. Youngblood said. "It's hard to do it twice."

"He told me not to expect him for supper. He said he had some tests to run in the laboratory that would carry him through the evening. He took some sandwiches. Enough for dinner and supper. I told him the door would be unlocked. We always leave our doors unlocked. Something crossed my mind—a shadow. I cannot explain it, Curtis, but I *knew* something was wrong, and I did not act on my impulse. The next morning, when he did not come down to breakfast and when Mr. Farmer went up and saw that his bed had not been slept in, I worried a little more. I never dreamed he would kill himself— not even when Mr. Pinkerton came to tell me. He was such a kind man. I never heard him raise his voice. He was always laughing, always telling stories."

"You have to watch that kind," Dr. Youngblood said. "They're the ones who kill themselves."

A silence fell on the room. The cool October air came through the open window. It had the tang of autumn to it. Guy stood by the window, looking with disapproval over the town, and Bernal stood by my bed, looking at me with compassion. They vanished.

Darcy Coolidge and Dr. Youngblood were still talking when I drifted off to sleep.

9

I TOOK UP my duties in the laboratory the next day, feeling weak and nauseated.

The laboratory was a flimsy shed, warmed by the kilns at one end and by a potbellied coal stove in the middle. Its wooden walls were painted a gaudy yellow on the outside; all the buildings of the Dixie Railroad in those days were yellow. The lab had a door on each end and a door in the middle. The doors on the ends opened onto the outside. The door in the middle opened onto a little shed where we kept tools, including the drill press. With it I drilled out metal filings for the various tests I had to run in the lab. There was a toilet and a shower in there, too. The outside doors had glass panes in the top half, which rattled when you shut the doors.

It was dim inside. The windows had not been washed, it seemed, in years. Two huge oaks stood at the entrance to the laboratory nearest the main gate. On the brightest days they kept the sun at bay. On the morning I went to work they flamed red with autumn. They stood on high ground. When the swamp was cleared, they might have fallen to the impulse of Pinkerton's men to hew down every tree they saw, but these oaks impressed him, and he ordered them left intact. He loved them. "I tore down a lot of things so I could build, but I left some things—don't ever forget that—I didn't come in here and root out the whole town. Those trees prove that."

Against the walls of the laboratory stood shelves of bottles, boxes, and gear rising in labeled and dusty ranks to the ceiling. The kilns were for baking tiny porcelain crucibles for testing for silica and sulphur in the iron. There was a desk with a logbook on it. I recorded the tests in the logbook. I noted the strong hand of Sanders. On the day he hanged himself, he did all the tests, and his hand was as firm as engraving. Juliet Fisher's handwriting was more elegant and slanted to the left. I wondered if she might be left-handed.

There was a scales house in the middle of the building, glassed in to protect it from blowing dust and from any stray breeze that might disturb the scales. It rested on a deep concrete foundation to keep the scales from trembling with the heavy passage of the switch engine on the spur along one side of the laboratory that led to the loading dock of the wheel foundry. All day long the switch engine puffed back and forth, hauling gondolas and boxcars, rattling the windows and the doors, making the floor throb. I could sit in the scales house on that concrete column plunged deep into the earth and know that nothing would move it short of an earthquake. I sat there at times and remembered Delphi, navel of the world, where the earth sometimes shook and roared and great stones crashed down the purple sides of Mount Parnassos.

I walked into the laboratory for the first time, smelled its strong odors—and felt at home. They were unpleasant to others—acids and other reagents, chlorine, permanganate, the reek of things burned. To me they meant chemistry. Chemistry had not changed; mathematics had not changed. Not even the war could alter the predictable and regular order that held the universe together.

Pinkerton appeared a half hour after I came to work. He strode in and looked proudly around, wearing a grin under his ferocious mustache. He smelled of whiskey. "Feeling better, I guess?" he said.

"Yes," I said.

"I have that effect on people," Pinkerton said, looking smug.

"I beg your pardon?"

"I scare people. There's something about me. I don't know what it is. Haven't had many faint in my office, but what the hell—haven't had many who've been in the goddamned Belgian Army." He laughed.

"I do not understand."

"Not many people understand me. I don't ask people to understand me. Work hard, and you get along fine with me; lay down on the job, and out your ass goes."

"I have work to do now," I said.

"You can do the work here later. Right now, I want to walk you around, show you the place. Meant to do that yesterday, and you passed out on me. Well, don't worry about it. Get your hat."

"Where are we going?"

"I told you. To see the car works. Don't ask questions when you know the answer. I guess you've seen a lot of heavy industry in Europe?"

"Yes," I said.

"Krupps and all that stuff," Pinkerton said.

"Yes," I said vaguely.

"Guess you look down on a little chickenshit operation like this one, don't you?"

"No," I said. "No, of course not."

"I don't like folks looking down on my work."

"I have not thought of looking down on it. I give you my word."

"You better not. I've given my life for it. You mock the Bourbonville Car Works, and you mock me. Let's go. When I say jump, I mean for you to jump."

Before I could get my hat, a wiry black man wearing a billed cap and carrying a block of hot steel with a huge set of tongs came through the door.

He was there with a sample from the first heat of the morning. He brought the chunk of steel in so I could drill a sample out of it and test it.

Pinkerton's eyes lit up. "Frankie!"

"Yassuh, Cap'n!"

"Dance, Frankie. Show Mr. Alexander here how you can dance. Dance!" Pinkerton yelled at him, a friendly yell but a yell nevertheless, full of command.

Frankie danced. Yes, holding the chunk of steel in one strong arm, this middle-aged black man did a rhythmic little step and danced. And while he danced, he sang:

> *Frankie and Johnnie was sweethearts*
> *And oh, what a couple in love.*
> *Frankie loved Johnnie more than*
> *The skies and the stars above.*
> *He was her man*
> *But he was doing her wrong.*

He went on. Pinkerton was rapt, and at the end he clapped and gave Frankie a nickel. Frankie laughed, dropped the chunk of steel back in the drill room, tipped his cap to me and to Pinkerton, and went away humming his tune, the tune he was named for.

"By God they love me, these niggers!" Pinkerton said. "They love me more than anybody else in town." His face was expansive and rapt in the contemplation of himself. "Get your hat, Alexander. You saw the nigger. When I give a command around here, my men obey—black or white. Get your goddamned hat and let's get moving. The morning's half gone."

I took my hat and followed him out the door. He walked along looking jaunty, sweeping his hands around like a museum guide to show me the masterpieces.

"New man needs to know the force. I never have had a strike. Do you know what that means in this day and age? You won't find many executives who can say that when they've been on the job as long as I have. All this union stuff, all these IWW people and the anarchists and suchlike crawling around and raising hell, and I have never had a strike. I tell you what the secret is: be firm, but stay close to the men. Walk around. Talk to them about their work, their women, their children. Learn what they like to do in their off days. Hell, I hate rooting around in the dirt. Eula gardens in our family if you want to know the truth. But do I tell the men that? Hell no. In summertime I talk about cabbages and beans and how far apart you plant corn seeds and how to hill potatoes and grow pumpkins and all them dirt things. I make these men think I got a garden from here to Chattanooga, and the ones that garden, they eat it up. That's pretty good, don't you think? 'The ones that garden, they eat it up.' " He laughed at his little play on words. He very much admired himself.

He walked along with his chin jutted out. "Managing men is a science. I'm the best you'll ever see. I'm fair—fair to the niggers, fair to every piece of white trash that works for me, fair to scholars like yourself." He clapped me on the back so that my eyes watered. "Come on," he said. "I'll show you my empire."

He walked me over the car works that morning, through the foundries, up slick steel catwalks and across railroad tracks, and climbed up into the little switch engine to talk to the respectful white engineer and the equally respectful black fireman. We walked out on the loading dock. We climbed up the steel ladder to the overhead crane in the wheel foundry, where an elderly white man named Scott sat in a suspended cage and put gloved hands on shining steel levers and lifted the cherry-red iron wheels out of the sand molds and with his great steel hook hauled them one by one down the length of the building to the annealing pits, where with surgical deftness he dropped them into the deep holes where they would cool slowly for two days.

It was a giddy distance above the wheel floor, where the molds lay in rows, and the heat rising under the high roof of the building was like a wave. Pinkerton, sweating and grinning and wiping his face frequently with a red bandana, was a boy at play. Men took off their hats when he spoke to them. He introduced me with a flourish: "This is Paul Alexander. He's been in the war. A genuine fighting hero of the Belgian Army. Look at that scar on his forehead—that's where he was wounded. Man's been through hell. Belgian infantry. It takes guts to be an infantry soldier. You people treat him right, now." He laughed, throwing his head back. I felt faint. I willed myself not to collapse. My intestines felt precarious, the way they felt when a headache was coming on. *One, two, three, four,* I said to myself. *One, two, three, four.*

After the wheel foundry, we hiked through the brass foundry and looked at its rotating furnace; the steel foundry with its open-hearth furnace that Pinkerton cursed; and the long shed where the carpenters built the wooden boxcars. "We make five hundred gray iron wheels a day and fifty boxcars. Hard to think the railroad soaks all that up, but it does. Sometimes we're three weeks behind in filling orders. That's what a war does."

We visited the pattern shop and the machine shop and went back to the wheel foundry. "Time to tap the furnace," he shouted at me in jubilation. "First iron heat of the day. It's the thing I like best."

I have said that the furnace was one of those old-fashioned cupola towers that Pinkerton and everybody else called "the cupulo." "I don't know much about chemistry," Pinkerton said, "but I know what happens in a foundry. You know about iron, don't you?"

"Yes," I said. "Everything goes to iron in the end. It is the ash of the universe."

"Jesus Christ—a philosopher!" Pinkerton said. "You're a smart man, Paul Alexander. You and me will do all right. I like smart men. We're going to do swell."

"I hope so," I said.

"Hell yes. Well, you're a chemist. You know about iron. Common stuff. It's everywhere. It's in your body. It's in your blood. It's in the leaves out there. It's in the dirt under our feet. Iron is a whore. Iron will copulate with almost anything. It takes fire and limestone and coke to make it pure, by God. Then the foundryman makes it useful. Founding iron is one of the miracles. It it wasn't for founding iron, we couldn't have progress. You talk about Houdini. Hell, the real magician is the foundryman. He's cousin to the devil and bastard son of God. You know how hot the iron is in the cupulo when we tap it?"

"About sixteen hundred degrees," I said.

Pinkerton glared at me. "What kind of chemist are you? Sixteen hundred degrees, hell! That will roast a wienie, but it won't melt iron. It's twenty-eight hundred degrees."

"I was speaking of Celsius," I said.

"Fuck Celsius," Pinkerton said. "I'm talking about Fahrenheit. If Fahrenheit was good enough for Ben Franklin, it ought to be good enough for you."

"I am sorry," I said.

"Aw hell," he said, slapping me again on the back so that it stung. "I know what you mean. I'm not stupid. Celsius, hellsius. I tell you, when I think that man can control something that's twenty-eight hundred degrees Fahrenheit, it makes me proud to be a human being. Do you believe in evolution?"

"I do not know much about it," I said.

"I believe in it. I believe we're going up. Today is better than yesterday. Tomorrow will be better than today. Our children will be better than we are. I'm glad to be alive now. Only one thing I'd like more."

I thought he wanted me to ask him what that might be, and I did.

"I'd like to live a century from now. God knows what we'll be then. God knows."

We saw the cupola tapped. We wore thick blue glasses, and the incandescent iron gushed out as an explosion of liquid light. When it erupted from the bottom of the furnace, Pinkerton said, "Haaaaaaa." Afterwards he had nothing more to say to me. *Post coitum, tristitia,* I thought. One of Guy's sayings.

I went back to the laboratory and had a headache. I put my head down on the cool marble counter and tried to bring the coolness into my brain.

"You must work," Guy whispered. "If you are going to be in this place, you cannot sit around feeling sorry for yourself because of a headache."

One, two, three, four, I said. *One, two, three, four.* I got control of myself.

Bernal lounged in a chair; Guy walked around with me. "He is a strange man," I said aloud.

"The black man is afraid of him," Guy said.

"Frankie?" I said.

"Yes, Frankie," Guy said.

"He admires you," Bernal said.

"What does that matter?" I said.

"It matters," Bernal said.

"It is everything," Guy said.

"Here are the kilns, and here are the crucibles," I said. "Here is the hydrochloric acid, and here is the sulphuric acid. Sulphuric acid is H_2SO_4, and hydrochloric acid is HCl."

"You remember," Guy said. "You are not mad."

"No," I said. "I am not mad."

10

IN THE AFTERNOON Pinkerton came back. "I thought I'd see how you're doing," he said. "Put a new man on the job and you want to see how he's doing. It's part of management science."

"Thank you," I said.

Despite his knowledge of iron, the laboratory and its mysteries were as foreign to him as the tribal languages of Outer Mongolia. He followed me around complacently, talking at me. I worked. I had nothing to say. I could tell he was trying to find out things about me so he could talk to me about those things in the same spirit with which he talked to men about gardening.

"I envy you, my boy."

"Why should you envy me?"

"Your wounds. You can go the rest of your life knowing you did your bit, knowing you were brave, having everybody else in the world know you were brave."

"I was not brave. I was terribly afraid."

"Tell him you dream of shell fire," Guy said.

"No," Bernal said. "Tell him nothing."

One, two, three, four, I thought. *One, two, three, four.*

"You were afraid, but you did your duty, and you've got your whole life to show off your wounds. I had some military experience, you know. It didn't work out."

"I have not heard about it," I said.

"You've been in this town a day, and you haven't heard about me in Cuba?" He laughed unpleasantly.

"No," I said. I thought of the telegrapher. I decided not to mention him.

"I don't believe you. Everybody talks about me and Cuba. They'll all tell you about it. I walk down the street and I know what they're saying. They're saying, 'Do you remember about Moreland Pinkerton and Cuba?' Now that's God's own truth, isn't it?"

"I do not know," I said.

"You're lying. It's written all over your face. I did the best I could. You and me know what it's like, don't we?"

"What?"

"What?! War, that's what. Hell, you and me know what war's like."

I was silent.

"You can't pay attention to what people say."

I bowed slightly.

"Hell, you do that real good. You come out of good stock, Alexander. . . . I had a son die when he was a baby."

"I am sorry," I said.

"I am, too," Pinkerton said, his voice changing. "He'd be about your age. He'd be out there at the front if he was alive. He'd be that kind of boy. He'd be a hero, but he's dead. I got nobody to carry on my name."

I could think of nothing to say.

"What the hell," Pinkerton said. "A man's got work to do. You leave your work behind when you die. It's your monument. I got my little kingdom here in the car works. Do your job and fuck the world." He laughed in his savage, humorless way.

"I was in the Spanish thing, you know. I raised a company of volunteers here in the county. We beat the living shit out of the Spanish. Just like we're going to beat the shit out of the Germans. Culture or no culture, it don't make no difference. Goddamned snobs with culture, they got to shit, too, and we're going to beat the shit out of them Germans. We'll wipe their Hun asses with their arty paintings, and we'll piss on their libraries. You can get too damned educated, if you ask me. That's what all you folks over there have done. Too much culture, not enough horse sense. You can't finish a war. You can't finish nothing."

He paused and retreated into a gentler mood. "Now Americans, by God, we don't have much book learning, but we can do things. We think of products in America—goods, solid things, things you make with iron and steel. We think of what a man can do. We don't ask a man to talk like the Duke of Puke. We ask him to *produce*. By God, we can produce better than anybody else on earth. We can fight better, too. The Spanish found that out.

You hold a dictionary full of big words up before an American Navy gun, by God. That gun will take you from *a* to *z* pretty damn quick, I tell you. That's what the Huns will find out. You've read about our Spanish war?"

"I believe so," I said, lying.

"It was a good little war," he said. "I raised a company of volunteers here in the county. Lots of men that worked for me. Most of them boys trusted me because I built this place, and they figured if I did that, I could beat the shit out of the Spanish. I went around the county and recruited them. I said, 'Boys, come along with me, and you'll have glory. Some of you will die, but you'll die in glory. You'll never forget it. And folks won't ever forget you.'

He stopped and gave me a look of hostile inquiry. "Do you know the name Virgil Weaver?"

"No," I said.

"You sure?"

"I have been here a day," I said, wearying of him. "I do not know anybody."

"You know Doc Youngblood."

"The doctor who came to my room."

"He's a friend to Virgil Weaver."

"We did not talk about Virgil Weaver."

"It don't matter to me. Virgil Weaver won't have anything to do with you. You know why?"

"I have no idea."

"You're a railroad man. Virgil Weaver won't have nothing, anything, to do with a railroad man."

"Then he does not matter," I said.

"He does matter. He matters one hell of a lot. Do you understand that? He matters one hell of a lot."

I looked up at him. His face burned, and he had clenched his fists. I thought he might hit me, and I drew back.

"Hey, I didn't mean to scare you," he said. He grinned.

"I am sorry if I made you angry."

"You didn't make me angry. Virgil Weaver makes me angry. I think about him and I get mad enough to kill him. I'm acting like a damned fool. Virgil Weaver makes me act crazy. All these years, too." He laughed again, harsh and bitter. "His stepdaddy fired a shotgun over my head when I was building the car works. I told you that."

"Yes," I said.

"Virgil Weaver is the old man's stepson. One of them. There're five of those Weaver boys—a goddamned clan. Used to be six, but one died when he wasn't nothing but a kid. Another one's gone off. An engineer in some goddamn foreign place. Virgil's the oldest. He's a lawyer. A smart lawyer. Hell, he's rich, too. That's the damnedest thing. Virgil Weaver is rich."

He paused, swallowing his rage, pacing up and down.

"Virgil Weaver spoke out against me, against the country. He said the war was immoral. He said we didn't need an empire! Even after the *Maine*, he said that. He said I was tricking the boys that was going with me. He said they was going to die for nothing. Town like to of tore him in two. Lord, I was a hero in those days. I was a hero because this town hated Virgil Weaver! But what happens? He speculates in the stock market. And Lord, he's rich as . . . as . . . hell, I don't know what. I don't want to talk about Virgil Weaver."

"You were speaking of Cuba," I said.

"Yes, Cuba," he said. "I thought if they turned me loose down there in Cuba, I'd be a general in two weeks. I can lead men! I know I can lead men. I could have led them like Teddy Roosevelt. I could have led them like Robert E. Lee. I had it in me; I've got it in me now."

He paused again, breathing hard, his eyes beyond me. "But my company and me, we landed down there on the tip of Cuba, and they came down with the yellow fever. They couldn't fight. I knew it was going to be over soon, and my men couldn't fight. You can't lead men if they can't follow. I thought the whole bunch was pretending. I thought they was afraid. Then they started to die."

I listened while the roar of the wheel foundry went on like the chant of a dark god. Pinkerton put his hand to his head to emphasize the heat, the terrible heat in Cuba that broke him out in a gluelike sweat and clung to him until he thought he would choke. He could not escape it, could find no shade to protect him during the day; and when night fell, the heat went on, and the wind blowing off the sea was hot and stank of rotting fish.

He developed an excruciating rash. He clawed it until the blood came. The rash became infected and ran with pus. Pus ran down his back, and he could not wear his heavy shirt with its captain's bars. He went naked from the waist up. Without the symbol of his rank, he did not feel like a captain. "I felt like a nigger pushing a wheelbarrow," he said. "I felt so goddamned helpless."

It rained every afternoon. He remembered the tropical rains thundering down on the tents and how the tents leaked and how the water ran in greasy streamlets onto the beds. He remembered boys who had toiled with him in the swamp, boys who had marched in the courthouse square in Bourbonville before they took the train south and all the county turned out to cheer. Sons of rebels, sons of Union men put the county back together after their fathers had torn it apart. Pinkerton imagined he was helping build a country anew as he had built the car works. His men would get glory; the greatest glory would belong to him. "Tell you what I thought! I thought there'd be a statue of me in the square one of these days." But when the yellow fever came on his men, they vomited syrupy black blood and turned yellow and lay in their cots glassy-eyed and motionless until they died like flames turned down.

The corridors between the cots stank of excrement and vomit, sweat, urine, and iodine. The flies were everywhere. So were mosquitoes. A doctor said he thought you had yellow fever wherever you had mosquitoes. His theory was still unproved, but Pinkerton believed it. No matter. The doctors were helpless. Some of them sank to their knees and died like the men. You heard a mosquito buzz, Pinkerton said, and you knew death was calling. He let the mosquitoes bite him. He looked at them standing on his skin, and he felt them draw blood. He saw them swell and swell until they were so full of his life that they could not fly away. He smashed them and saw his blood spurt out of their crushed bodies. He did not get sick. He did not die.

Finally he went berserk. The war had begun like the car works—men working together, men sweating together, singing, marching, loving each other, doing the job. Getting the job done. Now his men sat down and they could not get up again. They dropped their rifles in the mud and forgot them. Stretcher bearers picked the men up and lifted them roughly onto canvas cots. No one had time to be gentle. The men lay staring up at the canvas ceilings with listless eyes, and nobody sang.

He ran up and down the aisles between the beds screaming at them to get up. The voice was not his. It was the voice of his demon. He pulled men out of bed. He slapped them. He beat at them with his fists. He commanded them to rise, to charge the enemy with him, to be heroes, to trust him and to give him their hearts.

Doctors seized him, threw him down over a cot. Someone stuck a needle in his arm. The doctor was tired and frantic, and the needle slid in too far, and just before Pinkerton sank into blackness, he heard the tiny *tock* of the needle against bone.

He woke up strapped to a cot with leather belts. He could not scratch an itch or wipe himself. The doctors spoke to him soothingly, as if he had been a naughty child. He was ashamed, and he cried. They told him there was no reason to cry. The doctors went away, embarrassed by his tears.

Afterwards, Pinkerton and the survivors came home by train, winding slowly through the hot, pine barrens of Georgia in the broiling summer. The roadbed was rough. The train lurched along, and the windows of the flimsy wooden cars were all open. The hot summer air and the coal smoke from the locomotive blew in on him and blackened his face. He did not care. He could feel the rocking of the train like the rocking of that sea which rolls far down in things and finally takes them all away. He got sick and leaned out the window and vomited on the land rolling languidly by under the slow wheels of the wheeling train. No one spoke to him. He wiped his mouth with his sleeve, and the sleeve stank. People avoided him. No one looked at him. No one accused him.

His bosses in Washington were sympathetic. They gave him a month's continuance on his furlough for the war. He went over to Flat Rock, North Carolina, where an ebullient lawyer friend of his had a summer house on a little lake. The fish jumped and made rings that widened slowly in the still water. Sometimes he tried to count the rings. He always lost track.

He had his job. The railroad owed him that. "When I came back here, I joked about it," he said. "I said I lost my head. I said I'd done a fool thing. I told people I just wanted to be in it, you see. I guess I was sick, I said. Out of my head. I didn't realize how sick I was. I went around and apologized. I went to see the families of the dead ones. God amighty, that was hard! I didn't shirk anything. Some of them never forgave me.

"Virgil Weaver, he keeps it alive. He got to say 'I told you so.' The town hated him, you see; so he made sure that the town hated me, too. Fair exchange, you might say! Fact is, the town hates both of us. Ain't that something? It worked out so this little shithole of a town hates us both, and we hate each other. Things don't turn out like you think they will, do they?"

Talk was his consolation, and he talked to me, the stranger—endless, repetitious monologues spoken not just then but again and again. He wanted out of Bourbonville as a drowning man wants out of water. But he knew that there was a little tag by his name in the railroad's thick files up in Washington: "Pinkerton, Moreland J. Bourbonville, Tennessee. Manager of the Bourbonville Car Works. Unfortunate incident in Cuba." He knew that people looking over the files when they needed a man said, " 'Unfortunate incident'? What was that?" Always, he supposed, there was someone to tell the story—apologetically, of course, excusing him, telling with measured and sober praise of the fine work he had done in Bourbonville. But always someone would say in a final sort of way, "Oh well, we can't risk it happening again. There are other men." He imagined the scene as vividly as if he remembered it.

"You know what they say?" he said. "When somebody steps on your grave, on the ground where you're going to be buried, you feel a chill run down your back, and you shiver? Well, I feel like that when they're talking about me up there. I can see somebody open that damned file drawer, and I can see him take out my folder, and I can see all those sons of bitches standing around and looking at it, and I can hear their fucking snobby voices, and when they put the folder up and shut the file drawer, I can't hardly breathe. I feel that drawer shutting up on *me*. That's what it feels like—like I'm in there, and I can't do anything about it, and I feel the air get thick, and I see the dark. That's the worst thing. I see the dark inside that drawer, and I feel the papers shut down on me, and it's like being buried alive. I can't breathe. I can't breathe."

11

I BATTLED my own despair. At meals in the boardinghouse I nibbled at my food while around me a clatter of talk and laughter went on. People talked at me. Dale Farmer, the portly accountant at the car works, a vaguely effeminate man with a forced manner of speaking and an officious, mocking grin and a bad word to say about everybody.

DeShane Dugan, foreman of the wheel foundry. His room was filled with potted plants, which he watered conscientiously, and he gardened out back—tomatoes and cucumbers, flowers and bushes, and in the wintertime he read seed catalogues and talked about hybrids and Luther Burbank. He had a few acres in the country, and on weekends he went out there and puttered in his greenhouse or, in warm weather, in his gardens.

Ted Devlin, editor of the *Bourbonville News,* the paper that came out on Mondays and Thursdays—nights when he was always late for dinner. He filled its columns with the boosting of Bourbonville and small-town American life and the Garden Club and the Clionian Women's Club and the local high school and the achievements of its students, who were going to make Bourbonville proud of them, and the social news from the little communities in the country gathered around their forlorn little churches—Paw Paw Plains, New Providence, and Browders, and Varner's Cross Roads, and Martel. He chain-smoked, and he could talk about anything. "What the hell can I do?" he asked me once. "If I don't brag on the goddamned place, these stupid assholes won't buy my newspapers."

He was friendly in a boisterous, male way, but no one knew him very well. He wore bay rum shaving lotion, and beneath the smell of the lotion one could smell Bourbon whiskey. He conveyed a cynical face to everyone, mocking Dale Farmer sometimes, taking the opposite of whatever was the prevailing view at the table. He asked me one day if I believed in God. I thought for a moment that the question was frivolous, but then I saw the deep seriousness in his eyes, and I faltered. "I'm always wondering if there's anything to it," he said. His thoughts seemed to drift away as if he was embarrassed by them. His wife had died four years before; he did not have time to cook for himself, and he had moved into the boardinghouse. He rented his house out. It was up in the country. "I'll move back in when I quit this goddamned piss-ant paper," he said. He missed his wife.

The other men at the boardinghouse were bachelors. Six of us in all. Jack Robinette was foreman of the carpenters who built the boxcars. A tall, quiet man with watery blue eyes, he kept to himself most of the time, reading the papers and the *Literary Digest* and sometimes staring off into space as if his mind were a million miles away. W. D. Boling, whom everybody called "Dub," was the stationmaster of the depot and the daytime telegrapher— not the night man I had seen on my arrival. He was a dignified man who pretended to know all the secrets of the line because he understood the code that none of the rest of us knew. He was never surprised, and his favorite expression was "I could have told you that." Henry Morgan was foreman of the pattern shop, in charge of making the oak patterns that, pressed into the damp sand, made the molds for the iron and the steel and the brass. He loved to dog Dub Boling. "If you knew that all along, why didn't you tell us?"

"I know how to keep a secret," Dub Boling would say, nodding his head solemnly. "I don't have time to tell everything I know. I'd never get anything else done."

Seven men, and Darcy Coolidge presided over our long table. A black woman named Lucy helped cook and serve. She lived in Bucktown and walked to the boardinghouse before first light and walked home alone every night after she washed the dishes. She was strong and voluptuous, with broad hips and plump breasts and skin as sleek as black ivory. She seldom spoke in our presence, and she carried herself in aloof and sullen dignity. Darcy Coolidge confided that she paid Lucy ten cents an hour. "She can't say I'm not good to her."

Bourbonvillians were proud of themselves because of Lucy. She was in town after sundown, when blacks by law were not allowed to appear in the streets. No one gave her any grief. She was going home, minding her own business, and people in the village said it was just fine for her to do that as long as she moved along smartly and got out of town as fast as she could.

We had a sitting room with rocking chairs and easy chairs and two sofas and tables and lamps, and after supper the men sat around reading the papers or playing dominoes or talking. Darcy Coolidge sat with us for a little while, retiring promptly when the tall clock in the corner struck eight. Her departure was the signal that we could smoke.

There was an old upright piano in the sitting room. Often at night someone would call for a song from Darcy Coolidge, and she—protesting and red-faced—would say, "Well, just one, if Mr. Farmer will be so kind as to play." Dale Farmer gallantly stepped to the piano, seated himself with a little bow, and ran his plump fingers over the keys. He played astonishingly well. Darcy Coolidge stood beside him, folded her hands in front of herself, and sang, her voice quavering and ascending through the house and bringing into our midst in a domesticated fashion the primordial sadness of humankind. Her false teeth clicked faintly, but she had a sweet voice that must have been beautiful once. She sang songs like "Annie Laurie" and "Thou Wilt Come No More, Gentle Annie" and "Jeannie with the Light

Brown Hair." She reminded me of Stephanos, and I listened with the melancholy that is not stranger to peace.

I had nothing to say, and when they tried to have conversations with me, I did poorly. They talked about my accent. They wanted to know about my past. They asked me questions, endless questions, and I told them as little as I could, often nothing. My presence at first created interest, then discomfort. I fell into the habit of excusing myself as soon as Darcy Coolidge withdrew and often earlier. I went to my room feeling the relief of one who has discharged an obligation. I could sit there and talk softly to Bernal and to Guy, and we could look out over the little town. I have some photographs of me from that period, taken by Darcy Coolidge with her little Kodak, and they show an emaciated young man with sunken eyes and a solemn expression. "Smile, Mr. Alexander. Can't you give me just a little smile?" I look at the photographs and hear her voice and remember the bright sun in my eyes as we stood in front of the boardinghouse while she fondled her camera as Guy once fondled his pigeons. I am of middle height, and I look stiff and uncomfortable.

Darcy Coolidge took me to church one Sunday. Trinity Methodist—the Southern Methodist church. I told her I was Catholic, but she said I could at least *visit* her church. I think she wanted me to be so overwhelmed by the wisdom of her young minister that I would be converted. His name was Ware, and he was the leader of the Prohibition Party in that part of Tennessee. The Sunday I went, men in cheap suits at the door handed out little tin American flags to affix to our lapels, and Mr. Ware preached on how noble the war was and said that people who opposed the war should be put in jail. America was fighting for temperance, he said, by which he meant prohibition, and after good American boys had won the victory, they would demand the prohibition of alcohol throughout all Europe as we soon would ban it in this country by constitutional amendment. The French would drink milk and water; the Germans would break up their beer barrels; and the world would turn to Jesus. All around me people nodded solemnly, and I thought of how smug they looked, how ignorant, how clean—and how horrified they would be if someone machine-gunned Mr. Ware in front of their eyes and they should see his body almost cut in two and the scarlet blood gushing from him in torrents. The human body contains a great deal of blood. All these people supposed that war was a very fine thing, and Mr. Ware looked valiant and as heroic as the wooden Indian that stood in front of the drugstore that sold tobacco on Broadway in Bourbonville.

I was asked to stand up because I was a wounded veteran, and people applauded, and Darcy Coolidge glowed, and she was disappointed when I would not go with her again. "Mr. Alexander, *everybody* in Bourbonville goes to church somewhere," she said. I pointed out that there was no Catholic church. She did not know how to respond. "He is Catholic, but he's nice anyway," I heard her say one time to a visitor.

The last time I had been inside a church was when we fell back on Louvain before the Germans. We had lost our cannon. A Flemish sergeant gave us rifles.

The Belgian Army fought in lines and retreated in steps. A front line held the Germans as long as possible while another line formed a mile or so behind. The front line retreated through the rear line and formed another behind it. So we fell back towards Antwerp.

A single bullet killed our friend Huys. It made a hole the size of a fist in his chest. We saw his shattered heart, the gray tissue of his lungs. He was Flemish, too—shy, willing, and friendly. He felt proud to fight alongside university students, although he scarcely understood our French. He drove the mules because he was a peasant. Guy would not leave his body behind. He carried it, slung over his back like a sack of potatoes. "He was one of us," Guy said. "The Germans will desecrate his body." Huys's blood soaked the back of Guy's shirt.

We came upon an ancient church in a small town. The church was stone and cool and dark. It was now hospital and morgue. I do not remember what town it was. A makeshift white flag flew above the single Gothic steeple. We arrived at twilight. Behind us the thudding of the guns went on. In my war we never had silence, and to this day my sweetest moments are like this, when I sit in almost perfect stillness and the droning of a truck rolling on the highway makes the quiet all the more profound when it is gone. We went in the big open door under the tower, walking under a primitive carved Judgment of Christ, his hands uplifted over the damned and the redeemed, an expression of extreme detachment on his stone face, and we came into the melancholy gloom shed by the Gothic arches high above.

The wounded and the dead were laid out in rows on the stone floor. Frantic doctors and nurses ministered to them with a subdued murmuring. The doctors and the nurses were dressed in white and wore red crosses on their arms, and they were filthy with gore. Men groaned—an irregular, harsh chorus of pain—and some wept softly. Some were screaming. The sounds rose and tumbled against one another and reverberated off the impervious stone. The interior of the church seemed to be a gathering point for the misery of the universe.

One blank-faced priest wandered aimlessly up and down, chanting a mindless miserere. That sound rose somehow above the groaning and the weeping and the screaming and made a dismal threnody in the dusk. Finding a place, Guy laid Huys gently down, and we stood for a moment to ask for the priest's blessing. We took off our dark cloth hats and bowed. The priest blessed us absentmindedly, not ceasing his baffled litany.

The heat was abominable, and the fetid air was close. We stank, and our clothes clung to us and rubbed us raw, and on Guy's back spread the dark stain of the blood of our comrade. The priest was sweating as profusely as we were; his stench was rank in his woolen gown. It was hard to breathe, and I craved the open air. Guy said, "We must go, Father. The Germans are only a half hour behind us. Be well."

The priest went on chanting, and we walked out into the gathering night where the guns were louder, where a red glow burned in the darkening eastern sky, and we fell in with the file of beaten troops shuffling in mortal fatigue towards the rear.

In my room I talked about those days. The shades of my friends listened and spoke to me. We were very quiet. Sometimes I begged them to tell me how they had died. Then they were mute, gazing at me with silent and moody reproach.

Because of Guy and Bernal, I met Virgil Weaver.

12

FROM MY ROOM I could see the rooftops of the houses and the shallow valley floor where the railroad tracks gleamed in moonshine when the moon was full. Beyond, the river showed silver in the night, and beyond it the wild land ran to the mountains, black against the starry sky.

Then it seemed that I could see every detail of Bernal's room high on the fourth floor of the Institute St. Valéry in Ghent, and I could imagine his hard, narrow bed in the corner and the simple wooden chairs and the hideous crucifix with its tormented and bloody Jesus in agony on the wall over the foot of the bed so that it was the first thing Bernal saw when he awoke in the morning.

We sat there on many a night when we came in from the tavern, and we looked down on the cobblestoned streets where the yellow trams clanked by. I remembered how the snows fell in winter sometimes and how the workmen came out sweeping and shoveling the snow away from the tracks, their breath steaming in the soft light of the gas lamps along the sidewalks, the trams rolling by at last, lights flashing against the profound and radiant white, noise muffled by the blanket of snow.

We drank wine. We smoked. We talked. Guy was going to marry Leonora because she had tricked him. "It was her breasts," he said, his voice full of woe. "I dangled the promise of marriage before her because she dangled her breasts before me. I never once dreamed that she would take me seriously."

"Women take promises seriously," Bernal said. "In all countries and among all peoples, the sacred quality of a promise is fully recognized. Promises belong to the natural law. You have fondled the breasts and done more besides; now the natural law requires you to marry the woman."

"Ah, but you do not understand that Leonora is indissolubly *attached* to those breasts," Guy said in exasperation. "Could I but enjoy them in detachment, I should imagine nothing more pleasant. Could I keep those breasts in a drawer with my underwear and my stockings and my tennis racket, I should love them forever. But attached to the breasts is a woman I now detest. A woman who tells me constantly that she adores me, that she has sacrificed to me her most special and irretrievable treasure—her sacred virginity. She will cherish me forever, she says. And while she cherishes me forever, she expects to inherit our house in Dinant and to furnish it with those absurd paintings she adores and that I abhor—those Cézannes, those Renoirs."

"Virginity is a treasure," Bernal said gravely. "It is so recognized by all the fathers of the church, and the greatest of the saints have been virgins." Bernal believed the stories of the saints.

Guy waved him off. "I will admit that virginity is a treasure," he said. "But I pose a question and demand a true answer. Do *you* think that Leonora was a virgin when I penetrated her exquisite little temple for the first time? Do *you* believe that I was the culprit who robbed her of this inexpressible prize?"

We found the question difficult.

On the day we went to war, we formed at the barracks in response to the herald who came through the streets ringing his bell and reading the proclamation of mobilization on every corner. We marched to the railroad station in our dark blue uniforms, supposing that we looked brave and gallant. The people of Ghent packed the streets, filled the windows above us, cheering, waving flags, drunk with war, blissful at the release of something terrible. The regimental drums pounded. We put our feet down and the earth trembled. A roar of singing filled the air—the Belgian national anthem, the "Marseillaise," even "God Save the King."

Near the university Leonora rushed out of the throng, screaming and flinging herself on Guy. She embraced him, clung to him, kissed him, ran her hands over him until she was pulled off by two policemen. They tried to console her as they led her away. We could hear her keening long after we could no longer see her.

Guy was mortified, and we laughed at him. Leonora was the wise one. She knew what none of us could suspect even then: that the war would destroy the architecture of a predictable life where one might plan and toil with methodical care to build a future. Nothing worked out the way we thought it would. Everything turned out to be different. Now in Bourbonville, we did not talk about America or of this untidy town or of the river we could see from my room, running in its wide valley and sometimes reflecting the moon. We talked about the strangeness of our lost life in Belgium, how ordinary it had been, how sweet and how dear. One night Darcy Coolidge heard us.

13

AN UNSEASONABLE STORM led to her discovery. It burst in after a warm Indian-summer day. I sat at midnight by my open window and sniffed the dank smell of rain and heard the rattle of thunder and saw the lightning dancing beyond the river. Black clouds roiled overhead, and the storm burst with a fury that shook the world.

The wind shrieked around the house. Guy, Bernal, and I talked with each other, not in our usual whispers but—because of the storm—in our normal voices, though we were very quiet. The tempest raged as if a great hole had been torn in the sky, sucking the world into itself. About two in the morning, the lightning and thunder retreated, leaving only the sound of the cascading rain.

I do not know if I was aware that the lightning had knocked out the electric power in Bourbonville. I did not know then that Darcy Coolidge was also an insomniac, that she lay awake worrying about herself and calling up, in her fashion, her own ghosts from the past. Bits of her story came to me later, on cold Saturday afternoons when she did me the special honor of having me to tea in her private sitting room because she thought I was dying and needed her motherly attentions.

She had been a plain girl, she told me, born and brought up in Knoxville, only daughter of a real estate speculator and agent who lived on the expansion of the city after the Civil War. Her father drove fine horses and spent lavishly—so his daughter was desirable despite her plainness. Young men courted her. "None of them liked me for myself," she said. "They made no bones about it. They acted like somebody as ugly as I was ought to be glad to marry any of them. One of my girlfriends told me they made jokes about me. I never let on that it mattered, but it hurt, I can tell you that."

Perhaps the worst of it was that she, too, believed that her father was wealthy, that she would have a fortune, and that married or not she could be an independent woman.

The Colonel turned up, an older man down on some obscure business that kept him in Knoxville for weeks. He brought a proper letter of introduction to someone. He was invited to dinners and to parties in the great houses with columns overlooking the river on the eastern edge of town. He could quote Milton and Shakespeare and Tennyson. He spoke with a rich Virginia accent. He said "hoose" for "house" and "aboot" for "about." He bowed and kissed the hands of the ladies, and he spoke modestly now and then of having been in the war with General Lee, and though he smiled, he never laughed. He disliked speaking of the war, he said softly, because his side had lost, and with defeat, the chance had gone out of the world for the society where a man like himself could feel at home. There was also about him an aura of tragic memory and heroic loss. To see him standing tall in his fine gray coat, surrounded by people who talked more than he did, was to hear the trumpets summoning brave men to die in a noble cause now perished from the earth.

I knew him only by the portrait photograph that hung in Darcy Coolidge's sitting room. He had a fine look—slender, a long head, piercing eyes above his high, stiff collar. His mouth was firm and straight under a white mustache. He looked aristocratic, gravely dignified. Many times when I paused alone in that room on a lazy Sunday afternoon when a Sabbath calm hung over the house like the odor of cut flowers at a funeral, I looked at the portrait and supposed that had Guy grown old, he would have resembled this Colonel.

"He said he never wanted to know anything about my money," Darcy Coolidge told me. "He seemed to be the only man I ever knew who stood above pecuniary considerations."

Her father offered to talk to him about money. The Colonel refused. It had never been the part of his family, he said, to barter for its women. He stressed the word "family." He said he was marrying Darcy MacIntosh (her maiden name) because her company alone was sufficient to make his life complete.

The Colonel's reluctance to talk about money meant that he did not talk about his own. Occasionally he let slip some casual remark, as modest as his rare recollections of battle, that allowed people to know he was well fixed. In his splendid gray suits and neatly brushed gray coats, he gave an impression of comfortable wealth. They were married, and soon afterwards Darcy Coolidge's father died of an apoplexy. Everyone was astonished at how little money was left to the estate once his debts were paid. Darcy Coolidge thought it did not matter. She had the Colonel. Husbands were supposed to support their wives. He never reproached her father—"not with a single word," she said. He did say that he felt the man might have been remembered more happily if he had kept control over his accounts and lived within his means—a reserved remark (so Darcy Coolidge told me) uttered in sorrow and not in recrimination.

He confided that his own money was tied up in trust. He said he had a strong aversion to spending capital. He thought they should try to get along on the small sum bequeathed to her by her father. "My ancestry is Scots," he said in his mellow, Virginia voice. "I believe we can live well if we are thrifty. My dear, when I die, you will be rich. I will not tell you how much you will inherit because you would not believe it." He mentioned his will and tapped his coat as if the will reposed in an inside pocket. He spoke of it as if it were a sacred text inspired by a spirit even more noble than his own.

Darcy Coolidge disagreed with the Colonel's perception of the world. "There's more of my daddy in me than you may think," she said, nodding vigorously to me over her delicate cup. "I believe if you have it, spend it. Life's short. I wanted to see Paris, Rome, London, New York, all those foreign places. Do you know what I like to read? Books about travel, books about little out-of-the way places by the blue sea where you can look out and see sailboats. If I hadn't married the Colonel, I might have gone to the mission field. I mean, I didn't have the call; but I sure did like to travel, and that's half of being a missionary, if you ask me. If I had to preach a little to the heathen to pay my way, I was ready to pitch in, just as long as I got to go somewhere."

She could not contradict the Colonel. "I loved him, you see." Her eyes glistened. "After the shock of finding out just how poor my daddy was, I didn't believe I had any brains. I mean, how could I have any brains being the daughter of a man like that? I figured the Colonel was protecting me from myself."

It was not moral to spend money when a spouse—particularly a male spouse—wanted to save. The Colonel heard of the building of the car works. "The people there will need a boardinghouse," he said. "We could make it like a mountain inn I once visited in the Alps."

"I don't reckon it has ever looked like what he wanted it to look like," she said. "One of those mountain inns. But we did all right with it. We made a living out of it."

Darcy Coolidge vowed that her success came because the Colonel had such good business sense. "He gave such a fine tone to things," she said.

The Colonel told Darcy Coolidge that he would die before she did, and he did. "I trust you will grieve for me, my dear. But I trust also that when you read my will, a slight smile of love and satisfaction will crease your beloved face."

But where was the will? As he lay dying, she asked him that question tentatively, reluctantly. It was always bad taste to inquire about money, she said. "I never let people stay in my boardinghouse after I have to ask them the second time about the rent. And on his deathbed. I tell you, it seemed barbaric to mention it." It was not, she told me, the money in itself, although she admitted that the money was important. "I didn't want it to go to waste," she said. "If I didn't get what was my due, it was going to sit in some bank somewhere and pay interest to a bunch of bankers who were not even my kinfolks. They were going to be steaming back and forth from New York to Paris on those big steamboats, and I was going to be stuck here in Bourbonville when I could be going first class. It wasn't right!"

She bent over his bed and asked the Colonel about his will. At the mention of the word "will," he said something long and complicated, something mixed with his struggle for breath and his desire to speak. "What?" she cried. "What?" With a furious look of desire and effort, he said, "The money! The money! It's . . ." He fell back on his pillow and died with the location of the will gargling in his throat, his eyes open to the ceiling and glazing over with the film of death.

Darcy Coolidge could not find the will anywhere. Nor could she discover any trace of the Colonel's past. She could not recall who had written the letter to introduce him to Knoxville society. She could not reconstruct the means by which the Colonel had appeared at the party where she met him. When she inquired of those families who had had the Colonel to dinner in their fine homes, they told her either that they could not remember how they had become acquainted with him or else that her father had made the introductions because he knew that the Colonel would be a good catch. The Colonel was reticent about his family. "We came to a parting of the ways," he said without explanation.

"He seemed so sad when he mentioned his family, I just never could make myself force any more out of him," she told me.

Perhaps worse was her inability to find any mention of him in what records existed of the Army of Northern Virginia. There were Coolidges, but no Colonel Henry Cushman Coolidge IV, as he styled himself. "I thought I might get a pension from the State of Virginia," she said. "Maybe if I could find his army records, I might have had a clue to find out more about him."

There was nothing. She wrote to former comrades of General Lee. "He so often said he was standing next to Lee on the afternoon of the third day at Gettysburg," she said. "He said Lee turned to him when Pickett's Charge failed and said, 'It's all my fault! It's all my fault!' " Most men who had been near Lee that day were dead. The few survivors could tell her nothing. No one remembered the Colonel. No one had heard of him. Jubal Early wrote with regret, saying he knew the Colonel must have been a noble Confederate soldier, but perhaps he had exaggerated. Darcy Coolidge tore up his letter in anger. "Jubal Early might have been General Lee's friend," she said, "but I don't have any use for him."

She lay awake at night thinking about the Colonel. She went back over all his conversations, trying with all her might to remember something that she might have forgotten, something to reveal the secrets that had clanged shut in front of her with his death.

Perhaps he deceived her and everybody else from the beginning? I phrase the question as Darcy Coolidge phrased it to me, so tentatively that it was scarcely a thought. She trusted me. She wanted me to make some thunder-ous affirmation of the Colonel's honor since she took me to be one of his advocates, assuming—as so many did in Bourbonville—that since I was a foreigner, I brought a dispassionate wisdom to every problem. "The Colonel hated foreigners," she confided to me. "That was because he did not know any foreigners. He would have loved you, my dear Paul. And how you would have admired him! Both of you military men! You would have got on so well together! The Colonel could have explained your war to you. He read a lot. I've never seen a man read so much. He read all the memoirs of the generals he had known in the war. He used to tell me how this one was right and this one was wrong."

14

THE STORM blew itself out. The thunder and lightning receded, and I watched the rain pour down in the darkness, making the few lights of the town dance in a watery glow. I talked with Guy and Bernal about the rains during the retreat and the mud and how it came up above our ankles and pulled our shoes off our feet. We had heavy high-topped shoes, the kind peasants wore.

Darcy Coolidge heard my voice. At first she thought it a murmuring of the wind. Very slowly she picked it out for what it was. She looked at the radium dial on her clock and saw that it was past two in the morning. She was at first indignant that anyone would be up at that hour, having a conversation. Then (as she told Dr. Youngblood later on), she thought it might be a ghost. When Dr. Youngblood repeated this remark to me, chuckling around the stem of his pipe, I wanted to tell him that the house was filled with ghosts. If Darcy Coolidge had spoken to the Colonel, he would have spoken back.

She got up and pushed the light switch. Nothing happened. The power had been knocked out by the storm. She lit a candle. "She told me that the shadows of things looked alive when she struck the match, and suddenly she was afraid of her own room," Dr. Youngblood said in a ruminating way, as if it were not terribly important. "I've known that sort of fear—in my prac-tice, I mean—the terror of the familiar. It comes on lots of people who never say anything about it. Did you ever know anybody with it?"

"No," I said.

"Hah," Dr. Youngblood said thoughtfully. "Well, maybe you are not old enough."

She crept out of the bedroom and advanced through the empty darkness to the stairway. I can imagine her there, gripping her long night-robe around her, head cocked, listening to the irregular chorus of snoring from the rooms of her boarders and hearing the rain and the voice underneath it all, a voice in conversation, speaking a strange language (Guy, Bernal, and I spoke French together), although the voice was so low that she knew its strangeness not by hearing the words but by some unfathomable intuition. Clutching her candle, walking through the spurting shadows, she came stealthily and in terror to my door and knocked.

I was as terrified as she. I heard Guy whisper, "You must not let her stop you from talking with us." He told me that when I stopped talking with them, they would vanish from the earth. Bernal, bathed in a light only slightly less somber than the dark, looked sadly at me, and I imagined the dismal realm of the shades where the father of Odysseus waited to speak with his son.

"Mr. Alexander," Darcy Coolidge whispered urgently. "I know you're in there! Let me in at once."

I opened the door. She stood clutching her robe around her, the candle uplifted. The flame from the candle made her face ghastly. She had not put in her false teeth. Her mouth looked soft and old.

She pushed by me without a word, holding her candle aloft. She looked all around, seeing no one but me, no motion except the waving shadows and the faint reflection of the candle's yellow flame in the window glass, a reflection as liquid and unstable as the rain outside. She went to the closet and looked in and came back to me.

I was fully dressed. My chair stood alone at the window. She saw that I was the only living soul in the room. She lifted the candle to my face and stared at me, her eyes narrowing as she strained with all her might to understand. The candle threw shadows onto her face and showed the skull under her skin and made her look like one of the Furies. She was frightened out of her wits.

I waited for some question. Nothing. She stared at me, her soft mouth partly open, her eyes widening, narrowing, widening again. Then she turned abruptly and left, leaving the door for me to shut. I heard her slippered feet fleeing down the hallway and down the stairs. Never as long as I lived in her house did she speak to me of the incident.

That was not the end of it. She made her way the next morning to the office of Curtis Youngblood, M.D., and she told him everything. He told me about her visit, his voice deliberately amused to put me at ease.

I can yet imagine Dr. Youngblood, his white smock buttoned over his ample belly, puffing on his pipe, listening, nodding his balding head in the patient nonchalance that I have seen so many times. He was never shocked, seldom surprised. He heard Darcy Coolidge out and said at last, "Darcy, there's no law on the books that says a man can't talk to himself if he wants to."

"He's crazy. He killed people in the war. You never know if he's going to rise up in the middle of the night and murder all of us in our beds."

"How many old folks from the Civil War go around killing people in their beds?" Dr. Youngblood asked.

"There was Mr. Simson," Darcy Coolidge said. Mr. Simson had been a farmer in the county who, years before, had murdered his wife in her bed. He was hanged in the courthouse yard. It happened five years before Pinkerton built the car works, six years before Darcy Coolidge moved to Bourbonville, ten years before Curtis Youngblood arrived. It had passed into the collective memory of the county. Those who had not been born then believed they had seen it all. Darcy Coolidge called up the spectre of Mr. Simson as if she had known him and his wife, witnessed the murder, and seen the vengeance of the law.

The mention of Mr. Simson was sufficient. On the next Saturday afternoon, Dr. Youngblood appeared at the boardinghouse as though on a casual visit to inquire after my health. Just as casually he invited me to take a drive with him and to have supper with him that evening. I did not want to go.

"Oh, you just *must* go," Darcy Coolidge said, too sweetly. "You *need* to get out. You need to *meet* people. Dr. Youngblood so admires you. He's told me so himself. How *much* he wants to get acquainted with you! He is from Harvard, you know." Her teeth clicked softly. She smiled. Her eyes looked frantic. I knew she was saying this: "Dr. Youngblood must certify your sanity, young man, or I am not going to let you stay here one more week." I knew that if Darcy Coolidge made me leave her house, no one else would take me in. I went, and my friendship with Curtis Youngblood began.

He loved trains. We drove out on the Martel Pike alongside the railroad track. When train number 42, bound for Washington and New York out of New Orleans, pulled away from the Bourbonville station, we were waiting at the edge of town. For nearly four miles we sped along, abreast of the great locomotive, at times rolling upwards of fifty miles an hour, flinging rocks and dust up behind us and hurtling through the dun autumn landscape.

The engineer blew the whistle and waved. Dr. Youngblood, reaching out of the open Model T Ford, blew his horn by squeezing the rubber ball at its base. All the while he puffed his pipe and chuckled. I gathered that this was ritual, that the engineer and the fireman waving from the cab of the great steam engine knew him by habit if not by name. When the train left us behind, Dr. Youngblood subsided. The mirth drained from his ruddy face, replaced by something like sadness, and we drove slowly back to Bourbonville.

"Early tomorrow morning, before the sun is up, that train—those very cars—will stop in Baltimore," he said. Baltimore was his home. Forty-two's daily passage made him think he should go back where he belonged. "I will go back sometime," he said defiantly. His face mellowed, and he shook his head, as if he had forgotten about me. "But then who would take care of the county?"

He was a bachelor. He lived upstairs in a rambling frame house at the corner of First Avenue and Kingston Street just down the street from the boardinghouse. It was a comfortable place, built in no discernible style, featuring large windows and a verandah across the front and wrapped around one side. His office was on the first floor. These rooms smelled of disinfectant and medicines. The reek made me stop on the dark stairway leading to the second floor, remembering the hospital, listening instinctively for the groaning of the wounded. Silence. Utter silence, except for the faint sounds of a country town going to sleep early—a dog somewhere, a voice from far away, the whisper of tires on a dirt street. I saw Guy's face in the heavy gloom. He was jealous. Dr. Youngblood, leading the way, turned and asked, "Is something wrong?"

"No," I said.

The second floor of his house was his private museum. Civil War cavalry swords and Japanese ceremonial swords hung on the walls. Old photographs from Harvard hung in dark frames, looking out from a world of eternal obscurity. The Harvard baseball team of 1892 stood in a row, dressed in suits and bowler hats, young men with fierce black mustaches staring steel-still and gallant at the vanished camera lens, reminding me of the military photographs that we had made of ourselves in Belgium in the unreal July of 1914, when we tried to look eternally brave and chivalrous and sent the pictures off to our families to show them, I suppose, that the coming war had made us men.

There were darkening photographs of Harvard clubs with young men posing on steps rising to clubhouses. There was a fine old photograph of the Harvard Square with horses pulling dray wagons and a trolley in front of an exquisitely focused but nondescript building. In the hallway that led back to the kitchen hung a photograph of a voluptuous woman shockingly naked, turned slightly to one side so that a fleshy hip concealed her private parts, looking out with an untroubled expression. It was autographed, "To Curtis Youngblood from his friend, Little Egypt. St. Louis, 1904." He never explained how he got it or why she had signed it.

Over the large fireplace in his sitting room hung a handsome photograph that (I discovered later on when I knew American history better) represented General George Armstrong Custer, who had come to a bad end among the Indians in 1876. A rusting suit of armor stood in one corner, looking like a warrior in the shadows, arms slightly akimbo, watching us intently through the visor of his helmet. Dusty military helmets from various wars reposed on tables and lay in chairs. Other treasures, including books old and new, were heaped everywhere so that you had to move something before you could sit down.

It was a chilly day. He stirred up the coal fire in the grate, threw on more coal from a bucket, fixed ham sandwiches, poured wine, and sat us both down at his hearth. The wine was abominable. I expected Dr. Youngblood to make some apology for it, alleging the difficulties of the times—the war, prohibition in Tennessee. He drank contentedly as if it had been a fine Bordeaux, and he kept my glass full. After a while it did not matter that it was vile. I saw Bernal's yearning face loom out of the dimness and look at the wine.

"Darcy thinks you may be crazy," Dr. Youngblood said after a long time. "She says you talk to yourself in the middle of the night."

He told me the story of her anguished visit, slowly, often repeating himself, chuckling, dismissing her terror, explaining in detail the reference to Mr. Simson. I expected him to ask, "Do you talk to yourself? Are you crazy?" He did not.

We sat silently when he had finished. He charged another pipe, struck a match to it with preoccupied deliberation, and drew the tobacco alight. I smoked a cigarette. Cigarettes reminded me of Stephanos. Dr. Youngblood said, "I don't know why people get so upset when they hear somebody talking to himself. I talk to myself all the time.

"I go out and see somebody who's sick. I take down his symptoms—cough, no appetite, general weakness, something not right in the eyes, fever that comes and goes. I drive off, and I say to myself, 'Tuberculosis! It's got to be tuberculosis. What am I going to do? I must prevent him from giving it to somebody else in the house. Got to make him rest. Now the best thing he can do is go to a sanitarium. Up in the mountains somewhere. Good water. Fresh air. Rest for a year. Bed rest. Eat well. Let the body get strong enough to heal itself. But hell. He's poor as blue john milk from a starved cow. He can't even afford a train ticket to the sanitarium. So what do I do? Nobody can cure TB with a medicine. Not much of anything a doctor can do with medicine. You can vaccinate people if they'll let you. Keep people from getting sick. But we can't cure anybody once the sickness comes. Sometimes we can cut something off or out. We can't give them a medicine to make them well. You see a doctor giving nostrums to cure people, and you know he is a fraud. Might as well be out at the fairgrounds hawking tonic at a dollar a bottle.' "

I could not tell whether he was talking to himself or to me. "So I say to myself, I say, 'If there are children in the house, they ought to go live with somebody else.' But then I say, 'Hellfire, nobody in this goddamned county is going to send his children off to live somewhere else just because somebody in the house has a little cough.' Finally I say, 'Damn! We're going to have a family with chronic TB. There's not a thing in the world I can do about it.' I talk like that all the time. All the time. It doesn't do any good. It makes me *feel* better. It gets it out of my system. I do it when I'm alone. I reckon Darcy would think I was crazy, too, if she heard me." He laughed—a drawn-out chuckle of gentle mirth, uttered to the fire.

That was the end of any discussion with Dr. Youngblood about my talking in solitude in the middle of the night. By telling me of his experience, he gallantly relieved me of explaining my own. I am not sure to this day whether he believed they were really similar. To me they were as different as sanity and lunacy. That evening my fears sank peacefully into the fire, the wine, the gentle drone of Dr. Youngblood telling me about Bourbon County, weaving a spell.

The moon is full tonight. It casts a soft light over all the great world, and I hear the insects loud in the forest. I doubt that in the end my life means more to the universe than one of those katydids calling there, or if in the grand sweep of things, the years that I have lived count more than the summer that they flourish. Once that thought threw me into the pit. Now it is only a thought, and it carries something akin to the peace I felt with Dr. Youngblood and his wine on that first night when we sat together before his fire.

15

I BELIEVE it was that night that Dr. Youngblood told me how Bourbon County was divided between Moreland Pinkerton and Virgil Weaver. I heard the story again and again—as I heard everything in that place, where people fed on the repetition of incidents as if in telling things over and over they might find some meaning that made us more than insects.

"I try to mend things," Dr. Youngblood said. "When I was a little boy, I liked to glue broken dishes together. I kept my toys, and I glued *them* together when they got broken. When I broke something, I always fixed it. But those two men! They love to tear things apart. Virgil's my friend. Pinkerton . . . you never get to know Pinkerton. He doesn't entertain. He's married to a nutty wife. Religious fanatic, and she doesn't drink, and . . . Well, it's sad. She can't help . . . But it's a different story.

"It was the Spanish War. Virgil was a young lawyer—not twenty-five years old in 1898 when some damned thing blew up the battleship *Maine* in Havana harbor. He went to the university in Knoxville. His stepfather, old Brian Ledbetter—Brian's as proud of Virgil as if he'd been his own son—he made sure Virgil got an education. If it hadn't been for that good old man, Virgil would have been a farmer. His brother Gilly, too. I'll tell you about Gilly later. He's the engineer. Gilly's in India! Married to an English wife! He'd have been a farmer, too, if it hadn't been for the old man.

"Virgil went up to the University of Tennessee. Then he read law in Mr. Neal's office and passed the bar exam and came back here to practice.

"People say Virgil was religious when he was a child. I don't know about that. He doesn't talk to me about religion. Wait till Clyde comes home! That's another of Virgil's brothers. Lord, nobody talks about religion like Clyde does! . . . Anyway, something made Virgil moral. He is the most moral person I've ever known. He thinks about things. He makes up his mind. He's made a fortune in the stock market. He's a genius when it comes to thinking about the future, about business. It's all part of that *morality* of his. You work hard at what you're good at. Virgil's good at making money, and he makes money because he thinks that's what he's supposed to do. It's a sin if he doesn't make money. If you ask me. . . . But nobody asks me.

"Well, when the Spanish War started, Moreland Pinkerton raised his company. Just about every young man in the country but Virgil joined up. Pinkerton had bad blood with Brian Ledbetter. Brian took a shotgun to Pinkerton. Drove him off his place. I don't know if that's what started Virgil. Virgil thought that war—any war—was wrong, and he started making speeches against it. He told people that what they were doing was sinful, that America would not be America if it had an empire. Well, he was not the only person in the country to think so, but he was the only one in Bourbon County to speak out about it. Talk like that now, with this war, and that son of a bitch Woodrow Wilson will put you in jail. It wasn't that way then. Virgil got away with it.

"Now when you hear Virgil Weaver make a speech, you hear something grand. Go over to the courthouse when Virgil has a case he believes in. Sit there when somebody down at the car works has lost a thumb or an eye or a hand in an accident and sues the company, and Virgil's his lawyer.

"Anyway, the Spanish War came along, and Virgil made speeches against it. Back then, back in 1898, he was almost as good as he is now.

"One Saturday afternoon he made a speech down there in front of the courthouse. I never will forget it. He stood up on a stepladder and spoke to a square that was as packed as you'll ever see it in your life. I think people came to hear him because they could not believe that one of their own kind was against a war they loved like a pet mean dog. Moreland Pinkerton had his commission, and he drilled his troops in town in the morning, and Virgil Weaver put up posters to promise he would speak in the afternoon, and people came to hear him from three counties away. They came because they hated him because he was against the war they had all decided was *them.* The war was their child, their mirror of themselves, their estimate of their own nobility and their plain, dog-faced meanness. Virgil was against all that, and they despised him because they thought he despised them, and they thought he might be right.

"I'll tell you what I think. I think just because Virgil Weaver could make such a speech, he made people mad enough to kill him. I use the word 'mad' advisedly. He drove people crazy. They wanted the war. They wanted to stop being bored. They wanted something to cheer about. You live here long enough, and you find out that people in Bourbon County don't have much of anything to cheer about. It's a damn dull place. A dirt poor place. Look at all the people you see on the street with one eye or one hand or one leg or God knows what else missing. Look at their mouths. They don't have any teeth. They're poor folks. Look at the sunk-in chests of women who work in the cotton mill. They have TB. Give them a war, and you give them life.

"An American empire! That's something the poorest dirt farmer in a red-clay briar patch can cheer about. People wanted the flags waving and the guns booming and the drums beating. Hell, you know what I heard some of the rip-roaring Baptists say? They said they had to have revenge against the Spaniards because of the Armada! I'm not joking. They talked like the Spanish Armada was day before yesterday and that if you let the Spanish stay in Cuba one more year you'd have the Pope sitting in the White House and burning good Baptists at the stake in the courthouse square and closing down the public schools. Hell, a Baptist is too goddamned *wet* to burn, and if the Baptists did burn, they're so dumb they wouldn't give off any light. They lusted after the war; they hungered and thirsted for the war.

"And there was young Virgil Weaver standing up on a stepladder with that big strong voice of his, and he picked apart the rationale for the war the way you see a child pull the petals off a daisy. Maybe the metaphor is wrong. Maybe Virgil was like a child pulling legs off a spider or feathers out of a live chicken. Anyway . . . Virgil took on the announced war aims, and he made President William McKinley, the Congress of the United States, the United States Army, and the United States Navy look like a bunch of brown bandits with towels around their heads and knives in their teeth and pistols in their hands and rings in their noses.

"What could the good people of Bourbon County do? They couldn't *argue* against Virgil Weaver. For them to argue against Virgil Weaver was like setting up those little wooden Spanish boats in front of the guns of Admiral Dewey's fleet later on in Manila Bay. So they hated Virgil Weaver the way people can hate their own when they realize all of a sudden that their own are not like them anymore. That's hatred, my friend. That's what this town can do. This quiet little country town can hate you like fire hates a barn."

We sat without speaking in the great silence of a November Saturday night in Bourbonville, Tennessee, in the dark chill of early evening, this remote county surrounding us, cupping us, holding us, and I remember the patient ticking of the clock in the corner, a ticking that went indifferently on and on, telling us that time would tick like that through any of the horrors that we could devise for ourselves and would go on marching solemnly away even when all the clocks were dust. Dr. Youngblood replenished the fire, and he replenished my glass. I felt a warm disinterest, and to one side I saw Guy and Bernal sitting together, hands quietly on their knees, watching me, their faces as calm as the incised faces of the gods on the ancient pottery that I saw in the museum in Athens when I was a child.

"I remember it like yesterday," Dr. Youngblood resumed. "April 1898, and Virgil was up on that goddamned stepladder speaking, and that ugly crowd. You could feel the violence in the air like the electricity you feel in a summer storm. You walk, and it crackles. You bend your arm, and the sparks fly off your fingers. Then there was a murmuring, a whispering, and then something louder, and people were shouting, and somebody yelled, 'Let's get him, by God. Let's hang him!' And all those people pushed forward. They were one thing, one huge beast pushing forward to pull him off that ladder, and I thought to myself, 'It's over, by God. You have been in the South for two months, and you are going to see a man lynched.'

"But then Hub Delaney made his move. Hub was sheriff then, and he was Brian Ledbetter's best friend. He is still Brian Ledbetter's best friend. He was standing not ten feet away from Virgil. He was leaning up against the courthouse wall with his hat pulled down over his face like he wasn't even listening to what Virgil was saying. When the crowd started forward, that hat went up, and his pistol came out of his holster. A great big old U.S. Navy five-shot revolver, and he fired it two quick times in the air! Bang! Bang! That pistol sounded like a cannon. And the crowd stopped, and Hub moved over to Virgil, holding that pistol in front of him, sticking it in stomachs, pushing people back, and when the ones in front went back, the ones behind had to go back, too. I was standing on the porch of a store down there, and I could see that crowd back up like an animal with two thousand, three thousand legs, back and back, and down there was Hub Delaney coming to Virgil with his pistol swinging back and forth, back and forth, and the crowd moving back and back, and Virgil rubbing his face where somebody had hit him, Virgil just standing there looking bewildered, maybe scared.

"They could have piled all over Hub. They could have killed him like they wanted to kill Virgil. But Hub would have shot three of them dead first, and they all knew it. Bang, bang, bang, and three of them would have been worm food, and nobody wanted to be a martyr to America in the courthouse square of Bourbonville, Tennessee.

"Hub walked up to Virgil, still swinging that pistol, looking those sons of bitches in the eye, and he spoke very gently, and he said, 'Son, you better come along with me.' Virgil went. He knew what Hub knew, what I knew, that if he stayed there, he was a dead man. He told me once that was his big mistake—letting Hub take him off like that. 'I acted like a coward,' he told me. 'I should have died then.'

"Now for about six months, Virgil Weaver was the most hated man in Bourbon County. He never has got over that. He remembers every face in the crowd. Get him a little drunk—and you have to work like hell to do that, because he is not a drinking man—but get him just a little drunk, and he can start calling off names. You can see what I mean when I say Virgil is a *moral* man, not necessarily a *good* man, and the trouble with a moral man is that he doesn't forget anything. In particular he does not forget the people who are *immoral.*"

The fire made a crackling noise, licking at the coal in the grate. It was the only illumination in the room. Outside, it had grown very dark, and Dr. Youngblood had not lit a lamp. The light from the fire seemed to soak into the wine bottle, which gave it off again in a scarlet glow, and Guy—who would never taste wine again—looked at it with a yearning that, in my inebriated condition, threatened to make me weep with hopelessness and grief. I averted my eyes and saw Bernal standing to one side in a corner of the room where the shadows fell so dark that the walls were scarcely visible, and he murmured, "How strange! These people in this remote little place have their history!"

Bernal spoke so distinctly that his quiet voice seemed to shout in the room. I looked at Dr. Youngblood, sure that he had heard. He made no sign.

"Then Pinkerton's company got the yellow fever, and we heard that Pinkerton had gone crazy. Slapped some dying boys, people said. They had to strap him to a bed. Complete nervous breakdown, people said. That was the end of Moreland Pinkerton in Bourbonville. His glow went out like he'd been dipped in a pond. When he came home, he didn't give off fire anymore. People did not hate Pinkerton. They knew the yellow fever wasn't his fault, and they didn't blame him for going crazy. Hell, in a town like this, crazy's normal. But the magic was gone. When they saw Pinkerton, they thought of whatever it was that made them send their children off to war, and they were ashamed of it, ashamed of themselves, I guess, and Pinkerton reminded them of that thing they wanted to forget, the thing in themselves they couldn't look at.

"But I ask you this. Why did Virgil stay? Virgil could have left. He's rich now. I guess Virgil Weaver is a millionaire. I don't know. He doesn't show me his bank book. Why does he stay in Bourbonville?

"He told me once that if he left, it would be like Pinkerton had run him out of his own town. He was here first, he said. Pinkerton and the barbarians were not going to run him off. Well, why didn't he stay two or three years or ten years and leave? Nobody could have thought that Pinkerton had anything to do with it by then. But no. He stays here. He's built a mansion up on that hill of his outside of town, and he stays here where he can look down on the whole damned county. He studies the stock market. He goes to New York sometimes, and he talks to people. He's got friends I've never heard about. He comes back with knowledge from the inside. Something happens in the market, and Virgil seems to know about it before anybody else, and he's richer than he was before. Now and then he argues a case in court, especially if it's against Pinkerton and the railroad. He will make you a will or draw you up a contract and search a deed just like any lawyer if he likes you. It's playacting. The law's not what made him rich. He's got the magic touch, and his real business is making money out of money."

He shook his head and filled my glass and his yet again. "Virgil could go and won't, and Pinkerton wants to go and can't, and the two of them stay right here to hate each other. And what they've done! Lord, what they've done to each other and to this town! Each of them exists to hate the other one and to force this four-by-five cesspool of a place to be the audience to their tragedy and decide between them. If you're the friend of one of them, you're the enemy of the other one."

I sat looking into the red flames leaping in the coals, and I saw the mysterious world of Bourbonville, an unknown world fading into darkness with figures walking across its dim stage, gesturing, telling their stories. I heard Guy whisper. "Do not listen to his stories; you have our stories. Do not listen to his."

16

MY FATHER set things in motion, and once they began, everything happened, one thing after another, a chain of relentless cause and inevitable effect that gave me an improbable destiny. But all destinies are improbable.

My father was somewhere in America. Dead or alive, I did not know. Did I come looking for him? The incident in London with the coin . . . I tell that story to people who ask. I do not say I came in search of my father. Perhaps I did not. When I thought of my father, my heart filled with anger, with grief, and with choking shame.

When I was a young child, I thought my father was Herakles and Achilles or maybe Zeus the immortal. On the night he fled, I was terrified. "I love you, Paulos! I love you! No matter what it seemed, I always loved you, and I wanted you to love me." He hugged me with strong arms. I felt myself suffocating. Then he was gone, fleeing through the house and over the marble terrace where the leather heels of his fine English shoes made a clacking noise, and thence into the unknown.

The police came soon afterwards. I heard the insistent clanging of the brass bell at the wrought-iron gate, a gate locked now before the steep, unpaved road that sloped down to the Bay of Faliron. Ours was one of only three great houses built on the promontory of Kastella. We had the salt sea breeze and the quiet of country life within a short ride to the harbor.

The police stood in the moonlit night, dressed in their official black. The captain led the way onto the terrace when the gate was opened—a terrace illuminated now by oil lamps borne by hurrying and confused servants, stirred out of their slumber.

My mother, straight and tall and as beautiful as I had ever seen her, lied magnificently. "My husband has not been here," she said with icy composure. "Of course you may search the house." She gathered her long night-robe about her and looked unflinchingly at the police captain. "I believe that I am entitled to know the reason for this visit."

My father, cowardly to the last, had told her nothing. "Your husband has murdered Mr. Papagotis," the officer said.

My mother remained outwardly calm. Mr. Papagotis and his wife came to tea at our house on Sunday afternoons. He was thin and quarrelsome, not successful in business, jealous of my father, sometimes insulting him because my father did business with the Turks. Mrs. Papagotis was voluptuous and dark, with big breasts. She often had beads of moisture on her upper lip, and she laughed too loud. I heard my mother say once, "Madame Papagotis is not a lady." My father boisterously agreed.

"Mrs. Kephalopoulos, your husband was having a clandestine love affair with the wife of Mr. Papagotis. Your husband and the adulterous wife were to have had a tryst tonight at your husband's warehouse. Mr. Papagotis was supposedly on a journey for his business, but he had only pretended to depart. When his wife slipped out of the house, he accosted her and beat her until she confessed her destination. He went there himself to face your husband and to accuse him. Unfortunately, Mr. Kephalopoulos held a pistol in the pocket of his coat, and as Mr. Papagotis advanced on him, your husband fired two shots and killed him. Mr. Papagotis apparently did not see the gun. Your husband fired through the pocket of his coat, which he threw off, and fled."

The words of the police captain—spoken, of course, in a vulgar Greek—ring at me tonight all these decades afterwards.

The first words spoken after the captain's announcement came from

Eleutheria, my mother's maid, a plump, devoted girl from the country. She admired the fine clothes we wore and felt proud to be in our household. Now she threw both hands to her face and cried, "Oh, that beautiful new coat! Ruined! Ruined!"

My mother froze her with a look. Eleutheria fled sobbing into the kitchen.

I believe that the captain of police desired my mother to dissolve into a similar helpless emotion so that he might enjoy a kind of rape against a woman he would never dare touch. She did not change her expression. Her voice was a blade fashioned out of subterranean ice. She said, "You must search the house."

I understood that she was delaying the police while my father escaped. The captain paused before me, sure he was making an impression. He looked me in the eyes, keenly searching for any hint of a lie. "Is your father here, my child?"

I said stoutly that he was not. The captain hesitated. He did not want to make a fool of himself. Like all Greek men, he was fond of young boys. He spoke gently. "Has he been here?" I could feel my mother's steady, silent gaze. I lied with an energy that might have persuaded the angels and all the saints and perhaps a God who had been asleep while my father brought ruin on our heads. "No sir. I have been asleep. He has not been here. I would know if he had been here. He would have waked me up to tell me goodbye." I was dressed in my English pajamas, and my eyes were still swollen with sleep. The captain believed me.

He and his men searched methodically through the house. My father got down to the harbor, to the home of Dr. Sumaris, our friend and friend also to the fishermen, whose bones he mended and whose children he birthed. Dr. Sumaris found a fisherman to hide my father under the nets of a boat and to sail with him out into international waters before dawn, there to signal a Russian ship and to flee first to Italy and then to America. He escaped the implacable justice of Greek law, and he escaped from us, too.

These few pages have been the hardest so far for me to write. I have bled them out drop by drop, and now I see the dawn beginning to pale down the long green slope of the hill where my house is built, and I hear the woodland birds starting to sing, and I see the mist standing in the lower field where hay ripens in the summer heat. I have passed away this night without sensing the flow of time across the earth, and now the sun is somewhere in the near distance, just beyond the eastern mountains. I write slowly when the subject is so painful, and memory fills my words and makes them burn on the page, and the words make me live again all those hard days. I discover that I can live them over without dying the death, and that is consolation.

Fathers do terrible things to their sons; God have mercy on my father's soul; God forgive him for his sins.

17

IN NOVEMBER I was invited to Virgil Weaver's house for the holiday that Americans call Thanksgiving. So much came from that dinner that in looking back, I feel the destiny that has ruled my life and the lives of those whose stories I tell here. One is not destined alone, but destiny lies in the million strands that bind us to a world around us, equally fated to what will come.

The invitation created an uproar in Bourbonville: Virgil Weaver had invited a railroad man to his house! The town thrilled with a curious and uncertain mixture of astonishment, delight, terror, and wild curiosity.

Dale Farmer and I walked out together at 6:30 to be at work when the whistle blasted out over the town at seven. We saw Virgil Weaver from a distance several times. On the Monday before Thanksgiving a raw mistiness hung in the air. We saw him come down the steps of his office and move deliberately towards us. He ignored Dale Farmer as if the man were a dunghill. He tipped his hat and held out his hand. "Good morning, Mr. Alexander, I am Virgil Weaver, and at the request of my friend Dr. Curtis Youngblood, I should like to invite you to my home for dinner this coming Thursday. Dr. Youngblood will be one of my guests. He will pick you up about twelve o'clock and bring you in his car."

He put his hat back on as if the matter were settled and walked away without another word. He did not wait for a reply. Dale Farmer said something jovial and put out his hand, but Virgil did not even glance at him.

"I'll be damned," Dale Farmer said, his hand still outstretched on emptiness.

Dale Farmer told Pinkerton about the invitation, and within a half hour Pinkerton was in the laboratory.

"What is this?" he said. "It is disloyal of you to go to that man's house."

"I mean no disloyalty," I said.

"The hell you say."

"Please do not shout at me. He invited me."

"If you have to go out for Thanksgiving dinner, you can come to my house. I'll tell Eula. Hell, you can join me and her nutty friends from Knoxville. They all get together every holiday so they can preach me into hell. You can come along and get preached at yourself."

"I am sorry," I said. "I have accepted Mr. Weaver's invitation."

"Why? Give me one good reason why!"

"Courtesy," I said. "One attends functions to which one has been invited."

"Goddamn, you talk like a fucking book. Send him a note. Tell him that I've ordered you to eat with me."

"I cannot do that."

"Why the hell not?"

"It is not done!"

" 'It is not done'!" Pinkerton's face turned as red as fire. "What is done in this town is what I say ought to be done!" Pinkerton paced the floor. "He's trying to get at me. He will tell you I'm crazy. He thinks you're one of these hoity-toity college men, and he wants to get you to take sides against me."

"I did not get my diploma from the university," I said. I had told him this before.

"He's telling me you're good enough to sit down at his table. He don't think I'm good enough. Not that I'd accept one of Virgil Weaver's fucking invitations if I got one engraved in gold, you understand. I wouldn't accept an invitation from Virgil Weaver if he was the goddamned sultan and asked me in to fuck all his wives."

"I did not want to accept this one."

"Let me tell you something, bub. You talk about politeness. Hell, being polite's just another word for being weak." He paced the floor. "If we'd gone to Washington, Eula and me would have entertained all the big shots." He stood in front of me, his face only inches from mine. "You think you can take my place, don't you?"

"No," I said, drawing back in horror. "No."

"That's it. Virgil Weaver thinks you're going to take my place. The railroad sent you down here to see if the old man is losing his mind. That's it, isn't it? You're in line for my job." I stepped back. He followed me. His face was like fire.

"No," I said.

"You're lying," he shouted. "You want my job! You want to take over the car works!"

"Mr. Pinkerton, I am working here only until the war is over and I can go back to my home. I have a mother and two sisters to support. I must return to them. I want nothing but to get along with people here as well as I can until I can leave." I felt on the verge of tears.

"Then why in hell did you come if you're planning to leave?" he said, but his voice was softer. He paced. I saw an aura around him, the bright light that signaled my worst headaches. I was afraid to move. I did not want to faint in front of him again.

"I ran for mayor here once," Pinkerton said. "We didn't use to have a mayor in this shithole of a town. Didn't need one. All of a sudden folks decided they had to have a mayor. I ran. I wanted to make another try, you see. Show people that I could make up to them for what happened in Cuba. It wouldn't have hurt Virgil Weaver to let me be mayor. Hell, Virgil Weaver don't even live in the city limits. You know that? He lives *outside* the city. I live outside the city myself now. Back then I lived right here, and I could have been mayor. But no, Virgil Weaver put up the money for a man named Charley Meyers. Charley Meyers is a cantankerous fool. One of the people in Cuba with me. I grant you, he suffered. He had the yellow fever, and he lived to tell about it. But the truth is, I don't think his head's been right since then. Fever will do that to you sometimes. Charley had a fever of a hundred and six for six days. It'll turn you yellow and make you vomit black blood, and it will run your brains out the top of your head like when you boil a thermometer.

"Virgil Weaver, he put up the money for Charley Meyers to run for mayor, and you know what he did? He printed cards up. The cards said, 'Charley Meyers has never been crazy.' You see how clever it was? He couldn't tell people I was crazy. I could have sued him for libel. He said, 'Charley Meyers has never been crazy.' He papered this goddamn town with posters saying 'Charley Meyers has never been crazy.' I couldn't do a thing about it. I might have killed him. What good would that have done? That's the man you're going to have your Thanksgiving dinner with."

He broke off abruptly in mid-sentence, pounded me on the back, and said, "Hell, I'm sorry. Go eat with the son of a bitch. Choke on his food. What do I care?"

Not waiting for me to reply, he strode away, slamming the laboratory door so hard that a pane of glass broke and fell splintering on the floor. The glass in the door was filthy, and through it the world looked blurred, distorted, and dirty except for the one vacant frame where the shattered pane had left an opening for clear light. I could see Pinkerton moving away on the other side of the door, his shape hardly discernible except in that empty rectangle where the glass had been.

18

VIRGIL WEAVER'S HOUSE stood on a commanding hill outside Bourbonville to the east. It was a frame mansion, painted white, two stories high, with columns that did not fit the proportions of the house. It stood amid a grove of chestnut trees and oaks. Around it lay a yard fringed by a neatly tended flower garden.

From the tall windows you could see the river below and the wild, forested mountains to the east. On the western side you could look down to the macadam Martel Pike and the railroad running alongside and over to a rolling meadow lately bought up, so Dr. Youngblood told me, by one of Virgil's brothers in the mortuary business. It had become a commercial graveyard, the first in the county. A few white stones marked graves of the recent and prosperous dead.

Dr. Youngblood and I arrived. Virgil Weaver strode out to meet us, dressed in his unvarying black. I noticed how beautifully his suit was cut, how expensive it was. Guy would have loved it. His breath blew white in the cold air. He did not wear an overcoat. He greeted me with grave courtesy, bowing slightly as he shook my hand.

Dr. Youngblood climbed stiffly out of the car. In those days automobiles did not have heaters. The hard chill had eaten to our bones. Dr. Youngblood was bundled up in a thick red scarf that he had wrapped around his head to cover his ears, a heavy overcoat, thick boots, and a large fur hat. "I hope we're not too early, Virgil," Dr. Youngblood said. "I thought if I stayed close to home, some son of a bitch would shoot his best friend, and I'd miss my dinner. So here we are."

"Quite right," Virgil said. He looked uncomfortably at me and cleared his throat.

We made small talk. I did not know what to say to him; he did not know what to say to me. My awkwardness made others awkward and made me an island apart. People heard my strange accent, and I think they imagined that I was like a deaf person with whom conversation was bound to be difficult and so was to be avoided.

We were saved from each other by the arrival of Brian Ledbetter and Virgil's mother. They came flying up the hill in an open Model T Ford, the old man sitting straight behind the wheel, gripping it with both hands as if he were trying to choke it to death. The woman sat stiffly beside him, her hands folded in her lap, oblivious to the cold and the speed.

The car careened into the yard, and the old man threw on the brakes so that it skidded sideways, leaning violently, and the woman sat sternly unruffled, leaning against the lean of the car, a stiff, black wicker hat pinned to her braided and coiled hair.

Dr. Youngblood and Virgil ran to get out of the way. I had never seen Dr. Youngblood move so fast. Virgil seemed suddenly improbable—elegant reserve in flight. I stood stupefied by the apparition of the man and the woman and the car, which came to a rocking halt, the engine dying with an abrupt, terminal cough. The old man flung open the thin metal door and hurtled to earth with a shout of triumph that sounded like "Heeee-e-e-e-e-eee-HO!" I saw that a wooden peg formed the lower part of his right leg. He hobbled joyfully to the front of the car and kicked one of the tires in triumph. "That'll hold ye," he said. It was as if he and the car had once again taken up an ancient feud, and he had again demonstrated the superiority of humankind itself over the machine. The peg leg made him swagger. He made me think of proud Greek sailors in rough seas.

Virgil was furious. "You are going to kill yourself and my mother and the Lord God only knows what poor defenseless child and maybe widow woman with a house full of children who happens to be in the road when you kill yourself. You think you are Eddie Rickenbacker. You think you are Barney Oldfield. But you are an old man. Old men should not drive the way you drive. If I had any courage, I would take out an injunction to keep you from ever getting behind the wheel of a car again."

The old man looked at him with an amused smile and put out a gloved hand to pat Virgil on the back as if he were a child. "You ought to be thankful for your good health, Virgil," the old man said. "You run just then like you was still a boy. Not many folks your age can take off so fast. Ain't that right, Doc?"

"I am telling you something important," Virgil said, his face deeply flushed.

"Oh, Virgil, hush up," Mrs. Ledbetter said, fixing her hat. "You know Mr. Ledbetter just does that to get your goat. If you'd stop fussing at him, he'd lose the pleasure of it. He drives real good on the road. It's just when he comes up here that he shows off."

The old man turned to me. "I reckon this here is the foreigner. Well, you look right normal to me. From all I've heard, I thought you might have a fire in your forehead and a hickey on your nose and hoofs instead of shoes. How do, son. My name's Ledbetter. Brian Elisha Ledbetter. And you're Paul Alexander, only I don't know what your middle name is, if you got one, and I'm proud to make your acquaintance." Mrs. Ledbetter said something welcoming and smiled and offered me her hand, and for a moment I thought I was supposed to kiss it, but before I could do anything, she was shaking mine with the vigor of a woman pumping water.

We made our way inside. A black man dressed in a black suit opened the door for us. Brian Ledbetter grinned at him, and the black man glanced uncertainly at Virgil and allowed himself to grin back at the old man. "What do you say, Newt?" the old man said.

"I say all right," the black man said with a huge smile.

"That's the boy," Brian said. "I say all right, too. Why'd you let it get so cold?"

"I wasn't paying no attention, Mr. Ledbetter," the black man said. "I was just taking me a little nap in the sun, and that thieving cold snuck up on me. I swear it did. I'll work on it, though. I'll have this here cold drove out of the county by Sunday morning early, you wait and see."

The two of them laughed loud. Virgil looked displeased. "That's enough, Newt," he said.

"Yassuh," Newt said, bowing with a spastic jerk and pulling his head back high and tight so that he really did look like a respectable butler, the smile fading as though the sun had disappeared.

"I wish you wouldn't be so familiar with the help," Virgil said to Brian Ledbetter. Brian's only response was to put a large, gnarled hand on Virgil's shoulder, hold it there briefly, and take it away.

Virgil's son came down the big stairway as we entered, his hand stretched out, his upper body bent forward, and a big smile on his face. He approached me first. "Hello there, I'm D. B. Weaver. Dothan Brian. Everybody calls me D.B. Named for my grandmother's two husbands. I'm glad to meet you, Mr. Alexander. I've heard so much about you, and it's all been good." He spoke intensely and with a disingenuous cheer, cloying and false. He hugged his grandmother and kissed her stiffly on the cheek. He kissed his grandfather in the same way, oblivious to the effort the old man made to fend him off. A nettled Brian Ledbetter wiped the kiss away with the back of his hand and muttered, "D.B. has got the slobberingest kisses I ever seen."

D.B. turned back to me. "You've been in the army," he said. "Is that right?"

"Yes," I said.

"I'm joining the army myself. Two days after Christmas. That's my birthday. I'm joining the army on my eighteenth birthday."

I caught a glimpse of Virgil's face. He looked bleak and hurt and old.

19

VIRGIL'S DAUGHTER, Daisy, was barely sixteen when I met her that day. She was tall for a woman, chubby, with prominent but perfect teeth and dark hair. She shook hands with me uneasily and blushed and stared at me. "I've just been dying to meet you," she said.

"Thank you very much," I said.

"There's never been anybody like you in Bourbonville," she said.

I did not know what to say. She stared at me, seemingly at a loss for words herself.

I was saved by the epiphany of Melvina Weaver descending the long staircase. Her expensive dress was bright yellow and far too young for her. There was much kissing and hugging and whooping, punctuated with many repetitions of the word "wonderful."

"So *this* is the foreigner," she said, taking me by both hands and leaning back as if to bring me into better focus. "Why, young man, I feel just like you and I had been friends for a *lifetime*. Oh, I've heard *so* much about you, and it's just all been *wonderful*. I can see right now, Mister . . . Oh, what is your name?"

"Alexander," I said, bowing slightly. "Paul Alexander."

"Oh yes. Alexander. It's funny, Alexander don't *seem* foreign. I have some cousins in Kingsport named Alexander. You don't know them, of course. They're all full-blooded Americans. Well, I'm sure you're going to give the single women in this county heartthrobs, Mr. Alexander. David, is it?"

"My conscience, Melly," Mrs. Ledbetter said. "The man said his name was Paul. Just like the Bible."

"Oh yes. Well, I *knew* it was a Bible name. It is so comforting to have a Bible name, especially the Apostle Paul's name. You know his name was Saul, but he changed it to Paul when he was born again. I hope you've been born again, Mr. Alexander. But I guess you Catholics don't believe in all that." Big tears came to her eyes, and she squeezed my hands.

"Now, Paul—may I call you Paul?—welcome to Bourbonville. Welcome! Welcome!" Melvina said. "It's just *swell* to have you with we simple country folk. I do so *hope* we won't bore the life out of you."

We sat in the living room while two black servants prepared the meal. We talked uncomfortably. The black man solemnly brought in a silver tray and offered drinks. He managed to avoid looking any of us in the eye—except the old man. I saw the old man wink at him, and Newt looked quickly away.

The men took Bourbon whiskey. The women took fruit juices. I took a glass of Bourbon. It was like fire.

"Virgil, you drink the real bonded stuff," Brian said in appreciation, taking a big swallow from his glass and sighing lustily.

"It's hard to get good whiskey now with prohibition in Tennessee," Virgil said with a laugh that made his face seem suddenly warm. "The Women's Christian Temperance Union has made criminals out of all of us."

"My husband is making a comment about his wife," Melvina said with false gaiety. "I am a member of the WCTU. We disagree about alcoholic beverages. With all the drunks who beat their wives and let their children starve, I think we can all do without liquor." She shook her head; the corkscrew ringlets of her hair trembled like metal springs. I expected someone to challenge her, but no one did.

There was far too much furniture in the room—huge overstuffed chairs, sofas, oak tables, lamp stands, and one enormous wooden chair that looked like a throne. Nobody sat in it. The only variety came from a number of rocking chairs. Brian Ledbetter rocked contentedly back and forth in one, sipping at his whiskey.

Dale Farmer had spoken contemptuously of Melvina's taste. The chairs were upholstered in crimson velvet. The walls inside were painted a brutal blue. They were hung with reproductions of old masters and sentimental scenes of lighted cabins beside moonlit lakes, knickknack shelves crammed with porcelain figurines of cheerful little fat people.

Dominating all the other art was a large colored print of a guardian angel in white robes bending with a sugary smile over two little children, a ruddy boy and a moon-eyed older girl, both barefoot. They had just stepped over a broken plank in a wooden bridge in the dark, thanks to the protection of the angel. The bridge arched over an abyss.

Abruptly Bernal stood there, looking at the print. He wore his uniform and looked exhausted and dirty. I started. He vanished. I looked for mud on the rug.

Melvina saw my stare. "I just *adore* that picture," she said. "Don't it make you just want to *cry?* When I think that each and every one of us have a guardian angel, it just makes me feel *so* thankful. I look at that picture every day, and I say, 'O Lord, don't let my little boy and my little girl fall into the valley of the shadow of death.' " The big tears welled up again.

I did not know what to say. I was a stick making other people sticks. Guy could have walked into this room and charmed them all. Now I saw him by the tall eastern windows, looking out to the mountains that rolled against the horizon. I did not want to be here. These people did not want me here. I wanted to walk with Guy and Bernal, to be alone with them to talk the day away.

20

GRADUALLY, FUELED by whiskey, talk came. There was much to talk about. The Bolsheviks had taken over Petrograd and Moscow. Some people said that they would sign a separate peace with the Germans, allowing the Kaiser to throw all his army onto the Western Front. The newspapers gushed headline optimism about the invincibility of Americans in battle. Brian Ledbetter shook his head. "We might be whipped before you get out of the country," he said to D.B.

"Oh no," the boy said, with a superiority grating in one so young. "You're not going to beat American soldiers that easily."

"Anybody can be whipped," Brian Ledbetter said.

"The Germans are not going to run over Jim Ed and Willy," the boy said.

The old man snorted and looked into his glass of whiskey. "You don't know nothing, D.B."

"I think we should talk about something pleasant," Melvina said. "Thanksgiving is a time to count our blessings. I'm just so glad that all of us are here together. That's a blessing to me. It's *so* good to have you, Mr. Alexander. I'm sure you would rather be spending Thanksgiving with your own family. What do you have for Thanksgiving dinner? I do hope and pray you like what we have."

I said that we did not have Thanksgiving.

Melvina was astounded. "No Thanksgiving! Well, no wonder all you foreigners have gone to war," she said, shaking her head so that again her tightly curled ringlets quivered. "They have forgotten God. You know, Mr. Alexander, if you'll permit me to say so, if you forget God, he forgets you. We remember God in this country, and look at all the differences between us and you." She flashed a radiant smile.

"I do not believe we need to preach to Mr. Alexander," Virgil said. "History develops in different ways. I am disappointed with Mr. Wilson. He promised us to keep us out of war. And now . . ."

"Virgil," Brian Ledbetter said, "you should of took my advice, and that's a real true fact. You shouldn't never vote for a Democrat. I always vote Republican. It don't do no good in this state, except for the Congress, but I do what's right. If you'd voted Republican, and if enough of the country had voted Republican, things would of been different."

"I think the Republicans would have been even more eager for war than Mr. Wilson," Virgil said. "Mr. Wilson is not the man I thought he was. The one thing that he has done that I approve is segregate the Civil Service," Virgil said, turning to me. "I know you people in Europe don't understand our ways, but believe me, it's best."

"Daddy, please," Daisy whispered. "Newt and Victoria will hear you. You shouldn't say such things in front of the help."

"Daisy, I am saying only that I applaud Mr. Wilson's efforts to reduce friction by separating the races in the workplace. Do you realize," he said, turning again to me, "that before Mr. Wilson you had a situation where Negro men were bossing white women? That is against nature."

"I stand shoulder to shoulder with my dear husband on that one," Melvina said.

Brian Ledbetter looked down into his whiskey glass and shook his head. "You get to be as old as I am, Virgil, and you don't know what nature is. You change your mind about some things."

An expressionless black woman wearing a white apron appeared in the doorway and spoke to Melvina. Melvina leaped up. "Dinner is served," she said brightly, holding her hands palms up as if she had just discovered something wonderful.

She led us into a large dining room. The long table was covered with a stiff linen cloth and set with heavy, expensive china and silver. A turkey and a ham reposed on platters, and the smells were heavy. I felt nauseated. Melvina arranged us, putting me between Daisy and Dr. Youngblood. Mr. and Mrs. Ledbetter and D.B. sat across from me. Virgil and Melvina sat at opposite ends of the table. The black woman poured red wine from a decanter. She did it awkwardly. She filled Melvina's glass.

Melvina asked the blessing, speaking to God as if they were old friends. At the end I heard Bernal whisper "Amen."

"How are Jim Ed and Willy getting along?" D.B. asked when the prayer was over.

"They're up near Verdun," Brian Ledbetter said. "Jim Ed says there ain't nothing happening at Verdun now. The war's gone off somewheres else, he says. If the war's gone off somewheres else, I don't know why he's still living in a hole in the ground."

"It ain't a hole in the ground, Mr. Ledbetter," Mrs. Ledbetter said. "It's called a trench."

"In my war we put up *works,*" the old man said. "We didn't crawl in no hole in the ground. We didn't sit in cold, muddy water up to our knees. We killed each other civilized." He tried to laugh, but the effort failed.

"Let's don't talk about things like this old war," Melvina said. "Don't you think Virgil's just doing a great job with that turkey, Dr. Youngblood? You'd better thank your lucky stars that he didn't decide to be a doctor. He'd be the best doctor in the county if he wanted to be. So steady. So sure with the knife."

"We could use another doctor," Dr. Youngblood said.

"Pass the cranberry sauce, Mother Ledbetter," Melvina said. "Do take the creamed potatoes, Mr. Alexander. Do you have creamed potatoes where you come from? D.B., please see that the gravy starts around. Would anybody have a roll? We have biscuits. Father Ledbetter, I know you want biscuits. Victoria! Bring Father Ledbetter some biscuits. Won't you have a roll, Dr. Youngblood? Leave some room for your green beans. Remember, we have sweet potatoes. Don't forget the salad. I put orange slices in it just because I know how much D.B. likes oranges. Do you have oranges where you come from, Mr. Alexander? You ought to try the hominy. Pass the peas, please, Mother Ledbetter. Dr. Youngblood, would you put some food on Virgil's plate? I don't want my dear husband to go hungry when he's working so hard for the rest of us."

Plates of food went around in a whirlwind of arms and hands. I wondered why Melvina did not use her servants to serve. We passed things, and we passed things, and the food piled up on our plates and got cold. Virgil scarcely spoke. After Virgil had served everyone, he put his napkin in his lap and sat down.

Daisy turned to me with the inevitable question "How do you like Bourbonville?"

I made some bland response. She said, "Nobody could like Bourbonville who has seen anything else."

"Daisy believes she is wasted here in Bourbonville," D.B. said.

"Daisy, I do wish you wasn't so stuck-up," Melvina said. "If you are stuck-up, you will have trouble catching a man. You understand, Mr. Alexander, Daisy is too young to be married now, but the habits we form in our youth stay with us all our lives, and I am so afraid that if she stays stuck-up, she will turn eligible young men away from her. I say to Daisy all the time that if she is going to be stuck-up, she may end up an old maid."

"Stuck-up," Daisy said bitterly. "That's the worst sin you can commit in a town like this—being stuck-up. You're the least bit different and people say, 'Look at Daisy. She's stuck-up.' You like to read books and people say, 'Look at Daisy. She reads books. She's stuck-up.' You can't stand to go to parties where stupid boys sweat when they speak to you and talk about breeding horses and hunting, and people say, 'Oh, don't invite Daisy Weaver to your party. She's stuck-up.' "

"Daisy," Mrs. Ledbetter said gently. "It ain't so bad here in Bourbon County."

"That's because you never have been anywhere else," Daisy said with a toss of her head.

"I just can't bear to hear you talk like this," Melvina said, turning red with the first true emotion she had expressed. "You're going to ruin yourself."

"I don't care," Daisy said. "I don't care. You're supposed to apologize for being yourself in a town like Bourbonville. Pretty soon, when you've apologized and apologized, you've forgotten who you are. You're not anybody. You're just the common mud that gets ground underfoot. But at least you're not stuck-up. You're stuck *down*."

"Daisy! How you talk," Mrs. Ledbetter said gently.

I glanced over at Dr. Youngblood. His face was grave. He looked at me and looked away and poured himself more wine.

D.B. took it on himself to relieve the tension. "I warn you," he said, grinning his empty grin, "Daisy has been talking about you like you might be the prince to wake up the Sleeping Beauty and carry her off to your castle in fairyland."

"I am not going to fairyland," Daisy said angrily. "I am going to California. I am going to have a house overlooking the ocean. I am going to walk along the beach. I am going to swim naked in the ocean."

Melvina blushed scarlet. D.B. laughed much too hard. Virgil held his knife and his fork, looking at his daughter with weary impatience. Melvina patted her lips with a napkin and said, "To talk about being *naked* before a foreigner!"

"Well, if you ask me," Mrs. Ledbetter said with a genuine laugh, "most folks looks lots better with their clothes on than they do with their clothes off. Besides that, if you run around naked, you'll get poison ivy and sunburn, and you'll get your name in the papers."

Virgil spoke softly. "Daisy, it would be a shame to make you leave the table on Thanksgiving Day. Please do not embarrass yourself and us when we have company."

I am sure that had I not been there, Daisy would have risen from the table and stalked away.

"You're not eating enough to keep a *bird* alive," Melvina said, looking at my plate. "Oh, my! I *do* hope you like our cooking. Some people don't like Southern cooking, you know. It's all right if you don't like it. I *do* wish you'd *told* me what you like. I could have fixed a special plate just for you. Unless you wanted snails or frogs or something awful like that. I couldn't bear to touch a snail. Do you French people eat the whole frog, or just the legs like our men do?"

"Melly dear," Mrs. Ledbetter said, "these sweet potatoes melts in your mouth." I discovered much later that her name was Evelyn.

"I just *soak* them in butter," Melvina said. "Do you have sweet potatoes in France, Mr. Alexander?"

"He is not from France," Dr. Youngblood said. "He is from Belgium. Belgium is not the same as France."

"Well, it's all the same to me," Melvina said. "A foreigner's a foreigner." Then, as though remembering herself, she smiled sweetly at me. "Present company excepted, of course. Now personally, I don't mind foreigners—I mean foreigners of a higher class, like you, Mr. Alexander. I'm a *very* tolerant person. Everybody knows how tolerant I am. But it's *awful* to think of all those horrible Jews and Greeks and Eyetalians and Poles pouring into our country like . . . like . . . well, just like trash. We're becoming the garbage dump for all the world. They will pollute our native stock before you know it—the Jews opening pawnshops and the Greeks opening restaurants and the Eyetalians robbing people at gunpoint and selling innocent young girls into white slavery. They say there are places in New York City where a lady can't walk alone on the street without being leered at, and it's all because of foreigners." Melvina shook her head angrily, and the light danced in the thousands of stiffly coiled ringlets in her hair.

"Well," Brian Ledbetter said, "ole Paul here ain't no Jew, and he ain't no Greek, and he ain't no Eyetalian. So he ain't going to carry off your jewelry or poison you with his eats or sell you into white slavery, Melvina."

"I was not speaking of myself, Father Ledbetter," Melvina sniffed. "I do hope you don't take my remarks personally. I am an honest woman. I believe we ought to stand up for what we believe. Don't you think so, Mr. Alexander?"

I heard Guy laugh loudly somewhere nearby. I must have turned pale.

Melvina said in alarm, "Why, Mr. Alexander, are you all right?" She rose half out of her chair. Everyone stared at me.

"Is it a headache?" Dr. Youngblood asked in a soft undertone.

"No," I said. "No, I am all right. I felt dizzy for a moment. Please, I am quite all right."

"Mr. Alexander was wounded in the head," Dr. Youngblood said in his low, gravelly voice. "He has periodic headaches of great intensity."

"Oh my!" Daisy said. She touched me on the arm.

"Daisy, please!" Melvina said. Daisy took her hand away.

I was embarrassed and frightened.

Daisy turned fiercely on her brother. "You see what happens when you go to war? You see why Daddy doesn't believe in war? You see how . . . how *insane* you are?"

D.B. gave her a dismissive smile. "What branch of the army were you in?" he asked me affably.

"I began in the artillery," I said. "Then I was in the infantry."

"Why did you change?" D.B. said. "Did you like rifles better?"

"The Germans captured our gun," I said.

"Oh," he said, lifting his eyebrows. "They were that close, were they?"

"Yes, they were that close," I said.

"Interesting," D.B. said. "Did you kill anybody?"

I stared at him, unable to say a word.

Brian Ledbetter put down his knife and fork. "That's a question you don't never ask a soldier, D.B. For God's sake, shut up!"

"Oh," the boy said quickly, his brittle face crumbling for a moment. "Well, I just thought . . . I didn't mean any harm."

"Well, shut up," Brian Ledbetter said.

"Ah, me," Dr. Youngblood said.

"I'm so sorry you were hurt," Daisy said. "I don't see why people have to fight wars. It's stupid. Does it hurt now?"

"No," I lied. "No, I am fine."

"Daisy, don't pester the foreigner. Just mind your own business," Melvina said. "Won't you have some more sweet potatoes, Mother Ledbetter?"

"I'm not pestering him," Daisy said. "I just want him to be well."

The curtains of the tall windows were drawn back, and we could look out onto a day that had cleared to deceptive sunshine. I could see the muddy river like a brown snake sunning itself on the valley floor. Beyond, the primitive and forested land rolled eastward to the great wall of the mountains so clear and blue in the brilliant light that I thought I could see the crenellations of trees along the distant summits.

I thought of how the sun shone on the blue waters of the Bay of Faliron when Stephanos and I used to have our thick coffee on summer mornings after my father had gone off to his warehouse. When the wind blew slightly, the morning light, caught in myriads of small waves, looked like a hundred million mirrors briefly catching the sun. "We are all like the waves," Stephanos said. "We catch the light for a moment, and it shifts, and we are lost in the sea for all eternity." I never knew what to say to him in these moods.

Stephanos loved archaeology. I went with him on long walking trips, both of us dressed in the navy jackets and white duck trousers that he affected, wearing yachting caps and white gloves and viewing archaeological sites like the gentlemen we were, expressing a dilettantish support for science. It was hardly more than that except that Stephanos brooded deeply over the relics brought up out of the earth. He could stare at a fragment of broken pot inscribed with stylized human figures and not speak for a half hour, so lost was he in the contemplation of the work of anonymous men who had lived for a time in the sun and then, as he said, "descended into the shades forever."

"I would be so much happier," he said, "if I believed that the dead had even the miserable existence of the father of Odysseus. Then at least there would be *something,* an eternity for the mind to work things out and to understand what the world is. We could spend eternity remembering this life. I would remember you, Paulos. I would remember all our happy times, and I would be happy. But I do not believe there is anything after death. I think our soul rots into our bones."

21

MELVINA WEAVER SAID, "I am put out with myself for what I said a while ago, Mr. Alexander. I want you to know we don't have any prejudices in this house. We think foreigners are just swell. We truly do. Personally I think it puts Bourbonville on the map to have a man as smart as you to stay with we small-town folks for a while. And how long *will* you be staying?"

"When the war is over, I shall return home," I said.

"Oh, you won't be living here afterwards?" Her relief was palpable.

"No."

"How sad!" Daisy said. "But why should anybody stay in Bourbonville? The longer people stay here, the duller they get."

They asked questions about my family; I lied or told just enough of the truth to fend them off.

"Mr. Alexander, when you get back to your home, will you please write us and tell us that you found your family safe and sound? I'll be so *worried* until

I know they're all right. *Do* give them our regards. Won't you have just a *little* more turkey?"

"I cannot eat any more," I said.

"Oh my," Melvina said, making a woeful face. "I'm sure it's because you don't like my cooking."

Dr. Youngblood said, "Let him alone, Melvina. He is not well."

People talked on. I looked through the window to the brown river, to the forested land and the naked trees, and beyond to the blue mountains cut like etchings on the far sky, and I tried to think peaceful thoughts. Deep down in my skull I felt a headache coming.

I thought of Ghent and how clean it was and how happy I was to stroll with Guy and Bernal along the washed, cobblestoned streets for blocks and never to see a scrap of paper in the gutter. I remembered how snow rounded off the sharp lines of the town, and how, while snow was falling, we walked in it, and how Guy sang, his voice rolling carelessly through the streets, making men look at him in irritation, making women smile.

Melvina Weaver reminded me of Madame Conrad, our concierge's wife, and I recalled the snowy twilight once when Guy and I sat in our room over the great archway that led through tall wooden doors into the courtyard of the Institute St. Valéry in Ghent, and how old Madame Conrad looked as black as a crow beneath our window when she shuffled querulously through the snow carrying an iron pot across to the kitchen, and how she returned hugging herself, wrapped in her black shawl, scowling up at the bleak sky and the drifting flakes as if God had insulted her, had committed some atrocious vulgarity, without regard to how faithful she had been. She bathed on Saturday night and put on clean clothes every Sunday morning. She went to mass, hobbling painfully to church despite her arthritis, and everyone knew how painful it was and how noble she was because she told everybody about the pain and her devotion and likened herself to those saints grilled alive on fires or tortured with tongs that ripped their teeth out of their heads. No one spoke more faithfully than she of the virtues of priests or more angrily of the evils of Socialists.

Still it snowed.

Daisy said something to me, calling my name. "What?" I said. "I beg your pardon."

"Don't jump so!" she said. "You're so high-strung! I said I'll drive you around in Daddy's car and show you things. The land is beautiful here; it is just the town that's ugly."

Melvina said, "Hush, child. You can't drive around by yourself with a strange man in the car. I've always said that the automobile is going to be the end of decency in this country."

"Oh, Melvina, be still," Mrs. Ledbetter said. "I've been riding in cars since they was invented, and it ain't hurt my decency yet."

Melvina looked brightly at me. "You do understand, don't you, Mr. Alexander. A young girl's most precious possession is her reputation, and if Daisy was to go riding around the country with a stranger. . . . " Again the welling tears.

"Mr. Alexander is not a stranger," Mrs. Ledbetter said. "He is at our table. He is not going to do anything to harm Daisy's reputation. My stars, if you ask me, he might do her reputation some good."

"I can drive you over to the mountains," Daisy said. "I've been there lots of times."

"Daisy!" Melvina said.

"I hear the Smoky Mountains is just filled up with Eyetalians selling young girls off into white slavery," Brian Ledbetter said.

"Mr. Ledbetter, hush," Mrs. Ledbetter said. "Melly, dear, if you're scared to let them go out together, Mr. Ledbetter and I can drive them. We can take them on a little expedition one of these days."

Melvina summoned up her talent for changing subjects. She looked cheerfully at me. "Why don't you tell us about France?" she said.

"My God, woman!" Brian Ledbetter said. "The man ain't from *France.* Can't you get that into your head? He's from *Belgium.* Don't you know we're in this war because of Belgium? Don't you read the newspapers?"

"Well of *course* I don't read the newspapers!" Melvina said in an outburst. "Why should any *woman* read the papers? All you read about is this awful war. I don't know how you can sit there when you've got a boy at the front. How can you sleep at night?"

"Melvina, that is enough," Virgil said quietly. "Please stop." Melvina looked beseechingly at her son. D.B. wore his unchanged expression of bland and remote cheer.

Brian Ledbetter went gently back to her question. "I don't sleep too good at night, and that's a real true fact. But I don't figure it does much good to carry on about it. I get up in the morning, and I go my way. I think that's what folks has got to do."

"God's will be done," Mrs. Ledbetter said. I expected her to cross herself. I recalled Father Medulous and how he crossed himself over his fat belly when he said, "God's will be done." I supposed he lived now under the occupation, still saying mass in the mornings before the high, bare altar in the school while the German field gray held the streets outside. I wondered if the Germans had shelled the school.

I could hear the strong voice of the priest ring through the cold chapel during early morning mass. *Hoc est enim corpus meum.* The black-robed arms reached skyward. The priest was like a raven, soaring towards heaven, and the empty sky absorbed his pleas.

"So many folks have told me how they just *love* to hear you pronounce

'Bourbonville,' Mr. Alexander," Melvina said. "Won't you say it for me? Pretty please?"

"Bourbonville?" I said, pronouncing it as I usually did, baffled at her question, unconscious that I was giving it the soft French pronunciation.

"Oh, *there*. It's so *cute* the way he says it!" She looked around the table with an incandescent grin. "Well, I think it's just swell that you're here, and I just wish you could settle down like Virgil and I to spend the rest of your days in this wonderful little town. We'll miss you when you go back to where you belong, Mr. Alexander. It may not be an exciting place like your gay Paree, but it's a warm and such a *friendly* little spot, and it's all I want in life. Just between you and I, I'm a foreigner, too."

"Oh, Mamma, you're no such thing," Daisy said.

"Oh yes I am. Being from Knoxville, Bourbonville was a great trial when I first came down here with my husband in '97, Mr. Alexander. It was the last place in the world I wanted to go. But the Bible says, 'Whither thou goest . . . ,' you know. Of course you Catholics don't read the Bible. The story of Ruth? A wife's duty is to follow her husband. Don't you think so, Mr. Alexander? And my husband wanted me to be right here. So here I am, and now I wouldn't live anyplace else on earth."

She turned towards me, and her eyes welled. "Virgil walked me home from church one night in the snow," she said. "He was reading law in Mr. Neal's office up in Knoxville, and we'd known each other for a month, and he was so shy. Oh, you wouldn't *believe* how shy he was! The snow had fallen all that day, and Virgil and me went to the youth group at church, and he asked if he could walk me home, and I said of course he could because I really did like him, and we talked, and everything was so still and white and beautiful, and I can still remember how our footsteps sounded in the snow. We got to my house, and when I turned around on the porch to say goodbye, he suddenly kissed me goodnight. I didn't expect it. I never have kissed anybody else since, and I never will kiss any man again as long as I live. I just wish everybody could be happy like we've been."

Virgil stared at her with no expression. No smile. No grimace. Nothing. His face was like a steel door. I heard the soft clanking of silverware on plates. Dr. Youngblood poured more wine into my glass.

"Virgil was lucky to find you, Melly dear," Mrs. Ledbetter finally said. "You're such a good cook."

"She ain't as good as you, Mrs. Ledbetter," Brian Ledbetter said. He stifled a belch.

"Well," Mrs. Ledbetter said, "I don't reckon either one of my husbands can say I don't set a good table."

"Being as how one of them is dead, I don't reckon he better complain about nothing," Brian Ledbetter said.

"Dothan is in heaven," Mrs. Ledbetter said, patting her mouth with a napkin. "Won't none of us complain about being in heaven's bright city."

"My father's father died," D.B. said. "Grandfather Ledbetter and my real grandfather both fought in the Civil War."

"Dothan called it the War Between the States," Mrs. Ledbetter said. "I don't care, but for his sake we'd better not call it the Civil War. My first husband fought for the 'Federacy, Mr. Alexander. Mr. Ledbetter here fought for the Union, but we've all forgive him for that." She smiled at her husband, and I saw with blinding suddenness how much she loved him.

"It was one humdinger of a war, and that's a real true fact," Brian Ledbetter said. He took a deep, contented breath. "Didn't eat so good in the war as I've eat today, Melvina. You're second-best cook in the county, I reckon."

"Grandfather Ledbetter knows some dandy stories," D.B. said in a leading way.

"Aw, my stories ain't changed in fifty years," the old man said, looking hopefully over the table at me. "I'm sick and tired of telling them."

"Grandfather Ledbetter was at Gettysburg," D.B. said. "I guess you know all about it, Mr. Alexander?"

I said that I did not. I had never heard the name Gettysburg in my life.

The old man looked startled and troubled. "You don't know nothing about Gettysburg?"

"No," I said. "I am sorry."

"But you don't study about . . . you ain't never heard people talk about . . . ?" The old man looked uncharacteristically dazed.

"We didn't study much about . . . I did not study much history. I did mathematics."

"You folks over there . . . We're fighting over there for folks that don't know nothing about Gettysburg," the old man said, shaking his head in a troubled laugh. "Well, it just goes to show . . . Hell, I don't know what it just goes to show."

"Father Ledbetter," Melvina said. "I know you have your own way of speaking, but I do wish you would not use profanity in front of the children."

"Is it a town?" I said.

" 'Is it a town?' " Brian Ledbetter said.

"It's all right," Virgil said abruptly. "Why should he know about Gettysburg? Mr. Campbell used to say we've got too many memories in this county. I say it'd be a good thing to let some of them die."

"Don't be impatient," Brian Ledbetter said. "It won't be long till they're all dead."

"I didn't mean . . ." Virgil said. It was not clear what he did not mean. He looked suddenly bereft.

"My husband does not believe in war," Melvina said.

"You might could say I don't believe in it neither," the old man said.

"I know he's right," Melvina said. She looked at her son, sitting just to her left, and she squeezed his hand, and her eyes yet again filled with tears.

"You truly don't know nothing about Gettysburg?" the old man said, brightening a little.

"Mr. Ledbetter goes to reunions," Evelyn Ledbetter said. "He spends good money to sit up all night long on a train and go back to Gettysburg and stand around talking to the old coots that tried to kill him."

"Well, I was trying to kill *them!* Say, I heard a good story when I went to the last one, the one in 1913? Did you hear about the backwoods Baptist that said to an old yokel, 'Do you believe in infant Baptism?' And the other feller said, 'Believe in it hell, I've *seen* it!'"

"I don't know why you have to tell profane jokes," Evelyn Ledbetter said.

"Looky there, Mrs. Ledbetter! You laughed."

"Well, the Baptists is so pig-headed about Baptism. Them and the Campbellites."

"I don't reckon we'll have another reunion," the old man said. "Last time I went, you had folks fainting all over the place, old men all wore out by the heat. It wasn't as hot as it was on that day. They was just older, that's all. All them old codgers."

"You ain't so young no more yourself, Mr. Ledbetter," Mrs. Ledbetter said.

"I didn't faint, Mrs. Ledbetter. I didn't even come close." He turned back to me. "And you don't know nothing about Gettysburg?"

"No, he don't, and don't you tell him," Evelyn Ledbetter said. "I think we've heard all they is to say about that war. I don't know why we have to sit through all these stories again and again."

She patted her mouth with her napkin, and just for an instant I thought she was angry, but her eyes were bright. I saw Virgil smile, and then I understood that she was singing the opening words of a litany in an ancient ritual. I knew suddenly that she had said these things many times and that her protest was a prologue, a gathering of unconsciously memorized lines, one inexorably calling forth the next until it all came out.

I was at the edge of sanity, and my senses were so acute that the smells of food were suffocating, and it hurt to hear and taste and feel, and the sight of the carved mountains against the sky cut my eyes. I felt a headache forming, and the shapes of things were enveloped in an aura of dizzying light, and as the old man laughed and started to talk, I felt an eerie compression in the air, a shrinking at the back of my neck.

I remembered how clear the light was on the blue water of the Bay of Argos as you come down the dirt road from Mycenae and see it in the distance spread out still and flat under the summer sun, and somewhere in the great, great distance where memory dissolves and time falls into a sunny and mysterious haze, I heard a faint liquid chord of music, and I heard the old blind harper's voice sigh and begin:

> *An angry man! So my tale, the bitter*
> *Wrath of Achilleus, Master of the house of Peleus,*
> *That brought a thousand woes upon the Achaian host . . .*

And dead children gathered in silent and expectant wonder out of the deeps of earth, and from the crevices of the high, naked rock, their spirits summoned by the old enchantment.

"Go ahead and tell him about it," D.B. said.

Daisy looked around and rolled her eyes upward. "I'm afraid we're in for it now," she said. But that was part of the ritual, too.

"Daisy, don't be disrespectful," Mrs. Ledbetter said. "If Mr. Alexander ain't heard about Gettysburg, well, I reckon he's got a right to know."

"I could tell him a thing or two," Brian Ledbetter said.

He looked happily around in his aged brightness, unable for a moment to believe the good fortune of having someone to hear his story for the first time. He fastened his sharp eyes on me and cleared his throat and spoke carefully, like a man just remembering something not thought of in a long while, as if he had just decided to tell a tale never framed in words before, carving it all anew and taking care to get it exactly right, for if he did not get it exactly right, something would die.

It was all there, in lines honed and polished and stacked in clean rows in his mind so that to move one was to set them all in motion.

> *Well now, I'll tell you what's a real true fact,*
> *At Gettysburg on a summer day*
> *In the green fields that was all hazy with heat*
> *Amongst the wheat that was yellow and bending ripe*
> *And the peach orchard*
> *And a lot of big rocks that made walls*
> *And made it hell for the common soldier*
> *When the sharpshooters got up in there,*
> *We had us one hell of a fight.*
> *I was in the Sixty-ninth Pennsylvanie,*
> *And that's a story all by itself,*
> *And I'll tell it to you*
> *One of these Saturday afternoons in town*
> *When you ain't got nothing better to do*
> *Than listen to an old man talk*
> *For maybe two hours or three.*

But what you got to understand now
About the Sixty-ninth Pennsylvanie
Is that on July the Third, Eighteen-hundred and Sixty-three,
Ole Bobby Lee done his damnedest
To build hisself a rebel kingdom.
We was the nail his hammer hit.
And we didn't bend, and we didn't break,
And by God, we didn't sink down.
We taken every blow Marse Bob Lee give us that day,
And we broke his hammer in his hand.
We was the Sixty-ninth Pennsylvanie!
We broke his hammer in pieces,
And ole Marse Bobby Lee
Drawed back his arm,
And he found his hand full of blood.

It was not the last time that I heard the story. When he told it, Brian Ledbetter was young again, no more than a boy, and a quiet boy at that, far from home and so scared that he urinated in his trousers, and he did not know what he had done till after the fight. He was lying behind the stone wall, a wall just high enough to keep a cow from stepping over it into the wheat, and the grass directly in front of him was tall and green from the rainy weeks just past, and the black smoke from the Rebel artillery rolled in lazy clouds over the rolling land, and he could smell the grass and the earth and the smoke and the hot day and his fear.

There was a forest on the opposing ridge, dark with summer, and the Rebels were there. He felt again the furious immobile blast of the sun on his back, the sweat soaking his clothes, and he smelled the stench of himself, and he heard the Rebel guns go on and on and on, and they stopped, and a terrible silence ached in his head, and the sudden fixity of a windless summer day framed the boys who came walking up on the rounded hills to kill him.

His voice rolled on and on, awed at the memory of who he had been and venerable with the amazing years he had survived. Here and there he rose on the laughter of unbelief, and in other places he fell into the sadness of old men telling stories about the distant dead. We moved into the living room, and Virgil brought out brandy, and still the old man went on, and we listened, rapt in his words. And suddenly, he came to an end, and the sun had fallen far to the west, and the shadows outside were long and melancholy, and Dr. Youngblood was rising to go. I rose, too, all in a daze. My headache was gone.

Now I sit in another daze and see that the sun has lifted itself above the eastern rim of the world, and that down in the lower field the dew shines in the grass. It is Sunday morning, all calm and glorious, still cool, though it will be hot this afternoon, and I feel a deep peace with the world.

22

DR. YOUNGBLOOD told me the story of the Fourth of July Incident. A dozen others told me the same story. Pinkerton told it himself. The incident was named in Bourbonville like some war or natural disaster.

July 4, 1911. The world locked in the thrall of heat, the mountains a haze lost on the horizon.

The Fourth of July came around with a celebration in the courthouse square. The volunteer firemen had a brass band—still there when I came—a collection of five or seven corpulent men who blew horns to the accompaniment of another who beat a drum. You could more or less tell the difference between their renditions of "America the Beautiful" and "The Star-Spangled Banner."

On that Fourth of July, Bourbonville had the district congressman to make the principal address. The congressman was a Republican. He had endeared himself to Virgil Weaver by opposing the Spanish War in the Congress. He had endeared himself to the war party by resigning his seat at the outbreak of hostilities to join the army. The war was over before he could fight.

Virgil walked into town for the celebration with D.B. The boy was not yet twelve. The two of them stood in the deep shade near the edge of the great crowd. Charlie Meyers was still mayor then. He made an introductory speech for the congressman, a speech interminable and, by some accounts, intoxicated. People said the speech did Charley Meyers in. He lost the next election. Virgil dropped him. Pinkerton had been humiliated; Virgil had no more use for Charley Meyers.

Pinkerton was there. I can imagine him suffering in that crowd which fell into obscene humor and fidgeting discomfort as Charley Meyers went on and on. People were finally shouting, "Sit down, Charley! Shut up!"

The congressman spoke well, and the band played, and people dispersed in a murmur of good nature to await the evening fireworks. Virgil's son wanted "bought ice cream." Virgil walked with him to the drugstore at the corner of B Street. It had little marble ice cream tables. Electric ceiling fans stirred the thick air. Virgil and his son were sitting inside eating ice cream when Moreland Pinkerton found them.

The place was packed. Many sat outside on the porch. People lounged under the stately chestnut trees in the square nearby: a small-town crowd in its straw hats and suspenders, print dresses and kerchiefs. A drunken Moreland Pinkerton pushed through the crowd shouting in false cheer, "Virgil! Virgil Weaver!"

Virgil Weaver looked up at him, and you could see an expression on Virgil's face—wary, surprised, ugly. Had it not been for the child, Virgil might have thought faster. The child made him hesitate, and Moreland Pinkerton was standing over him, leering at him, shouting in mock good cheer.

"Virgil Weaver! Virgil Weaver himself. I am flabbergasted. Here you are, out on the Fourth of July, pretending you love your country. What's got into you, Virgil? You think you can make people forget by coming out here on the Fourth of July with all your neighbors? We know what Virgil Weaver thinks of the United States of America, don't we, folks? We know how he felt during the Spanish War. That right, folks?"

He swept his eyes around to the great, watching, silent crowd, to people crowding in at windows and doors and others rushing across the square because they heard something was going on at the drugstore. The sun broiled the world, and sweaty bodies gave off heat, and the air was humid enough to drown in.

Dr. Youngblood was not there. "I was out in the country patching up what was left of the hand of a child that had played with a dynamite cap. If I'd been there . . ."

Darcy Coolidge was there, eating ice cream with a woman friend. "I did not know I was holding my breath. I forgot to breathe, and everything began to go black, and I realized that I had to breathe or I would faint. I thought I would die. I did not see how I could endure seeing what I was seeing."

Virgil sat still. The boy sat there, too, looking blankly at his father, at Moreland Pinkerton, back again. Pinkerton let the silence lie there a moment. Then he turned to the boy. "Now, son," he said. "I'm real sorry your daddy is a coward. Your daddy sat back here at home and got rich while a lot of us went off to risk our lives because we loved this country. Let me tell you something, son. I done the best I knew how to do. It didn't turn out right. I admit that. I done my best.

"This man, he didn't do anything. You know why? Because he didn't want to *die!* That's why he didn't want an American empire! He didn't want to *die!* Sonny, you get your daddy to take off that black suit of his some of these nights—you'll find a big yellow stripe running straight down his back."

In every account I heard of the Fourth of July Incident, Pinkerton put his hands down on the white marble table and hissed at Virgil's son so that the boy drew back and started to cry. In every account, Virgil Weaver jumped up and slapped Pinkerton across the face. Virgil was slender, almost frail.

Pinkerton was strong and hard. The alcohol had not yet softened him then.

Pinkerton didn't even rub his face. "Well, well, WELL! Look what this sweet pacifist has done! He don't believe in violence, folks. He preached sermons right out there on the courthouse lawn against war—remember that, folks? I thought he had wings under his coat, and he was going to fly away to Jesus. Here he is, Mr. Lying Hypocrite. He just proved he believes in war. He just proved he's been a liar all his life. Sonny, I could break your daddy in two pieces. I don't have to do anything to him now. He's just broke himself in two."

Even now, very, very late on a hot, humid night, when not a breeze stirs in all the festering world, I can imagine Moreland Pinkerton swaying there, reeking of alcohol, swinging his wild red eyes around the silent drugstore, where people sat stupefied over their melting ice cream. Nothing broke the silence except the weeping of the terrified boy. Pinkerton staggered away and fell unconscious in the square and had to be loaded onto a wagon and driven to the house he had bought in the country because he would not live in the town that would not elect him mayor.

"D.B.," Dr. Youngblood said, sitting in long reflection and looking at the fire in his grate. "Two years later he came to see me in my office. I never will forget it. He was skinny and blond, and he came in like he had thought for a long time about what he had to do and just worked up the courage to do it. He came in and sat out in my waiting room with the sick and the near sick and with people bleeding through bedsheet bandages, and when I had time to see him, he sat there on a little stool and looked at me, and I knew he wanted to say something that didn't have a damned thing to do with the kind of medicine I practice. I remember looking at him, seeing those eyes, and thinking, 'Boy, be silent! Don't speak! I don't want to hear what you have to say.' But hell, it's un-American for a doctor not to listen to people, and I had to listen to him.

"What he had to say was this: 'Dr. Youngblood, is my daddy a coward like everybody says?' I played the Jesuit. I said, 'Hell, son. In the first place, everybody doesn't say your daddy is a coward. Ted Devlin is somebody, and Ted Devlin doesn't say he's a coward. I'm somebody, and I don't say your daddy's a coward. Douglas Kinlaw doesn't say he's a coward. Most folks in Bourbon County don't think your daddy's a coward.

"' 'Now, in the second place, he's *not* a coward. Your daddy's got convictions, and they happen to be pretty good convictions, and he stood up for them and proved himself a man. People told him they would kill him, and he still stood up for what he believed. You can't call a man like that a coward.' "

Dr. Youngblood sighed. "I knew it wasn't any use. That is why D.B. is going to join the army."

I thought of the summer of 1911 and wondered if all the calamities of that year had come about because of the comet of the year before. People in Bourbonville said so. My mother said so, too. I knew that was nonsense.

23

IN THE SUMMER of 1911, my father killed a man and fled Greece and his wife and children.

My father, Vasilis Kephalopoulos, was the oldest of three brothers. My uncle Georgios was second, and Stephanos was third. When my grandfather died at a great age, my father as first son, according to Greek law, inherited the tobacco business that had made our family wealthy.

My grandfather had an eye and a nose for tobacco. Though he had carried a rifle and led men against the Turks, tobacco was his true nationality. He traveled over the Ottoman Empire looking for the best tobacco he could find, speaking Turkish like a man born in a fez. He also spoke Bulgar, Macedonian, and Servian—the languages of tobacco.

He was proud. I remember how he swaggered when he walked, even as an old man with a cane, a lean, handsome man; his cheerful brown face, his large head with its shock of thick white hair. In the harbor men rushed to do him favors.

He did business in Italy and could speak Italian like the Pope. There he met the owners of one of the great merchant companies of Bologna and encountered the only child of the household, a daughter. He decided that she must be his wife. The negotiations were long and complicated. In the end he prevailed in courtship as he did in everything else, and they were married. She died when Stephanos was born; I never knew her. She had done her duty; she had given my grandfather three sons and her dowry. It contributed much to the stability of wealth in our family.

Our old servants told me that my grandmother was a beautiful woman with olive skin and an unblemished face and a thin waist, a woman who obeyed her husband. People praised her honorable quiet. Her older sons adored her. Stephanos remembered her not at all. Even my father venerated her. When he mentioned her name, tears came to his eyes, and he crossed himself.

Her father remained adamantine about religion; he would not marry her to anyone not a Catholic. The prospect of her dowry inspired my grandfather to mystical transports, and he converted to the papal church. This transmogrification left most of my Greek relations hostile to my family even when I was growing up. To be Greek was to be Orthodox. But we were so wealthy that we could have been Mohammedans.

My grandfather said, "We're all going to the same place. What does it matter what we call ourselves?" My father said he preferred the Catholic Church because of its celibate priesthood: "I do not want to take the Eucharist from the damp fingers of a man who has just had his fingers in his wife's cunt." He was a great lover of women. He also held them in contempt.

My grandfather died old and venerable when I was six. My father had been directing the firm for years; now he was chief in law as well as in fact. His brothers were junior partners. My father inherited his father's amazing talent for judging tobacco. He inherited also his business sense and the furious energy that carried with it a diabolical devotion to work. He did not inherit his father's good humor. He and his brother Georgios quarreled.

My father slapped Georgios with an open hand. They never spoke again. Georgios departed for Russia a week afterwards. Like many other Greeks, he took a position in the Russian bureaucracy at Sebastopol, and he married a fabulously wealthy Russian woman. Part of the luck of the Kephalopoulos family lay in its ability to find women of great wealth to be their wives.

Stephanos stayed in the firm. He was handsome and elegant, almost beautiful. He had a full-length mirror in his room. When I was a little boy, I saw him pose often before it, holding his cane at various angles, lifting his chin, cocking his head, practicing expressions—humor, gallantry, surprise—sometimes stroking his mustache, laughing gaily at nothing, appraising his performance.

"I must make the best of what I have, for I do not have very much," he said. When he walked along the quais, he looked debonair—like my grandfather, people said; tall for a Greek, and handsome. No one who knew him well took him seriously—except me.

My father wanted him to marry. "If you cannot do anything to help the business, you can at least bring in a dowry. A rich wife would be something. Suppose she is as fat as butter and her breath smells like the cesspools of Macedonia. If she brings a dowry to the firm, I may forgive you for being more worthless than garbage."

Stephanos tried. I saw him striding along with this woman or that gently on his arm at the yacht club on the Turkolimani, her parents walking discreetly and expectantly behind them, everyone dressed up, stiff and formal.

He was almost to the church with one of them, for he liked her, though he confessed to me that she frightened him. Finally he managed to find an excuse or else to create such doubts in the minds of the young woman and her family that the engagement and the marriage were called off. I remember a night when from my room upstairs I heard my father shouting at

Stephanos and making unspeakable accusations, and I heard Stephanos crying. We never spoke of it.

Stephanos took his comfort in harmless pleasures. I have mentioned archaeology. He also played the bouzouki. It is of some importance to this story that he taught me to play as well. My father did not know that I learned to make music from the instrument. We never played in his presence.

When Stephanos and I traveled, we took our instruments in our luggage, wrapping our clothing around them. I had the gift to tune them exactly.

We played at home when my father was away at the warehouse, and the servants—who feared and disliked my father and loved our music—never tattled. I watched the slender fingers of Stephanos fly over the strings, and my fingers followed his. I cannot explain it. I could never teach anyone else to do what I could do—what I can still do—with the bouzouki. Stephanos taught me. Something in me leaped to his teaching, and I played in a way that to him seemed miraculous.

We played together atop the high tumulus of Mycenae, where the wind blew up from the Gulf of Argos and where the naked hills rose on each side of the ruins of the house of Atreus. We played on the patio of the Hotel Castalia at Delphi and looked down the Pleistos Gorge onto the fragile green of the olive grove. People gathered silently and listened as though they were in church. All during the Turkish times, Greeks played the bouzouki. It was the sound of our freedom. When we played at Delphi, a professor of some sort rushed up to us with tears in his eyes. "You are true Greeks," he said. "As long as we play the bouzouki, Greece will be free. The Turks could stop us from writing. They could stop us from speaking. But they could never stop our music. Bravo! Bravo!" He sobbed. We wept, too. I do not know why.

In those days I had fancies about the old gods. The God we worshipped in the Eucharist when we knelt in abject submission in the tiny Catholic church in Piraeus was distant, immaterial, holy, and forbidding. Apollo at Delphi seemed closer, more like me, grateful for the offering of my music. I never supposed that Jehovah danced. But when Stephanos and I fell into our music at Delphi, I imagined that Apollo wakened from his long slumber on Mount Parnassos and came down to listen, and that as our music rose and became a storm, he danced, leaping over the naked rocks, naked himself save for his fiery cloak of light, doing cartwheels over the purple peaks above the village and the deep gorge. Stephanos loved to welcome the sun spilling over the bare granite mountains from the east of Delphi and to exult in the clear light that poured down on the delicate green of the ancient olive grove far below.

Sometimes we walked with our bouzoukis and played as the sun rose in stately fire over the great land, and I pretended that Apollo drove his chariot in exchange for our performance and that if we did not play, the world would be plunged into darkness. When the flaming disk of the rising sun appeared over the purple wall of rock to the east, I felt the power of creation in my fingers.

A part of me realized how jealous my father was of the love I felt for Stephanos. My sisters, Helen and Anna, shared that love. We were afraid of our father, accustomed to his rages, to his abiding frown over the long table late in the evenings when we ate, to his criticism of how we dressed or how we spoke French or how we did in school. I think I saw that beneath his hardness my father loved us and felt himself cheated out of the love we owed him. He worked for us. He saw to it that we dressed well, that we had French governesses to teach us the language that let us move in the best circles around the Mediterranean, that we lived in luxury. "Stephanos killed your grandmother," Lukas, our coachman, told me once. "Your father has never forgiven him." I have thought much about that statement. Stephanos took my grandmother from my father; he took us away, too.

My father took vengeance against Stephanos; with the cunning of childhood, my sisters and I took vengeance on our father. I think I was pleased to suppose that my father was hurt when he came home in the evening and found Stephanos and me sitting together on one of the benches on the curved terrace before the view of the bay and the faint lights of Athens glittering across the water. I believe that I was wise enough to know that my father felt injured and that perhaps I meant to injure him.

Maybe that is why he criticized us, insulted us, cursed us, and told us how ungrateful we were—a campaign he waged to liberate himself from the burden of loving us. If he could make us hate him, he could hate us in return. There is liberty in the renunciation of hope.

I wonder now that neither my father nor I ever thought to throw ourselves on our knees before the other and to say, "Can we break this circle? Must it always be so?" That was, I suppose, exactly what my father did on the fatal night when he fled. He threw his arms around me and wept, and I felt amazed at this collapse of hard, interior walls, and I rushed blindly to meet his love. I hardly had time to speak before he was gone headlong into the dark. I do not recall that I said anything at all. I believe that I hugged him as he hugged me. He may have been too frantic to notice.

I wondered afterwards, when he vanished from our lives, if he remembered me only as the son who avoided him and stubbornly refused to be grateful for all he gave me, the son who chose to love Stephanos more. When we remember the distant past, we recall those things that make a great impression at the time and seldom can re-create subtleties in the relations of people with one another. In the end our memories become broken mosaics strewn amid the blackness of what is forgotten, and our distorted recollections lose the varied tones of flesh and blood that made the original event—which we never quite knew anyway.

24

MY FATHER ARRIVED in Naples and went to our company's factor there and drew money. The factor telegraphed this information routinely to the firm in Piraeus, and a secretary came with the telegram at night. The police came soon after with many questions; they had seen the telegram before it arrived at the firm. Where was my father going? We did not know. As it turned out, he found his way to America, and a cousin in Chicago wrote mysteriously with gossip about people we knew nothing about and asked for money to help a Greek family in need. My mother understood instantly, and Stephanos wired her money. Later the cousin—one of my mother's relations—wrote that my father indeed had visited her, filled with prospects and optimism and with the bizarre tale that he had killed a Turk who had tried to destroy the warehouse and that for that reason he had had to flee Greece. She announced with great indignation that he had tried to seduce her and that she had ordered him out of the house. She did not know where he had gone. Later she wrote that a Greek who was a friend of a friend had seen him in Alabama. We studied a map of the United States and found Alabama. We could not find him. My mother's cousin could tell us no more.

Stephanos took over the business. He changed. Suddenly he was up early and out of the house and to the warehouse. At lunch he came home in the family carriage and sat at the table, talking importantly about accounts and visitors and his plans for the firm. My mother praised him extravagantly. Sometimes she said to me, "Your uncle is amazing. I never would have believed that he could become so serious about the business. He is going to do well. I am proud of him."

Stephanos sent word to Uncle Georgios. Uncle Georgios hurried from Sebastopol, arriving grandly on a Russian ship, marching slowly down the gangplank in his splendid uniform with its double rows of brass buttons, holding a fine cigar, looking around the harbor and his old haunts with an air that told us how proud he was to have risen above them.

He coldly shook hands with Stephanos, and they kissed in the Greek manner. He kissed my mother on the cheek and allowed her to kiss him in return. He presented his cheek to me; I smelled cologne on his smooth skin. He kissed me drily in return. He was a statue. Some men in the harbor recognized him and came respectfully to speak to him. There were murmurings and noddings of heads.

He rode in our carriage to our house and walked stiffly around the terrace with a small cup of coffee, looking out across the great blue bay to the white ruin of the Acropolis shining in the late afternoon sun. He sat in a large chair and stared at me. He sipped his coffee. He said, "The boy must go abroad to get an education."

My mother gasped. "Paulos?"

"Yes. To school. If the business fails, someone must provide for you."

"The business will not fail," my mother said. "Stephanos . . ."

My uncle gestured impatiently. "Vasilis is no longer here to direct the business."

"I am here," Stephanos said.

"Yes, you are here," Uncle Georgios said.

"The business is flourishing," my mother said.

"Yes, the business is flourishing," Uncle Georgios said.

"Paulos has opportunity here," Stephanos said. "He can work with me in the business. He can learn. He can educate himself about tobacco the way we all have learned. We can learn together."

"Yes, of course. You can learn together," Uncle Georgios said. His contempt was unbearable. He turned to me.

"Tell me, boy—do you speak German?"

I said that I did not.

"I thought not. Greeks do not learn German. A pity. The Germans are the most brilliant people in the world. If Germany and Russia and the Dual Monarchy could all unite, we could save the world from revolution. We could maintain peace for a thousand years. Perhaps it will happen."

He looked thoughtful for a moment. He scowled at me. "If you had had the sense to learn German, you might go to Germany to school. That is where I shall send my own sons. The University of Leipzig. A wonderful place, Leipzig."

"Perhaps he could learn German," my mother said.

Uncle Georgios waved her suggestion away. "There is no time. He must go to school in a French-speaking land, for he speaks only French. He must do the best he can with his limitations."

We were speaking French at the time. It was an affectation of our level of society. I attended a French school. I read French books. I spoke French with my mother and my sisters at home. Usually I spoke Greek with Stephanos and my father. Georgios, hating Greece as he hated my father, would speak only French.

My mother broke in. "Georgios, I understand your affection for Paulos and your brotherly desire for the well-being of all of us. But my son cannot go to school in France. The Socialists. The atheists. The Republicans. The morals of the women. I would not sleep at night."

Uncle Georgios impatiently waved off her plea. "France! I would not send a cur to school in France! Every French woman is a whore. Every French

writer is an atheist. Every French university is a breeding ground for Socialists. French artists paint pictures of naked women in immoral poses. It turns
my stomach. The Socialists and the atheists deserve to go to the wall, to be
shot. I would not send a nephew of mine to France, woman. I am still a
Christian."

"But where, then?" my mother said.

"To Belgium. The Belgians speak French. They are a safe, decent people.
Catholic. Perhaps a little dull. Nothing ever happens in Belgium. A young
man should grow up in a dull country."

"Belgium!" my mother said. She scarcely knew where Belgium was.

"Paulos should stay here," Stephanos cried. "We can take care of the
business together. We can be rich and happy. He should stay here where he
belongs." I thought he would weep.

"I have already taken the liberty to make the arrangements," Georgios
said, as if Stephanos had not spoken. "I sent a telegram to the school that
was highly recommended to me in Sebastopol, the Institute St. Valéry in
Ghent. It is a proper place, a very proper place. A Father Medulous is in
charge. He has telegraphed me that he will receive Paulos as a student on
the payment of his fees. The fees are exorbitant, but they must be paid. In
advance. The Belgians think always about money. A very good sign. People
who work hard at making money have little time to be immoral with women
or to entertain fantasies of revolution. I have telegraphed Father Medulous
that you will come."

He paused and looked at us with cold finality, drawing at his cigar.

"I have, to be sure, not revealed to the good father the circumstances that
make it necessary for Paulos to go abroad. A reputable religious school
would not receive the son of a murderer, especially one who murdered a
husband he had wronged. I must be frank, Maria. Vasilis has committed a
detestable crime. I have not spoken of it; I have—" Here Uncle Georgios
cleared his throat delicately. "I have not precisely lied to the good father, but
I have implied that Vasilis is dead. I would suggest, Paulos, that you convey
that impression to the priest. I believe . . . ah . . . that there is some . . . ah
. . . justification for this view. To us Vasilis is dead. We will not see him
again."

"Oh, Georgios," my mother cried. "Oh, no—no."

Uncle Georgios raised his right hand in a gesture that said "Halt!" "Hear
me out, Maria. I speak the truth. Vasilis is dead to us. He will never return.
He cannot return. We cannot go to him."

My mother arose and went swiftly into the house so the servants would not
see her cry. Georgios looked pleased. He had the pleasure in virtue that I saw
later on in Virgil Weaver—though without the torment. But then I did not
see Georgios after the war and the revolution, when he lost everything and
came back to Greece a broken man.

He tossed his cigar away and lit another. He drew on it, expelled pungent smoke, and looked at me. "Belgium!" he said with great satisfaction. "You will be very happy in Belgium."

25

SO IT WAS THAT in the late summer of 1911, I found myself aboard an ancient steamer, painted white long before, now rusting away, the name *Agamemnon* painted on the bow, chugging out of the port of Piraeus and making for the Corinth Canal and the narrow gulf between the mountains that lay beyond. I disembarked at Brindisi and took the train north to Bologna and to Milan and thence through the Alps and across a fringe of Germany and into Belgium and Brussels, where the dense smoke of a coal-burning city dimmed the sun, and thence to Ghent across flat land and marshes and water-soaked earth and canals and finally to the spare gray walls of the Institute of St. Valéry, where—timid, lonely, brokenhearted, and innocent of worldly knowledge—I was assigned by Father Medulous to share a room with one Guy Bruyère, only son of a brewer from Dinant, taking his college preparatory work at the Institute, intending to enter the university in the autumn of 1912.

Even now, here in this remote and silent place a little before ten in the evening, tears come to my eyes when I think of that first meeting.

I had traveled far with the memory of my mother and Stephanos and my sisters waving their white handkerchiefs on the quai for as long as I could see human forms against the outline of the wharfs in the harbor. They vanished. With them vanished my old, sure world. I came a stranger to a strange land.

There was Guy, dressed in a green silk robe that swept the floor, nonchalantly smoking a cigarette, literally looking down his delicate nose at me since he was tall and stood very straight, speaking in an accent pompously affected.

The porter carried my bags up to the room, dropped them on the floor, scowled at the tip I gave him, and went out muttering under his breath. I put out my hand to Guy. "I am Paul Kephalopoulos," I said in careful French. "I am from Greece."

"Of course you are from Greece, *mon enfant,*" Guy said, disdaining my hand and turning his back on me. "Where else could a type like yourself be from? I can smell the olive oil in your skin." He walked as far from me as he could get. "The world is come to a very strange place, *mon enfant,* when

Greeks come to Catholic schools to prepare for a university education. I want you to know that you are being forced on me. Why are you here? I supposed that Greeks need know nothing but the recipes for boiled goat meat for their poisonous restaurants."

Someone else might have struck him. I could only stare at him. When I realized what he had said, I began to cry.

Guy did not change his expression immediately, though he told me afterwards that he had been shaken by my weeping. "I had heard that you were very rich and proud and that your family owned many ships, and I was sure you would scorn me," he said. That was much later on when we were friends. Now, instead of apologizing, he rushed forward, holding his hand out to take mine, which I gave him without knowing quite what I did. He called me *"mon vieux"* and clapped me on the shoulder and laughed loudly as if everything had been a joke. As I tried to fist away my tears, he offered to help me unpack, which he did to the accompaniment of a storm of talk.

"You are bound to be disappointed in the school," he said. "It is a dreary place, *mon vieux*. Mass in the morning at six. Father Medulous will give you demerits if you are late and more demerits if you are absent without a good excuse, and it is said that ten of his demerits will cost you a hundred years in purgatory, where you will listen daily to his homilies on venereal disease. Father Droos is the only worthwhile priest. Father Medulous? The man is a fool. He teaches mathematics. He believes the kingdom of God will come in when six-year-olds can do calculus. Most priests are fools. They spend their time lusting after nuns, you know. They decide they want to be priests because they are afraid of sex. 'Shy boy, old priest.' That's what they say.

"Then they are ordained and they hear confessions from those adorable little virgin nuns. What do the nuns confess? Why, *mon vieux,* they confess to the priests that they think of sex all the time. They confess to the priests that they lust after them. They pant in the confessional. 'Oh, Father, I so lust for your manly body. I yearn to look up your cassock. I have sinned, Father. I have sinned. Father, forgive me. Oh, forgive me." Here Guy lifted his voice to falsetto and imitated the passionate effusions of his imaginary nuns. I laughed. I was laughing, and the tears were not yet dry on my cheeks. Guy looked at me solemnly and lifted an admonishing finger.

"You laugh! You think I am joking. No, my friend. No. I tell only the truth. The nuns confess, and the priests tell them that truly lust is a little sin, a mere peccadillo, something so slight that it is hardly worth confessing, that lust comes from love and that love is blessed by God and that perhaps it would make the little nuns feel better if they had sexual intercourse, not out of desire, you see, but simply to satisfy their curiosity. I know why the confessional box has a wire netting nailed across the little window inside. It is so the priests cannot put their hands through and fondle the nuns' breasts when the poor little dears are confessing how they lust at night and how they stroke those very private parts that they have vowed to keep sacrosanct for Jesus."

I was laughing so hard that I had to sit down. Guy sat on his bed and plunged on, waving his cigarette, drawing deeply from it now and then as if to inspire himself, blowing smoke through his nose in what he evidently supposed to be a manly gesture.

"Now, Father Medulous may not spend his time lusting after nuns. To be frank, I believe he lusts for boys. He likes to gather the very young ones about him and run his fingers through their hair. It revolts me, *mon vieux*. But I am tolerant. He has never mistreated me, but I am rich, and were he to mistreat me, he might lose the benevolences that I may give later for the school. Perhaps I shall build a new dormitory—to be named after me, of course. Perhaps if I choose a religious vocation and become Pope, I may make Father Medulous a cardinal. Or if he is dead, a saint. A fine joke, that! No, he has never troubled me, and I have been here six years. In fact, he is not bad. Everyone else loves him. I am hard to please, you see. I withhold my love from all but the most worthy."

"Six years," I said.

"Six years! My God, six years!" He put the back of his hand to his forehead in a gesture of theatrical tragedy and shut his eyes momentarily. "I entered very young. I am eighteen years old now, and I have been a student here since I was twelve. Devilish long time to be in one place, especially in a place like this. I do not perhaps have the religious vocation. Indeed, at heart I am a Socialist. I do not confess my socialism to the world now. It would break my dear mother's heart. Perhaps I shall go to the Congo after graduation from the university. Bear the white man's burden. Do you know Kipling? British poet. Very advanced. I shall of course write about my experiences, and even before I write about them, people will know of them because they will read them in the newspapers. I shall be famous. My destiny is to be famous.

"If there is a revolution in Germany, I shall go there. The revolution is coming, *mon vieux*. When my mother dies, I shall confess my socialism before the world. If I am by then Pope, it will be inconvenient. No matter. I shall be the first Socialist atheist Pope. Will you have a cigarette?"

I took a cigarette—the first I had ever smoked. I did not like it, but it did not matter. Guy rattled on and on. That very evening he took me to the Vieux Gand, the "Old Ghent," though I can never think of it by that dull English name. This was the tavern where the university students gathered. We took a table in a dark corner and drank wine and watched them smoke and drink brown Belgian beer and laugh and call to each other in a clamor of good cheer.

I have mentioned that Madame Boschnagel owned the Vieux Gand. There were many Germans in Ghent in those days. They ran hotels and taverns and restaurants. Madame Boschnagel was huge. She wore a wide, fixed smile. Yet somehow her brightly painted smile with its large white teeth was sincere. Her eyes flashed above it, and everyone could believe that she loved the world and the students who came to drink at her tables. She played a pump organ installed in a place of honor to one side of the dance floor. At various times during the evening, to the cheers of her clientele, she seated herself on the tiny oak bench, her great bottom pouring over it like an overflow of yeasty dough, and with her fat legs she would pump vigorously and run her plump fingers over the ivory keyboard, her head thrown back with that bright, fixed smile, and at the first triumphant notes of a familiar tune, the place would roar with song. Father Droos ignored us when he saw us in the Vieux Gand. He sang. I can see him now, waving his cigarette and singing as loud as anybody else.

She was invariably accompanied by an emaciated man wearing a green vest with sequins that flashed in the light as he played his accordion. I remember how the strong rush of the instruments and the harmony of male voices rose through the smoke-filled air, pounded against the heavy wooden walls, and rolled over the dark ceiling where sooty oaken beams held up the roof. Two tall photographic portraits hung side by side against one wall. One showed young King Albert of the Belgians, the other was of Kaiser Wilhelm II of the German Empire, both rigid in military uniforms.

We were observers. "Next year, when we are in the university," Guy said in an awed voice, "all this will be ours."

26

I TOOK CHRISTMAS DINNER of 1917 in the home of Virgil Weaver and remembered Uncle Georgios. Virgil was thin; Uncle Georgios was heavy. But both looked down on the world from a commanding height. It was a tense and unhappy meal, and I do not know why I was asked. Perhaps Melvina thought that with Dr. Youngblood and me present, we might talk about something besides D.B.'s imminent departure for the army. The talk alternated between unnatural liveliness and a morose recollection of Christmases past, the mention of names unfamiliar to me, half-told tales, and silences when, as people say, an angel passed over the table amid the clinking of silver and porcelain.

Melvina's prattle made a barricade against unpleasantness, and her son contributed his bland, smiling effort to talk about trivial things as if he had given them years of thought. I could see the pain in Virgil's eyes when he looked at D.B., and I saw other emotions, complex and unfathomable. I had a father, but at that time I had not had sons.

Brian Ledbetter and Dr. Youngblood always visited Hub Delaney on Christmas Day after dinner. They excused themselves as Newt set out the coffee pot and the cups. They invited me to come along, and I went.

Brian Ledbetter drove us in his open Model T Ford. Daisy came out as Dr. Youngblood and I were arranging ourselves in the car, Brian Ledbetter crouched in front of the brass radiator, preparing to crank the engine. She said, "I want to go, too. I don't want to sit here on Christmas Day waiting for D.B.'s funeral."

"It ain't D.B.'s funeral," the old man said. "He ain't dead yet. He ain't even in the army. Listen, when one of them army doctors takes a look in D.B.'s ear, he's going to see straight through, and he's going to say, 'Boy, you can't serve in the army, but you will be a whiz-bang in the circus.' "

"I want to get out of this house," Daisy said. "I am tired of worrying about D.B. I am tired of seeing Daddy look at D.B. like he's already dead. I am tired of seeing Mamma cry about D.B. And I am tired of thinking about this war. I want to go see Hub Delaney."

"Honey, you can't go see Hub Delaney. It wouldn't be fitting."

"I don't know what all the fuss is about," Daisy said.

"The fuss is about because Hub Delaney is a moonshiner," Brian Ledbetter said. "Ladies don't go to see moonshiners. Leastways, they don't go with Brian Elisha Ledbetter."

"I never planned to be a lady," Daisy said.

"Honey, you might could try," Brian said. "It'd make your daddy and mamma proud of you if you was to turn out to be a lady after all."

"I would rather drink whiskey and smoke cigarettes," Daisy said.

Brian Ledbetter shook his head. "Honey, what makes you want to talk thataway? You will bust your daddy's heart if you keep on like that," Brian said.

"I couldn't bust Daddy's heart with a nine-pound hammer. Daddy doesn't care about what I do. The only thing on earth Daddy cares for is D.B. Daddy breaks hearts, but his heart is never broken."

"Daisy!" Brian said.

"He broke Hub Delaney's heart, didn't he? Didn't Daddy do that? Hub Delaney is your best friend, but I can't go see him because Daddy turned him into a moonshine man."

"I ain't going to talk about that," Brian said. "You ought not to talk about it neither."

"Cause and effect," Daisy said defiantly. "Daddy was the cause, and Hub Delaney's sitting up there in the hills right now so's no lady can come call on him. That's the effect."

"It ain't the way it was," Brian said doggedly.

"I wish I had a penis," Daisy said. "That'd take care of everything."

"Good God!" Dr. Youngblood said.

"I don't mean I wish I had one all the time," Daisy said, pulling a shawl tight around her shoulders and standing straight and defiant and turning her gaze on me. "I'd just strap it on now and then. Somebody would tell me to go do the dishes, and I'd grab my penis quick as lightning and strap it on, and I'd say, 'Nope! No dishes for me. Look, I have a penis! If you have a penis, you don't wash dishes.' Somebody would say, 'A lady can't smoke cigarettes and drink whiskey,' and I'd haul out my penis and I'd say, 'Have I shown you my penis? I can smoke if I want to.' Somebody'd say, 'A lady can't chase after a man and ask him to marry her,' and I'd wave my penis right under that person's nose, and I'd say, 'See here! I have my very own penis, and I can do anything I want.' "

Brian's face turned purple. The veins on his neck swelled up. He whirled around as if to see if we had heard. He made a helpless gesture towards me, as if he thought Daisy might have forgotten my presence though she was looking me in the eye, but he could not speak. Finally he squeezed out one word in infinite pain. "Daisy!"

Dr. Youngblood, settled in the backseat of the Ford, was lighting his pipe and grinning around the pipe stem. Brian looked at him, looked again at me, and gave the crank a terrific whirl. The engine coughed to life. Brian came around and swung himself up behind the wheel, still looking at Daisy, who kept her shawl wrapped around herself, her arms folded, her dark eyes looking up at him with amusement and love.

"Hey!" she shouted above the engine noise.

"What?" Brian said.

"I write Jim Ed every week," Daisy said. "I tell him everything."

"He's glad to hear it," Brian shouted.

"Daddy never says anything about Jim Ed. All Daddy can think about is D.B., and D.B. is right here, safe as a cat on a couch."

Brian shifted the Ford into reverse and began to ease backwards to turn around. "Let's not talk about that," he said.

"Does Daddy love Jim Ed?" Daisy said.

"Damn right he loves Jim Ed," Brian shouted. "My God, girl—they're brothers."

"They're half-brothers," Daisy said.

"It don't matter," Brian said. "I raised them both, and they're brothers. If I say they're brothers, they're brothers, goddammit. Listen here, young lady. You need to watch your tongue. If you was my daughter, I wouldn't let you do the things you do. I'd whale the tar out of you for that dirty mouth of your'n."

Daisy smiled. "If I was your daughter, you'd let me go with you to see Hub Delaney."

"I wouldn't do no such thing," the old man said without conviction, more to himself than to her. With that he pulled down on the gas lever, and the car jumped, and the back wheels threw gravel up. I looked back and saw Daisy looking after us, her face fixed in a smile.

27

OLD BRIAN LEDBETTER gripped the wheel of the Ford and leaned forward, peering with a resolute squint through the high, split windshield at the land flying by—a land primitive and vast. The wind was freezing.

The land and the cold seemed to bring up in the old man both anticipation and exaltation. I sat bundled in the front seat. Dr. Youngblood sat miserably behind, dressed in his shabby overcoat, his round face almost as red as the old red scarf wrapped tightly around his neck. He wore a heavy wool cap pulled over his ears. He smoked his pipe with the joyless resolution of a martyr forced to endure tribulation for a glory not yet revealed.

Guy and Bernal appeared beside him. They wore the gray suits and the stiff straw hats and the black slippers they had worn to the summer party Monsieur and Madame Grutyer had given in Dinant to celebrate the engagement of Guy and Leonora. The band had played light music, and young men in striped coats and women in long white dresses strolled on the grass and laughed and talked. The women wore straw hats with large brims. Leonora was overdressed and looked old—older at least than the young women Guy's age. She looked fretfully around to see if any woman there might be flirting with Guy. It was early July, 1914.

We followed the macadam pike towards Knoxville along the railroad tracks. In a few miles we passed under a viaduct and drove up into the forested hills. Most of the hardwood trees were bare. Dead leaves clung to the oaks. Naked branches reached into a sky thick with clouds portending snow. Pines and cedars showed a somber green. I could smell the cedars. The cold squeezed the earth.

The road climbed more steeply, and Brian put the Model T Ford into its lower gear and made the gearbox sing. At a fork the trees opened onto a clearing. A stark church, unpainted and bleak, stood against the woods. Beside the church lay a graveyard, overgrown with dead grass, the grass blowing fitfully in the cold wind. Most of the tombstones were unhewn rocks. A few were slabs with inscriptions scratched on them, leaning and rotting in the raw afternoon.

Brian braked to a halt. The engine of the Ford ticked in the windy silence.

"That there is the Friendly Pentecostal Church in Jesus Name Only," he hollered. "Don't never go to church there, or they'll hand you a rattlesnake to test your faith." His voice was thrown back to us by the church and the woods, and we heard its echo crash around us. I imagined the dead, startled by this intrusion, rising slightly, looking out at us, settling down, grumbling, sleeping again.

Dr. Youngblood chuckled. I did not understand. Nobody explained. We drove on. The trees closed in again. The road became dirt. At the top of the ridge the road leveled out, but Brian drove in almost surreptitious languor. Pine needles covered the road, and the tires went softly. Now and then we could look to the right and glimpse through the trees the gray sheen of the river far below. The trees came closer. Very distinctly, high in the naked branches overhead, a crow cawed. I looked up and saw black wings against the wintry sky. I could hear the wind rise and whisper in the cedars, a cold and lonely sound like a chorus of phantoms straining for words, hopelessly murmuring. The cold worked down my back, up my arms and legs, into my gloves and shoes. My fingers and toes became numb.

The track ended in a small clearing. Brian stopped. Against the dark cedars and pines sat a tightly built cabin made of logs and caulked with white plaster. A small window gaped at us from beside the door. A large shed with a loft stood nearby. Two black dogs as big as wolves rushed out of the shed, baring their teeth, barking ferociously. We cringed. They leaped against the sides of the car and snapped at us. I heard their teeth click and felt dog breath on my face, and Brian Ledbetter jerked me back.

"Goddamn you sons of bitches, git back, or I'll run the hell over you!" Brian shouted. His voice sank into the quiet and made no echo. He turned off the engine. White smoke rose from the stone chimney of the cabin. The world smelled of cedars and of cold wind and of burning wood.

"This is it," Brian hollered over the barking dogs. His face was alight with pleasure. The dogs had fallen back from the car, recognizing a sincerity in Brian. "Hey there! Hub? Hub Delaney!"

The door of the cabin cracked open. A voice called from within, cautious and uncertain. "That you, Brian?"

"Who the hell you think it is—Santy Claus? Call these shit-eating dogs off."

"They won't bite," Hub called. "Not lessen I tell them to bite. You ain't never been bit, have you? If you was to come around more, they wouldn't even bark at you."

"I was here last week, goddammit," Brian hollered. "What kind of shit-eating dogs has got such nose trouble that they can't recollect what I smell like from one week to the next!"

"You, dogs!" Hub hollered. "Get back. Get back." He stepped out into the yard, carrying a rifle cradled in an arm. He moved slowly in the slow little steps of an old man. He went on shouting at the dogs and waving them back with his free hand. They backed away but kept on barking, bellies low, ready to spring. He came out to the car and peered up at me. His hair was snowy white, like Brian's. Unlike Brian, he was bald on top.

"If you was a revenue agent or a sheriff or a preacher, these here dogs would of cut you in two," Hub said. "But they ain't never bit no good customer."

We climbed down. I had no feeling in my feet or hands. I could scarcely walk. Brian seemed oblivious of the cold. "Hub's one of the leading citizens in Bourbon County," he shouted. "He makes the best whiskey around."

"Hello, Doc," Hub said. He put out a hand, and I could see that the arm was stiff.

"I'm going inside," Dr. Youngblood said, making for the cabin.

Brian was as leisurely as summer. "This here's the foreigner I told you about, Hub. Name of Paul Alexander."

"What do you say?" Hub said. We shook hands, both of us bewildered and uncomfortable. His rifle was a lever-action Winchester. A friend of Guy's father had shown us one once. He hunted wild boars with it in the Ardennes.

"What?" I said.

"What do you say?" Brian said.

"I do not understand," I said.

Brian suddenly comprehended my discomfort. "It's the way we say hello," he said. "We say 'What do you say?' Why the hell do we say that, Hub?"

"Damned if I know," Hub said. "Come on. It's colder than a witch's cunt out here."

The two old men moved slowly. "Hub was shot by a preacher once," Brian Ledbetter said. He did not explain.

Dr. Youngblood waited at the door. "I don't know why I was fool enough to let anybody talk me into coming up here in an open car," he grumbled.

"Your blood's too thin, Doc," Brian said. "You ain't sleeping enough. It shows in your eyes. Take my word for it, Doc. They was folks dying in Bourbon County before you ever come here. They's going to be folks dying after you've fell down dead yourself. You can't save them all, Doc. Better not kill yourself trying."

"Merry Christmas," Dr. Youngblood said sarcastically. But he grinned, and his eyes shone. He was always pleased when people took note of how hard he worked and how much the sick in Bourbon County depended on him. When we got inside, he took off his heavy mittens and held his hands towards the fire. After a long time he removed his hat, his scarf, and his overcoat.

The cabin had a main room and another room off to the back. A bed with high, thick wooden posts stood in a corner. It was neatly made, piled with blankets and covered with a quilt. Near the bed stood a small oak table with a tall kerosene lamp, unlit, on it. Beside the lamp was an alarm clock with a luminous green dial. Beside it lay a worn Bible. Everything was immaculately neat.

We stood in front of the fireplace holding out our hands. The fireplace was made of fieldstones, held together with mortar. I wondered if these old men had once been able to lift those stones, heft them into place, and cement them together. There was no light in the room except the fire on the hearth and the dimness of a declining afternoon filtering through the small windows.

Dr. Youngblood muttered that it was the coldest winter he had ever seen. Brian said every winter was the coldest one Dr. Youngblood had ever seen. "Well, it's true," Dr. Youngblood said. "I think we're entering a new Ice Age myself. You won't laugh when one of these springs the river doesn't melt and a glacier comes down from Knoxville."

"It wouldn't surprise me none," Hub Delaney said. "We ain't never got nothing good out of Knoxville, and I don't reckon there's nothing to stop Knoxville from sending us a glacier."

Over the mantel, between two rusty old swords with crossed blades, hung a gaudy lithograph of a square-looking man with chestnut hair. He had clear blue eyes, and he wore a dark blue uniform with two rows of yellow buttons on the front of his tunic.

"That there is Sam Grant," Brian said. "Hub and me, we foughten under him in the War of the Rebellion. Not that we knowed him personal, you understand. But we seen him lots of times, and that's a real true fact." I had never seen any of my generals.

"He died in the summer of '85," Hub said reverently.

"We're still alive," Brian said. "He didn't give a shit for us. I thought he'd kill us all and live forever. But he's long dead, and we're still alive."

"What do you hear from Jim Ed?" Hub said.

"We had a letter two weeks ago. Him and Willy's up near Verdun. He didn't tell me nothing about the fighting. Said it was raining and how he missed his guitar and the water from our spring and said he'd won a hundred and four dollars playing poker."

"That Jim Ed," Hub said. "And Clyde? Does anybody hear from Clyde?"

"He writes Joab. I reckon Joab's the only one in the family that takes him seriously. Clyde's decided that Christians don't need to speak in tongues. I thought you'd be glad to know that. Lord knows what Clyde's going to come home with next. I swear, Clyde runs through religions like some folks wears through pants."

"I pray for all of them ever night," Hub said.

"Hub's the Christianest moonshiner you'll ever meet," Brian said.

"God knows my heart," Hub said.

"You might could say we didn't come up here for no prayer meeting," Brian said.

"Where's Caleb?" Hub said. "Caleb always comes to see me on Christmas. He ain't been here today."

"Christmas ain't over yet," Brian said. "I vow he'll be here."

"Folks neglects me now. They don't come round like they should," Hub said.

"Hub, when did you see Caleb last?" Brian said.

"Well, I ain't seen him much. I ain't seen him in at least a couple of days."

"Jesus Christ, Hub Delaney, you are crazy. You're sitting up here all alone, and your brain is getting soft. We all come to see you all the time, and you talk like we see you once a year."

Hub fetched glasses and disappeared into the room in back and returned with a crockery pitcher of whiskey. He poured whiskey for all of us, and we drank. Outside, the afternoon light dissolved and drained away, and we could hear the wind trying itself against the house.

28

I HAD NEVER TASTED anything like Hub's whiskey. It looked like water, but it burned all the way down. After a while the burning felt good. We sat in rocking chairs before the fire. The talk went on to the accompaniment of a rhythmic thumping of wood against wood. A comfortable sound.

I knew that Guy and Bernal were behind me in the shadows. I refused to turn around. Brian and Hub talked languidly after the energy of their first meeting was spent. After all the years of their friendship, they had little new to tell, and they were often silent, looking into the fire, puffing their pipes, sipping the whiskey, listening to the wind sing in the chimney. If Dr. Youngblood had not been there, they might have sat away the afternoon and perhaps the night as well in the thoughtless and peaceful intimacy of wind, fire, tobacco, whiskey, and silence.

Dr. Youngblood provoked them to talk. He seemed content to listen to their stories and to tell none of his own. I was a new audience; by being present I made something new of old tales. He was a man without the simplest envy, and he delighted in the people he loved as some might have delighted in jewels or in coins or in stocks and bonds. He wanted to give his friends to me with a generosity that might have caused others to give food to strangers, the act being a hospitality that, he felt, he owed as much as he owed his medical powers to the sick and the maimed. He had long since heard all the stories that Brian and Hub could tell, and he could have told them himself. He wanted me to hear them, but he wanted Brian and Hub to tell them.

So he said "Tell Paul the one about . . ." and the two old men leaped to draw up their tales from that great pool where all our stories lie patiently still, one old voice beginning, the other adding, the first adding again, sometimes disputing, a squeaking of old ropes and pulleys, tugging upward until a time and place stood solid in the room.

Dr. Youngblood sat puffing softly at his pipe, his round and kindly face red with whiskey and contentment, and he laughed in his languorous way with the anticipation some feel when a singer begins a dear old song.

"You should never listen to stories about this place," Bernal whispered at the back of my neck. "They will make you forget ours." His whisper fell into the wind gusting in the chimney and sighing beyond the cabin walls and in the forest beyond waving for miles in its dance with the cold air.

So while the last of the afternoon light thinned and paled and faded into a dusk that slowly extinguished the trees beyond the window of the cabin, I heard of the black midnight when Buster Abernathy's wife, Abigail, became convinced that Buster had a woman hiding in the outdoor privy and how she took a ten-gauge shotgun and blazed away at the outhouse with buckshot and filled it full of holes so that a decent man could not relieve himself there without being on public display to anybody who passed by in the road, and how Buster did indeed have a woman but how she hid in the hay in the barn at milking time and how once in their thrashing around they stirred up the fresh milk so much that they churned it into butter and how Buster explained to his wife that the cow had run around all over the place that day and churned it inside herself so that milking her had taken twice as long as it usually did since what came out of her teats was pure butter in long strips.

I heard how Molly Montgomery Clanton, daughter of the preacher at the Tabernacle Baptist Church on Second Avenue, eloped in the spring of '93 with Roy Tom Blankenship and how she discovered, after they had said the proper words and signed the proper papers before a proper justice of the peace in Rossville, Georgia, where you could get married without having to wait three days after procuring a marriage license, and after they had checked into room 238 of the Grand Plaza Hotel in Chattanooga, Tennessee, and locked and chained the door and pinned their brand-new Georgia marriage license to the flowered wallpaper over the bed—how Molly Montgomery Clanton learned that Roy Tom, when seized by great excitement, as, for example, in the anticipation of sexual union, was afflicted by abdominal convulsions that in some people produce the hiccups but that in Roy Tom produced uncontrollable and suffocating farts, and how Molly Montgomery

Clanton's undying love for Roy Tom, who sported a fine little mustache, dissolved like sugar in castor oil and made the marriage bed and the marital experience repulsive and how she leaped out of bed and grabbed her clothes and covered her thin nakedness as best she could and ran away, still less than half dressed, out into the empty streets and came home sobbing from Chattanooga in a caboose because there were no eastbound passenger trains at one o'clock in the morning, and how she walked all the way from the depot to her father's house behind the church whence she had run off with a cardboard suitcase on the previous afternoon, and wept on her forgiving father's loving shoulder and told him that she could never, never bear the children of a man who cared so little for her as to lose all control of his lower abdominal functions and produce the foul-smelling gunpowder blasts of Roy Tom Blankenship but that because she had seen Roy Tom's nakedness (a nakedness reported to be unremarkable by others unknown to Molly Montgomery Clanton but experienced in the matter) and because he had seen her nakedness and had devoured her with his lustful eyes, she could never, she said, never honorably live with another man in Christian matrimony because she had been defiled and her virgin conscience deflowered so that she could *never* bring the purity the Lord Jesus Christ demanded to the marriage sheets of a deserving and fartless man, so she became a spinster missionary schoolteacher and went out with the China Inland Mission to Nanking, China, and never came back to Bourbonville again, and the two old men, taking turns with the lines, told how Preacher George Montgomery Clanton, her father, had explained and excused his daughter by declaiming the real true facts of the case in a sermon to the biggest Sunday-morning congregation that the Tabernacle Baptist Church had ever held within its sagging walls and how he had given a private and much more detailed account of the story to others who for unaccountable reasons did not make it to preaching that day, including Hub Delaney, then sheriff of Bourbon County, who never went to church but who received a visit from Preacher George Montgomery Clanton so that Hub could spread the truth around on his official business just in case anyone asked, and how the tale provoked Bourbon Countians to indecent laughter in the presence of pale, angry, silent Roy Tom Blankenship who, they said, would be the only man since Creation to get his heavenly reward for sending to the heathens his very own missionary, paying for her with an intestinal malfunction that had been used by the merciful and mysterious providence of God to be the instrument of salvation for untold thousands and perhaps millions of Chinamen who on the Great White Throne Judgment Day would mill around Roy Tom Blankenship and sniff at his nether parts with abject Oriental gratitude, joyfully chattering in their heavenly China talk, exalting him as the divine censer pot of all the ages, and they told how Roy Tom finally in frustration and in exasperation and in incandescent fury at the unanimous, unceasing, and inescapable mockery of the town one morning during the July heat wave of '03 took the early train to Knoxville where resided the nearest known (though tiny) congregation of Chinamen and walked into the Wong Lee Laundry on Market Square and introduced himself as if his name—Roy Tom Blankenship—pronounced at the top of his voice and with a marked separation of the syllables, would bring a flash of instant recognition to the yellow face of any Chinaman in the world and how, having shouted his name a second time as though in explanation sufficient for what he was about to do, proceeded to try to dunk the laundry's head Chinaman, Mr. Wong Lee himself, into a galvanized iron washtub full of boiling bedsheets from the King Cotton Hotel, and how the Chinaman's wife picked up a hot flat iron and commenced to beat Roy Tom in the head with it, and how he didn't even feel it, he said later, and how the Knoxville police had to come rushing to rescue the squawking and indignant and thoroughly terrified Chinaman, and how they dragged Roy Tom bleeding and bruised and partly scalded himself and still shouting and unapologetic off to jail and kept him overnight and fined him ten dollars for public drunkenness the next morning in court, and how he risked contempt by protesting to the baffled judge that he had never swallowed so much as a drop of liquor in his entire life and how his defense was his decision to become a missionary for the Hindoo religion and to baptize Chinamen in scalding water to save them from ignorant East Tennessee Christianity, and how after it was all in the newspapers, he had to leave town, and how he ended (so some said) in Detroit, Michigan, where he went to work for Henry Ford and was never heard of again—except that Brian Ledbetter swore that when you got three brand-new Ford cars together, you could sniff very carefully, and something indefinable, so faint under the new-car smell you could scarcely tell it was there, something maybe in the cloth upholstery Henry was putting in some of his cars now, would hover in the air, and whatever it was just made you naturally think of Roy Tom Blankenship.

And Dr. Youngblood, who had heard the story a dozen or maybe three dozen times, laughed and laughed and turned a deeper shade of red and shut his eyes down until they became fine, straight lines in his face and, as he always did at the end, asked the only question that a Harvard-educated man from Baltimore, Maryland, a man who remembered (as he told me) the ordered brick streets and the ordered brick houses built wall to wall with the white marble steps and the black maids in white dresses scrubbing the steps in the morning light so that the world seemed rectangular and precise as a brick abacus, *had* to ask in Bourbon County, Tennessee, where nothing was exactly straight at the corners and where the world, except for the brick courthouse, was wood and all the clocks told a different time: "Is it really true? Is that damned story *really* true?"

And Brian Ledbetter, looking solemn and venerable, lifted his big right hand as if to take an oath binding his immortal soul, and he nodded gravely, slowly, and he said in a low and reverent voice, "That's gospel, Doc. I swear it's gospel. On my sacred mother's honor, it's gospel."

"I don't believe it," Dr. Youngblood said. "I never believe it."

Brian solemnly shook his head. "Doc, you think I could make up a story like that? You think I could make up all them *details*? You think somebody like old Hub there could make up a story like *that*?"

"It makes me want to be a Christian," Dr. Youngblood said. "Anybody that can believe that story can believe anything."

"By faith you can move mountains," Hub said solemnly. And as he spoke he sat up straight and motioned for silence. "Listen!" he said.

29

WE HEARD A CAR chugging softly through the dark woods. A yellow ripple of headlights washed through the window and over the opposite wall of the cabin. The dogs outside set up a wild clamor. Hub got up stiffly and took his rifle down from pegs along the wall. The rest of us sat still.

The engine stopped. The headlights went out. The dogs began a joyful whimpering.

"Do you reckon . . . ?" Hub said.

"Hub! Hub Delaney! You home, Hub! Stepdaddy?"

"By God, it is!" Hub said joyfully, and his soft old mouth made a smile.

"It *sure* is," Brian said, hobbling out of his chair. "It's Caleb. Caleb's one of the boys, Paul. He's second after Virgil."

Hub pulled the door back, and the winter air poured in. Caleb came sweeping after it. I had never before seen anyone like Caleb. He was large, jowly, going to fat, although something about him seemed powerful. He was in his forties, and he resembled Virgil, except that the lines in his face were blunter and more blurred. He had a heavy shock of unruly hair going gray. He wore a new black sealskin coat that gleamed in the firelight, and he carried a rakish fur hat with large ear flaps. All his gestures were large. When he took off his coat and tossed it onto a chair, he revealed a gabardine suit woven in enormous, alternating patches of black and white; he resembled a man who had rolled in a giant checkerboard and run off with it.

Caleb was not alone. He was timidly followed by a slender woman in a cheap coat. She wore a velvet hat of faded green, and she looked anxiously around and smiled frantically, all crouched over as if trying to make herself as small a target as she could. She kept her lips tightly shut when she smiled.

She wore bright rouge on her cheeks, and she had blackened her eyebrows. Altogether she looked tacky and used.

"This here is Gladys," Caleb said. "She is a waitress, a very fine and polite waitress in the Hotel St. James up at Knoxville, and I give her boss twenty dollars to let her be off for the day. Gladys and me, we're special friends, don't you know." He winked broadly and hugged the woman in a jovial way and grinned down at her as if he had just paid fifty cents for her to a man who had not realized that he owned a five-dollar dog.

The woman was embarrassed. She resisted him ineffectually. "Gladys's modest," Caleb said approvingly. "Gladys, say hidy to the folks."

"Pleased to meet you," she said faintly, and she blushed through all her rouge. She had dark and lovely eyes and high cheekbones and a thin face that might have been elegant except that when she spoke, she showed rotting black teeth. She seemed to be thinking "teeth" every minute, keeping her lips pressed tightly together even when she smiled.

"I told Gladys if we come down here to see you, Hub, we might get something stronger than orange juice and apples to make Christmas go away faster. By God, Stepdaddy, I see you done got the jump on me." He gave Brian an affectionate bearhug.

"Not by more than forty years, you old dog you," Brian said, clumsily clapping Caleb on the back in unmitigated joy.

"Har, har, har!" Caleb said.

"It sure is good to see you, Caleb," Hub said. "I was thinking maybe you had forgot me this year. Lots of folks forget me nowadays."

"I always come down Christmas, don't I, Hub? I told you I'd be here. Don't I always come down Christmas? Doc, it sure is good to see you, you old pussy puller you. I thought you might be out squeezing another kid into the world. Put her there."

Dr. Youngblood laughed. The two men shook hands.

Brian was embarrassed. "Caleb, I swear. You might could talk better in front of a lady."

"Hell, Stepdaddy, Gladys ain't no lady. She's a friend. A damned good friend, ain't you, Gladys?" He hugged her again in his overpowering way, and she looked up at him, this time not resisting. She smiled, her mouth shut, but a flicker of hurt went through her eyes.

Caleb did not notice. He turned on me like a friendly bull. "I reckon you must be the foreigner. Well, you don't look like no Bolshevik to me. Put her there." He wrung my hand. "You know, you've scared the living shit out of this county. You make old women pee in their drawers when you walk by in the street."

I made some stumbling reply.

Caleb drew himself back and inspected me and kept on in a loud voice. "Well he has, ain't he, Stepdaddy? All them Bolsheviks running around in

Russia like fleas on a rat's ass, and they's lots of folks that wonders if this here foreigner might be one of them spies they got all over the world, and my brother Virgil gives him an invite for Thanksgiving, and that clinches it. If they was a Bolshevik within a thousand miles, Virgil would give him an invite just to show this town a thing or two. Ain't that right, Stepdaddy?"

"He had him to Christmas dinner today, too," Dr. Youngblood said.

"It goes to show," Caleb said. "If the circus was to show up with a three-headed man with a harem of sheep-headed women with three titties each, Virgil would have them all in to dinner just to show the good folks of Bourbon County what he thinks of them."

"Caleb, you're going too far," Dr. Youngblood said, glancing at Gladys.

Gladys grinned as hard as she could.

"So Virgil has had this young Bolshevik to dinner, and I reckon that rubbed the chicken shit on Bourbonville's face," Caleb said. "Ain't you scared to be with this foreigner, Stepdaddy?"

"Let him alone, Caleb," Dr. Youngblood said softly.

"Aw hell, I reckon you ain't no Bolshevik," Caleb said, clapping me hard on the back. "Shit, I talk to folks, don't you know? I mean, when I'm going up and down the streets of my little hometown, I drum up business, and I palaver with folks, and about all they're talking about nowadays is the foreigner. They've got a bee stinging them up their ass to know what he thinks about them. He's seen so much, don't you know? He's so educated, don't you know? He's been to Paris goddamn France, don't you know? They all figure he can tell them what Bourbonville's like compared to all them other places. They think he can tell them how they stack up. And Brother," he said addressing me, "I reckon you've got these folks scared to death because you might tell them all the truth, that we're all a bunch of hillbillies that can't tell our ass from a caboose. What's your name, anyhow, Brother?"

"His name is Paul Alexander, Caleb," Dr. Youngblood said. "Don't give him any trouble."

"Aw hell, Doc. I don't mean to give nobody no trouble. Paul Alexander, eh? I bet that ain't your real name. But what the hell. If I could change my name, I'd do it. Most everybody that comes to America changes their god-damned name. I ain't meaning to give you no trouble, Paul Alexander. I just tell you something. You're damned lucky. Bourbonville could of decided you *was* a Bolshevik. But they've decided you're some kind of god. They ain't going to run you out of town. Hell no. They want *you* to approve of *them*. Count your lucky stars, Mr. Frenchman. Few more months, and you'll be the goddamn king of Bourbon County."

"I am Belgian," I said.

I heard Guy whisper, "This man is not unintelligent." It was a warning.

"I say the Belgiums is all right," Caleb said, clapping me on the back again. "What do you hear from Jim Ed?" Caleb said to Brian.

"He's all right. We got a letter a little while back. Him and Willy is still up near Verdun. They say it's quiet."

"Well shit, of course he's all right. Jim Ed's always going to be all right. Long as he don't crawl up in no tree. He's funny, he is. I ain't never seen nobody scared of high places like Jim Ed is."

"We have the right to be afraid of some things," Dr. Youngblood said.

"I'm just glad Jim Ed ain't seven foot tall. He'd get dizzy looking down at his feet," Caleb said.

"That's a real true fact," Brian said.

"Hub, they ought to of took you up in the army. You could still be a soldier to whup all soldiers. Hub here was a soldier once," Caleb said, turning back to me. "Did you know he used to be sheriff of Bourbon County?"

I said that I had heard.

"Sure you did," Caleb said. "Everybody's heard about Hub Delaney. Best damned sheriff we ever had in the county. Ain't that right, Hub?"

"I was pretty good," Hub said. "I had the job thirty years, and I reckon I done all right." Hub was grinning with pleasure.

"Then my brother Virgil, he made a goddamn ass out of hisself, and Hub here had to run in and save his life," Caleb said.

"Oh, I probably didn't save his life," Hub said uncomfortably.

"Sure you did," Caleb said. "Ain't it so, Stepdaddy?"

"It's so," Brian said.

"And the patriotic voters of Bourbon County turned Hub out the next election. Goddamn preacher of the First Baptist Church led the charge. He said we needed us a moral sheriff. I reckon that's one that'd of let Virgil be lynched."

"That did surprise me," Hub said very softly. "I'd done good for the county, I thought. I never figured they'd turn me out like they done. I should of gone west when I was young. That's what I wanted to do. I should of done it."

"He ain't never gone back to Bourbonville since the day he lost that election. Ain't that right, Hub?" Caleb said.

"That's right," Hub said.

"Tell you something about Hub, Gladys. He can still hit a marble with his pistol if I was to throw one up in the air. Ain't that right, Hub?"

"Aw, I can't shoot my pistol no more," Hub said. "I'm too stiff in the arm. And I never was that good, Caleb. I could do it with a rifle, but not with no pistol." He grinned happily.

"Sure you was," Caleb said. He rubbed his hands and held them out to the fire. "Goddamn," he said. "I hate Christmas. You and Mamma had a good time, I reckon, Stepdaddy? You eat with Virgil and Melvina, I reckon. You was there, too, Doc?"

"You should of come over, Caleb," Brian said. "Virgil always wants you to come. Your mamma was hurt when you didn't show up."

"Yep, and if I'd of come, Mamma would of spent the whole time talking about how poor Aaron wasn't with us on this Christmas Day."

"She didn't mention him," Brian Ledbetter said. "Cross my heart and hope to die. She didn't call his name, not even to me."

"Well, she thought about him," Caleb said. "She's always thinking about him, and if I was there, she'd of thought about him a lot more. Hell, I know Mamma. Aaron was her favorite."

"You got to make allowances, Caleb," Brian said.

"She ain't never forgive me," Caleb said.

"You're doing your mamma wrong," Brian said. "It was a long time ago."

"You're damn right it was a long time ago, Stepdaddy. It was August 23, eighteen hundert and ninety-one."

Brian took a deep, weary breath. "That was when Caleb's brother Aaron died," he said to Gladys and me.

"Mamma ain't never forgive me for it," Caleb said.

"Let's talk about something else," Brian said. "You might could say she still feels sad about Aaron. But she loves you. You ought to come see her more than you do."

"I know she loves me, and I know I ought to come see her more. But I know that at Christmastime she always used to talk about how poor little Aaron ain't with us no more, and she used to cry and carry on, and talk about how we was all together on such and such Christmas Day. Hell, you'd think I taken and shot him on Christmas."

"She wants to see you, Caleb. She's getting old."

"Aw, I'll come out and see you both tomorrow, Stepdaddy. I got so much to do. I got three graveyards now, don't you know. It takes a lot of work to make a graveyard pay. Sometimes I wonder if I'll ever make 'em pay like I thought they would."

30

CALEB HAD BEEN DRINKING. The smell of old whiskey came through his skin. His face was puffy in the firelight. He looked tired. When he talked an electric energy surged through him. When others spoke and he listened, the electricity stopped as though a switch had been turned off.

"Caleb charges fifty dollars to be buried in his graveyards," Brian said.

"It's cheap at the price," Caleb said with a dour laugh. "Where the hell else can you rent a room for eternity and not pay more than fifty dollars for it and it with all the heat, water, and lights you'll ever need? Now, in case you're interested, Brother Alexander, that fifty simoleons includes the embalsaming and a genuine rosewood coffin. If you want a concrete vault to keep the water from rotting your loved one's body, well, that comes extry. If you love your loved one, you'll buy the vault. Keep him dry forever, don't you know. Well, to hell with that. . . . I reckon D.B.'s still planning to join up?"

"Day after tomorrow," Brian said. "The day he's eighteen years old."

"Eighteen years old and you got to tie a rope around his neck to pull him out of the rain. He's trying to get at Virgil; that's what he's doing."

There was an uncomfortable silence. We stood like blocks of wood scattered and forgotten by someone who had planned to do something with us.

Caleb walked back and forth. The planks on the floor creaked under his steps.

"Virgil done what he done in the Spanish thing just because of Aaron," Caleb said. "You name me five other brothers in the world that is more fucked up than us. Well, I take it back. Joab's normal. He's the only one. Gilly's left the country. Where the hell is he now? China? He don't want nothing to do with us, and it's because of Aaron. Clyde's running around after first one damn religion and then another because of Aaron. I was reading in the papers the other day that a lot of them damned Algerians in the French army are Mohammedans, and I thought, 'Oh my God, Clyde's going to come home wearing a fez and crouching down to Mecca five times a day.' "

Brian laughed uncomfortably again and stared into the fire. "I'm glad he got over speaking in tongues. Jesus Christ! That made me nervous."

"It's all connected," Caleb said. "That's the thing about life—it's all connected. You can't get away from none of it."

"You can't never tell," Brian said vaguely.

"It was my fault," Caleb said. "Everybody knows it was my fault."

Brian started to say something and changed his mind.

"It ain't something you will or you don't will, don't you know?" Caleb said. "It ain't nothing that has anything to do with you. I was the one that said, 'Let's go play in the flour mill.' It don't matter whether you think I'm guilty of something or not. I'm the one that started it. From what I started, everything else has come."

"You can't think like that, Caleb. Goddamn. Scuse me, ma'am. I don't mean to cuss around a lady. But Caleb . . . Caleb's like a mule. He works hard, but the only way you get his attention is to cuss him or kick him. He don't understand nothing else sometimes."

"I was the oldest in the bunch that went to the mill," Caleb said. "You remember how Aaron was, Stepdaddy. He loved me. I was his favorite."

"Oh my God," Brian said. "Shut up, Caleb. Don't bring it back. Let it lie. Let it lie."

"Aaron's been lying in the grave all this time," Caleb said. "He was dead and rotted away during the Spanish thing, and Virgil said God told him we didn't have no right to kill people just because a bunch of lunatics like Teddy Roosevelt wanted an American empire. And they all said he was a coward. They still say it."

"They don't say it around me," Brian said.

"By God, they don't say it around me neither," Hub said. The two old men stood side by side, and they might have been young again, and they might have made somebody afraid.

"I always thought Virgil said all them things about how wicked the Spanish War was just to remind me that I'd kilt my brother," Caleb said.

The room was deathly quiet. Gladys looked frightened. Caleb looked at her as if he suddenly recalled that she was there. His voice roared. "You just sit down there, honey. We need something to drink, Hub. Something to make us feel good."

Hub brought out the clear whiskey. Caleb downed a glass, and Hub poured another. Caleb perched on the edge of a wooden chair, his thick legs spread wide. The fire leaped across his face and made it strange, and the shadows nodded around us on the walls like memories come in out of the night to whisper to us and to each other.

"Does the young lady want a drink?" Hub said.

"You want a drink?" Caleb said.

"I don't care if I do," Gladys said, holding a hand up to her mouth and looking timidly around.

"That's the spirit," Caleb said. "Gladys is all right."

Hub poured her a glass. He offered it with a courtly bow. Gladys sipped the whiskey and winced when it hit her teeth.

"Gladys's a good girl," Caleb said. "I feel monstrous comfortable around Gladys. That's the main thing about a woman, ain't it?"

Gladys had black hair, and the fire made lights in it. Caleb tossed off his second glass, and Hub poured a third. Caleb's face glowed. The fire brought out fat bags under his eyes.

"Hey, you know what we done today, Gladys and me?" Caleb said. "We had us a first-class Christmas. I mean *railroad* first class. I bought two Pullman tickets for Bristol, and we rode up there on the train this morning, and we had us one hell of a dinner in the dining car with nigger waiters crawling all over the place and white tablecloths as stiff as planks and silver so bright and heavy. . . . It was one good meal. We got off in Bristol, and we walked around the big graveyard over the depot, the one back up on the hill there? Aw hell, you don't know. I love old tombstones. I want my graveyards to have pretty tombstones in them. I go to an old graveyard, and I get ideas, don't you know?" He stretched his legs towards the fire, and he looked almost content.

"This afternoon we come back on the train, and we had one hell of a supper. God, what food. Roast turkey for dinner and Virginia ham for supper. I'm sure glad the trains keep running on Christmas. It makes it a hell of a lot easier on folks like me. I ain't never going to like Christmas. Christmas is when the sky falls."

"I don't like it much myself," Brian said.

"Damn right," Hub said gloomily. The fire leaped and fell in the logs. We heard the wind suck at the chimney. I looked around. Guy and Bernal stood in the ulterior dimness of the cabin, their arms folded, their faces dark. The fire burned low, and the shadows crept in. Hub threw on more wood. "I'm going out to fetch some more logs," he said.

"Let me do it, Hub," Caleb said. He made an insincere effort to rise.

Hub laughed. "In that suit?"

"Oh, all right," Caleb said, sinking gratefully back. "All these folks heard me make the offer."

Hub put on his heavy jacket and his gloves and went out. The cold swept through the door and lingered like a ghost in the room when the door had been shut.

Caleb drained his glass and went into the back room and returned with the glass full. His face burned like the fire.

"Gladys wants to get married," he said. "Don't you, Gladys?"

Gladys looked away and said nothing.

"You're a bachelor, Doc. You got to be on my side. Just like old Hub there. If you get married, you will more than likely have children, and your children will grow up, and they will treat you like you was simpleminded, and they will spend all your money, and you won't have nothing left when you get old, and they will not give a damn for you, and they will not come down and be with you on Christmas Day no matter what all you done for them." He laughed harshly and drank deeply and seemed to fall further back into time and space.

"I don't know," Dr. Youngblood said wistfully. He sat in his rocking chair and rocked gently. "If you get married, you have somebody to talk to in the middle of the night."

"How many women talk to their husbands in the middle of the night, Doc? If any woman was to talk to me in the middle of the night, I'd bop her one. Middle of the night's made for sleeping off drunks. Ain't that right now?" He laughed.

"Maybe so," Dr. Youngblood said. He looked at the fire.

"Hey you—Paul!" Caleb said in a loud voice. "How long you reckon you're going to stay here amongst us hillbillies?"

I was startled out of a haze of rumination. I did not know what to say. Caleb started to say something else. Dr. Youngblood quelled him.

"Let him alone," Dr. Youngblood said. "He's not a talker."

"Aw, it's all right with me if he don't talk," Caleb said, subsiding into a laugh again. "Hell, if you ask me, we all talk too damned much. All of us excepting Gladys here. She don't talk too much, do you, girl?" Caleb clapped her on the knee with his big, heavy hand, and she jumped.

"I ain't got nothing much to say," Gladys said.

"I like it that way," Caleb said, clapping her again on the knee and making her cringe.

Hub came staggering back with a load of firewood in his arms. The cold stood in the door. He kicked the door shut with a bang. He was breathing hard, all bent over. He looked triumphant. He dumped the wood in a clatter in the dark beside the fireplace and let it lie without stacking it. He tossed a couple of logs on the fire and sat down heavily and sighed an old man's sigh.

"Tell you one thing about this old feller," Caleb said expansively, nodding at Brian and addressing Gladys. "He married our mamma when I wasn't more than nine year old, and he raised all of us and his own boy, too. Worked our asses off, but he never one time got mad at us. I ain't never seen this man in a fume. What do you think about that?"

"That's nice," Gladys said. She put her hand over her decayed and twisted teeth and looked at Brian with amazement.

Brian chuckled. "Why'd I want to get mad? Hell, we was happier than pigs in mud. Lots of times now I get out with Joab and his girls, and we put up hay and bring in the corn. I drive the wagon. I can't throw hay like I used to. But I do my bestest, and I sit up there thinking about what used to be, and I wish it was all back the way it was. I wish we had it all to do over again."

"Before Aaron died," Caleb said.

"I didn't say that, Caleb," Brian said. "I didn't even think that."

"It's why Gilly went off," Caleb said. "He wanted to get as far as he could away from here after Aaron died."

"Gilly went off to make his fortune," Brian said.

"He didn't know he was going to make a fortune. He went off, and the fortune come." Caleb seemed to get confused. "Gilly. He ain't one of us no more. Last time he was here, he was somebody else."

There was a tense and gloomy quiet, and the fire made the shadows leap back against the log walls.

"How did Aaron die?" Gladys said. She was a little tipsy; her voice didn't sound just right.

The silence came back. We could hear the wind in the chimney, and the flames danced in step to the wind's voice. Beyond the walls of the cabin, we could feel the enormous dark of the woods and miles and miles of icy silence and the cold river pouring down through the cold night.

"We don't want to talk about that," Brian said.

"I want to talk about it," Caleb said.

"You always want to talk about it," Brian said. "I'm sick of hearing you talk about it."

"Let him talk about it," Hub said wearily. "He's going to talk about it anyway."

"It was a Sunday afternoon," Caleb said. His voice was thick. "Mamma and Stepdaddy was off at a funeral."

"It was Clarence Jackson's funeral," Brian said. "He used to be the telegrapher here, and he was our friend. He was like you, Doc. He was from Baltimore, Maryland. We called him a carpetbagger."

"I know," Dr. Youngblood said. "I've heard it all before."

"I was there," Hub said quietly.

"They was all at the funeral," Caleb said. "And Virgil got to go to the funeral because he was bigger than the rest of us, and he thought men went to funerals. Well, I taken the boys, 'cepting Jim Ed of course because he wasn't nothing but a little kid, and Stepdaddy here had took him to the funeral, too. Jim Ed is our half-brother." Caleb looked at me, the stranger, for whom genealogies had to be explained. "Mamma had six boys by my daddy, and she had one more by Stepdaddy here. That's the way it was.

"Anyway, the rest of us, we snuck off to the old flour mill on Town Creek. That flour mill, it was run by a feller named Hodgson, and it had this great big bin of bran—you know, the stuff you give cows for feed when you're milking. And this bin was maybe twenty feet acrost, and it had bran in it ten foot deep.

"We was climbing up onto the rafters and jumping off into the bran. It was maybe twelve, fifteen foot up there, but hell. It was like jumping into a mattress. All of us 'cepting Aaron was jumping. Aaron crawled up into the rafters, but he wouldn't jump because he was scared. I shamed him. I hollered up, 'Shamey, shamey, shamey! Aaron's a baby. Aaron's a baby. Aaron won't jump. Aaron's a baby.' And Aaron, he got to crying. I remember him hanging up there onto the rafters with his little brown hands, and he was crying and scared and looking down at me. He wasn't more than eight years old, and he had the yellowest hair. It was like wheat straw, don't you know? He was the onliest one of us that was pretty, and he was the closest one of the bunch to me. I always looked after Aaron on account of how he looked up to me so much, and I wanted him to be a man because he was so close to me, but hell, he was just eight years old.

"And he was hanging up there with the fat tears running down his face, and his face was all dusty, and the tears was washing through the dust, and he was looking down at me like he couldn't believe that I was the one making fun of him like that. And I was out on the floor of the mill and all covered over with bran myself and looking like some wild Indian, I reckon, and I was mad at him because I loved him so much, and he wouldn't jump, and I wanted him to be a man. Maybe them rafters was high. But I didn't figure they was no way he could be hurt. And he looked at me and I shouted 'JUMP,' and all of a sudden he done it. He didn't say nothing. He just jumped.

"Only, he dove off headfirst like he was diving off a rock into water. But he wasn't supposed to dive into bran like you dive into water, because you can't swim up out of bran. And he drownded in it. He drownded in the bran. We couldn't get him out in time. We tried. But the bran was all in his lungs, and when we dug him out, they wasn't nothing we could do. Nothing. I held him, and he kicked hisself to death and turned blue and looked up at me and died and never said a word. Never a word."

Caleb stopped. The tears were running down his face. Gladys put both hands over her mouth. "My God!" she whispered. Dr. Youngblood and Brian and Hub looked into the fire. Dr. Youngblood lit his pipe with elaborate concentration and puffed at it. They had heard Caleb tell the story again and again, and they had nothing else to say about it.

"You see, it was all my fault," Caleb said. His voice had lost its slur. It was low, distinct, regular, and somehow strange, like a hammer falling far, far away, a thing you hear in the summer woods sometimes when it is very, very still, and somebody is driving a hammer off on the edge of silence, and you hear it striking and know that somebody is living out there and you don't know who it is.

"It wasn't nobody's fault," Brian said with a weary sigh.

"How about a drop more, Hub?" Caleb said, his words sugared with artificial gaiety. "I'm too damned comfortable to move." He looked spent, and the fire threw old age into the caverns of his face.

Hub got up stiffly and poured him more whiskey. "Caleb always was a hard worker," Brian said, speaking in the false lightness that had come onto the talk like some luminous moss on rotting wood.

"I still work hard," Caleb said. "But Stepdaddy and Mamma don't like my job."

"I never said that," Brian said.

"You don't have to say it," Caleb said in a flash of anger. "But I know what you're thinking—what everbody's thinking. It don't matter. I'm man enough to take what folks thinks, don't matter if they say it to me or not. It don't matter if some of them is in my own family. I decided way back when that I was going to get paid for what I did. I seen all them folks working so hard—like ole Stepdaddy here—and all us boys in the fields like slaves with the sun coming down. Stepdaddy here, he loves to thresh wheat. It's a party for him. All it ever was for me was wheat dust down my back so I'd come home at night looking like a goddamn raw beet."

"You could always take a bath," Brian said.

"In a number-three tin washtub? Hell no. I decided the best way to get rich was to find something nobody likes to do very much, something that has got to be done, something you don't find many folks doing. I thought about going into the garbage trucking business. But then I'd of had to have partners and men driving trucks and that big stink, and I didn't want to fool with it. So I went into the undertaking business. That's what people call it, but we like to call ourselves embalsamers."

"In my day we laid out the corpse in his Sunday best and planted him in the ground before he began to rot," Brian said.

"We didn't get Aaron in the ground in time," Caleb said. "Do you remember that, Stepdaddy?"

Brian sighed in resignation. "It was August."

"August, and he stunk," Caleb said. "I smelled him. We all smelled him. It made me puke."

"He looked so pure and white," Brian said wistfully. He had drunk a lot of whiskey.

"That's the thing about modern embalsaming," Caleb said. "Pretty soon we're going to have a whole generation that don't know what it's like to smell a corpse. We embalsamers are taking all the disgusting things out of death. Folks ought to be grateful, but they ain't. They just complain about the bills."

He shook his head and drank. "Only damn thing bothers me is I never can get the stink of formaldehyde off of my hands. You can't smell it, but I can. I lift my glass to take a little drink, and I smell formaldehyde. Just a sniff, don't you know? But I can't wash it out. No matter what soap I use, it's always there. I wear gloves when I work, *rubber* gloves, goddamnit. And it still gets into my skin."

He sniffed gingerly at the back of one hand and shook his head in disgust. "That's the way it goes. You got to do what other folks don't want to do if you're going to make it in this old world."

I was thinking that formaldehyde was HCHO, hydrogen, carbon, oxygen, the same in all the universe, unchanged by death or war or time, when Gladys screamed.

The scream rang in the room. I thought it would make my head explode. Her scream drove needles into my eyes. She jumped up and leaped backwards in terror, and her chair crashed onto the floor behind her. She nearly fell. Caleb, leaping from his own chair with a speed that I could not have believed in him, grabbed her. We were all on our feet, utterly uncomprehending. Glasses dropped to the floor and broke, and Brian was shouting, "What is it? What is it?" His face was slack and old and pale like the horsemen of dreams.

"A snake!" she shrieked. "A *snake!* Right here in the *house* with us!" She screamed again, both hands pressed to her wasted mouth. Following her horror-stricken gaze to the floor, we all saw it.

A black snake with white markings, heavy and long of body, sluggishly flowed out of the woodpile Hub had dropped near the fireplace. It poured slowly and gracefully over the smooth plank floor towards us in the red firelight, its forked tongue licking at the air.

"It ain't nothing but a goddamn king snake," Caleb hollered, holding Gladys, looking down.

Gladys went on shrieking and wrestling, trying to free herself and run away. "He carried it *in!* He had it in his *hands!*"

Hub ran unsteadily back to the storeroom and brought back a double-headed axe, almost too heavy for him to carry; but, staggering under the effort, unnerved, he threw it up, and the axe flashed overhead in the dark gathered underneath the roof. The sound was a heavy THUNK.

He cut the snake in two and left the axe embedded in the floor. The snake writhed violently, both long parts in hideous, flopping motion, trying and failing to coil, flinging a spray of dark blood from each severed part of itself. Gladys shrieked again, and now she did tear herself away from Caleb and went flying to the opposite wall and cowered there, sobbing hysterically in the near-dark. Caleb did not follow her. We were all in the spell of the dying snake.

Brian shouted suddenly, "Git a *shovel*, goddammit, Hub! Throw the goddamn thing *out* of here! Look what it's done to your goddamn *floor!* Damn! *Damn!* DAMN!"

I was too weak to stand, and I sat down. The others stood in stupefaction, and the room fell into a silence broken only by Gladys's shrieking, which died away into a crazed whimpering back in the dimness. The snake twitched and died, its lidless eyes staring, its white mouth opening and shutting, its forked tongue doing a wild and impotent stabbing at air it could no longer breathe.

"He was asleep in the wood," Bernal whispered. "He was asleep, and something waked him up. The heat. He thought it was spring, and the axe fell on him. I was walking in a green field."

"Forgive me," I whispered. "Forgive me."

No one paid any attention to me. I felt the tears on my face. The others stood with their eyes fixed on the vile thing that lay slowly twisting in two severed parts on the floor, and in the back of the cabin Gladys's helpless sobbing went on and on.

31

IN THE SUMMER of 1912, I finished my preparation for the university, taking my examinations at the Institute Saint Valéry, finishing at the head of my class. Father Medulous rubbed his plump hands together at my triumph. Guy finished, too, but he was near the bottom.

"Why do you do so poorly?" I said. "You are so much more intelligent than I am."

"What does it matter?" Guy said, shrugging his shoulders in indifference. "No matter what marks I make, I am doomed to be a brewer. Besides, people who finish first in their class are never heard from again. Do not be proud, my friend."

"I am not proud," I said.

"Of course you are proud," Guy said.

He was right. I was proud. He took away my joy.

The *Titanic* sank in the North Atlantic in April. My mother became frightened of ships—even the old tubs that steamed across the Adriatic Sea between the heel of the Italian boot and Greece. I went home in August, traveling by train not through Italy but across the Dual Monarchy and Servia, sitting transfixed at the window of my first-class compartment and watching a green and primitive world undulate, expand, and shrink again within the magic frame of glass, whitewashed villages with mosques, the fertile valleys, the mountains, the plastered minarets rising white above twisting streets, the swarthy Moslem peasants in baggy trousers and shoes with toes curved up standing by the tracks as the train shouted its sovereignty over their land. Finally we wound slowly through the naked mountains of Greece, and I drank in the familiarity of the homeland. In Athens I stepped off the train into my mother's arms, and my two sisters flung themselves on us both. We wept with joy.

"Stephanos cannot be here," my mother said. "He is in his office. Very important business, Paul. He is making everything work. Paul, you are so large. You have grown. Is Belgian food so much better than ours? I am so proud of you. I am proud of Stephanos. You cannot imagine the hidden strength the man has. Your father—may God and all the saints bless him wherever he is—never gave him enough credit. Things go on as they always did. Perhaps they are even better than they were. Yes, God forgive me for saying it. I mean no disloyalty to your father. But it may be true. Things may be better than they were."

My sisters asked a thousand questions about Belgium, as if I had not written them every week telling them everything. Lukas, our coachman, greeted me with a smile and a bow, and he drove our carriage swiftly down the long, tree-lined avenue that led from Piraeus to Athens and with grand solemnity turned up the avenue that led to our house on Kastella.

When I passed through the iron gate and came up onto the terrace, a thousand details that I had not thought of in months came rushing back, and I climbed to my old room and found my bed looking just as it did on the morning that I had departed for Belgium the year before. I felt the mystery of how it is that our lives are supported by a thousand or a million small details and that the details in my old life were still in place. For just a moment I imagined my father's step at the gate, and I wondered if he would be pleased when he came in and discovered that I was home.

My mother had heard nothing from him. The police had ceased their inquiries. "I am sure he does not write because he does not want to get us in trouble with the authorities," my mother said. "When he is sure that we will not be harmed by his letters, he will get word to us somehow. He will find another Greek in America to bring us word."

Stephanos came in at seven. He greeted me by kissing me on the cheek, throwing his arms around me, then holding me back by the shoulders to get a better look at my face. He spoke in a loud and contrived voice. He turned to my mother and sisters and said, "Look at him. He went away a boy; he returns a man." He embraced me again.

Without pausing for breath, he began telling me of his successes in the business, of what people had said about those successes, of a trip he was soon making to Crete to look at tobacco there, of the political situation and the war between Turkey and Italy, giving me his own opinion that the injustices of the centuries were about to be undone and that the Greeks would recover their empire and rule in Turkey as the Turks had ruled in Greece. "We will burn them as they burned us," he said.

I saw that he was trying to be like my father—to talk like him, to imitate his gestures, his way of walking, even the way my father held his coffee. His face was drawn behind his smile.

Time passed. We sat at the dinner table late at night on the terrace. We ate and talked and laughed, and as the candles burned down, we watched a faint twinkling in the distance where Athens lay, a small town, not as important as Piraeus. We saw an occasional hazy light bobbing in the vast dark sea, and sometimes a larger ship passed by. One night my mother said wistfully, "I see the great ships, and I wonder if any of them might be bringing Vasilis back to us. He might shave his mustache and come under an assumed name and knock on our door some night. How glad I should be to see him!"

"If I know Vasilis at all, he is in America getting rich," Stephanos said gloomily. "He will build a fortune worthy of his family, worthy of you, my dear Maria, and he will send for all of you, and you will go to America and leave me here alone."

"I am sure he is doing well," my mother said.

"He has the power," Stephanos said.

"He is talented," my mother said. "But no more than you, Stephanos. No more than you. You have proved that."

Stephanos had slept late in the old days. Now he was up at six, as my father had been, walking out onto the terrace, looking across the bay to glimpse the white ruins of the Parthenon on the Akropolis, and if the mist was too thick, he muttered as my father had done, "Ah, it will be hot! It will be hot! *Tha kanei zesti! Tha kanei zesti!*"

He drank his coffee quickly, affecting an expression of resolution; and off he went to his office—my father's office—at the warehouse.

He wanted me to come with him, and I did on many days. I saw him hurrying about, giving orders. I saw the silent contempt of his workers as he changed his mind again and again. He berated them. When tobacco came in from Egypt or from Turkey, where trade went on despite the Turkish war with Italy, Stephanos did as my father had done: he picked up tied bundles of cured brown leaf and smelled them with a professional expression, sometimes putting a few fragments into his delicate mouth and chewing them up, rejecting this lot and accepting that. I wondered if he could tell the good from the bad.

Yet the trappings of success were everywhere. He had always been a fancy dresser. Now his clothes were splendid. We had a new carriage, brightly trimmed with the blue and red colors of the house. He insisted on wearing white gloves whenever he walked in the streets. He carried himself proudly, and when he took me to lunch at a restaurant in the harbor or took us all to dinner in the evening at the Turkolimani, he chose the most expensive items and ordered the waiters about with a domineering tone and tipped lavishly at the end.

I do not think he deceived anyone but my mother.

Our best times that summer were when we played the bouzouki together at night after dinner. Then he seemed like the old Stephanos. I could see the music, not as notes but as colors dancing in my mind. Something in the shifting of the colors told me where to put my fingers. When I let myself float with them, my fingers followed magically, and our music poured out into the night. The terror left his eyes as he played. With the music, I could believe that all was well.

Guy wrote me regularly. He was at home in Dinant, and he was bored. I wrote him, too. One night at table, my sister Helen said, "Paul, you seem so happy in Belgium that you may never come back to us. We are so uninteresting. Your friends are so much more interesting than we are."

"Of course he will come back," Stephanos said. "He will finish the university, and he will return, and he will help me run the business. Isn't that right, Paul? Will you come back?"

"Yes," I said. "Of course I shall come back. Where else would I go?"

"Do you play the bouzouki in Belgium?" Stephanos said.

"I do not have a bouzouki in Belgium," I said.

"You should have taken it with you," Stephanos said. "Why did you not take it with you? Are you ashamed of the bouzouki?"

"Stephanos!" my mother said.

"I am asking if he is ashamed of being Greek, Maria. It is not impossible. Why did he not take the bouzouki with him?"

"I did not think about it," I said. I could not tell Stephanos that yes, I was deeply ashamed of being Greek, that in Belgium Greeks were the scum of society, a laughingstock, and when I thought of Greeks, I thought of my father and that when I passed a Greek restaurant, I feared to look inside lest my father be there, surrounded by people like himself who thought nothing of their families.

"How could you not think about it?" he said.

"Stephanos!" my mother said uneasily.

"Maria, I tell you the matter touches me to the heart. The boy is gifted. He can play the bouzouki as no one else. I have never heard anyone play as Paul can play."

"You can play beautifully, Stephanos," my mother said.

"I cannot play like Paul."

"Do not be angry with him. Surely you knew he did not have the bouzouki," my mother said.

"If I had known, I would have made him take it with him. If he does not play, he will lose his gift. He will forget that he is Greek."

"Stephanos, he can never forget that he is Greek."

"If he forgets that he is Greek, he will not come back to us. We need him in the business. All of us must stay together. We are a family."

My mother tried to calm him with laughter. "But it has nothing to do with the bouzouki, Stephanos. You cannot make our family depend on the instrument."

"It has everything to do with the bouzouki, Maria. Everything," Stephanos said.

I went back to school in October, this time taking the boat over to Italy and the train from Brindisi because there were rumors of a Turkish attack on Greece from the north, where the rail line went. The Turks had no navy, and everyone said the sea between Greece and Italy was safe, and my mother surrendered her lesser fear of ships to her greater fear of the Turkish army.

Stephanos came to the harbor with a long box wrapped in white paper and tied with a blue ribbon. "You must take this with you and open it only on the boat," he said. I knew what the box held. He was barely able to contain his pleasure.

In the Gulf of Corinth, the ship under full steam for Patras and for Italy beyond, the sun sinking to the water through flaming clouds, I opened the package from Stephanos. It was an antique bouzouki, the most beautiful bouzouki I had ever seen. The polished wood shone.

"Remember that you are Greek and that we love you and that you must come back to us." Stephanos had inscribed the message on the card that he had enclosed in the box.

I sat alone in the stateroom and looked at the instrument. Very tentatively I tuned it and ran my hands over the strings. My fingers found the music. Softly I played for myself. I thought of Guy. I imagined his mockery when I returned from Greece with a bouzouki. I thought of the filthy Greek restaurant in Ghent, everyone shouting. I thought of my father and wondered where he had gone.

I sat at the little desk and wrote Stephanos a long letter. I thanked him for the beautiful gift. I told him that I would always be Greek, that I could be nothing else. I promised him to play the bouzouki and never to forget him or who I was. I promised to return to live in Greece always.

Very deep in the night, I slipped out onto the deck with the bouzouki in my hands. I held it and strummed it softly, and the music came gently in the darkness. All around the sea stretched in a blackness to the horizon, where thousands of stars shone on the water. At the stern a party of poor people, traveling deck class, chattered away, trying to keep warm. I walked to the prow and stood with my bouzouki, watching the dull white gleaming of the water parting before the ship in a rush of foam. Very gently, as though letting a beloved corpse down into the grave, I held the bouzouki out away from the railing of the ship and let it fall. I heard the almost inaudible splash as it struck the water; I saw a momentary swirl of blackness on the foam; and then the sea carried it away, and we went on.

32

I SAT HERE last night in my kitchen weeping silently over what I had written. I went to bed and slept the sleep of exhaustion, and this morning awoke in a strange peace. The sunlight lay in the grass beyond my window, and the trees were lush, and the roses in the garden caught the dawning light and glowed so that for a moment I was in rapture.

Two days after Christmas D.B. Weaver went down to the depot and boarded the morning train to Knoxville to join the army. That night Dr. Youngblood came for me after supper and we walked to his house. Virgil sat by the fire looking bereft. We drank whiskey until far into the night.

D.B. departed in impenetrable good cheer. "I thought at the last that we might talk," Virgil said.

"He's only gone to Virginia," Dr. Youngblood said.

"He's gone to the next world," Virgil said. His restrained tongue was loosened by the whiskey. Maybe he thought of me as others did—the oracle who could bring wisdom.

"My father was a carpenter," he said. "He built things. A good carpenter. Do you know what I remember about him?"

"No," I said.

"I remember how he smelled and the sound of his voice. He was a singer. Tenor. It was a nice voice. I never heard one nicer. When I hear a tenor to this day it makes me want to cry. He rocked us to sleep at night—me first because I was the oldest—and he sang to us. All sorts of old ballads. He held me in his arms, and I smelled tobacco and wood dust and sweat. We took baths once a week in those days."

"I wish some of my patients would take them that often," Dr. Youngblood said with a chuckle.

"He never did talk very much. Not like Brian Ledbetter."

"Brian is a good man," Dr. Youngblood said.

"One of the best," Virgil said, a little too stoutly. "Oh, he scared me to death when he married Mamma. Taking Daddy's place like that. I can't tell you how I felt when I realized that he was going to sleep in Mamma's bed. That they were going to sleep together the way Mamma and Daddy did. I didn't understand sex. I knew about cows and bulls, but I didn't understand how human beings did it."

"They seem to come by it naturally," Dr. Youngblood said.

"I missed Daddy. I've missed him all my life. Back when I was doing those things against the stupid Spanish madness, I used to think that Daddy would approve. Daddy and John Wesley Campbell."

"They would have, too," Dr. Youngblood said.

"Oh, I don't know. Who can tell? I used to think about them both—my dead father and the dead lawyer who'd been a giant in this town."

The cold pressed itself against the windows and slid across the floor and washed at our ankles.

"You know what I did once?" he said to me.

"No," I said.

"I went around to ten, fifteen houses my father had built. They're all over the place. Not fancy houses. Just plain old houses. He built them. Designed them and built them. I can tell you what one of his houses looks like. I can look off in a field somewhere or back up in the woods behind a dirt driveway, and I can tell that's one of my daddy's houses. Something in the style. The man had a style, and I can tell what it was."

"Yes," I said.

"I went and felt the nails he'd driven in. That's a pretty intimate thing, don't you think?"

"I do not understand," I said.

"A bad carpenter drives a nail in, and when it's totally sunk in, he keeps hitting it with his hammer. You know what that does?" Virgil said.

"I suppose it leaves a dent," I said.

"Exactly! My daddy didn't do that. You can feel the nails my daddy drove, run your finger over the nail head, and you won't feel any dents in the wood. His nail heads are flush with the surface of the wood. He had a delicate stroke. He must have been the best carpenter that ever was."

We were silent. Virgil said, "People write about lovers. That's the kind of book Daisy reads. Love stories about men and women. I tell you the most important story. It's the story about fathers and sons. Fathers and sons can mess up more things than men and women ever can. That is the truth, my friends. That is the truth."

33

ON DECEMBER 26, 1917, the federal government of the United States nationalized the American railroads.

Pinkerton got the news by telegraph in the late afternoon. The papers the next morning carried the story in black headlines. A former Knoxvillian, William Gibbs McAdoo, was made czar of the railroads. "The goddamn Bolsheviks have taken over the country," he shouted. "Just like in Russia. I never trusted that goddamned Wilson. Now look what he's done." He imagined, I suppose, that strangers would re-examine the operation of the railroad and decide that he was dispensable.

As it turned out, the federal takeover meant that a couple of inspectors came down from Washington to supervise the running of the Bourbonville Car Works to see that our production fed the war effort.

They arrived on the afternoon train from Washington in the middle of January. Pinkerton took Dale Farmer and me to the depot to meet them. "I want people who look good in suits," he growled. "I want those shitheads to know we go first-class."

It was a clear, cold day. Everything seemed carved out of glass. The sky was as blue as ice at sea. I wore a new overcoat. It cost twelve dollars. Even so, the chill ate into my bones. Pinkerton never wore an overcoat. He paced up and down beside the tracks, his face red with cold he pretended not to notice, his hands rammed into the pockets of his trousers. His suit needed pressing.

"Listen," he said suddenly. "There he is! There he is!" His face lit up.

I could not hear anything at first. Then from far away I heard the locomotive whistle, rising in the icy afternoon air, dying away, rising again, dying again. Above us the semaphore signal cranked down to a forty-five-degree angle.

"He's on the block at Martel!" Pinkerton said joyfully. "It's the sweetest sound in the world, Alexander." He stood with his hands deep in his pockets, his feet wide apart, looking up the track with a rapt grin, and in time the train swept around the bend by the brick cotton mill and bore down on us. It was number 41, bound for New Orleans, pulled by two powerful steam locomotives trimmed the green and white of the Dixie Railroad and gushing coal-black smoke and white steam into the vivid sky, side rods moving in tandem, catching the winter light. Pinkerton yelled happily at me. I could not hear what he said.

When I saw the inspectors, I knew they were third-rate men. They wore cheap clothes and cheap grins. Each had a railroad watch in his vest, a silver chain stretched across a big stomach. They smelled of cheap cigars and cheap cologne. Their hair was slicked down with brilliantine under their hats.

Pinkerton strode forward and shook hands with them and introduced them to Dale Farmer and to me. Within an hour we were walking around the car shops, Pinkerton pointing here and there, talking about the operation as if nothing else on earth could be so interesting, so full of wonder, so glorious. He was the king showing visiting ambassadors his fertile valleys, his vineyards, his fields, his orchards, his rivers. He told them how he had built the car works where a swamp had been. The inspectors exclaimed their appreciation.

Their names were Joe Vissing and Dick Shaw. Vissing had bulging eyes and wore an expression of studious calm over a vacant smile. He puffed habitually on a pipe and spoke slowly and wisely, as if every word cost him great effort and should be closely attended. He had traveled, though I never learned why. He had been in Mexico and in Panama, and at times when he had had a little to drink he could speak with great energy about the beauties of those lands. Yet he remained dull and commonplace. "If you take nothing with you, you find nothing there." A proverb. Vissing reminded me of it.

To Pinkerton he was a marvel. "The man's deep," he exulted to me. "Such thoughts! Such sentiments! What experience!"

Dick Shaw, the other inspector, was preposterously overweight. He wore in turn two frayed old suits so tight that they looked like discolored skin. His stomach hung over his belt. How did he manage to buckle that belt? How did he fasten his trousers every morning?

Everything seemed simple to Dick Shaw. "I've just had to realize it," he said to me. "I'm smarter than other people. I see things other people don't see. That's the way it is."

He belonged to that human type that can never confess ignorance. He spoke with a measured and delicate caution, floating his words on cushions of air, politely conscious that his prodigious learning might crush ordinary mortals. While he spoke, a restrained and haughty smile twitched over his face. His eyes never smiled. They watched and calculated.

Like Vissing, Shaw told stories about people he had known and deeds he had done. He mentioned speeches he had made at important meetings. He called the President "Woodrow" as if they were old friends who had advanced equally in life. He did not quite say that Woodrow had consulted with him about the declaration of war against Germany, but he left that impression. "I said that we couldn't take the sinking of our ships lying down," he declared. "I felt like Woodrow felt; I hate war. I didn't think we could get into this war without changing a lot of things that ought not to be changed. The niggers, for example. The Civil War upset the way whites and niggers lived together. This war might do even more harm than that if we ain't careful. But I said we had to fight. We can take care of the niggers afterwards if they get uppity. I know Woodrow feels the same way."

We became accustomed to the three of them—Pinkerton, Shaw, and Vissing—parading about the car works together. I saw how Pinkerton was seduced by them and that his old fantasies were reborn by the appearance of these nonentities in our midst.

"I tell you," he told me, "I've been in Bourbonville too long. It's a limiting town. These fellows . . . can't you just smell the fresh air blowing in their talk? It makes me want to take a deep breath. That's the thing about a good war! It shakes things up, raises the dust a little, makes people move. I tell you what I think, Alexander! I'm going to Washington City when this shindig is over. Maybe before it's over. Hell, now that we're at war, a war like this one, the goddamn railroad can't afford to hold something against me that happened twenty years ago. I've had a perfect record since then. No labor unrest here. No strikes. Everything runs like an Elgin watch. Now I'm being seen. And by what men! I'm not as young as I used to be. But it's never too late so long as you're alive, and I'm *alive!*"

34

THERE BEGAN THEN a tragicomic drama that played itself out over the next months. Shaw and Vissing, delegates from the federal government while good men were otherwise engaged, came to Bourbonville, a remote outpost, to administer the colony, and they found it advantageous to make an alliance with the local chief, Pinkerton. The chief, imagining that these nobodies were plenipotentiaries of a divine authority, regarded their vulgar tricks as miracles.

"Pinkerton puts a lot of store by you," Shaw told me gravely. "He says you're the smartest man around. Now myself, I think folks are smart in different ways. I reckon you're *book* smart. But that fellow Pinkerton, the man's *people* smart."

Shaw ambled into the laboratory at odd hours. I decided early on that neither he nor Vissing had any idea of what they should be doing. They had papers to fill out. They wrote letters. Otherwise they had nothing to do but endorse the bills of lading and other instruments that Dale Farmer prepared for them in his efficient and energetic way. The car works, operating like some eighteenth-century metaphor for the universe, ran like a great machine after its creation. Vissing sat for hours in the room assigned to them in the main office building, reading the newspapers and taking careful notes in a large black notebook. "A man in my position has to know what's going on in the world," Vissing said, as though instructing me in the secrets of success that had made him great.

Shaw liked to poke about "to see how things are getting along," he told me. Sometimes he waxed reflective. "Must be great to be somebody in a little burg like this. Be known by name to people you meet in the street. Tell you what's the worst thing in the world—walk down the street of a town where you'd like to know folks and not have nobody speak to you. Not have nobody even look at you. That's the way it is in a big city. Have you ever been to New York? Nobody speaks to you on the streets in New York. Here folks already call me by name. 'Hello, Mr. Shaw.' 'Good morning, Mr. Shaw.' 'How's it going today, Mr. Shaw?' That's nice."

He clasped his hands behind his large bottom as though for balance and walked slowly up and down, nodding in agreement with himself. "This here's a family town. I like to see it. Husbands going to work. Wives sticking to home and doing their duty, not bellyaching about wanting to vote and all that shit. Never did get married myself. Still haven't given up hope. Might find a little widow somewhere. Don't think a man ought to get married till he can support a wife and family. Husband ought to provide, you know. You ain't married yourself—you must agree with me, right? I thought so. One of a kind, you and me. Knowed it from the first time we met. Want you to call me Dick. All my friends call me Dick. Shake on it?"

We shook hands.

"Tell you the truth, just between you and I. Wouldn't mind seeing this war go on a while. Don't think I'm bad for thinking about . . . Well, what the hell does it matter what I want? My wanting something ain't going to make it happen. It's just that the war has . . ."

He paused, thinking of how to continue. "You see, lots of folks I've worked with, they've been jealous. You don't have many friends in this old world if you're a go-getter. Folks like to see you chopped down. You won't believe what folks have done to me, the lies they've told. You're my friend. I can tell you things. Shake on that."

We shook hands.

"Well, tell you the truth. Been kept back from things I should have had. But the war . . . Well, look at me now. Look what the war has done for me."

35

I SIT HERE at night in the placid calm of an East Tennessee summer, the daytime heat lifted from the earth, the world still, and I feel two silent streams pouring together on this tabletop, both from the past—one Greece and Belgium, the other East Tennessee, Pinkerton, and the rest. It is all improbable. But is it a bromide to say that every life is improbable? An ancestor killed accidentally by a falling rock two thousand years ago, failing to produce the heir he did produce that stands in our anonymous genealogical line, and we might never have been! Or would we have been some slightly different person? Where does our consciousness originate? What infinitesimal part of ourselves is essential? I cannot say. I can only report my memories here so that they look up at me from my words, and I wonder if anyone on earth can ever see in these lines what I intend to put them in. A puzzle it is not my responsibility to solve.

The Greeks of old believed in fate. I have stood in the hot road where Oidipous, abandoned by his father and cast out into the world, killed him whom he did not know near Hagios Loukas. "Why did it have to be?" Stephanos said, almost in a whisper. "What did he do to deserve the fate that overwhelmed him? Can anyone have deserved such punishment? Either Laios, who abandoned his child to the wilderness, or Oidipous, who killed the man he was bound to love? If Laios had paused somewhere else to repose himself, Oidipous would have passed by the fatal place without encountering him, and the two would never have seen each other, and all the subsequent history of the terrible affair would not have been." Many times I have walked here at night under the moon, my mind filled with a thousand incidents. If any of them had been different, my life would have been different, unimaginably different. It was destiny; if any of it happened, all of it had to happen.

I went back to Ghent in October of 1912 to enter the university and to study mathematics and engineering. I boarded still at the Institute St. Valéry, because universities had no dormitories in those days in Belgium and we lived where we could. Devout parents wanted their children to live under the pious supervision of priests, and so the Institute rented rooms to its graduates who went on to the university.

Father Medulous taught mathematics. Father Medulous could be cloying as celibate headmasters sometimes are when they see their lives wrapped up in an adopted progeny. He proclaimed me a genius. His loud and frequent praise embarrassed me and made me worship him, and the other boys joked with me about it; but they respected me, and Guy proudly claimed me as his best friend, and we did everything together—concerts, the opera, the theatre, long walks on Sunday afternoons, endless parties given by Guy's friends (who seemed to be all the rich people in Belgium), even a week in Paris. Above all we went at night to the Vieux Gand, and we drank wine and smoked and talked with our friends.

Guy seduced women. Ghent was a cloth town. Peasant girls came from the country to work in the shops and mills. Some were lovely, and they came to the Vieux Gand at night to sit at the edges of the crowd. Since they had no money, they had to barter themselves to young men like Guy. He looked like a young Apollo, and in the tavern where light poured down on his head, he drew women as if he promised the gift of eternal youth and grace.

Sometimes three or four young women sat with us, and Guy entertained them all. Often he would depart with one, leaving me to amuse the others as best I could. I was tempted by their eyes, the softness of their skin, their scents of soap, of cheap perfume, their wet young mouths, their eagerness, the breasts their clothing revealed and hid. My mother's image came to me in those moments, a stern and reproachful vision that made me withdraw and become even more tedious than usual. Guy sometimes returned to our room in the first light of dawn. He wanted to tell me about how he had slipped his hands into their dresses, their ritual protests, their halfhearted resistance, their panting, the relentless progress of his fingers to the tops of their legs, and how slowly, inevitably they parted their thighs and yielded to him with gasps of passion, his sense of victory at that, their arms around his neck, their hesitation overcome by desire, and how he undressed them while they clung to him, and what they whispered in his ears as he pumped away at their responding bodies.

In his view, he came to them briefly from their most romantic dreams. For one night or for two or three or for a week, he was substantial and real, in their arms and in them. They came to him with their eyes, their arms, their moist thighs all open, knowing he would put them aside but that until then they would have pleasure and excitement, and afterwards memories that would warm them when they were old and forgotten.

A few days after I came back to Belgium, Greece went to war with the Ottoman Empire. I was troubled. Should I go home and enlist in the battle against the Turk? Stephanos telegraphed me at once to stay in Belgium. "We are in no danger," he said. "The war is being fought in the north. If you come home, you may be killed, and the family depends on you to get an education. Do not come home. I repeat. Do not come home."

My mother wrote me long letters. They came punctually every two weeks, despite the war, fat in their pale-blue envelopes, their regular appearance testimony to the orderly way she conducted her life. She wrote every other Sunday night, apparently setting aside the entire evening for her task, for me, telling me the things people were talking about, reciting the unimportant details of the house. She reassured me about the war. It was not coming to much. People in Greece were not suffering.

She wrote pages of advice, especially about women. Do not let women deceive you. Keep your body pure. Indecent women lurk everywhere, waiting to lead a clean boy astray. Pray to the Virgin Mary; she will protect you from foul women. Pray to St. John the Baptist; he will wash you in the pure water of life. Combat the desire that Satan implants in the heart of a boy your age.

My mother had always been devout. Now her intensity embarrassed me, and I hid her letters lest Guy read them. Still, they brought Greece back to me, and always I stood for a moment holding them to my mouth and nose as if the crisp paper could somehow convey to me all the smells and tastes of home.

The letters were carried to the post office in Piraeus early on Monday morning. The thick pale-blue envelope, bearing her neat and familiar hand, was on the shelf outside the concierge's window at the Institute by the following Friday afternoon.

The terrible letter arrived on a Wednesday in early December. I had received the customary formal epistle with my monthly bank draft the previous Friday. This was a thin missive, containing only one folded sheet of pale-blue writing paper. I opened it impatiently and saw my mother's familiar hand, as firm as a copper engraving. I stared at the single terse sentence like a man struck in the head suddenly, not knowing what struck him, hardly knowing that he has been struck. Stephanos had killed himself.

How? She did not say. I stood in the open and read it again and again, seeking to squeeze some larger knowledge from the naked words. The air was chill. Low, dark clouds scudded overhead. The cobblestones glistened with the damp. Within the courtyard of the school, tall windows, going up four floors, looked blankly down on me. Life on the street beyond the great portal went on. Boys came and went and spoke to me. I heard the rattle of crockery and pans in the kitchen across the courtyard. I could hear in the distance the murmur of the town. And Stephanos was dead.

I supposed he had shot himself. I wept at the thought of what the bullet did to his beautiful head. I went up to my room without replying to Madame Conrad, who rushed after me, asking me for the stamps, which she sold. I heard her muttering indignantly when I went away without speaking. I pulled the shutters over the windows and sat all afternoon in the dark. I thought of the bouzouki Stephanos had given me, thought of it rotting down in the sea, and I wept bitterly. Finally I could not weep anymore. I sat. The iron radiator popped and gargled. It gave little heat. I did not feel the cold.

Guy came in at six, turned on the light, and jumped when he saw me sitting there.

"What is wrong with you? What . . . ?"

"My uncle has killed himself."

"Your uncle? The one in . . . ? What was his name?"

"Stephanos," I said.

"Well, I never can remember names. Killed? Well, I don't . . . Terrible, my dear friend. Simply terrible."

"Yes," I said.

"I am desolate," Guy said, using the conventional French politeness. "I do—"

"You did not know him," I said.

"Well, I am devastated nevertheless. Truly I am."

"Please go away and leave me alone. I beg you, Guy. Go away."

He left, and I turned out the light. In a few minutes I could hear the boys singing grace downstairs in the long refectory, where they were sitting down for supper. The sound seemed to come from a great distance, muffled and somehow grand and harmonious because of the distance, rising and falling in hearty waves. The words were indistinct, but I knew them by heart.

> *Toi qui dispose*
> *De toute chose*
> *Et nous les donne chaque jour,*
> *Reçois, O Père,*
> *Notre prière*
> *De reconnaissance et d'amour.*

The sound made me ache inside, and I wept again. Then I was empty and could cry no more.

Father Medulous rushed into the room after supper. "My dear boy!" he said. "Guy has told me. What a terrible, terrible thing." Father Medulous sat down on the edge of the hard bed and took me clumsily in his arms. He smelled vaguely of onions and old sweat. My face pressed into his rough cassock. I was as still as death. When I looked up, Guy was standing in the door, doing his best to look compassionate.

Two days later Father Medulous said a mass for the soul of Stephanos. It was a kind gesture—strictly against the church doctrine. Suicide was a mortal sin, worse than murder because the sinner could not confess and gain absolution. Stephanos was in hell. Hell was a place of black fire, and it went on for eternity. A mass said for souls in hell accomplished no good. It might be blasphemy, like praying for the salvation of the devil.

"We cannot know what went through your poor uncle's mind in his last moments," Father Medulous told me. My ignorance about how Stephanos had died allowed Father Medulous to speculate. "Perhaps he took some sort of drug, something that put him to sleep. At the last instant, when he had no strength to move or cry out or save himself, he regretted what he had done and prayed one final prayer for forgiveness. That is all it would take to get him safely into purgatory—one prayer at the moment of his death. No matter how low he is in purgatory, no matter how many thousands of years of pain he must suffer, it is enough to put him within reach of the mass and the help that the Holy Catholic Church on earth can give him."

The mass was sung at dawn, and nearly every boy in the school came and sat in unusual stillness and silence. Father Medulous sang the ancient rites in his rough, strong voice. The pale light of a new, cold day brightened outside, making the stately figure of the serene Virgin glow hot in the stained-glass window over the altar.

I sat in front next to Guy. I heard the litany and thought of Stephanos, remembering the little perfumed Turkish cigarettes, and remembering, too, the sound of his voice, so familiar, feeling a quiet and unreal astonishment at the finality of death, which took familiar things away forever.

On my other side that morning sat Bernal Díaz y Aguela, newly arrived that year, veteran of other universities, native of Argentina, fabulously wealthy, inordinately devout, occasionally drunk and dissipated. He greeted me with profound sadness after the requiem. I saw with a start that his sadness was genuine. He held my hand for a moment, looking at me with his steady brown eyes, and I believed that he felt my grief more than anyone else in that place felt it. It was the first time that we spoke, and we did not immediately become friends, for he quickly withdrew into the aloofness and silence that kept him isolated from the rest of us. But that was the beginning.

36

I PASSED INTO a period when I could think of nothing but death. Sometimes at night when Guy was with a woman, I lay insomniac and thought of the infinitesimal point that is the present, and the thought would strike me that at some present moment, a moment that would be as present as this one, I would die. Often I lay listening to the bells toll the hours. Every bell had a different tone. I knew them all and lay waiting for them to come one after another. When Guy came in, making his clumsy efforts not to waken me, I pretended to be asleep. Soon his deep, regular breathing indicated that he slept, untroubled and thoughtless, dreaming happy dreams. I lay still and miserable, waiting for dawn, listening to the bells.

My evenings at the Vieux Gand became more and more rare. I could not bear company. I sat at one of the big tables looking at happy people, and I could not understand them. They were going to die. Did they not know that they were going to die? Why were they so happy? I walked alone hour after hour on some nights, sometimes into the countryside by empty fields, bundling myself against the dank chill of the Belgian winter, walking, walking, feeling no sense of fatigue or drowsiness, impervious to the cold that crept into my clothes, returning at last at first light to sleep fitfully for an hour or so before rising for the Holy Eucharist which comforted my soul.

Guy took me home with him for the three weeks of Christmas vacation. Dinant was covered with snow. He and and I tramped around together, and under the continual force of his bantering goodwill, some of my gloom dissipated.

"If a man wants to kill himself, what are we to do?" he asked, shrugging his shoulders and lifting his eyes towards heaven in an imploring gesture meant to call on God to witness his innocence and helplessness before events.

"It is a sovereign right, one we all possess. Now, my friend, suppose you come to me, and suppose you say, 'My dear friend Guy, I am going to shoot myself.' What should I do? I should of course attempt to persuade you that you are following a course of action that could lead to no progressive result. I would point out that suicide is contrary to the optimistic spirit of the age. I should declare that suicide leads one to a fate of great uncertainty and that on the whole, uncertainty is to be avoided by the prudent. I would tell you that suicide would distress and inconvenience your friends, of whom—without meaning to presume—I count myself chief. I should express my sincere conviction that we would all miss you extremely.

"But now suppose that after due deliberation you remained resolved to put an end to your life no matter what I said or did. At a certain moment I should recognize your sovereign right to make the proper decisions about your own life—or in this example, your own death. I should bid you a most fond farewell. I should embrace you as a brother. Then I should politely leave the room, assuming that you had procured for yourself a pistol of sufficient calibre to make your death instantaneous or, better still, some painless narcotic or some other more imaginative device for doing the job with dispatch and . . . ah . . . hygiene. I should urge you not to hang yourself. I find hanging a vulgar way to die, and I hope that for my sake you would avoid hanging yourself, especially in our room. Yes, I should feel affronted, my dear Paul, if you were to hang yourself.

"But whatever means you chose to end your life, I should depart from you and after a decent interval, I should telephone the police and report to them where the remains might be found. That night in the Vieux Gand, I should order the finest champagne, and I should lift a glass and call for a moment of reverent silence in sad memory of my dear friend now departed. I should be considerably put out if anyone were to laugh or speak or belch or even pick his nose during that moment. Madame Boschnagel would play some appropriate dirge on the organ. Father Droos would perhaps say a prayer— in incomprehensible but reverent Latin, of course. We would all weep. Then I should begin my search for another person to share my room. I must go on living, you see."

He put both his hands out in a gesture of finality and satisfaction. Then he lit a cigar. Then he grinned, giving me a sidelong glance of mirth. I believe that I grinned back.

"Now my friendly and entirely disinterested counsel to you, my dearest friend, is that you must go on living. Your uncle has chosen a course that distresses us both. But you are still alive, and you must make the decisions that are appropriate to life. Let us drink to life."

37

THE HOLIDAYS ENDED on January 6, 1913, a Monday, and we returned to Ghent that evening on the train. I expected two letters from my mother, and a bank draft with my allowance. There was nothing.

I had only a few francs. Guy wanted to go immediately to the Vieux Gand. I made an excuse. I did not have enough money. Two days later a letter came. It was long, detailed, and impersonal. The business was gone. Stephanos had made debts no one in the family had known about. They would have to be paid; our grand old house would have to be sold.

The servants had been let go. They wept much in parting. Eleutheria was hysterical. She wanted to keep working for my mother for nothing. That was not possible. My mother and my sisters moved into the house of her father, old Iannis Pedakis. Grandfather Pedakis was wild with anger. He had given his daughter a handsome dowry, supposing that the marriage he had made for her with Vasilis Kephalopoulos was worth any expense. Now she was back in his house, and the dowry was gone. I could imagine him—old, bald, and bent, wiry as a stick figure, his voice shrill. He would blame his daughter. In his world every bad thing happened because someone had been either criminal or irresponsible. He would tell my mother that she had not been a good wife. That is why my father had taken a lover, he would say. If Vasilis had killed his lover's husband, my mother was to blame.

My mother would withdraw into dignified silence, head bowed in the submission that a Greek daughter owed her father, even a daughter who had presided over her own household and mothered children now nearly grown. In her father's house, she would be a child again, and she would wrap her silence around her like a garment and obey him.

Her father had issued commands about me. He allowed me to remain in Belgium to the end of the school year because my fees were already paid. At the end of that time, I should return to Greece and assume responsibility for my mother and my sisters. Grandfather Pedakis had friends in the postal service. I could start work as a clerk. In a few years I might become a supervisor. It was far from the position everyone had hoped for me. But life was life. We must bow to the will of God.

In the meantime my grandfather had forbidden my mother to send me money for incidental expenses. I read my mother's careful, dispassionate prose, and I could see the scene—my grandfather standing behind his little desk with the heavy ledger books open before him. He would be shouting, pointing to the irrefutable evidence penned in the hand of Stephanos. From time to time he would stride back and forth, waving his bony hands, cursing my father, painting me as a parasite absorbing vast sums from a destitute family, giving nothing in return. The post office was to be my punishment.

My mother's letter was formal and dry. But at the very end she wrote, "Oh my dear boy! I am sorry that things have come down to this state. I so wanted more for you in life."

I held the letter and felt tears come. I dried them quickly. Tears were futile. I sat looking out the window. It was a gray day and very cold.

I had no money. I have never forgotten that feeling. I could no longer go with Guy to the Vieux Gand. I could no longer follow his occasional whim to take our meals in a restaurant rather than in the refectory. I could no longer buy any clothing.

"I will not go with you to the Vieux Gand anymore," I told him that evening.

"But why?"

"I am tired of the place. I must study. I cannot waste time."

"You cannot study all the time, every night. It is not natural."

"I am sorry. I have made a resolution. I will not go with you anymore."

"You are offended with me," Guy said. "My dear friend, I have done something to offend you."

"You have done nothing to offend me. I do not want to go to the tavern anymore."

"Let us have a quiet meal somewhere and discuss this over a bottle of French wine," Guy said.

"No," I said. "There is nothing to discuss. I am going to stay here from now on and study."

He argued and apologized, certain that he had done something offensive. He lay at the center of his universe, and he could not think that anything that had happened to me was not somehow related to him. So we fell into a sullen and aggrieved silence. He was deeply hurt. He assumed a tone of elaborate courtesy when he addressed me, the mark of those wanting nothing to do with each other beyond the necessary. We tried to ignore each other.

There was a library on the second floor of the Institute. There I spent many evenings while Guy went to the Vieux Gand. The library was not large or popular. It was not heated well, and to read there in the winter one had to wear a heavy coat and sometimes gloves. Often I sat alone with the books, and I discovered a talent for solitude.

I sold my overcoat. I had paid 200 francs for it—a prodigious sum in those days. It had a sealskin collar and fell almost to the floor when I wore it. I bartered it away for forty francs.

The sale bought me time. For the moment I had enough money to pay for my laundry. I no longer walked with Guy to the university. If we had classes at the same time, I left early. Sometimes I took long detours to avoid him at the end of the class day. When I walked swiftly, I warded off the dank chill of the Belgian winter. Sometimes the wind tormented me, and I suffered in the snow.

After all these years I dream sometimes about walking those long blocks through the cold streets of the early-winter dark in Ghent, and I am once more without money and without an overcoat, wearing several shirts, and in a world where Guy and so many others had all the money they could spend. I felt like trash. A pity to be so materialistic? And so noxiously self-pitying? Yes, but I was very young, and I had had everything.

38

GRANDFATHER PEDAKIS made a mistake that undid his vengeance. Late in January Father Medulous sent for me. He stood nervously with his hands folded as he motioned me to a chair in his tiny office. "Your grandfather has written me a letter," he said gravely. "A very disturbing letter. Your grandfather has told me some terrible things."

"I am sorry, Father."

"A vulgar letter, I might add. In my life I have not received a communication like this one, and I have often heard from irate parents. The life of a headmaster is not easy."

"I am sorry, Father," I whispered. My cheeks burned.

"Yes. Well, we are not responsible for the sins of our families. I have a brother . . ." Father Medulous cleared his throat and looked grim. "Your grandfather berates me for our fees."

"I am sorry, Father." In my mind I was folding tents, packing bags, preparing to return immediately to Greece to escape my shame.

"You have a . . . what shall I say? A *complex* history, according to your grandfather."

I forced myself to look him in the eye. "You did not know that my father had killed a man," I said.

"No," Father Medulous said.

"And that my father was having an adulterous affair with that man's wife," I said.

"We should not speak of such things," the priest said. He reddened. "The most important fact that I did not know was that your father is alive."

"I do not know whether he is alive or dead, Father," I said.

"Where is he?"

"We heard that he was in America," I said.

"America," Father Medulous said. "Everyone goes to America." He cleared his throat again. "I took the distinct impression from your uncle when he wrote me from Russia that . . . *eh bien!* I thought your father had been killed in an accident."

I made myself stand quietly. I could have died of shame. "I will leave the school. I shall not subject you to embarrassment. I shall write my grandfather and ask him to send me enough money to return to Greece."

"But my dear boy! You are a mathematician, a genius in mathematics. You have something to do in the world, something important, perhaps something historical. We have never had a student equal to you in all the years that I have been here. We are proud of you. We have so many hopes."

His sudden outburst of praise, becoming more fervent as he went on, nearly broke down my defenses. I felt ready to cry again. "I must go home, Father. There can be no discussion."

"You do not have to go home until the summer. Between now and summer something may happen," Father Medulous said. For a moment I thought he was going to reach out to me, to touch me, and then surely I would have wept. But he made only a vague motion with his hand and let it fall back onto the desk.

"But I thought . . ."

"It is up to me to do the thinking, my boy. I am older. I can think better than you can. Not about mathematics, understand. But about practical things. I am going to write your grandfather. A short letter, I promise you. 'Sir, I have received your communication. Yours very truly.' Something like that. I do not believe in dignifying such vulgarity with a long letter."

"Yes, Father," I said.

He picked the letter up and quickly let it drop again. He looked at it with distaste.

I knew that Grandfather Pedakis had hired a French-language scribe to write it. Such men hawked their talents at booths in the streets of the harbor near the post office. I could imagine the vile old man sitting on a stool under an umbrella before the scribe's little table. It would have cost him more to hire the scribe to come into his house. Besides, if anyone entered his house, a Greek host was obliged to offer something sweet and cool to drink.

Grandfather Pedakis would have gone down to sit on the stool in front of the scribe's table on the street, to howl his complaint, speaking not merely to the scribe who must compose the diatribe in the form of a letter, but declaiming to idlers gathered to enjoy the performance.

"It is a selfish thought," Father Medulous said, "but I have never sent a student to the university for whom I had hoped so much. I am not immune to the sin of pride. I wanted people in the university to know that you were ours, that I had taught you at least something of what you know. Already Professor Kooning has spoken to me about your prowess, and I took great pleasure to hear him praise you. Ah," he said with another great, sad sigh. "St. Augustine tells us *'superbia mater omnium peccatorum est,'* and he is of course true in this as he is in all else. We shall see. We shall see."

We stood and said goodbye in common discomfort. Father Medulous was preoccupied. I felt sad, but I also felt released from a burden. I told Guy that in the summer I should return to Greece forever.

He heard the news with reserved formality and with scarcely a comment. He bowed in polite acceptance. We were no longer friends.

39

I WITHDREW into mathematics, into the spirals of forms rolling upward from the papers where in the library at night I conjured equations. The equations hypnotized me and comforted me.

When I went to bed, I imagined myself in the shabby uniform of the royal Greek government, perched on my tall stool behind the counter in the post office in Piraeus, selling stamps and weighing packages. I supposed that I would start drinking too much wine at night. I would marry a stupid woman. We would have stupid children. I could not sleep and could not take walks because I had no overcoat, and the weather was too cold.

March came, and winter broke up in a gush of melting ice and green things and the sweet, dank smell of the fertile fields and the canals. The nights were still cold, but flowers bloomed. In early April Father Medulous called me back to his office. I went in dread. He wore a radiant smile. He walked around his desk and shook hands with me.

"My boy, I have something to tell you. Please sit down. Sit down."

I sat, and he went back to his chair and sat there glowing at me. A stack of letters lay on his desk. He picked one up and waved it in the air.

"I have been corresponding with your Uncle Georgios in Russia," he said.

"Uncle Georgios," I said.

"I have taken the liberty of explaining your situation in detail. I have taken the even greater liberty of sending him the letters—alas, I have received several now—from your grandfather Pedakis. I have suggested to your uncle that he is an affluent man, that Almighty God by his own inscrutable will made you his charge, and that it is his duty to support you in the university."

I sucked in my breath. The thought of asking Uncle Georgios for charity never entered my mind. I knew he would refuse. Father Medulous turned grave and nodded his large round head.

"Your uncle was at first unwilling to undertake this obligation," he said. "He was decidedly blunt in his response." The priest sighed. "The male members of your family appear to be a stiff-necked lot. As St. Augustine might have said—"

"What did he say, Father?"

"Ah! As I have told you, we exchanged letters. Several letters in fact. I regret very much to tell you that these letters have not always been friendly, neither on your uncle's side or on mine." Father Medulous crossed himself and looked briefly skyward. "I am afraid I have spoken to him about the providence of God and the wheel of fortune and the divine uncertainty of life. I have fulfilled my priestly duties by speaking of judgment, heaven, hell, and purgatory. In our communications I have seen that your uncle is, alas, more swayed by the fear of financial punishment in this world than of spiritual judgment in the world to come. God wills that we approach human beings in the language that they understand. One does not speak to a cow in Ciceronian phrases; one shouts and perhaps uses a whip. So I have done with your uncle. I have told him that if he did not help you, God might take away all his property and make his sons ashamed of him."

Father Medulous smiled. I smiled for the first time since entering his office. I almost laughed. Father Medulous was looking at me, and I was looking at him, and we were happy together, and I thought he was one of the grandest human beings I had ever known. My family was superstitiously religious. Despite his contempt for priests and his ridicule of my mother's piety, my father had always done his Easter duties. He attended mass with a great show of reverence. "It's good business to be religious," he said offhandedly now and then. "I let God know that I respect him, and God lets me be rich. A fair trade."

Father Medulous had somehow penetrated that mentality. "The long and short of it is that your uncle has consented to pay your fees with us and with the university. He refuses to provide any spending money for you. We must arrange for that ourselves. He has consented to make it possible for you to complete your education. After you have received your diploma, you will go to Russia and work for him to repay him for his kindness. I have agreed to his terms. I have sentenced you to a period of servitude in Russia. You may leave Russia when your debt is paid. The experience will be rewarding. You will work only a few years for your uncle, and you will meet Russian mathematicians, and you will do good deeds—for yourself *and* for Russia. Russia needs you, my boy. Russia is Christian, but she is not *Catholic.* You may be the man to change Russia back to Mother Church."

He was in earnest. He believed that if anyone applied energy and good will to a problem, it could be solved. I loved Father Medulous in that moment for his absurdity. It had made it possible for me to stay in school. He had redeemed my life.

We sat for a few moments in a glow of mutual esteem. I thought of my mother. My mood changed.

"My mother expects me to come back to Greece this summer," I said. "Her father has commanded it. My mother lives in his house and must obey him. I must obey her."

Father Medulous frowned. "I supposed naturally that you would make such an argument." He cleared his throat uncomfortably. "I have taken the liberty to write to your mother and to tell her that it is my judgment that you should stay here with us."

"Father—" I said.

He hushed me with an upraised finger. "What will you do if you return to Greece, my son? Your mother has written to me that her father has secured for you a job in the postal service. Why not clean toilets instead? Do you think you can help your mother, increase her happiness, by working at a menial job in the post office? Or will you make her more proud, more happy by becoming a mathematician, a professor? That is what you will be, my son. One of the most renowned professors ever to hold a university chair." He mused happily and smiled. "A university chair. It is like the Pope's chair. When you speak ex cathedra, you speak with the voice of God. At least in mathematics. I believe God speaks to us more absolutely in mathematics than by any other way."

I almost laughed with delight.

Father Medulous leaned forward and clasped his large peasant hands in front of him. His eyes glowed. For a moment he was not dreaming; he was looking on a gloriously accomplished fact. Outside, the spring was coming to Belgium.

"Now, you will require spending money," Father Medulous said in a businesslike way. "You cannot stay in your room like a nail in the floor. You cannot live in the library. Yes, my son, I know what you have been doing. The priest always knows. I have a solution to this problem. You must tutor other students. Yes, I know it may seem demeaning to you. Look at it this way. We have many rich students from all over the world. They have parents willing to pay whatever it costs to get them an education. Some of them . . . My boy, how can I say this? You must never tell anyone that I have said this to you. But some of the richest of them are stupid beyond belief. A terrible thing for a headmaster to admit, but I am a priest as well as a headmaster. I must speak the truth. God has arranged the world so that there are few evils without their corresponding blessings. The stupid ones are also the profitable ones. Their parents will pay anything to get them educated. Why should they not pay you, my son? I shall arrange it."

40

I WROTE TO MY MOTHER. Her reply was a single line: "You must do what you must."

Grandfather Pedakis gushed out a sewer of letters. I did not reply. My silence drove him to more fury. Finally I threw the letters into the trash unopened.

I began my career as tutor. Students came to me. Some of them were young children, far from home. Sometimes they cried, not because I was harsh but because they were overcome with what they must learn to please parents they scarcely knew. They struggled with their lessons to make their parents love them; they knew the futility of their enterprise, and they pursued it in terror. Some were older than I, students in the university, bashful at their ignorance and my knowledge. I lived frugally. My reputation spread, and I had much to do, and I began to enjoy a modest prosperity.

I wrote regularly to my uncle Georgios, thanking him for his generosity, repeating the good things Father Medulous said about me and the good things my teachers said about my work. He wrote that he would appreciate it if my letters were shorter.

One evening in May when spring was full in Ghent and the damp smell of the canal and the fields hung in the air, I looked up at Guy as he started to walk out the door to the Vieux Gand. "If you do not mind," I said, "I believe I will go with you this evening."

He stopped in his tracks. A great smile broke over his face. "Mind?" he said. "My dear friend, of course I do not mind. I assure you, I shall be delighted."

We returned to our old ways as if they had never been interrupted. I expected Guy to ask questions. Why had I withdrawn? Why was I tutoring students? Why did I return with him to the Vieux Gand? But he was not a questioning sort.

About that time, Father Medulous summoned me again to his office. "It is a most desperate case," he said, smoking a cigarette with a frown. "We have in the Institute a university student from Argentina, Bernal Columbo Díaz y Aguela. I believe that you have met him."

"Yes, Father. He came to the mass for my uncle."

"Your uncle. Yes, poor man," Father Medulous said, crossing himself absentmindedly.

"He promised to pray for me."

"Yes, he is devout. A very devout young man." Father Medulous frowned more deeply.

"It is rumored that he weeps at night," I said.

Father Medulous cleared his throat. "Yes, I have spoken to him. . . . Others have reported. . . . It is the crucifix, you see. That horrid crucifix. He lives in his room with a bloody crucifix. He is Spanish, you see. It makes me shudder. He prays before it and weeps. In the Middle Ages he would have been regarded as a saint."

"I suppose we should be honored to have a saint among us," I said, I think innocently.

Father Medulous gave me a sharp look and cleared his throat again. "His . . . ah . . . sanctity is not my affair. God takes care of that. I have another charge—to take care of his mind." He finished his cigarette and lit another. I had never seen him smoke.

"He refuses to study," Father Medulous said at last.

I said nothing. Father Medulous puffed. "I do not know what to do. The examinations come in July. His head is as empty as a drum. He says he does not want to know anything. He goes to the university only because his father in Argentina vows that he must have a European education. He failed his examinations last year. He had an apartment in the town. His father made him come to us this year. The father supposed that the son would do better if he lived in the Institute, where life is disciplined. He trusted me, you see. I have failed. If the boy fails, well . . . My own pride does not matter, I know. It is a sinful emotion, but . . . the father trusted me."

Father Medulous's eyes pleaded for understanding. "You know how it is. If the son fails the examinations the second time, he must leave the university. Before he came to us, he was at the Sorbonne two years. He failed there. Before he was at the Sorbonne, he was at Oxford two years. He failed there. He tells me that next year he will go to Berlin. He will fail there. He thinks that if he fails his examinations at every university he attends, his father will let him return to Argentina. His father writes me that he is resolved for his son to receive a diploma or spend his life in exile. Where will it end? He is amiable. I am certain that he is intelligent. I have experience in these things. But he will not study. Never in all the years I have been teaching have I met anyone like him. I turn to you, my child. I beg you to do what you can to help him. For his sake. For my sake. For the sake of his father. For the sake of the Lord Christ who has told us that it is death to bury our talents in the earth."

I was embarrassed to be thrust on Bernal Díaz y Aguela. He was the only student who had a private room in the Institute. Rumors flew that he was granted this privilege because his father paid double fees. He dressed in an elegance that surpassed even Guy's. He walked among us, aloof and silent, smiling formally without quite seeing us, making no friends. He was older: ten years older than I was, eight years older than Guy. We felt bashful in his presence.

I believe that I have already written here that I saw him once kneeling at the Cathedral of St. Bavon before the van Eyck altarpiece, the Adoration of the Mystic Lamb. He was weeping silently, his face contorted in grief, eyes uplifted towards the great seated figure of God with His hand upraised in judgment above the scene where the saints and the prophets gather in worship on a green plain before the Mystic Lamb. I saw him and fled.

He loved the color green. He never appeared in public without something green showing in his clothes—a cravat, a handkerchief. I have always loved green, and sometimes when I hear music, the color green sweeps through my mind. The color was all we had in common.

41

FATHER MEDULOUS led me up the dark wooden steps to the fourth floor, where Bernal lived. Bernal expected us. He greeted us with formal courtesy, bowing slightly from the waist and showing us to hard chairs. He took one himself and sat facing us, crossing his legs carefully and nodding to me. "How is your mother?" he said.

"She is very well," I said. "Thank you for asking."

"She has suffered great grief," he said.

"She will be grateful for your sympathy," I said.

"I regret that I do not know her so that I might extend that sympathy in some personal way," he said.

I looked at the bloody crucifix on the wall, turned away, felt my face grow red, and had to look back at it. I had never seen a more horrifying object. Father Medulous glanced at it and averted his eyes.

"Monsieur Díaz y Aguela," Father Medulous said, "I believe that God has given you a mind, a talent, and that you, like the cursed man in the Gospels, are burying your talent in the earth. God will judge you for your neglect. The judgments of God are true and righteous altogether."

Bernal looked grave. "I know that God's judgment against me is harsh," he said with crushing conviction.

Father Medulous did not expect this response. "Yes, of course," he said nervously. "To be sure. Well, I mean that those judgments are harsh against all of us. Monsieur Díaz y Aguela, I speak to you of an opportunity to redeem yourself. I have brought with me this brilliant young man. He it is who may save your mind and your soul. Your mind is a gift of God, and if you do not use it, God will damn you to an eternal hell."

Bernal shifted uncomfortably. "The sins that concern me," he said slowly, "are not the sins of the mind but the horrible sins that I find lying in my body."

"Tush," Father Medulous said. "The body is the temple of the Holy Spirit. The sins of the body are more notorious. But as a priest I assure you that the sins of the mind are worse. The sin of sloth, for example."

Bernal was silent.

"God watches the sparrow's fall," Father Medulous said sternly. "He knows that you are engaged in an unworthy conflict of wills with your father. Your father pays your bills. He laments your sloth. He asks me to pray for him, to pray for you. I pray for you both. But I tell you this: if you neglect your mind, God will damn you for sloth as surely as he will damn you for any sin of the body that you can commit."

I was embarrassed. The priest's peasant upbringing showed in his coarse hands, in his strong Flemish accent, in his unrestrained emotion. Bernal was handsome, cultivated, restrained, and wealthy. But Father Medulous was a priest. That gave him a great advantage.

I became Bernal's tutor in mathematics. I went to his room every day and sat at his desk, my back to the crucifix, and we worked. I should say that I worked, and he looked on benignly as I drew circles and triangles and other figures and set down numbers and letters and drew lines with a straightedge and explained problems.

"My life is in Argentina," he said. "My father owns thousands of hectares of land and thousands of cattle. My life is to ride horseback in the wind, to love the pampas and the tall grass. Alas, my father believes that his only son must visit Buenos Aires and make small talk with the wealthy and cultivated people who will invite him into their houses. I say that I shall never visit Buenos Aires. My father says I must. He will not let me come home until I have a university degree. He is a practical man. He believes that mathematics will lead to some practical good. He is very bad in mathematics. I think that he is determined that his son will succeed where he has failed. What am I to do with mathematics? If I wish to know the number of cubic centimeters in a funnel and to calculate the rate at which a liquid flows through it into a jar, I can hire someone to do it. Why should I know the rate of flow? I can hire a servant to stand by the jar until it is filled, and neither he nor I will consider the rate of flow to be important."

"Mathematics is beautiful," I said. "And if my father were interested in anything that I did, I would do everything I could to please him."

"I understood that your father is dead," Bernal said.

"No, he is alive," I said. "I do not care to discuss it."

"Then we shall never speak of your father again," Bernal said, bowing in extreme gravity.

"I want to teach you mathematics," I said.

"My dear friend," Bernal said in his most formal way, "let us go on."

I sat with him night after night and attempted to trace out for him the mysteries of calculus. He looked on, always smiling and nodding politely as if I were a child reciting a memorized piece in school to a courteously indifferent audience. Father Medulous asked me impatiently, "How is your pupil doing?" I shook my head, and he looked disappointed in me, in the world. "I do not know what I shall say to his father," he said.

The weather warmed, and the world smelled damp and sweet. I labored on with Bernal, trying to tell myself that all I cared about was the money. But I cared about Bernal, too, and I wanted to make Father Medulous happy.

"I think I might be content in Berlin," Bernal said. "They are a fine people, the Germans."

"Father Medulous loves the Germans," I said. "He says that the French are evil but that the Germans will save Christian civilization."

"Many Germans are Protestant," Bernal said. "At least the Kaiser is Protestant."

"The French government is atheist," I said.

"No one is an atheist," Bernal said.

"Father Medulous says that if there is a war, the French will attack Belgium, and the Germans will come to our rescue," I said.

Bernal laughed. "War is against the spirit of the age."

"Father Medulous says there will be a war."

"Priests know only things of heaven," Bernal said. "They know nothing of the things of earth."

I repeat these words now because they were spoken and because they were more foolish than most things from that foolish time. There were hundreds, perhaps thousands of Germans in Ghent, including dear Madame Boschnagel. The great photographic portrait of the Kaiser in the central room of her tavern seemed as normal to us as the portrait of Albert, king of the Belgians, that hung next to it. If Bernal planned to go to the University of Berlin the following year, that seemed natural, too. German students came to our university. Belgians went to German universities. Why should an Argentine not go to Berlin?

Because I was teaching him mathematics. Because if he went to Berlin, I would fail.

42

GUY HAD BEEN FASCINATED by Bernal's conspicuous wealth. But somehow Bernal's aloof bearing, his age, his solitary dignity had prevented Guy from making any but the most superficial approaches to him. Now that I was Bernal's tutor, Guy saw an opportunity. He pestered me to bring Bernal to the tavern. One evening I timidly suggested to Bernal that we conclude our evening with a glass of wine at the Vieux Gand, and to my astonishment he accepted my invitation. I was frustrated. Once again I had explained problems and principles patiently and carefully, and Bernal had looked on with an expression of amusement as though he found my earnestness some childish quirk. I needed a glass of wine—perhaps two or three.

Guy greeted Bernal effusively. The young women at our table shifted their attention to Bernal. He was very dark, very handsome, slender, with a thick mustache and dark eyes set deep in his head, giving him a profoundly thoughtful expression that women found romantic. His age made him seem more manly than Guy or I could possibly be.

"We are honored to have you with us," Guy said, scarcely able to contain his enthusiasm.

"But it is I who am honored to be invited to join your company," Bernal said.

"You are too kind," Guy said. "Far too kind."

"Introduce us, Guy," one of the women said.

"Ladies, my dear friend Bernal Díaz y Aguela from Argentina. We welcome you here, sir. Welcome."

Bernal inclined his head gravely at the women but did not put out his hand. They were captivated with him.

"Will you have some wine?" Guy said. "Of course you will have wine. A gentleman of your distinction would not touch beer, especially the poisonous brew made here in Belgium. Champagne. For you we shall order champagne. Waiter! Champagne for the gentleman."

"No," Bernal said quickly and signaling the waiter to come back. "I love beer. I especially like Belgian beer." The waiter bowed respectfully. Bernal ordered the beer made by Guy's father in Dinant.

"You truly like that beer?" Guy said in astonishment.

"It is my favorite," Bernal said.

"My father makes that beer," Guy said.

"My compliments to your father," Bernal said. He seemed genuinely impressed. "I am happy to be able to convey those sincere sentiments to him through a son who doubtless must feel proud of his parent's talent."

"You like my father's beer," Guy said. "He will be so proud. I am proud. I thank you, my friend. I do hope you will be my friend." Guy put out his hand, and Bernal took it briefly.

"Of course I shall be your friend," Bernal said.

"I am so grateful," Guy said. "So very grateful."

43

I EXPLAINED PROBLEMS to Bernal until my head roared. He listened benignly, nodding politely when I said, "Do you understand?" I said, "If you understand, please take a sheet of paper and work out the problem as I have done so I may be certain that you understand."

"My dear friend," Bernal replied. "Why should *I* work the problem again? You have already worked it out! It would be an insult to you if I were to work out the problem as if I did not believe you."

"It is not a question of courtesy," I said wearily. "*You* must work out the problem to demonstrate to me that you understand it."

"My dear friend, I know that you take me at my word as I take you at your word. If I tell you that I understand, you as a gentleman are bound to believe me. I would insult our friendship if I should presume on your sense of honor to do the problem myself as if I did not believe you."

"You *must* prove to the examiners that you can work the problem."

"The examiners are not my friends, and I am led to believe that they are not gentlemen. I cannot ask them to take my word for anything. I shall work the problems for them because I hold them in contempt. I honor you by refusing such a scornful act."

"It is hopeless," I told Guy. "Hopeless."

"My friend," Guy said, "I am sure that you will rise in the world despite being Greek. I feel certain that I shall read about you in the newspapers, that you will win prizes and have an entry in the encylopedias under your name. But for the moment . . . oh, how shall I say it without insulting you? You do not understand Bernal. He is a genius. I can tell that he is a genius."

"He may be a genius, but he must pass his examinations, or he will be expelled from school."

"Oh yes," Guy said, frowning. "That is a problem with men of genius. They must often prove themselves to lesser men. To priests. To examiners. Sometimes they cannot lower themselves. It is up to you, my friend. If he fails his examinations and is banished from the school, it will be entirely your fault."

"Thank you for such comfort." But I, too, thought it was my fault. Father Medulous would be unhappy with me. Bernal would soon pass out of our lives forever. That possibility consoled me sometimes. He would be gone, like a serious childhood disease. I wanted to forget him.

44

IN LATE JULY the examiners came, and for a week one by one we were summoned to their long wooden table in the Salle des Grandes Etudes. The examiners in mathematics sat on one side, five of them. The student was directed to sit in a hard chair opposite them. It was hot, and we sweated in floods. They dressed in wool suits and wore horn-rimmed glasses and expressions of impassive sobriety. They wiped their faces with a succession of handkerchiefs and held onto their dignity while sweat dripped off their noses and their chins.

I may say in digression and braggadocio here in my quiet kitchen on an evening when the August heat is almost unbearable and I am old that I passed my first-year examinations with the highest honors and that the examiners stood up when I had explained the last problem on the blackboard. I trust that my unknown and future readers will forgive me for the pride with which I recount my academic accomplishments. They came to nothing in the end, you see, but when I recall them even now, I am once again the foreign lad in a foreign land, making his way perilously and discovering with wonder that I had something hidden within me that I did not suspect. Put yourself in my place and look kindly on my boasting.

Yet to continue: The chief examiner wiped his face a last time and put out a wet hand and took mine with torpid enthusiasm. The examination had ranged far beyond the courses I had taken. The examiners kept trying to find some problem that might baffle me, and they did not succeed. The chief examiner told me that I had done "brilliantly." He repeated the word several times, though I feared that each time he said it the strain of his exertion might be too much for him. I should be teaching others already, he said. One by one the examiners bowed and shook my hand, and I went out into the scalding sunshine feeling a delicious coolness. I crossed myself and thanked God for his many gifts.

My ebullient mood did not last. I was devoured with anxiety for Bernal. Guy stood before the examiners in literature, a different group of men, and passed without distinction. Bernal's examinations were the next day. We accompanied him to the university early that morning before the awful heat of midday had built up, and I could see that my pessimism had infected Guy. He seemed gloomy and silent.

"Do you know what I have been thinking of?" Bernal asked, looking at us both with luminous enthusiasm.

"I hope you have been thinking of discovering the center of gravity of a triangle by using calculus," I said.

"Oh, nothing so ordinary as that," Bernal said.

"What have you been thinking about?" Guy said.

"Croissants," Bernal said. "I awoke this morning thinking of croissants. I have tried to put croissants out of my mind, to tell myself that before my examination, I should abstain from all thoughts of luxury. I thought that I might promise croissants to myself as a reward for when I had completed this distasteful task. I think I made a mistake. I should have gone to the bakery and purchased nine or ten croissants. I should have eaten them to purge my mind of desire. It is one way to avoid temptation."

"How?" I said.

"To yield to it," Bernal said, abruptly morose. "If one yields to most temptations, one discovers that the reality is not as satisfying as one had hoped. One is tempted less thereafter."

"Croissants," Guy said, looking at Bernal in exasperation. "You are at one of the most important moments in your life, and you think of croissants."

Bernal laughed. "I admit that my reflections on croissants are more important to me than my thoughts of other things."

Guy took a deep breath and looked gravely at me. We marched towards the university in a mood of a little procession moving towards the guillotine with a madly cheerful victim. I looked at the ground.

"When you are through, we shall have croissants," Guy said sarcastically. "That will make this a day to remember."

"Indeed it will," Bernal said. He laughed, and we shook hands. He disappeared inside the great hall.

"We shall eat croissants for his farewell lunch. All that wasted time!" I said bitterly.

"I must admit, my friend, that the prospects are discouraging," Guy said. "I shall miss him terribly. You should have worked harder."

"Guy, your kindness and generosity are enough to make the saints gasp," I said.

We went over to the flowered park in front of the casino and sat on a bench and looked out at the canal. It was a beautiful day—hot, with steamy clouds floating overhead. The minutes passed, and then an hour had gone. The shade where we were sitting floated beyond us, and the sun crashed down on our backs. We moved, hardly speaking to one another. I knew that peasants were working in their fields. The thought made me miserable. We found another bench in the shade. The benches were made of wood, and they were painted green. We sweated, and our shirts stuck to the wood.

"I should have believed you," Guy said. "Now I am going to lose the bets I made on our friend."

"You have bet on him?" I said.

"Yes, I bet Johannes Dubler fifty francs that Bernal would pass."

"Dubler bet against Bernal? But Bernal has been so kind to him!"

"My dear friend, you are so damnably *innocent!* Yes, Dubler bet against Bernal. Everyone is betting. I would not be at all surprised to discover that some of the priests are betting. Some are betting on you and Bernal; some are betting on the examiners. I have bet on you. I hope it is not immodest of me to say that had I not bet on you, no one else would have bet at all. Remember this, my friend. I am so loyal to you that I have bet on you. You are doing this to me."

"My God, Guy!" I put my head in my hands, imagining the examiners posing their relentless questions. I imagined Bernal shrugging, being excessively polite. "None of this matters to me, gentlemen," Bernal would say. "I have enjoyed myself in your splendid little country, and I am profoundly sorry to tell you goodbye and even more sorry that I have displeased you by not passing your examination. Gentlemen, why should we prolong this exercise? I believe that few things can be of so little importance as mathematics. Gentlemen, I believe that you are even less important than your paltry discipline. If you will excuse me? I am hungry for croissants."

The examination began at ten o'clock, and the bells of the city had scarcely ceased striking noon when Bernal appeared. He wore his easy smile and looked serene. We stood up, unable to speak.

"I am so very happy to see you both," he said. "Are you well?"

"We have been broiled like English beef," I said irritably. "Why did the examination take so long?"

He rubbed his stomach gingerly and ignored my question. "I am so hungry," he said. "I have seldom been so hungry. I believe it has something to do with intellectual activity. When I am forced to concentrate on disagreeable and meaningless examinations, my body reacts by becoming ravenously hungry. I have thought only of croissants for the past two hours. I tell you, it has been agony. I was sure my stomach was going to begin growling. Thanks be to God it did not humiliate me before the examiners. I find the bodily functions embarrassing at times. Do you not think it so? Now we can eat. We can eat mounds of croissants. I have been released from my purgatory, and we can enjoy paradise."

He started to walk towards a little restaurant that we both knew, and Guy and I followed dumbly. I had tears in my eyes.

"In all of Argentina I do not believe we have a single croissant made with hot butter and wound in such fine layers of pastry as one can obtain here and in Paris. In Paris the croissants are better. I must confess that, though, my dear Guy, I am afraid my statement may affront your national honor. Ah, what a relief to be in the open air again!"

"You will be returning to Argentina soon?" Guy said.

"Yes, of course. In three days. I shall miss the croissants. And the two of you, of course. I have no friends like you in Argentina. You must come to visit me there. We shall eat good beef. I promise you that."

Guy and I were walking a little behind because Bernal's eagerness carried him swiftly towards the cafe. My legs felt like cement. We exchanged glances. Guy's face was deeply troubled. He shrugged wordlessly and shook his head.

I wiped clumsily at my tears. "So, you are going back to Argentina," I said finally. "You did not tell us that you were going back to Argentina."

Bernal did not look around. He had only one thing on his mind—croissants. "But my dear friend, I return to Argentina every summer. My father demands it. I go to school in the winter as he desires, and I return to him in the summer as he desires, and I ride horseback on the pampas alone as I desire. I could not leave before the examinations, but now I must depart. After we have eaten croissants and drunk coffee, let us drink some of your father's beer, Guy. It is such a hot day."

I was angry now. "You are going home, and next year you will go to Berlin. You will forget us. You do not care that I have worked so hard for you. You do not care about anything. You were here, and next year you will be at the University of Berlin."

Now Bernal did stop short in the street. He turned around and looked at me in astonishment, perhaps even confusion. "But why should I go to the University of Berlin? What do you mean?"

"Perhaps you are not going to Berlin," I said. "Perhaps you have decided to go to another university. Bologna, perhaps. Cambridge—Zurich. The Swiss are dull, I hear, but they have several universities. Perhaps you should go to Heidelberg. You can drink German beer and sing songs all night long at Heidelberg. You can forget all about us."

I tramped on, leaving Bernal standing amazed in the street. I thought I was going to start sobbing.

"But my dear friend," he said, following me. "Why should I go to Berlin? I shall return here. In the month of October I shall return in time for school."

"How can you return here when you have failed your examinations?" I cried. "When you have failed your examinations twice, you are not allowed to return."

"But I did not fail my examinations," Bernal said. "I passed my examinations. Thanks to your help I passed with 'very great distinction.' The examiners were amazed. They remembered me from last year. Last year they nearly ordered me out of the room. This year they rose and shook my hand. I am coming back to Ghent. I am going to finish the university. Next year I shall work even harder. Who knows, my friend, I may surpass you!"

We stood there looking at each other. I could not believe what I was hearing. Very slowly I did believe.

"You passed," I whispered. "You did say that you passed the examinations? The examinations you took this morning?"

"But of course I passed," Bernal said. "You are my friend, and you wanted me to pass. So I passed. I did it for you, my friend." He spoke in his usual mild way, as if what he had to say was so evident that I should never have doubted it. I recall shaking his hand again and again. We did not embrace. We were both too formal for such things.

I was responsible for Bernal's decision to stay in Ghent. It was the summer of 1913. None of us could know then that these were the last examinations we would ever take. After he died, I never did mathematics again.

45

LAST NIGHT after sitting here for hours, I went out with the dog into the warm dark and urinated in the yard before I went to bed. The stars overhead swam in a hazy sky. Far away, heat lightning danced on the horizon. I felt stiff and exhausted. I lay awake a long time remembering Guy and Bernal and that lost year.

It was only a year and a few months. To me it was an epoch—the year of our friendship. Our idyll. Our Arcadia.

I wanted to speak to them last night. I knew that they would not come. I thought that perhaps somewhere some parts of their bones still exist—a skull perhaps, a tooth, a thighbone, picked up casually by a peasant unborn when they died, meditated upon for a moment, flung away. I have heard that at Verdun bones are still being picked up on the field of battle and piled in vaults under the great monument called the Ossuaire. You can peer down into the vaults and see piles of white bone that were once human beings who drank in taverns and walked in streets and sat in classrooms and loved women. I half dreamed that I walked across a grassy field and came upon some particle of them, and that like some relic of a saint, the bone spoke to me.

Last night the recollection of that year came back like a tide rolling in from a vast, dark sea. I lay tossing in the late-summer heat, sweating profusely, listening to the choir of insects singing by the million in the nearby woods, and the weight of death and oblivion fell upon me. In the deep of night, I had a resurgence of the darkness in the soul that once left me passive in the world, hardly able to live.

I arose and walked back out into the yard in my bare feet. I considered the far, impersonal stars wheeling overhead. I felt a strange comfort in the occasional passage of a car or a truck on the highway. Someone was alive. The dog barked at something in the woods. I felt better, and afterwards I slept.

Tonight I shall return to Bourbonville. My stories converge as they will.

At the end of his basic military training and before he went to France, D.B. came home. I saw him walking with Virgil in the streets, the boy tall and muscular in his close-fitting uniform. Virgil was tall, too, and held himself stiffly erect. They looked uncomfortable together. They made me uncomfortable when I spoke to them. D.B. forced out his words and bragged in an offhand way, a boy reading brave lines.

"Yes, I'm the best shot in my company. The captain tells me I'll be a lieutenant before this thing is over. I hope so. I suppose I have a talent for the army."

"When will you go to France?" I said.

"It can't be too soon for me. I'm ready to go now. But probably not until late February. I hope the Huns aren't licked by then. I want to get in on it. It's all going to be over soon, you know. We'll have a world safe for democracy, just like the President says."

He prattled on. Virgil said little and looked dour and older.

Pinkerton came up to the laboratory, followed by Vissing and Shaw.

"I saw Virgil and his son walking around town," Pinkerton said, an unusual tone of wistfulness in his voice. "I wish I had a son to send off to war. I wish things had turned out different for me."

"You don't have any children?" Shaw said in a restrained sort of way.

"I had a child. He died," Pinkerton said. "Lived two months and died. A boy. I called him after me—Moreland James Pinkerton. He's buried down in the Methodist burying ground south of town." For a moment I thought Pinkerton's voice would break.

"Terrible, terrible," Shaw said.

"How you've suffered!" Vissing said. He stoked his pipe carefully and looked at Pinkerton in pop-eyed contemplation.

"Addled my wife's brain," Pinkerton said. "She's never been the same since we lost our boy. Never had another child. Ah, well, you play the hand fate deals you."

"That's the way I see it," Shaw said, trying to look dolorous.

"Virgil Weaver's got a son to go fight. Hell, even that damned old fool that fired the shotgun over my head has got a son in uniform."

"It's a strange world," Shaw said.

"If I had a boy, if my boy had lived to be a soldier, I'd be so proud of him," Pinkerton said wistfully. "But Virgil, he's different." I noted the lack of animosity in Pinkerton's voice. Shaw did not.

"He was a coward in the war," Shaw said. He said the words as though by rote.

"Maybe his boy will make him different," Pinkerton said. "If Virgil had ever said to me, 'Maybe I was wrong, Moreland. Maybe you and me were both wrong,' I might have been friends with him. You never know."

"You never know," Shaw said safely.

In late February D.B. sailed for France. Virgil withdrew into a higher room of isolation. He went about the town scarcely speaking to anyone, eyes straight ahead. I was not invited to dinner with him again.

Old Brian Ledbetter greeted me warmly in town on Saturdays when the streets swarmed with farmers in from the country on their day of leisure. He sat in Douglas Kinlaw's hardware store by the potbellied stove, surrounded by friends, swapping tales, smoking his pipe. Sometimes we drank coffee together in Bessie May Hancock's cafe.

"Virgil wasn't as foolish as I was when Jim Ed left for the war," the old man said with an uncustomary sigh. "I taken the train to New York City. That's where him and Willy left from. Jim Ed, he wrote me how he missed the water from our spring. So I filled a couple of gallon jars with spring water. I bought me a train ticket to New York City, and when I'd sat up all day and all night long on the train with them two gallon jars of spring water in a box at my feet, they wouldn't let me down to the dock where he was leaving from. They told me, they said this here was war. Daddies couldn't be running around looking for their boys like it was a Sunday-school picnic.

"Well, I went down to the Statue of Liberty. She's on this island, don't you know, and you can get out there on a ferry boat. I taken and went out there with my two gallon jars of water, and I waited till Jim Ed's ship come down. It was a ship called the *American Traveler*, and it was packed right up to the smokestacks with men in khaki uniforms, and I knowed that one of them was Jim Ed, and I poured them two gallon jars of water in the harbor. I figured it this way: maybe part of that water from home might run out there to that ship and get around it some way and keep him safe. Then I got back on the train, and I come home again. Leastways Virgil didn't do no damn fool thing like that."

It was a hard winter. In early February the river froze. To show how brave he was, Pinkerton walked across the river on the ice. To show how agreeable they were, Vissing and Shaw walked with him.

One day Pinkerton came up to the laboratory by himself. He talked while I worked.

"They admire me," he said. He might have broken into song. "They see what I'm doing here; they see what a leader I am, how this place runs like an Elgin watch. Yesterday Shaw said to me, he said, 'Captain, you have a gift for leadership, a gift for making men see a problem like you see it and making them see that your way is the only way to settle it. You know something else? The men in this foundry love you. I've never seen anything like it, like the devotion your men give their captain. If the businesses of America could be led by people like you, Moreland Pinkerton, Bolshevism would vanish from the face of the earth.' That's exactly what he said."

Pinkerton's face shone. I bent to my work. I saw Guy's still, dark shape in a corner, a foreboding presence. I prayed that he would not laugh aloud.

"What do you think of our inspectors?" Dale Farmer said cautiously.

"I do not think anything of them," I said.

"The Captain is under their spell," he said.

"Yes," I said.

"The Captain does not have much experience with the world. He has lived too much of his life here in Bourbonville. He does not know people beyond the borders of our little county. It is troubling. Very troubling." We were walking back to the boardinghouse, down Broadway. Dale Farmer looked anxiously around to see if anyone was listening.

Pinkerton knew he would be summoned to Washington, because someone up there had to read the reports Vissing and Shaw wrote about him and realize that he could not be left in a backwater. The war effort required this man to be at the center of things. Every day he expected a telegram asking him to take the next train. Day after day no telegram came. He was not daunted. His anticipation rose as his salvation was deferred.

Dr. Youngblood sought me out; we spent much time together. Guy and Bernal were jealous of him. "He sees us," Guy whispered. "You may think he does not see us because he is so slow, so calm. I am sure he sees me. I look at him, and he looks back at me, and I am sure he believes he is fighting us for your soul. My dear Paul, I do beg you—do not let him take you away from us. We are not demons; we are the only friends you have in the world."

"No one will ever take me away from you," I said. "No one. No one."

"Do not underestimate him," Guy said. "He is an easy man to underestimate. I know he sees us."

46

DR. YOUNGBLOOD was in Bourbonville by accident, he said, laughing in his slow, chuckling way as if the tale mystified and amused even him, like a stranger's epic told at fireside all night long in an inn where the road came out of the forest and vanished again and the traveler would vanish with it in the morning, taking his tale with him. He told his story to beguile himself and perhaps to still his restlessness and regret.

He had had an uncle, a Dr. Jeremiah Cogill, who had ended by equal accident as the physician ministering to the ills of Bourbon County. Dr. Youngblood studied at Harvard College and at the Harvard Medical School, and when he had taken his last diploma, he was uncertain about what to do with himself. He thought of going to Germany. "They see medicine as a science over there, you see. Here it is still an apprenticeship, something you learn by seeing other doctors work. In Germany they see medicine as a science, and they do research in laboratories. I thought I might do research. Maybe study contagious diseases. But . . ."

His uncle, visiting his sister, Dr. Youngblood's mother, a displaced Tennessean, invited him to come down to Bourbonville because Doc Cogill, as everyone called him, was the only physician in the county. "He was getting old and tired," Dr. Youngblood recalled. "He said he needed help." Doc Cogill said it was a good place to learn about stab wounds and the peculiar holes made in bodies by shotguns and pistols and the compound fractures made by falling out of barns or from being dragged behind a runaway horse when a plowman had tied the reins around himself to avoid the trouble of having to hold them and the plow handles at the same time.

It was a good place to see what happened to mothers who bore too many children and to study the choking effects of diphtheria on little boys and girls who coughed themselves to death with it. No laboratory could provide a better demonstration of the effects of malnutrition in tenant farmers, and Bourbon County obliged medical practice every year by providing a dozen or so cases of pellagra. It was a fine place to study the damage to the brain that might be inflicted by a drunken husband when he beat up his wife, and an equally excellent laboratory for the practice of sewing up holes made by pitchforks, which men and women alike fell on during haying time. Doc Cogill commented that the young physician would also gain much practice in amputating hands and arms and sometimes legs mangled by farm machinery. "You can learn how to be a doctor down here," Doc Cogill said. "After you've been here a couple of years, you'll know everything you need to get rich back there in Boston. You can even go to Germany and teach those folks a thing or two. You can talk all you want to about laboratories and science and microscopes and chemicals and all those things. But a real doctor has got his hands on human flesh and human bones, and he's got to dip his fingers in human blood."

"I never planned to go back to Boston," Dr. Youngblood said. "I wanted to go back to Baltimore, if you really want to know. Baltimore's my real home. I never have called home any place but Baltimore." He spoke slowly, thoughtfully, looking into the fire burning against the chill of a late winter night. "Sometimes when it rains here, I can smell rain on the brick streets back there. Sometimes I can shut my eyes and see people scrubbing the white marble steps in front of the brick row houses. It's a beautiful place, Baltimore. All so neat compared to here. You know what is hardest of all for me to get used to down here? The way people throw garbage into the streets. The way they put up with trash. The way they dump an old icebox in the backyard and let it lie there until it rots away. Baltimore is clean and neat."

One night Doc Cogill was called to the home of a family named Reesor, where an old man lay dying. The death rattle was in the old man's throat, gargling through the dimly lit cabin so that when he opened the door, Dr. Youngblood surmised, Doc Cogill could have told everybody there was nothing a doctor could do. People fetched doctors in the middle of the night because they thought a doctor might do *something*. If he might do something, they called him, because otherwise they were not doing their duty to kith and kin.

He went out as he did on so many nights when he was already bone weary, and the comatose old man was noisily dying in a darkened back room, a very old man who so far as anybody knew had never been to Knoxville or any other city and perhaps never outside of Bourbon County in eighty or ninety years, and Doc Cogill was barely able to stay awake, and he went yawning into the kitchen and asked for black coffee, and Clara Reesor, the old man's daughter-in-law, poured him a cup, and he took it and stood there swaying for a moment and said, "I feel strange," and without another word fell dead on the floor, and the old man in the back room was still alive, with the death rattle in his throat but alive, and Doc Cogill was dead.

"I should have gone out there myself," Dr. Youngblood said sadly. "He always told me he was used to it. He told me to stay in bed. Hell, you never get used to it. After that there wasn't another doctor in the county. Just me. I couldn't walk out and leave all these folks without a doctor. I had to stay and take care of them. You understand that, don't you? It's a damn fool thing. But here I am!"

He spoke with his familiar chuckle. He poured another glass of wine and puffed on his pipe and looked into the fire. Behind him I saw the shapes of Guy and Bernal against the draperies. They were afraid.

47

PEOPLE OFTEN CAME to fetch Dr. Youngblood in the evenings. One night in March we heard a car pull to a stop before the door. In a moment we heard a soft knock. "That'll be somebody here in town," Dr. Youngblood said wearily. "They could have called on the telephone. They don't trust the telephone. They come to be sure that I'll go back with them." He pulled himself out of his chair and shuffled downstairs, and I heard him open the door.

"Why, Miss Daisy," he said. "Come in! Come in! Is anything wrong? Is your mamma sick?"

"Of course she's not sick, Curtis. Daddy told me you two sit down here at night. I decided I'd come and sit with you."

"Don't you have homework? Shouldn't you be studying?"

"I don't have to study. I know more than my teachers, Curtis. Girls at Bourbonville High take home economics. They learn how to boil water without burning it. I can do that."

I heard Daisy's quick step ascending. She strode into the room, plump, triumphant, her black hair parted in the middle and swept back. She grinned at me.

"Everybody at my house goes to bed at 9:30," she said. "Daddy gets up at five. He says he works best in the morning. He gets up and writes his history of Bourbon County. Why does he want to write a history of the county that hates his soul, Curtis? You tell me that if you can. Mamma does what Daddy does. If he went to bed at five o'clock in the afternoon, she'd go to bed with him. So here I am." She sat down.

"It seems dangerous for a young woman like you to drive a car by herself at night," Dr. Youngblood said. "Aren't you scared?"

"Scared! What's there to be scared of? I'm sixteen years old. Almost seventeen."

"I don't know," Dr. Youngblood said.

"Nothing ever happens in Bourbon County."

"Well . . ." Dr. Youngblood said vaguely. He smiled. She sat with her lips slightly parted, and I could see her bright teeth.

I felt Bernal nearby and looked around. Daisy looked around to see what I was looking for in the dimness behind our chairs.

"What is it?" she said. "Did you hear something?"

"Nothing," I said in confusion. "Yes. I thought I heard a noise."

"Mice," Daisy said, sitting back. "Curtis, you need a cat."

"I don't like cats," Dr. Youngblood said. "I prefer dogs."

"Then get a dog."

"I can't keep a dog because of my hours," Dr. Youngblood said. "I can't take care of a dog."

"You don't have to take care of a cat," Daisy said. "Cats take care of themselves."

"Did you tell your daddy you were coming here?" Dr. Youngblood said.

"He won't mind," she said.

"He will be worried," Dr. Youngblood said. "Maybe I ought to ring him on the telephone."

"You'll just wake him up," Daisy said. "He doesn't worry about me. He spends all his time worrying about D.B. If you call up, you'll just have Mrs. Flint listening in and telling the whole town that I'm over here doing something bad."

Dr. Youngblood chuckled. Mrs. Flint was the night operator at the telephone company. Bourbonville had few night telephone calls, and Mrs. Flint listened in on all of them.

"Can I have some wine? I'm cold. Some wine would warm me up."

Dr. Youngblood hesitated.

"I am not a child." She looked like a child—an overweight, pretty child. "Come on," she said.

Dr. Youngblood relented. "Wahl, Miss Daisy," he said, affecting a false southern drawl that he thought clever, "if y'all want some wine, then I just reckon I'll have to po' you a little drop. Course, I hope I ain't going to be accused of corrupting your morals, Miss Daisy. I sholey don't want to be accused of that."

"You can't do that, Curtis," Daisy said with a laugh. "They're already corrupt." She looked boldly at me. "Can I smoke?"

Dr. Youngblood looked at me as if for help. "It's all right with me," he said uneasily. He handed her a glass of wine. I lit her cigarette. She looked at me happily and drew the smoke deep into her lungs.

Her energy made the dark old room waken and blink. She made the fire gleam more warmly on the crossed cavalry swords rusting on the wall. She reconditioned the old rifles and muskets. She illuminated the photographs of London and Paris and the poster announcing the appearance of Sarah Bernhardt at the Odéon.

I smoked a cigarette. I remembered Stephanos, how in the morning he had walked out onto the terrace at home and looked across the bay, across the yellow grain fields that lay between Athens and the port, the dirt road winding around the bay, and through groves of trees in the direction of the city, how in smoking Stephanos gathered strength for the day in imitation of my father.

"I guess you haven't heard anything from D.B.," Dr. Youngblood said.

"Not since the little note he wrote before he got on the ship. You know D.B. He won't write much, especially not to Daddy. I write to Jim Ed all the time, and Jim Ed writes me. I tell Jim Ed everything. I won't write to D.B. I know he won't write me back."

"He can't mail a letter off the ship," Dr. Youngblood said.

"He won't write me. D.B. doesn't like me."

"Don't let this stuff go to your head," Dr. Youngblood said. "You can sip at wine, and first thing you know, you're drunk. I don't want you to run off the side of the road going home," Dr. Youngblood said.

"I'm old enough to take care of myself," she said. "I have a question. Do you understand my father?"

"I understand him well enough," Dr. Youngblood said uneasily. "He's my friend."

"Daddy talks about small farms and how terrible the idea of progress is, and he says America is going to lose its soul if it dives into industrialization and . . . Well, you know how he talks."

"Yes, I know your father's ideas."

"But he makes money hand over fist. He studies the newspapers and stocks, and he invests. He bought stock in oil companies that struck it rich in Oklahoma. It was the first stock Daddy ever bought. Then he bought stock in steel and rubber just when Henry Ford was starting to build cars. He's buying stock in plumbing fixtures now. Did you know that?"

"He told me," Dr. Youngblood said.

"Daddy says there's going to be a lot of building when the war ends. Buildings have to have bathrooms and toilets and bathtubs. So he's buying plumbing fixtures. Toilets. My daddy is going to make a pile of money on toilets. He says the era of the outhouse is over."

"That depends," Dr. Youngblood said, chuckling.

"He's like Midas—he's got the golden touch," Daisy said.

"He has that," Dr. Youngblood said.

"Midas kissed his daughter, and she turned to gold," Daisy said.

"There are lots of people who envy his judgment," Dr. Youngblood said. "He's done well for you."

"I feel like a gold statue. There's more to life than money and a big house."

"That's a fact," Dr. Youngblood said. "But it's nice to have money and a big house."

"Daddy talks about the goodness of farm life, but he means for other people. He doesn't mean for himself."

"He told me once he never wanted to put up hay again as along as he lives," Dr. Youngblood said. "I don't blame him. I see people doing it, and I'm glad I just cut off legs and hands and sew up pitchfork wounds. I'm glad I don't put up hay in summertime."

"He's writing a history of Bourbon County and talking about farmers and the independent life. He says he can go back to it. He can be poor again. Daddy wasn't really poor, was he, Curtis?"

"It all depends," Dr. Youngblood said uncomfortably.

"It all depends!" Daisy said. She laughed and tossed her head and blew out smoke. She threw the butt of her cigarette into the fire.

"Your father is a complicated man," Dr. Youngblood said.

"He's making money out of the war," Daisy said. "He's a pacifist, but he's got stock in all these companies that are making money out of the war."

"You get started doing some things, and you can't stop," Dr. Youngblood said.

Daisy looked around at the cluttered room. "I haven't been in your house in years. Not since I was a little girl."

"You should come here more often."

"What is that picture?"

"That is a print of Trafalgar Square in London."

"Have you been there? Have you been to England?"

"Yes, I've been to England."

"When did you go?"

"In the summer between my junior and senior year at Harvard. I went to Europe. I did a short version of the grand tour."

"You went to Europe for one summer? I thought people went to Europe for years and years."

"No, you can go in the summer. With steamships you can cross the Atlantic in a week."

"You've been on a big steamer!" Daisy said admiringly. "With a band and everything like that?"

"Yes, with a band."

"And you danced?"

"Oh yes, I danced."

"You danced. I'd love to see you dance. I'd love to dance with you."

Dr. Youngblood blushed. "I wasn't very good. No sense of rhythm. Still . . ."

I believe I looked at Dr. Youngblood in mild surprise. He had never mentioned England to me. I had no idea that he had been abroad.

"You've been to England, too, haven't you, Paul? Is it all right to call you Paul? Everybody else calls you Paul. Except Daddy. He is determined to call you Mr. Alexander. May I call you Paul?"

"Oh yes," I said.

"Will you call me Daisy and not Miss Weaver?"

"If you want."

"I bet you won't. You've been to England?"

"He was three years in the hospital in London," Dr. Youngblood said gently.

"Three years!" Daisy said. "Of course! I forgot! You poor man. How terrible it was! I'm so sorry."

These were the first artless words she had spoken since she entered the room. Everything else had been studied, a little too much like lines practiced by an actress resolved to make an impression. She put out a hand and touched me gently on the knee and let her fingers linger there just a moment.

"I am well now," I said.

"Three years in a hospital. Three years in bed?"

"I was not in bed all that time," I said. "I walked around during the second and third years. A nurse walked with us. I do not remember much about it."

"You lie," Guy whispered from somewhere close by. It might have been a gust of March wind at the windows.

"Poor thing," Daisy said. "Poor thing."

"I would like to visit England again," Dr. Youngblood said in a dreamy way.

"Can I have some more wine, Curtis?" Daisy said.

"No," Dr. Youngblood said.

"You still think I'm a little girl," she said.

"I know you have to drive back home tonight," he said.

"I've never been anywhere," Daisy said. "Daddy goes to New York. Do you suppose he has a sweetheart in New York?"

Dr. Youngblood looked aghast. "I am sure he does not."

"Oh, you're not sure at all. He doesn't love Mamma. Everybody can see that. He must have a sweetheart. That's why he doesn't take me with him when he goes. Old Grandfather Ledbetter has been to New York. He didn't see anything. He went up to see Jim Ed off to the war, and when he couldn't, he came right back home. Has he told you that, Paul?"

"Yes," I said.

"Of course," Daisy said. "We tell you all our secrets."

"It wasn't a secret," Dr. Youngblood said.

She lit another cigarette. We smoked, and the haze of tobacco smoke rose in the air.

"I'll tell you what," Daisy said after a while. "As soon as the war is over, let's all three go to England. We can go together. We won't tell people we are going. We will just disappear for a while. Wouldn't that be nice? Maybe we will never come back. Please let me have some more wine, Curtis. I promise I'm not drunk."

Dr. Youngblood relented. He poured her a half glass.

"I've read lots of books about England," she said. "I've studied a map of London. I know that the biggest street is called the Strand."

"I know a stamp shop in the Strand," Dr. Youngblood said. "You can buy stamps there from all over the world. The clerks are very polite. You have an interest in stamps, you see, and they think you're quality."

"We'll buy tons of stamps," Daisy said. "I've always wanted to collect stamps."

"I collect them," Dr. Youngblood said. "But I don't mount them the way I should."

"We can drink tea in London," Daisy said. "Can't we drink tea?"

"We can drink all the tea you want, Miss Daisy. Chinese or Indian," Dr. Youngblood said. He grinned so much that his eyes nearly shut.

"We can look in windows. We can shop in the Strand," Daisy said.

"There is a small art gallery in the Strand," I said. "It is very quiet. When I was convalescing, I went in there sometimes with my nurse. The pictures were bright and sunny. I used to look at them until the nurse said we must go."

Dr. Youngblood smiled around the stem of his pipe and looked at me. "I have never heard you put so many sentences together at one time," he said.

I stammered something in reply, embarrassed.

Daisy smiled at me. "If we really want to go, we can go," she said. "We can do what we want to do no matter what people think. Isn't that right, Paul? I think we ought to go and not tell anybody. They will look for us one day, and we'll be gone."

"The theatre," Dr. Youngblood said dreamily. "I have not been to the theatre in years. The West End is lined with theatres. We can see plays and eat supper afterwards with the theatre crowd."

"Every night," Daisy said. "Every night we'll go to the theatre. We will do it. We will do it." She got up and spun around with delight, her skirts swirling, and ended in front of me, standing over me, putting her hands down on my shoulders.

Suddenly, lightly, she leaned down and kissed me quickly on the mouth.

I heard Guy moan—a terrible sound. It seemed to come from very close by. Daisy bent over me, grinning and pleased with herself, pleased with me.

"I will marry you, Paul Alexander. You don't know it now. But I will marry you someday." She laughed and backed away.

Dr. Youngblood chuckled uneasily. I heard the far-off sigh of wind blowing over a valley of dry bones.

48

THE WORLD turned green. Rain whispered in the fields and woods. I heard it drumming on the shingle roof of the boardinghouse at night and on the laboratory by day. The air smelled of rain. When Dale Farmer and I walked to the car works carrying umbrellas in the morning, our feet stuck in the mud along the streets.

The sun warmed, and in April the daffodils bloomed, and the grass shone, and rose bushes put out tendrils, and the world seemed soft. At night fireplaces stayed cold. Men stood in shirtsleeves and suspenders in yards and talked with each other, and though it was a wet spring, they watered their grass with rubber hoses and looked proprietary, as if the hoses were sceptres granting them sovereignty over a green empire.

I slept badly. I dreamed. I was falling. I was under bombardment. I was alone in the dark, and the Germans were coming to kill me. I lay down late and got up early. People told me I looked tired. Darcy Coolidge worried aloud about me. "If you don't take care of yourself, you can get sick and die," she said. I knew she was thinking of Mr. Sanders.

My first pleasures with Bourbonville came in that time—sunrise over the mountains, the sky turning liquid gray, then pink, then fiery orange, then incandescent as the sun serenely climbed the eastern sky.

Dr. Youngblood fetched me often after supper, and Daisy sat with us, and rumors multiplied.

Darcy Coolidge said, "I hear you're sweet on the Weaver girl."

"I am not," I said.

"You don't have to fib to me, Mr. Alexander. I wasn't born yesterday, you know. I know a few things about the world. A young man's fancy turns to love in the spring. I loved the Colonel; the Colonel loved me. Love makes the world go round." She exuded a nostalgic and sentimental happiness. "I'll miss you when you leave my boardinghouse," she said. "But to be in love! Oh, it's so wonderful!"

"I am not in love, Mrs. Coolidge."

"Oh, we're so shy. I do not want to inquire into your personal affairs, my dear Mr. Alexander. I am not a prying woman. But I see things. Yes, yes, yes. I see how you look at Daisy Weaver. Yes I do." She pointed a finger at me in a teasing, girlish gesture.

I knew it would do no good to protest. Darcy Coolidge saw what she wanted to see.

"Now I wouldn't say a bad thing about anybody in the world, Mr. Alexander. But Daisy Weaver has a bad reputation. I would as soon let a man see me naked as see me smoking. But the other things people say about her? I don't believe half of them are true. At least I hope they are not true."

"I am sure they are not," I said.

"Of course," Darcy Coolidge said, looking at me as if she had suddenly collected herself. She looked out the window onto the bright spring day. "Ah me, I grieve for all the mothers of the world whose daughters do not live up to their expectations, Mr. Alexander. I grieve for poor young husbands who bring purity to marriage and then have their wives' impurity rub off on them."

"Mrs. Coolidge," I said.

"But you can't resist love. When I fell in love with the Colonel, I was hopeless."

"Mrs. Coolidge," I said wearily. "Daisy Weaver means nothing to me. She comes to speak with Dr. Youngblood when I am there. I have no interest in her."

"Well, she's telling everybody in town that you two are going to be married," Darcy Coolidge said, suddenly cross.

"She is making that up," I said. "She is a young girl, Mrs. Coolidge. She is romantic, and she imagines things. I have never said a word to her about marriage." We were in Darcy Coolidge's private parlor. Lucy had served us tea. I saw a shadow where no shadow should be, falling the wrong way into the light. I knew it was Guy. I refused to look at him.

Darcy Coolidge shook her head in disappointment. "Well, you might get married yet. You don't know."

"That will not happen," I said. "She is a child."

"You aren't so old yourself, Mr. Alexander. Just because you've been in the army don't mean you're so old. There are girls as old as Daisy Weaver in Bourbon County who are already mothers. If the two of you should get married, it'd be a grand thing in a way. I mean, you'd probably be miserable for the rest of your life, but you could do a lot of good for the county. Virgil Weaver's daughter married to a railroad man. It would help patch things up."

"I do not want to 'patch things up,' as you put it," I said.

Darcy Coolidge stared at me thoughtfully. "I reckon Bourbonville isn't good enough for a quality person like you," she said, without reproach.

"I did not mean that," I said.

"I never have cared much about it myself," she said, looking vaguely upward as if to avoid my eyes. "But what's a body to do? How could I move my boardinghouse? I would leave if I could. I don't think anybody would stay in Bourbonville who could go somewhere else."

"Mrs. Coolidge, I did not mean anything like that."

"You do not have to apologize," she said. "We all think Daisy Weaver is special. She's a little fat. But you want a woman strong enough to bear children. Skinny women don't do so good. You need big hips to have children, and Daisy Weaver has big hips. Maybe you've seen prettier women than Daisy. I just know what's here in Bourbon County. I've never been much of anywhere. I don't know what the world is like. Once the Colonel and me, we went to Atlanta. The Colonel said he'd heard so much about Atlanta, he wanted to see it. We went down there and stayed in a cheap boardinghouse and saw how Atlanta folks did things. Let me tell you, I don't think they did things all that great. But it was the only trip I ever had. Oh, life's so short, Mr. Alexander. Take love when you can get it. Take it. If Daisy Weaver is your pick, I say it's all right. She wouldn't be my pick, but I'm not a young gentleman who needs a wife. You do what you think best."

49

DAISY BROUGHT Palmyre back to me. Part of the chemistry of recollection was size. They were both large. Palmyre was almost six feet tall, big-boned and strong like one of the Karyatides on the Akropolis. I told her that once, and she laughed. In that way she was not like Daisy. Palmyre was full of good-natured mirth, and I never heard her utter a word of self-pity.

I met Palmyre because of Leonora.

Leonora was an actress. Guy loved the theatre. On weekends we went to the theatre and came to the Vieux Gand afterwards, where Guy explained the play to us. One night in the spring of 1913, we saw Leonora play the Virgin Mary in Maeterlinck's *Sister Beatrice*. She appeared at the beginning of the second act as a statue of the Virgin that came to life and descended to speak some sentimental lines. She delivered her speech with far too much passion, a declamation unsuited to the tone of the play, making the Virgin not the meek and mild Mother of God but a loud harpy devouring sweet thoughts.

Guy was captivated by her thin good looks, by her breasts uncommonly large for so slender a frame and shown to great effect by the filmy gown she wore; and (I suppose) by the role she played, of a virgin.

Guy and I waited for Leonora by the stage door. When Leonora emerged, wrapped in a dark cloak with a hood that enveloped her head, Guy begged her to accompany us to the Vieux Gand. She studied him coldly. "No," she said. "Let me alone."

"My beautiful young woman," Guy cried, "I beg you to reconsider. Do me the honor. I will buy you champagne. Have you had supper? We can have a nice roast beef at the tavern."

He followed her, pouring out an elaboration of compliments, promises, and declarations of harmlessness. She held her head aloof and strode on, gathering her cloak around her. Finally she turned and looked at him.

I realized later how she must have appraised Guy. There he stood under a gaslight, a handsome and rich young man dressed in elegant evening clothes, carrying a cane, looking wealthy and above all *promising*. I stood nervously behind, and Leonora relented—or seemed to relent. She would come to the Vieux Gand the next night—a Saturday—if she could bring a friend. "I must have a chaperone," she said coldly. I could see that Leonora was older than she seemed on the stage.

The friend she brought was Palmyre. Bernal came, too, after our tutoring session of the day. "I am in love," Guy had said. "I need my friends to witness this moment. Fifty years from now we shall sit around and remember how it was when I met her. You must come, Bernal. You must be a part of this moment."

After the performance we went to the Vieux Gand and sat at one of the round oak tables. Guy paid. He smoked an expensive cigar. He ordered an icy bottle of excellent champagne, then another, then another still. It was unseasonably warm, and we drank until we were all tipsy. He flourished his cigar. He tilted his chin upward as he talked and half closed his eyes.

Leonora saw his money. He looked at her and saw only himself. All his women were like that to him.

She told us that she had been named Leonora after the heroine in *Il Trovatore*. She said that her mother had been a soprano, her father a baritone. "They never sang in Paris because my mother refused to sleep with conductors. That is how the great divas make it to the great opera houses. They sleep with conductors."

She said she had always been in the theatre. "I also refuse to sleep with conductors or directors," she said. "It is the same everywhere. When you see an actress get the great parts, you know that she has been in a dozen, perhaps a hundred beds. Only those who love the theatre for itself and play the minor roles are truly virtuous. I am saving myself for the man I shall marry. I am faithful to him now, though I do not know him."

"Oh, my poor beauty!" Guy said. He was drunk, and he had tears in his eyes. Blue tobacco smoke hung over us, a jinn that made us all new creatures.

Leonora spoke in the grand manner, making grand gestures. I studied her face, trying to guess how old she was. All I could tell was that she was older than we were. She painted her face and dusted her eyes with dark powder, and she wore a strong perfume.

"A woman's most precious possession is her virtue," Leonora said. "The next is her reputation. It has been difficult for me to remain pure in the acting profession. But I have done so. My husband will have a treasure that no other man has ever possessed."

"She is magnificent," Guy said, waving his walking stick as we went home that evening.

I was alarmed. I had seen him infatuated before, but never like this. He walked in exaltation, and he was sad as young men are sad when they are first struck by love, believing the universe bends to listen to their lament at the passing of time. "Think of the stories that die when we die," he said, reeling with the champagne. "Think of the dreams that have been. Walk through a cemetery. See the epitaphs, and think of how little they tell us. Think of the connections that once existed between people, the web that held the living together. Think of how death breaks the web and makes of us nothing but disconnected atoms. I wish I could know all the stories. I would write them down. They perish as we perish, and when people tell no more stories about us, we are truly dead."

He embraced Bernal, his voice breaking, and I believe we wept, too. We were very drunk. "Promise that when I am dead, you two will tell my story. Promise to keep me alive as long as you live by telling my story again and again. Be Horatio to my Hamlet."

We assured him that we would all live together into deep old age. That night he believed that his bliss meant that he would soon die.

Then there was Palmyre. "So you are Greek," she said pleasantly while Leonora and Guy were absorbed in each other on the other side of the table. "I have always wanted to visit Greece." To Bernal she said, "You are Argentine. I am ashamed of my ignorance. I know nothing about Argentina."

These were commonplace statements. In setting them down now, I am not able to convey the impression they made on Bernal and me. She had no artifice. She met the world with the ease of water poured in a glass, taking the shape of her surroundings but maintaining herself distinct and clear.

Now Guy went to the Vieux Gand every night to meet Leonora. Bernal and I went to see Palmyre. We talked to her about everything. She ran a dress shop for rich women. Now and then, walking home late in the gloomy afternoons from the university where I had been transcribing lectures to duplicate and to sell, I stopped by and spoke with her. In her presence I became talkative. She and Bernal and I laughed so much that people at adjacent tables looked at us and smiled.

She catered to the wives of the merchants and industrialists of Ghent.

Leonora came, too. An actress needed the proper clothing. Palmyre gave her a reduction in price. "Leonora insists on designing the clothes I make for her. I would dress her in another fashion if she would let me. But then it is an honor to make clothing for an actress," Palmyre said. "She is an artist. I am only an artisan. The artisan should serve the artist. She tells me how she wants me to make her clothes, and I do the best I can." This was the only bad judgment I ever knew Palmyre to make. The style Leonora chose was Bohemian; it made her look like a slut.

I supposed that like Leonora, Palmyre thought that only the thin were beautiful. "You are beautiful," I said fervently. Another woman might have taken the compliment by patting her hair and by denying my praise in a false tone that might have required me to speak it again. Palmyre only said, "My dear friend, you have no experience with women; you do not know what beauty is. Leonora is beautiful. I am not." She did not mean to rebuke me. She told the truth as she understood it. She no longer had any interest in the subject.

"My clothes are beautiful," she said. "I make my clothing. That is all about me that is pretty."

She was wrong. She was strong and beautiful, and very early I loved her.

50

IN AUGUST when Bernal took ship for Argentina after the examinations, Guy and I went to Dinant. He took me to parties where crowds of formally dressed people stood about on lawns and made polite conversation. I felt out of place, for by now my clothes were showing their wear, and I could not buy others. I wore the same things again and again. No one seemed to notice my frayed cuffs sticking out of the sleeves of an increasingly worn jacket. We went to parties, and when we dined at home, we dressed for dinner, sitting at the long, candlelit table much too large for the four of us, and we listened with covert amusement but with outward respect while Monsieur and Madame Bruyère discussed the Socialists, whom they abhorred, and the Catholic Church, to which they were touchingly devoted. Madame Bruyère had gone on a pilgrimage to Lourdes. She returned with jars of holy water, and she put drops of it into the cut flowers that filled the tables and the corners. "I am convinced that it keeps them alive longer," she said.

I remember the flowers by candlelight, the servants standing behind us, silent as columns while we ate and talked. They wore white gloves buttoned at the wrists. They called me "Monsieur." They inclined their heads when they served or removed the plates from the table.

When I recall those days, I think of the flowers, but my memory also fills with brown and amber—the wood paneling of the room, the wooden table, the oak chests against the wall, the beamed ceilings, the carefully waxed parquet floors, the touch of Scotch whiskey that Monsieur Bruyère poured us before the meals. "Candy," he called the Scotch in a display of humor. "*Un bonbon.*"

It was a rich, happy life, despite Guy's professed gloom about his future. I imagined Russia and the immense flat sweep of the Russian steppe, a destiny that bound my life as implacably as the outer planets were bound in orbits in the cold void of space, and I envied Guy.

I knew that he did not truly dread his future. He assumed that interesting people were tormented. Here he was like Daisy, and sometimes when memories of them collide in my mind, I think of how well suited they would have been for one another.

I was a romantic, too. I was the retiring young foreigner from an exotic land, enjoying the faint air of mystery and romance that my distant origins gave me. At parties where Guy told how brilliant I was, young women gathered, inquiring with their eyes what my future might be. Guy's praise embarrassed me, though I understood well enough that in praising me he was praising himself for having a friend with the impossible attributes he gave to me. I was pleased with perfume and white bosoms barely suppressed by party dresses showing bare at the top where the breasts separate, the innocent willingness of young feminine eyes. I had fantasies of the cleft female bottoms under the thin, flowered dresses, and I, who had never seen a woman naked, sometimes went to bed in misery because my lusts could not be satisfied. I was happy to play the dark, romantic, brilliant gentleman from a distant land. Yes, it was a time for theatre, and I chose my part and acted it well.

Guy and I took long walks along the river and into the hilly countryside, and we never tired of talking or each other. I discovered that he had not given Leonora his address, and he had told her not to write him. She was hurt, he said. But he had delicately persuaded her that his parents needed time to become accustomed to the idea that he was in love with an actress. "I tell her that if she forces herself onto me at this point, my parents may forbid me to see her again, and of course if they do that, I shall have to obey," he said, without giving an impression that he was depriving himself of any great treasure. Surrounded as he was by adoring and rich young women, he seemed to think of Leonora as we think of interesting strangers with whom we have chatted in trains on long journeys long ago.

I thought of Palmyre even as I lusted for the virgins of Dinant. I missed her easy ways, her self-confidence, her spontaneous and gentle laughter.

Bernal wrote us funny letters. It always seemed strange to me that in his letters Bernal was funny. He adopted an absurdly ironic style that made Guy and me wrestle to be first to open his frequent epistles. In late September he joined us at Guy's home, returning early from Argentina to be with us before school began, and the three of us fell into an idyll of contentment. I recall mass early on Sunday morning as the cool light of autumn broke through the stained-glass windows and shone on the altar in the church of Nôtre Dame de Dinant, Bernal kneeling in abject silence and woe as though he could never be happy again. But afterwards we often climbed the stairway cut into the barren cliffs behind the church, and from that eminence we looked down upon the town in its narrow valley and the river running in the valley floor.

Bernal decided to become an expert in trees. "I can recognize the difference between an oak and a pine at a glance," he said. "I believe it is time to make more discriminating scientific judgments." He bought books about trees. He bought a magnifying glass and a leaf press. Sometimes he was up before dawn, tramping out in his English plus fours and sometimes cycling into the countryside, armed with his books and his glass, collecting leaves, making notes in an elegant little notebook. Guy and I were amused by his inexplicable dedication. Often he spread his leaves on the table before us and showed us how they differed from one another and what qualities allowed him to identify the trees whence they came.

"I can understand a passion for women," Guy marveled. "I can understand a passion for money. I can understand a passion for alcohol, for tobacco, and even for books. But trees? How can I understand a passion for trees?"

Bernal shrugged and smiled. "I want to know everything I can about trees," he said.

"But why?" Guy said. "What will you do with it?"

"Do with it?" Bernal said, just as amazed as Guy. "I shall enjoy it."

"Ah, perhaps you will write a book about leaves, about trees," Guy said.

"Oh no, I could never write a book about anything," Bernal said. "Besides, why should I write a book about trees when there are so many excellent books about them already?"

"Well, to make money. To be famous as a botanist."

"I have all the money I can ever use, and I have never heard of a famous botanist," Bernal said.

Guy looked bewildered. "There was Mr. Charles Darwin," he said. "The Englishman? He was famous. Was he a botanist?"

Bernal shrugged again in his grandly indifferent way. "If I wanted to be famous, I would not choose to be a botanist," he said.

"You might receive a university chair," Guy said.

"Surely you jest," Bernal said with a laugh. "I am not that dull."

"But my dear friend," Guy said, "professors do something with their knowledge. They hand it on to us. Why bother to have such knowledge if you cannot do anything with it?"

"I *told* you what I want to do with it," Bernal said. "I intend to enjoy it."

"Bernal, you *cannot* spend so much time studying botany merely for the sake of enjoying it," Guy said. "That would be a sin. Truly a sin."

Bernal laughed again. He went on taking his voluminous notes about trees, studying them in books, taking leaves from them, making drawings, preserving the leaves with his press, so absorbed in trees that he might have been a Druid, worshipping them.

The women at parties flocked around us when Bernal came. He was so handsome, so calm, so certain of himself that when he entered a room, attention blew on him from every side. He was courteous to them; that was all.

Everyone knew that Guy was wealthy and that he would soon take a wife. One of the young women was named Yvette. I do not recall her last name. She wore muslin dresses with tiny flowers embroidered on them. She looked properly pale and beautiful. She carried herself with exquisite dignity, and she had a lovely bosom and clear skin. "My parents are talking with her parents about marriage," Guy sighed.

"She is very nice," Bernal said.

"She is very nice and very dull," Guy said. "Perhaps I could settle down with the little thing in five years. But now I want excitement." He cast a theatrical glance skyward, and I half expected an equally theatrical sob.

Yvette suffered from the mania for polite and innocuous conversation that afflicted all the young women, and for that matter, all the young men, at those parties. Unlike others, she was witty. She made happy little jokes and teased Guy for thinking so highly of himself. She laughed in an unaffected, lighthearted way, seeing much delight in the world. I remember thinking that when she grew older she would have laughter lines around her mouth and her eyes. She loved Guy. She looked at him with the pleasure of someone in possession of a marvelous thing that she delights in showing off to others even while she remains humble and unaffected by her ownership. She knew of the discussions between parents. She radiated delight, and other young women treated her with envy, respect, and affection. I liked her very much.

Guy played the tragic hero, fated to spend his life in unwanted wealth, carrying on the inescapable responsibilities laid on him by birth. "It is not mine to have a real life," he sighed to Bernal and me. "If I had a choice, I would have lived as a simple Bohemian, making his way in a garret in Paris, writing books to make me famous after my death. But I can never enjoy that life. Never." His voice seemed ready to break.

Bernal and I supposed that he might be able to bear the heavy destiny that birth and wealth had given him. We saw, too, that when he spoke to Yvette, especially when they stood apart from the rest of us, he seemed even more animated than usual and that his smile was expansive and warmly sincere. I can see them yet—Yvette looking up at him, listening, adoring him with a generosity that now brings tears to my eyes as I write these words. I suppose that if Yvette is still alive, she is old and wrinkled and remembers Guy with a bitterness cooled by decades and that she probably does not recall my name.

I can write no more tonight.

51

BEGINNINGS AND ENDINGS and beginnings again. The cycle of life. The university term began, and we went back to Ghent. Leonora fell on Guy like a cormorant.

"You did not write me once," she said fiercely. "How can you tell me you love me if you do not write in months?"

"My little chicken," Guy said, "I was so busy. My friends can tell you how busy I was. My parents arranged so many dull visits to cousins, to aunts and uncles, to grandparents. I worked late into the night with my father. My friends can tell you that I neglected them shamefully. Ask them. I pined for you every day."

"You went to parties. You spent your time with rich women. You look down on me, Guy. But an actress has a noble soul. We feel the parts we play. We absorb our souls from the greatest writers in the world." We sat in the tavern. She performed these lines in a histrionic voice that drew amused attention from other tables.

Guy leaned forward and spoke in his most placating tone. "Parties? What parties? I care nothing for parties. I will not attend parties when I am in love with you. My love for you makes me faithful in heart and in mind, in body and in soul. I spoke of you every waking moment. Ask my friends."

"Well?" Leonora said, flashing her dark, angry eyes at us. "Is it true? Did he speak of me every moment?"

Bernal smiled, unable to tell an untruth. I lied volubly. "Oh, yes indeed," I said. "At each party we attended, Guy said he wished you were there."

"Party! Each party." Leonora shrieked. "You said you did not go to parties."

"My little mouse," Guy said. He threw me a fierce look. "Now and then I was obligated to go to a party. In my circle it is a mortal insult to refuse an invitation. My dear friends can tell you how I pined for you on those occasions. I was courteous, nothing more."

"Did he pine for me?" Leonora said.

"Oh, yes," I said. Bernal looked at me, and I looked at my hands on the table.

Another month in Dinant, and Guy might have lost interest in Leonora. But here she was in Ghent, beautiful in her eccentric way, with those adorable breasts hanging under her blouse, showing just enough to entice curiosity and desire. In Leonora a sexual fire smoldered. But she refused to go to bed with Guy.

Guy marveled. No one else had refused him. Leonora became his Holy Grail, his Jerusalem. "She says she will sleep only with the man she will marry." Guy uttered these words in incredulity, respect, and challenge.

"Perhaps she fears pregnancy," I said.

"No," Guy said. "I am convinced that she is innocent, virtuous. No one need have a baby who does not want to have a baby. This is the modern age, my friend. The condom liberates us from the old fears. An unwanted baby? People who have unwanted babies are illiterate. No, Leonora is a shy little mouse. I am sure she has never been naked with a man."

"Do you truly think not?" I said cautiously. I supposed she had been naked with dozens.

"Truly, I think not. She is a child."

Sexual fire did not smolder in Yvette. She belonged to a circle where passions were decently restrained. Guy's mother would be proud of her. Who knows what she would have been alone in a bed with a man she loved? She had thoughts. She was so superior to Leonora that I felt confident. Nothing Guy did with Leonora would have any lasting effect. It was a play, enacted on the stage of our tiny community in Ghent. Guy would get what he desired from Leonora; the curtain would fall; we would walk out into a street where a rain had left things clean. It would be over. I knew Guy.

I did not know Leonora.

52

TWO WEEKS AFTER the *rentrée* of classes, Guy and I found ourselves one night with Palmyre and Leonora at the tavern. Bernal was not with us. He was in one of his moods. He may have been praying alone before the Adoration of the Mystic Lamb in the candlelit chapel.

It was Friday. The tavern was packed, and a thin rain fell outside. The room smelled of wet clothing. Leonora was talking about art, prattling about painters whose work she had seen in Paris. Guy nodded impatiently as she talked on. "I tell you," he had said as we walked to the tavern, "I begin to find Leonora tiresome. Why must she always be instructing me about art? Why must she always be showing me how learned and superior she is? Tell me—what do you think of her?"

"It is not for me to say," I said.

"You are my friend. You are obligated to say *something*."

"A friend cannot tell another about love."

"Oh, it is not love. It is infatuation. All these weeks, these months, and I have not advanced one centimeter up her skirt, and she talks incessantly, and I am bored with her talk. I am famished for love, my friend. Famished, and there are others willing to feed me. I put my hand on Leonora's leg, and her fingers grip my wrist like a steel trap and push me away."

I laughed as I did when I was embarrassed.

"I must tell her it is all over," he said with finality. "There is a time for everything, and my time for Leonora is gone."

"Perhaps she knows that," I said. "Perhaps that is why she has been so excitable of late."

"Her excitement is embarrassing," Guy said. "Do you believe it is sincere?"

"She is an actress," I said. "She believes her roles."

Guy laughed. "I shall tell her it is over," he said. In that mood we joined Leonora and Palmyre. I thought Leonora looked unusually fine this evening. She seemed less gaudy, and her perfume was not so strong. Madame Boschnagel came out and sat at her pump organ, her huge bulk quivering. The students cheered and clapped when she played. She looked happily about with her wide smile fixed on her glistening face, a face so fat and sleek that it seemed molded in porcelain, a Dresden china figurine moved by one of those clockwork mechanisms at which the Germans excelled. Her accordion player came out, too, cadaverous and unsmiling, carrying his instrument, wearing his inevitable green vest. They swung into a German song for the many German students at the university. They began to sing: *"Die Gedanken sind frei."* Palmyre turned to me and said, "Would you like to dance?"

"I do not dance well," I said.

"It does not matter. No one will be watching you."

She led me by the hand onto the crowded floor. It swirled with the dancers. Palmyre turned to me and put out her arms, and we were softly together, our bodies pressed against each other. Soon the organ trilled. Madame Boschnagel and the accordionist coasted down together in tempo, and they began to play another song, very slowly. The dancing became not an engine pulsating with power but rather a pool flowing softly in the green woods. Palmyre and I floated on the stream. I thought of blue skies seen through radiant leaves and, incongruously, of violet clouds standing over Parnassos in the dry summer and the high purple rocks over Delphi.

"You dance well enough," she said.

"I love music," I said.

"You have a nice face. I like your hair," she said. "I do not see hair so dark here often in Belgium." She was breathing hard, and her words seemed thick.

"I am Greek, remember."

"Yes. You are very nice. So polite. You are the most polite person I know." She put her head on my shoulder. She pressed herself against me. I felt her all the way down to her knees. I trembled with excitement and held her tighter.

I had never felt a woman so close before. Our knees moved in time, and I was hypnotized with desire and the sudden sense of possibility. I felt her hair against my cheek. I smelled her body, a fragrance of soap and delicate perfume. We danced on, her legs moving against mine, her body pressed to mine.

Some stern admonition from my mother rang in my head, faintly, like the voice of a forest sprite above the music, a voice wild and carrying far but muted by time and distance so that the words were not quite distinguishable. I thought the beating of my heart was louder. My mother was an abstraction in my mind, not a person but something that had happened long ago.

The music stopped. If it had gone on, I would have been undone. Madame Boschnagel stood, bowing her head with her fixed smile while the crowd applauded and cheered. There was a languid movement back to the tables. The air was blue with tobacco smoke. Our table was empty. We sat down, not looking at each other. We were silent. I lit a cigarette and drew on it. Our eyes met. My hand trembled. Palmyre looked at it and smiled. I realized that Guy and Leonora would not return. I looked over a litter of wine glasses and empty beer steins. People were leaving. The waiter came with his brows raised with interrogation. He wanted to go.

"Would you like another?" I asked Palmyre.

"Oh no," she said. "Come with me for a walk. We will have some fresh air."

"Your friend paid the bill," the waiter said. He began picking up the empty steins and the glasses, wiping the table with his towel, acting now as if Palmyre and I did not exist.

We went outside, wrapping our coats around us. We could see our breath. I felt the damp cold creep up my sleeves and down my back under my collar. The sky was overcast and low, and the rain had turned to drizzle. My teeth chattered. I had not replaced my overcoat. Overcoats were expensive.

"Leonora wants to marry your friend," Palmyre said.

"Ah, she should not take Guy so seriously. He is sincere, you understand. But today he is sincere about one thing, and tomorrow about another." My voice was unsteady, and my teeth chattered. Palmyre took my arm.

"He has a fiancée in Dinant?"

"There is a woman he plans to marry there. Her name is Yvette."

"Yvette. Of course he would marry someone named Yvette. It is so French."

"Yes. Leonora will be disappointed in the end."

Palmyre, her hands deep in her pockets and her face down, bent against the cold, said, "Oh yes, she will be disappointed one way or another. I cannot tell her anything. I have told her that he is not serious. She will not believe me. She is like me. She comes from nowhere, and she will return to nowhere in the end, sooner or later, as they say. But no, she says. This is the age of equality, she says. She thinks that if he loves her, he will marry her. She thinks that they will have happiness in barrels."

"Leonora truly expects to marry him?" I said.

"She says she will marry him this summer."

"That is impossible. He will not be graduated from the university this summer."

"She is talking about how she will change the house in Dinant."

"She has not seen the house in Dinant. She will never see the house in Dinant except from the outside if she visits there. She will never be invited inside."

"She has made him tell her about all the decorations, you see. The rugs and the curtains and what sort of furniture there is in the salon. It is all too old-fashioned, she says."

"Preposterous." I was frightfully cold. Palmyre seemed serene.

"No matter. She has made her decision."

"That is madness."

"It is determination. She will go to Paris. She will buy art, and she will run the finest artistic salon in Dinant."

"There is no art in Dinant. There is no salon there. Dinant is . . . it is *Dinant*. Dull."

"She worries about her origins, you see. She thinks that people scorn her for being an actress, but if she brings art to Dinant, everyone will admire her."

"It will never happen," I said.

"She has such energy. She believes she can make it happen. She will sleep with him tonight. She will give herself to him at last. Then she will have him."

"What?"

"She knows he is becoming tired of her. She also knows that he cannot resist love when it is offered. She is going to make him believe that he has seduced her against her will, that she is carried away by her passion for him, her trust, her love."

I stopped and stared at her. Our breath blew clouds in the cold air.

"Why are you telling me this?" I said.

"You are his friend."

"I must warn him."

"It is too late," she said.

"This is a conspiracy," I said. "It is evil."

"Is it worse than what he has been doing to her?"

"Well . . ." I wanted to say that Leonora was Leonora and that Guy was Guy and that what he was seeking to do to her was not conspiracy but that what she was now doing to him represented a plot. Even as I started to frame this argument, I felt it collapse. What was the difference between Guy and Leonora? He was rich; she was poor. He was a man; she was a woman.

"She has taken him to a hotel?" I said.

"Oh no. My dear little cabbage, Leonora would not go to a hotel. She said a hotel would make her feel like a whore—and besides, if Guy takes her to a hotel, it will be as if she has consented to make love to him already. She wants to be seduced."

"Then where are they going?"

"To your room."

"To my room . . . to *our* room! In the Institute?" I was horrified.

"Yes, of course, in the Institute. It will all seem accidental there."

"But Father Medulous . . ."

"I am sure they are there now."

"If Father Medulous discovered such a thing, he would turn Guy into the streets, into . . ."

"That is the charm of the situation," Palmyre said. "Leonora wants to make Guy feel guilty. By going with him to your room, she offers a whiff of scandal. It is nice, do you not think? Leonora would have been a fine general. It is too bad that women cannot be generals."

"She has told you all these things?"

"She has told me some of them; I have worked out the rest of them for myself."

"Why did you not tell Guy?"

"He is not my friend," she said.

"I must go to him."

She laughed. "It will all work out." She took my arm, and I allowed her to lead me along. I shivered violently.

"You are cold," she said.

I laughed. "I shall go to the railroad station," I said. "I can pretend to wait for a train until morning."

"No," she said. "You are to come home with me," Palmyre said calmly. "I promised Leonora that I would keep you for the night. It is something I would like to do. There is no conspiracy on my part. I want to sleep with you. If you want to sleep with me, you are welcome. If you do not, I can make you a bed on the floor."

I heard the shriek of my mother's voice like the sound of wind around the stony peak of a mountain far away. Palmyre was there, her face turned up, smiling in a night illuminated by gas lamps, and I wanted her more than I had ever wanted anything else in the world.

53

SHE WAS MY FIRST LOVER and perhaps the one I always loved best. Who can tell about such things? I had never seen a naked woman. I had never had the freedom of a woman's body, and I did not know how a woman could embrace a man with arms and legs and mouth. I assumed that a woman who did such things loved the man who made her tremble and groan. I was far more romantic than Guy. It seems very foolish now.

Palmyre was passionate. I did not know what to do. Her body, her hands, taught me. When I finished in her, she seemed to feel some signal that made her finish, too, and her head jerked uncontrollably. She held me tight and kissed me and said I was good to her. We fell back in peaceful fatigue. Quickly strength and desire built up in me. We made love again. And again. And again. Deep in the night we slept, and I awoke later in a horror of darkness.

Yes, a horror. I thought that I had lost some dream of myself. I do not know what; I did not know then—some illusion about who I was and who I would become, perhaps the common illusion of young men that they can live up to their mothers' expectations.

I dozed fitfully, and thought of the sea rolling against the shore of Faliron in the middle of the night when the beach was empty and of all the centuries that had looked on the sea, and death seemed large and near. I thought of Stephanos and how he had laughed at Delphi, and of how sweet April had been when the round bare hills behind Athens turned green, and I thought that what Palmyre and I had done meant that everything that had been hoped for me, everything that I had hoped for myself in the distant kingdom called childhood was lost forever. *Post coitum, tristitia.* I did not know the proverb then.

Before dawn I reached for her, and we made love again, her legs drawn back, her feet over my head, her mouth raised, groaning slightly and coming in rhythm to my frantic pulsating at her with all my body.

"I love you," I said. "I love you."

We lay in the pale dark, my arm over her breasts, my mouth at her ear. "I love you," I said again and again.

"You are too young to know what love is." She laughed and kissed me gently.

I knew she was wrong. I had given up an old world for her. Now I had nothing else. We slept again, and when we awoke, it was day, a Saturday morning, and I wondered if Father Medulous had missed me at mass and what lie I would tell of where I had passed the night. I wondered if Guy had got Leonora out of our room.

54

I NEVER KNEW if Palmyre loved me. I loved her so much that I believed she had to love me in return. I supposed that love was like fire that when hot enough would make anything burn. It was Leonora's error with Guy, but I thought I was different from Leonora, different from Guy. Superior to him. Yes, I am ashamed now to confess that my night with Palmyre filled me with pride at what an honorable person I was compared with Guy, and that pride made the distant keening of my mother's voice seem like nothing but the winter wind.

In what did my superiority consist? Honorable intentions! From the morning of that first day, when I got out of her bed and stood naked by the window and looked out across the tile roofs of Ghent, I wanted to marry her. I had not *merely* seduced her; I loved her. Note that in my mind, I had seduced *her;* she had not seduced me. That was how it was in my world; men seduced women, and women were seduced and were then dependent on the man's goodwill. Palmyre could count on my faithfulness. I was not merely honorable; I was noble! I knew that when she recognized my sincerity, she would gratefully adore me. I stood in the bright, cool morning, scratching myself and feeling myself a man, proud because I was going to do the right thing, make Palmyre an honest woman, as they say here in Tennessee.

It did not turn out that way.

She accepted my passion and her own as naturally as she would have accepted a meal or a drink of water. Sometimes in the days that followed, I could not contain myself. I remembered her legs drawn back, her thighs pressing against me, her body moving in response to mine, her eyes rolled back in her head, her spasms at the end, and I could think of nothing else. I rushed to her shop in mid-afternoon. Often she was speaking gravely with some thick-bottomed matron done up in feathers and furs.

I came in and stood there, childishly eager and embarrassed. Palmyre looked up, an amused look of benign condescension. I suppose that she was no more than thirty. But her wisdom was beyond calculation.

I waited in frenzied silence until her business with the matron was done. Then she would smile almost absentmindedly at me. Not speaking, she would lower the shade on her door, lock the door itself, and we would climb the steep stairway to her living quarters under her roof. She led. I followed, my eyes on her delicious rear, seeing it naked already. As soon as we entered her bedroom, I began removing her clothes. I was a man dying of thirst, and water was in my grasp.

She regarded my frenzy with tolerant amusement. "Please, my little rabbit. Do not tear my clothes. What will people think? No, no. Let me do it for you. Ah, you do not know how to undo a button. It is unseemly to be doing this. Good people are working. They are not going to bed with each other." She spoke in a mild tone of reproach, but she raised her arms so I could lift her undergarments over her head.

She gave herself to me. I gave myself to her, and we were passionate together. Afterwards, sticky and embraced by her smells, I felt a contentment as deep as the granite under the mountains.

She knew that I adored her. At first she was merely amused, then she became troubled. "Paul, my dear little cabbage, listen to me. People like you and me, they do not get married. I am older than you. I come from a different class. You would quickly tire of me. I would be an outcast in your world. You could not live in mine."

"No," I said. "I will never stop loving you. You must marry me."

"My dear little gentleman," she said. "Marriage is for a very long time. I do not think that I will ever marry. Why should I marry? I have everything I want without a husband."

"Don't you want me?"

"Of course I want you. But in a certain way. I want you to go to bed with me."

"Then you can have me to go to bed with you for the rest of my life. Marry me. You must marry me, and we shall go to bed forever."

"Nothing is forever," she said. "Life passes."

"We can love each other until we die. That will be forever enough."

"People who go to bed with each other should do it for the moment," she said then with gravity. "When they start thinking about doing it for the rest of their lives, they ruin the moment."

"You mock me," I said. "You think that I am too young."

"I do not mock you," she said. "You must take what we have and be content."

I could not understand. In the midst of making love, I sometimes whispered, "I love you! I love you!" But she never said, "I love you, too." Never once.

She seemed strangely withdrawn into a world of passion where she thought only of our bodies and our commingling in their wondrous motions so that she was unable to think of such abstract things as love. Love brings all the past into the moment and carries the moment into the unlimited future. Everything lovers do becomes part of a great chain of being spread across an infinity of time. Palmyre was violently passionate. But in her passion, everything else was distant. I think she found my frantic protestations of love distracting. She could not respond to them while she was consumed by what our bodies were doing. When our bodies were finished, she came back to herself, to her tranquil self-possession, and she refused to tell me that she loved me.

The weeks slipped by and my world was filled with events that I shall describe in their place. But through them all, I was consumed by my love for Palmyre.

In early December, Bernal discovered that Palmyre and I were lovers. We were sitting in the tavern, and suddenly he knew. "I had no idea," he said later as we walked together, bundled up against a falling snow. "Why did you not tell me?"

"I thought you would reproach me."

He laughed gently. "I? I reproach you? My dear friend, you do not know my heart. I can reproach no one. No one on earth."

"I was afraid," I said.

"You need not be afraid. Do you want to marry her?"

"Yes, with all my heart," I said.

"Then it is all right."

"No—she does not want to marry me."

"Ah," Bernal said.

We walked. The snow crunched under our feet. Everything seemed hazy in the snow, the gas lamps along the street throwing out soft and magical light. The world was quiet, so very quiet.

"I love her," I said.

"It is grave," Bernal said. "Very grave. I am sorry, my friend. Very sorry."

55

I DID NOT SPEAK to Guy about his night with Leonora in our room, and he did not speak to me about it. Now that they were lovers, Guy could take her to hotels. At first he even boasted of how eager she was to enjoy him every night. Quickly his mood changed. As the woman he had clamored to possess now spoke of possessing him, he began to think of escape.

"She waits for me everywhere," he said. "She is like a hunter, and I am the prey."

"She loves you," Bernal said.

"Oh, Bernal," Guy said.

In December, Guy came in late one night looking dismayed and sick. We were alone. "Do you know what Leonora told me tonight?" he said, his voice quavering.

I had no idea.

"Tonight," he said, "I told her that we were becoming too deeply involved. I told her that our passions were burning away our reason and that on the whole it was better to live with reason than without it."

"I am sure she was captivated by your concern for her," I said.

"I am telling you something serious, very serious," he said impatiently. "I told her that I did her wrong by monopolizing her time, that I was hindering her growth as a human being."

"I am sure you made her grateful for your generosity," I said.

"Mockery ill becomes you, my friend. My feelings were sincere," he said. "She should *want* to be with someone else. She is still young. I mean, she is younger than my mother. I must confess that I believe my enthusiasm for her at an earlier time robbed me of my judgment to a degree, and I do not think she is as attractive as I once thought. But she is not ugly. She is intelligent. You know how intelligent she is. I am not intelligent. I am merely the son of a brewer, and I know my station in life. Books and art, that sort of thing. . . . Well, it is very fine, to be sure. But I am not as interested as she is in talking about these matters all the time, and I am of the opinion that she would be better off by seeking fulfillment in another quarter. I told her from the bottom of my heart how much it would hurt me never to see her again, but I could no longer bear to stunt the growth of her soul."

"Your generosity would melt the heart of an iron statue," I said.

"Oh, do not talk to me like that," Guy said. "You are supposed to be my friend. Why are you becoming so witty? I liked you better when you were dull."

"I did not know you considered me dull," I said, deeply hurt.

Guy sat down on the side of the bed and put his head in his hands. "I am sorry."

He sighed deeply and looked at me, his eyes hollow and mournful, dark pits in his face.

"You look ill," I said.

He shook his head. "You do not know how bad it is. She said tonight that our present situation is too ambiguous for her reputation. It is creating too much tension, she said. That is one of her favorite words—'tension.' You would think that she had been manufactured by a Swiss watchmaker who filled her with springs and wound her up like a music box. She says that if we should now marry, she could relax. Life would become orderly. We could dispense with seeing each other at the tavern. She knows how you look down on her."

"I never said that," I said.

"But of course you look down on her. I look down on her, and if I look down on her, you must look down on her, too." He shook his head again in unbelief. "She says that if we were married we could spend evenings in bed together, having sex and talking. Especially talking. Leonora says talking is much more important than sex."

"You could learn much about art," I said.

"Oh, hush," Guy said miserably. "You have no compassion. You do not see the point of it. *Leonora is serious.*" Guy looked at me with his eyes brimming. "She wants me to marry her this summer!"

I felt cold. "So soon," I said.

"Yes, so soon!"

"There is no law that says you must marry Leonora."

Guy shook his head. "I told her, very patiently, very carefully, that we could not possibly be married this summer. I am a student. I told her that I had no means to support her. I told her that my father and my mother would never permit it."

"What did she say?"

"What did she say?" Guy laughed. His laughter had a note of hysteria in it. He swallowed suddenly and looked at me with tears running down his cheeks. "She told me that she would go to Dinant and talk to my father and my mother and that she would arrange everything with them. They will see what an intelligent girl she is, how *uncommon* she is, what a talented actress, and my father will increase my allowance, and we can live together legally for the rest of my student days."

"What a horror!" I said.

"In our own flat, she says. She says we can stop moving in the low society of students. We can spend our evenings in candlelight dinners with professors and with officials of the town. She finds only professors and attorneys and perhaps a few very wealthy merchants and industrialists and perhaps some city officials to be worthy of her brilliant attention."

Guy lit a cigarette and paced the floor. "She believes that professors will find her brilliant and indispensable at their parties and that she will become the social leader of Ghent and that when at last we remove ourselves to Dinant, crowds of weeping professors and their sorrowing wives and the mayor himself will accompany us to the station to kiss us goodbye before my special train departs. She does not suspect that professors never find *anyone* brilliant! *They* are not brilliant. Expecting a professor to be brilliant is like expecting an egg to sing."

I took all this in with gloomy amazement. I should have told Guy everything that Palmyre had told me. Then I would have had to tell Guy every-thing about Palmyre, everything about that night when she first took me home. After these weeks he did not dream that Palmyre and I were lovers. I could not make myself tell him what I knew. Something would happen, I thought. Guy's future did not depend on me. He needed to be humbled—at least for a little while. Then perhaps I would free him from the curse Leonora was putting on him. "She is going to tell your mother," I said stupidly.

"She believes that she talks invincibly," Guy said. "I should have listened to you, my friend. You should have insisted. You should have flung your arms around me and made me stop. Why were you not more bold? Why did you give up on me so easily? It is your fault. Completely your fault."

He did not know how truly he spoke. Why did I remain silent? I have always been afraid of the answer to that question.

"She will not dare come to your house," I said. "Even Leonora has some taste, some tact. She will not come."

56

WHILE GUY SPENT the holidays with his parents in Dinant, Bernal, Palmyre, and I ate Christmas Eve dinner in her flat, and we were happy. His face turned ruddy with wine, and he sang gay Spanish carols, and we laughed.

Bernal had found a card of three little angels announcing Noel, two blowing trumpets, one pulling a bell rope, all of them sitting high against the night in what looked like the belfry of a church. The caption said, *"Es kam die wunderbare Nacht."* I imagined the heavenly realm full of music and starry skies, warmth blowing through space. I saw colors dancing to celestial music.

I looked at Bernal, and he was beautiful, and I looked at Palmyre, and she was beautiful, and I looked at the colored print of the angels, and it was beautiful, and the candlelight was beautiful, and I was immersed in the beauty of all that was and all that had been and all that would be. I could imagine the Christ Child in the straw of the manger and hear angels singing high over cold fields and see the animals on their knees at midnight. I could feel the glory of a world transformed.

A little past midnight, amid the pealing of bells all over the city, Bernal left us. He was very drunk, and I think he was sad at the end. Afterward the desire that had built in Palmyre and me burst out, and we tumbled into bed.

Later we lay naked and spent and warm and wrapped in each other, and we listened to the pecking of snow against the windows and the whoosh of the wind across the city and the great silence above it all.

My mind wandered. As though in a dream I thought of my mother and sisters and how Mother prayed in church, her face composed and beautiful. I remembered the midnight mass on Christmas Eve in the tiny Catholic church in Athens, my father impatient with the long service, my mother rapt in her prayers. I thought of Christmas feasts gone by. I murmured, "I wish you could go to Greece with me, to meet my mother."

"You know, my dear friend, your mother would not allow my mother to sit in her presence."

"I do not want to marry your mother," I said.

"I am my mother's daughter. I am a peasant woman."

"You are not a peasant woman. You are Palmyre. You own a dress shop, and you make masterpieces."

"I own a dress shop, but at heart and soul I am a peasant woman," she said.

"I want you to marry me," I said. "Your mother and my mother have nothing to do with it."

"It is not that simple," she said.

"It is that simple."

"My little cabbage," she said. "You are too young, far too young, to talk about marrying me or anyone else. You will have many lovers and finally a wife. It will take time—much time—to find the one who will be best for you. Life is long, so very long."

"Life is short," I said. "Please do not speak to me in that tone of voice."

She kissed me softly and lay naked and close. She was wet where we had made love. "Do not talk to me about marriage, and I will not be bad to you."

We were silent, and I thought she had fallen asleep. But when I raised my head and looked at her in the soft reflected light from the snow, her eyes were open.

"Perhaps I will marry when I am old," she said.

"Then I will wait for you," I said.

She lifted herself and lay on her stomach, propped up on her elbows, her large breasts pendulous beneath her. She looked at me with great seriousness.

"Do you know why I will not marry when I am young?" she asked softly.

"No," I said.

"Because when I was a little girl, my father used to go to church on Sunday and pray. Then a Sunday came—every month, every six weeks, one Sunday would come—he would come home from church and drink apple brandy until he was drunk and he would beat my mother until she was nearly dead. He did not scream at her. He did not seem angry. He took her by the arms and dragged her into their bedroom. My father was very strong. He had arms like iron! Oh, I have never seen a man so strong!

"My mother begged him not to take her into the bedroom. She did not scream. She did not weep or cry out. She was very quiet. She did not want to frighten her children, you see. 'Please! Please!' she said. That was all. 'Please! Please!' My father dragged her into the bedroom and shut the door, and then he beat her.

"She did not cry out even then. Her silence was for us. We could hear his fists falling against her flesh. He did not hit her in the face. He beat her in the body, all over the body, and we could hear him, through the door, breathing hard, and we could hear her choking and trying not to cry out. Once a month, once every six weeks, he was like that. My mother was in bed for days afterwards, horribly bruised, and we took care of the house. I took care of my father. Of the children."

She was silent a long time before she resumed. "My father went to the priest. He confessed, you see. He was a good Catholic. The priest forgave him. My father never asked my mother to forgive him. He asked the priest, you see. The priest forgave him because a priest can think of nothing to do with a woman but humiliate her because a woman brought sin into the world by creating desire in men. To a priest, beating a woman is like a sacrament. All that is necessary is to perform the sacrament for the right reasons, and surely there can be no wrong reason for beating a woman!" She made a bitter, chuckling noise.

"The priest absolved my father and told him to say some Ave Marias and some Pater Nosters, and my father said them, and he looked glum and guilty for a while, and he was tender and loving with my mother—until he drank apple brandy again. On Sundays. Always on Sundays."

She lay on her back then, and I held her and wondered if she would cry. I did not think I could bear it if she cried. She did not cry. I heard a horse go by, steel horseshoes beating the cobblestones, muffled by snow. My ears fixed on the sound and followed it until it dwindled and died away, and I wondered who might be abroad on Christmas Eve when everyone should be at home.

"I decided," she said at last, "it was not good to do what everyone thinks a woman should do. If you do as the priests say, your husband will beat you, and a priest will forgive him. If you have children, you will stuff blankets in your mouth to keep from screaming, for if you scream, you will frighten your children."

She pressed against me, and I held her tight. "I was more frightened to hear my mother groan behind the closed door and to hear the blows falling on her soft flesh and to hear my father breathing hard with the exertion of beating her . . . I was more frightened than if she had screamed until the roof cracked."

The silence in the room was like a thousand years. I thought of moonlight shining on naked hills somewhere, all cold in the winter dark, and black ice in the Arctic voids, and the god of Christmas departed from the earth.

57

THAT NIGHT I told Palmyre about my father, about Georgios and Stephanos, and about my mother and my sisters and Grandfather Pedakis. We lay holding one another and hearing the bells toll away the hours, night settling on the earth like a nesting fowl, feathery soft, and we felt the winter silence deepen, and at some time that neither of us quite knew, we slept in each other's arms.

Christmas came on Thursday, and the city lay silent and shut up in the snow that had fallen over the previous days. We arose late and drank coffee and sat looking out the window onto a white world with clouds lowering above the tiled roofs and threatening to deliver more snow.

"We have been through much together," I said, trying to seem old and wise and trying, too, to make the night we had passed a seal between us that could not be broken.

She smiled distantly and said nothing.

"Do you care for me at all?" I said, feeling utterly bleak all at once.

"I do care for you," she said slowly. "I do not love you. There is a difference. You should know that."

"Then you are in love with someone else," I said.

"No, I do not love anyone else."

"There *must* be someone else," I cried, sure as men are that a woman *must* be in love with someone.

"Oh, there is someone else," she said indifferently. "But I do not love him, either."

Her easy admission was like a blow. She laid a hand gently on my arm. I shook it away.

"I am an independent woman," she said softly. "You know that about me. I have always told you the truth."

"You have not told me about another man," I said.

"You have not asked about him," she said.

"Then I ask about him now," I said. "Tell me about him. Tell me about this rival. I never dreamed of him. I thought . . . I thought . . . Tell me about him."

"Are you sure you want to know?" she said.

I lied. "I want, I demand to know everything."

I was angry. She smiled as though I were a child.

"I came to Ghent as the maid for a banker and his wife," she began, speaking carefully. "I was eighteen years old. He was forty-five, very successful and handsome and charming. He was kind and good, too. I had never known a kind, good man. He seduced me on a pile of dirty laundry. I cried. It hurts so much for a woman the first time. A man, it is nothing. But a woman, it is like being burned in your most private place with a red-hot iron, and I could not help it. I cried because it hurt worse than anything had ever hurt.

"He consoled me and petted me. He thought I was weeping for emotion, because I loved him. I deceived him, you see. He wanted to be deceived, and I cried because it hurt so much and because I was embarrassed, and at that moment it was easy to say that I loved him. It did not injure me to tell him so.

"I was only eighteen. I began with very little feeling for him. I supposed that if I did not submit, I would lose my place in the house. I gave myself to him when he wanted me, and slowly I came to care for him. It was not what I expected."

"You fell in love with him," I said bitterly.

"Oh no—I cared for him. But I did not love him."

"What is the difference?" I said.

"There is a difference," she said.

"You could have had a child!"

"A child? Oh, my dear boy, you do not know anything. You do not know anything at all."

My face grew hot.

She touched me on the arm. "I am fortunate to have a lover who does not know everything already," she said.

"You mock me," I said, my voice husky. She took no notice. She seemed to have moved into her memories.

"I suppose we went in opposite directions," she said. "I did not start by caring for him, but I ended by caring for him very much. He began by loving me, but his passion lessened. At the first all I had to do was lie on my back naked and spread my legs and shut my eyes, and he thought that I had unlocked the gates of paradise. He used to caress me afterwards with his hands, even when I did not cry anymore. I grew to love his touch, to love the way we talked afterwards more than the thing itself. I was eighteen, then nineteen, and when we are that age, everything is new."

"What about his wife?" I said.

"Oh, she was as cold as carved ivory. She walked so carefully that you would think she was about to break, and I was sure that when they made love, she was like a piece of Venetian glass. She did not give him much, and I gave him everything I could. I did enjoy him. Forty-five years old and as impetuous as a boy. Yes, there was something very sweet about him. Very sweet."

She lapsed into silence again. I thought she was dreaming about this lover, and jealousy devoured me. I said harshly, "Go on. Tell me all of it."

"It all ended suddenly," Palmyre said. "I must confess that I missed him when we had to separate. It was necessary. It could not have been any other way. I did miss him. Truly I did. But all things end, and I did not complain. When you leave me, my little cabbage, I will not complain."

"Ah," I said. "His wife discovered that you were having an affair. She made him choose between you and her. He abandoned you. He showed what a cowardly man he was by choosing her."

Suddenly it all began to seem bearable. Of course Palmyre had had a lover. I could not be the first for a woman of her age and experience and her . . . social class. Even now I have trouble admitting that such things did play a part in my own thoughts. I have no reason to lie now. At that moment I felt myself immeasurably superior to this contemptible man. He lacked the courage to follow his feelings to an honorable end; I had courage. I wanted Palmyre to marry me. He had turned her into the streets.

Palmyre laughed again in her superior way—a superiority that bit like a coarse steel file across the tops of my teeth. She seemed distant and serene. "Oh, my dear little friend! You do not understand anything. His wife never knew about us. She died, you see. I thought about it afterwards—her white, aristocratic skin, her still, quiet ways, her stiff walk, the aloof way she scarcely spoke to me. The poor woman was ill, and no one quite knew it because the illness had become her character, and she had become her illness. People who knew her supposed that she and the illness were the same. Such pain, and we did not know.

"She was a magnificent actress, you see—far superior to Leonora. Although I was jealous of her while she lived, I admired her when she was dead." Palmyre's voice dropped to whisper a horror. "The doctors said it was cancer of the bone."

I shuddered. "He left you then?" I said, bewildered. "When he was free to marry you, he left you?"

"Free to marry me! My poor little cabbage! He was never free to marry me. Never, never, never. Oh, forgive me for laughing. You look so hurt. But a banker in our world would *never* be free to marry his maid."

"But his wife was dead, and you were . . ."

"I was his maid. He and I were making love in piles of dirty sheets and sometimes in a bedroom reserved for company. When we made love in a real bed, I changed the sheets afterwards and washed them myself and made it seem that no one had been there. You do not think that such things gave me the right to marry him! Ah, you have so much to learn, my little rabbit. It is a good thing that you have me to teach you."

"But why? It is . . . In our world, we are . . . Leonora says . . . It is a democratic world. People can do anything they want. Leonora—"

"Leonora is a fool," Palmyre said with sudden and uncharacteristic brutality. "It is a pity to say so, but she is a fool. Just imagine how embarrassed he would be to introduce me as his wife at large parties. People would naturally inquire about my father. I would say to them that he is a peasant in the village of Wyssel near Oudenaarde. I would tell them that he used to beat his wife and that she died and that he now lives in a house with her photograph above the fireplace. He has a candle on each side of the photograph, and he kneels in front of it and prays, and the tears run down his cheeks, and people in the village speak of his devotion to his dead wife as though he were a saint in heaven. I would tell people those things, and they would flee. They would never invite me again. I could not bear to invite them, either. I know what they would be thinking."

"You would not tell people all those things," I said gently. "If you love someone, such things . . . the things you are telling me, they do not matter."

"Such things always matter, my sweet little cabbage. After a few experiences with me in public, everyone would know. Then he would stop loving me. He would begin to hate me. Perhaps then he would beat me. You think only peasants beat their wives. But it is not so. Women talk to their dressmakers, my little one. Of course, if he had beaten me, I would have killed him." She laughed without rancor at the foolishness of great feelings.

We were silent. My thoughts were in turmoil.

"No, it is good how things turned out," she said in dreamy tranquility. "He gave me this shop. I suppose it was guilt, but he wanted to do it, and what could I do? I could not stay in his house after his wife died. I am clever with my needle and my prices, and I have a good eye for design. I speak with proper humility to the rich matrons who come to me. I listen to the stories they tell me about their husbands, about their husbands' lovers, about their own lovers. Sometimes I make dresses for the lover and for the wife of the same man. I am discreet. I have done well. I am independent. I have never had to ask him for anything else."

"Is he . . . is he here, in Ghent?"

"Of course he is here in Ghent."

"And you still . . . you see him?"

"Yes, I see him. He is guilty about what happened, and he still cares for me. That is a nice thing about our love affair. It went on just long enough that he looks back on it with nostalgia and affection. Sometimes he comes by. Once a year, perhaps. Sometimes twice. He wants to know how I am getting along. He has even brought his new wife to have me make her a fine dress. I liked her very much. Very beautiful and young, and she has a nice, firm little body. I make the women undress, you see, and stand naked before me while I measure them, and she liked that. Many of them do. I looked at her, and I approved. He has good taste."

"He comes to see you now," I said, so slowly that my words seemed wrenched out by tongs, words too big for my throat and so sharp that they tore at my gullet. I felt a darkness gathering. "What do you do when he comes?"

"Why, my little cabbage—I do as we do when you come. I close up my shop, and we come up here, and we make love again—just as we did, except in my bed, and here I am in charge."

I could scarcely speak. My voice was husky, and it hurt to talk, and I could not look her in the face. "Has he been here . . . recently?"

"Yes, my sweet one," she said sweetly. "Yes, he was with me only three days ago. He comes around Christmastime. He thinks no one will notice when there are crowds in the streets. He is very well known now, you see. One of the wealthiest bankers in Ghent. Older now, very distinguished, with white hair."

"And you . . ."

"Of course I did, my sweet."

I could not think of anything else to say. I felt the hot tears come and looked away, not wanting to shame myself by rubbing at my eyes. "But," I said after a long time, "you slept with me last night."

"Of course I did," Palmyre said. "Did I not give you everything you wanted? Can you ask of me anything that I will not give you?"

I formed my lips to say "No," but the word would not come, and I could only shake my head in dumb negation.

It seems strange and foolish after all these years that recalling that conversation now, with the hush of a mild September night on the earth, the faint smell of autumn vaguely in the air, as it is this time of year, gives me a pain that I can scarcely bear. I suppose it is a memory akin to an ache in an amputated leg of the sort that Brian Ledbetter used to describe. The leg hurts, and yet it is not there. On the day Palmyre told me these things, I nearly died with pain. Now, so long afterwards in a different place, the pain is still there.

58

LEONORA FOOLED US ALL. Guy came back from Dinant shaken to the bone, thin and pale, as miserable as I ever saw him in his life.

He smoked cigarettes one after the other, sitting on the edge of his bed, his eyes red. He wore his black suit with its black vest and its gold chain across the front. He wore his polished black shoes. He smoked with rapid flourishes of his delicate hand, and he poured out his woes. We agreed that the situation was grave.

"Leonora and I are now engaged," he said with a colossal and incredulous sigh, ending with an insane laugh. "My father will hardly speak to me. My mother has taken to her bed and must swallow little white pills to sleep. Yvette's father has been to see me and to tell me in the presence of my parents that I am worse than a cur and that were the laws of Belgium not so strict, he would challenge me to a duel and kill me with such pleasure that it would be the unpardonable sin.

"Leonora insists on sitting with my mother. Every time my fiancée looks at my dear mother, my mother turns her head to the wall. But Leonora stays in the room with her to keep her company. You should see Leonora smile over her. Imagine a jackal with wings, a veritable Pegasus of a jackal with wings like a rapacious vulture, and think of how that jackal would smile to see a herd of elephants dying of thirst on the African plain, and you will have a tiny part of the essence of Leonora's smile over my mother while my poor mother lies abed, a handkerchief over her eyes, wanting Leonora to withdraw.

"But my mother and my father agree with her. Our solicitor agrees. The only honorable thing I can do is marry her. Well, if it is not honorable it is safe—safe for the entire family, safe for the business. Leonora threatens legal action, you see. The woman has no shame. She threatens to sue me for breach of contract. We shall marry in August. Come join me, my friends. You cannot miss such a festive occasion!"

By the time he came to the end of this speech, Guy was shouting at us, and tears were running down his face.

"She has won," I marveled. "Leonora has won her wager."

"You are not married yet," Bernal said. "But if you are betrothed . . . the canon law holds that—"

"I *fuck* the canon law," Guy said. "Leonora is above the canon law. She is above all the laws of God. She is herself, the one and only. I beg you, imagine Leonora, imagine her coming to my house, ringing the bell in her imperious way. I heard the ringing, and I knew. Oh, my friends, I knew. Something about it. . . . Well, you know Gustav, our butler. He is proper. He grew up in the house. He was astounded. Speechless. He showed her into the main salon, but he could not believe his eyes. He came to fetch me from my room. Out of breath and red in the face and looking as if he had seen fire burning in the middle of one of our Persian rugs. When I saw him, I knew Leonora was downstairs.

"Poor Gustav! You know how scornful servants can be towards people they do not think belong. He was the first to reproach me with his eyes. When I think of how terrible it will be to have a wife who will be scorned by the servants. . . . To think of them laughing at me behind my back . . ."

He began to laugh hysterically himself.

"Please, silence. . . . Silence!" Bernal commanded. "The priests will be knocking at our door."

"Let them come! They should be in raptures of happiness," Guy sobbed. "I am about to participate in two of the sacraments. Should not a priest leap for joy when a Christian observes the sacraments? The sacrament of matrimony! And then the last rites. For as soon as I am married to Leonora, I shall shoot myself."

"This is preposterous," I cried. "You do not have to marry her. This is the twentieth century! Deny everything. Tell people that she lied."

Guy, wiping his eyes with a large white handkerchief and taking charge of himself, gave me a look balefully wise. "My dear fellow, you do not understand society. Society in Dinant. My parents. Their religion. Leonora. They know. . . . My solicitors know, we *all* know that Leonora will create a scandal if I do not marry her. She has my letters, you see. . . ."

"Letters?" Bernal said in astonishment. "Leonora has letters? But you never wrote her when . . . ."

"I wrote her last spring. At the very beginning of our romance. I was in love, you see. A man in love will do anything, and I wrote Leonora. . . . I told her that . . ."

"That you would marry her," I said.

"A lawyer may read that promise into my letters." His voice caught in his throat, a huge hiccup, and for a long time he could not go on. He sat in misery, trying to regain control of himself. "One could say that I promised her marriage." His voice choked on a huge sob.

Bernal looked gravely at me. "He wrote letters," Bernal said.

"Do not sound so *reproachful,*" Guy said. "Have you never written a love letter to a woman?"

"As a matter of fact, no," Bernal said.

"You have no feeling then," Guy said angrily. "It would be a scandal, a terrible scandal. There would be damages. My parents cannot . . ." He could not go on.

After a long time he uttered a long and pathetic sigh that seemed almost to crack his ribs. "Poor Gustav. He was shocked because he knew . . . Gustav *knew* that I had broken one of the most important rules of all: I had become seriously involved with an embarrassing woman. 'Monsieur Guy,' he said, 'there is a woman calling herself your *fiancée* downstairs in the grand salon, and she insists on seeing you.' He wanted me to look puzzled, you see. 'Fiancée?' he wanted me to say. 'Fiancée? Gustav, do not be mad. If there is a woman claiming to be my fiancée in the grand salon, call the police. Tell them we have a madwoman here. Tell them to take her away. Be gentle. She is harmless. But take her away nonetheless.' Perhaps he wanted me to laugh. All those things he wanted. I could see them in his face. I could not say them. I knew it was Leonora.

"I must have looked like a mouse caught in a trap. Because Gustav put on his correct face again—the servants' face that hides what they are thinking.

"I went downstairs. If I walk to the guillotine for killing her, that journey will not be as difficult as my walk downstairs to see Leonora. I was weak. I was dizzy. I prayed. Dear God, Bernal, I prayed."

"Sometimes calamity turns us to meekness and repentance," Bernal said softly.

"Oh, Bernal—I did not pray for what you want me to pray for. I prayed that lightning would strike through our house and kill Leonora on the spot. I prayed that she would be incinerated by spontaneous combustion. I prayed that she would be dragged down to hell through a crack in the floor, screaming in the talons of demons, and that I might watch her fall. I said, 'God, strike her dead right now, and I will go as a missionary to Africa for five years, and I shall not have sex during all that time, and I shall live out my life in gratitude to your almighty will and purpose.' Nothing happened. No lightning fell. I entered the grand salon, and there she stood by the great fireplace.

"Have you noticed how thin she is? Despite her big breasts, she is thin. She stood there looking around the room like the triumph of Death. One of Bosch's demons. That's what she was. She puts that dark makeup on her eyes—horrible stuff that makes her look consumptive. She was inspecting the walls, the draperies, the paintings, and the windows—all with that expression on her face. You know the one I mean! The one that seems to ask, 'How much does this cost?' At the same time it seems to say, 'This is not good enough for me.' She was standing there, looking around, and she said to me, 'Guy, these portraits of King Leopold and King Albert—they should not hang in the grand salon. They make it look like a vulgar public gallery. We must take them down.'

"I begged her to leave. I wept. I confess it. I wept before a woman. . . . No, Leonora is not a woman. She is a vampire!" He delivered himself of a hysterical laugh, which broke into a sob. He paused to recover. " 'Leave!' I cried. 'For the love of God, leave me in peace.'

" 'Nonsense,' she said. 'I have come to meet my fiancé's parents. You are being rude to me, Guy. I do not know why you imagine you have a right to a place in society, rude as you are!'

"She turned to Gustav. Poor Gustav had followed me into the room. He hovered there, rubbing his hands in perplexity. I think he was hoping for a miracle—like me, the lightning bolt. I thought an earthquake would be fully acceptable even if it destroyed the house if only it killed Leonora. She turned to Gustav and said, 'Who are you, my good man?' She called him 'My good man'! Oh, he was polite to her. He bowed and said, 'I am Gustav, mademoiselle. I have been in this house forty-three years.' Leonora said, 'I did not come here for a history lesson, *mon bon homme*. If you want to stay in the house another year, please be so kind as to inform Monsieur and Madame Bruyère that their future daughter-in-law is here to meet them. Please have the maid draw me a bath. I have had a dirty journey by train, and as soon as I have met my new family, I want to bathe. Be quick!' She had come third-class, you see. Imagine! I am to marry a woman who travels third-class!

Poor Gustav's eyes pleaded with me. 'The lady will be staying here?' he said. His voice was incredulous. Before I had a chance to reply, Leonora said in her angry tone, 'Of course I shall be staying here! Do you think I am going to visit my fiancé in a house like this and stay in a hotel?' I could have died on the spot."

I poured Guy some brandy. He gulped it down and asked for more.

"You should have called the police and had her carried off to jail," I said. "Fight fire with fire. You should have been bold. We would have sworn that we had never seen Leonora in our lives."

Bernal looked gravely up at me. He would never have sworn a lie. And there were the letters.

"You do not know Leonora," Guy said. "She would have made a scene with the police. She would have fought and screamed. The scandal would have been in the papers. My mother would have died. Our marriage may kill her slowly. The scandal would have killed her instantly."

He smoked. He drank more brandy. "No one saw you sleep with her. With the letters only, you may escape." I thought there had to be a way out. I did not tell what I knew. I thought that it was hopeless.

Guy glared at me as if I were a complete fool. "My dear Paul, I could not have allowed Leonora to crawl over the wall as we do after hours. I invited her in through the door, and I escorted her out through the door when she left. I paid Madame Conrad handsomely to open the door on both occasions. Madame Conrad would tell all to the police, to journalists, to my parents, to the king, to all the priests of the church, to the Pope himself."

I was speechless. Bernal did not appear as surprised as I.

Guy shook his head. "Leonora calculated everything with exquisite precision. My parents are exactly the kind of people she thinks they are. They are devout. They are honorable. They are wealthy. They are not noble. The nobles can do anything they want. But people in business . . . ah, that is another matter. *We* must be circumspect. *We* cannot get our names in the papers.

"When my mother saw Leonora . . . that was the worst of all. My mother could not understand why such a low person dared to be standing in our grand salon. I truly believe that my mother thought she was dealing with a lunatic, someone who had wandered into the house in a delirium. Leonora was wearing her rust-colored skirt. She is not entirely ugly when she is naked. But in the clothes she wears, she looks like a Gypsy. She has seen *La Bohème,* you see. She thinks she must look Bohemian, and she looks like a tramp.

"My mother came in looking stern and puzzled. Gustav had not told her why Leonora was there. Some things are too terrible even for butlers. My father came in looking perplexed. He is an orderly man; he thinks everyone is orderly. He looked as if he had once known why this woman should be in our house, but he had forgotten the reason, and he thought that he should make amends. He is a polite man, a very polite man, my father.

"Leonora has no sense of decorum, no sense of what is correct. She greeted them with her horrible smile. It would turn a Medusa to stone. It would make a harpy vomit, that smile. She put out one of her hands and did a curtsy! Just like a parlor maid! She said to my father, 'Oh, Father, you are every bit as handsome as your son! I hope our children look just like you. Your son wanted it to be a surprise. That is why he looks so confused. I have come to tell you that we are engaged. We are going to be married.' "

"God and all the saints!" I said, crossing myself and losing hope. Bernal remained silent and grave.

"She told them everything," Guy whispered. "Everything. She told about our making love here in this bed. In the many hotels. My mother assumed that I was a virgin. She wept. She gasped in shame and gave me a look. It was a spike in my heart, that look! There was Leonora. . . . She told about bribing Madame Conrad. She said she gave me her virginity. Her *sacred* virginity. I cannot talk about it. So vulgar. Once I heard my father tell a slightly obscene joke. He was in the brewery with his brewmaster and some of the assistants, and they had been drinking some of the beer. It was summer and very hot, and the men were telling stories, and you know how it is. When someone tells a funny story, you want to tell a funny story, too.

"My father told his story. It was not very funny. But he was the chief, and the story was slightly off-color. The men laughed, and suddenly my father remembered that I was there, sitting on a box behind him and being still because I was small and happy to be with the men, and I was afraid to make a sound because someone might make me leave. My father looked around and saw me, and he was embarrassed. His face turned as red as Burgundy wine because he had told a slightly vulgar joke in my presence."

"I am sure Leonora did not give you her virginity," I said. "You must find other men who have slept with her, and you will not have to marry her."

Guy laughed bitterly. "Be careful, my friend. You and Bernal must witness for me in August. You must not slander my bride."

"In August," Bernal said. "I must be sure to be here."

"Of course you must be here," Guy said with a bitter laugh. "Saturday, August 29, 1914. Leonora and I are to be married in Dinant."

I could have told him then about Palmyre, about all the things she had told me about Leonora. Would it have made a difference? I shall never know. I kept my peace and said nothing. I am not sure to this day why I was silent. Now it does not matter. Surely it does not matter. Surely the God in whom I do not believe has forgiven me for that.

59

I HAD TAKEN GUY to be frivolous. Now he surprised me. His father had commanded him to marry Leonora. He obeyed. Gradually his desperate talk stopped. I think he said something to Leonora about what she wore and her cosmetics, or perhaps it was Palmyre. She cleaned up her face and stopped wearing the dark powder that shadowed her large and reproachful eyes. She had Palmyre make her other clothes, like those worn by wealthy matrons in Ghent. Guy paid for them. I began to think that Leonora was almost pretty. At least she looked normal.

Palmyre marveled. We lay abed and talked in a desultory way on the nights I slept with her. "I begged her not to do this terrible thing. I told her that he does not love her, that she will be a fool to force him to marry her. He will hate her. She will be miserable."

"What did she say?" I said.

"She is a romantic. She still believes everything Guy told her when he was trying to get her to bed with him last spring. She thinks he will love her again as he did then. I tell her love never returns. It is like life, or childhood, or youth: when it is gone, it is gone forever. I tell her that, and she gets angry. She says that he will see her for what she is and for what they are together. Then he will adore her. She is certain that she will conquer Dinant. It is such a small place. The Belgians are so dull, she says. She will beguile them because she is so smart."

"Who knows?" I sighed. "With the new clothes that you have made her, maybe people will accept her."

Palmyre rolled against me and kissed me on the neck. "Let us never get married," she whispered. "Marriage destroys people."

"I want to marry you," I said, taking a sudden hope because she had spoken of marriage as if it might still be something under discussion.

"Do not speak of it," she said, laughing. She rolled me over onto herself, and we made love in the abandoned way that made me whisper frantically at the end, "I love you! I love you!"

Something changed with her. I do not know even now what it was, though

I have pondered it through the many years that have passed since the spring of 1914. We saw something happening to Guy and to Leonora. Everything seemed to be working out. I copied more lectures at the university in all sorts of courses, and printing them on a simple machine, the ancestor of the American Mimeograph, and I sold them to students. We had no thought of copyright; I am sure the concept existed, but I ignored it. The professors seemed pleased to have their lectures put out in accurate copies. My little business flourished, and I had money. I transferred my little printing operation to Palmyre's flat, and I worked hour after hour in the late afternoons. I had many subscribers, and I sent my mother more money than I had dreamed possible, and life seemed full of promise. I was optimistic about my world, and despite what Palmyre said, I was optimistic about Guy's world, too, and Leonora's. Everything seemed settled and ordinary and . . . *happy!*

When the engagement was announced, Leonora and Guy went on the train to Dinant for a weekend to a small dinner party at the home of Monsieur and Madame Bruyère. She wore one of the new dresses that Palmyre had made for her, and without her atrocious makeup she looked almost attractive. When she did not talk but stood by the railway carriage in the station looking still and thoughtful while Guy chattered away, I thought, "Maybe it will work." With even more astonishment I thought, "Maybe she truly loves him."

Now in the long retrospect of years I believe that she did love him. Yes, she was greedy for Guy's possessions. The love and the greed perhaps fed on each other. The love of men and women for each other has greed at its core, and Leonora was greedy for all of Guy, including the world of luxury and society that had created him. I descend into thoughts of such complexity that my expression of them risks becoming banal. It is a pity that the truth about human beings is so often banal.

She returned from their weekend speaking of plans. The wedding would be a considerable social event, and there would be parties throughout the month of August, and we were all to be involved, and when she talked about them Leonora seemed radiant. Guy wore a new white suit at the reception where the coming marriage was made public. He tried it on when it came from the tailor's in Ghent, and Bernal and I admired it. "White for my virginity," Guy said with a laugh. "White for the lilies that are put on the grave at funerals. White for the fear that I have before this ghastly marriage." His tone was surprisingly gentle and self-mocking, a talent I had never observed in Guy before.

"It is a mistake," Palmyre said to me. "When the wedding is over, when they look at each other and see that they are truly married and cannot escape, everything will change."

Yet Palmyre, like the rest of us, was caught up in the sweep of things. There was a large garden party on a Saturday afternoon, and we went—

Bernal, Guy, Palmyre, and I. We were absorbed in the whirling crowd, captivated by the sweep and dash of the occasion, the air of happy expectancy that hangs over the approach of a great wedding, the romance and the promise that weddings give to the future. Palmyre was stunned and honored when Leonora announced that she would be her chief *témoine,* what we call the maid of honor now in America. "We will tell people that you are descended from Flemish nobility," Leonora said. "They will not know the difference. Just try not to talk too much."

"I will be silent," Palmyre told me. "You will see. I shall be aloof and cold and pretend not to enjoy myself. People will think I am a great lady."

"You are a great lady," I said.

"No, it is not true. But we will have good times to remember. I think the marriage is a mistake. Still, we are not prophets. The future is in the hand of God."

"Yes," I said enthusiastically. "In the hand of God."

60

ALTHOUGH GUY accepted his fate, he rebelled against the image of himself that Leonora pushed on him. In the late winter and spring of 1914 he began to drag us to working-class taverns in the poor sections of Ghent. He began to cultivate friends who were probably very much like Leonora's true family and for that reason much against her taste.

"I may go into politics," he said. "If I go into politics, I must have friends everywhere. Do you not agree, my dear?"

"I do not see why we must have such friends now," she said. "I find them boring. I find them vulgar."

"Every political figure must cater to the vulgar," Guy said. "If I am to be prime minister of Belgium, I need the vulgar to vote for me."

She accompanied him on one or two of these excursions, but refused to go again. She met us later at the Vieux Gand, sullen and impatient. He gaily pretended not to notice.

In the working-class taverns, his charm was irresistible. His greatest triumphs were not over me or Bernal or even the crowds of women that used to gather around him at the Vieux Gand, but over the workmen who greeted him at first with scorn and suspicion and swiftly grew to admire and cherish him. When the weather warmed, Guy began to race pigeons.

I feel slightly ridiculous in trying to describe the enthusiasm for pigeon racing that agitated parts of the Belgian populace in those days. Pigeons generated an excitement that seems so remote and preposterous that even as I bend here over this page in this crisp autumn night, I pause for a moment and laugh at Guy and at myself. Yes, at myself. For the races excited me, too.

The pigeons' one talent was to return as fast as their wings could carry them to their cages where they lived as prisoners. In a race, people took them to some field far in the country and released them on a signal, and the pigeons rose up in a fluttering swarm and wheeled about, taking their bearings by some magical impulse, and they sped away towards those cages. Each pigeon carried a tiny medallion around its neck. When the pigeons arrived at their cages, someone—usually the owner—removed the medallion and put it into a little machine called the *constateur*. The *constateur* was a sealed clock, and when the medallion was dropped into it, it recorded the exact time. So were the races scientifically determined. Guy thought it was a miracle of the modern age.

When he discovered pigeon racing, he fell headlong into the great passion of the working class. He had an aptitude for judging birds. It seems absurd to recall how proud he was of this talent and how much admiration it aroused from his new friends. They spoke Flemish. I was astounded to learn that Guy spoke Flemish fluently. "If you run a brewery, you must speak Flemish," he said impatiently.

He found that he could talk pigeons by the hour with beer drinkers in smoky bistros. He never confessed to them that some of the beer they drank came from his father's brewery in Dinant. They saw him only as a student who had more money than they did; but somehow, in the drollery of pigeon fancying, his wealth did not matter. They gave him advice. Had he absorbed lectures in the university as he sopped up the advice of these workingmen in blue, he would have stood beyond us all.

Guy raced his birds every Sunday. From the first races, Palmyre and I took the pigeons to the starting place for him. We boarded the train in the South Station or the Central Station in Ghent and rode into the country with dozens of others on the identical mission. Guides led us to the starting field, and we waited for the official in charge to blow his whistle. At that moment we released Guy's birds by opening the doors to their wooden cages. They wheeled up and up in a great whirring of wings, and off they went. Our task done, Palmyre and I idled our way through the day, had lunch somewhere, and returned to Ghent in the afternoon or evening.

Everything was leisurely. We had beautiful Sundays that year. Bernal went with us sometimes, and he gloried in the wondrous greens of the land, and on our walks he added to his collection of leaves. He was not loquacious except when he had drunk too much wine, but the colors of that spring created in him an eloquence that made the words pour out and embrace all that he saw, including us. We had lunch in tiny restaurants in villages. We sat in the shade of faded umbrellas and drank wine and ate chops and drank coffee afterwards, sometimes with a glass of rough brandy, and we were as happy as the shepherds in Arcadia, and I recall the ring of Palmyre's laughter.

Late in June, very early on a Sunday morning while it was still dark, Palmyre and I took the train some forty kilometers from Ghent to a small town whose name has escaped me entirely. We went in a third-class carriage, not because we could not afford second class but because everyone who raced pigeons traveled to the starting ground in third class. We sat on wooden seats pressed against each other thigh to thigh in a crowded compartment that smelled of old sweat and garlic and food, and we laughed and shouted with strangers who carried their pigeons in wooden cages as we did. Most people spoke Flemish, and Palmyre felt at home with them and spoke with them in that language. I felt her warm body against mine, her hip against my hip, her thigh against my thigh, and when we looked at each other, we paused and were silent amid the uproar.

The train made a special stop for us a little after dawn, and we stepped down into the fresh, pure light of a clear June day. We walked out with the large crowd to the starting field, and on the signal released our birds. While they sped away towards Ghent, the crowd noisily dispersed, and we had the day to ourselves. We gave Guy's cages to someone who promised to take them back for us. The dew was still on the grass. Our feet made dark prints in it. We were happy in our Sunday peace.

Not far away was a village built against a long curve in the macadam road. The red tile of its roofs shone in the early sunshine. We went there for breakfast and found a woman with a towel wrapped around her head cleaning up in a little bistro. It smelled of soap. She brought us bread and coffee, and we sat at a wooden table and watched the day come full on the green earth.

We walked. I thought I could walk forever. I remember cows and the damp fields and windmills turning slowly in the gentle air. Palmyre spoke to people, and I nodded. They did not smile. It was Sunday, and they were going to mass, and we heard bells ringing, a harsh clanging of country church bells pounding over the land summoning people to the body of Christ.

"The Flemish are so glum," I said.

"They have a hard life," Palmyre said.

People wore their Sunday clothes, and they looked hot. Some women wore flowers on their dresses, and some men wore flowers in their hats. We heard the softer sound of cowbells.

"When I was a little girl, I used to see the peasant women in my village wearing their bonnets and going to church on Sunday, and something in me cried out at how dull their lives were. The same thing, day after day, year after year, and suddenly life was over, and it had all been the same, and people walked behind the hearse on the way to the graveyard, pretending to be sad. All the dull days, and life passes quickly just the same."

I laughed. "You are unkind. People are sad when others die."

"Oh, I suppose," she said. "They get over it soon enough. Life goes on. There are not many people who truly love each other."

"I love you," I said.

She laughed in her dismissing way. "I believe you do," she said.

I do not remember all we said. Strange now that that lost morning remains so clear, and I can recall the sights and the sounds and even the smells. Sometimes when I think of that morning—as I do now—it seems so near that I imagine that I can step magically into it again and that we could make everything different. A foolish romanticism, but I feel it now. I feel it so strongly that I think I might look up and find Palmyre smiling at me in this strange place, young as she was then. I look up and see only beyond my kitchen into the dimness giving way to darkness in my house. I remember walking, holding her hand. How firm, and yet how smooth it was! We talked about many things. We felt at peace.

Or at least *I* felt at peace, and joined to her by a bond flowing out of my soul and drawing her to me. I do not know what she felt. The largest illusion of humankind is to imagine that we know what another is thinking or feeling. Under that illusion there is something real and powerful which in a moment can bind lovers to each other and the moment to their memories as long as they live.

In another village we took lunch. The church bells had ceased. The day was heating, and we were hot from our walk. We sat outside a tiny cafe under a faded awning and had a plate of ham with beer and thick country bread. A peasant girl with a white apron served us. The world seemed ready to go to sleep, and when we resumed our walk, I felt drowsy. Young men were nursing drinks at tables before a small tavern. They looked gallant and proud and eyed us with arrogant suspicion. We knew that their lives were hard and that on Sundays they gave themselves the right to look heroic and to pretend to noble thoughts as they sat sipping one beer for hours and posing. We walked on.

We found a meadow near a woodland. The clover in the meadow danced in a scarcely tangible breeze, reflecting the light in undulations so delicate that they were like a dream of sunshine in the mind of God. We walked to the deep shade of a tree, and we sat down and lay in the grass, and I held her in my arms, and all the world hung suspended in stillness.

"I love you," I said.

"You do not know what love is," she said. For once she did not laugh.

"Do not patronize me," I said. "I know enough to know that I love you. Please marry me."

"You want to be married because your friend Guy is going to be married. I have seen that all my life. One girl in the village gets married, and all the girls her age want to get married, too, and the unmarried girls who are older than she is lament their misfortune."

"I am not a girl in the village," I said.

"I would do you wrong to marry you," she said.

"You would do me all the right in the world," I said.

"Where would we live? What would we do?"

"We would go to Russia," I said. "Russia is huge and promising. My uncle in Russia will give me a job. Who knows what we can do there?" I raised myself on an elbow and looked down at her face. She seemed as tranquil as the day itself.

"Russia," she said dreamily. "I wonder if Russian women would buy my dresses?"

"Of course they would buy your dresses," I said. "The Russian women buy clothes that come from Paris. They dress in fashion. I have been in Russia. I went there with Stephanos once, when I was very young."

Unaccountably at the mention of Stephanos my voice broke.

"It is all right," she said. "He is at peace."

"We were happy in Russia," I said.

"Where does your uncle live in Russia?"

"Sebastopol," I said. "It is the only place in Russia I know."

"He will give you a position? You are sure?"

"Of course I am sure. He expects me there. He must give me a position so I can repay him for my tuition here in the university."

"Ah," she said. "You will go to Russia no matter what."

"It is decreed by fate." I laughed. "The gods know everything, and they ordain our fate, and we must accept it."

"How strange Russia is!" she said. In those days Russia seemed more mysterious than any country can be now. Russia was enormous and terrible. It loomed in our minds tremendous, unfathomable, and—above all—promising. *Something* would happen in Russia. Whatever it was would purge the world and restore something lost for centuries, lost perhaps since the Golden Age when humankind fell from bliss to barbarism. Palmyre grasped the outlines of the hope.

"If I marry you, I will have to be faithful to you," she said. "Is that not so?"

I believe my mouth went dry. She had never before said, "If I marry you. . . ."

"Yes," I said in a whisper. I cleared my throat and said it again, still not loud. "Yes, you will have to be faithful to me."

"You are jealous, my little cabbage," she said, stroking my cheek gently with a hand.

"Yes, I am terribly jealous," I said.

"I am older than you," she said. "I will get fat and ugly while you are still attractive to younger women. You will become more handsome as you grow older. I know it. I will not. I will become ugly."

"You will never be ugly to me," I said. "Never. Never."

She smiled and stroked my hair. "You are so young; you do not know what you will be, and you cannot imagine what I will be," she said.

"I am not a child," I said.

"I know you are not a child," she said quietly. "It is just that . . . I do not know what to do with you."

"You can marry me," I said. "That is what you can do with me. We can be with each other forever. That is what you can do."

"You are serious," she said. "You mean it. You truly mean it."

"Of course I mean it. Why else would I bring the subject up again and again and again?"

She looked up at me, and her face was soft and warm. She had brown eyes. I remember her eyes more than I remember anything else about her face. Her fingers lingered in my hair.

"All right," she said. "I will marry you."

I drew back and sat up and stared at her in wonder and unbelief bursting into joy as I repeated in my mind the simple syllables of her promise. "I will marry you. *Eh bien! Je t'épouserai, moi.*" I felt a joy that I cannot describe. I was a candle held up to the sun, and my light and the sun's light were one.

"I love you," I said. "I love you more than I have ever loved anyone else in my life. I will always be good to you."

She did not say she loved me. We kissed and held each other, and she stroked my hair.

I know now that I duplicated the foolishness of Leonora by supposing that if someone lived with me for a very long time, she would love me. Palmyre would love me in time. We were not like Guy and Leonora. We were not like anyone else on earth. It is the foolishness of love to suppose always that no one else in creation shares the experience two lovers share, that no one else has ever quite known it before. Only with many years does it appear that all loves are alike and that some immutable law of similarity governs them from beginning to end. Had I known how ordinary my passion was and how I might in the great remove of years have looked back on myself (as I do now), seeing an awkward boy clumsily attempting to be old and wise, I still would not have stopped loving Palmyre. I would not have forsaken her. I would have married her.

Our blissful Sunday passed, and we were happy. The world seemed so good that I believed all life had conspired to give me this glory. I thought of the chain of accidents that had brought me to her, and they fell together as destiny, and destiny made all bad things not good but comprehensible—

my father's act, my long journey to Belgium, the failure of the business and the suicide of Stephanos, my grandfather Pedakis's wrath, my disobedience and my exile, my Uncle Georgios, and now my future in Russia. These things had to be if I was to be who I was; and though, like Odysseus in his frail ship pummeled by the wine-dark sea, I found the voyage hard and dangerous, I knew it lay in the lap of the gods, concluding at my destiny, leaving me not only at peace but wise in the knowledge of what had brought me home.

Yes, the wisdom I felt filled me with a delicious tranquility. I had grown up. I was a man. Men could see the wisdom of things, be wise, and if wise, unmoved by the buffetings of the temporary waves. Palmyre and I walked aimlessly and said little, and the intoxication I felt at first fell quickly into the serenity of accomplishment that I have described, and in the bright sunshine of that glorious day I saw in my mind the foamy flash of water on the raft of Odysseus bringing him safely home to Ithaka.

It was late in the long June twilight when we took the train back to Ghent from a little town where we had taken supper. It was past the time when most people had returned to prepare for the day's work on the morrow, and we had a compartment to ourselves, and we sat holding each other and kissing and watching the darkening countryside roll by like a pattern of dreams.

It was late when we arrived in Ghent, and we went to the Vieux Gand to see if our friends were there so we could tell them our news. They were sitting at our accustomed table, a table crowded with others. Guy saw us and leaped to his feet with an expression of wild pleasure. I thought, "Somehow he has guessed; he knows we are going to be married." He shouted, "My pigeon won! My little Shakespeare beat every other pigeon in the race." (He had named his pigeons after great writers.) He clumsily hugged me and kissed Palmyre on the cheek. He was drunk and deliriously happy.

Bernal was happy, too, and I saw that he also had been drinking much wine, and I wondered if he might soon retreat into one of those dark spells of abnegation and penance that would put him on his knees in sorrow before the painting of the Mystic Lamb. He was smoking a cigar. I had never seen him smoke before.

I tried to tell Guy and Bernal about Palmyre and me, but people were pressed around the table, drinking, smoking, congratulating Guy again and again over the victory of his Shakespeare. Several times I started to speak, but no one paid any attention, and I could not be heard. I waited for an opportunity, but Palmyre looked at me, smiling silently, and shook her head. We would tell them later. I leaned against her, my heart so full that it could scarcely contain my joy.

I do not know how long we sat there, but suddenly the raucous talk about pigeons was interrupted by a crash of sound from the pump organ on the dance floor. Madame Boschnagel sat at her instrument with an expression of the most terrible anguish on her huge face. She had been weeping. Her large eyes were swollen and blood red, and her heavy skin had gone slack over her skull. The accordion player in the green vest marched gravely onto the floor. He did not carry his accordion. He clapped his hands for silence, and kept clapping in a steady rhythm, and slowly, slowly the room quieted down and became completely still. When silence had fallen over everything, the accordion player turned to Madame Boschnagel and bowed solemnly.

She spoke from her bench, very slowly, in a voice breaking on almost every syllable, with the tears flowing down her cheeks. She struggled to go on, and her heavy German accent rang unnaturally in the room, giving her words even more feeling.

"This morning, in Sarajevo, the Archduke Franz Ferdinand, royal heir to the throne of the Dual Monarchy of Austria and Hungary, was murdered by a cowardly brigand. The archduke's beloved wife, Sophia, was murdered with him. I should like to play a hymn of praise to God for the lives of these two glorious martyrs, and when the hymn is concluded, I must ask that you depart. The Vieux Gand will be closed for mourning until the funeral is complete."

A murmur of excitement ran through the crowd. Guy and others at our table had heard the news. They dismissed it. Guy was saying that it was all too bad, really too bad, making a conventional and insincere offering to the grief of the moment. Someone said it might mean war. Guy rejected the thought with an almighty shrug. "My dear fellow," he said, "Sarajevo is in the *Balkans*. It is an affair for Austria and Servia. It has nothing to do with us. Nothing at all."

"Do not forget Russia," someone murmured.

These whispered conversations flew in fragments, and the roar of the organ silenced them. Madame Boschnagel began to sing in German, a high, melodious, surprising voice, and we stood and sang with her as best we could.

> *Lobe den Herren, den mächtigen König der Ehren*
> *Meine geliebete Seele, das ist mein Begehren. . . .*

None of us could comprehend what these deaths meant. We joined in the song not because we felt compassion for the victims of a distant calamity but because we loved Madame Boschnagel for presiding over a place where we were happy. We departed into the warm night, more sad that the tavern was closed than that two people had died. We did not imagine that those murders in a wild, remote, and dreary land like Bosnia could touch us in any way.

61

IN THE SPRING of 1918 my headaches got worse again. They came almost every night. Some days I could scarcely see, but I worked anyway. After I ate, I often vomited; so I ate little and lost weight. "You look like a skeleton," Darcy Coolidge said. She seemed frightened.

Dr. Youngblood gave me no medicine. "I don't believe in giving medicine when I don't know what's wrong with you," he said. Sometimes, out of the habit we had formed, I went to sit with him but felt so miserable that I left early and walked back to the boardinghouse on the dimly lit and empty street, half blind with pain. He watched me in grave silence and smoked his pipe, now and then asking an oblique question.

Walking helped. No one in Bourbonville locked a door. I came and went as I liked, and often I walked through Bourbonville slowly in the middle of the night, whispering to Guy and Bernal, and feeling the solace of their companionship. "You should come to us," Guy said. "It is not bad here. You would be happy."

We had much rain that spring, and the sun sank to the west amid purple clouds that stood in high columns illuminated by ever-changing light in the damp air. Sometimes we had rainbows. I made pictures in the clouds and thought of floating there, happy with my friends high above the earth. Dr. Youngblood told me much later on that he thought I would die.

Late in May the Germans attacked on the Marne. The papers blazed with headlines. People talked about battle in a land so far away that it seemed lost in a mystic haze like the lands of the Bible, where miracles glittered in coruscating light. The Germans were trying to win the war before the weight of the American Army could be thrown into the scales. Already that weight was there. On Sunday morning, June 2, the papers exultantly reported the first great American engagement of the war. On June 1, near a riverside town called Château-Thierry, the American Third Division had met the German attack.

D. B. Weaver was a corporal in the Third Division.

The effect of the battle on Bourbonville was prodigious. Something huge was happening over there, something tremendous and unfathomable like nothing known to anyone younger than sixty.

Brian Ledbetter told me later that he could see dark horsemen riding down the immense sky and that he thought he could hear the roar of artillery in the Sabbath calm when he went out to milk. The old man shook his head and made a face. He said that at Cold Harbor he had written his name on a piece of paper and pinned it to his tunic. "I was sure I was going to die," he said. "We was all sure we was going to die, and we didn't want folks back home not to know we was dead. So we pinned our names to our tunics." He did not die. He lost a leg, and he came home.

"I come home a storyteller," he said. He told his stories of battle again and again and told always how terrified he had been. "I think I tell them stories so they won't happen to me no more," he said. "I mean, if I tell them stories, maybe I'll never have nobody shoot at me again. You know what I mean? Feller's afraid of something. What does he do? He talks about it. Talks about it all the time so it won't happen no more. Think about it like this. You're afraid of high places, like Jim Ed is. Well, you talk about them high places all the time and being afraid of them, and it's like . . . Aw, you can't understand. Can't nobody understand. If Jim Ed would talk about being afraid of them high places, he'd . . . Aw, hell, I don't know."

I understood his incantations. Those old men who had endured the ancient war now receding into haze and legend and melting in senescence had told their stories, repeated them to each other and to the young and to strangers like me and perhaps mostly to themselves alone in the middle of twenty thousand insomniac nights departed since their war stopped, and now the stories were dying like a distant echo of trumpets fading on far hills. Brian Ledbetter told me about the petty things he remembered—the design on the grips of an officer's revolver he had found and carried for a while, the scrollwork on a cavalry sword he picked up in the dust on the march out of the Wilderness, the peculiar heft of his long-barreled rifle. As he spoke of these details and a thousand others, his stories became spells he cast against terror. He told them, and he had not been under cannon fire again. He had not seen again the plume of brown dust rising over roads hidden by green hills in the muggy summer heat, dust announcing that a column of enemy infantry was marching up to fight.

On this cool Sabbath with the lacy shadows of trees waving in the spring breeze over the sandy streets, with the tranquil shadows of piled clouds floating over the still green fields, and with the brown river winding peacefully down from the high mountains, old men who had told their tales and with the telling purged themselves of horror found these horrors uncoiling from the hidden places and gliding out into the sunshine where they might coil and strike again. There was something in the spirit of the day, something in the titanic phantoms whose faces showed in the great and shifting clouds, *something* that made them imagine (so Brian Ledbetter said) that perhaps the earth, winding mysteriously around the sun, had blown through some veil of time and whirled to life dead days that now must be lived again with all the old lethal menace and sinister mystery intact.

"I didn't go to church," Brian Ledbetter told me later. "I ain't never been to no church since the war, since *my* war. I mean, I go to funerals, but not to church. Mrs. Ledbetter, she gets her way about most everything. But she don't get me to church. I walked around out at my place, and I wondered what it'd all meant, what good we'd done, and I worried about my boy. I worried about Jim Ed. D.B., I didn't worry none about him. God judge me if I don't tell the truth. I figured D.B. was some kind of stranger. I don't think I ever did know that boy. I don't think nobody did. He'd run off to be what he wanted to be. My boy, Jim Ed. . . . Hell, I done a heap of thinking about Jim Ed that morning. I didn't pray. I swear I didn't pray. But Lord God, how I thought!"

62

MOST BOURBON COUNTIANS did go to church that morning. I remained asleep in the boardinghouse, exhausted from days of not sleeping. I remember the dream I was having—a strangely peaceful dream. In it I lay soaking in the marble tub in the public bathhouse in Ghent before the war. I went there every Friday afternoon. For a few sous I could soap myself and lie in the hot water in the cracked marble while a thin, dry woman in a blue smock waited patiently outside to tap on the door when my half hour was up.

I do not remember how my dream progressed. I lay in profound sleep and felt the soft June air stir over my body. I woke up, realizing that someone was in the room with me. It was Daisy. She sat in my chair looking at me, her legs stretched out. She smoked a cigarette. The smoke smell had wakened me.

"Good morning," she said. "It is a beautiful day. I have come to take you for a drive."

I was naked under the sheet, and I sat up, gathering the sheet around me. "How did you get in here?"

"I walked through the door like a normal human being. I wanted to see you. I just took Daddy and Mamma to church. They need God. I need you."

"To church," I said.

"Yes, to church. Strange, isn't it? I don't remember Daddy ever going to church before."

I could not think of anything to say. I had a stark and unpleasant recollection of Leonora, her pursuit of Guy. I felt trapped and almost angry.

"Did you pray during the war? When they were shooting at you, did you pray?"

"Yes, I prayed," I said.

"Did it do any good?"

"I am alive," I said.

"I suppose those who died never prayed," she said.

"That is not true," I said.

"Let's go somewhere," she said. She took a final pull on her cigarette and threw it out the window. I thought of how horrified Darcy Coolidge would be about all this—Daisy in my room, smoking a cigarette.

"I do not want to take a drive," I said. "You should leave."

"Well, if you don't want to take a drive, I'll get into bed with you," she said. She stood up suddenly and began taking off her shoes. She smiled at me, and I thought of how childish and sweet the smile was and how bold the gesture she was making by starting to undress.

"Please," I said. "Please go away." I could almost see Leonora in the room with me, Leonora leering at me and forcing me to do what she wanted.

She tossed her shoes on the floor and hiked up her dress and slid her garters off. She had long, plump legs. "I've always wanted to sleep with you," she said. "I'd rather do that than go for a drive anyway."

I gathered the sheet around me like a foolish virgin. "Please," I said.

"You have to lose your virginity sometime," she said. "I think virginity's a burden myself. I've had mine too long. Everybody thinks I've lost it already. Let this be the morning."

She reached around behind herself and unbuttoned her skirt and started to slide it down her legs.

"Please," I said, almost shouting at her. "I will go with you. Put your clothes back on. Please."

She stopped and looked at me. I think she was testing herself.

"May I watch you dress?" she whispered.

"No," I said. "Please go downstairs, and I will come to you. Did anyone see you come in?"

"I suppose the whole town saw me come in," she said. "Are you afraid to be naked before me?"

"No," I said. "Well, yes. It is not . . ."

"Have you ever been naked before a woman?"

"That is not your affair," I said.

"Then you have been," she said, looking suddenly hurt. "I was hoping it might be the first time for both of us. I am a virgin. Do you believe that?"

"Of course I believe it," I said.

"Lots of people in town don't," she said. "I am. I swear I am. I hoped you were a virgin, too. It doesn't matter. I don't want to be a virgin. It's just that until you, I never have seen anybody I wanted to give myself to. There's something about it, you know. In spite of everything. A woman has only one virginity to give to a man. The man who takes it always has something nobody else has. He has something over her husband if she marries somebody else. Don't you believe that?"

I thought of Palmyre's lover. "No," I said.

"I'm romantic, I guess. Do you think I'm romantic?"

"Please go downstairs," I said. "I will dress and come downstairs."

She stood, looking at me tentatively. Her words were bold, but her expression was timid and questioning, and I saw anew how young she was. She stood with her hands still behind her, as though ready to let her skirt drop to her ankles. I felt no desire. I had had no desire since Palmyre, no stirring of lust for a woman since Guy and Bernal died. In the blackness of my continuing melancholy, a still, hard weight lay on my heart, a weight palpable beneath my ribs as though the war and death and the meaninglessness of every human act had settled there. To this day when I look back on that awful time, I do not know what kept me from killing myself as Stephanos had killed himself, and I had no desire at all to risk bringing more life into a world where I wished I had never been born. I can explain none of this; I can only say that I looked at Daisy and felt then none of the emotion that I feel now in remembering how she stood there, so young, so eager, so willing to give me anything she imagined a man might want of her.

"No, please," I said. "Please go downstairs, and I will come to you. I promise."

She hesitated, shrugged, and deftly rebuttoned her skirt. She picked up her garters and sat down and slowly put them back on, showing me the curves of her long legs. We looked at each other without speaking. I listened for the door downstairs, for Darcy Coolidge's voice.

When she had arranged herself, she took out another cigarette, but she did not light it. "The thing in itself is nothing," she said. "I used to think I would take the train somewhere, some town where nobody knew me, and I would give my virginity to a complete stranger. Maybe a preacher. I'd walk into an empty church, back to his office where he was preparing the sermon, and I'd tell him I needed help with my soul, and I'd talk to him about sex, about the things I thought about it, and when I'd heated him up, I'd make him sleep with me. Wouldn't that be fun? I'd make him sweat all over me on the carpet in his office. He could never prepare a sermon again without thinking of me lying there under him with my legs all around him."

"Please," I said.

She laughed. "Who can tell? Maybe he'd save millions of souls because when he prepared his sermons, he'd be thinking about that strange young girl who once gave him her virginity and vanished without a trace. Maybe he'd think I was a miracle."

"Please," I said.

"Do you think Jesus had sex?" she said.

"No," I said.

"Why not? He was a man. My Sunday-school teacher said Jesus was thirty when he began to preach. Do you think it's normal for a man thirty years old never to have had sex?"

"Jesus was not normal," I said.

"That's the first thing we've agreed on," she said.

"Daisy, please go downstairs."

"Do I embarrass you?" she said.

"Of course you do," I said.

"Are you afraid of my father?"

"Why should I be afraid of your father?"

"If I told him you tried to attack me, he would sue you. He would put you in jail."

"I have not tried to attack you."

"Suppose I told people you tried to attack me. Who would believe you if you said you did not?"

I had no answer but sat dumbly looking at her and trying to decide how serious she was.

Suddenly she burst out with laughter, unnatural and forced. "I am not Potiphar's wife," she said.

"I wish you would go downstairs," I said.

"Listen," she said with deep earnestness. "I could get into bed with you right now, and you could take my virginity, and I would be better for it. I know you would never brag about it. Please let me do it. Do it to me."

"No," I whispered. "I cannot. You are young, and you do not know what you are saying."

"Oh, pooh," she said. "That is the coward's way out. I *do* know what I am saying. I know that right now, while we sit in this room, people are dying. It's morning here; it's afternoon over there. It's the same world. The same sun." She stopped and groped for some grand words to express the grand and hopeless feelings that swept over her face. "Do you understand?" she said.

Then, shaking her head and bringing back a bewildered smile, she said, "No, of course you don't understand. I sound crazy. It's just that right now, my brother may be dying. Some German may be shooting him in the head or bayoneting him in the stomach this very minute. While so many people are dying, why don't we make life? Why don't we love each other? Why don't we have a baby?"

"I could not," I said. "I could not."

"I could give you pleasure. I never have done it. But I have talked to people. I know what people do. I went to see a colored whore down at Sweetwater once."

"Why?" I said.

"I wanted to find out all about it. About sex. About fucking. About sexual intercourse or whatever you want to call it. About love."

"You went to a prostitute to find out about . . . ?"

"Where else was I going to go? My father always says to go see the experts. Go to a lawyer about the law, a preacher about the Bible, a farmer about crops. Why not a whore about fucking?"

"Well," I said, discovering that I could not finish the sentence I began.

"Isn't that the American way?"

"Your mother," I said, faltering badly and feeling beyond my depth. "You could have asked your mother."

Daisy whooped with laughter. "My mother! Do you think my mother is going to tell me about such things? Do you think she is going to draw me aside and say, 'Uh, Daisy, I, uh, want to . . . oh, my *dear,* I want to tell you how *sweet* it is to *fuck* the one you *love.'* She and Daddy never do it. How should she know what to tell me?"

"Well," I said, "she has had two children," and then I stopped because I felt foolish.

"That's twice," she said. She lit her cigarette and inhaled deeply and held the package out to me, punching me to make me open my eyes. I refused it. I thought that if I smoked, all this would take longer.

"I heard about this colored whorehouse down in Sweetwater. I took the local train down there one day when I was supposed to be in school, and I found the place, and I knocked on the door, and I told the colored lady in charge that I would pay her the price she usually charged to a man if she would tell me about sex."

I remained silent.

"You ought to try that place out," she said. "It's called Estelle's, and it would do you a world of good."

"Did the woman let you in?"

"She sure did. Estelle was pretty swell. She thought it was funny to talk to a white girl like me. She said she'd never met up with anybody like me, and I said she never would in her sweet life meet anybody else like me, and she laughed. Do you believe me?"

"I believe you," I said.

"She talked to me pretty straight, and she told me lots of things. I asked her if I could watch her do it. She said no, that would be dangerous for her and me. It's all right for black girls to be whores, she said, but since most of their clients are white men, she said I might be surprised by whoever it was that had her, and then I might tell somebody. I said I wouldn't, but she said I couldn't promise what I might tell."

"You left," I said.

"Not before we had some coffee and upside-down cake and she told me all I could think of to ask and a lot more besides. I bet I know more than you do, Paul Alexander. I mean, I know you've done it, and I haven't done it. But I know all about it."

"If you will please wait for me outside, I will get dressed, and I will take a ride with you," I said.

"You promise?"

"I promise."

"All right," she said. She got up and flipped her skirts around her and went out of the room, slamming the door, and I heard her footsteps diminish on the stairs. I had a fleeting vision of Bernal in the morning light filtering through the gauzy curtains that fluttered quietly at my window, the merest suggestion of a shape or perhaps only a shadow, moving across my sight, quickly gone.

63

DAISY WAS SITTING behind the wheel of the open car in the sunshine. She had lit another cigarette. If Darcy Coolidge found out that Daisy was smoking in the street outside the boardinghouse, she would think it had been disgraced.

"Can you crank the car?"

"Yes," I said. I turned the crank. It took all my strength. The engine popped. I worked harder and the world swam before my eyes. The engine fired. I stood up, staggering and blind from the exertion, holding the crank in my hand. She grinned and gestured for me to get in beside her. My head slowly cleared. We descended the hill and made our turn around the empty square. The sun was bright and mild, building to be hot. We headed for open country along the Martel Pike.

I am not certain to this day where she took me. Now and then out of the whimsy of restlessness on a lazy summer Sunday, I have driven off into the mountains in search of the place. I have not recognized it. It is as lost to me as one of those fairylands that people in stories walk into unawares and never find again.

We drove for a time without speaking. She bent silently over the wheel, and her dark hair whirled in the wind. The trees thickened on each side of the road. Here and there shabby, unpainted houses squatted gray and black in ragged fields. On the ridges, the thick forest brooded in the sunshine. We turned beneath the underpass of the railroad viaduct at Martel and headed in the direction of Knoxville. To the right a stately brick house rose on a low hill. It had a sweeping porch, framed in a white railing, a gallery behind it, and it reposed amid an immense grove of oaks. Its beauty in this poor land was stunning. "It was built before the war," Daisy shouted. "Before the *Civil War*."

It made me recall the stone house with the high casement windows, a manor, set off by itself amid carefully kept lawns and hedges, in Belgium, four years before. I remembered the stillness, the desolate emptiness of the broad abandoned lawns and the trees. "Don't think of such things," Guy whispered from the backseat or perhaps from some indefinable point above my head. "They will make you sick."

"One, two, three, four," I whispered. "One, two, three, four."

"What?" Daisy shouted over the noise of the wind and the engine.

"Nothing," I said.

The house reposed in its great garden behind a stone wall with an open iron gate. We trudged along, sweat-soaked, stinking, fatigued, and lost, moving west, looking for our unit. Faint on the air we heard the high, pure notes of a single violin playing something from romance—a sonata, something I recognized but could not name, something in the key of E.

Drawn by the music, we paused. We were filthy and exhausted and famished, and our throats burned with dust and thirst. We did not know where the Germans were. They followed somewhere behind us, where we heard the heaving of artillery—always artillery. Here was almost silence except for the single trilling sound of the solitary violin rising and falling in sweeps of music.

We went up to the house where the huge door stood ajar. The downstairs was furnished in expensive elegance. The violin was somewhere above us. Stealthily we crept upstairs, holding our rifles at the ready. We had lost our cannon by then. We had killed the mules and eaten them.

Following the music down an oak-paneled corridor, we opened a door onto a sunny room, tall windows flung open onto the hot summer day, summer curtains hanging motionless beside them, framing the deep green of the countryside.

A man in formal evening dress sat playing a violin. He was bathed in light from the brilliant day. His clothing was heavy wool, and sweat coursed down his face and dripped steadily off his nose. He glanced up at us and looked quickly away. He played on, the sound rolling rhythmically away and away, the music filling our space like some sweet, clear song of happy gods. The tall window behind him threw him into a sort of silhouette, and the curtains were nearly transparent and pure white.

Through the window we could see the forest, a preserve of some sort. We could look over the trees from this coign of vantage and in the distance see the slow, oily billowing of black smoke from something burning—smoke horribly opaque against the luminous August sky. We stood reverently, abashed in the presence of music that flowed on like an almighty river, rich and full.

The violinist did not look at us again. Guy spoke, excruciatingly polite, raising his voice. *"Pardon, monsieur, nous sommes des soldats belges, et les Allemands sont très proches. . . ."* But the violinist turned with a jerk in his chair and sat with his back to us, facing the open window and playing on. The daylight gleamed on his elegant black shoes. Guy's voice sounded inharmonious, an intrusion amid this perfection of music. In my mind the notes poured out in a symphony of color, blending in hues never seen by the physical eye.

Guy looked wearily at Bernal and me and shrugged. His eyes were sunk into his face with fatigue. We were filthy. I stared through the window at the smoke. What precious thing was burning out there? I supposed this house would burn.

We left without speaking again, carefully shutting the door to the room as if we had been leaving a theatre shamefully early and did not wish to call attention to ourselves. We shut the front door, too. We went through the empty grounds and back out onto the road. The music followed us. It died away as we tramped on, and behind us we could hear the continuous desultory murmur of the artillery.

"He is insane," Guy said.

"No more than we," I said.

"Why are you with Dale Farmer every day?" Daisy shouted.

"He lives in the boardinghouse. We walk to work every day."

"He is a sodomite," Daisy said.

"A what?" I said. I understood her well enough.

"Everybody knows it. You know it, too."

"I do not think about such things," I said.

"Look at the prissy way he walks. Listen to how he talks. Look at the way he sits in a chair. Estelle down in Sweetwater told me all about sodomites. She said that's the kind of man a woman doesn't ever want to get mixed up with."

"I do not know anything about Mr. Farmer," I said.

"You can't tell me you don't know what he is."

"He has done nothing to me," I said.

"Are you a sodomite yourself?" she asked.

"You mock me," I said.

"I am not mocking you," she said. "I want to know. I want to understand you. Are you a sodomite?"

"No," I said.

"I'm very tolerant. I'm not like other people. It's just that . . . well, if you're a sodomite, I think it's a shame. A waste."

"I am not a sodomite," I said, shouting over the sound of the engine and wondering how my voice carried over this quiet land behind the sound of the car.

We drove on for a while in silence.

"Well, what *am* I to think?" she cried. "I offer you my body. I don't ask you to marry me. I want the experience, that's all. You can do anything you want to me, and I'll never tell anybody. They could stick red-hot spikes into my skin, and I wouldn't tell anybody. I'll let you do anything you want. Touch me anywhere. You can even hurt me if you want, and I promise not to tell. But you refuse me. And I see you with Dale Farmer every day. Everybody knows what he is."

I could feel Guy and Bernal, sitting stone-still behind me. I took out my watch. It was 11:30. "We should go back," I said. "Your parents will be worried."

"Let them worry," she said. "Let them think about something besides D.B."

She kept doggedly on, pressing the gas lever to get more speed. We hurtled through the land, dust spinning behind us. She spoke again, her voice loud, strained, taut. "If D.B. is killed, it will be my fault."

"How could it be your fault?"

"I have been so jealous of him. Daddy loves him. Daddy does not love me. I've let horrible thoughts enter my head. They torture me at night before I go to sleep."

"Whatever you think, you are not responsible for anything that happens to D.B.," I said.

"I'm a very honest person, you see. Honest people have bad thoughts just like everybody else. Don't you agree?"

"Of course," I said. My head ached dully. I shut my eyes. The swaying and bouncing of the car nauseated me.

"Honest people often have bad thoughts and don't try to drive them away because if they have the thoughts, they *have* to have them. Do you know what I mean? No, you don't. You don't understand."

"Yes I do," I said. "I do understand."

"When I have bad thoughts, I know they are a part of me. I want to let them run free so I can recognize them and do something about them. I have thought—I have thought and thought and thought—that if D.B. is killed, Daddy may love me. He will have to depend on me. It would be sad, but I would be there to comfort him. Do you understand?"

"Yes, I understand. But if he gets killed, you have nothing to do with it. You are here, and he is there."

I thought she was going to cry. "We should go back," I said.

"I don't want to go back. I want to be with you. I want you to be happy with me. I want you to save me from myself. I am a terrible person. You can save me."

"I cannot do that," I said.

"If you can't save me, nobody can," she said.

64

WE CROSSED the river on a ferry. We got out of the car and stood leaning together on the wooden railing of the ferry, a railing crude and weathered. My headache receded. I recall looking down at my hands and thinking how thin they were, supposing that they had as little life left in them as the railing they gripped. I watched the brown water come down, the water reflecting the white clouds, and I thought of death.

Guy and Bernal leaned weightlessly against the railing, looking silently into the water rolling against the side of the ferry. I saw them as clearly as I saw Daisy, their features etched into the bright sunshine, the light flashing on Guy's thick black hair. He looked at me as though in contemplation of a stranger.

"Maybe we were sodomites and did not know it," he said. He faded and vanished.

On the other side, a red dirt road rose out of the river, and we drove up it and went on, and the country became more wild. Poor cabins and shanties, weatherworn and unpainted, sat tentatively on wretched fields fenced with crisscrossing rails. Sometimes the railings had collapsed and lay rotting on the ground, overgrown with briars and weeds, snaky and forbidding. It looked like land that you could work and get nothing from, land too much for its people, land that devoured their hopes. They wrestled with it like Jacob wrestling with the angel in the dark, and it touched them and left them lame and beaten and gave them no blessing.

Everything was still, empty, the land suspended in the blue enchantment of the Sabbath midday sun, and as we drove, the afternoon heat came on heavy and thick, and the mild morning flew away into the mystery where Sunday mornings go.

Somewhere Daisy pulled the car to a halt in a grassy grove. At the edge of it, a small river came down out of the mountains above us. The river washed over a rocky bed, eddied, and whispered in the shadows and hollows of the great rocks. Here and there it tumbled with a soft singing, and near us it poured into a deep pool, and beyond in the middle distance fell into a small cascade that sang the river's gentle way down the hills to the larger river that we had crossed on the ferry.

I heard a voice in the singing, or voices, something confused and far away, a crying of multitudes all maddeningly indistinct, so that I could not under-stand a word but so audible that I felt at the threshold of being able to hear one voice above all the others. A confabulation of dark fairies saying dark things.

We sat in the grass, and I strained to hear the voices, and terror engulfed me. If I went mad, I would be shut in a room naked, my arms pinned to my sides, and people would come and stare at me, and I would try to beat my brains out against the walls of my blindingly white cell. I could imagine the loss of coherence, the breaking up of orderly syllables that made words and the roaring of sound in my head as all the syllables in the universe strove with each other there.

In the deep place in the river, small fish jumped and splashed when they fell back into the water. Tall oak trees grew near us, and white birches and one enormous American chestnut stood across the river. It was cool here.

My uneasiness grew. The sun blazed on the mountain crests, and the light hurt my mind. An artillery observer up there with a good map and field glasses could send shells on us from miles and miles away. There was no artillery. The world was profoundly quiet except for the voices in the water. There was no artillery. No artillery. I write the words as I spoke them to myself at the time. No artillery. No danger. No artillery.

Daisy lay back and stretched and sighed. "It's nice up here," she said, "even in the hottest part of the summer. I've been as far as you can go in an automobile. If you cross over into North Carolina, you have to walk. Only you'd get lost. People get lost in these mountains all the time. They just disappear. You can find black bears and bobcats and lynxes. God knows what else. It's isolated from all the bad things. Someday I will cross the mountains and never come back to Tennessee."

"Where will you go?" I said. I wanted to talk. I wanted to drown out the voices.

"Why, to whatever is beyond," she said. "I don't know what it will be. It will be somewhere else."

I was silent. She sat up, her legs stretched in front of her. For once she did not smoke.

"Daddy would be angry if he knew how often I come here. I want to paint it all on my mind. When it gets too hard for me at home, I come here. It's like the night we went to England in our minds, when we were sitting with Curtis in his house? Do you remember?"

"Of course," I said.

"We were walking along the broad street in London? What was it called?"

"The Strand," I said.

"Yes, the Strand. We were walking by the river," she said.

"The Thames," I said. "It runs not far from the Strand."

"Curtis never intended to go," she said.

"I suppose not," I said.

"What's wrong with you?" she said.

"Nothing is wrong with me."

"You look pale. Are you all right?"

"Yes, I am all right."

"I have not been to England," Daisy said. "But I have been here—again and again. When I am at home, I imagine every tree, every stone in the water, the different ways the water laps against the banks here. I have built myself a house on that little knoll up there. I can see it; you can see it if you try. It has a red cedar roof and a porch with screens to keep out the flies and mosquitoes in summer, and it has a fireplace that's so big a man can stand inside it, and there is a boar's head hanging over the mantelpiece, and through the windows in the evening you can see the sunset turn the sky to fire and thousands of stars come out, more than we can ever see in the flatland. The house is all in my mind. But it is all there. Every plank. Every nail. Every window. Sometimes I have been swimming here, in this deep place, stark naked, and I have felt the water running free in every part of my body. Sometimes I have lain here on this rock, my whole body open to the skies, and I have hoped there was some man in the trees to see me and to take pleasure from me. I wish you wanted to see me naked. You don't have to touch me. I will undress for you right here if it will give you pleasure."

I was sure I saw a rustling in the foliage across the river.

"Why don't you pay attention to me?" she said.

"I am sorry," I said. I watched the foliage.

She hugged her knees. "Do you know what I do sometimes? I look at myself in the mirror in our bathroom to see if I am ugly. Sometimes when I get out of the tub, I stand there naked and look at myself all over, and I ask myself if you can find me beautiful. Do you think I am even pretty?"

"You are very pretty," I said.

The voices in the water were getting louder and louder, and something was moving in the woods beyond. Something terrible. I stared across the river, and Daisy might as well have been a thousand miles away.

65

WE JOINED the army because everyone joined the army. We joined the army because Guy was seized by a fit of patriotism. We joined the army because Father Medulous told us that the French would invade Belgium. We joined the army because we loved each other, and if Guy was resolved to be a soldier, we would be soldiers, too. We joined the army because the trumpets and the drums called us. We joined the army because the university told us that all students who enlisted would have their examinations suspended until the end of the national emergency. We joined the army because we were stupid and ignorant. We joined the army because we were young. We joined the army because the war clarified all the complicated, insoluble things and made them simple. We joined the army because the thought of death for a noble cause filled us with such sweetness that it was as if every recumbent effigy of knights with folded arms and faithful dogs at their feet in every stone church raised in Europe for a millennium gave off an essence that, concentrated and poured out on us in the storm of that summer, drugged us with unspeakable bliss.

We drilled in the daytime in the fields outside of Ghent, grain fields newly harvested, hot and dusty, the sunlight brilliant on trampled stubble, and we had great fun. Our officers, beefy in the Belgian way, redfaced, loud and obscene, walked up and down cursing us, as if their blasphemy made us soldiers and them brave. We laughed at them behind their backs.

The three of us and Huys manned an artillery piece, working at it with the pleasure of boys shooting off fireworks to celebrate a birthday. The Belgians had very little artillery. The old army scorned artillery. It held soldiers back, officers said. Someone thought university students, especially one like me, trained in mathematics, would be better at artillery than at being infantry-men. At first we expected to fight the French—if we fought anyone. With the weeks of crisis, the idea of war became more and more unreal. Everything was so calm, so orderly. The sun rose every day. The yellow streetcars clanked along their tracks in the winding streets of Ghent. People went to work precisely, dressed in the stuffy Belgian way—an imitation of the stuffy German way and the stuffy English way and the stuffy French way. We reported to our officers at six-thirty in the morning, and precisely at six o'clock, the end of the working day, the stuffy office people of northern Europe filed out of their offices, their stores and their factories, and they went home through crowded streets. We drilled until dinnertime. We took two hours for lunch and drank strong red wine and took naps. There were not enough officers. Since the barracks were not large enough to house the new recruits, we went home at night.

A Saturday morning came. I slept that Friday night in Palmyre's arms. We sweated on each other, lying atop the sheets, the windows opened on the muggy night air where not a breath stirred. Palmyre slept peacefully, and dawn came, and with it a loud knocking at the door downstairs. I roused Palmyre, and she got up grumbling, throwing her robe around her, her rump so fine, her breasts big as gourds, and down she tramped, complaining at the indecency of a knock so early on a Saturday when she did not open her shop until ten o'clock, and I heard the door open, and a boy's voice, earnest and sympathetic, speaking in Flemish, then Palmyre uttering a ritual cry of pain. "The poor one! The poor one! Ah, the poor one! Dead! Dead!"

The tramping of two pairs of feet upstairs, one shod, and in she came leading her nephew, a sunburned, dark-haired boy with deep brown eyes and a shy look. He stood with a large peasant hat of thick yellow straw in his hand and nodded uncomfortably at me, I who lay naked in the bed, carelessly covered with a sheet, smoking my first cigarette of the morning, looking at him with all the annoyance that I could muster. He was embarrassed, and turned his hat in his hands. My uniform was flung over the back of a chair. He looked at it and said with a terrible Flemish accent, "You are in the army, monsieur?" I said with enormous self-importance, "Yes, I am in the army."

"I wish I could be with you," he said fervently.

"Wars are for men," I said pompously. I was perhaps five years older than this child.

Palmyre fussed in her wardrobe. What should she wear! The question took on huge importance. She was returning to her village, to people who knew her and knew her family. She found a long, black silk dress she had made for someone else and held it up to the pale light brightening before the sun.

"Ah!" she said.

"That is an evening gown," I said.

"The crazy woman I made it for agreed with you," she said. "She said it did not look right for mourning. She said it was more for dancing."

"She was right," I said, laughing. "It is not appropriate for a village funeral."

"Nonsense," she said. "What do you know about my village?"

I wrapped the sheet around me in a gesture of impatience before the gawking boy and went into the other room and put on mufti. I went down to the street to buy a newspaper and saw that her nephew had come in a large wooden cart pulled by a huge draft horse. The horse stood there placidly sweating, switching his heavy tail lethargically against legions of flies. I came back up, reading black headlines, thinking that things looked serious, and she had put on the silk dress. "You should not wear the dress in the cart," I said. "At least wait to put it on until you are in your mother's house."

"I want to make a good impression as soon as they see me," she said. "I want people in the village to know who I am!"

"You will not make a good impression if your dress is dusty and sweaty," I said.

"Oh, my little cabbage," Palmyre said in her jocular tone of condescension. "My people live in dust and sweat. They will see that it is silk. Silk. The important thing is not the dust and the sweat but that the dress is silk. Oh, the poor one! The poor one! Dead at eighty-eight! Life is so short. So short." The "poor one" was an uncle of some kind.

She had packed other clothes in a flowered carpetbag. I carried it downstairs and loaded it in the back of the cart. She took enough clothes to last four days. She pecked me lightly on the cheek and pushed me away when I tried to kiss her on the mouth.

"Not in front of the boy," she whispered.

"He found us in bed together," I said.

"He did not see us in bed together," she said, shaking her head vigorously. "A woman must keep up appearances."

With that the two of them were gone, the iron-bound wheels of the cart pounding over the cobblestones and the horse's shod hooves ringing in the tranquil morning of an ordinary Saturday in a hot summer. Palmyre sat stiff and proud beside her nephew. She turned once and waved at me, a formal and restrained gesture that made her seem like a distant acquaintance. I stood in the doorway and watched them disappear around the great curve of the street near the cathedral. She was to return Wednesday. I did not dream that I would never see her again.

The royal herald appeared in the streets early that afternoon. I heard him coming a long way off. He paused on every street corner. He held a heavy brass bell with a wooden handle, ringing it vigorously, and the sound crashed against the stone walls. People poured into the streets to listen to his proclamation. Mobilization. Troops to the barracks. In the name of the king. War. Placards went up on the walls. I went up to the basket where Palmyre put her dirty clothes, and I found a silk stocking. I put it in my pocket and carried it every day of the seven weeks I was in the war. When I awoke in the hospital and discovered that my clothes had been cut away and that my last relic of her was gone, I wept.

66

I WAS TELLING how Daisy and I sat by the mountain stream on that day of blue sky and sunshine and the quiet sound of the woods and the great rise of the mountains and the smells of late spring and of my growing terror.

"I want you," she said. "I want to marry you. I have been waiting for you all my life. If you don't want to marry me right now, we can live in sin. Look at all the people who have lived in sin and been interesting. Lord Byron, for instance. Mary Shelley."

I saw something moving across the stream. It moved, and the trees swayed. I heard a moaning in the treetops. Something terrible was coming, something with a human form but not human. Something dark was passing overhead, a terror out of the abyss where the collected terrors of all our primitive history lie caged and hidden so that we can make illusions and live according to them and imagine until almost the last moment of life that the illusions are real and that the horror is no more substantial than the nightmares of childhood. But the horror is the real.

"I want you to take me back to Europe with you," Daisy said. "I will leave everything here and never look back. I promise I'll never be homesick. I want you to show me the world and teach me things. I can't love you so much and let you go. You will love me in time; I love you so much that you will learn to love me."

I believe that some slight residue of rational recollection told me even then that Daisy was speaking to me as I had once spoken to Palmyre, and I have wondered in the intervening years if the great abyss I felt between Daisy and me revealed in unmistakable horror the foolishness, the absurdity of what had been the most powerful desire and purpose of my life and perhaps of the despair seemingly destined to attach itself to any illusion of enduring love. I wonder if this faint, far-off, and bitter comparison coming to my mind like another of the whispering voices in this mountain glade was in fact the cause of the mounting terror that I felt. For whatever it was, her words were like an unbearable sound of bells crashing in a windowless room with cement walls. I was shut in the room with the bells; they throbbed in my head; I wanted to scream. If I started screaming, I would never stop. The thing was moving through the trees beyond the river.

"You think I am young," she said, looking at me in her grave way. "I am younger than you are. I am older than other women my age. I will get older. That's an advantage, you see. I won't get younger. You are twenty-four, and I am seventeen. It's a big difference now. But many men are older than their wives. Daddy is three years older than Mamma. I know a man who is twenty years older than his wife. When we go back to Europe, I will lie about my age. I will grow up to you."

I was panting. I could not get enough air. I was suffocating.

Why did Guy run away?

"You have been hurt," Daisy said. "I do not know how you have been hurt. The wounds. There is something more. I don't know what it is. Maybe I never have to know. I do know that I have never seen a man I wanted to marry until I met you. Now I know I never will see another man I want so much. I want to marry you, to take care of you. . . ." She stopped talking. I stared across the river, straining to see what terrible thing was coming through the trees.

"What is it?" she said. "What are you looking at?"

I turned blankly to see her. "Nothing," I said.

"Why were you staring at the trees?" she said.

"There is something over there," I whispered.

"There's *nothing* over there," she said. "Nothing."

"There's something over there," I said. "Can't you hear it?"

"There's nothing anywhere. Nothing! Nothing!"

"I want to leave," I said, staggering to my feet. I was sick and dizzy, and the world whirled around me, and the dark thing passed overhead. Dark wings.

We were lying in a meadow on a hillside. The sun was shining. It had rained, and we were wet. The sun had broken through the clouds. My legs ached from so much walking. We lay there drinking in the sun and feeling it drying our clothes. I wanted to sleep. The army was falling back in steps towards Antwerp. We thought we were behind our defensive line. We stank. I hated the stench. We could not get away from it. In the sun, in the grass, everything was good. We could hear the artillery, a dull, irregular muttering like summer thunder in the distance.

Guy was complaining about our stink. He was talking about baths and soap and good wine and a good bed, lying there making fantasies, creating a world of words when reality would not do. I was the one who, moved by some instinct, lifted my head and saw the field gray in the copse of trees at the foot of the meadow. I shouted, *"Les Allemands!"* Guy jumped up and started to run just as the German machine gun opened fire, raking our meadow like a scythe. The machine gun ripped him across the back and hurled him to earth. I heard him groan, a terrible, suffocating groan, and I crawled to him. He lay there with his eyes open, his mouth pouring blood. The machine gun swept back and forth over the meadow, and Guy's mouth poured blood. Red blood. I heard the stream of bullets buzz like hornets over my head. The sunshine made the blood look divine, pouring out of his mouth, feeding the green earth. My comrades were firing back at the machine gun now, using their rifles. Guy was dead.

We had to leave him there.

I thought—I still think—that if I had not cried out, he might not have jumped up to run away. I have relived the moment a thousand or a hundred thousand times. Did I cry out before the machine gun started? Or did the Germans begin firing a split second before I shouted that they were there? I cannot tell. Why did Guy bolt and run? For years I could not hear the crash of a screen door in the Tennessee summer without forcing myself to resist the impulse to leap onto the ground and to try to make a hole for myself against enemy fire. I developed that instinct in one week of war. Guy had it, too. Why did he run?

"What is wrong with you?" Daisy was shouting at me.

I saw Guy standing across the river where he had walked out of the forest. I heard the wind howling overhead, but the trees did not move. He was looking across the river at me, as solid as the tree trunks, as present as Daisy. His face was rotten. His skeletal arms hung out of his uniform tunic. Maggots crawled in his eyes. The flies swarmed around his corrupt flesh. He held skeletal arms out to me, and his skull grinned.

I shut my eyes and sobbed. "We must get away from here," I said. "We must go home."

"Come to me," Guy called. "You loved me once. If you love me still, you will not be afraid. Come to me." I could not keep my eyes shut against his voice. I stared at him and sobbed, "No. No. No." He laughed and lifted his arms. "Do not be afraid. Come to me." A bony hand fell off an arm. The skin fell away from his face. Only his black hair covered his shining skull, and a snake looked out of the empty socket of one eye and crawled slowly down the front of his rotting tunic. I closed my eyes against the horror.

"We must go home," I said.

Daisy was standing. She shouted, "Do you think I am going to attack you? Am I so terrible?"

I felt the world spinning. A headache erupted inside my skull. Every pulse was a hammer.

"I wasn't going to rape you," she screamed. "Of course I will take you home. I would not dream of forcing you to stay in my company." I pressed my hands to my eyes.

"Don't stand there looking like a baboon! Get back in the car. No, you can crank the goddamned engine first. You might as well be good for something!"

I opened my eyes and stared at her. I could not understand. She climbed behind the wooden steering wheel and grasped it with both hands. She was weeping, the tears running down her face, making streaks where the dust had settled on her skin.

"Listen, Mr. Alexander. Do you know the difference between me and other women, between me and all those other women you *could* marry? Other women don't cause trouble. They take hints. They leap gratefully at any opportunity to be slaves. They wallow before men. When a man gives them the slightest sign of dismissal, why, they scurry away like cockroaches when you turn a light on in the kitchen.

"Well, you listen to me! I wanted to be with you today. I wanted you to comfort me. I wanted you to tell me I'm not a bad person because of what I feel about my brother, my father. I wanted to ask you to marry me because no matter what you think, we are very much alike. If you don't want to be here with me, I am hurt to my bones. I am hurt, hurt, hurt, and I hate you for hurting me. I hate you now as much as I loved you. Now get in the goddamned car, and I will take you home."

Guy stood on the other side of the stream, all bones and rotting flesh, maggots crawling in his corpse, and a snake sliding out of the socket in his skull where an eye had been. I could not see Bernal. But I remembered how he died. Guy held out his arms. "Come with me!" he shouted.

I stumbled against the front of the car and fell forward, throwing my hands out. The brass radiator in front of the car caught me. I stood there with my head lowered, vomiting yellow bile. I had not eaten in more than a day. I had nothing to vomit but bile. I heaved until I thought my chest would break. I cranked the engine.

On the way back we had two flat tires. Both times I staggered down to help. Both times Daisy pushed me away. "I know everything there is to know about a car!" she screamed. "I am strong enough to use a jack. I don't need a foreign gentleman to fix my tires. Get the hell out of the way."

Both times I dropped in the shade of trees beside the dusty road. It was hot. My clothes were soaked with sweat and filthy with dust. I shut my eyes to keep from looking into the cutting sun. My pulse thundered in my head. I was dizzy and felt the ground turning beneath me. I was on the point of vomiting again. Daisy jacked the car up and wrestled the wheel off and replaced the first flat with a spare. When the second tire went flat, she expertly removed the wheel and flipped it on the ground, took the tools out of the box on the running board, and removed the tire from its rim. She worked quickly, with furious concentration.

A car stopped. I opened my eyes and saw an earnest, fat young man with straw-colored hair and a round, pink face getting down. He wore a starched white shirt with a high collar and a bright red necktie and red suspenders. He wore a hard straw boater hat against the scalding sun. The sweat darkened out from his suspenders and under his arms, making wet semicircles. His face dripped. He glared at me in indignation and made for Daisy with an expression of smug arrogance and reached for the tire tool, looking incandescently cheerful and authoritative.

Daisy's hair was an oily mess. Her hands were black with oil and dirt. Her long skirt fanned out around her in the dirt, and it was filthy. The starched young man said, "Here, little lady, that there's a man's job, and now you're lucky enough to have a man to do it for you." His plump shape and his ice-cream clothes swam in the brilliant light.

He was reaching for the tire tool when Daisy leaped up and swung it at him. She meant to hurt him for life. Some instinct saved him. He jumped back just in time to keep his hands from being broken off at the wrists. The tire tool buzzed through the air. Daisy shook the tool like a club and screamed at him. "Get the hell out of here, you fucking fat prick, before I stick this thing up your ass and give you another hole to shit with."

The pink boy turned white. His mouth fell open. It was a large mouth, much too large for his face. When it was open, he looked extremely stupid. He started to say something, but no words came. Daisy lunged forward with a choppy step and swung the tire tool at his head. He scrambled away, his eyes popping in terror. Daisy glared at him and advanced another couple of steps, sizing up the place where she would hit him, waving the tire tool. "I could knock your balls off with this thing," she screamed. "But you probably don't have any balls. I bet you don't have anything down there but a little red rubber hose to piss with."

The pink boy's mouth fluttered dumbly. Then he bolted for his car. His nice boater hat with its bright red band fell off and rolled in the dirt. He had to bend up and down to crank his engine. His head bobbed over the brass radiator. His pop eyes came up frantic, disappeared, came up again, disappeared, came up—all so fast that he looked as if the engine were cranking him.

Safely behind his steering wheel at last with the engine running and the car easing out of her reach, he found the presence of mind to begin reconstructing his vision of chivalry. His voice trembled uncontrollably. "Young woman," he cried, "you are a disgrace to your sex."

"Go fuck a drain pipe, you pervert," she screamed.

"Give me my hat," the young man cried. "You don't have no right to steal my hat. I was just trying to help. I didn't know you was crazy."

Daisy picked the hat out of the dust and sailed it into the back of his car. "I don't want your fucking hat. I wouldn't let my dog wear your fucking hat. You probably have fleas on your head. And ticks. I bet you have ticks, too. Why don't you shave your prick and walk on your hands? You'd look better."

All this was beyond the young man's experience. He pushed down on the gas and roared away. A storm of flying gravel and dust came up behind his car. Daisy stood in the empty road, glaring after him. She held the tire tool in her hands. She looked down at it, and she looked over at me. She began to laugh. She bent double with laughter.

I lay back against the tree, hot, sick, and exhausted. My breath was so shallow that I thought I could not keep on breathing. I could not stand up. When I shut my eyes, the world resumed its sick turning. I heaved, but nothing came up. My mouth had a foul taste.

Daisy came over and collapsed beside me and took me in her arms. "My poor baby," she whispered, kissing me on my dirty face, stroking me with her dirty hands, finally embracing me and putting her face close to mine. "My poor sweet baby. We're both crazy, Paul Alexander. Do you know that? We're both crazy. We're in the wrong world, the wrong world. We're bluebirds in the snow."

67

D. B. WEAVER was not killed in June. He was recommended for the Congressional Medal of Honor. He captured a German machine gun, killing its two-man crew with his bayonet, turned the gun on the Germans, rallied his men when his captain fell dead with a bullet through the head in the Bois de Belleau. He held his ground until reinforcements arrived. Some said his action was the turning point of the battle. It was quickly said in Bourbonville that the American victory was the turning point of the war.

Virgil Weaver learned these details from a young reporter with tuberculosis who landed gasping and coughing in Bourbonville from Knoxville, having hitched a ride on the caboose of a freight train just after he had seen the report come over the telegraph from Washington.

Other reporters poured into Bourbonville. They talked with Virgil and Melvina and with everybody in town they could find who knew D.B. They took notes furiously. They drank lemonade and Coca-Cola and whiskey and admired Bourbonville, and they wrote about D.B. Weaver, the Fighting Volunteer.

All three of the Knoxville papers published long stories, and D.B.'s photograph in uniform appeared in the Sunday rotogravure along with the photograph he had had made for his high school class, when he posed in a high-collared white shirt with a necktie and an uncomfortable expression. Photographs that Melvina had made with the Kodak camera appeared, too. Everybody in Bourbonville was proud of him. People believed he had taken from them something that made him a hero.

The culmination came on a Saturday afternoon when Pinkerton ran into Virgil in the square. It was scalding hot and humid, and the square was crowded with farmers in from the country to sit around the courthouse spitting and whittling and talking and watching. Pinkerton was in his shirtsleeves. Dick Shaw was with him, and Dick Shaw was in *his* shirtsleeves. Virgil was in his habitual dark lawyer's suit, lightweight, exquisitely tailored, slightly out of fashion.

The two of them, Virgil pale and Pinkerton hale and ruddy, collided in the square under the giant chestnut trees and the oaks, and they stood face-to-face in the hot shade. I was walking through the square. I saw Pinkerton rush up and seize Virgil's hand.

"I just want you to know how proud we are of your son, Virgil. Goddamn, we're proud of *you*. I mean hell, you raised him, didn't you? He's got your spunk, Virgil. You did good! You did real good! Listen, all that trouble we had? Hell, it was way back then. It's over. It's all over, Virgil. Hell, we're old men! Good God, it's time we stopped all this stuff! It's time we buried the hatchet and forgot about it. I'm sorry for my part of it. I was right; you were right; I was wrong; you were wrong. What do you say, Virgil? What do you say?"

Virgil looked astounded. He let Pinkerton take him by the arm—an amazing act of familiarity—and steer him off to one side, and we all watched as Pinkerton talked earnestly to a slowly nodding Virgil in a low voice. People applauded. I will never forget that. The square rang with applause and cheers. Virgil looked around in embarrassment. He lost control, and he smiled. Pinkerton grabbed Virgil's hand, shook it hard again and hugged him. The applause rolled on and on. People rushed up and shook hands with both of them and clapped them on the back. I was deeply moved. And I applauded, too.

Much later Dale Farmer told me what Pinkerton said. Dale Farmer's pink face glowed. He believed he was next in command at the car works, that when Pinkerton left, he would take charge. That is why Dale Farmer had stayed at the car works all those years.

Pinkerton was soon going to leave Bourbonville. That is what he told Virgil. He was going to Washington, to the main offices of the railroad. When D.B. came home from the war, Pinkerton promised, a job would be waiting for him. Because Pinkerton was leaving, going up to a new step in life, he and Virgil should stop their quarrel and be friends. Virgil thanked him. Virgil said yes, they should be friends. That is what they said to each other, and the town made it a peace treaty that would last as long as the world.

68

THE NIGHTS grow cooler. This morning I went outside with my coffee and the dog and stood in the grass at the side of the house and looked towards the upper field, saw the flaming trees, and smelled autumn at the full—tangy and dank at once, sharp with a hint of melancholy and triumph. It is warm at midday. But autumn is here, the leaves are brilliant, and we have endured.

During the summer of 1918, while Bourbonville was still rapt in its adoration of D. B. Weaver, the silent pestilence called the Spanish influenza mowed people down. It swept through Bourbon County and the car works and sent men to bed and the grave. I wonder yet that Dr. Youngblood did not die of fatigue during that terrible summer. His eyes became more red, his steps more slow, his face more drawn. He began to look old and sick. He passed from youth into middle age.

We seldom had time to talk. He came to the boardinghouse to treat Darcy Coolidge, who nearly died. He came down to the car works on the morning Vissing collapsed. Dick Shaw turned pale when he saw Vissing lying there, struggling for breath, scarcely conscious, his face ghastly. Shaw refused to touch him. "Call that hillbilly doctor," he was reported to have said. "I ain't going to risk my life by laying a hand on him."

Someone ran for Pinkerton, who was in the steel foundry helping tap the furnace there. So many men were out sick that Pinkerton often did the work of a laborer, resolved to keep the car works going. Dale Farmer struggled up through the summer heat to fetch me. I do not know why. He was undone. I could smell the sweat and fear. "Where is it going to end?" he sobbed. "Who's going to be next?"

I arrived in the office as Pinkerton rushed in. No one had loosened

Vissing's necktie. Pinkerton ripped it off of him, opened the man's shirt, and commanded Dale Farmer to bring cold water. Dr. Youngblood came and said there was nothing to do but to put him to bed and keep him comfortable. Pinkerton took Vissing back to the King Bourbon Hotel and nursed him through the night. It was said that Pinkerton was holding Vissing's hand when Vissing gave a little sigh and a shudder and died. I learned that Vissing was from Connecticut. Caleb embalmed the body and shipped it off in a coffin on the train. Vissing had a brother and sister back there. I tried and failed to imagine anyone grieving for him.

Pinkerton accompanied the coffin to the station and stood with his hat over his heart as the train pulled out. Shaw was nowhere to be seen. He was sure he was coming down with the flu himself. Dr. Youngblood said the death rate in the county went up seven times during the epidemic. Caleb's funeral parlor on Broadway sometimes put on three funerals on the same day.

That summer Pinkerton seemed elevated and changed. He stopped drinking. He paid attention to details at the car works. He worked tirelessly. He came to call on Darcy Coolidge when she was recovering and brought her a bouquet of flowers. "You've been loyal to the railroad, Darcy," he said. "You and the Colonel. You are the kind of people who made this country great."

Darcy Coolidge feebly clasped my hands and whispered, "What you are seeing now is the Moreland J. Pinkerton who came here years ago. That's the man who built the car works."

Pinkerton made rounds like a doctor, nursing his sick men, sitting by their beds, comforting them, giving them hope. Throughout the county you could hear a rumble of approval. A man in the car works went down. He had to be taken home because there was no clinic in Bourbon County to take care of him. Pinkerton appeared, driving up to the house in his dusty black Ford, jumping down, walking inside. He organized the care of the patient. He stayed until he saw that the organization was working. Then he went on to his next charge. "You're my men," he said at bedsides. "I take care of my men." He was as gentle as sleep.

Dr. Youngblood had Ted Devlin print up a list of things not to do for flu patients, and Pinkerton took dozens of copies of it around in his car. Don't give them alcohol or patent medicines or tonics. Don't let them drink coffee, though they might take a little tea. Don't let them get cold. Don't give them ice water, but let them drink cool water out of springs or out of cisterns or wells. Don't give them purgatives like castor oil or any of the dozens of other remedies designed to open the bowels. "We don't know what's causing this thing," Dr. Youngblood said wearily again and again. "The best we can do is make the body comfortable while it tries to heal itself. If you pump a lot of patent medicines into the body, you get in its way. All we can do is not to get in the body's way." He sighed and told me, "But nobody's going to pay any damned attention to anything I say."

Dr. Youngblood reckoned without Pinkerton. Pinkerton read the printed sheets to the families of victims. He read with a voice that brooked no contradiction. "Now I'm telling you this one time. You keep the whiskey and the patent medicines and the roots and the herbs and all that shit out of his mouth. You hear me? You give him that stuff, and you're going to kill him dead as a shoat in November. You hear me? You give him castor oil, and his death will be on your head. You'll be a murderer before God." Pinkerton ruled by terror and by command. People cowered and obeyed. "We've got a lot of folks dying," Dr. Youngblood said. "But we don't have so many killing themselves. That's because Pinkerton's out there giving commandments like God Almighty."

Sometimes Pinkerton appeared to me in his new incarnation, usually late in the day when a silence had fallen over the car works and the men were finding their quiet way home. "How are things going?" he would say. I might tell him that there had been only two heats of iron during the day instead of five because there were so few men able to work that everything had slowed down. "No help for it," he said, showing no trace of impatience. "It's not our fault. It's in the hand of God." Even this unexpected religious allusion did not seem strange now.

"Tell you something, Paul Alexander," he said once in a ruminative way. "I've been wondering who can run this place when I move up to Washington." He laughed. "It's my kingdom, you know, and I don't have a son to leave it to. I might leave it to you."

He looked at me so earnestly that I felt moved with compassion for him. I do not know why. I suppose that when men want something with all their hearts, they become children again. We are most helpless when we desire. I wanted all his dreams to come true.

I told him that I could not stay after the war, that I must go home.

"No, you won't do it," he said softly. "Not if you've got a kingdom to run. There's power here. It's not power like the President of the United States or even the president of the railroad. But it's power in its own little world. Power's like a new suit: you don't think you want it till you try it on, and then you find out that it fits you just fine, and you don't ever want to take it off. You can do this job. The men think you're some kind of foreign god. You could lead them. Damned if you couldn't." The idea seemed to grow on him as he talked.

I protested. Pinkerton shook his head. "Hell, they're already telling tales about you—how many languages you know, how you were wounded in the war, the medals you've got for heroism. They tell me you're some kind of count."

"A count! That is not true, Mr. Pinkerton. That is not true."

"That's what I've heard," Pinkerton said. "Why not be a count for them? Hell, if you're as far away from home as you say you are, you can be any goddamned thing you want. Why not be a count?"

"But it is not true," I said.

He laughed and slapped me on the back. "What are you going to tell them, then? That you're no count?" He laughed at his little pun, which I did not then understand.

Abruptly he turned serious again, as if he had just convinced himself of a new thought. "I'm glad Virgil and me made peace. It was too long a fight. If I was going to stay in this town, he'd be my friend now. Maybe he was right back there in '98. I sure as hell didn't get anything out of that war. If I'd done what Virgil said—stayed here and minded my own business—I never would have got in the trouble I did. They's been lots of times I've laid awake nights thinking about that. Maybe that's why I was mad at Virgil for so long. If I hadn't gone off to that damn fool war, I'd have been in Washington years before now."

69

I SHOULD TELL how Bernal died. It was after Guy's death. Bernal and I walked through a field not far from Antwerp. We could see the spire of the cathedral. We thought Antwerp meant safety. It was hot, September, and a moist haze lay over the world. The haze softened things. We were in a field, and there was a tree in the middle of it, and when we passed near the tree, Bernal reached up out of habit to take a leaf.

We heard the shell coming. You could hear them roaring in like an approaching train, *chka-chka-chka-chka-chka,* and when you heard that sound, it was probably too late. I dived into a small declivity as the roaring got louder, and I had scarcely hit the ground when the shell exploded with a deafening roar seemingly right on top of me. With the roar came a big *whump,* a hard blow across my body that I thought was shrapnel. But it was not hot or metallic, and later I realized that I felt only the concussion and the earth that the blast threw on top of me. Shrapnel whizzed overhead. I thought I was wounded. In terror of suffocation, I dug myself out of the dirt and found that I was only bruised.

For a moment I lay flat. The shell might mean the beginning of a barrage. But it was only a random shot. Maybe a battery checking range. It might have been a Belgian battery.

The randomness made me angry. Yes, when I finally decided that there would be no shell to follow that one, I felt angry. I got up and shook the loose dirt off my filthy uniform—as if the dirt mattered—and raged at the insult spoken against us by meaningless terror.

I looked around for Bernal. I could not find him. I called him. He did not answer. The ceaseless firing behind us came closer. I began screaming for Bernal. Finally I looked up. There was the tree: a large tree, still with the branches and the leaves on it, and he had put out his hand to take some of the leaves. There he was—not floating like an angel in the air, but pitched wildly into the tree. He hung there, arms and legs across a branch. His head was gone. His beautiful head was gone. The headless body hung there in the tree. The blood dripped out of the stump of his neck, and the white bone of his spine gleamed like a broken stalk in the blood and sunshine.

My first thought was madness. I would find the head and put it back. I began to look for it. I was frantic. I never found it. Someone found me and led me away. I was hysterical.

Bernal was dead, and Guy was dead. After that day by the river with Daisy, I remembered how they died—a release of sorts. All the muck stopped up in my brain gushed out through a plug that had been removed. I cannot write any more tonight.

70

SEPTEMBER CAME on clear and bright, and then October. The torrid summer released its grip slowly, then fled in the middle of the night. The Spanish flu faded. Pinkerton contracted with Caleb to put up a bronze plaque in memory of Vissing on the wall of the main office, and the day Caleb came down and screwed it to the woodwork, we had a little ceremony, and Pinkerton made a brief speech, and some of the women typists wept. The plaque is still there; we kept it polished as long as I stayed at the car works. Shaw wiped his eyes with a great grubbing-about of his handkerchief. I saw no tears there.

Shaw and Pinkerton seemed to be the closest friends. Wherever you saw one of them, you saw the other. Shaw told me he was invited to dinner at Pinkerton's house. "You ever been there?" he said.

"No," I said.

"Strange sort of house. Big photographs of a rebel soldier hanging on the wall. His eyes are on you everywhere you look. Can't get away from it. Do you know the Captain's wife?"

"No," I said.

"Odd person. He loves her. God, that man loves his wife! Treats her like a baby. She's crazy as a loon, of course. She dresses all in black. Beautiful voice when she speaks. Only it sounds like something . . . like something out of a ghost story. She can't talk about nothing but the Bible. Poor man. He's got his tribulations. Way she starts out talking to you, you think she's one of the nicest people in the world. Friendly. Asks you a lot of questions. Then she starts talking about the Bible, and my God, the woman's crazy."

Shaw cleared his throat. "Of course I ain't criticizing the woman. You won't tell the Captain that I've been talking about his wife, will you? All this is in strictest confidence, and if you say I said these things, I'll deny it."

"Of course," I said.

"Good for you. It's like the Captain says, Paul. You're smart, and you're loyal. You ain't going to regret being loyal to me. I'll fix you up one of these days. You wait and see. We're friends, ain't we?"

"Of course," I said.

He shook my hand. His flesh was soft and damp. "Funny how it was," he said. "It was like he was trying to show me she was okay even if she had all these crazy ideas. Lord God, it made my head swim! The millennium. The Antichrist. That woman knows Bible prophecy up and down. Do you believe that shit?"

"No," I said.

"I never have paid no attention to it myself. I'm not a reading man, you know. But hell, the Bible's the Bible. Ain't that right?"

"I am sure it is," I said.

"She knows it backwards and forwards. Did you know that the Bolsheviks are in the Book of Ezekiel?"

"No," I said.

"I didn't even know there was a Book of Ezekiel. She got her Bible down and showed me, and the way she explained it, well, you'd just have to think about it. She's either awful smart, or she's—"

Shaw's tongue froze on the word. I knew he had been going to say "crazy" again. He looked at me mistrustfully and went off with his sentence incomplete. I imagined Pinkerton's wife as a young woman, her skirt hiked up to her waist, Pinkerton on top of her, her legs wrapped around his body. It was not a sensual thought. It was a random image, and I could make nothing of it.

71

THE GERMANS were everywhere in retreat, a field-gray tide rushing out to a dark sea. The papers predicted an invasion of Germany by Christmas. Berlin in the spring, they said. On Sundays the rotogravures showed American soldiers marching to the front singing. The papers never showed photographs of American corpses.

Dale Farmer read the news aloud, his plump red face beaming with excitement. "You see what happens when Americans get into the war!" he said. "We're fighters. We don't fool around." I tried to imagine him carrying a rifle, muddy to his hair, stinking of weeks-old sweat, hauling a corpse on his back.

When I stopped in the cafe, Bessie May Hancock said, "I reckon you'll be leaving here when the war's over, Mr. Alexander?"

"Yes, I shall go home," I said.

"I'm going to miss you," she said. "Ain't you going to miss him, too, Doc?"

"I think he ought to stay here," Dr. Youngblood said.

" 'Everbody to her own taste,' said the lady as she kissed the cow," Bessie May said. "I just got to say that it ain't been near as bad having you in Bourbonville as I figured it was going to be."

"She means that as a compliment," Dr. Youngblood said.

"Thank you," I said.

"I mean, we got all these foreigners coming in with the moving pictures nowadays. Why not have them in real life? It's the same thing, ain't it, Doc?"

Dr. Youngblood chuckled and drank his coffee.

"I mean, just look at Rudolph Valentino. Who's more foreign than that, and he's right here at the Grand Theatre when he's got a picture show on. Not in the flesh but twenty foot high. Did you see *My Official Wife?*"

"I think I missed that one," Dr. Youngblood said.

"Oh, Curtis, you don't never go to the picture show. I'm asking Mr. Alexander here."

"No," I said. "I didn't."

"Well it's just scandalous, and *Isle of Love* ain't much better. He just kisses women right and left. Right on the mouth, like they was all married to him. But he ain't married to none of them. I've never seen the like. My dear departed mamma saw just one Rudolph Valentino moving picture, and it carried her off."

"You mean she liked it?" Dr. Youngblood said.

"No, I don't mean she liked it, Doc. I mean she died. It got her so excited."

"Which one was it?" Dr. Youngblood asked vaguely, in a tone he might have used to inquire about the symptoms of a new but not serious disease.

"It was *Ambition.* Oh, I tell you, my dear departed mamma's heart beat so fast in that show she died two weeks after she seen it. No, I take that back. She come through *Ambition* all right. She died after we seen *Patria.*" Bessie May wiped a tear from her eye.

"I missed that one, too," Dr. Youngblood said.

"Tell me something, Doc. Have you ever seen Rudolph Valentino in *anything?*"

"I know who he is," Dr. Youngblood said defensively.

"Mamma said if she was married to a man like Rudolph Valentino she'd make him change his ways in a hurry," Bessie May said.

"I'm sure she would have," Dr. Youngblood said. "How old was your mamma when she died?"

"She was eighty-five years young, Doc."

"I thought it was something like that," Dr. Youngblood said.

"Just think about kissing all them women on the mouth with a camera pointing at you. I couldn't let a man kiss me on the mouth if I looked around his head and seen a camera pointing at me like a gun. And a moving-picture camera at that! Could you, Doc?"

"Well, in general, I don't let men kiss me no matter what," Dr. Youngblood said.

"Oh, you know what I mean—Lord, a mercy, Doc! But tell me now. How would you like it if you was, say, married to a moving-picture actress, and she was to come home at night, and you was to say, 'Well now, wifey beloved, what you been doing all day long?' And she was to say back to you, 'Well, hubby dear, I've been kissing Rudolph Valentino on the mouth all day long.' How'd you like that, Doc?"

"I'd say it would depend on whether Rudolph Valentino was eating garlic that day," Dr. Youngblood said. "I wouldn't want my wife to smell like garlic when she got home."

"Oh, Doc. You can't be serious about nothing but cutting people's arms off and having babies," Bessie May said. "I just say every time I see a Rudolph Valentino moving picture, I say the country's going to the dogs, and he's a foreigner—and, Mr. Alexander, I don't see you running around kissing people on the street, and I say that means you're all right. If we got to have flesh-and-blood foreigners here in Bourbonville, I'm glad it's you and not Rudolph Valentino."

"Thank you very much," I said.

Daisy and I saw each other only at a distance. She no longer made any effort to talk with me, though she seemed to pass by in her father's car every time I walked down the street. She drove swiftly, throwing up dust and rocks and annoying people.

"That girl's going to kill herself," Darcy Coolidge said. "Driving like a demon and smoking in public! That's the worst thing yet. I've had several of my friends in the Clionian Club tell me they've seen Daisy Weaver smoking in public. What is the world coming to? Her poor mother! Her poor mother! I tell you, if the Colonel was still alive, he would go to see her father."

Virgil Weaver came to his office in the square almost every day, and Darcy Coolidge might have gone to see him herself. She did not.

Darcy Coolidge smoked a cigarette now and then, but always in the privacy of her own parlor. She would not dream of smoking in public, just as she would not dream of defecating on the courthouse lawn. There were some things that a woman kept to herself.

72

OCTOBER FLOWED on with milky blue skies and scarlet leaves on the oaks and gold on the maples, and farmers harvested corn and made shocks, and the air smelled pungent and clean, and the Germans fell back. The Balkans were crumbling. Ecstatic headlines.

In October news came that Joab's son Willy was wounded. The telegram arrived in the middle of the afternoon on an Indian-summer day when the morning papers had been filled with good news. People in Bourbon County were astounded.

"It's awful," Darcy Coolidge said. "The Germans about ready to quit, and the poor boy gets himself shot! There isn't any justice in the world." She was in a daze, and her voice broke. No false emotion there. The war was almost over. People should not be wounded now.

The telegram said his wounds were in the head and "serious." "That could mean anything," Dr. Youngblood said. He took me out to see Joab and his wife, Mary, and Willy's five sisters on the night the telegram came. Joab was tall and lean. He was Virgil's brother, and you could see the resemblance in the shape of the face, the eyes. But they were different. Joab was quiet, content to listen to others talk, and he laughed at Brian Ledbetter's stories. He was the only one of the six Weaver children to stay on the farm. Like the old man, he worked hard—up early in the morning, finding something to do all day long, to bed early. He always greeted me courteously but not effusively, and he wanted to be sure that I was well. Now he stood around trying to see that everyone was comfortable while people talked about Willy and wondered how badly he was hurt.

Neighbors gathered, and the older daughters made coffee and acted as if everyone who came to call was a guest who had to be taken care of. They were healthy, energetic girls. Joab's wife, Mary, was a plain country woman. Her eyes were red, but she would not sit down. "It's nice of you to come, Mr. Alexander," she said. "I see you walking, and it's good to see somebody looking around just to enjoy things and not to shoot the squirrels and the rabbits."

"I am very sorry about your son."

"It's in the hands of the Lord. I pray for him. You pray for him, too." Her voice broke, but she recovered.

"Barbara, see that Mr. Alexander has a cup of coffee. We have some cake, Mr. Alexander. Will you have a piece, Dr. Youngblood? It's so good of you to come."

"No, thank you," Dr. Youngblood said. "A cup of coffee will be good. When do you think you will hear something about Willy? Did the government say?"

"It was just a telegram. That nice young Armstrong boy brought it out here on his bicycle when it came to town. He wouldn't take nothing for his trouble. Such a nice boy. Blood will tell, you know. His father was such a nice man. Too bad he died so young, but Bonnie Armstrong seems to be raising those children just fine."

The conversation went on. The old man came and sat by the stove and drank coffee and was silent. He shook my hand warmly. Mrs. Ledbetter sat with her husband, her hands folded in her lap, and the old man reached out and held her hand.

"You was wounded in the head, wasn't you?" he said to me hopefully.

Every eye turned on me. "Yes," I said.

"You got over it," he said. It was not a question. Everybody nodded.

I thought of the headaches, how pain threaded its way up and exploded in my skull. I said, "Yes, I got over it."

"See there?" the old man said. I expected him to tell of somebody he knew who was wounded in the head at Gettysburg and recovered. He did not. He fell back into revery and silence and drank his coffee.

Virgil, Melvina, and Daisy came out. Daisy barely spoke to me. Melvina threw herself onto Mary and Joab and wept and told them how sorry she was. They seemed embarrassed. Mary comforted her. Grief was interspersed with food. "Have some chicken, Melvina. This was brought by Mrs. Shanks, and it's just *so* good. Won't you have a little coffee? We got more coffee pots around here than Carter has pills. This lemon pie melts in your mouth."

"Oh, Mary," Melvina sobbed. "You're so *brave!*" Melvina burst into a renewed flood of tears.

Virgil greeted me with a vague air of preoccupation. "Did you see many head wounds during the war?" he said.

"He was shot in the head hisself," Brian Ledbetter said impatiently.

"Oh yes," Virgil said. "I forgot."

"It's all right," I said.

Daisy talked warmly with everyone except me. She seemed almost beside herself with good cheer.

Joab stayed outside with the men. Dr. Youngblood and I went out, and we stood in a murmurous conversation, Dr. Youngblood puffing his pipe, giving laconic answers to questions about head injuries.

Douglas Kinlaw drove up in his car and greeted us in his shy and quiet way. More and more people came, all of them bringing food, and by the time Dr. Youngblood and I left, people were there for a long night together, and somebody had built a fire outside, and men were standing around it warming their hands and talking in low voices. I had been in Bourbonville a year.

"It's not a bad county," Dr. Youngblood said as we were driving back. "Not a bad place to make a life."

"It is not my home," I said.

Dr. Youngblood was silent to that.

Two weeks later Joab and Mary got a letter from Jim Ed saying that Willy was blind.

73

IN NOVEMBER the Armistice came. The news that the war would end came down by telegram on Sunday evening—that on the next day, Monday, November 11, 1918, firing would cease on the Western Front. Newspaper extras came down on the train from Knoxville. Bourbonvillians devoured them.

Church bells rang until far into the night. People poured into the streets, though it was a dull, drizzly evening with more than a twitch of winter cold in the air. The great steam whistle at the car works blew again and again. You could hear it for miles. Jubilant people shook my hand. "It's over," they said. "You must be glad."

On Monday morning, everything stopped. The wheel foundry did not make a heat. Douglas Kinlaw, Dale Farmer, and I walked through a milling, cheerful crowd. Everybody wanted to shake hands—a Te Deum of touching.

"It's the beginning of the American century," Dale Farmer gushed. "If you want to get rich, buy stock in American business. I'm putting everything I can beg, borrow, or steal into stocks. There's no way but up. I can give you some dandy tips."

He confided that Pinkerton would be moving to Washington. "I'll take over, of course. Don't worry, my young friend. I'll take good care of you."

"I'll be going home," I said.

"Oh, now," Douglas Kinlaw said, sincerely surprised.

"He keeps saying he wants to go home," Dale Farmer said. "What are we going to do with him? The boy's got a good life here, and he wants to go home. This *is* his home now!"

"I guess you have only one home," Douglas Kinlaw said. "I just hate to see you go."

I thought of my father and wondered where he was. Walking in some town square in Alabama right now, savoring the damp smell of autumn, savoring the victory? Where was he? The thought banged in my head and went away. Dead, I thought. He would have tried to get in touch with me if he were alive. I thought of my mother sometimes and wept for her. I sent her money. Hers was the only love I had in the world.

People made bonfires with fallen leaves. The smoke rose in blue clouds and drifted through town. I smell leaves burning to this day and think of Armistice Day, 1918—children roaming about, screaming with happiness for the unexpected holiday, people standing in doorways, and greetings everywhere.

Shaw and Pinkerton walked through the crowd, shaking hands. Shaw looked absurd in his little derby hat, his mask of dignity pierced at the mouth by his emotionless smile. His belly seemed grander than ever. Nothing mattered to me. I would be going home where I belonged, to the clear light, the wild highlands of Greece, to the horizon filled with sea.

For the first time in memory crowds of black men came into the square on a weekday morning. Somebody called for a spiritual, and molders' helpers, wheel jockeys, lifters and haulers sang on the courthouse lawn: "Burden down, Lord, burden down, Lord, when I lay my burden down. . . ." Everybody hushed and listened. The bells were ringing in all the churches in town, an irregular, clangorous hymn of jubilation, distant, dissonant, and pounding. But here were male voices singing in rolling cadences, strong and harmonious and constant—exuberantly orderly—and sounding together like the choirs that sang at Creation in celebration of the unvarying firmament that God spoke into being out of chaos and boiling darkness.

When the singing died away, white preachers took turns standing on a flatbed wagon, praising God for victory. The noise from the crowd started up again, and the preachers hollered in waves of voices, and nobody paid any attention to what they were saying, but the preachers preached on anyway.

A cold sun broke through the overcast, and I saw Guy standing in the crowd, still and unmoved amidst the ceaseless motion, wearing his green velvet vest. A large silk cravat encircled his starched collar. He wore his black tails, and he held a top hat in one hand. With the other he gestured and said something to me. I could not hear him. I blinked and he was gone. Our war was over.

74

TWO WEEKS AFTER the Armistice, the telegram came from the War Department announcing that D.B. was dead.

It arrived in the afternoon. I learned of it as Dale Farmer and I walked into the square at quitting time. The day was raw and overcast. A crowd stood before the house where Virgil kept his office. D.B. had been killed on the last morning of the war.

Dub Boling, the daytime telegrapher, took the message, read what his fingers had automatically written in response to the clicking of the key, put on his coat, and went to see Dr. Youngblood. He found him cleaning out the gashed thumb of a farmer named Cedric Minge who had cut himself to the bone while sharpening a saw. "It's Virgil's boy," Dub said.

Dr. Youngblood looked at the telegram, said not a word, took a deep breath, and finished sewing up Cedric Minge's thumb. He went into the waiting room and told everybody he had to go out. He did not know when he would be back. He took the telegram and walked down to Virgil's office. He forgot to put on his coat.

Virgil was studying a New York newspaper when Dr. Youngblood came through the door. "What the hell are you doing down here on a day like this without your coat? What are you going to do if you catch pneumonia?" Dr. Youngblood could not speak. Virgil's smile faded; he saw the telegram, and he understood.

Within an hour the town knew, and the news spread into the county. Douglas Kinlaw came down and pushed his way through the crowd and went inside. The crowd waited. The sky threatened snow, and people stamped their feet and smoked or chewed and murmured to each other. While Dale Farmer and I stood there, Dr. Youngblood and Douglas Kinlaw and Virgil came out. Men took off their hats, and a vast silence fell. You could hear the wind breathing in the leafless trees.

They walked to Virgil's car, parked at a slant against the side of the street. The crowd folded back to let them pass. Virgil's eyes were red. He started to the front of his Model T to crank the engine. A young man in work clothes rushed to take the crank and did the job for him. Virgil's face was as blank as death. When the engine spun to life, he muttered,

"Thank you." The young man touched his hand to his forehead, as if he had seen pictures in the papers of soldiers saluting. Virgil got behind the wheel of his car and put it in reverse, Dr. Youngblood hauled himself up beside him, Douglas Kinlaw climbed into the backseat, and they drove away to Virgil's house.

By that time people had rushed out to tell Melvina. Preacher Ware got there first. He had been leaving the barbershop, freshly shaved and reeking of pomade, when somebody told him. Melvina was one of his most faithful members. He climbed into his new Chevrolet and drove out to Weaver Hill to comfort her. He was the first to speak to Melvina and Daisy, the first to don the appropriately solemn expression that shouted "death" as soon as he got out of the car, the first to tell them that D.B.'s death was the will of God.

He was on the point of clearing his large, fat throat to pray over them when Daisy cursed him and his mother and the foul act of intercourse that had brought him into the cur's litter where he had been born in slime and puke. When he said, "See here, young lady," Daisy went screaming into the kitchen announcing that she was going to get a butcher knife and hack him to death.

He decided that she was sincere. Everybody knew that Preacher Ware wanted to become a bishop. He retreated with indecorous speed.

Others arrived. Some of the women of Bourbon County went in to sit with Melvina, and they were in the living room when Virgil and Dr. Youngblood drove up. The yard was by then filled with men standing speechless and bundled against the hard chill, and it was starting to snow—an early, November snow with tiny flakes spitting out of the gray sky, and it would keep falling, and it would be deep by seven o'clock. The men stamped their feet and smoked and chewed, coat collars turned up, snow on their shoulders and on their hats, their faces red with frost, wearing the expressions they reserved for funerals. They took off their hats and cupped their cigarettes and held them behind them when Virgil and Dr. Youngblood and Douglas Kinlaw got down out of Virgil's car, and some of them murmured expressions of sympathy. Most of them remained silent. Virgil nodded vaguely at them, and he went into the house.

The house was filled with women with eyes red from weeping and with the silence that had fallen over the world. Melvina was sitting in the living room. Her face was swollen and flushed. When Virgil came in, she did not get out of her chair. The women of Bourbon County parted, and Virgil and his wife looked at each other across a short aisle opened by female bodies. For a moment the silence held. Then Melvina spoke.

"It's your fault," she cried, choking with rage. "If you had not been a coward, our boy would not have died."

75

JANUARY CAME on cold. Coal smoke hung over Bourbonville. You could put on a clean shirt in the morning and by afternoon it was black inside the collar. You could wipe a damp cloth across a table and it came away black. We had intermittent snow. It did not stay on the ground long. When it fell, Bourbonville seemed almost beautiful, the shapes rounded and muted and the light brilliant and the town buried underneath the brilliance. People went around bundled up and blowing steam and talking about the weather. They wondered when the first boys from the county would come home from the war. They wondered if the Bolsheviks were going to win in Russia. Preachers said Lenin was the Antichrist.

A train hanging with icicles brought Captain John S. Tomlinson, D.B.'s commanding officer, to Bourbonville. He came because D.B. was news all over America. The War Department had to make a gesture for a Congressional Medal of Honor winner killed on the last day of the war.

Bourbonville declared a memorial day, and stores closed with a printed sign pasted on the doors: "Closed in Memory of D. B. Weaver, the Fighting Volunteer." Pinkerton, grim and sad, shut down the car works. He and Shaw wore black arm bands and black neckties and stood close to the captain. They are in all the photographs. You might have thought Pinkerton was D.B.'s father. Emotions are not simple.

Hundreds of us were there when Captain Tomlinson in full-dress uniform and his United States Army overcoat and polished brown boots stepped down off the train at 2:30 in the afternoon. The captain was rawboned and boyish, with a red farmer's face, awkward, with clear blue eyes and an expression of earnest innocence that made him look like a child untempted by evil. He was followed by an entourage of reporters.

At first I barely noticed the woman reporter who stepped down from the train and looked at Bourbonville and the crowd. She was a little older than I. She wore a long gray coat with a fur collar that came up high around her neck, a hat with a wide brim pulled down low over her eyes, and feminine boots. Under the hat her blond hair was done up in a bun at the back of her neck. My attention did linger on her a moment; I saw how blue and direct her eyes were. But I was looking at the captain, who was greeting Douglas Kinlaw and Sheriff Hardison and shaking hands in an attitude of official grief.

Unexpectedly she turned up at my elbow. She asked my name and wrote it down in a little notebook and asked where I was from, and when I said

Belgium, she wrote that down, too, and with a certain satisfaction told me that she knew I was not from Bourbonville. "I'm good at fitting people in," she said. "I want to talk to you."

There was no time then, because Captain Tomlinson, led by Douglas Kinlaw, went up the steps to a little porch on one side of the courthouse and made a speech.

Captain Tomlinson was thirty-one, from Kansas. Later the woman reporter told me that he had never been out of Kansas before he went to war. Standing on the little side porch above the winter-dead grass beneath the naked limbs of the trees, he made an oration, his breath steaming in the hard winter air. Ted Devlin took it down in shorthand and published it in the *Bourbonville News*, and I have a withering copy here on the kitchen table before me tonight. The captain's earnest young face, darkened by the bill of his military cap and blurred by the millions of dots that compose the engraving, looks out at me. D.B.'s face is next to it, bareheaded, eyes looking directly at the camera, his military collar high and stiff, his boy's face fixed in the immemorial calm of a soldier posing for the photographer who will record his bravery before death.

"That boy was the hardest fighter I ever saw in the war," Captain Tomlinson said, his voice high and thin in the open air. "We had to drag him back sometimes. Any time your normal soldier hears a Hun machine gun open up, his first thought is this: 'How can I save my hide?' But not Corporal Weaver. No siree bob! When Corporal Weaver heard a machine gun, he said, 'How can I kill that Hun?'

"Now on the last morning of the war, we were ordered to send out patrols right up until eleven o'clock. That was when the Armistice was to take effect, you know. Our generals thought we had to have patrols because the Hun is so devilish fiendish, you see. Us soldiers in the trenches, we thought all this Armistice business might be hogwash. The Hun might be trying to rock us to sleep and *wham*—he might have socked us with one last offensive. Roll up our flanks. Break through. Be in Paris before we could say Jack Robinson. Strike us out in the last of the ninth. We had to stay awake. Keep on our toes. Send out patrols. Patrols are the eyes of the army."

It struck me that the captain was acting in a play. He had been brave. He had obeyed orders at the risk of his life. But he talked as though he were reading a script—badly. Saying the expected thing, the thing he wanted to believe, not only about D.B. but about himself, the war, the United States, life and death.

"I asked for volunteers. Corporal Weaver was the first man to step forward. I said to him, I said, 'Looky here, Corporal. You've done enough for this war. You've done enough for ten men. You've earned the right to let somebody else take the last patrol. You deserve to go back to your mamma and your daddy in one piece.' Now that boy really did admire his daddy.

Talked about him all the time. Said he wanted to make his daddy proud of him more than he wanted anything in the world. That was why he volunteered, he said. He said his daddy wouldn't expect nothing else. Well now, I told him he'd done enough to make a thousand daddies proud. I told him he couldn't go on that patrol. I put my foot down. I promise you I did.

"Well now, friends. You'd have thought I'd accused him of being a coward. He jumped at me with a look in his eyes that meant business, I'll tell you. He told me I had to let him go, or he'd hate me the rest of his life. I owed him this one last chance, he said. He carried on like a . . . Well, if I'd told him he couldn't go, he'd have gone anyway. So I gave in to him. Maybe it was his time. If it's your time, you have to go. It's all God's will, my friends.

"You've read all about it in the papers. He was between the lines with his patrol, and a Hun sniper dropped him. One bullet through the heart. He never knew what hit him. For a few minutes all hell broke loose, if you'll pardon my French. The patrol had to leave the body behind and get out of there. I reckon they were in the very last engagement of the Great War.

"The Armistice came along at eleven o'clock. Two Hun stretcher bearers came over to our lines bringing back Corporal Weaver's body. There wasn't much blood. They'd put a blanket over him, and he looked like he was asleep. We all stood there and admired him. He looked so peaceful, so handsome. One of the Huns who brought him in took off his helmet and bowed his head and said, *'Schönes Kind, schönes Kind!'* That's Hun talk for 'Beautiful child, beautiful child.' He was an old geezer with a gray mustache. At the end the Huns were throwing old men and children at us. They didn't have any young men left, I guess. We stood there, the Huns and us, and we just looked at him."

At that moment Captain Tomlinson's flat Kansas voice broke. "I tell you the truth. His face was so beautiful, so innocent, that I'm sure as I'm standing here under these trees that the angels carried Corporal Weaver's soul away. I know he's with Jesus, my friends. I hope to be with him there someday with our Lord. I hope we'll be sending out patrols all over heaven, looking for you, my friends. Looking to lead you back to the heavenly lines and to safety in Jesus Christ forever more."

The captain cried then. Ted Devlin was standing near me, taking it all down, his head bowed studiously over his note pad, but he muttered out of the side of his mouth, "Jesus fucking Christ! I can't believe this asshole." Most of the people in the audience cried with the captain. Pinkerton's eyes were moist. Pinkerton started the clapping. It became a thunder of applause.

Virgil Weaver did not see the captain. When he got the telegram telling him that Captain Tomlinson was coming down on the afternoon train, Virgil drove up to Hub Delaney's and got very drunk and sat in Hub's cabin for three days. Dr. Youngblood went up to see him and came back looking solemn and sad. "Hub's got cancer," he said. "He can't control his bowels."

"Cancer?" I said. The word was death.

"He's had it awhile. He didn't tell me. He thought it would stop."

"Could you have done something?" I said.

"Probably not," Dr. Youngblood said.

The woman reporter took notes on Captain Tomlinson's speech. "What did you think of it?" she asked me.

"I suppose it means that D.B. Weaver was a very brave young man."

"Or a fool? I can't write that, of course. But don't you think what he did was foolish? And please don't respond with a bromide like 'Well, young woman, war is very foolish.' "

"I was about to say just that," I said.

"Surely you can do better than that," she said.

"I have said everything I have to say," I said.

"Have I offended you?" she said.

"Not at all," I said. "I do not know what to say about the captain. I do not know what to say about D.B."

"Would you have done what he did?"

"No," I said.

"Well, it's queer. That's all I can say. The patrols are queer. Why didn't they wait till eleven o'clock? It seems so stupid."

I opened my mouth and shut it again. "You were about to say that war is stupid," she said.

"Yes," I said with a smile.

"I'm glad the war's over," she said. "It was about to ruin language."

"Would you like a cigarette?" I said.

"Oh no," she said. "I don't smoke. My mother would have a fit if I came in smelling of tobacco. It's a terrible habit, you know. Tobacco is a filthy weed. Do you think I can talk with Virgil Weaver and—what's his wife's name?"

"Melvina," I said. "I do not think so."

"I'm supposed to get the family angle on this thing. You know, a headline for the women's page. 'Dead Soldier's Mother Gives Recipe for Apple Pie.' . . . My name is Mary Eugenia Curry."

"I am very pleased to meet you, Miss Curry," I said. We did not shake hands. I bowed slightly to her.

"Where is Virgil Weaver?"

"I do not know," I said.

"You do know," she said. "You won't tell me. I can tell when people are lying," she said.

I laughed. "That is a great talent," I said.

"I can see you are not going to talk to me," she said, a little sadly.

"I am sorry," I said.

"So am I," she said. "You could help me."

She went out to see Melvina, but Melvina would not come out of the house. Captain Tomlinson came to the door and knocked with maybe half of Bourbon County trailing behind him and the woman reporter closer than anybody else and a photographer behind her with a huge box of a camera on a tripod to "shoot" Melvina, as he said somewhat indelicately. A woman later found to be Melvina's sister, the one from Chattanooga, answered the door and told the captain to go away.

Captain Tomlinson apologized to everyone he could find for having offended Mrs. Weaver, and later that day nearly everybody, including Captain Tomlinson, went back to Knoxville on the local train. A certain dull resentment spread in Bourbonville because the Weaver family had not done better with the press.

"People were just trying to be nice to them," Dale Farmer said. "They'll make the whole world think Bourbonville is a crude and impolite place."

76

DR. YOUNGBLOOD was losing his hair. He let it grow long on the sides and combed it over the top of his head to hide the baldness. His large eyes looked red and doleful, and his cheeks sagged. He was always tired. He told me what was happening in the Weaver household.

Melvina Weaver now slept in D.B.'s room. She gathered pictures of him and lined them up on tables and chairs around the bed. She hung some on the wall and put others on tables. She slept with twenty pairs of his eyes looking at her. She awoke to a panorama of his faces, from babyhood to the Congressional Medal of Honor—given after his death. She would not let Virgil enter the room. "This is his shrine," she cried. "You would profane it."

Melvina's sister Beatrice (which everyone pronounced "BeACTrice") came up from Chattanooga in February, and the two women were closeted for days. Dr. Youngblood called on them, although they had not sent for him. "It is my duty," he said. They received him, and Melvina talked. I am not sure he told me everything she said. He and Beatrice talked Melvina into going off to Chattanooga for a rest. Beatrice was the wife of a preacher, and they lived in a parsonage down there.

Melvina left the door to the bedroom locked. The night after she departed Virgil kicked the door down. He made a fire in the fireplace and burned all the photographs of his son. Daisy told us everything. She came to sit with us the next night and sobbed out the story, detail by bitter detail.

D.B. had been a methodical sort. He had kept everything—his examinations, his prizes from school, his letters. The papers were bundled by subjects—his Latin exercises, his algebra, his plane geometry, the botany, the French lessons, the compositions in rhetoric, the orations from American history. Daisy had heard him give these orations. "He could have been a great preacher," she said, the tears running down her cheeks. All the bundles were neatly tied together with flat red ribbon.

"He wanted to keep everything because people said high school was the happiest time in anybody's life," Daisy said. D.B. had intended to keep his memories in perfect order and never forget anything.

Virgil threw the bundles into the fire. He burned D.B.'s clothes in the furnace, heaping them up with coal to make the fire hot enough to consume everything.

"It was all ashes," she said, sobbing. "Daddy washed up, and he looked at me with an expression on his face that . . . I can't describe it."

"Was he angry?" Dr. Youngblood said.

"No, he was *peaceful*. That was the awful thing."

A week later Melvina came home and went up to the shrine and found an empty room. Virgil had given away D.B.'s furniture. He had had painters in to do the walls. Even the curtains were gone, and the closet was empty. He had a carpenter hang a new door. Melvina put her hands over her eyes and screamed. Daisy tried to console her, but Melvina would not be consoled.

She ran down to the living room, where Virgil stood silently waiting for her. She beat at him, but he seized her hands and held her. She tore herself away and flung herself on the floor, beating the rug with her fists.

"What have you done? What have you done?" she cried.

"I have exorcised a demon," Virgil said. "I have cast out the spirit of a dead man, a son who will not come to us again."

Melvina cried until she could not cry anymore. Her bags were still packed. She picked them up and hurried them out to the car, and she made Daisy drive her to the depot. She sat in the depot, in the white waiting room, for hours until the next train to Chattanooga, and she got on it and never set foot in Bourbonville again. She never saw Virgil again, either.

Virgil sat in the house for two days. Daisy made him dinner and supper, but he did not eat or drink anything. "I did not see him take a drink of water in all that time," she said. It was cold outside, but it did not snow. The skies were clear and bright like tempered steel. Dr. Youngblood went up to see him and came back troubled. Daisy said, "He just sits there. Hour after hour he just sits there."

Then one night she came into Dr. Youngblood's sitting room and collapsed on the old leather sofa before the fire. "I need a drink of whiskey," she said.

Dr. Youngblood gave her the whiskey. She drank it and shook her head.

She was in a daze. "I'm going to leave all this," she said. "Daddy is going to sell his office. He is going to move away from Bourbonville. He is going to California. I'm going to go with him. California. Think of that. Los Angeles, California."

77

PINKERTON FELT REMORSE. "I feel like it's my fault," he said to me. "If I hadn't been drunk that day, hell! I didn't mean to say those things. The boy was there, and I was drunk and mad, and I wanted to hurt Virgil. I didn't want to kill the boy. You don't know what you're doing sometimes. You don't figure a child is going to grow up. That's what you never figure."

"I'll be leaving Bourbonville now," he said. "Virgil's going to be leaving Bourbonville, too. We both should have left here long ago. This shitty little town poisoned both of us. It's poisoned me; it's poisoned poor Eula; it's poisoned Virgil. If Eula and me had gone to Washington, she'd have had different friends, and I'd have had friends like Dick Shaw. Important folks. Folks that can do something for you. That's all behind me now. I'm not going to stay here any longer than it takes the damned railroad folks to get things straightened out, and then I'm going to Washington. I should have gone long ago. Maybe that boy would still be alive if he hadn't been trying to prove that I was wrong about his daddy. I've never been so sorry for anything in my life."

None of this concerned me. I planned to return to Greece in the late summer of 1919, when I would have money saved for my passage and a little laid by for a new start in the homeland. I wanted no more of America. I daydreamed of Greece and the magical light, and I thought of tramping Sundays along the barren highlands of Thessaly, talking to Guy and Bernal, perhaps Stephanos, too. Everything would be peaceful in Greece. I would find some work; there had to be some work. Perhaps I could devise a way to finish university in Greece.

The rumor that Pinkerton was moving to Washington swirled through town. Ted Devlin, smoking his perpetual cigarette—and coughing his perpetual cough—his rough gray hair unkempt and his ruddy Irish face huge with interest, told me, "Let me know as soon as the official date for his leaving is fixed up," he said. "He's an asshole, but he happens to be the asshole that made this town. I guess that means the town's a piece of shit. What the hell. When he leaves, I'll do him up good." Ted Devlin had a wonderful ironic laugh.

Dale Farmer quizzed me on our morning hike to work. "What's the Captain said to you?" he said eagerly.

"He has not said anything to me," I said.

"You don't have to be so coy," Dale Farmer said with a rotund little laugh. "Everybody knows how much he likes you. You're like a son to him. I thought he might give you a hint about when he's going to leave."

"No, he has not told me anything," I said.

"Don't you worry now," Dale Farmer said, becoming expansive. "When he leaves, I'll take care of you. You don't have a thing to fear from your good friend Dale Farmer. Bourbonville needs a handsome young man like you around. You do look like Rudolph Valentino, you know. Everybody says it. Oh, if you only had a sweetheart. I'm going to run this place like a good ship, and there's a place for you on my crew. The Captain's a great man. You understand I'm not saying one word against him. But I'm going to be good for the car works, and I'll be good to you, too."

Dick Shaw took on stature in people's minds. No matter how preposterous a man may be, he gains respect when others imagine that he has authority. Shaw seemed to be the key to everything. It was as if Pinkerton, having placed his trust in Dick Shaw, had purveyed his faith to the town and the county so that everyone shared it and believed that Dick Shaw was one of the great men of industrial history. Shaw became more monumentally fat, as if he recognized the confidence placed in him and felt that he ought to be a bigger man so there would be more of him to appreciate. He continued to stand painfully straight and to thrust his jaw out when he talked so that he seemed to be in charge of all he surveyed. He was the agency to translate Pinkerton to the heavenly Jerusalem, and everyone waited for a word from his lips, a word with the power of prophecy and the gift of creation.

Lacking any useful work to do, Shaw frequently stopped by the laboratory to talk about himself. "I'm not a man to turn my back on my mistakes," he said. "It's useless to try to change old Dick Shaw. Lord knows I've tried to change him! But old Dick Shaw will be what he is! If you want la-di-da stuff and nonsense, you have to find somebody else besides plain old Dick Shaw to give it to you. He's as honest as a shovel, Dick Shaw is. If you want flattery, Dick Shaw won't give it to you. Dick Shaw will give you *compliments,* but only if you *deserve* compliments, my friend. If you don't like what he says, well, you can go to the devil. It'll be a pity, because you won't *find* a friend as loyal as old Dick Shaw. Dick Shaw ain't never seen the inside of a college, and he's proud of it. Dick Shaw is one of the common people, Dick Shaw is. The kind that made America great."

He shook his large head in sadness. "But that's not what this old world wants. Take heed, my friend. You pay a price for being honest. Old Dick Shaw's paid that price. You see him now in his glory. It ain't always been that way. But through thick and thin, Dick Shaw's always been plain old Dick Shaw."

78

ONE DAY in the third week of March 1919, when we had heavy rain at dawn and mild sunshine by nine o'clock, Pinkerton rushed into the laboratory about nine-thirty in the morning, breathless and wildly excited. "Dick Shaw has asked to see me at ten," he cried. "He says he wants a *formal* appointment because he has something formal to say to me. This is it! This is the job in Washington! He's going to offer me the job in Washington!"

"I hope that it is so," I murmured. "If that is what you want."

"Well, of course it's what I want, you fool!" he said, black rage rolling suddenly across his face. "What the hell do you think I want!" I looked at him apprehensively.

The ecstasy returned, and he seized both my hands. "I'm sorry," he said. "I apologize. I have sworn never to get mad again. I know what you mean to say to me. I'll be leaving a place that's been my home. But I was meant for more than this. It's going to be such a great thing for Eula, too. Eula, she always thought God taken our child away because I knocked her up on a church bench before we got married. Did I ever tell you about that? I don't mean while church was going on, you understand. I ain't no goddamn animal, and you can bet your life you'd never see Eula letting me pull her drawers down in front of no preacher and a house full of folks singing hymns. I mean, I knowed she was religious, and we was out riding in my buggy on a Saturday night, coming home from some damned party, and I got her into one of them country churches that don't never lock their doors up because I told her I wanted to meditate a minute, and I got to kissing her and feeling her, and I got her so hot she let me do it to her. God, you know, there ain't nothing in the world like putting it to a woman that's out of control.

"Tell you the truth, Paul Alexander. You get a religious woman's drawers off, and she'll take you from Christmas to Easter so fast you'll think Jesus invented the express train. Afterwards she found out she was pregnant, and she cried and took on something awful. I done the right thing. I made her an honest woman. By God, she was the beautifulest woman you ever seen in your life, but when the baby died, she turned into a goddamn religious fanatic. I figured if I get her up into Washington City, she ain't going to be that way no more. They'll be so much for us to do—going to plays and concerts and taking long walks by all the historic buildings and by the river and being with all them smart people. I'll have her back like she used to be, by God. You come and see us, Alexander. You'll be my guest."

"I should not hear such things, Mr. Pinkerton."

Pinkerton laughed. "Why the hell not? You're family, Alexander. My boy died, and here you are, the kind of boy I could have wanted and just about the same age. I've got plans for you. Listen, I want you to be there in Washington with me some of these days. You and me, we're going to work together."

"I do not want to go to Washington," I said. "I want to go home."

"Don't talk like a woman!" he cried. "What have you got waiting for you in the old country? A Bolshevik revolution? You listen to me. In three years the goddamned Bolsheviks will own everything from Moscow to the Atlantic Ocean, and they're going to shut down all the churches and put the preachers up against a wall and shoot them, and they won't let anybody own so much as a dog or a set of long-handle underwear. It's going to be the goddamn Dark Ages all over again, only this time it's going to be Lenin instead of the nun-fucking Pope. You won't have paper to wipe your ass on back where you come from. Europe's used up like an empty can of beans. You've got something here. I'm going to see to it that you get more. You've got a hand on the lowest branches of the goddamned tree of life, and the only thing for a *man* to do is climb! Tear out your fingernails, by God. But grit your teeth and climb!"

He took me by the arm. "Come on," he said. "You're my best friend. I want you to be with me when Dick Shaw comes in and offers me the job in Washington."

"No," I said. "No, I am sure Mr. Shaw wants a private meeting. I should not be there."

"Come on," Pinkerton said softly, pulling me towards the door. "You're like my son. I want you to see it."

79

So I was in Pinkerton's office, smoking one cigarette after another, when Dick Shaw swaggered in. Pinkerton, smoking an expensive cigar, leaped up to meet him, extending his hand in a big American motion to clasp Dick Shaw's. Shaw was wearing a cheap new suit that did not fit. He had buckled the belt of his trousers under the mighty overhang of his belly. His face seemed dangerously red—perhaps because the cruel belt had squeezed so much blood to his head. It struck me that he had bought the suit for this moment. It was made of coarse brown wool, and he was sweating.

He greeted me uncomfortably. He had no idea why I was there. When he saw that Pinkerton wanted me there, he shook hands with me with false cordiality and managed to give me a significant look and a grin, as if he and I shared some secret understanding.

He sat down in one of Pinkerton's leather chairs, carefully crossed his fat legs, accepted the cigar that Pinkerton offered him, accepted also the light that Pinkerton came around the desk to give, took a couple of deep puffs, removed the cigar from his mouth and inspected the burning end of it and nodded gravely over the fineness of the smoke, cleared his throat, looked with fleeting anxiety at me, cleared his throat again, and asked Pinkerton for a job.

Pinkerton's world fell like the walls of Jericho, roiling in clouds of dust and smoke and fire.

Pinkerton had been powerful as a youth, and he was still strong. In that moment he became a Cyclops flinging death around the cave where he roared in blind agony. He did what no humane person should ever do to another: he told Dick Shaw exactly what he thought of him. I did not realize until then that some lower and perhaps unconscious or subconscious awareness in Moreland Pinkerton had seen Dick Shaw more clearly than I had supposed. Or perhaps, in that catastrophic revelation, Pinkerton saw Shaw for the first time as all of us at the great day of judgment may see God and ourselves and all history in blinding clarity.

Pinkerton stood up, the cigar fallen from his lips and alive on the desk, scorching the polished cherry wood and releasing a stench of burning paint and wood. He leaned onto his knotted fists, which rested on the desktop. The veins in his face swelled and turned purple. He shouted about Shaw's belly and how Shaw resembled a swollen bag of pig shit shaped like a man but that, in bursting, would put enough raw excrement in the Tennessee River to kill fish in Chattanooga a hundred miles downstream. Pinkerton discussed Shaw's cowlike face, his cocklike arrogance, his chicken brain. He mimicked Shaw's affected voice and observed that Shaw's digestive tract was so marvelously arranged that he farted through his mouth and called it speech.

I tried to flee, but Pinkerton shouted me back into my chair with a horrible curse and a threat of violence.

Shaw was dumbfounded. He sat there for a moment, his cigar forgotten in his mouth. Somehow the cigar disappeared shortly. I wondered afterwards if he had swallowed it. He staggered to his feet and tried to speak, his face flaming with outrage. He had his grievances against Pinkerton, and in some mad faith in fair play, he supposed it was now his turn to recite them. "You're a crazy drunk," he shouted. "I'll report you in Washington, and they'll come down here and put you in a straitjacket, and I'll come to the asylum every Sunday afternoon to spit in your face."

He could not imagine, I believe, that Pinkerton would do anything but shout back at him, and I think Shaw supposed that he would whirl and depart in a flourish of trumpets while Pinkerton fumed ineffectually behind him, defeated. This was Shaw's second mistake of the morning. It was almost fatal.

For like some predatory beast from our worst nightmares, Pinkerton lunged around the desk, crouched over, his hands become raised claws, and made for Shaw, intending, I think, to tear him to pieces. "Don't you touch me," Shaw cried, his voice becoming a falsetto squeal. "I'll sue. I swear to God I'll sue. Keep back! Keep back!" He backed away, circling the desk but Pinkerton stalked him. Shaw backed up more, keeping the desk between himself and Pinkerton, Pinkerton coming after him one step at a time, wearing a tiger's grin, his big hands up. Both men had stopped talking. Shaw's thick lower lip trembled. Once he looked beseechingly at me. I stood up, but I was frozen at my chair. I smelled Shaw's terror. Pinkerton came on. Shaw whimpered—a low, whining cry deep in the throat, like a whipped dog about to be killed. By that time he had backed all the way around the desk, and he looked at the frosted glass door that opened into the outer office, and he bolted for it, flinging a chair in front of Pinkerton to slow him down.

Pinkerton brushed the chair aside and leaped for him, and as Shaw arrived at the door, Pinkerton kicked him—a hard, precisely aimed kick that caught Shaw in the middle of the lower part of his buttocks with such force that I could swear that he was lifted slightly off the ground. Shaw screamed with pain. He suffered agonies from hemorrhoids and was always on the lookout for a salve that would cure them. Once he had asked me to mix something up for him. I declined. I heard Guy whispering to me to mix up something with sulphuric acid in it and to tell Shaw to apply it liberally to his nether parts. Now Shaw crashed against the door, and the frosted glass panel gave way and fell in shards to the floor, and he rushed through to the other side, where he blundered into a desk that must have bruised him terribly, though it kept him from falling. If he had fallen there, I think, Pinkerton would have killed him.

He turned briefly, his eyes imploring Pinkerton to stop his assault. There was no mercy in Pinkerton then. Three bookkeepers, a secretary, a payroll clerk, a black janitor named Harvey, and a ghastly Dale Farmer looked on in stupefaction. Shaw cried something—an inarticulate combination of scream and appeal, perhaps a plea to bear witness to the injustice of the world.

In the wink of time that any half-formed thoughts of speech may have flickered through Shaw's brain, Pinkerton kicked him again. He fled through the office, knocking over chairs, scattering papers, shoving people aside, making for the outside door and sunshine and open air and escape. We followed, mesmerized with horror.

The outer door opened onto three wooden steps that descended to the oval driveway between the brass foundry and the wheel foundry. The door, by some carpenter's mistake, opened inward. As Shaw first tried to push it out and then fought to pull it back, Pinkerton kicked him again. As he wrestled the door open and squeezed through it, Pinkerton kicked him yet a fourth time. Shaw was off balance, and with this last blow expertly delivered to his anus, he lost his footing completely and toppled through the air like a barrel falling off a wagon. He fell on his face in the brown mud of a puddle left from the hard morning rain.

He gave up. He knew that he was a dead man, that he could no longer flee his destiny. He rolled over in the mud and sat up, uncaring about his ruined suit, uncaring about the mud, weeping with terror and shame, and probably trying to recite some childhood prayer to prepare himself to meet God, and he looked up at Moreland Pinkerton expecting (I believe) to see a sword or a pistol and to meet death.

Pinkerton had no sword or pistol, and he did not murder Dick Shaw. He did deliberately unbutton his own trousers, and just as deliberately, he urinated on him. I do not think Shaw understood what was happening. He did not lift his hands. He sat gaping upward, his mouth open, the urine falling full in his face, washing the mud off it in chunks, and he did not even shut his eyes. He sat there blinking slowly, the yellow fluid streaming into his dazed face, and once he ran his heavy tongue over his lips as if in blank curiosity at an ammoniac taste he had never known before.

Pinkerton had a copious bladder that was at the moment remarkably full from his steady, nervous drinking of morning coffee. He stood there holding his penis with both hands, directing the stream for maximum effect, and looking as calm as a man pissing in a woods. At last he finished. Very deliberately he came down to the lowest step and shook the last drops off onto Shaw's uplifted, uncomprehending face. Then he slowly buttoned his trousers and went back to the top step, where we had gathered like birds on a wire, and he paused a moment to make a final comment before he returned to his office.

"The answer," he said, "is no."

80

FOR A WHILE the talk around the boardinghouse table dwelled on Pinkerton as it might have hung on some great disaster—the sinking of the *Titanic* or the San Francisco earthquake. "I think it's time he stepped down," Darcy Coolidge said. "He's worked long enough. Hard enough. It's time he retired."

Dale Farmer nodded gravely and cleared his throat. "It is disturbing," he muttered. "The man has been a great leader. He's given Bourbonville a place in the sun. He's a remarkable man. But perhaps . . . Well, it isn't for me to say, of course." He swallowed his thoughts and looked bleak.

After Dick Shaw vanished from Bourbonville, Pinkerton started drinking heavily again. We saw him drunk at mid-morning, his eyes hardly focused on anything. Dale Farmer found him unconscious once, sprawled over his desk in an alcoholic stupor. "I was afraid to leave him there, and I was afraid to try to wake him up," Dale Farmer said miserably. He weighed his two fears and left Pinkerton alone.

"He is going to kill himself," Dr. Youngblood said. "He is committing suicide."

People asked what I thought. I thought nothing. I was leaving Bourbonville. I thought already of the pleasure of the long sea voyage. Bourbonville was beginning to smother me. I knew so much about Pinkerton, so much about Dick Shaw, so much about Virgil Weaver, so much about Darcy Coolidge, so much about Dale Farmer that their stories threatened to drown the memories of who I had been. Without my memories I would be nothing, a formless gas swirling in a universe of horrifying infinity. Often Guy whispered his threnody of reproach: "We died, and you lived. It was not fair. You must remember us. You can never forget us. We live only in you."

I told Dr. Youngblood that I was going to leave. He looked into his fire built against the rainy chill of the season and did not say anything for a long time.

"I hoped you would stay," he said.

"It is not my home," I said.

"It is not my home, either," he said. "But I have lived here a long time."

"You could leave," I said.

"Who would take care of all these people?"

"That would not be your concern if you leave."

"Yes it would. I know them. It would be my concern even if I never heard of them again."

"It is not like that with me," I said. "I am not their doctor."

"No," Dr. Youngblood said. We were silent, and I could hear water dripping somewhere. "Ah me!" he said at last. "You don't want to be trapped here, I guess. I guess that's what happened to Pinkerton. Poor man. You don't want that. I guess it's happened to me, too."

I started to reply, but I said nothing. What was there to say? I was going to sit at night by the sea and watch the lights of distant ships rise and fall in the great dark; I was going to listen to the songs of fishermen; I was going to hear the surf rolling in slow cadences on the rocky shores of my homeland; I was going to be with Bernal and Guy until I joined them wherever they were.

81

VIRGIL'S DECISION to leave shook the town. A neat, black "For Sale" sign went up on the porch of the large white house on the square that he kept as an office. "It was John Wesley Campbell's house," Brian Ledbetter told me one Saturday afternoon when he and Ted Devlin and Douglas Kinlaw and I sat in Bessie May's cafe drinking coffee. The old man was dejected, and his thoughts wandered backwards so that it was hard to follow them.

"John Wesley Campbell was the bestest lawyer that ever did live. He was a good man, my best friend. I've set in that house many a day. He built it, built it for him and his wife. Her name was Charlotte. I remember her. Just barely, like she was a shadow. I was so young. She died in the night, and he wasn't never the same after that. They had a boy, and in the war, in the Rebellion, the boy disappeared. Nobody knowed what happened to him. Never did.

"J.W., he always thought his boy might come riding up that street some of these days. J.W. died up there, right behind that window there, the one with the white shade pulled halfway down? They found him lying in his nightshirt like he was standing by the window when death took him. Somehow, I always figured he was there in the middle of the night looking at something down in the street. What the hell could it of been? Did he hear something and get out of bed? Did he think his boy was coming home after all those years? When I think about how J.W. died, the chills runs down my back. I recollect it all like it was yesterday. Hell, it *was* yesterday to my way of thinking. He seemed like he was old, J.W. did. Now I'm older than he ever got to be. I tell you, it's a mystery, Paul Alexander. It's the damnedest mystery on earth how what we recollect is more real than what is."

John Wesley Campbell was the long-dead lawyer whose brooding spirit lingered in Brian Ledbetter's memory, as in Virgil's, distant and familiar like a place where one lived long ago in another country. To me the fragmentary story of Mr. Campbell was one of the many unfinished and half-forgotten tales that provided Bourbon County its somewhat shapeless definition and its past. Mr. Campbell, who had been Brian Ledbetter's best friend, dead for years, was unknown to most people in the county where once he had been prophet and potentate, conscience and sage. I understood what the old man was doing—pondering the losses that fall on us one by one, each bearable at the moment, even expected and ordinary, but that erode life as a river will tear away one small bank today and another tomorrow in cumulative, enlarging compass until its course and all the banks and the whole valley have been changed beyond the imagining of any casual traveler on a long-ago journey who might have supposed that the forests he observed idly, while smoking a cigar at the rail, had been there for eons. The changes never arrive at finality, completion, perfection, but go on and on as long as the river called time keeps flowing. The river carries away one man today, another tomorrow—actors essential to the daily translation of our lives from momentary and disconnected sensation into extension and design and destiny, the accidental acquaintances who seem in a while to be part of us like our eyes or our arms, though immediately after they are gone we readjust our perception and decide that they were exterior, peripheral, bound on a journey different from ours, but still they people our memories. Then at a further moment, we understand abruptly that they have taken with them our own location in time and place, our belonging, and we waken to dream in subdued, quiet terror, to discover that the present has become strange, darker, and more amorphous than the past, that indeed the past is the only place we are at home, and we know with final, implacable certainty that we, too, will be gone and that neither we nor any creation that we have made can have any claim to stay.

I thought of my father, and I wondered if he ever stood by a window in the night and hoped that I might come riding up a moonstruck street. Did he wonder where I was or what had become of me? Or had he, like the mysterious Mr. Campbell, already been found dead in a lonely room, leaving others to wonder why he was there when death struck him down? I had no answers to these questions, and because no answer was possible, I brooded over them and felt a helpless sadness that made me sit silently and listen to the talk as though I were unmoved by what anyone said.

Daisy came in one evening, knocking, admitting herself before Dr. Youngblood could descend to let her in. I heard them meet on the steps, heard her breathless voice: "Well, guess what? Daddy's sold his office to a doctor." I remember the light falling on her face in that moment, an image as sharp as any that I have of her, a girl, excited, afraid, and eager.

"A doctor?" Dr. Youngblood said. "A doctor, sure enough?"

"Another doctor. Bourbonville is going to have another doctor. Do you think there'll be room for both of you?"

Dr. Youngblood laughed. "We could have five more doctors and it wouldn't be enough," he said.

"This one's not like you."

"What is his name?" Dr. Youngblood said.

"Dr. Cameron Bulkely. His wife calls him 'Buck.' Right to his face."

Dr. Youngblood smiled.

"He's been down several times to talk to Daddy. He says this town needs the kind of care he can give."

"Well," Dr. Youngblood said.

It was a mild night. We had no fire, and the windows were open on the spring dark. The air was soft and still. I had booked passage from New York to Athens in September.

"He's going to have a clinic where Daddy's office is. This is really going to surprise you! He's going to tear Daddy's office down. Tear down the whole house."

"Why is he going to do that?" Dr. Youngblood asked.

"He's going to put up a brick clinic with all sorts of modern things. He's got one of those new X-ray machines."

"I have an X-ray machine," Dr. Youngblood said. "I don't use it much. I can usually feel how to set a bone. I don't trust X-rays."

"Daddy told Dr. Bulkely you're old-fashioned," Daisy said. Dr. Youngblood looked hurt. He puffed his pipe thoughtfully.

"I guess I just don't believe in medicine," Dr. Youngblood said. "He's been down to look at Bourbonville, has he?"

"Several times. Daddy drove him around the county. He says it's just the place where a man can settle down and live a healthy life. He says cities aren't healthy. To be healthy you have to live in the country."

"I'm surprised your daddy didn't bring him by to see me," Dr. Youngblood said.

"He tried," Daisy said. "Honest he did, Curtis. Daddy said he thought it would be a courtesy if Dr. Bulkely called on you." Daisy lowered her eyes. "Well, Curtis, I'll have to tell you the truth. He doesn't think much of you. He's a temperance man, you see. He's for prohibition."

"We have prohibition in Tennessee," Dr. Youngblood said. "Pretty soon we're going to have a constitutional amendment and have it everywhere."

"Tell that to Hub Delaney," Daisy said.

"Hub Delaney will not be here very long," Dr. Youngblood said. "He has cancer. He cannot control his bowels. He was passing blood for a long time before he told me. When he told me, it was too late."

"Can't you do anything to help him?" Daisy said. For a moment she looked startled.

"There's no way you can cure cancer except cut it out, and Hub's too far gone for that," Dr. Youngblood said.

"You can x-ray it," Daisy said. "Dr. Bulkely can put Hub under the X-ray machine and burn it out of him."

"You cannot cure cancer by X-ray when it has gone as far as it has with Hub Delaney," Dr. Youngblood said.

"Maybe you don't know, Curtis," she protested. "Maybe it's just because you're old-fashioned. Dr. Bulkely has all these new ideas."

"New ideas won't cure cancer," Dr. Youngblood said.

"Well, he's your friend and not mine," Daisy said, dismissing her emotion for Hub as quickly as it had come on her. "Anyway, Dr. Bulkely said he heard that you drink alcoholic beverages and smoke a pipe, and he said he thought it was a bad example for a doctor to smoke and drink before the young people in the county."

"I suppose it is," Dr. Youngblood said.

"To tell the truth, he talked so much about prohibition that he annoyed Daddy. You know what Daddy thinks. He thinks prohibition is a foolishness."

"It is a foolishness," Dr. Youngblood said.

"Daddy wanted to sell the house, so he kept quiet. Can you believe that Daddy didn't want an argument?"

"Oh yes," Dr. Youngblood said, chuckling a little too eagerly, I thought, as if to assuage her discomfort.

"Dr. Bulkely believes that we should take deep breaths and drink a glass of hot water every morning and chew our food thoroughly so the body can digest it. If you do all that, you won't get sick. He says doctors ought to be examples to the whole community because they're like priests."

"Jesus Christ," Dr. Youngblood said.

"It doesn't matter to me," she said, shaking her head. "We're leaving. I'm leaving Bourbonville. I've always hated Bourbonville, and now I don't have to live here anymore. Good riddance, I say."

"Everybody's leaving," Dr. Youngblood said. "Paul's leaving, too. He's going in September."

Daisy looked at me with dismay. "You are leaving? Where are you going?"

"Home," I said.

"You are going back to your mother and your sisters," Daisy said.

"Yes," I said.

"And your fiancée," she said.

"Oh yes, my fiancée," I said, thinking of Palmyre with an almost overwhelming nostalgia.

"You will get married," Daisy said.

"Perhaps she has forgotten me."

"I hoped you might move to California," Daisy said. "People say it goes for weeks in Los Angeles without raining. Daddy's bought some property there. It's all going up, he says. He says there is a lot of money to be made there."

"Your father has a lot of money already," Dr. Youngblood said.

"You always want more," Daisy said. "That's what money's for—so you can use it to get more. Even I know that, Curtis," she said bitterly. She turned back to me. "Have you thought of going to California?"

"No," I said.

"Have you written your fiancée?" she asked.

"Yes," I said. "But I have not received a reply."

"She may be dead," Daisy said.

I sat silently for a moment, and I felt the foolish tears come to my face. "Yes," I said at last. "She may be dead."

Daisy looked sympathetic and uncertain for a moment, but her face hardened. "You are wrong if you go back to Europe, Paul Alexander. You should stay here. There are millions of people in Europe who wish they had your chance in life."

"I must go home," I said.

"America is your home now," she said.

"No," I said. "I have a real home. I must go to it."

"You are a fool," she said. "A fool. I'm leaving. I am not going to stay here."

With that she got up and flung herself down the stairs and out the door without a backward glance. Dr. Youngblood and I sat without looking at each other, listening to her steps descend, hearing the door slam, hearing the violent rattle of the Model T Ford crank, the engine begin, the car depart, its sound dying slowly in the great emptiness of the spring night.

"A new doctor," Dr. Youngblood said. "A prohibitionist doctor." He chuckled. "Times are changing."

82

I HAD WRITTEN to Palmyre as soon as mail service was restored between Belgium and the United States, letters sent to the several addresses where she might be—variations on the same letter, written again and again. Was her promise still good? Would she marry me? I cannot now untangle the emotions that drove me on this quest. They were more complicated than you or I can imagine. I felt dead inside, unmoved by any emotion except perhaps guilt, and most of the time, I think, I cultivated the deadness to shut out the guilt. I sought Palmyre because she had made me feel supremely alive, and in some upper chamber of my mind, I could not bear the deadness that I had become. But I was also afraid to find her, because I did not know if I could live if the deadness in my heart lifted. As I say, my reasons were not simple.

The week after Daisy had fled into the night, I came home from work, and Darcy Coolidge was waving a letter at me. "You have mail," she said. "You have foreign mail." Her face glowed. "Your mother perhaps?"

My heart jumped. The address on the envelope was in Palmyre's hand. I tore the letter open, and I have it before me now. She wrote in French. I translate her words and fold the original within these pages.

Heidelberg, March 14, 1919

My dear Paul,

My sister sent me the letter which you sent to me at our village. I rejoiced that you survived the terrible war, and I grieve that Guy and Bernal are dead. May God grant them eternal peace. May God grant also that such horrors never again come upon the earth. I supposed that you all were dead, and I could not get word of you because we were behind the German lines for such a long time.

Now I hope you can find it in your heart to forgive me, dearest Paul, because I have married someone else. My husband, Hans Stotheim, was in the occupying forces. He is a kind man, a very good man, older than I am, an excellent automobile mechanic, and we are opening a garage here in Heidelberg. Hans says that the automobile is the true emperor of the future. We have two sons now, little Hänschen and Bruno. I know you would love them if you could see them. Bruno was born only last month. They are so small, so dear!

I could write a very long letter explaining myself and asking for forgiveness. But you would know that such a letter would not truly be the sentiments of the Palmyre you knew in Ghent. I need scarcely tell you that my family was horrified when I married a German soldier. But war is a passing thing, and families go on and on through the years. We must have families to make up for all the death that war deals. You would like Hans very much. He is a very jolly man. He reminds me very much of Guy, though of course he does not have Guy's money or Guy's way with the world. If you could meet Hans, you would know what I mean. He loves to make jokes.

Leonora vanished from Ghent during the occupation. I never saw her again after I left you on that terrible weekend. God have mercy on her soul. She may be dead. So many are dead. Every year on August 29 I go to church, and I hear mass, and I pray for the souls of all those who were to be in her wedding. I have been praying for your soul; now I will pray for your happiness and trust that you will always hold a special place in your heart for your

Palmyre. What I have done is for the best—for me and for you.
You would have tired of me. You are so young and so intelligent,
and I am nothing but Palmyre. I am fat now. You would not
recognize me. I will never forget you. I hope you will never forget me.

My love always,
Palmyre

I read the letter swiftly and took it to my room and read it again. I have
read it a thousand, perhaps ten thousand times. Its ironies can still crush me,
though I am old enough to live with them now.

Darcy Coolidge ached to know what the letter said. Finally I told her that
my fiancée had married another. She expressed conventional regret. "My
dear young man, do not give the matter a second thought!" she said. "You
can find hundreds of women to marry you. Maybe you should marry the
Weaver girl. You'd do her a world of good, and she loves you. Everyone
knows that."

I went out that evening for a long walk under the stars. The air blowing
up from the south was softening nightly. The smell of flowers hung around
me. The silence of Bourbonville and Bourbon County after dark amazed me.
No bells tolled the hours. No trams clanked by. No drunks staggered home
singing in the streets. No freight wagons lumbered along, pulled by behe-
moth horses, shod hoofs clanging on cobblestones. At night, the world of
Bourbon County slept like death. A dog barked. A train passed, its whistle
screaming across the dark, the rumble of its journey reduced by distance.
But beyond these brief and feeble eruptions of sound stretched the silence,
like a spell cast by the sky.

I was free to return to Greece and to be with Guy and Bernal, the only
company I wanted. I still had no sexual desire. I had had no desire for so
long that I expected never to have it again, supposing that it was like a
childhood disease that, having once infected me, left me immune so that I
thought about sex as little as I pondered measles or whooping cough or the
mumps. I wanted only solitude and my friends. I thought of the uplands of
Thessaly. I had been there once. Stephanos and I, on the same trip that led
us to Delphi, continued to Larisa, and we walked together, and I saw how
wild and barren the country was, the ragged shepherds, the white rocks
dazzling in the brilliant sun.

Palmyre had married a man who reminded her of Guy. She did not marry
someone like me. He was like Guy. Guy had seduced her as he had seduced
everyone else. Not in a physical way; he had not taken her to bed. He had
spread the net of his charm, and she had been ensnared without quite
knowing it. I had not understood. But it was all right. He had ensnared
me, too.

83

THEN CAME ANOTHER letter, this one from my mother. Her letters had become more and more formal. I felt that she hid behind the tedious factuality of her epistles, those dry chronicles of her life and the lives of my sisters. I felt that I was reading about people I scarcely knew. I went to Knoxville on the train to the postal box that I rented there; I removed the letters that came as regularly as the rotation of the weeks. I went in warm weather to Market Square, which on Saturday afternoon filled with farmers in town to sell their produce, and I went into a steamy little cafe and ordered coffee and opened her letter and read it. I never read it twice. I folded it away in my pocket and put it with the others in a drawer in the chest in my room at the boardinghouse.

When I wrote that I was returning to Greece, my mother replied with cool reserve that the family would be happy to have me home. I did not expect an outpouring of feeling from her, but I expected more than she gave. Then in May I received a letter that did betray emotion. It, too, lies here beside me on this cool autumn night. I translate it from the careful French in which the original is written on its fine blue paper.

My dearest son,

We have looked forward with joy to your return to us after so many years. My father is old and feeble, and must soon pay his debt to nature and die. His house will be sold for the benefit of my brothers, and since everything he owed to me was delivered to your father in my dowry, and since my dowry was devoured in the settlement of your father's affairs after he left us, I shall receive nothing more from my father's estate. Naturally your sisters will receive nothing, either; we may be cast as waifs on the world.

Your sister Helen has received a proposal of marriage from an officer of high rank in the Greek postal service. He is an older man, and his table manners are not what I might wish them to be. He has not had the advantages of good family and an education. It is not the marriage that I would have preferred for her, but the world changes. We have changed more than I ever dreamed. Who can tell what changes may yet come? We must bow ourselves to the will of God and utter no complaints lest we offend Him and bring down His wrath upon our sinful heads.

Only one thing stands between Helen and her marriage. That is agreement on her dowry. My father will naturally contribute nothing. He owes nothing to me or to Helen, and he will give nothing. Yet I must do something, and I have proposed the following terms. Her husband should receive a thousand American dollars on their marriage, which will then take place in the late summer of 1920. We depend on you, my son. Mr. Pelykes, the gentleman who has proposed marriage to Helen, has said that he will wait two months for a reply before withdrawing his offer. I beg you to write to him in care of me and to assent.

I must tell you that times in Greece are very bad. Nothing you can get here will pay you as much money as you are making in your wonderful position in America. Will you, my dear son, postpone your return to us and stay in your job there until you can provide a dowry for Helen? Mr. Pelykes tells me that he will be happy for me and for Anna to come to live with Helen and him in their house overlooking the port in Piraeus where there is some new building going on. I have told him that you will contribute to our expenses and that if you finally return to Greece, we will dwell with you. Of course Anna must be married in time, but we shall deal with her dowry when the necessity arises. You, my son, can solve our problems if only you can stay where you are for another year or two.

Please reply at once if you can make this agreement. Perhaps you must make a loan. If you will do so, I can reply immediately to Mr. Pelykes and accept his proposal. Considering your father's deed, I believe Mr. Pelykes's offer to be the act of a gentleman of honor and courage. To bind himself to our family will not be beneficial to him in his career, though perhaps people in his circles do not think so much of such things as do people in ours. I do ask you to come to our aid if you love us as we love you.

Always,

Your loving mother

I thought of Helen's dark, voluptuous beauty and of how young she had been when I had seen her last. I supposed that Mr. Pelykes must be in full middle age and that he would rape her in the marriage bed. He could treat her like a servant he had redeemed from shame. I looked at my mother's firm script, almost printed, and demonstrating the self-control that allowed her to rule her own life and my life as well.

Everything swam before me. The little cafe became suffocating. I stumbled blindly into the street and vomited. People rushed to help me. A barefoot young man in deeply worn and faded cotton clothes helped me to the train station when I said that that was where I wanted to go. He was shy and withdrawn, and when I tried to give him a dollar, he refused it and turned red with embarrassment. When I got off the train in Bourbonville, someone called Dr. Youngblood because I sat down in the depot and could not move.

He came in as much of a hurry as I had ever seen him and drove me home. He sat for a long time beside my bed, but I could not look at him. I could not think of anything. I shut my eyes and tried to wish him away, tried to wish life away. But I lacked the will to sustain even that primitive desire. When I opened my eyes, the world went slowly round and round, and I was dizzy and nauseated again. Dr. Youngblood told me later that he had begun to have hope for me, to assume that I would begin to thrive. But when he saw me lying in my bed that day, my face pale and my mind distracted, the conviction came to him once more that I would surely die soon.

84

I WROTE MY MOTHER that I would obey, and I wrote to Mr. Pelykes. For the first time in my life with her, I made a demand. She must tell me how Stephanos had died. She had not told me, and I had not been able to ask. I think I wanted to cause her pain. The memory must have been so terrible that she could not reply at once, for her next communication with me came weeks later. It, too, lies here before me, neatly written on her fine blue linen paper. She never sacrificed that part of herself.

My dearest Paul,

We received your last letter with gratitude and joy. Helen sends you a thousand kisses, and Mr. Pelykes sends his respects and invites you to visit us in Piraeus as soon as you can.

How difficult is the task you set for me! May God rest the soul of your poor uncle. You have a right to know how he died. I have not been able to bring myself to tell you or to speak about it to either of your sisters. They still do not know the details. I could not tell them; I would not let anyone else tell them. God forgive him for what he did.

I did not expect his death. He seemed unusually cheerful and happy for several days before it happened. I believed that things in the firm had taken a turn for the better and that all was well. For a while, you see, he had been silent and even more nervous than usual. He had frequently lost his temper with the servants, and he had even spoken harshly to Helen and to Anna, so that we were all worried about him. I suspected (though it is not a woman's place to inquire about such things) that things were not going well in the business.

But then he recovered his spirits all in a night. He became as calm and as loving as a man could be. I had never seen him so at peace with himself or with others. He joked and told us that everything was going to be splendid and that we were all going to have good lives, and one morning he told me that he would be forced to be away overnight on an important trip. He did not tell me where he was going, and I supposed that he might be traveling somewhere for business.

Later we discovered that he took the train to Livadhia and rented a carriage to Delphi and stayed there in the hotel with the terrace overlooking the gorge. In the early morning he appeared on the terrace and had his morning coffee. He carried his bouzouki with him, and he sat at his table and played it, much to the joy of several foreign tourists also staying at the hotel. He played for a little while, and then he stood up and carefully placed the bouzouki on the table, bowed to the people applauding him at the tables, walked to the edge of the terrace, and leaped into the gorge.

It happened so quickly that no one could stop him. Most did not know what he was doing even as they saw him do it. They supposed that there was some pathway perhaps beneath him. Only a few realized that he would fall so very far. Someone said he held his hands straight out from his body. I do not know why he did that.

That is all there is to the story, my dear son. His body was badly broken by the fall. I had to identify it, of course. It was very hard for me. I would have preferred not to tell you. Since you wanted to know, I had to bow to your request. Do not think about it. I think about it every day. You should not. It is a curse to think about it.

Your loving mother

I did not get a headache when I read this letter. I sat on a wooden bench in the sunshine of Market Square in Knoxville in the midst of a crowd of the poor on a Saturday afternoon, and I read about Stephanos and how he had died. I knew that he had been thinking of me. He had fallen like Ikaros to his death.

85

One Saturday morning Darcy Coolidge wakened me by tapping urgently on my door. "Mr. Alexander! Mr. Alexander! The Weaver girl insists on seeing you. She is sitting out there in broad daylight *smoking.* Someone may think she has been here all night long! *Everyone* can see her. Please go down to her. Get her away from here. Why can't she be a lady? Why can't she paint pottery or do watercolors or stay at home and read decent Christian books? Why does she have to parade around in her father's car with a cigarette in her mouth like a hussy? When I smoke, I smoke in my *kitchen* where nobody can see me. Thank *God* she's leaving; thank God she and her father are *both* leaving. They've put this town under a *curse.* Get out there and make her go away. I trust you to save the reputation of my boardinghouse."

I dressed quickly and went downstairs.

It was a perfect day. The birds were singing, and everything smelled of spring on the cusp of summer. Every object wore a garment of light. The sun had risen, and great puffs of white cloud floated serenely overhead. Everything—the white frame houses, the great trees, the wooden fences in their various states of repair, the untraveled street—radiated light.

"We are leaving tomorrow afternoon," Daisy said in her peremptory way. "We're going to New Orleans. From New Orleans we'll take another train to Los Angeles. I want you to take one last ride with me."

I hesitated. "I'm going away," she said softly. "You won't have to put up with me again. Give me today."

Her talk floats back to me now, borne on winds that blow from nowhere into silence.

"Daddy has burned his manuscript," she said. She drove slowly. Her long cotton dress clung to her body. She had become thinner.

"His manuscript," I said.

"His manuscript of the history of Bourbon County. He worked on it for years. It's all ashes."

"I am sorry," I said.

"He had copies of so many records. He burned everything. He said he never wanted to think about Bourbon County again as long as he lives."

I was silent.

"Your fiancée is not going to marry you," she said, with an air of both inquiry and finality. "You don't have to look surprised. There are no secrets in Bourbonville. Will you still go back to your home now?"

"No," I said. "I will stay here. At least for a little while."

"She married someone else."

"Yes, she married someone else."

"Was he somebody you knew?"

I paused at the question. Yes, in a way Palmyre had married someone I knew. When we fought in vain to save our cannon, I killed a German in hand-to-hand combat. He was blond and very young, and I bayoneted him in the stomach as he was drawing back his rifle to club me. I recall the surprise that came into his face when out of sheer terror I put the bayonet all the way through his body.

I looked off into the unkempt fields, high with pale green grass. It was called sedge grass, and it would soon turn yellow. There was a forest beyond the field, brooding and still in the sunlight. Guy appeared in the field and waved at me. I looked away.

"I do not want to talk about it," I said.

She tossed her head. "I am going to leave you behind in this vile little town," she said.

"People are nice here," I said.

She shook her head. "Bourbonville is a sewer of quicksand. You walk out into it, and it drags you down until you smother to death. You must pull yourself out of it, the way I am doing. You're staying here just because your heart is broken and you don't want to go back to your home to see your fiancée married to . . . I bet she married your best friend." Daisy's eyes widened, and I could imagine the romantic novel unfolding page by page in her mind.

"My best friends are dead," I said.

Her expression changed. "I'm sorry," she said. "I'm always saying the wrong thing."

"No," I said. "It is all right."

"Don't you feel angry at her?"

"She thought I was dead," I said.

Now Daisy stopped and put a hand to her face and looked ready to weep. "Oh, that is terrible. I read a book about something like that once."

"I am sure you did," I said.

"You still love her even though she married someone else. You can't bear to see the woman you love every day and know that every night she sleeps in the arms of another man. I understand everything, Paul. Everything!" I thought she might cry.

I wanted to change the subject. "Is your father going to practice law in California?" I said.

"No, he says he doesn't believe in the law anymore. He's going into real estate."

"Real estate?"

"Speculation on land. Daddy says Los Angeles is the coming town in America. He has a knack, you know. Daddy has always known how to make money."

"Yes," I said.

"He's free now. He was a slave to D.B. while D.B. was alive. Now D.B. is dead."

I could think of no response.

"You think I am being mean," she said in a while. "You have to accept things. Poor fool. Poor dead fool. I loved him, you know. I dearly loved him."

She shook her head in an expression of prolonged melancholy. "It's like D.B. had walked into a dark room, and Daddy shut the door after him and locked him up and won't let him out again."

"Your father will always remember him," I said.

"Yes, but what is memory? D.B. is gone; he is nothing. We'll be nothing with him in time. How many times can you talk to a memory? Unless you can talk to the dead. Do you believe in spiritualism? A lot of people do. I don't myself. But maybe there's something to it. What do you think?"

I looked at her in anguish.

"What's wrong?" she said impatiently. "Are you sick again?"

"No," I said. "No. I am not sick."

"You need a woman," she said. "I am a woman."

"You are too young," I said.

She looked at me with a flash of anger. "I am not much younger than you are."

"Yes you are," I said.

She turned away from me in silence, and I thought again that she was on the verge of tears.

86

SHE DROVE ON, her black hair flying in the wind, an expression of meditation on her face.

"We should have Grandfather Ledbetter with us," she said. "This road leads down to the old Methodist church. It used to be *the* Methodist church in Bourbon County. Grandfather Ledbetter drove D.B. and me down here in a wagon lots of times when I was a little girl. He was always good to us. He's sad now about Mr. Delaney."

She turned down the road and stopped, and the motor whirled idly in the gentle morning.

"I've written Jim Ed about you," she said. "I've told him I love you."

"Please do not talk like that. You do not know me well enough to love me," I said.

"I know enough to know I love you," she said.

I started to speak, but it seemed fruitless. I took a deep breath and looked away.

She drove down the dirt road, and the tires whispered softly.

"See that house? That old ruin? You can hardly tell it's a house now, all grown up with honeysuckle like it is." Her voice had a metallic brightness to it, and she gestured with too much energy. "Smell the mint," she said. "Can you smell it? I love the smell of mint."

She stopped, and we took deep breaths, her eyes theatrically closed. The fragrance of mint hung thick in the air. I had walked here.

"Grandfather Ledbetter told me all about that house. He said it was lived in by a couple of old colored women. Grandfather Ledbetter calls them the hags. Grandfather Ledbetter said the hags told fortunes. Do you believe people can see the future?"

I distinctly heard Guy laugh. "No," I said.

"You don't have to shout," she said. "If the hags were still alive, I'd get them to tell my fortune. What will happen to you. To you and me. I'd do anything to know."

"You should not seek to know such things," I said. I heard Bernal's voice in my own. What if Guy or Bernal took over my body and lived through me? I shuddered.

"What is wrong?" she said.

"Nothing," I said.

"Well, you're right, I guess," she said softly. "Just think what it would have been if we'd all known what was going to happen—to D.B., to Daddy, to Mamma, known it for years and years before it happened. Maybe the only thing that makes life bearable is not knowing what will happen. We all end badly. All of us. If the hags were alive, maybe they could bring D.B. back. What would he be then?"

"We would not want to see," I said.

We went on. The little road ended at a neat white church that reposed amid its graves in a large clearing on a slight hill that below the church became a graveyard in front of the forest. I had been here.

"Here's the church," she said. "The Southern Methodists used to meet out here every Sunday. Then they built in town. Trinity, the black and white church on the hill near the school? That's the Southern Methodist church. Central, down near the square on B Street, that's the Northern Methodist church. My grandmother is a Southern Methodist, and this is where she came to church when she was a girl. Now they just have one meeting a year out here. They have funerals. Lots of the old people want to be buried out here. My grandmother will be buried here sometime. It's what she wants. Next to my real grandfather. I never knew him, of course. Daddy's daddy. He's buried over there. Daddy comes to his grave a lot. I don't think his brothers care much about it."

"Your father was older when his father died," I said.

"You remember something we've told you," she said with a wry smile.

"I remember more than you may think," I said.

She laughed. "They have all-day singing and dinner on the ground for homecoming once a year. That's when all the people who used to come here come back. It happens in July. I'll miss it this year. I love homecoming. Jim Ed plays the guitar for it. Jim Ed's the best guitar player you'll ever know. And the banjo. And the dulcimer. And the mandolin. He can play anything. Do they have guitars in Europe? Do they have instruments you can strum like that with your fingers?"

"Of course," I said. I thought of Stephanos and turned away as if to look around.

"Well, if there's a guitar in all of Europe, Jim Ed will find it, and he'll play it to Willy. Willy's blind, you know. He was so much fun! He had the deepest blue eyes. I never loved him as much as I loved Jim Ed. But I loved him. They're coming home in a few weeks, and we won't be here to see them."

"You should stay," I said.

"I think it's deliberate in a way," Daisy said pensively. "Daddy never did like Jim Ed. He denies it, of course. He says of course he likes Jim Ed, that Jim Ed's just so much younger than he is. They never had the time to be together, Daddy says. I know it's more than that."

"Mrs. Ledbetter cannot understand why your father will not stay," I said.

"I think she can understand," Daisy said. "That's why her heart's broken. Daddy just says it's time to go, and we're going. I know what he's thinking. Jim Ed went all the way through the war without a scratch, and D.B. was killed on the last day. Jim Ed has won again."

She turned off the engine and climbed down out of the car. I got down, too. "There're so many connections in a small place like this. Grandfather Ledbetter says Jim Ed used to follow around after Daddy like a pet dog. Jim Ed thought Daddy hung the moon and the stars. Daddy never did like him. Do you understand things like that?"

"No," I said.

"Connections. They're the main thing. Everything that happens to anybody in a place like this happens to everybody before it's over. We're all tied up together, the living and the dead. Out in California, the things that happen to me won't matter to anybody else; the things that happen to anybody else won't matter to me. I'll be free. Daddy will be free. Do you understand?"

"I think so," I said.

She drew another deep breath. "Aren't the smells wonderful? I'll miss the smells here—the hills, the river, the flowers. Can you smell the river? It's just over there, through that little screen of trees. The graveyard here is so peaceful. The Methodists keep it clean and pure. Uncle Caleb runs his own graveyards, you know. He has to hire people to mow the grass. He's in debt, you know. Uncle Caleb is in debt up to his ears. He's trying to be rich like Daddy."

"That is sad," I said.

"He doesn't have the knack. That's what it is, you know. A knack. The Methodists keep the grass cut in summer. It's the way they respect their dead."

"It is very pretty," I said.

We walked among the graves. I saw a vase of spring flowers against one of the tombstones before I read the name: John Wesley Campbell. It was a small, plain stone. Nothing on it but the name, the date of birth, and the date of death. Daisy looked at it wistfully. "Grandfather Ledbetter has been here. He has never forgot Mr. Campbell. Neither has Daddy. Grandfather Ledbetter is the one who brings flowers to his grave."

We walked on. "Grandfather Ledbetter knows all the stories. When we used to come down here together, Grandfather Ledbetter told them one after the other. I can remember some of them. I can't remember them all." She fished in the pocket of her dress and brought out a package of cigarettes. She offered me one, and I took it, and we went through the rituals of lighting them.

"Look over here. This is the grave of Samuel Atkins Beckwith. He came here at the end of the Civil War and stayed. He was a rebel, but he was a great friend of Mr. Campbell's. Mr. Campbell was a Union man, but they were friends anyway. Grandfather Ledbetter says Mr. Campbell's own son disappeared in the war, and Mr. Beckwith was almost like a different son. It doesn't matter now, does it? I've heard about him from Grandfather Ledbetter hundreds of times. He's been dead a long time—1870. Grandfather Ledbetter can talk about him by the hour. The stone's marble, you see. It should be granite, Grandfather Ledbetter says. The inscription is wearing away. In another fifty years, you won't be able to read it. He used to live in the house where Mr. Pinkerton lives now. I've never been there. It's just a little way from here, but of course I've never been invited, and I wouldn't go. I hear that Mr. Pinkerton still has Mr. Beckwith's photograph hanging in his living room. Grandfather Ledbetter says it's huge. The picture, I mean. Mr.

Beckwith's wife had it made from a little picture after he died. You can make photographs as big as a house now. She went crazy. She died in the lunatic asylum up in Knoxville. Why do you suppose people go crazy?"

I had no answer. Guy and Bernal stood in the forest shadows, watching me with intense concentration.

"Here's Uncle Aaron's grave," she said, pointing to a small stone with a reclining lamb carved on top of it. "It seems funny to call him 'Uncle.' He died when he was a child. You've heard the story."

"Yes, I've heard it," I said.

"Uncle Caleb never lets you forget it."

"No," I said.

"Sometimes I think all the connections in my family run back to him. Who can say?"

I said nothing.

"I don't suppose there's much left now," Daisy said. "They're all buried in oak and pine coffins. Uncle Caleb says that a wood coffin doesn't last long. I wonder about the resurrection, how all the dead will stand up here dressed in their funeral clothes. Do you think the dead will be raised? If God can resurrect the dead, he can gather up all the dirt from the earth and put them back together like they were, I guess. But why should he bother? The preachers talk like God doesn't have anything better to do than create a world like this and watch us like he was watching a play. Only he's backstage fixing it so it will turn out to be a joke on us and everybody else. I think there could be a God. But it's stupid to think he is so bored with himself that he has to have us to keep him company. Why are you looking at me like that? What's wrong?"

I stared at her and in a moment saw that I had frightened her. "Nothing," I murmured. "Nothing is wrong. I have had such thoughts. That is all."

"You see how much alike we are," she said with a hopeful smile. "We think the same thoughts. From the first day I saw you, I knew we were alike. Two peas in a pod. Do you know the expression?"

"No," I said.

We were silent, and the faintest of breezes stirred the grass. It smelled sweet and mild, and there was life in the air. We heard bird song and the languid hum of insects. Guy and Bernal stood fifty meters away, looking at me, their arms folded. I tried not to look at them.

"The sad thing," Daisy said as if she were speaking the last of a thought she had not spoken aloud, "is the stories don't matter unless they happen to us. If it hasn't happened to us, we might as well stop talking about it. What good is it to talk about Samuel Atkins Beckwith? He's just a story. He doesn't mean anything to me."

I looked at a small granite stone. "It had the name Moreland James Pinkerton, Jr., carved on it and an epitaph: "Asleep in Jesus." I realized that this was the grave of Pinkerton's son. He had lived from February to April in 1893.

Daisy turned towards the thin line of trees that stood between the grave-yard and the river. I could see through the trees to the water. It was like a mirror, reflecting the blue sky and the clouds. It seemed serenely powerful, motionless in its wide valley, but its current moved beneath the surface, carrying this part of the continent away. Here and there a piece of drift-wood—the limb of a tree, a log—rushed downstream.

She turned abruptly to face me, and she was very close. The scent of her perfume enveloped us; it was an expensive perfume.

"I am doing my best not to say anything important," she said. "I am tired of it, tired of myself, and there is no time left. I am tired of trying to keep my dignity. What is dignity anyway? I never could hold on to dignity in the night. It never spoke to me when I was sad. It never told me it loved me. Mamma always tells me—always *told* me—to keep my dignity. I don't know what dignity is, unless it's a word to keep people from knowing how hurt you are or how hopeless you feel." The tears came up in her eyes. Her face was close to mine, looking up.

"You have no reason to feel hopeless," I said.

"Oh," she said with a bitter laugh. "I know there is hope. I am a strong person, you see. I'm going to be happy in California. I'm going to be happy as a lark. I'm going to sing all day long. It's not going to matter in California that you rejected me in Tennessee."

"I have not rejected you," I said.

"Yes you have," she cried.

"No," I said. "No. You cannot understand."

"I understand everything that I should understand," she said. "I under-stand that you don't love me."

We stood confronting each other strangely in this graveyard far from anyone else. The tears were running down her face. Finally she shook her head.

"I have thought that without you my heart would stop beating. But you know what will happen? Time will keep on passing, and I will live. I have been thinking about how I am going to look when I'm forty. Once you're twenty, people say the next twenty years fly away like the wind. Gone in a wink, and you're forty, standing knee-deep in middle age. I think that then I'll hear your name, and I'll think back on how much I have loved you, and do you know what I hope I'll do?"

I could not think of a response.

"I hope I laugh. I truly hope I laugh. I hope I laugh at myself, at how young I was, how foolish."

She reached up and kissed me on the mouth, her mouth slightly open and wet, and pulled away. She had discarded her cigarette, but her mouth tasted like tobacco.

"I will take you home," she said. "It's all right. Everything is all right." She tried to smile and gave up the effort. She seemed very, very young.

When she pulled the car to a dusty halt before the boardinghouse, she sat for a moment looking at me. "I may never see you again," she said. "I will tell you one thing. If you ever want me, send for me. You will always know where to find me. I'll see to that. Send me one word by telegraph. 'Come.' That's all you need to say. I will drop everything and I will come. If I have a job, I will quit it. If I have a husband, I will leave him. If I have children, I will abandon them. All you have to do is want me, and I will come."

I stood there in the bright sunshine before the boardinghouse and saw her drive down the hill. I thought of Leonora and of Palmyre, and I thought of Daisy's body beneath her dress and of how it had been offered to me, and I felt a stirring of hunger—hunger for what Palmyre and I had. I thought that if she looked back I would wave to her, signal her to return; and who knows what might have happened then? But she did not look back. She turned through the square and was gone.

87

PINKERTON MARCHED like a sleepwalker through the car shops every day. We avoided him. He did not come into the laboratory.

Shaw lodged a protest in Washington. The railroads continued under the nominal supervision of the government. The company's officers, its civil service, had never been truly displaced; now they were recovering their old responsibilities. One of them came down to investigate. His name was Philip Drodge, a thin, balding, energetic man with sharp features, a sharp voice, which he controlled with diamond-cutting precision, and intelligent eyes. He walked with a slight stoop. He was in his early thirties, immaculately dressed in the slender style that would continue to be the preferred masculine fashion through the twenties. Such hair as he had was parted in the middle and slicked back on the sides of his head.

"Mr. Davis told me about you. He thought you could tell me what's going on." The statement was somehow a challenge.

"I know only what I have seen," I said.

"That's probably enough," Philip Drodge said with a steely smile. He stood in the laboratory with his arms folded loosely across his chest, impeccably self-controlled. "Pinkerton says you were there. I need an eyewitness report."

"I do not wish to add to Mr. Pinkerton's difficulties," I said.

"Look," he said in a mood of weary confidence. "I don't give a damn for Richard Shaw. It serves the government right for hiring a preposterous, pontificating fraud like him to be an inspector. I talked with the man, you know. With fools like that trying to run the railroads, we're lucky the trains didn't stop altogether and that we didn't lose the war. Why couldn't he have the decency to die in the flu epidemic like the other one—what was his name?"

"Vissing," I said.

"Vissing," he said. "Did you know him?"

"Yes," I said.

"Stupid, I'll bet."

"Yes, I think so," I said.

I did not intend the remark to be humorous, but Drodge laughed, and leaned back against one of the long counters, his arms folded, grinning.

"You're an honest man. I like that. Well, Wilson's a fool, and McAdoo's a fool even if he is from Tennessee, and he brought fools in to run the railroads. We could have done it by ourselves. But still . . . it's hard to ignore government bureaucrats who tell us that one of our people peed in the face of one of their people. McAdoo's from down here, you know, and the hypocritical son of a bitch wants to be President, and he's not happy that one of his men got peed on in his own backyard, so to speak. He can make trouble. Now, tell me about it."

"Mr. Shaw asked Mr. Pinkerton for a job," I said.

"A job?" Drodge made an incredulous face. "Hell! Why should that make Pinkerton mad? There're going to be six million men home from the war asking for jobs. Is Pinkerton going to chuck all of them out the door and pee in their faces?" Drodge broke into his stiff laughter. "You know, that *was* an accomplishment. I don't think I could do it. Could you do it? Could you pee in somebody's face when you wanted to? With a crowd of people looking on?"

"I have never considered it," I said.

Drodge laughed again. "I suppose not," he said. "Well, go on. Explain this mess to me."

"Mr. Pinkerton expected Shaw to offer *him* a job," I said. "Mr. Pinkerton longs to go to Washington, to work in the company up there."

I expounded all this carefully—Pinkerton's dreams. Drodge only slowly understood. I had to repeat myself several times.

"Pinkerton thinks he might have gone to Washington!" Drodge said. "Good God! He thought Richard Shaw could give him a job in Washington! Why, he's crazy." He laughed his hard laugh. "There has never been a chance that Moreland Pinkerton would go to Washington to work up there. My God, what would he do?"

"He thought he deserved it," I said. "He built the car works. There was a swamp here before he came. He thought he deserved to be promoted. He thought he would be one of the senior officers in Washington. He talked about it all the time." I faltered.

"That was his *job*. The railroad paid him just like it pays those carpenters out there in the car sheds. It pays him just like it pays those colored men out there spinning wheels around the wheel dock. That is the only obligation the railroad had to Moreland Pinkerton—to pay him an honest day's wage for an honest day's work."

"He thought he would have been summoned up to Washington if it had not been for the Cuban business, the trouble he had down there."

"What Cuban business?" Drodge said. "I never heard of any Cuban business."

"It is in his file," I said, plodding on in this dreary and impossible fantasy. Suddenly the story Hub Delaney and Brian Ledbetter had told about Molly Montgomery Clanton seemed perfectly plausible compared with the tale I was spinning about Moreland J. Pinkerton. "Mr. Pinkerton thought it was in his file. His disgrace in Cuba."

"I looked in his file before I came down here," Drodge said. "I met Pinkerton once or twice before last year. I was here several times, down to inspect things, you know. His payroll records are there. We pay him well. And yes, he was on leave during the Spanish War. So were a lot of others. He was sick for a while afterwards. That's in the file, too—a carbon copy of a letter extending his leave. No details. I thought maybe he had a touch of the fever everybody got down there. Do you smoke? Here, have a cigarette."

"Thank you," I said.

"I used to smoke cigars, but I think cigarettes are better for you," he said. "I think a man ought to take care of his health. Did Pinkerton have the yellow fever?"

"No," I said. "It was something else. I do not know the details."

"A disciplinary problem? Cowardice?"

"No," I said. "Some form of hysteria."

"Shell shock?"

"I think it was something like that," I said.

"We wouldn't hold that against him," Drodge said with a thoughtful grunt, shaking his head as if somehow the righteousness of the railroad had been impugned and he had to defend it. "There's not a damned thing in his file about any trouble in Cuba."

I was flustered. "Mr. Pinkerton always thought that there was something in his file about the Cuban business, that it kept him from going to Washington."

"Oh, come now," Drodge said. "You can see what the man is. Limited. He would be out of place in Washington. A joke. He wouldn't belong. Do you think Pinkerton could be a chemist?"

"Chemistry is not difficult," I said.

"It's not difficult for you. I asked you a question: could Pinkerton be a chemist?"

"He could learn. Anybody can learn chemistry."

"All right. I am not going to ask you to be disloyal. Let's just say this. There is a sort who comes to Washington and a sort who doesn't. Pinkerton is the sort who doesn't. He doesn't have any education. He's crude. He's loud. No table manners. He doesn't fit. Imagine him at a formal affair in morning dress, top hat and tails. It's as simple as that. Can't you see that?"

"I never thought about it," I said.

Drodge clapped his hands to his head and laughed. "You never thought about it. Swell! Think about it now, and listen to me. Trust me. You are not telling me anything that will hurt Pinkerton any more than he has hurt himself already. You're amazing. The world's last loyal man. Say, I want you on my side."

I thought that to convince Drodge that I was not amazing or loyal would not be worth the effort.

"He thought Dick Shaw could give him a job! Shaw was a hack, a nobody. He probably knew somebody who knew somebody, maybe McAdoo himself. Hell, McAdoo's a Klansman, or pretty close to it. He hobnobs with all sorts of trash. I suppose that's how Shaw got this job. But hell, Shaw couldn't have known anybody very important if he landed in a place like this. It's funny. And Pinkerton . . . Good God!" Drodge laughed again, shaking his head at the folly of it.

"Pinkerton thought that Shaw would see what a good job he was doing here at the car works, and Pinkerton would be elevated to Washington. We all thought so."

"Elevated to Washington," Drodge said. "Where did you learn English?"

"In school," I said carefully. "I was also in England three years."

"In school in England," Drodge said. "Oxford, was it? Cambridge? What in hell are you doing in a little burg like this! I can do better for you. You can't waste your time down here."

"It is a peaceful place," I said. He had misunderstood me again. It was tedious to correct him.

"So's a graveyard," Drodge said with another carefully controlled laugh. "Tell me this. Do you think Pinkerton's crazy? Do you think the man is dangerous?"

"He is very unhappy. I cannot see how he could be dangerous."

"I guess not. Poor fool! We get what we deserve in this old world. Don't you think that's true in the end?"

I felt Guy and Bernal in the room. "I was in the war," I said. "It's hard to think people got what they deserved in the war."

He frowned and straightened himself and tossed his cigarette butt into an ashtray. He reminded me of the blade of a pocket knife being unfolded.

"All right, here's what we're going to do. I'm going to write a report of this affair. I've talked to a lot of people in town. Hell, I've investigated this case like a treasury agent! I'm going to have to tell how Shaw made an indecent proposition to that thirteen-year-old girl in the Baptist church."

"I beg your pardon?"

"You didn't know about that, did you?" Drodge laughed.

"No," I said.

"You're not as well informed as you should be about the affairs of your town," he said with a smirk.

"It is not my town," I said.

"And I suppose you have also not heard about Mr. Shaw's clandestine affair with the wife of one of the prominent ministers here in Bourbonville?"

"No," I said.

"Not surprising," Drodge said with a conspiratorial wink. "We've had to fight hard to keep scandal from destroying the reputation of the federal government in this little burg. Thank God for a moral hero and Christian gentleman like Moreland J. Pinkerton, who will not let indecency and evil go on right under his nose."

"Are you making all this up?" I said.

Drodge gave me a look of mock horror. "Making it up! How could a respectable man like me do a terrible thing like that to a gentleman like Richard Shaw?"

I opened my mouth to say something and then closed it again.

"Of course there was also the affair of the young man on a dark night as he was coming home from church. The plump gentleman who offered him candy to go with him into the nearby woods. I believe the young man was twelve. I don't think we ought to have both a thirteen-year-old girl and a thirteen-year-old boy in the same report, you see. Variety lends a certain plausibility. The young man who reported the plump man to the sheriff did not identify him positively, but the description could fit Richard Shaw."

"I have not heard that story, either," I said drily.

"According to my information, Moreland J. Pinkerton summoned Mr. Shaw to his office for a reckoning about his morals, and Mr. Shaw created a disturbance."

"Did Pinkerton say that?"

"Of course not. The surprising thing about your employer is that he remains almost completely silent. And you need not worry about yourself. I shall not require you to lie. I have the feeling you wouldn't. If I know men like Richard Shaw, he will read my report, understand the stakes, and fade into oblivion like a fart in a crowd." He laughed and looked very wise.

"I'm going to recommend that we write Pinkerton a letter thanking him for upholding the moral reputation of the railroad at a time of grave national emergency. The man's worked hard down here. We owe him something. You don't toss a crazy old coot onto the scrap heap after all that. The railroad's humane, you know—merciful, when you think about it. We'll ease him out in time. We'll make some changes when this all blows over. To think that he expected to come to Washington because of Richard Shaw! That's funny. Curious how success is. It just came to me. I worked hard, but I became successful as easily as a man walking upstairs."

"It depends on whether a man has legs or not," I said.

Drodge's thin face brightened. "Yes. That's a very good way of putting it. Very good! Thank you for the compliment." He smiled like a child. I had to guess what the compliment was.

"Pinkerton doesn't have the legs for the climb, poor old coot. He may have been a giant here at one time, but he's a pygmy everywhere else. A man hurts himself when he won't recognize his limits, where he belongs."

"Very true," I said.

"At least he's harmless. He did pee in Shaw's face, but Shaw didn't die of it. I don't see an old man like him causing anybody trouble. Do you?"

"No," I said.

"We'll fix him if he does," Drodge said.

88

MORE SOLDIERS from the county came home every week. Spring broadened on the land—my second spring in Bourbonville—and people were happy. If you looked at the flowers, the roses growing in fence rows, the lilies in gardens, looked at the grass flourishing, looked at the hardwoods turning pale green; if you smelled the air, felt the mild warmth on your face like gentleness itself, if you kept your eyes averted from every human-made thing in the town, Bourbonville was beautiful in the spring.

The town passed into exaltation. The war was over; victory was complete; something grand would come of it. Woodrow Wilson would make peace in Paris, a peace that would end all wars and make the world safe for democracy.

Late in May Jim Ed came home with Willy. Dr. Youngblood went with Brian Ledbetter and a crowd of others to the railroad station to meet their train. The train pulled in, and the conductor, in navy blue with brass buttons, stepped down and put his hands up as though reaching for a child, and slowly, slowly came Willy descending, his blank, shattered face turning first this way and then that, his eyelids stitched shut, his scars raw and red, but the most horrible thing was that broken face turning, turning, looking sightlessly for someone. They were around him in a moment—tall Joab and Mary, the five daughters, Barbara first, Mrs. Ledbetter—and Willy was kissed and kissed and hugged and hugged and cried over, and slowly you could see him smile and cough, and people were shouting at him, and he was silent in their midst.

Dr. Youngblood and the old man stood back, Dr. Youngblood puffing his pipe; and behind Willy two big khaki duffel bags appeared and behind and above the duffel bags came Jim Ed, swinging down in a little gap of space and quiet as everyone else flocked around Willy.

"Hey, Bub!" the old man said, and Jim Ed looked at his father.

"Hey yourself," Jim Ed said.

"You look thin," the old man said.

"Don't know why. Haven't done much of anything but eat for the last six months."

"It's that frog food," the old man said. "It don't stick to your bones."

"Ain't had a good lard biscuit forever," Jim Ed said.

"I reckon we can fix you up some," the old man said.

All the time this laconic conversation was going on, tears were pouring down the old man's face.

Mrs. Ledbetter fell on her son, and he hugged her and kissed her on the cheek, and she kissed him on his cheek. She looked him up and down and said, "Jim Ed, brown just ain't your color. It never was."

"I tried to tell the officers that, Mamma, but they didn't much care."

"Brown is the color of dirt," Mrs. Ledbetter said. "I guess that's why they make army uniforms out of it."

"I sure have seen my share of dirt," Jim Ed said.

"We wore blue," the old man said.

"You didn't have machine guns," Jim Ed said.

Jim Ed expected Daisy to be there. Dr. Youngblood said he was hurt and puzzled that she was not.

There was to be a welcoming party at the Ledbetter home on a Saturday afternoon later on. Dr. Youngblood said I must go. Brian Ledbetter invited the world—except Moreland Pinkerton. "I can't forgive the man," Brian said. "As God is my witness I've tried, but I can't forgive him."

Clyde would be back in two weeks. He was visiting cathedrals in France. They would not have the party until he came home.

"Lord, I hope Clyde don't come home a Catholic," Brian Ledbetter said. "I served with a bunch of Irish Catholics in the war. I think of all that incense stinking up the house, and I don't see how I can take it. I'm just thankful for one thing about Clyde: he ain't gone through snake handling yet. I swear, if he was to bring a snake into my house, that'd be the end." Clyde was a chaplain in the army. He was always looking for the right religion.

89

A COUPLE OF DAYS after Jim Ed's homecoming, a black man I did not recognize brought the morning heat into the laboratory from the wheel foundry.

I do not think I have explained about the heats. Every batch of metal fired in a foundry furnace was called a heat. By the rules of the Interstate Commerce Commission, the chemist had to test a chunk of every heat from the wheel foundry for sulphur and silica. Too much sulphur or silica could make the iron brittle, and brittle iron could cause a broken wheel, throwing the car off the track and the train down a ravine, splintering the wooden box-cars, splitting open tank cars filled with chemicals or gasoline, causing fire and destruction. A block of iron from each heat was set aside, cooled, numbered with chalk, and brought into the laboratory. I recorded the number in a book, drilled out a sample, ran my tests on the filings, and recorded what I found. If the heat failed the tests, I had to order it turned into scrap.

Anyway, one morning about this time a new black man brought in the first heat of the day, swinging the chunk of iron with tongs as though it were a wad of paper. He dropped the iron on the concrete floor with a clang and stood leaning against the counter, his huge arms crossed in front of his chest.

"Good morning there, boss. It *sure* is a good morning now, ain't it? It's just the kind of morning that makes a man glad to be alive, now ain't it? I sure am glad to be alive, and I'm glad to have this here job, and I'm right glad to make your acquaintance, boss. Does you want me to dance?" He grinned and showed exceptionally white teeth.

"What?" I said.

"Dance, boss! Dance! Like Frankie. He's the little nigger that brings in the heats from the steel foundry. You seen Frankie dance, ain't you?"

Pinkerton had ordered Frankie to dance the first day I worked in the laboratory and repeated the order whenever he saw Frankie. Frankie obeyed Pinkerton. With me he was silent and morose. He brought the chunks of steel in from the steel heats, dropped them in the shed, and left, usually without a word. I did not order him to dance.

"I know the man of whom you speak," I said.

"The man of whom you speak," this black man said, mocking me. "Lord God, boss. You gonter give white folks around here conniption fits talking like that. 'The man of whom you speak.' Whooooo-eeee! But I bet you ain't never seen Frankie dance like this, has you?" He did a swift little galloping dance step, and his shoes clacked energetically against the cement floor. He was large and muscular, one of the blackest black men I had ever seen. He danced a moment or two, whispering some active little melody to himself and snapping his fingers. He abruptly stopped. His eyes impaled me. I must have looked amazed.

"You call that there the buck and wing, white boss. I can sing, too. You want me to sing and dance at the same time? I'll do it, by God. I can play the mouth organ, too. I got all the regular nigger talents."

"What are you talking about?" I said.

"Just what I says, boss. You need a shoe shine? I can make your brogan shoes shine like mirrors. You give me a pair of black shoes to shine, and when I gets through with them, you'll see your reflection in the toes and think you've turned nigger yourself. I preach a little on the side, and I sings spirituals. I knows all twenty verses of all the spirituals that has ever been sung by any nigger on the face of God's green earth. But maybe you be the mammy kind."

"The what?"

"The kind that loves stories about how good nigger mammies has been to little white children who loved them mammies up a storm. If you loved your nigger mammy, that means you love all the niggers. You may shoot one or two now and then, or maybe stomp one or two for not taking off their hats when they passes you in the street, or maybe you string one up to a lamppost because he wasn't more than six miles away when some white woman say she been raped by a nigger. But if you love your nigger mammy, that means you love all us black folks. Love your nigger mammy, and you one hell of a good Christian."

"I do not understand," I said.

"Maybe you's the dog kind."

"The what?"

"The dog kind, boss, the—"

"The kind that likes stories about dogs."

"You got it, boss. Go to the head of the class! I heard you was smart. You be the foreign gentleman, ain't you? A real live Frenchman, I hears."

"Belgian," I said.

"Belgian. You don't look Belgian to me, boss. Not that I'm disputing your word. No siree. This nigger wouldn't be dumb enough to dispute no white boss's word, even if that white man was some foreigner that don't know nothing about how we does things here in Tennessee. I seen a lot of Belgians in the war. Got home two weeks ago. Don't you want to know my name, white boss?"

"You have not given me time to ask," I said.

"Hey, that's right, white boss. I'd send you to the head of the class again, but by God, you already there. Well, I'll tell you what my name is. Standing right here before you is Moreland Pinkerton. That's me, boss. Moreland Pinkerton." He delivered himself of a large, false laugh and slapped his knee.

"Please," I said. "I have work to do. I do not have time to stand here and make foolish talk."

"Boss, this ain't foolish talk. I'm telling you the gospel sure-enough fourteen-carat-gold truth. Does I look like the kind of person who'd tell a nice white boss like you a lie?"

"I do not care whether you tell me a lie or the truth," I said.

"Oh, boss, I've hurt your feelings. Well, you listen to me. My name *is* Moreland Pinkerton. But it's Moreland Pinkerton Brown. Folks just calls me M.P. for short."

His face shone with sweat, and his perfect teeth made a brilliant contrast with his skin. His chest looked like a torso you might see in a museum or in the ruins of a classical site, only it was black.

"Your name truly is Moreland Pinkerton Brown?" I said.

"Ah, look at him. He believes me, and by God he's interested. Yes sir," he said with a deep bow. The words came out as "Yassuh," and I did not at first know what they meant. "My daddy, he come up here with the Captain when the car works was being built. My daddy helped drain the swamp. You know this place is built on what was a swamp?"

"Yes, I know," I said.

"Sure you do. I hears tell that you're one smart white foreign gentleman. Most foreign gentlemen I know has information, and information makes the world go round."

"Who told you I was foreign?"

"I ask questions, boss. That is how you get information. I knows all about you, but you don't know nothing about me. It don't seem hardly fair, does it?"

I looked at him. By now I vaguely understood that he was trying to intimidate me, that this outpouring of scarcely comprehensible thoughts, spoken in a loud, jovial tone as if we both understood perfectly what he was talking about, was an attack, intended to put me on the defensive.

"I have work to do," I said.

"You've said that, boss. But I'm telling you if it wasn't for the black folks like my daddy, you wouldn't have no place to work. You wouldn't have no car works. My daddy died here. He fell into one of them annealing pits. My daddy was roasted alive."

"How horrible," I said.

"Burned up like a chicken in a fire," the black man said with sudden tenderness.

"I am sorry," I said.

"I was, too," M.P. said. "It was bad."

"Your father named you after Mr. Pinkerton."

"You got it, boss. I was born in 1893. You know how old that makes me. I'm just about as old as the car works."

We looked at each other for a moment. "So, what do you think about niggers?" he said.

"I do not think anything about them," I said.

"You don't think nothing about us? Come on, boss. You're lying to this poor old nigger. Every white man in the world thinks something about niggers. You think we're hewers of wood and drawers of water? Ain't that right? You think we ain't more than one and a half step above the gorilla— ain't that right? You think uppity niggers ought to be strung up—ain't that right?" His voice came at me like a machine gun.

"I do not," I said, confused and annoyed.

"You don't think them things? Well, you got to think *something*, boss. You can't live down here in good old Bourbonville, Tennessee, without thinking something about the niggers. But maybe you ain't quite telling me all you knows, white boss. Maybe you got to give this old nigger some more information. What do you know about Mr. Vladimir Lenin?"

"I know only what I read in the newspapers."

"Mr. Vladimir Lenin is one smart man," M.P. said. "I knowed some froggies that thought Mr. V. I. Lenin was the smartest man in the world. What do you think? You can tell me the truth." He narrowed his eyes and searched my face.

"I know little about him." I felt uncomfortable.

"You know folks that knowed him?"

"I had a friend before the war who was a Socialist. He is dead. I never heard him mention Lenin."

I saw Guy standing behind M.P., looking with skeptical curiosity at this bizarre black man.

M.P. looked disappointed. "Let me tell you, boss. You gonter hear lots about Mr. Vladimir Lenin before all this is over. Time's gonter come, boss, when they gonter be a statue of Mr. Vladimir Lenin right here on the courthouse lawn."

"You're going to have to kill a few people before that will happen," I said.

He leaned forward, speaking quietly with the volubility of conviction. The transformation was unsettling. "We may have to kill some folks, boss. But not many. Times is gonter be so bad that everybody's gonter want the revolution like hungry folks wants food. We're gonter have a big boom, and then we're gonter have a big bust, and when the big bust comes, the revolution is gonter come like lightning."

"How can you seriously believe in a revolution?"

"You read the Bible, boss?"

"I wish you would not call me 'boss,' " I said. "No, I do not read the Bible."

"Well now, you is missing out on a lot of good information, boss. Read the Bible, and you'll see. We're in the last days, boss. New day coming. The day of Jubilee. Mr. Vladimir Lenin is gonter take us to the day of Jubilee. White folks, black folks. We're all going to Jubilee together."

"Lenin does not believe in God. He is an atheist."

"Hell, boss! I don't believe in that old-timey God that the nigger preachers talk about. That old sweet-Jesus licky-my-shoe God ain't good for nothing. The real God ain't got no white beard, and he don't wear no halo. That God has got judgment in his hand and blood up to his knees and Vladimir Lenin in his vest pocket. That's the God that wanted Saul to kill the Amalekites. You know that God, boss?"

"I do not know what you are talking about!"

M.P. gave me another searching and critical look. "Begging your pardon then, boss. I thought that being as how you come from the froggie lands, you might know Mr. Vladimir Lenin. I thought you might even be one of his people. I thought maybe you'd been sent."

"I do not know what you are talking about," I said.

The false accent came back. "Hey there, boss. You sure am smart. You speaking the truth there, boss. I sure better shut my mouth. But I tell you something, white man. The day is coming when everything will be made plain. Then you see, boss. Then you see."

"I can wait," I said. I turned away. I wondered if this man might be dangerously crazy.

"Et vous parlez français très bien, n'est-ce pas?" he said suddenly in perfect French.

I whirled and looked at him with astonishment. He was grinning broadly, his immaculate white teeth gleaming in his ebony face. .

"Alors, vous me comprenez," he said, looking pleased.

I replied to him in French without thinking of what I was doing. "Of course I understand," I said. "But how do you speak French?"

"I was in the French army."

"The French army? How could you have been in the French army?"

"I volunteered," he said. "I left Bourbon County in 1912," he said. "I wanted to see the world. I rode freight trains to New York, and I shipped out to sea on a merchantman. A stoker—*un chauffeur!* I shoveled coal like a machine two years."

"Two years."

"It made me a man. On a big ship a stoker works eight hours a day shoveling coal. You work two hours, and you sleep two hours. It pays good wages, and nobody bothers you. It is hard work—very hard work. You meet people, too. When the war came in 1914, my ship was in Le Havre in early August. I got permission to leave and join the French Army."

It made a splendid kind of sense. Black soldiers from French Africa fought on the Western Front. Congolese troops fought in the Belgian army. Why not an American?

"They put me to repairing truck engines. Then they moved me to airplanes. I was there four years. I learned a thing or two."

"I can see you did," I said.

"Well, you just recollect that now, boss." He shifted abruptly to English. "It ain't too good for you and me to be standing around here making frog talk like we been doing. I's just your general dumb old nigger to most of these white folks, and if you ask me, it's better to stay that way. See you around, white folks. You forget what I said about Vladimir Lenin, you hear? You forget all about it. See you around."

He took his tongs, pointed them at me with an ambiguous gesture, waved, and went out through the door of the laboratory in the direction of the wheel foundry, the light gleaming on his bare shoulders, and I could hear his laughter come and go until it was finally absorbed in the roar of the foundry.

"Hephaistos," I thought suddenly.

But M.P. was not lame.

Every day he came bringing the heats; every day we talked. He was self-educated—the typical autodidact, with contradictory opinions passionately held. I was uninformed about politics because I did not read the newspapers, but even I could see the foolishness of a man who believed the Bible and V. I. Lenin with equal conviction. I thought he was a harmless and good-natured eccentric.

90

CLYDE CAME HOME in June, and Dr. Youngblood took me to the party the Ledbetters gave for their children.

The car works had stopped working its Saturday-morning shift—a temporary cessation, Dale Farmer said. He put the best face on things, but he worried. The economy was slowing down; fewer trains were running. On the Saturday of the party, the car works lay silent. Dr. Youngblood came by the boardinghouse in the afternoon to pick me up.

"I should not go," I said.

"Nonsense," he said.

"It is not nonsense. I do not belong."

"If Brian Ledbetter says you belong, you belong."

He was happy as he turned the car south of town, and his face glowed. "It's going to be a wonderful party," he said. "I sewed up all the bloody ones that came to the office this morning. I took care of a broken finger and a broken leg. I told the folks with summer colds and headaches to see Dr. Bulkely." He laughed.

"Has he spoken to you yet?" I said.

"I made him," Dr. Youngblood said with a chuckle. "I went to call on him."

"Was he friendly?"

"He was correct. He told me we should work together to prevent disease before it happens. It was kind of like a speech to a graduating class at medical school."

"What did you tell him?"

"I said that unfortunately we had a lot of diseases we had to take care of because nobody had prevented them yet."

"What did he say?"

"He said he thought people brought their sicknesses on themselves. If you get sick, it's because you do something wrong. If you chew your food and don't smoke or drink and if you take exercise every day and drink hot water first thing in the morning and think optimistic thoughts, you won't get sick. He told me you could smile your way through just about anything. He said you ought to smile even when you don't feel like it because a smile makes you feel good when you do it."

"A comfort for the afflicted," I said.

"Well, he is young," Dr. Youngblood said. "Doctors can learn. You may not believe it, but they can."

"When is he going to tear down Virgil's office?"

"I asked him. He was vague. I don't think he has any money now. He was irritated that I knew his plans. He does not understand a small town yet."

"I hope he waits for a while," I said.

"Until Brian dies," Dr. Youngblood said.

"Yes," I said uncomfortably.

"You are beginning to think like me," Dr. Youngblood said with another of his gravelly chuckles.

"Tell you one thing," he said after a while. "This is going to be a nice party. But if D.B. had lived, Virgil would have given a homecoming for him that people would be talking about when your grandchildren are in their dotage."

"Yes," I said.

I heard Guy whisper, "If I had lived through the war, my parents would have given a party that would have been studied by scholars a thousand years from now." His voice was like the wind blowing by the open windows of the car.

"You are not going to leave us after all," Dr. Youngblood said cautiously, not looking at me.

"No," I said. "Not now. I will leave later on, but not now." I paused, considering how much to tell him. "My sister is getting married. She must have a dowry."

"You still do that, do you?"

"Yes," I said.

He drove thoughtfully for a time, watching the road. "You will not go home," he said. "I will not go back to Baltimore, and you will not go back to your home."

"You will see," I said.

"So will you," he said. We spoke no more about it.

When we arrived, a crowd had already gathered. A few dusty cars were parked along the driveway. Wagons, horses, and mules were everywhere—wagons parked in a field, horses and mules unhitched and led into the shade of a woods, where they stood patiently switching their tails. We parked and walked up a curving gravel driveway shaded by apple trees laden with ripening fruit. The Ledbetter house was neat white frame with a verandah across the front and tall shade trees in the yard.

It was a country crowd, a country holiday. The smell of meat roasting over an open fire filled the air. Unexpectedly I felt hungry.

Dr. Youngblood was greeted everywhere with affection. He shuffled from one group to another, beaming, smoking his pipe, chuckling, receiving adulation, looking like some benign Buddha with a ruddy face enlightened with the knowledge that he had, all unknowing, created a lovely world. Anecdotes of his deeds clustered around him like the nimbus of a saint. Our passage provided an excuse for the storytellers of the county to construct a pageant of disorganized biography ordered by their conviction that some good men lived in creation, that Dr. Youngblood was one.

One man, holding up the smooth stump of an arm, told how Dr. Youngblood had come to his house at three in the morning to amputate a hand that had been mauled by a machine.

"I was dead drunk, if you want to know the facts of the business," he said. "When I done it, I didn't know how bad it was. I figured I could wait till next day, and I reckon I thought that the goddamned thing would get better on its own, and I wouldn't have to pay Doc here no bill. But hell, when the whiskey wore off, I like to of went crazy, it hurt so bad. When I tried to move, I couldn't do nothing but scream. The old woman, she laid wet sheets on me to keep the fever down, and I'll tell you what's God's own truth: you could of boiled an egg in my mouth. That's how bad my fever was. My oldest—that was little Cephas that wasn't more than eight year old at the time—he taken and rode into town on the mule we called Frank to fetch the doc here. Goddamn if the doc wasn't out there by dawn on horseback. That was afore he got rich enough to have a car, you see. He was young, too, wasn't you, Doc? Had all your hair. This man had curly hair when he come down here. We've snatched him bald-headed. Anyhow, he cut my hand off slick as a chicken's head. Put me to sleep with chloroform, and when I come to, I didn't have that hand. I didn't have no pain neither, and my fever was broke. Lordy, I was sweating like a hog."

He held up the stump. People admired it as they might have revered a religious relic. Some touched it in amazement. Dr. Youngblood grinned around his pipe. "You get the credit, Mack," he said. "You'd lost so much blood, I figured you'd die. You've got the constitution of a mule, and here we are."

"Here we are," Mack said. He was a little drunk and very happy. There was a barrel of whiskey out back with a metal dipper hanging next to it. Hub Delaney's best.

Hub Delaney was there, too feeble to sit up. He lay dozing on a long garden chair covered with a red blanket, his skin yellow as an onion and thin over his bones. His eyes were sunk in his head. The outline of his skull was clear. When I spoke to him, he knew me at once, opened his eyes, and made an effort to smile.

"I ain't like I was," he whispered.

"No," I said.

"You seen Willy?" he said.

"Not yet," I said.

"He's blind," Hub said.

"I know," I said.

"Tell you the truth, Doc. If you'd been over there in France with Willy, he wouldn't be blind now."

"There're some things a doctor can't do," Dr. Youngblood said.

"Ain't much *you* can't do, Doc," Hub murmured.

"There're many things I can't do," Dr. Youngblood said.

"There's sure lots of things *I* can't do," Hub said, shutting his eyes. "Brian had to tote me down here like a baby. He said I had to come. I wanted to come, too. Lordy, it's something when a growed man like me has to be carried around by the likes of Brian Ledbetter. You want to know what's truly funny? I'm wearing a big diaper. Brian Ledbetter put . . ." With that his voice trailed away, and he took shallow breaths. His mouth was open. I thought he had gone to sleep. Dr. Youngblood checked his pulse and looked at me. We went quietly away. Hub smelled bad. We did not mention it.

Willy was sitting in a wooden lawn chair in the shade of a maple tree.

People gathered around him. They did not know how to talk to him, but they tried. He sat blank-faced, returning greetings laconically. "They have to take out the whole eye in cases like this," Dr. Youngblood told me. "That's why they sew the eyelids shut. You don't want infections getting up in there. Too close to the brain. Besides, folks don't want to be looking into somebody's skull." Dr. Youngblood stood in front of Willy, smoking his pipe, holding it with one hand, the other arm folded across his chest, and I realized that he was making a quiet judgment on how good Willy's doctors had been.

I felt Bernal near me and turned around to look for him. I could not see him.

Dr. Youngblood introduced me; Willy's mouth flickered. He put out a tentative hand, and I took it. "I've heard about you. You're the foreigner. Everybody talks about you. I reckon you're the most exciting thing that's happened to Bourbonville since we've been gone." He spoke slowly, and we were silent. Then he said, "I reckon you and me both wishes we'd stayed home."

"Yes," I said. "I wish I had stayed home."

"I didn't think it'd end up like this," Willy said.

"I did not, either," I said.

"That's the way it is," Willy said.

"Yes," I said.

"At least we wasn't kilt like some," Willy said.

"No," I said.

"You and me ought to talk sometime," Willy said. "I bet we got a lot to talk about."

I murmured an insincere assent. I did not want to talk about the war.

91

JIM ED LEDBETTER stood on the verandah at the top of the steps, a slender man with sandy hair, tall, with freckles, stooped shoulders, a pleasant, open face with intelligent blue eyes, easy with people. He was about ten years older than I, with rawboned good looks. He wore baggy cotton trousers and a much-washed khaki army shirt open at the neck. I saw him and had a sudden, vivid image of how the old man must have looked when he was young.

People crowded up to shake hands with him, people full of respect, even reverence, good cheer, love. He had something to say to each of them. Now and then he burst out with laughter, bending his tall body back at the waist, and people around him laughed, too.

We waited our turn at the bottom of the steps and moved ceremonially upwards as the line moved. Brian Ledbetter, stumping out of the house, saw us. I had never seen him so happy.

"Doc! Paul! Come on up! Come on up!"

The old man pushed us in front of Jim Ed, and Jim Ed first saw Dr. Youngblood, putting out his hand, smiling like the sky. "Hey, Doc! I didn't get to say much of anything to you at the train. It *sure* is good to see you." He pounded Dr. Youngblood affectionately on the shoulder, and Dr. Youngblood grinned and turned red, and his eyes went down to little slits in his head, and he remarked on how fine Jim Ed was looking.

Somehow I was introduced. I was Paul Alexander. I was the foreigner. I put out my hand to take his. Jim Ed's smile died. He did not put out his hand. "I know all about you, mister."

"What do you know about him?" Brian Ledbetter asked, seeing something was wrong.

"Daisy wrote me all about him. He did her wrong."

Dr. Youngblood looked level and stern. "That is not true," he said. "Paul is an honorable man; he has not done Daisy or anybody else wrong."

"That's what she told me, and Daisy don't tell lies. She said this man told her he was going to marry her, and then she wrote that he'd broken his word. He did her wrong. I got the letters to prove it."

Brian Ledbetter put his hand on his son's shoulder. "Daisy don't know what's she's talking about, Jim Ed. She lives in fairyland. You ought to know that by now."

"I care a lot for Daisy," Jim Ed said. "I don't like to see her made a fool of. You promised to marry her."

I was angry. "I made no such promise," I said, my voice icy. "And *I* did not do *her* any harm." I turned to Dr. Youngblood. "I want to leave. I told you that I should not come here."

Brian Ledbetter looked stern and unhappy. "Jim Ed, son, I'm gladder that you're home than anything else I've been glad about since you was born. But this is my house, and Paul here is my friend, and he is our guest, and he is an honest man. He didn't do Daisy no harm. The girl like to of dogged him to death. Paul, if you leave now, I'll call this whole party off right this minute. I will walk down there in front, and I will ring the dinner bell, and I will tell folks to go home."

Jim Ed said, "The foreign son of a bitch can stay till hell freezes over for all I care. All I know is that Daisy isn't here because she wrote me that he did her wrong. She said she couldn't stand to be in Bourbonville anymore and be a laughingstock because of the way this man shamed her."

"Oh, now, Jim Ed, be reasonable!" Dr. Youngblood said, frowning and looking irate and exasperated. He started to say more, but Brian Ledbetter cut in.

"Daisy ain't here because Virgil went off like a damned fool to California. You know why Virgil left. You come home alive, and D.B. didn't come home at all, and Virgil can't bear it. That's the real true fact of the business. You know Daisy, too. You can't believe nothing Daisy says. She's read so many of them dime novels and such trash that she don't know the difference between what's real and what's in books. If I ordered a trainload of dumbbells, and they just sent me Daisy, I'd sign for the shipment."

"Daisy wrote me the truth," Jim Ed said.

"She did not tell you the truth about me," I said.

"I believe her," Jim Ed said.

I turned to Dr. Youngblood. "I want to leave."

"All right," Dr. Youngblood said. "I want to leave, too."

"Then the party's over," Brian Ledbetter said, his face full of wrath. "Mrs. Ledbetter! Mrs. Ledbetter!"

Mrs. Ledbetter put her head out the door. "What is wrong with you now, Mr. Ledbetter?"

"Get me the dinner bell. I'm calling off this party."

She looked at him and looked at us and looked around the vast host of people in the yard. She came out, wiping her hands on her apron. "What?"

"I am calling off the party because Jim Ed is acting a fool with Paul here. He believes the tomfool stuff Daisy wrote him about Paul."

Mrs. Ledbetter looked at her son. "I don't know what Daisy told you, but I can guess," she said. "Let me tell you a thing or two. Daisy like to of drove this poor boy crazy. She wouldn't give him no peace. She followed him around like a puppy dog. If you don't believe that, you're calling your own mamma a liar, Jim Ed Ledbetter. I hope it ain't come to that. If it has, I'll fetch the dinner bell for your daddy."

Jim Ed took a deep breath, clearly perplexed. "I said it don't matter to me," he muttered. "He can stay if he wants to stay."

"You tell him you're sorry," his mother said.

Jim Ed looked more and more exasperated. "All right," he growled. "I'm sorry. You stay, you hear? Doc? I'm sorry. Truly. I want you both to stay."

He ambled away without looking back, and his face became pleasant and relaxed talking to other people.

"I can walk back to town," I said. "I am accustomed to walking. I love to walk, and it will be no trouble."

"No, you cannot leave," Dr. Youngblood said.

"You're damned right," the old man said. "If you leave, the party's over."

"Why did Daisy tell him that I promised to marry her?"

"Because she wanted you to marry her," Dr. Youngblood said. "She thought that if she said you were going to marry her, you might do it."

"Daisy ain't got the sense of a pullet," Brian Ledbetter said.

"We all want you to stay, Mr. Alexander," Mrs. Ledbetter said. "Jim Ed's going to believe Mr. Ledbetter and me. We ain't never lied to him. If you go off and leave, and if we call the party off like we will, he's going to feel awful bad about it, and we'll have a bad memory that'll be like a rock in our shoes whenever we think about our boy coming home. He's a good boy. I'm begging you to stay."

I could not resist such a plea, though I was still puzzled and angry. "Why did she lie?" I said.

"She didn't know she was lying," Dr. Youngblood said. "She can't tell the difference."

"She don't know nothing," Brian Ledbetter said.

"She's a sad, mixed-up young woman," Mrs. Ledbetter said.

Dr. Youngblood took me by the arm. "Come on. Let's have some more whiskey. Not many times a man has an excuse to drink whiskey in the middle of the day. This is Hub's finest. We won't have him or it for very long."

92

CLYDE WEAVER. I met him that afternoon. Clyde bore a family resemblance to Jim Ed—slender, not quite so tall. They had the same mother, different fathers, and while something about Jim Ed instantly recalled Brian Ledbetter, Clyde resembled Virgil, and both of them, I suppose, resembled their long-dead father, of whom Clyde had no memory at all.

Clyde asked Dr. Youngblood to introduce us and shook hands with me with grave courtesy.

"You are a Catholic," Clyde said without preamble.

"I do not practice my religion."

"Ah," Clyde said. "You are then a lapsed Catholic."

"Let's get some whiskey," Dr. Youngblood said.

"I believe I should abstain," Clyde said carefully. "A minister should not break the law."

"You don't have a church right now," Dr. Youngblood said. We walked towards the whiskey barrel at the barn behind the house.

"I shall have a church when I'm sure I have the right one," Clyde said.

"A little tot might help you look for it," Dr. Youngblood said cheerfully.

"If people were to see a minister of the Gospel drinking an alcoholic beverage, especially since whiskey is against the law in Tennessee, it would hurt his influence," Clyde said.

"Most preachers I know would be better off under the influence now and then," Dr. Youngblood said.

"I believe that our most important question in life is this," Clyde said. "What happens to us after death?"

"I don't think much of anything happens to us after death," Dr. Youngblood said. "We just rot away."

"That is natural reason speaking," Clyde said. "The tradition of the Catholic Church stands against reason by providing a story of how God works within the world. If we believe the story, we do not have to explain it by reason. But to believe the story, we must believe the teller of the tale. So the second most important question after what happens after death is this one. Whose story do we believe?"

"A lot of storytellers lie like carnival pitchmen, Clyde," Dr. Youngblood said.

"True," Clyde said. "Very true. I am not sure that I believe that the Pope tells the story truly. But the Catholic Church claims miracles that validate its version of the story. But do the miracles happen, and if they do, what do they prove? I ask you, Dr. Youngblood, as a man of science, can you believe in the resurrection of Christ? If one of your patients was to rise from the dead before your eyes, what would you do?"

"I'd jump out of my skin," Dr. Youngblood said. "And then I'd go have a good stiff drink. Maybe I'd have a drink with the stiff himself." He chuckled.

"Yes, yes," Clyde mused without a smile. "The natural man speaks in your voice, Dr. Youngblood. We do not believe miracles even if we see them."

"Clyde, I don't want to talk about religion today," Dr. Youngblood said. "I want to drink whiskey. I want to celebrate your homecoming."

"I believe I can prove that God exists," Clyde said carefully. "I argue from the design in the universe. Do you think that something as miraculous as the human eyeball could have come about solely by the chance of evolution? I have studied Mr. Charles Darwin carefully. Even Mr. Charles Darwin cannot explain the human eyeball. I say there is only one rational explanation— God. Only God can create the eyeball." He paused and bit his lip and knotted his brow. "The only trouble is," he said with great hesitation, "I can appreciate his intelligence, but I do not know what he is like. I can't tell which religion tells the truest stories about him."

"Why don't you stop worrying about it, and everything will be all right," Dr. Youngblood said gently.

"If I stop worrying about it, I may go to hell," Clyde said.

"Jesus," Dr. Youngblood said.

"Do you believe in the divinity of Christ, Mr. Alexander?"

"I do not think about such questions," I said.

"Ah, then you are an atheist like Dr. Youngblood?" Clyde said.

"I suppose," I said uncomfortably.

"But what about the eyeball?" Clyde said.

"Willy's eyeballs are gone," I said.

"Ah," Clyde said, looking very troubled. "You are asking the reason for evil in the universe. That is another way of inquiring after the nature of God. That is the question I am trying to answer."

"I do not believe there is an answer," I said.

"That is a counsel of despair. If we give up on religion, there's nothing left to us but death."

"If death is all there is, believing in God cannot change it," I said.

"You must consider Cicero," Clyde said. "He said there has to be some truth to religion, or else we would not be religious. Thomas Aquinas held that we must have immortal souls because there is a natural desire for immortality, and natural desires must be fulfilled."

"Do you think if we want something we're going to get it?" Dr. Young-blood asked. "I'd take a dose of religion like that." He laughed.

Clyde's face glowed with the love of argument. "Of course not," he said. "But we desire only what exists. We are hungry. That is a natural desire. Our hunger indicates that there must be such a thing as food. Otherwise we would not be hungry. Do you follow me?"

"Clyde, I don't want to talk about it," Dr. Youngblood said.

Clyde could not be stopped. "We desire everlasting life. We desire it universally. Is that not true?"

"I am not sure that it is," Dr. Youngblood said.

"Of course it is," Clyde said impatiently. "Yes, the occasional sick person, the person sick in the mind such as the suicide, may for a moment wish to die. But that is a form of sickness. It is as though someone who has not eaten in a while has no desire to eat. The healthy person desires to live. No healthy person wants to die. Do you agree?"

"It may be that only when we are healthy do we wish to continue living," Dr. Youngblood said. "When we wish to die, it may be a sign that we have completed life and that we should surrender to death."

"Are you saying that Thomas Aquinas is wrong?"

"I am saying that perhaps he was healthy when he wrote about eternal life. If he had been sick, he might have written something else. If he could have written when he lay dying, he might have greeted death as the autumn leaves greet the earth when they fall."

"A poetic thought," Clyde said without irony or mockery. "But poetry is not theology. Theology is built upon logic—the iron laws of reason. I intend to prove that God exists and that we should worship him only the way that he approves. But alas! I am not sure of the way he approves." Clyde looked genuinely lost and sad, and I decided he must have in him some strain of craziness.

We stopped at the whiskey barrel near the barn. Dr. Youngblood filled two tumblers of whiskey with a tin dipper. He handed me one of them. "If you're going to talk about religion with Clyde, you need some nourishment," Dr. Youngblood said. I drank and felt the whiskey scald my throat and spread through my body. I felt much better.

93

I DRANK MUCH WHISKEY. Brian Ledbetter rescued us from Clyde, steering him off to set up tables and chairs. Caleb spoke to me with alcoholic warmth and hurried about giving orders, waving his arms like a field marshal presiding over dubious battle. He gave one command and rushed on to give another before he could see the first one obeyed. The old man plodded after him, in grim patience, making sure that everything was done.

Caleb saw everybody as a customer. He handed out business cards. "Let's hope the need is far off—*very* far off," he said. "But when there *is* a need, next to your minister the person you need most is your mortician. We can now preserve the body for a hundred years. By that time the great day of resurrection may have come." With that he bowed his head as though in a gesture of prayer, handed over his card, gave the recipient a solemn pat on the shoulder showing his deepest sympathy for future loss, and hurried on to the next client. Caleb smelled like an empty whiskey barrel left in a hot place.

We ate barbecued pork and beef and chicken. Dr. Youngblood and I took places on the wide verandah, sitting on kitchen chairs near the door. The broad valley north and west of the house lay in a summer haze. The woods a hundred meters away stood green and thick and still. People swarmed across the yard, eating, drinking, talking, and laughing. In the late afternoon Brian Ledbetter rang a bell for quiet and made a speech. His son was home. The war was over. Most boys from the county had survived. Many were here today. He was sad for those who had died. He was happy for the rest. His voice trembled, and he faltered, fighting the tears.

People started cheering and clapping, and Brian stopped, and Jim Ed appeared on the porch near Dr. Youngblood and me with a guitar and a mandolin, and around him other men with instruments collected themselves—a fiddle player (I still called it a violin then), a couple of banjo players, a tubercular-looking man with a dulcimer, three men besides Jim Ed with guitars—and I saw that according to a universal expectation, they would now play.

Jim Ed laid the mandolin on an empty chair near me, without giving me a glance. Its dark wood shone. He seated himself and stretched his long legs and tuned at his guitar. The other men sat down beside him, and people gathered at the foot of the steps and on the porch. Some sat in the grass, others brought benches and Caleb's folding chairs over, everyone looking up in anticipation.

"I ain't played for a long time here," Jim Ed said with a ritually modest laugh. "I played in the war when I could get to a guitar. They was nights when I wanted to play and couldn't. Sometimes I'd sit there in the trenches, listening to the big guns off in the distance and trying to hear if there was somebody sneaking up on me, and I'd move my fingers like I was playing, and I'll tell you something: I could hear the music in the dark. Even without a guitar in my hand, I could move my fingers, and I heard the music. Isn't that something?" His words dwindled to an embarrassed chuckle.

A murmur of assent, and silence settled over the uplifted faces.

"So it's real good to get back here and play real music whenever I want to. I just hope you folks are in a mood to listen. Boys?"

He looked around and nodded. Another murmur of approbation passed through the crowd, followed by a deeper silence. Jim Ed struck a G chord, and the men strummed briefly, listened, and tightened or loosened strings. The sun was a huge red disk low over the western trees. Twilight was stealing out of the woods. Shadows stretched across the earth, and in the quiet before the music began, you could hear the humming of bees and the singing of birds.

I am not so foolish as to describe music with words. I will say only that after all these years I remember the sudden, vital, and harmonious notes filling the thickening light. It sobered me and gave me unexpected delight.

Jim Ed took the lead. The others watched him with expressionless faces and picked up his tune and his rhythm. He played the melody. They played over it, under it, around it, and made variations on it. Always his line dominated the rest. They played old ballads. They were new to me then, haunting and melancholy. Their music was different from mine, but not so different that it failed to call up memories from the hidden places in my heart. I heard the shepherds singing in the treeless hills of Greece, and the eternal blind harper strumming his lyre to stories of love and war in an age before anyone knew how much time there was and how much time was yet to come and how long the dead are dead.

Jim Ed sang sometimes, his voice a piercing tenor, wavering and free, without the affectations of trained singers I had heard, a voice almost harsh, natural, deep with feeling. Often the others joined the chorus, melding in a wailing harmony that I had never heard before. They sang of love and loss, murder, betrayal, and death, and they sang of heaven and Jesus and sorrow and pilgrims in a rhythm regular as a drum. In some hymns, the assembly joined, and the slow, ponderous rolling of the music made it seem as if the earth itself sang in uplifting abnegation, as strong as the mountains. I was entranced by the spell of whiskey and music, the multitude of harmonies, crowding into a moment that dissolved the world into itself as some philoso- phers have said that God sees time, all beginnings and all endings in one prolonged and dreamless present moment, held in God's hand and known by his mind, the eternal now. I felt at peace, afloat above the earth.

The sun fell, and the twilight came, and in the dimness I could see the faint brightness of faces where people sat listening in a silence so deep that they were like phantoms. Someone lit a coal oil lamp and hung it on a hook from the porch ceiling. It shed a circle of yellow light and made the elon- gated shadows of the musicians move in surreal shapes against the house. Choirs of insects in the woods started to sing and became a chorus to the music of the men, rising and falling in a grand and primordial rhythm.

Out there in the dimness near the trees I could see Guy and Bernal illuminated by a spectral light just where the woods began, and as I yearned for them, my heart jumped, and knots rose on my flesh. There was a third man. It was Stephanos—dear, beloved, inept, dead Stephanos, come to the music like the shades from the underworld when they heard the lyre of Orpheus, Stephanos released by a dazed Apollyon, lord of the bottomless pit, beguiled by the magic of harmonies.

Stephanos was there, and I thought of how he had played in his last solitude on the terrace of the hotel in Delphi, the terrace looking down into the yellow and green Gorge of Pleistos, where he knew he would die. He must have thought of me as he sat there, playing his final melody. Now he was here, and I could not speak to him because he was beyond the reach of my voice, and had I rushed towards him, I could not touch him because the densely packed crowd was between us, and I knew that when I had pushed through them, he would be gone. Oh yes, it was insane and hopeless and all the other things that I can say now in the pleasant darkness of an autumn night long, long afterwards. I remember how vivid it was then, how filled with sweetness like the smell of honeysuckle in the spring evening.

Jim Ed played his mandolin a couple of times, but he preferred the guitar. At a moment I noticed the disused mandolin on the empty chair next to me. Looking out across the lake of dimly shining faces towards the brighter shining of Stephanos, I picked it up. Jim Ed was singing. He glanced at me in undisguised irritation. I paid no attention. I took up the mandolin, listening to their music but looking towards the spectral glow at the woods, and I ran my fingers experimentally over the strings and the frets, feeling the differences between the mandolin and the bouzouki, feeling also how much alike they were, my fingers remembering, and I believed that I heard a whisper of encouragement and pleasure from Stephanos, perhaps only a breeze from the gathering night.

I picked up the notes and the rhythms of the other players. I heard them all distinctly now—as a musician always hears music—and I played, slowly at first, feeling my way with infinite caution, striking one note out of every four that they struck, turning to watch Jim Ed's fingers on the frets of his guitar, and I became more sure, playing more notes, testing out the instrument, pausing once briefly to bring a string into perfect pitch, then suddenly, as though bursting from restraint, swimming in a current of sound all around me, feeling for my place, and an old and half-forgotten power came pouring back. My stiff fingers loosened. For the first time since 1914 I felt confidence, and I felt desire—desire to play. I cannot explain all that it was. I experienced it as a flood and a liberation, a spiritual outpouring, and the infallible harmonies danced in my head, and the colors I had once seen in time to music leaped to the rhythm and formed themselves into geometrical shapes of ethereal beauty. In my ecstasy, joined to earth by the music of the others, I played.

Jim Ed changed. I could not see clearly enough to know how he changed, but I could feel it—some loosening of his body, some special attention now turned on me. He sang. I played, and my harmonies embraced him, rushing around his voice, holding him up, holding his music up. He stopped singing, and we were playing together, my fingers floating effortlessly over the strings and the frets, my heart in my fingers, and all the world gathered in around us to hear the music. Slowly I heard the silence fall behind us as the others one by one stopped their playing, leaving us at last with the tall fiddle player, a thin man with a prominent Adam's apple, and finally he stopped, leaving Jim Ed and me playing alone, our hands racing together in the lamplight, our bodies close but not touching, our minds joined in the music beyond all worlds.

I followed his lead, and I made the music that he made, except that as he played I made his music more profound. At first he played as though trying to shake me off. He was a horse, I the rider. He resolved to fling me into the dust. I saw Stephanos as a phantom phosphorescence in the distant dark of the woods, and I thought of all our days. Jim Ed's music was the wind coming off the tops of the high, bare hills of home. I played like a harp hung in a mountain gorge, the wind rolling through me, making the glory come. Jim Ed stopped trying to fling me off, and we played as one, his music reaching to me, mine reaching back to him.

I do not know how long we played, except that at a moment we both knew it was time to stop. It was full night, and the moon rose high in the warm sky, casting its light over the theatre we had made of our little piece of earth. We came down together in one grand harmony that ended on the same note and left the silence all around the moonstruck audience and the house and the black woods. The silence remained for a long moment, and I distinctly recall how the insects in the trees filled it with their own rising and falling song. Then the storm broke.

People were standing, making sounds I did not know people could make.

They were in a frenzy of delight. Dionysos there, I thought vaguely. Somewhere in the dark the old god still lived, the vine leaves green around his head, dancing with joy and giving life to a dead world. The night filled with the cheering of the people below us and around us, and still they went on. Jim Ed and I stood, looking at each other in the golden lamplight, the spell broken, the shadows thrown over his face. Then he said softly, "I haven't shaken your hand."

We shook hands clumsily like men waking from a dream, and people were streaming wildly up onto the porch, shaking hands with both of us, pounding him and me on the back, their faces gleaming with fierce, ultimate pleasure, and some were in tears. Brian Ledbetter made his way to me and hugged me in a big, sweaty embrace and shouted in my ear, "By *God!* By *God!* I didn't know you could *do* that." The tears were rolling down his face. I thought that never in his life until the night he left me had my father taken me in his arms.

Much later on, Dr. Youngblood and I drove drunkenly back through the dark to Bourbonville, the headlamps yellow on the rough dirt road rolling beneath us.

For a long time we rode in silence. "I never heard anything like it," he said at last. "Nobody else did, either." He drove for a while and shook his head as though in a dream. "You are the one to put this town back together. I always knew it."

He was still collecting his thoughts, and I did not understand what he meant. I am not sure that he fully understood himself. The glimmering of Bourbonville's lights came up on the dark ridge where the town was built. I could not tell him that while I played I looked at Stephanos and that when we stopped I yearned for Stephanos to speak to me and to tell me that I had played well.

From then on Jim Ed and I were friends, and we played often together and spoke seldom of Daisy. I did not tell him of Stephanos.

Part Two

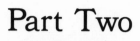

Part Two

94

HUB DELANEY died a week later, a night filled with the smell of flowers around his house and the forest alive with singing insects and the sky filled with stars. He slipped away while Jim Ed, Clyde, Brian Ledbetter, and I kept watch, sitting in the little room with him, the windows open on the gentle evening. Jim Ed and I played hymns as he sank away, Jim Ed singing quietly, Hub opening his milky eyes, looking at us, dying with his eyes open.

Brian, holding Hub's hand, realized that he was dead. He gently shut the eyes of his old comrade and pulled the blanket over Hub's face and walked outside to weep softly in the peaceful dark. Jim Ed drove down into Bourbonville to fetch Caleb, and in an hour Caleb came with his new hearse and took the body away.

Brian wanted to bury Hub in the woods behind Hub's cabin. "You can't do that to a man like Hub, Stepdaddy," Caleb said. "Hub deserves a real funeral. And hey, I want to show this town what I can do, don't you know? I won't charge a nickel, and I'll give him the best damned funeral you ever seen, Stepdaddy."

"I guess Virgil can come home for the funeral, then," Brian said. "Can you keep him till Virgil gets back?"

"I'll embalsam him and put him in my icebox. You didn't know I had an icebox, did you now, Stepdaddy? Hell, ever mortician worth his certificate has an icebox nowadays. I can tuck a corpse in there and keep it two weeks fresh as a side of beef. Virgil can get here in four days by train. I'll send the telegram myself."

Hub died on a Sunday night, and Ted Devlin was able to put a story about him on the front page of the *Bourbonville News* on Monday afternoon. "Civil War Veteran Succumbs," the headline said. In Ted Devlin's paper, people never died; they succumbed.

It was a good story. I learned that Hub's real name was Hubert Gresham Delaney and that he had been born in Bourbon County and that he had stayed there all his life except while he had been away during the Civil War. He had fought at Antietam and at Fredericksburg and at Chancellorsville and at Gettysburg and in the Wilderness and at Petersburg—misty names as unfamiliar to me as the battles of Senacherib. He had been in the army outside a house owned by a family named McLean in Virginia when Robert E. Lee rode up on horseback to surrender what was left of the Army of Northern Virginia to Ulysses S. Grant. Never once was he wounded.

Brian Ledbetter—he who had lost a leg at Cold Harbor—was amazed by Hub's luck. "He always said the Lord God was saving him to go west. The man was a fool about the West. Back then he figured you could go west and stake out a million acres of land and fight off the Indians and buy some cows and get rich and be free. Hub said that out west you had the chance to be somebody different. But hell! Why does anybody want to be different? I loved ole Hub like he was, and I told him he was a damn fool for talking about going west like it was the Promised Land. Maybe he was right. Maybe I should of let him go. He never did stop talking about it.

"When he wasn't nothing but a tad, him and his daddy and his daddy's brother was out chopping stove wood one morning in the spring, and a boy that had lived in the neighborhood rode by with a stranger, heading west. It was the gold rush time. Gold in California. Folks rushing out there to get rich, and . . . hell, you know.

"Boy's name was Adam Cloud, and I recollect him. He rode out of here one morning with this stranger, feller dressed up in a white suit. I reckon he was some kind of gambler off the river. I didn't see him myself. Hub seen him, and Hub always said the stranger looked like an angel. It was back around 1850, maybe 1851. He never did forget it.

"We always heard that Adam Cloud went out there and got rich. That's what folks said. He never come back here. Hub believed he got rich, and he talked about Adam Cloud off and on as long as he lived. He thought Adam Cloud was some kind of goddamned prophet. You know, like Joshua and Caleb—the Bible Caleb, you know. Prophets is called of God, and they got to do what God tells them. That's what Hub said, and I reckon he thought God passed him by because he never could pull his stakes and move on out of here. I told him I thought he'd be a fool for going. I thought he would of been sure enough. Who am I to say? Maybe I should of let him go. He stayed right here, and now he's going to be buried here."

Brian babbled in a daze of grief. Many times I heard about the young man Adam Cloud and the stranger in white and the departure through a sunny woods on a spring morning in the deeply receded past. Hub had seen some mystical significance in that strange passage westward, and he had spent his life yearning after it, working at it like some Talmudic scholar poring over an ancient and sacred text to find its secret meaning, feeling it always close but never making it come into the light he knew was there, believing that if he had followed Adam Cloud west, not only would all his life have been different but he would have understood something that in Bourbon County was never revealed. Whatever might have been Hub's destiny was moot, lost now in conjectures that were themselves fading.

Brian took pleasure in expecting Virgil. "I loved Virgil. I just never could get to him. I keep thinking that we'll have one more chance, that maybe Virgil and me can get together like I always wanted. He's got to come back to the funeral. Hub saved his life. That day in the square, that changed everthing for ole Hub, and Virgil knows it. The way Hub waded in there, drawing that pistol up over his head, shooting in the air. Lord God Amighty, I was glad to see him! I was out on the edge, not wanting to be there. I was clawing and fighting and trying to get to Virgil to help. Folks was holding me back, and I knowed he was going to die.

"Wouldn't of been no easy death, neither. Hell, them good Christian folks was fixing to tear him limb from limb. Then Hub come in, holding that navy revolver up, firing it a couple of times in the air. Lord, it sounded like a cannon, that thing did. That meant he had three shots left, and there wasn't nobody in the bunch that didn't know for sure and for certain that Hub Delaney wouldn't shoot him dead if he touched Virgil. Virgil knowed that Hub saved his life. All them folks that cowered back, they bided their time till the next election, and then they turned Hub out. They made him into a moonshine man because he couldn't do nothing else.

"Virgil . . . Well, tell the truth, I don't think Virgil ever did thank Hub enough. Virgil is proud, and he's quiet. He's got to come back. Four days. He can be here in four days. Hell, with trains this country ain't no bigger than the palm of your hand. Think of getting all the way out to California in four days! It's a miracle, that's what it is. I'm going to be so glad to see him. Even if it's to come home to Hub's funeral."

Caleb said Hub looked better than he had looked in years. It was the first time I heard the boast of morticians that they made people look better in death than they had looked in life. The funeral was set for Sunday afternoon. Caleb's telegram went off on Monday morning. Early Tuesday morning the return wire came. Virgil expressed "genuine sorrow" at Hub's passing but, he said, DISTANCE TOO GREAT FOR US TO COME. REGRETS.

We were at Brian's place when Caleb drove out with the telegram. He handed it over without a word. Brian read it with the aid of his spectacles. He handed it around, and we read it, too—a sheet of cheap yellow paper with "Western Union" printed at the top.

We sat away the afternoon and the evening. Dr. Youngblood came in late, silent, tired, and he studied the telegram and remained silent. Brian talked morosely, in disconnected bursts. We drank whiskey, and we listened.

"I'll never forget the day Hub shot dead the preacher that was trying to kill J. W. Campbell," Brian said. "It was the afternoon of the rain, the rain Simson predicted on the scaffold. The day after Simson was hanged. Hell, it was the day I decided to marry your mamma, Jim Ed. Virgil come to get me that morning. His mamma sent him to get me to come fetch her cow and bring her back to my bull. Lordy, they was so much that happened on that one day, and I didn't even know about Hub and the preacher and Mr. Campbell, not till that evening. They's lots that can happen in this old world that you don't never know about."

We smoked. We drank. We listened. Brian told the old story, the faded and patchy narrative that he alone in the room could tell. It was another link in the county's chain of legend, remembrance, history, fable, tradition—I do not know what.

By this time I knew of the long-dead Mr. Campbell as if he had been a neighbor of my childhood. I felt absorbed by the stories of the county like some liquid taken up by a sponge, and I was passive and exhausted of all feeling. Guy and Bernal sat in a darker corner of the room, hands on their knees, faces staring straight ahead, like Egyptian funereal monuments carved out of worn old basalt and half hidden by shadows.

95

WITH OR WITHOUT Virgil there had to be a funeral, and on Sunday afternoon Hub Delaney had the biggest funeral I had ever seen. The procession to the cemetery on the east side of town must have been two miles long. It took more than an hour to collect in the square and for the hearse to start its journey and for the crowd to fall in behind and to walk or ride out Broadway and to assemble around the open grave where Hub's gleaming coffin sat on the leather straps that would lower it and him into the earth.

Hub's death made middle-aged people in Bourbonville understand that they were losing their past. They had grown up on stories about "the war." There was only one war. They had heard its stories as children until they were bored and wished they never had to listen to a war story again. They had listened to a thousand tales in the same way that they had heard the call of a whippoorwill in the dark woods when they sat on the porch talking at night, when they dozed and dreamed of other things, and felt that the stories were pleasant in the way that a familiar night was pleasant with familiar sounds in the woods and the familiar stars overhead and the familiar, heavy smell of roses and jasmine in the air, a ritual sound of old tales spoken in rhythm to the thunking of a rocking chair on the plank floor, the passage of the white moon across the sky, and the revolving of the earth towards morning. They did not pay attention to the stories, because like the whippoorwill or the night insects singing in the dark, the stories were always there, a background to life, constant as nature itself.

Now they knew that they had never listened carefully enough. They remembered the stories in isolated fragments so that they could not get the sequence right, and the stories were confused, and details were vanishing like gray shapes at sea in the twilight, and their past was being overtaken by darkness.

To Bourbon County, Hub's death brought anew the old understanding that everyone now alive would die, and that memories of the scalding sun falling on the dry grass of fields where the acrid smoke of battle rolled in clouds, memories of burning thirst and fear and fatigue and hunger and the smell of earth and the reek of corpses would all fade into an unreal and impalpable world only vaguely symbolized by words and that the words themselves would dim and go out like guttering candles with the death of the generation that had made the memories. All that is, to be sure, a common-place knowledge, but one that comes to most of us only in moments, and then with a stark and suffocating weight, as it did to Xerxes weeping at the sight of his great army crossing the Hellespont on the way to Thermopylae because he knew that within a century all his great host would be dead. After Guy and Bernal died, I felt those moments so frequently that at times, such as the evening Virgil's telegram came, I felt empty of all feeling, a human shape obliged to continue life but already surrendered to death.

In Bourbonville and the county, the understanding of death fell on otherwise unreflective citizens with a peculiar and profound melancholy, the inexorable, intimate knowledge that something as tremendous as the Civil War could fade into thin air as the thousands and thousands of men who had fought its epic battles took their deeds into the grave with them, and that their own small lives in a remote community that seemed from day to day fixed and timeless were devoured by implacable change, that everything they knew was in flux, and that every common ritual was only a bubble on the surface of a dark and profound stream and that it would burst and that all of them would be carried away.

So when Hub was buried, men put on their hard, black funeral suits despite the heat. Men now old who had been too young to fight in that receding war came tottering out to recall him toothlessly as comrade and friend and to praise his virtues. To hear Bourbon County tell the story now, no one had been in the square that day when Hub saved Virgil's life, and no one had voted against him in the next election, and no one had treated him as a pariah who had to live by making whiskey in the hills. None of that had happened. The county and the little town accepted gratefully Ted Devlin's story in the long obituary, that after years of brave service as sheriff, Hub had "retired" and had withdrawn to the country to live on comfortably in a benign old age as the patriarch of the county in pleasant independence on financial resources not required to be mentioned because everyone knew them so well.

Reporters came down from Knoxville for the funeral, for by now the death of a Civil War veteran had become an event to be memorialized nostalgically in newspapers, a final and ceremonial outburst where might be felt the throb of mythic drums, the call of legendary trumpets out of distant misty mornings, and the steady tramp of thousands of marching feet from a vanished time that, in the summer of 1919, swelled with romance and passion lacking in the aftermath of another war whose glory was turning from gold to lead.

Those people who had lustily cheered their boys off to fight the Kaiser and his Huns now said that Woodrow Wilson had lied them into the war, or that he had been criminally deceived by the British and the French. The newspapers were running memoirs of German generals who had never made a mistake although they had somehow lost the war; the war had not been fought to make the world safe for democracy but to stuff the bank accounts of the munitions makers and other profiteers. The English and French would snatch the German colonies, and virtuous America would be left to pay the bills. The Germans in defeat were somehow heroic, as Confederates were now heroic, because they had lost another greedy war.

"We should have stayed home where we belonged," Jim Ed said. Others, who had not been to France, used stronger language. Gentle remembrance of the Civil War came drifting like an opiate over the general unease of the county, and Hub Delaney's death made spiraling fantasies out of the narcotic pipe of history, which for a moment could be inhaled by anyone who looked at Hub's skeletal corpse, which all Caleb's rouge and wax could not make natural or alive but which seemed noble anyway.

Eugenia Curry came down to write about the funeral, her dark blond hair shining over her white collar in the radiance of the afternoon. She spoke to me, extending her gloved hand. She had a natural easiness with people. I do not believe she ever pretended anything. She wore a severe suit, of a sort women bought to prove to the world that they meant business. The severity was mitigated by a very large-brimmed hat made of yellow straw. I thought of Renoir, whom Leonora had loved and Guy had scorned.

"I wanted to write about a Union soldier. The insurrectionaries get all the newspaper stories written about them down here."

"The insurrectionaries?"

"The rebels. My people fought for the Union," she said. She stood by me during the funeral, and I nodded and smelled the cleanliness of her dress and her skin and her hair. She wore no perfume.

People collected in a wide circle around the green awning that Caleb put up over the grave and in the place reserved for "family," where the Ledbetter and Weaver clan, adopted as Hub's kin, sat on wooden folding chairs. The fringed awning had "Weaver Funerals" in bold white letters on each side.

Willy sat to one side. He walked with a white cane now, tapping the ground in front of him, and he was getting fat. Brian sat in the front row, dressed in the gaudy uniform of the Grand Army of the Republic. Mrs. Ledbetter sat beside him, holding his hand during the service. An American flag covered the coffin.

For a ten-dollar fee, Caleb had secured the young Reverend Dr. Ware from the Trinity Methodist Church to do the preaching. Darcy Coolidge told me that Mr. Ware had said that anybody who sold liquor was guilty of the blood of those who bought it and that people who drank it were guilty of murder because they supported interests that killed others and guilty of suicide because they were surely killing themselves. "The Colonel always loved his little toddy in the evenings," she said. "If Mr. Ware had ever had his little toddy, he wouldn't talk that way. Now, I don't like saloons. But everybody who has a little toddy in the evening doesn't necessarily hang around at a saloon and beat his wife and children."

Preacher Ware, his hair greased down over his large head, savoring Caleb's ten-dollar fee and knowing about Hub only what he had read in Ted Devlin's paper, humbly decided it was his Christian duty to do his best. He gave his voice an even deeper affectation, pronouncing the word "God" as if it had six syllables.

Dr. Youngblood told me that the Methodists changed preachers every two to four years and that a preacher seldom stayed in any one community long enough to know people or what they did and that Dr. Ware, living in Bourbonville a little over two years, had been so absorbed in the campaign for prohibition that he had been less informed than he might have been about his parish. Caleb could be counted on to protect Hub's reputation, and so it was that Bourbon County's leading prohibitionist delivered the funeral oration for the county's late leading manufacturer of moonshine whiskey.

Dr. Ware stood by the grave and looked out over the sweating throng pressed in under the hard sunshine. After a portentous pause he shouted, "Abraham Lincoln!" Another long pause: "Jefferson Davis!" Another long pause: "Ulysses S. Grant!" Another long pause: "Robert E. Lee!" Then a longer and more dramatic pause. "All DEAD!" The preacher stood in his black suit, looking about in thunderous triumph. "History proves we *all* die! I could mention dozens of names, and you've heard of them, and they're *all* dead. Read your history, my friends. History *proves* we all die."

Ted Devlin, standing on my other side from Eugenia Curry, muttered, "Goddamn, I reckon Hub proved that." Eugenia heard him and laughed.

"The rumor is he's in line to be a bishop," Dr. Youngblood said.

"My father was a Methodist preacher," she said softly to me.

Dr. Ware steamed on and on until he ran out of fuel in the intense, hot sunlight. He had sweated through his clothes, and even on his black preacher's suit you could see a large wet spot in the middle of his back. Sweat rolled off his jowls. He wiped his face with a sodden handkerchief and nodded distastefully to Jim Ed, who had brought his guitar. Jim Ed walked to the head of the closed coffin and stood for a few moments looking around in the fiery sunshine. He had worn a hat to the funeral, but he took it off out of respect for Hub. He blinked as if to get his bearings. He looked sad and uncomfortable in a wrinkled cotton suit. He strummed and started the words to a hymn, and the crowd, which had been moved to whispering and murmuring at the end of Dr. Ware's absurd address, settled down into silence. Jim Ed's clear tenor voice poured out over them, wavering with sorrow.

> *I am a poor, wayfaring stranger,*
> *Now traveling through this world below;*
> *There is no sickness, toil, nor danger*
> *In that bright land to which I go.*
> *I'm going there to meet my father.*
> *He said he'd be there when I come.*
> *I am going over Jordan;*
> *I am just going over home.*

He sang verse after verse, his voice quavering and somber, and we listened in rapt silence under the still, hot sky. I could look up and see Virgil's house—not his anymore. Then it was over, and Mr. Ware prayed again, and the crowd broke up into knots of people who knot by knot moved towards the roads that would lead them home.

96

"I WISH YOU WOULD TALK to me," Eugenia Curry said as we were walking back to the turnpike in the crowd. "It would help me so much if I could do a story about your exploits in the war."

"Why would it help you?" I said.

She laughed. "Because I'm a *woman* reporter; I want to be a *real* reporter."

"I do not understand."

"A *woman* reporter writes about the garden club and bird-watching and weddings and recipes and parties. Sometimes I write obituaries, and I write about the women's tennis championships in Knoxville. My sister Bert won last summer, and I got to write about her. You would never have known I was her sister by the way I did it. I write about the doings at the YWCA. Oh yes, I get to write about happenings at church. Those are good, safe topics for a woman. My editor doesn't think it's ladylike for me to do anything else."

"What would you like to write about?" I said.

"A murder," she said.

"A murder!" I laughed.

"Don't laugh! A good murder. The kind of story where the victim deserved to be killed and the murderer is a saint and reporters come from miles around and the telegraphers are standing by and the whole country is waiting for every gory detail. You must have read about the trial of Henriette Caillaux?"

"Of course," I said. "Of course! Of course! I had a friend passionately interested in her trial. It was going on when we went to war. The day we got on the train to go to the front, he could hardly talk about anything else. He sat in the train reading to us out of a newspaper about her scandal!"

She looked at me with a warm smile. "Sometimes I think you are incapable of saying anything," she said. "Then you erupt in words."

"I am sorry to disappoint you," I said.

"You do not disappoint me. You surprise me. There is a great deal of difference."

"I recall the trial," I said. "In Paris. She killed a newspaper editor who threatened to publish the love letters her husband had written her."

"When she was his mistress," she said.

"Yes," I said.

"The editor had published Caillaux's letters to another mistress, and now he was going to publish his letters to Henriette, and her letters to him, I suppose. She shot him with a pistol. Nobody doubted that she shot him. The most famous trial of this decade."

"It had gone out of my mind," I said. "It all comes back! The jury found her not guilty. We talked about it more than we talked about the Germans. Then the shooting started, and we forgot Henriette Caillaux. I could not have recalled her name unless you had spoken it first."

"It was more important here than the war for a few weeks in 1914. It was in all the papers. I have read everything anybody wrote about Henriette Caillaux. I could have written a great story if I had been assigned to do it. I was completely on her side. It's good to shoot an editor once in a while. It makes the rest of them have second thoughts. If we find the right editor to shoot, you can use the pistol, and I'll write the story. Aha! I have made the redoubtable recluse Paul Alexander laugh again!"

"Do you think I am a recluse?"

"Everyone says you are a recluse," she said. "If I can get you to shoot an editor who threatens to publish your lover's letters, I shall make you a public man."

"It sounds ambitious," I said.

"I am ambitious," she said seriously. "I don't want to spend my life writing about flower arrangements. Have you ever talked to a member of a garden club?"

"I do not believe I have," I said.

"Well, if garden club ladies had been governing Germany and France and England and all the rest, they would have gone to war over who had the prettiest tulips or the best dry arrangement, and trench warfare would have seemed like a picnic in the country."

She laughed, and I felt pleasure.

"Now another treat allowed me by my editor is that I get to cover Ossoli Circle in Knoxville. Do you know about the exclusive Ossoli Circle?"

"I have not had the honor," I said.

"The well-to-do ladies who like to root around in the dirt belong to the Garden Club. The well-to-do ladies who like to stay in the shade and sip iced tea or mint juleps belong to Ossoli Circle. They read books and paint pots—inane books and gaudy pots. Ossoli Circle is named for a woman named Margaret Fuller who met an Italian in Italy and had his child. His name was Count Ossoli or Marquis Ossoli, something like that. It's not at all clear that she married him. They were on their way back to America when their ship wrecked, and all three of them died off the coast of New York. Very sad story. She was a wonderful woman. Probably not as coura-geous as Henriette Caillaux, but she did the best she could at the time. You have to make allowances. Anyway, somebody read about her in Knox-ville, and so we have Ossoli Circle. The joke is that the women of Ossoli Circle would never have permitted Margaret Fuller to join their club. 'A confessed adulteress in our club! Oh, the thought makes me ill! Think how gauche it's going to be if she makes all the rest of us confess. Hand me the smelling salts, Emma! I think I'm going to faint.' I'm glad women are going to get the suffrage. We ought to have it. But mark my words! It won't make politics in America one bit better. Anybody who has ever been to Ossoli Circle can tell you that. The suffrage will just spread the non-sense around."

"You are here to write about this funeral. That represents some progress in your efforts," I said.

"Yes, it does. My editor thinks I can write something to make my genteel lady readers cry. He thinks the only people who read what a woman writes are other women who want to cry while they eat their chocolates and have babies."

"Did you see anything here to make them cry?"

"Oh yes. But I want to do more than that. That preposterous minister didn't know he was preaching the funeral of a moonshiner. That won't make people cry." She laughed with delight.

"Will you write about that?" I said. I was beginning to see some possibili-ties in all this.

"Wait and see," she said. "What was the boy's name? The one who died on the last day of the war?"

"D. B. Weaver," I said.

"D. B. Weaver. Somebody known only by his initials and his death. I had forgotten his name. That story made people cry. I got a lot of compliments for it. Even my mother liked it." Her face turned solemn. "It's nothing to laugh about, is it? The poor boy is still dead. I think Americans had the idea that when the shooting stopped, all the dead soldiers would leap up and come home as if the whole affair had been a stage play. They would take their curtain calls, and everybody would clap. But they're still dead, aren't they?"

"Yes," I said. We walked in silence for a little while. "Does your mother live in Knoxville?"

"We all live in Knoxville. Except Bert. She lives in Maryville with her husband, Lionel."

"And your father?"

"My father is dead."

"You said he was a priest," I said.

"Not a priest, silly. Catholics have priests. Are you Catholic? Of course you are. Somebody told me that. You have priests; we have preachers. Evangelists. My father was an evangelist."

"I do not understand what an evangelist is," I said.

"It's a preacher who goes around saving souls from hell by shouting at them and threatening them with fire and brimstone," she said. "I never knew my father, but I think he might have embarrassed me. I don't mean to mock. My mother adored him. We ought to respect our parents. Are your mother and father alive?"

"My father is dead," I said. "My mother is alive."

"In Belgium?"

I hesitated. "Yes."

"Is she well?"

"Oh, yes."

"She survived the occupation. Good for her. She must be a tough woman."

"Yes," I said.

"Do you believe in hell?"

"No," I said.

"Neither do I," she said. "I couldn't worship a God who sent people to hell. Could you?"

I shrugged. "I don't believe any of it," I said.

"I guess I believe some of it," she said. "I'm just not sure what."

"Your father died," I said.

"He died of typhoid when he was preaching a revival out in Kingston. That's just over the way from here. In Roane County."

"I am very sorry," I said.

"I am, too," she said, shaking her head and looking sad. "Maybe if my father had lived, my mother would not have been so gloomy about the world. I don't know. He was pretty gloomy and fanatical himself. We have his diary. He kept it for three years. He worried about his soul every day. How did your father die?"

I hesitated. "His heart," I said.

"A heart attack? Did he die suddenly?"

"Yes," I said.

"No one expected it?"

"No," I said.

"We never really expect death, do we?"

People passed by and spoke to me and gave Eugenia a sharp and inquiring look and looked back to me in eager but silent interrogation.

"My mother thinks it's wicked for me to work on the newspaper," she said at last.

"Wicked?"

"She wanted me to be a missionary. She still does. It's all she talks about. She says God will punish me for not going to save the heathen."

"I have heard of missionaries," I said.

"I am sure the missionaries will be glad to hear that. But now the major question, the all-important question: do you *approve* of missionaries?"

"No," I said.

"How could anyone approve of them?" she said. "Why should we try to change all those people? My brother Alfred says that all religions are mountains pointing up to the same sky. Don't you think that's a beautiful thought?"

"I am not religious," I said.

"But you are Catholic," she said.

"I was baptized a Catholic, but I am not religious now. I do not practice."

"Practice? How do you practice religion? You either believe it or you don't."

I stammered. "I think it must be a difference in language," I said. "I mean that I do not go to mass."

"I don't blame you," she said. "I couldn't be a Catholic. How can you take orders from the Pope?"

"I do not think about the Pope," I said.

"I don't think about him, either," Eugenia said with a grin. "My mother thinks he's the Antichrist and that he's going to take over the world and that he will brand the numbers 666 in the foreheads of his people, but then Jesus will come back, and the skies will open, and the Pope will be cast into hell." She laughed again, not taking any of it seriously.

97

OUR CONVERSATION was interrupted by Pinkerton. He had been drinking. Since the affair with Shaw, he seemed to be drunk every day. His face looked like an eroded field. He grinned without humor when he saw me and came over and shook hands clumsily. I introduced him to Eugenia Curry.

"Miss Curry writes for the *Knoxville Guardian*," I said. "She is writing a story about Mr. Delaney's funeral."

"Reporter, eh?" Pinkerton said. "I didn't know they had woman reporters."

"It's something new," Eugenia said. "Like woman's suffrage and electric washing machines and toothpaste."

"Jesus! Next thing you know they'll be having woman lawyers and woman doctors."

"It is already being done," Eugenia said.

Pinkerton frowned. "You'll never see me take my clothes off in front of a woman doctor," he growled.

"I don't believe doctors sell tickets to the public to watch such performances," Eugenia said. "So it's very doubtful that I will see you when you do it."

Pinkerton was so drunk that Eugenia's words went over his head. "You're writing up old Hub. He deserves a write-up."

"Thank you," Eugenia said.

"I had my name in the papers once. Back in the Spanish thing. I raised troops here in town. I guess you've heard of me? Moreland J. Pinkerton? I was Captain Pinkerton then. The men at the shops still call me Captain. Not old sobersides here. Alexander just calls me 'Mr. Pinkerton'—'Mr. Pinkerton, Mr. Pinkerton.' "

"Perhaps you should make him salute. Then he would remember," Eugenia said.

"Salute. That's not a bad idea. I'm the most important man in Bourbon County," Pinkerton said, swaying uncertainly on his feet. "Not to brag, you know. It's a fact." He looked disheveled and sick, and the smell of whiskey came through his pores. "Good day for a funeral," he said. "All this sunshine. It'd be sad in the rain."

"Death is sad anytime," Eugenia said.

"Sure it is," Pinkerton said vaguely. "You don't know who I am, do you?"

"You just told me," she said.

"You hadn't heard of me before that?"

"I'm sorry, but no," Eugenia said.

"I built the car works here, in a swamp. You could write about that."

"Perhaps I could," she said.

"You could," Pinkerton said, warming to the subject. "It would be a good story. You could interview folks, folks all over this county that remember."

"I might do that," she said.

"You ought to," Pinkerton said. "You know, I made the county move into modern times. This county, this town, without me . . . It was just a swamp, and I got out there and . . ." He lost the thread again. "Hub Delaney was sheriff when I came here. He was always fair to me. Always fair."

"I could quote you on that," Eugenia said, taking out her notebook.

"Well, you could for a fact," Pinkerton said. "Hub Delaney was a good sheriff. He was always fair. You can say that."

Eugenia wrote in her notebook. "Would you spell your name for me, please?"

Pinkerton spelled his name.

"Do you have any interesting personal recollections of him?" Eugenia said, holding her notebook in the shade of her broad-brimmed hat.

"I do," Pinkerton said. He gave a garbled version of assaulting Mr. Mahoney. Mr. Mahoney was dead, and Pinkerton left out so many of the details that it was not clear why he had gone to attack Mr. Mahoney, and in the end, when he told of Hub's advice to the beaten and filthy proprietor of the hardware store, Eugenia was completely lost. She held her pencil up from her pad and looked painfully at him while he galloped to the end. "Isn't that a great story?" Pinkerton asked.

"It is very interesting," Eugenia said.

"Ah," Pinkerton said in a deeply disappointed way. "You won't get it right. I didn't tell it good enough. Maybe old Mahoney was right. Maybe I shouldn't have brought the niggers in here. What do you think about the niggers?"

Eugenia shrugged. "I don't know," she said.

"I've been thinking a lot about them," Pinkerton said. "A hell of a lot. Excuse me for cussing in front of a lady. I don't mean to cuss in front of a lady."

"It is all right," Eugenia said.

The sun was brilliant, and we had moved into the shade of a chestnut tree. Pinkerton looked up into its branches. "The chestnuts are dying. You know that?"

"I have heard that there is a disease," Eugenia said. "Surely they will find something to save them."

"Naw," Pinkerton said. "They're all going to die. It's something that comes from the Japs. Foreign things come in here, and they kill off the native American stock. Ain't that right, Alexander?" He tried to laugh.

"We're all foreigners unless we're American Indians," Eugenia said before I could reply.

"You ain't no foreigner. Not with that blond hair," Pinkerton said. "Are you two going to get married?"

Eugenia turned red, and I felt my own face get hot. "We scarcely know each other," I said.

Pinkerton grinned. "Well, you look here, miss. This boy's a good catch. I couldn't care any more for him if he was my son. I'm proud of him. I've made him what he is, and he's going places. I won't run the car works forever. There'll be a funeral for Moreland J. Pinkerton one of these days. This boy's in line to take over the whole shebang."

"I have no desire to take over anything," I said.

"Don't lie to me," Pinkerton said with sudden ferocity. "I can see ambition burning in your eyes like two coals of fire. You think I'm blind? You're biding your time, and when the time comes, you'll make your move, like a cat onto a bird."

"That is not true," I said quietly.

Just as suddenly as he had erupted, Pinkerton was grinning again. "Well, hell. I want to pass it on to you. Say, that Ware—he can preach up a storm, can't he? Wish Eula could of heard him. Eula's my wife, miss. She's big on preaching. Too bad about ole Hub. Old generation's dying off. New generation's coming on. Just like the chestnut trees." He looked around at the hills, and his eyes rested for a while on Virgil's house, looming above us in the Sabbath sunshine.

We were silent. I willed him to depart, my thoughts almost a prayer.

"Well, to hell with it," Pinkerton said. "I've kept you folks too long. Don't mind me, Alexander. Don't mind me at all." He wheeled off, staggering slightly under the scalding sun, looking bereft and friendless and beaten. People nodded at him and scurried away.

"He is a drunkard, poor man," Eugenia said.

"He is my superior," I said.

"He is your boss," she said. "He is not superior."

I smiled. "It is a way of speaking," I said. "He was once a powerful man."

"Alcohol," Eugenia said. "If he were not a drunk, he would still be a powerful man."

"It goes deeper than that," I said.

"Let me take you somewhere," she said. "I have to go back to Knoxville. I'll be up all night writing the story of this funeral. Where can I take you?"

"To the square," I said. "I do not mind walking."

"No. No, I will give you a ride. If I put you under obligation to me, maybe you will talk to me."

"You should write about Mr. Pinkerton," I said. "He deserves a story."

She shook her head impatiently. "I cannot write a story about a drunkard," she said. "I may quote him. But I cannot write a story about such a drunken man."

"He is better than he seems," I said.

"He could be that and still be awful," Eugenia said, and laughed.

I laughed, too.

98

GUY REPROACHED ME for filling my life with stories that were not our story, and after I basked in Eugenia's company that afternoon, I went to bed sick and depressed and afraid again for my sanity. I felt tempted to withdraw into a rapture of silence and to purge my mind of all thoughts. In that temptation the world appeared alien and detached, unreal, a creation merely of words and not things.

Words themselves sometimes became strange, as if I had never heard them before even when I knew them well. Their meanings seemed arbitrary, protean, disconnected, and the world they represented seemed arbitrary, too—and as nonsensical. I feared that I would forget how to use words as sometimes we may forget how to do a common act, repeated thousands of times in the past, such as tying a necktie or signing our names; that people might speak to me and I might have no idea of what they were saying, though I had known the words for years. I seemed on the point of losing the ability to connect words with what I saw or tasted or smelled or felt or touched. "This is a window," I sometimes whispered in an exercise of reassurance, feeling the glass in the frame. "This is a sill. This is a bed. This is a wall." I ran my fingers over those objects to comfort myself with their solidity, but the words sounded unfamiliar or, worse, nonsensical and menacing in whatever language I spoke them. I knew that the complete alienation of myself—whatever that was—from the outside world was going to come and that then there would be nothing to do but to sit in a corner and stare at the walls and be nothing.

I studied the Webster's dictionary in the parlor, telling Darcy Coolidge and the others that I wanted to improve my English. It seemed natural to them that a person with an accent as strong as mine should study the dictionary. In truth, I studied the dictionary because it was alphabetical, orderly, arranged. In working through it, I ordered my life with the neatly ordered words.

"A," I thought, looking at the single letter, much the same in English as it was in Greek. "An article that stands before a noun. I can think about things if I put 'a' before them. If I can put 'a' before a word, the word exists, and I exist along with it because I can say the word. I have a connection with anything that I can identify with an 'a.' "

"Aardvark," I read. "A nocturnal animal of southern Africa that digs burrows and eats ants, especially termites." Each of these words had associations. I tried to remember when I had first thought of them, when I first understood them. I had never been in southern Africa, but Guy and I had talked about Africa, and I knew the difference between north and south, and I had seen termites, and the network of associations created by the words comforted me. Patiently I studied words and disciplined my mind to resurrect and sort out every memory of them, to restore the sense of time and order that I had lost, and recover the assurance that I could connect them to memory and to the world. I could believe that my *self* (I dare not call it a *soul*) was intact.

Eugenia Curry's story of Hub Delaney's funeral made everybody in Bourbonville talk. "The young woman has no sense of decorum," Darcy Coolidge sniffed, shocked by the simple narrative. "She has ruined Preacher Ware."

"Everything she says is true," Dale Farmer observed, looking on the ruination of a Methodist preacher with rubicund pleasure.

"There are some times when truth should lie still," Darcy Coolidge said.

"How did she learn all that stuff?" DeShane Dugan said, his eyeglasses on his forehead, his expression nearsighted and perplexed.

"She ran around asking questions," Darcy Coolidge said. "Dr. Ware will be mortified."

"It will not help him become a bishop," DeShane Dugan said.

"Well, I think Dr. Ware's ambitions have been exaggerated," Darcy Coolidge said. "But yes, Mr. Dugan, this will not help him rise in the church."

"Perhaps he can go into another line of work," Dale Farmer said.

"How can he do that if God called him to preach?" DeShane Dugan said. He was serious, and Dale Farmer laughed.

"She makes his sermon sound so silly," Darcy Coolidge said.

"She must have written it in shorthand," Dale Farmer said. "It is exactly what he said."

"Many serious things that a man can say eloquently sound foolish when they are written down," Darcy Coolidge said.

"I thought it was silly when he said it," Ted Devlin said. "That's why I didn't print it. I swear, though, that woman can write."

"I applaud your discretion, Mr. Devlin," Darcy Coolidge said. "I've always loved to hear Dr. Ware preach. I will admit that perhaps he did get carried away at Mr. Delaney's funeral. It must have been the crowd."

"Undoubtedly," Ted Devlin said. "If there hadn't been anybody there to hear him, he would have sounded like one of the prophets."

"She makes Bourbonville look bad, telling all that stuff about Virgil," Dale Farmer said, trying to arrive at some critical consensus. "Even if it is true."

"Some things are better forgotten," Darcy Coolidge said. "I approved your courtship of Miss Curry, Mr. Alexander. I was wrong. She is not the kind of woman you want for a wife. A good wife must be able to forget details. You do not want to marry a woman who remembers details unless they are about recipes or money."

"Oh, are you courting her?" Dale Farmer said, looking surprised and perhaps a little disappointed. "Well, well, well. Will we be hearing wedding bells, Paul? I had no idea. You are a sly one."

"No, I have not been courting her," I said.

"But look how red he is in the face," Ted Devlin said.

"I get red in the face sometime when I work outside," DeShane Dugan said. "That's why I wear a hat."

"I agree with Darcy," Ted Devlin said. "If you don't print bad news, it isn't real. That's why Bourbonville is the garden of God."

"Well, I wouldn't go so far as to say that," Darcy Coolidge said.

"What do you reckon God plants in his garden?" DeShane Dugan said.

"If you are courting her, why didn't you tell me?" Dale Farmer said, looking injured.

"I am not courting her," I said.

"You don't tell me anything. I don't think that's friendly," Dale Farmer said in a pouting voice.

"There was nothing to tell," I said.

"Well," Darcy Coolidge said. "I'm sure that after this you'll not want to see her again."

"If you do, I hope you have the decency to tell me about it," Dale Farmer said.

"Let him alone, for Christ's sake," Ted Devlin said. "He didn't write the story. I say it's a good piece of work. The woman can write for me any time she's willing to work for nothing."

I have Eugenia's story here on the table beside me. It is moving and tasteful, an elegant piece of simple narrative, uncomfortably complete. Darcy Coolidge reported that Dr. Ware took it very hard. He spent the next Sunday morning's sermon denouncing Caleb Weaver from the pulpit for not telling him that Hub had been a moonshiner. Caleb gained a certain notoriety and a fair amount of business from Hub's funeral and Dr. Ware's attentions. Dr. Ware was so angry that he embarrassed his congregation. He turned to the subject three consecutive Sundays. His stewards suggested he find another topic. He refused and preached about Hub Delaney's wickedness another three Sundays. By this time the whole town thought he was silly and gullible. Finally the bishop transferred him out of Bourbonville before his term was up. I do not believe Dr. Ware ever became a bishop himself.

99

ONCE OR TWICE a week I spent an evening talking after supper with Dr. Youngblood, or rather sitting with him while he nodded and dozed and wakened and spoke briefly before his chin dropped onto his chest again.

"Why do you not go to bed?" I said.

"I am not sleepy," he said. "It is early yet."

Dr. Bulkely demanded cash payment on the spot, and he considered it beneath his dignity to accept chickens and potatoes in lieu of money. The healthy people in Bourbonville, who seldom needed doctors anyway but who had cash, went to him for their ailments because he seemed modern, and he used his X-ray machine for nearly everything. He told them that if they chewed their food thoroughly and ate carrots they would live to be ninety, and he flourished.

Dr. Youngblood worked as hard as ever. His eyes were perpetually rimmed with fatigue. He drank too much wine. He could sit for long periods saying nothing. When people came to fetch him at night because of birth or death or accident or fever, he wearily gathered up his black bag and went off to do what he could.

On Sunday afternoons he felt free to ramble about. Bourbon Countians did not generally stab, shoot, club, or gouge each other on Sundays, and since Christian sentiment frowned on breaking the Sabbath, farmers did not generally mangle themselves at work. We fell into the habit that summer of driving around with Brian Ledbetter and Jim Ed in Brian's Model T, which Jim Ed now drove.

Brian retreated more into himself. The drives brought him out a little and made him more talkative. Something was irrevocably changed in him. He had told his stories with the zeal of someone reliving them, surviving them. Now he seemed to tell them because he realized that life was short, and he wanted to get them all told once more so they would not vanish from the earth. He became tedious. No one complained.

Jim Ed listened patiently, hearing them all as if he had never heard any of them before, laughing at the right places, nodding in sympathy where sympathy was required. Once in a great while Jim Ed told stories of his own.

The old man was taken with racing cars and with airplanes. With the end of the war, car racing came back to Knoxville, and on some Sunday after-noons, in defiance of the Sabbath, we drove to a dirt track north of Knoxville and saw men with goggles over their eyes race cars. The engines screamed, and the dust flew up in gritty sheets, the oil burned in blue smoke at the exhausts, and happy Sabbath-breakers cheered, and the drivers, filthy with striving, looked like grease-anointed paladins from a new kind of romance.

On Sundays when there were no races, we went to the airport, taking the ferry across the river to a little hamlet called Greenback, driving on dirt roads to the new Knoxville airport, located not at Knoxville but near the company town of the Aluminum Company of America.

Jim Ed could not fathom the old man's fascination with airplanes. "An airplane is a flying coffin," he said. "You are never going to get me up in an airplane. The thought of it makes me sick." He was terrified of high places. "I proved I was brave in the war," he said. "I got the right to be scared of some things."

Dutifully he drove his father and Dr. Youngblood and me to the airport, and we watched flimsy little planes land and take off and saw pilots standing about self-importantly talking to each other. We joined the gawkers who had come out to gape at the miracle of flight. The pilots and mechanics, who could touch the planes—priests and acolytes granted contact with the sacred objects—clustered apart, bending to their work, talking, laughing, grandly ignoring the timid mass of worshippers.

"I tell you, if we'd had airplanes in my war, we'd of whipped them rebs in ten days," the old man said. "We could of knowed everything they was going to do. God, I wish we'd had airplanes at Chancellorsville!"

"We had airplanes in my war," Jim Ed said. "And it taken us more than ten days."

In some way that I do not quite remember, Dale Farmer started accompanying us. He had been morose and withdrawn for weeks after Pinkerton's episode with Shaw. He usually went to Knoxville on Saturdays and came back to the boardinghouse on Sunday evenings. Somebody said he had a boyfriend in Knoxville. Just before Hub Delaney's funeral, Dale Farmer quit making those weekend trips. He looked like death. His face was drawn, and he lost weight. On Sundays he read the papers again and again, seeming not to see what he read.

He hinted that he would like to go with me on the occasional evening that I spent with Dr. Youngblood. Dr. Youngblood, kind to the world, began inviting him. Dale Farmer talked of how nice it would be to go with us on our Sunday drives, and the next thing I knew he was squeezed into the backseat with Dr. Youngblood and me.

One Sunday afternoon we were standing at the grass air strip watching when a pilot ambled over. "You boys like airplanes? Seen you around here a lot," he said. He was tall and angular with a pockmarked face and some missing teeth. He wore high boots and a leather flying jacket and smoked a cigarette. His fingernails were black, and his fingers were yellow. He wore a smirk like a medal.

"I don't care for them myself," Jim Ed said.

"Our elderly friend loves them," Dale Farmer said.

"That mean you, Pop?" the pilot said with an insolent grin.

"I don't reckon you got the right to call me 'Pop' lessen I knowed your mamma when she was stepping out on your daddy," Brian Ledbetter said calmly.

The pilot looked at him a moment, an ugly expression coming into his eyes. Abruptly he laughed. "Hey, Pop. You're all right. That's pretty good. You like airplanes, huh?"

"I like to look at them," the old man said.

"Looking ain't flying, is it, Pop?"

"Man like you ought to teach in the university yonder in town," the old man said. "You can't talk without asking questions."

"I'll ask you another one," the pilot said, taking a deep draw on the cigarette and tossing it away. "You want to go up with me?"

"In the airplane?"

"I don't figure on flapping my arms and carrying you up on my back, Pop," the pilot said. "Three dollars and I'll give you a ride."

"Hey," Jim Ed said to his father. "You stay down here on the ground where you belong."

"What do you mean, where I belong?" the old man said. "How do you know where I belong?"

"I taken a good look at you, and I figured you belong on the ground like me. You don't have to go flying around all over the place like a buzzard."

"How much do you say it is?" the old man said.

"Pop, you're a gas," the pilot said with a laugh that was part cough. He lit another cigarette. "Three bucks. Three little George Washingtons, and you're an ace, Pop. If you ain't got three dollars, I might do it for two. What the hell."

"I reckon I got three dollars here someplace," the old man said. He removed a little snap purse from his trouser pocket, opened it, and dug out a roll of bills. The ones on top were hundreds, and he smoothed them out.

"Jesus, Pop!" the pilot said, his cigarette hanging on his lower lip and his eyes huge with the sight of the money.

The old man found some ones and counted three of them into the pilot's oily hand.

"Come on, Pop," the pilot said with a big laugh. "You're all right."

"Daddy!" Jim Ed said in desperation.

"Better not look up at us, Jim Ed," the old man said. "You might get sick."

While we watched anxiously, this veteran of Gettysburg and the Wilderness, wounded at Cold Harbor, a man with a peg leg and thick white hair, put on a leather flying cap with goggles and hauled himself up into the rear cockpit of a two-seater biplane, the hair bristling like a wild bush from under the cap held tight on his head by its chin strap. The pilot climbed up into the forward cockpit, the old man pulled his goggles down over his eyes, the pilot did the same, and another pilot smoking the inevitable, gallant cigarette whirled the propeller blade, and the engine sputtered to life, coughing foul-smelling exhaust under the wings, and the propeller spun in an almost invisible roaring circle, and the tiny thing made of canvas and wood bumped down the dirt runway on its hard rubber tires and lifted itself into the air, struggling against gravity, gaining altitude slowly, the sound of the engine receding to a hard buzz in the quiet afternoon air.

"I feel like I'm going to vomit," Jim Ed said.

"You look sick for a fact," Dr. Youngblood said.

The little plane cleared a forest at the end of the runway and climbed into a cloudy blue sky until it became a dot, devoid of color. We sauntered down to a fence along one side of the runway and leaned against it and watched.

"You wonder how it stays up," Jim Ed said.

"The laws of physics," Dr. Youngblood said placidly. He puffed his pipe, pleasantly absorbed.

"I look for the day when we'll see airplanes in the sky just as we see automobiles on the roads nowadays," Dale Farmer said.

"If we do there'll be airplanes falling on our roofs like bird shit," Jim Ed said. "If God had meant for us to fly, he wouldn't have thought up trains."

"I have read that there are now airplanes that can climb thousands of feet into the air," Dale Farmer said. "Sometimes a mile high."

"I don't like to climb up into a silo," Jim Ed said. "I get dizzy looking down."

The plane made broad circles. Above it, huge clouds billowed across the sky, white and soft. The plane was a dark and buzzing object against the clouds.

"I can't look," Jim Ed said. He lowered his eyes and rolled himself a cigarette.

The rest of us kept our faces turned upward. It was hypnotic. The plane went round and round in slow, lazy motions. We could hear the engine grinding away, high under the clouds.

"Hey, ain't that one of your colored men?" Jim Ed punched me in the ribs. "I know that fellow."

"I believe I know him, too," Dale Farmer said, looking in the direction Jim Ed was pointing.

Leaning on the fence down the way was M. P. Brown.

100

HE WAS THE ONLY black man around, and he had taken up a spot in unobtrusive isolation. He was wearing worn khakis and a straw hat, but the hat was pushed back so he could look up at the plane, and that is how we recognized him. We strolled towards him.

"How do you do?" I said.

My voice startled him, and his shape changed, a black Proteus going from stone to water in an instant. "I don't mean no harm, boss," he said, whirling about and throwing up his hands, palms out as though in supplication. His eyes were as steady as flint above his studied abnegation, and he observed us coldly.

"Hell, man—you don't have to jump like that," Jim Ed said. "We don't mean no harm, either."

"I'm minding my own business, boss. I ain't doing nothing to nobody, and if you white folks wants me to move on, I'll get out of here like greased lightning."

"Hell," Jim Ed said, "I don't want you to go away. We saw you were from home and came over. How did you get up here?"

M.P. looked at me, and his face changed subtly, a calculating face, staring at me, then at Jim Ed, then at Dr. Youngblood, then at Dale Farmer, then back at me.

"I got a car," M.P. said. "I paid for it with my own money."

"A car!" Jim Ed said. "You mean colored folks got cars now?"

"Ain't no law against it, is there?" M.P. said. "It's sitting over there, down the road a piece. Nineteen-fourteen Model T Ford. First year Mr. Henry turned them out on his assembly line. I didn't park in the white man's place. I ain't doing nobody no harm. Ain't nothing wrong with looking at the airplanes, is there?"

His clothes were soft with many washings, and they clung to his hard body as if every wrinkle had been tailored to fit him. A red bandana handkerchief hung from his hip pocket.

"I'm Jim Ed Ledbetter. That's my daddy up there flying around in that thing. . . . I knew you in France, didn't I?"

Now I was surprised.

"Deed you did, boss. I'm mighty proud you recollect that. I's just a poor old nigger, and I don't 'spect white folks to recollect nothing about me."

"Cut it out, dammit."

"Cut what out, boss?"

"That talk," Jim Ed said. "You didn't talk that mushy-mouth way in France."

"France is France," M.P. said. "I's in America, boss, the land of the free and the home of the brave. I ain't in no backward old country like France where niggers talk any which way."

"Shit," Jim Ed said. "You were in the French Army. That was the damnedest thing. An American colored man in the French Army. And from Bourbonville."

"Everbody's got to be someplace," M.P. said.

"You were at Soissons," Jim Ed said.

"Yassuh, Sergeant. I was at Soissons. He's doing a dive. Look up there!" In his excitement M.P. forgot his obsequious tone. He commanded us.

We looked up and the plane was swooping down like a hawk. While we watched, it nosed up again, and we heard its little engine grinding towards the clouds.

"It makes me sick," Jim Ed said.

"Hell, man, what you talking about? That's the biggest thrill in the world," M.P. said. "Whoo-eeee. Look at him go!" He seemed to have forgotten himself and us for a moment. "You get up there, and the land spinning round and round below you, and you take a dive and see the ground coming up, and you think you gonter die. But you ain't. Not most of the time. You pull back, and the nose comes up, and you see the horizon drop, and you get a feeling down in your sweet place, and I tell you something, it's a feeling."

" 'Your sweet place'!" Dale Farmer said.

"That's what I call it," M.P. said.

"That's pretty good," Dale Farmer said. "Your sweet place."

"You were in the French Army?" Dr. Youngblood said.

"Yassuh, boss. I joined the frogs in 1914. Got off the boat where I was stoking coal and joined up in Le Havre."

"The French Army took a colored man," Dale Farmer said in a wondering tone.

"They let me join the frog army like I was born with white skin and yellow hair," M.P. said.

"Were you a cook?" Dale Farmer said.

"Hell no. . . . Oh, shut my mouth, boss. I didn't mean to use no cuss words around you white gentlemens. I didn't mean no harm. But I wasn't no dumb cook. Hell no. I was a mechanic."

"A mechanic," Dale Farmer said. His eyes rolled like hands over M.P. Dale Farmer licked his lips.

"First on trucks, then on airplanes," M.P. said with sudden proud dignity.

"When we met, Sergeant, I was working on airplanes at Soissons. I was teetotally perfect with Spads."

"He was reading a book," Jim Ed said. "I hung around up there because that's where they had Willy in a field hospital. There was this colored man reading a book, and I wanted to see if he was holding it right side up, and damned if he wasn't from Bourbon County."

"An astounding coincidence," Dale Farmer said. He was grinning like a Halloween pumpkin.

"I like to read," M.P. said.

"You're the only colored man I ever saw reading a book," Jim Ed said.

"You ought to come to church with me one of these days, white boss. You'll see colored folks reading a book all over the place. We call it the Bible."

"It was something about airplane engines."

"Sure enough was. The frogs sent me over to Soissons to learn them new Curtiss Jennys from the Yanks. I was reading the factory manual on the Jenny."

"Did you become a pilot?" Dr. Youngblood said.

"I learned to fly, if that's what you mean, Doc. They was a French officer that taught me. I had the knack for it. I can fly one of them things as good as anybody you ever seen. You see somebody that can fly better than me, boss, and he's got wings and a harp."

"How about that?" Jim Ed said. "How we going to keep you colored folks in your place when you go flying around like a bunch of crows?" He laughed without malice.

"That's the trouble," M.P. said. "My money's good as any white man's. I bought a car. Cash down. That's the only way they'll let a nigger have a car—cash down. But I can't buy me no airplane. Not down here in Tennessee anyhow. Nobody will sell a nigger an airplane lessen he goes off to California or somewheres like that. I wanted to buy that Jenny over yonder, but them white folks, they told me they'd string me up if I tried to do it. They meant it, too. They're mean white folks."

We looked where he pointed. "It's the black one yonder," M.P. said. "It's for sale. Two hundred dollars. You can buy one new in the crate, never put together, for four hundred dollars army surplus. But they want two hundred dollars for that piece of junk, and they won't sell it to me."

"Hell, what's anybody need with an airplane?" said Jim Ed.

"I like to fly, that's why," M.P. said. "I dream about flying ever night and ever day. Ain't no day passes that I don't think about flying." M.P. looked skyward, rapt with desire. I think he had momentarily forgotten us.

"Why don't they come down?" Jim Ed said. "They've been up there long enough."

At last the little plane carrying Brian Ledbetter swooped towards the strip on a long and graceful arc and landed and bumped to a stop at the line of planes parked to one side. The old man tumbled out and stumped over to where we were standing.

"Feller over yonder's got a airplane for sale," the old man said. He seemed laconic, nonchalant.

"So what?" Jim Ed said.

"Maybe it's time I bought me a airplane," the old man said. "Let's go take a look."

"Hot dog!" M.P. yelled. "Hot dog!"

"Who are you?" the old man said.

"I is M.P. Brown," M.P. said, bowing and grinning. "And Mr. Ledbetter, I fly airplanes, and I's gonter be your chauffeur."

"Well, I reckon I need one, because it's hard to fly a airplane with a wood leg. I asked the feller, and he said it couldn't be done."

"Hot dog!" M.P. said.

"Goddamn," Jim Ed said.

101

IN A MOMENT we were walking across the field, M.P. leading us. He was almost beside himself with enthusiasm. "That plane you want to buy, it's a sure enough Curtiss Jenny," M.P. said. "It ain't in good shape, but it's the real McCoy. Nineteen seventeen. I know the year. They won't sell it to me. But hell, Mr. Ledbetter, you're *white*. You can do anything you wants to do, buy anything you wants to buy, and I'm the best airplane mechanic in the world, and I's gonter fix it up for you, and you and me is going to fly from here to kingdom come and back."

"I wish I wasn't so old," Brian Ledbetter said. "I wisht I'd been flying all my life."

"If you keep on flying, you will likely not grow much older," Jim Ed said.

"I will not grow much older in any case," the old man said. "I want to try this out."

"I am myself interested in all sorts of experiences," Dale Farmer said. "Perhaps I should reconsider. Perhaps I too should be willing to go aloft in an airplane." His face glowed, and he looked at M.P.

"Hell, you're too damn fat," M.P. said. "Put you in a Jenny, and the thing's going to fly with the tail hanging down like an old cowed hound dog. Come on, white folks. Let's go look at that thing. Whoo-eee."

"I am only temporarily fat," Dale Farmer said, deeply injured. "I plan to go on a diet. The real person that I am is thin. Almost emaciated, in fact."

No one listened to him. We were already walking towards the airplane, grass swishing around our ankles.

The Curtiss Jenny seemed to grow smaller as we got closer. It was a biplane with two open cockpits, one behind the other.

Around the aircraft several men stood in attitudes of nonchalant bravado. M.P. held back, and Brian Ledbetter went ahead, stumping with his wooden leg across the turf, his white hair blowing gently in the soft air.

Brian's pilot leaned against one of the airplanes. He said something to the others and they laughed. They were smoking in studied gestures. The brave cigarette: I have seen it since in the films. They eyed us as if we had been cattle walking across a pasture behind the determined plodding of an old lead bull.

"How about it, Pop?" Brian's pilot said. "You looking to take another ride? This ole coot's pretty good, fellers. He didn't holler once."

"Come up with *me*, Pop, and I'll make you shit all over the cockpit," another young pilot said. He had thin, sandy hair and clear blue eyes. "I mean, come up with me if you got another three bucks to spend."

"Hell," Brian's pilot muttered, "this old coot's got cash. Don't sell him short."

"But has he got guts?" one of the others said. He laughed, a voice hard like a marble floor where crockery breaks when it falls, and the others laughed, too.

We stood there not knowing what to do next, collectively uncertain and foolish, and I felt that we were making up our minds that this was a ridiculous enterprise and that we had best be getting back to the ordinary life where we belonged—on the dull earth among the wingless quadrupeds, our natural company.

All of us except M.P. He pushed his hands deep in his pockets, his head bowed so as not to meet the eyes of any white man. He shuffled to the black Curtiss Jenny and peered at the engine with mute, mild curiosity, as if he had never seen an engine before. He reached out to touch it, still with the respectful air of a man pondering something alien and hitherto unsuspected, to affirm to himself the existence of a strange apparatus whose purpose he did not understand.

"Hey, nigger! What the hell you doing, touching my airplane? I told you before—get the hell out of here." A bushy-haired man spoke, a growl primitive and hostile like a whipsaw tearing through live flesh. I can reproduce the words, but I cannot reproduce the hatred in every syllable. "That nigger come around here earlier wanting to *buy* that airplane. You figure that? A nigger wanting to buy an airplane. Jesus fucking Christ."

Nor can I reproduce the craven whine that came into M.P.'s voice, a voice that simultaneously relaxed the mortal tension and allowed M.P. to have his say. "Oh, lordy, boss. I didn't mean no harm. Swear to God I didn't. I's just a poor old country nigger that don't mean no harm to nobody."

"Then get your dirty black hands off my airplane." The bushy-haired man knotted his fists and advanced a step, and M.P. backed up. M.P. could have broken him like a dry stick.

"Yassuh. But you got a bad piston in this here engine. Maybe you got more than one. You better be mighty careful, boss. You likely to lose oil pressure three thousand foot up in the air, and then you're gonter burn up a piston or maybe throw a rod through the cylinder, and you'll come down hard, mister. Real hard. You can get kilt coming down as hard as you gonter come down when you lose oil pressure and the engine locks up and the prop up there just stops and wiggles a little and the wind starts whistling through them struts and you goes down like a tin can filled with rocks and throwed off a house, and you just as dead as a codfish."

M.P. did a little jig step backwards and bowed his head like a man striving to ward off a blow. The bushy-haired man was as startled as the rest of us by this unexpected outpouring of mechanical analysis, but he was stupid and slow, and his face twisted like half-hardened clay worked by an unseen hand.

"Listen here," he said. "I don't need no smart-ass nigger to tell me about my airplane."

He took another menacing step forward, but something had become uncertain in him, and he looked with a flicker of anxiety at his airplane. The sandy-haired pilot squinted at the engine and turned to the bushy-headed man. "Maybe the nigger's right, Gus. The oil there, around the exhaust. Maybe the piston's cracked. You might should look to it."

"I's just giving you information, boss. There ain't nothing so good as information in this wide, wide world. Information is what makes the world go round."

The man called Gus chewed his thoughts, looking at the engine, then at M.P., then at the sandy-haired man, and then spitefully around at all of us.

"I don't like niggers telling me what to do. I told you once to clear out of here, nigger." I could see tension quiver down his body, the sort of tension that takes over when one man is about to hit another.

Jim Ed turned red. Dale Farmer retreated, grinning, saying that he thought we had disturbed these kind gentlemen long enough and that we should go on back home. I think M.P. saw his last chance at flying the Curtiss Jenny dwindling like water out of a leaking pot.

But the old man took charge, raising his voice a little as an imperturbable teacher might to assert his authority over an unruly class. "Don't pay no attention to him," he said suddenly. "I want to buy this airplane."

"You!" the bushy-haired man said. "What's an old peg-legged coot like you going to do with an airplane?"

"I reckon I'll fly it around the country and look at the ground," the old man said.

"Jesus Christ!" the bushy-haired man said. "You can't fly no airplane with that stick you got for a leg."

"Hell," Brian's pilot murmured, "the old coot's got the money. This ain't no joke. He's got guts, too. I'll testify to that." He spoke softly, as though supposing that we might not hear him and that he might therefore conjure up a conspiracy with Gus. "Let him show you that bankroll he's got in his little pocketbook." The murmur with its delicate mention of gold clanged in the air, and Gus looked at the old man in a mingling of rapacity, wonder, and scorn. He disregarded M.P. as utterly as a thirsty man might disregard the design and architecture of a spigot after he has filled his glass and sated his thirst and belched and turned away to other things.

"Who's going to fly it for him?" Gus said. "Tell you one thing—I ain't letting no nigger fly my airplane. It don't matter how much this old pirate's going to pay me for it."

"It won't be your airplane if I buy it," Brian Ledbetter said.

"The hell you say," Gus said. "I ain't going to be the first white man that lets a nigger fly a plane. Thing like that might get in 'Believe It or Not!' "

"I ain't going to fly no plane," M.P. whined. "Lordy, mister, I ain't smart enough to fly no airplane. I's just a simple old mechanic. I know what makes these things work, but I can't fly one."

"Then why was you wanting to buy this plane earlier today?" Gus said.

"I just thought I'd fix it up and sell it," M.P. said. "But I wasn't going to fly it. Oh, lordy no, white boss. You can count on that. I knows my place."

Gus glowered at him. "And who's going to fly it if this old man buys it?"

"Why, Captain Paul Alexander here," M.P. said, turning with sudden inspiration on me.

I looked at him, wondering if he had gone mad.

"That's right," the old man said quickly. "I want you gents to meet Captain Paul Alexander of the French Air Corpse. He had thirty-five kills during the war."

I thought the men would burst out laughing, but they turned to me with respect.

"Sure enough?" Brian's pilot said. "The French Air Corps! Thirty-five kills! That's more than Eddie Rickenbacker. Jesus!"

"He was shot down three times, and here he is," M.P. said. "Ain't that right, Cap'n?"

"I beg your pardon," I said.

"Jesus, listen to that accent," Brian's pilot said. "You're the real thing."

"Thirty-five kills," the bushy-haired man said.

"Richthofen got eighty," another pilot said.

"But he's dead," M.P. said, somewhat jubilantly. "The captain here would of got lots more kills if he hadn't been wounded so much, but then he might be dead, too. After he was wounded, he taught Yanks how to fly."

"So you was wounded?" the other pilot said.

"Yes, I was wounded," I said. "But—"

"It's a wonder you wasn't killed," the bushy-haired man said. "Most of the boys I knowed that was shot down was killed."

M.P. had his hand on a pulse of truth. Wounded French aviators had taught Americans how to fly when the United States entered the war. It was something we saw in the newspapers—photographs of French officers in their fine uniforms and with their canes, helping young Americans learn about airplanes.

"Anyway," Brian Ledbetter said, "I reckon I'll just buy this airplane, and my friend the captain here can fly it down to my place in Bourbon County."

"And I'll just fly along in the backseat to make sure everything's all right with the engine," M.P. said. "Like I always done when we was testing out airplanes over there in the French Army Air Corpse."

"I don't know," Gus said. "I ain't got no hankering to let a nigger ride in my airplane. He'll stink it up something fierce."

"I'll be in the backseat, just like I is on the streetcars," M.P. said. "There ain't nothing wrong with a nigger sitting in the backseat, is there, white boss? That's where you white folks wants us to sit, and here's one nigger that don't mind at all sitting in the backseat of that airplane."

"Jesus," Brian's pilot said. "I never heard a nigger talk so much."

I looked at Brian and Jim Ed, expecting them to laugh and shrug their shoulders and to say at last, "You are right. This colored man is crazy." And I would say, "That is right. I was in the Belgian infantry. I have never flown an airplane in my life. I have never even been *in* an airplane. I once climbed the Tour Eiffel when I went to Paris with my friends Guy and Bernal on a lark. That is as high off the earth as I have ever been. The elevator frightened me."

But no. I stood there, probably with a blank expression that someone might take for confidence, and the old man and M.P. and even Jim Ed looked expectantly at me. We had all fallen under M.P.'s spell. Jim Ed told me later that he knew better but that when M.P. was telling this string of lies, he believed all of it. "The man sounded so *sure* about you," Jim Ed said. "I mean, you're the man who had played the mandolin better than anybody I ever heard play the mandolin before in my life, and I thought, 'Yes, this man can do anything. He can fly an airplane. Why should he not fly an airplane? If anybody can fly an airplane, this man can do it.' "

"Well," Gus said, running an oily hand absentmindedly through his thick hair. "I reckon you can take it up, Captain. I reckon if you're serious about buying it." He looked at the old man.

"How much you selling it for?" Brian Ledbetter said.

Gus hesitated, calculated, looked at me and squinted, looked down at the ground and spat contemplatively. "I was thinking about three hundred," he said. "That was what I was thinking about."

"Well, maybe we were thinking that we would go one hundred fifty," Jim Ed said. "With that burnt-out piston and all. You can get a new airplane for four hundred, still in the crate. We just have to put it together."

M.P. nodded and looked at Jim Ed appreciatively.

"Three hundred ain't a bad price for my airplane," Gus said, looking quietly desperate.

"It's not a bad price," Jim Ed said. "But you can understand if we want to get more for our money than that. Captain, come on, and we'll find something else. It's getting late. We've got to be getting back."

"Not so fast," Gus said. "How about two fifty? I'll come down fifty dollars?"

"No, I don't reckon my daddy could go no more than two hundred," Jim Ed said. "Sorry to take up so much of your time, fellows. Come on, Daddy. Let's go find another airplane."

I greeted this idea with relief and started to make my goodbyes to the pilots. But Gus said in a tone of jovial concession, "Well, I can see you're from East Tennessee. You know that's where the ten lost tribes came. Right here to East Tennessee. Har. Har. Har. All right, then. Two hundred."

The old man opened his little leather purse and took out his roll of bills. He licked his thumb and counted out two one-hundred-dollar bills. The pilots looked at the money with hungry eyes.

"Damn," Gus said.

"I told you," Brian's pilot said.

Dale Farmer looked on. "You will give us a receipt, of course," he said in his most officious way. "We don't do business without a receipt. It just so happens that I'm a notary public and an accountant. I can notarize the receipt to prove to God and man and any court of law that these clients of mine have truly paid you the two hundred dollars that we are talking about, and just to be certain, my good friend Dr. Curtis Youngblood will witness it. Isn't that right, Doctor?"

Dr. Youngblood chuckled. "All right," he said.

"God Amighty, you fellers come prepared," Gus said.

"Do you mind flying it home, Captain?" Brian Ledbetter said, turning to me.

"Ah . . . no. Oh no, of course not," I said.

"I reckon you've flown a Curtiss Jenny, then," Gus said, nodding at me.

"Boss, the cap'n here was called back from the military hospital to help design Curtiss Jennys. This man can put a Curtiss Jenny together blindfolded. It's something they make you do in the French Air Corpse. You got to put a whole airplane together blindfolded."

I looked at the little airplane, and I decided that I would not mind dying like this.

M.P. looked at me with implacable seriousness. "Don't you worry none about this piston. You know me, Cap'n. I can fix anything that rolls or flies or hops."

Gus said, "You really want to fly with that nigger?"

"I always fly with my mechanic," I said.

Gus shrugged. "Oh well, what the hell. I don't mind your nigger. I ain't no fucking bigot. Get him out of here before he talks us all to death."

It was the headiest moment of my life since Guy and Bernal died. I nodded.

"We'll meet you back home," Jim Ed said.

"You'll get there before we will," Brian Ledbetter said.

"The good Lord willing," M.P. said. He looked at the Jenny, and for the first time he showed a tremor of uncertainty. It passed quickly. He pulled out a pair of goggles from his trouser pocket. "I knew no white man would lend me his goggles. I came prepared." We had this conversation in French much later on.

"How did you know I had been wounded?"

"How do you think?" he said. "I ask questions, and I get information. Information is the key to the universe. This town knows all about you—that you do not eat anything, that you study the dictionary and take long walks and that Miss Daisy Weaver loved you and you did not love her, that you go to Knoxville every other Saturday, that Doc Youngblood and the Ledbetters like you, and that you play the mandolin like magic. You think you have any secrets in Bourbon County?" He laughed sardonically. He did not say, "And you talk to two ghosts, and people think you are as crazy as popcorn."

All this was later: now M.P. and I were to fly.

Another pair of goggles came from one of the fliers, and in a moment I had them on my head, and somebody was helping me into the front cockpit, and M.P. was clumsily and obsequiously climbing into the back cockpit, making noises about how he sure did hate to fly and he wouldn't do this for anybody else on earth, but I had saved his life during the war, and he was bound to me like a slave to his master, and many other preposterous things.

Gus stood in front of the plane ready to spin the propeller, and M.P. sat back there whimpering with his straw hat still on (though he put it down at his feet just before the engine caught), and he whispered urgently at me through the speaking tube that connected the dual cockpits, "Bend forward, goddammit. Look smart! Pretend you know what you are doing. Do not look off into the wind, white man. Look *interested,* for chrissakes."

"I do not know what I am doing," I whispered.

"Pretend, goddammit. Pretend."

I heard Guy laugh. I bent forward. Gus spun the propeller and shouted

"Contact!" The engine sputtered and stopped. Gus repeated the process and repeated it again. The engine coughed and belched a dense, black cloud of oil smoke from the exhaust under the top wing and caught and throbbed to life. The propwash (I did not know the term at that time) blew into my face and through my hair, mingling with the foul-smelling exhaust, and I was glad to have the goggles. The little plane vibrated violently.

M.P.'s voice rang at the back of my neck. He was whispering in a peculiar, shrill way so as not to be heard beyond the roar of an engine. "Grab the stick, Captain. Do not hold it tight. Keep your hands loose or we will die. Let me fly this cocksucker. You *pretend.* Look straight ahead."

Later I learned from the others that as we taxied off down the little grass runway, M.P. sat in the back with both hands clutching the sides of the cockpit. He was steering the plane with his knees, and as we went faster and faster he casually put one hand in the cockpit and grabbed the stick and pulled it back. We went bumping across the field, the green grass flashing by, and I held my hands loosely on the stick and felt it come back, and the bumping stopped, and we left the ground.

I was so caught up in the thrill of speed and flight that it took me a moment to realize that M.P. was screaming "Shit! Shit! Shit!" at the top of his voice. I looked around and saw his face in a rage.

"This damn engine!" he shouted at me. His eyes were frozen on something ahead of us. I turned to see what it was. The forest at the end of the runway was rushing to meet us. We were climbing too slowly. I could hear the engine laboring, grinding, ready to burst.

"Shit!" M.P. was shouting as though the energy of his voice could give power to the engine. Perhaps it did. With a slow, agonizing ascent we cleared the tallest chestnut trees by inches, and I looked over and saw the leaves and the branches so close that I could almost touch them, and I heard the propwash storm through the leaves. The plane, laboring, laboring, climbed up and up, slowly, slowly, and we banked, and the brown river fell away below us, the sun gleaming on it, and upstream I could see Knoxville and the spidery iron framework of the Gay Street Bridge and the leafy hill where the meager brick buildings of the university squatted dark red under the branches, and downstream I could see mansions under construction on Kingston Pike along the river, and to the east I could see the mountains, blue and solid and huge.

"We must rebuild this engine from the cylinders up. Our friend Gus, he is a shithead, *une tête de merde.* He has not spent two cents on this engine. I bet he has never flown it with a passenger. We had the good luck not to be a couple of broken eggs when we came off that runway." He shifted to English, his language of joy: "How about it, Captain? Are we flying or ain't we?"

"Like birds!" I shouted.

"Whoooo-eeeee!" M.P. shouted.

I felt wildly happy.

"It's gonter take a hell of a lot of work," he shouted. "These controls feel like they've been dipped in tar. Listen to that no-count engine. I've heard butter churns worked by old women sound better than that. I got to tear the whole thing down and put it all back together again."

I was rapt in the great green earth wheeling grandly below, the immense forest, broken here and there by meadows where cows grazed and fields where corn and hay grew, the incandescent flash of the summer sun on a pond or a patch of the river, the lines drawn by the roads over the land, the houses and the churches and water tanks and the stitching of railroads, the crawling of an occasional automobile. I sat mesmerized by the beauty of motion.

I realized how flimsy our support was, high aloft on this uncertain engine and on fabric stretched taut over wooden ribs and struts, and I knew how far and how violently we could fall. The prospect of such a death filled me with serenity, as though the radiance of the sun had impregnated my body and made me like light itself. I imagined riding the plane down to earth, the final crash an epiphany, Apollo's fiery darts at our presumption, and then a sunny peace. I did not see Guy or Bernal. I felt their presence as part of the serenity. We were part of one another up here; I flowed into them, and they into me, and we were one with light and earth and everything that was, and there was no more separateness. Everything in being was combined, and eternity was in this moment.

The mood was on M.P., too. He shouted at me over the engine noise. "Up here, it ain't like it is down below. Down there, I am a nigger. Up here I am a man! The angels up here are black people. They sit on the clouds and wave their old hats and jump up and down and shout 'Whoooo-eeeee!' Those black folks are all around us, Captain, watching a black man fly. Can you feel them?"

"Yes," I shouted. "Yes!"

"You must be part black man, Captain. Whoo-eeee."

"Whoooo-eeee!" I said.

"Whoo-eee," he said. He did slow turns, slipping the plane from side to side, doing as much as he could without killing us.

"It's in bad shape," he shouted. "I can fix it up. I can make it a new airplane." We laughed again. The world seemed young and free.

We winged over the hills and the L & N Railroad tracks and crossed the river and the Dixie Railroad and saw the village of Greenback on one side and Bourbonville on the other and found the Ledbetter farm below us in its hills and pastures and woods. M.P. brought us down in a swooping glide onto a meadow behind the barn. The wheels touched. We bounced, and rolled to a stop.

We were scarcely out of the plane when Mrs. Ledbetter came hurrying down through the field. She was frantic. "What is it? What's wrong?" she cried.

"Mr. Ledbetter's just bought hisself a airplane," M.P. said, bowing mightily. "I'm his new chauffeur and mechanic, and here we is."

"Lord have mercy," Mrs. Ledbetter said.

102

EVELYN LEDBETTER was irate. "You, Brian Elisha Ledbetter! A grown man! Playing with airplanes! Why don't you get you a jump rope? It don't cost as much, and you can't get high enough off the ground to fall down and hurt yourself. Men never grow up. If it wasn't for me you'd starve to death, but maybe before that the law would put you in the asylum for crazy folks."

"Mrs. Ledbetter," the old man said in patient placation, "you are going to love that airplane, and the colored man understands the airplane the way I understand a horse. That is why he is working on the airplane."

"If you ask me, he understands it a lot better than you understand a horse, because I ain't never seen you change the parts of a horse like he is changing the parts of that airplane."

"Mrs. Ledbetter, this is the age of progress. Pretty soon we're going to be able to go to the hardware store and say, 'Brother Kinlaw, I need me a new belly for my old wore-out horse,' and Brother Kinlaw is going to reach up on his shelf and pull down a box with a picture of a horse's belly on the outside, and he is going to say, 'One belly. That'll be one dollar and ninety-five cents. You need anything else while we're at it, Brian?' And I'll say, 'I reckon we need a horse's behind, Brother Kinlaw. My horse's behind is all wore out, too. You got any horse's behinds on them shelves?' And ole Douglas is going to look at me and say with a face about ten miles long, 'Brian, I had me a whole room full of horse's behinds, but they was all called to preach. You can't get a horse's behind nowhere lessen you go to the Methodist church on Sunday morning. As soon as he gets through taking up the collection and preaching his sermon, you can screw him right onto your old horse and hitch him up to your plow—but you ain't going to be happy, Brother Ledbetter, because by the time he's preached one sermon, he's forgot how to do a lick of honest-to-God work."

"How you talk," Mrs. Ledbetter said.

"You're laughing, Mrs. Ledbetter."

"I'm laughing at how foolish you're getting to be in your old age, Mr. Ledbetter. Spare parts for a horse!"

"Mrs. Ledbetter, if they's anybody in the country that can put spare parts in a horse, that colored man out there can do it. Right now he is fixing up my airplane."

"He's a very polite colored man," she said. "I'll say that for him. Lordy, lordy, I reckon if men wasn't crazy, women would have life too easy, and the good Lord didn't never mean for women to have life easy."

"The Lord God meant us to go up in our airplanes and look at heaven to see if we like it," the old man said.

"You better take a good look," Mrs. Ledbetter said. "You might not never get that close to it again."

The old man threw back his head and laughed.

At first M.P. treated the Ledbetters with distant and mute respect. On most afternoons after the whistle blew work to an end at the car works, he drove to the Ledbetters' in his car. He worked on the airplane until the light left the earth, and Mrs. Ledbetter fixed him a supper, which he ate out on the porch.

Sometimes after supper Dr. Youngblood drove over to get me at the boardinghouse, and we went to the Ledbetters'. Always Dr. Youngblood asked Jim Ed and me to play, and we played, and Jim Ed sang, and M.P. sang, too, after a while, and it was all tranquil and good.

M.P. made lists, carefully writing in a precise, copperplate hand. Jim Ed took time off from hoeing corn and tending pigs, cattle, chickens, and fields and drove to Knoxville with M.P.'s lists, sending orders by telegraph, taking heavy packages off trains, coming back to the farm, grunting and heaving and laughing about the whole foolish enterprise.

M.P. took the engine apart and studied everything. There was a cracked piston. He removed it, held it up, and pulled on it, and it came apart in his strong hands. He tossed the pieces into a pile of scrap. Brian Ledbetter came out and sat by the hour watching M.P. work, each hardly speaking to the other.

During the day, M.P. continued to bring the heats into the laboratory. When no one else was around, we spoke French. With Brian he was quiet. With me he was boisterous. In he would come, throwing the door open with a crash and a rumbling laugh. "How goes *mon capitaine* today?"

"I go very well," I said.

"You do not look as pale as you did," he said. "It was the flying. Flying even one time will make you ruddy. If you fly enough, you will turn dark. Fly six months, and no one will be able to tell the difference between you and me."

Pinkerton would have clapped me on the back. M.P. never touched me. Despite our French, despite our joviality, a distance remained between us—the distance of race at that time and place in the world. We both accepted it—just as we accepted his place on the porch when Mrs. Ledbetter fixed him supper and he ate there and we ate in the kitchen.

M.P. talked on and on to me about the revolution to come. I did not take him seriously. The obsessions of others are tedious.

"This is not a revolutionary country," I said. "Your people are not revolutionaries."

"That is because they do not yet have information," M.P. said. "I am giving them information. You must have information before you can want anything. When my people have information the revolution will come as day follows night. It is inevitable."

"What sort of information?"

"The information that they are human beings."

"Surely they know that," I said.

"No they do not, my white friend. My people imagine that they are cattle. The whites say that the blacks are a herd to be driven here and there, and the blacks believe it. I tell them they have the right to eat in restaurants and stay in hotels and piss in toilets and keep their hats on when they pass a white man on the sidewalk. I tell them they have the right to go to college and be doctors and lawyers and anything they want to be. I tell them first we have to show the white man that he cannot live without us now. And then we force the white man to give us our rights."

"And how will you do that?" I said.

"A general strike, all over America. Black men walk off their jobs. We start here, in Bourbonville. It spreads. State to state, then the whole country. Black people lay down their tools, walk out of the fields, off the jobs, out of the homes where they are cleaning toilets. Do you not see it, man?"

I was not sympathetic. "In Europe the general strike was supposed to keep war from coming. The German rail workers and the French rail workers pledged to throw down their tools and their weapons and meet each other at the borders in a great embrace. They sang the 'Internationale' and embraced each other and cried together. They promised to overthrow capitalism and bring in the new age."

"Exactly," M.P. said.

"Exactly," I said sarcastically. "The war came. The German rail workers and the French rail workers killed each other with bloody abandon."

"Blacks will not be so stupid, my friend. We are united by something far more powerful than economic class."

"What is that?"

"You are intelligent; you do not need to ask the question."

"Pretend I am stupid. What can unite you more than the Socialists were united?"

"Color," my friend. He held out his ebony arm. "This!"

"Forgive me, but I do not believe it."

"You are from Belgium?"

"Yes, Belgium."

"You do not look Belgian."

"It is complicated. Get on with it."

"The Socialist stoker in Belgium. He speaks of the revolution, but thinks about his children. He thinks about the possibilities of capitalism, and he ponders possibilities. He thinks that some accident may happen, and because of the accident, his children may climb. He knows that sometimes the son of a stoker becomes an opera singer or the daughter of a switch man on the railroad marries a banker. His revolutionary fervor is dampened just a little by that knowledge. He does not know how enfeebled it is until the moment of crisis."

"Like 1914."

"Like 1914. But your black man knows he will be black always. His children will be black. His grandchildren will be black."

"And?"

"When we call our general strike, black men will stand together. Nothing can break our unity. You wait and see."

"It is a dangerous dream," I said.

"Dangerous for whites. I will organize black people all over the South, and when I give the signal, they will stop work. The white people cannot live if the black people stop working."

"The black people cannot live, either," I said. "If they stop working, how are they going to live?"

"We have always lived on nothing. We can live on less than nothing."

In the late afternoon, when he worked on the airplane, he was a teacher of physics. Jim Ed did not trust the airplane. "I've seen it fly, but I don't believe it," he said with a laugh.

M.P. grinned. "If it wasn't for this curve . . . You see that? This curve on top of the wings? That makes the air wash up, see? That makes a vacuum. An airplane is sucked up in the air. The propeller pulls it forward fast, and the machine is sucked up in the air. The curve is everything. That's what the Wright Brothers discovered. That's why the Wright Brothers were geniuses. They had information, and they made something new out of it. You get information, and you have a revolution." He winked at me.

"Lordy," Jim Ed said, shaking his head.

"Ain't it something?" M.P. said.

"Yes," I said.

"Don't it make you believe in God?" he said, looking momentarily serious, as if he had been truly caught up in the aura of a divine miracle.

"It is the laws of physics," I said. "You do not have to believe in God."

"Jesus Christ, I've been flying with a goddamn atheist. I'm gonter get up there in the sky, and God is going to say, 'Why am I holding up this goddamn atheist,' and he's gonter throw you onto the ground. Only trouble is, I'm gonter be in the same damn airplane with you."

"We better call Clyde if you're going to talk about God," Jim Ed said. "You know what Clyde's decided to do now? Be a carpenter. None of the churches have the truth, he says; so he won't preach in any of them. He's going to be a carpenter like his daddy, and he can find God's truth without being responsible to some congregation that's all mixed up and wrong and won't learn any better."

"A carpenter!" M.P. said. "Hell, he ain't trying to be like his daddy. He's trying to be like Jesus Christ."

"At least he's not going to be running around from one church to another anymore. At least he's not going to go back to speaking tongues. When Clyde got off speaking in tongues, it gave me the goose bumps. I never heard anything so weird."

M.P. laughed. "That's what Paul and me does," he said. "We speaks in tongues."

I realized that he had called me by my first name. Jim Ed looked at me quizzically. I looked away.

103

ONE PLEASANTLY rainy morning in late August Pinkerton walked into the laboratory when M.P. and I were talking. I do not know if he heard us speaking French. The door opened, and we turned as though caught in an illegal act and saw Pinkerton out of breath and staring at us, his eyes red. M.P. started for the door, bowed down and looking as humble as he could.

"Loafing, are you, nigger?" Pinkerton growled.

"I's just brought the heat in from the wheel foundry, boss. I's just getting my black ass back to work. 'Deed I is, Cap'n. And a good day to you."

"I know you, don't I?" Pinkerton said.

"I reckon you knows all of us, Cap'n. Sure I do. You has the name for seeing everything, just like God."

The mockery was so obvious that I thought Pinkerton must feel it. But he looked at M.P. and smiled slowly.

"Like God," he said. "Do they say that about me?"

"Deed they does, Cap'n. They says you knows everything they is to know about folks that works in the foundry. My pappy said that about you, too, Cap'n."

"Your pappy," Pinkerton said.

"Hobart Brown," M.P. said. "You brought him up here from Sweetwater. He worked with you clearing the swamp. Hobart Brown was his name."

"Hobart Brown," Pinkerton said. A needle of memory pricked his brain. "Hobart Brown."

"He named me after you, Cap'n. I's named Moreland Pinkerton Brown. Folks calls me M.P. for short."

"M.P.," Pinkerton said.

"You remembers my daddy," M.P. said, gently now. "You remembers the way he died."

"Yes, I remember. In the annealing pit."

"That's the one," M.P. said, very softly.

"In the annealing pit. He died in the annealing pit." Pinkerton's face was illuminated.

"He did for a fact," M.P. said.

"This nigger's daddy fell into an annealing pit on top of red-hot wheels," Pinkerton said. "Jesus Christ! How could I forget it?"

"God rest his soul, Cap'n," M.P. said.

"The crane operator almost saved him," Pinkerton said.

"I've heard about it many a time," M.P. said.

"His name was Lonnie Blankenship," Pinkerton said. "You see how I remember things?"

"My daddy always did say you was the smartest man he ever knowed," M.P. said.

"Did he say that?" Pinkerton said, obviously pleased.

"He said it lots of times," M.P. said.

"Your daddy died for the car works. Lonnie Blankenship almost saved him."

"He done his best, Mr. Blankenship did. My mamma said he done the best he knowed how to do. He dropped the hook in the hole, right on top of my daddy."

Pinkerton turned to me. "Lonnie wasn't trying to hook the darky. The hooks on the crane, they was red hot from holding the red-hot wheels. Lonnie, he dropped the hook on top of the nigger, and the nigger's body stuck to it—because of the heat, you see. The nigger's body stuck to that red-hot crane hook, and Lonnie hauled him out. It almost worked. It damn near almost worked."

"My daddy died," M.P. said. "He lived a few minutes. But he died."

"He died," Pinkerton said. "Somebody come down to the office for me when it happened. I went running. I could smell your daddy's body frying, boy. I took one look at him, and I knowed there wasn't any hope. He was quivering, and his mouth was opening and shutting. His eyes were open, and he was looking at me, but he couldn't lift his head. That hook, it must of burnt three inches into his body. His body stuck to it, and you could smell it frying. And he was burnt all over from the wheels."

"It was hard," M.P. said.

"You must of been a baby," Pinkerton said.

"I was a little boy," M.P. said. He was not false now. His sadness was deep. A patter of raindrops rolled across the thin roof and passed on.

"That was a long time ago," Pinkerton said in a drunkenly dreamy tone. "Let's put it this way, nigger. I did wrong to bring your daddy up here. If I hadn't brought your daddy up here, he might still be alive, enjoying life like the rest of us down there in the Sweetwater Valley where he belonged." He laughed bitterly. "Just like the rest of us. We should have left you in Africa. Wouldn't you rather be in Africa than here? That's where you *really* belong."

"I ain't lost nothing in Africa," M.P. said.

"You see," Pinkerton said wearily, "you don't know what's good for you. Shit, we've all forgot what's good for us." He took a step and staggered. I thought he might fall. He caught himself.

"Can I help you, Cap'n?" M.P. said cautiously.

Pinkerton's face turned savage. "Hell no, you can't help me. Don't you put your black hands on me."

M.P. backed off. "Mr. Pinkerton . . ." I said, not knowing the predicate of my sentence.

"You shut up," Pinkerton said. He looked at M.P. "And you get on back to work."

M.P. looked at him. I felt defiance in the black man, but it passed. "Yassuh, Cap'n. I's going right on back to work this minute." He went, shuffling easily and not looking back.

Pinkerton and I were left alone.

"He did not mean any harm," I said. "He wanted only to help you."

"You think I'm drunk, don't you?"

I was silent.

"I'm not drunk. I just want to tell you, if I had my way, we'd send all the niggers back to Africa. We wouldn't never see niggers. They're polluting our society, our blood." He seemed to lose his thought.

"He is a good foundryman," I said.

Abruptly Pinkerton threw an arm heavily around me and put his face close to my ear. Even at his age, and drunk, he had enormous power in his arms. The reek of whiskey surrounded us. He spoke in my ear with a hoarse whisper, the words drawn out and mysterious, as if imparting some secret unknown to all but two or three. "I tell you just one thing, Alexander. When you take over the car works, get rid of the niggers. Fire them. Run them out of town. Exterminate them. They're under a curse. Eula tells me that. Noah cursed the niggers. You can read it in the Bible. You try to take them out from under that curse, and you're going to bring down the wrath of God on yourself. I didn't know that when I brought the niggers up here. I have finally understood it. God has been angry with me because I brought the niggers in here. It's the niggers' fault that I'm condemned to be here in hell for the rest of my life. You remember that when you run the car works."

"I am not going to take over the car works, Mr. Pinkerton," I said quietly.

He stopped and backed off from me a step, leaving one hand on my shoulder. He stared at me, his face a disk of white in the interior dimness of the building. "You're the one, Alexander. You're the only one I've seen that's worthy of the car works. I can leave it to you, and you're smart enough to keep it going. It's my monument, you see. Some of these days, the town will understand. . . . I want you to do something for me."

His hand was like a vise. "What?" I said.

"You put a statue of me up at the gate."

"A statue?" I said.

"A granite statue," he said. "You put up a statue of me right there in the vacant lot over from the main gate so the first thing people see when they come into the car works in the morning is me looking them over, and the last thing they see when they go home at night is me guarding the place—guarding the whole damned town. You understand that?"

"Yes."

"Good!" He released me suddenly. "You remember what I say. A statue. In granite, not marble. Marble wears away. I want my statue to be here five hundred years from now." He seemed to lose some of his confidence. "I trust you, Alexander. You're the only soul in this piss-ant town I trust. Do you know that?"

"Yes," I said.

"Good," he said. "I knew the first day you walked into the office you would be the one. I saw something. Something in your face. I knew you were the one to take my place. I don't fight with destiny, Alexander. You know what happens to people that fight against destiny?"

I knew.

"They lose," Pinkerton whispered. "They always lose. You're the last victory I can have in this town."

"Mr. Pinkerton—" I began, but he cut me off.

"You remember what I tell you," he said. He took out a cigar. He struck a match to it and stood puffing on the cigar so that the flame at the end alternately illuminated his face and darkened it so that he was a demonic figure coming and going in the gray morning.

Suddenly he laughed. "I fixed up ole Dick Shaw pretty good," he said. "Surprised him."

"You did that," I said. I think I smiled.

"I was a fool," he said. I said nothing. "I thought when he and the other one came . . . Shit!" He laughed, almost naturally. "I have a destiny," he said.

"You have yours, and I have mine. That's the thing, ain't it? Having a destiny. They's lots of folks that don't have one."

He went off into the gray morning, smoking his cigar, his shoulders humped, the blue smoke trailing behind him. The thin rain made a haze, softly sinking into everything. He seemed not to notice it.

104

THE AIRPLANE drew attention. People dropped everything to look up when an airplane passed overhead. Schoolchildren rushed to windows. Barnstormers made a living—and often died—flying from place to place and doing stunts. Men who had flight in their blood and who had fought in dogfights during the war came home and bought airplanes and re-enacted battles in the skies. So Brian's airplane (was it Brian's, or was it M.P.'s? Brian had paid for it, but somehow it became M.P.'s, and I think of it now as his) brought out the curious; and in the country, just about everybody is curious. Country people went visiting on warm Sunday afternoons. They dropped in unannounced and uninvited because in the country everybody felt invited everywhere on Sunday afternoons, and you made as if you had been dying to see them, offering them iced tea and a place on your porch in a rocking chair and your share of the county's gossip and maybe a walk to your barnyard to see a new calf or a litter of pigs, and before milking time they left and told you to come see them, and you said you would.

People came to see the airplane on Sundays. M.P. wanted to work on Sundays, but the taboo of the county was against it unless hay was down and a storm coming. M.P. sat in the shade with his straw hat pulled down, his eyes under the brim fixed on the plane, and people came and looked at it, scarcely noticing him, and they talked with Brian, and Brian talked to them and told them how it had been to fly and how when the plane was done he and his own pilot were going to take a trip north and see the battlefields where he had fought and how they looked from the air. Sunday afternoons passed away, and the summer slipped along. People thought I was his pilot, and they treated me like a god, and the rumor spread that I had been an ace many times over in the war.

All this irritated M.P. He came into the laboratory on Mondays fuming about the waste of time that Sundays were. "I thought you were a preacher," I said.

"I am a preacher for a new kind of religion," he said impatiently. "I do not have time for the kind of religion that people have around here. This religion is an opiate of the people."

I laughed.

A betting fever swept the county as people chose the date M.P.'s work would be finished and the little plane would take to the air. Pincher Eubanks, Bourbonville's loan shark, began speaking to me, asking questions about schedules and "the colored man" and other things. He strutted around carrying a notebook, writing figures. I saw him speaking to people in small groups and looking wise. He spoke to me effusively, tipping his hat, bending his body in a crooked bow. He was short and plump, as nearsighted as a mole.

When I swam into focus before his immutable squint, his face broke into an unpleasant smile—an expression crafty and defensive and malign. His real name was Earl Eubanks, but people called him Pincher because he stood outside the gates of the car works a week before payday and let you borrow five dollars on condition you pay him back six when you were paid. Pinkerton hated him. "If that loan shark sets foot on railroad property, throw his ass in jail"—instructions to Mr. Green, the gateman. Pincher stayed on the other side of the tracks. He bowed to Pinkerton; Pinkerton cursed him for a dog. Gossip said Pincher carried a small pistol in his pocket. It was also said that a white man had beaten him so badly once that he could not hear in one ear. Pincher preferred to deal with the colored men. No colored man who valued his life would hit a white man—not even Pincher Eubanks.

I did not understand about the betting until Dr. Youngblood told me about it. "But why?" I said.

Dr. Youngblood grinned around the stem of his pipe. "You don't know the South. You can always find somebody to bet on anything." I remembered Guy and Bernal and the day Bernal took his math exam.

People invited themselves to sit in the grass in the afternoons at the Ledbetters' and stared at us. An East Tennessee country stare is formidable. Illiterate farmers and their women can stare at you as if you were a post, a block, or an exotic animal. You nod at them, and they may turn red and look away, or they may try to speak and choke on their words, but most of the time they do not say anything. They stare, expressionless, supposing that your effort to communicate with them is part of the aberration that makes you who you are and makes you worth staring at. It is a discomfiting stare, a boring of eyes through your skin, the cumulative desolation of the ages there, less than human, waiting for *something* to happen, for you to do something. They reduce you to the subhuman by their fixity. They came, and they stared at us.

They stood with their arms folded, or else they squatted on their haunches and smoked or chewed tobacco or sat in the dust, respectful, curious, ignorant, murmuring to one another about our magic. What went through their minds? I felt as distant from them as I might have felt from some Chinese coolie trundling his burden through the streets of Shanghai, where I had never been. They could not understand any of it—the mysteries of the engine and aerodynamics and other arcane lore that decides whether something is a good bet. Sometimes money came out, and a buzz of talk rose like bees and subsided into the lethargic watchfulness that clung to us like the muggy heat of the dog days.

Ted Devlin wrote a story about the airplane and airmail, and he took a photograph of Jim Ed, the old man, and me standing by the plane, and to make the story better he called me "Captain Alexander." He did not exactly say that I was a pilot, because he knew I was not, but you could read his story and suppose that I had been a flier in the Belgian Air Corps because he juxtaposed a story of my wounds with a story about the airplane.

Daisy got Ted Devlin's paper in California. She wrote me letters. People were making movies in Southern California. She had a job in a Hollywood studio. She thought she could become an actress. She wanted me to come to California. Her father was dealing in real estate and getting richer. He could take me on as a partner. But she thought I would be a great actor. We might become famous together. Her letters were long and detailed and filled with fantasies. At first I did not respond. My silence did not keep her from writing. Her letters flowed on, and I read them. She was more interesting than my mother. I started writing her.

105

M.P. FLEW THE PLANE in September—a warm Saturday morning. Money changed hands among spectators when the frail little craft, M.P. behind and I in front, bounced down the grassy pasture at the Ledbetter farm and lifted off the ground behind its strong, rebuilt engine. I made no pretense at flying the plane myself.

"Whoo-eeee!" M.P. shouted. We swept up and wheeled in great circles. The world revolved under us, flattened out and made benign. M.P. was ecstatic; so was I.

We landed, and the old man went up with M.P. They were gone an hour. After that they flew every day when the weather was good. People were shocked to discover that M.P. was the pilot. They asked me if it was true— though they could see it was true. I told them it was. They asked if I had been in the French Air Corps, and I told them I had not. They muttered among themselves, and they looked ugly at me. They looked ugly at M.P., too, but he ignored them. He was too proud now to care what they said, and Brian Ledbetter owned the airplane.

Brian bought himself a fur-lined flying cap, wore goggles, and looked bizarre. Nothing daunted him. The leaves changed, and I went up with M.P. again. It was cold in the air now, and I shivered. The land beneath flamed with cool fire. I saw the colors as a symphony over the great land, and I heard the music.

The news that M.P. was the pilot spread like fire in dry wood. The little plane buzzed over Bourbonville, the old man sitting stoically in front and M.P. waving down at his friends in Bucktown. A current of hatred ran through the county. It came out in things people said to me on the street, in an almost palpable hostility that hung in the air whenever the subject of black men came up, especially when the subject of M.P. Brown came up, as it did every day. "What the hell is everybody so afraid of?" Ted Devlin said. "We've had Negroes as chauffeurs since we've had cars." The idea did not go down. Flying an airplane was different. Any idiot could drive a car. Besides, nobody in Bourbon County had a chauffeur.

All over America there were race riots and panicky stories about them in the newspapers. Early in September a race riot broke out in Knoxville, and the governor sent in the National Guard. A white officer was killed accidentally by his own men. It was said that several black men were shot down, but nobody had a number. Rumors and hatred swelled. Race riots blazed in Chicago, in New York, in Texas, in Oklahoma. Black men had been soldiers, real soldiers. They wore uniforms. They walked down the streets of Paris and London, and nobody yelled insults at them. They went into bars and restaurants and drank beer, and nobody ordered them out, and nobody told them to sit in the back of the bus or to ride in segregated railway carriages, and nobody except other Americans made anything special of their being black. They enjoyed the pleasures of French and English whores, and some of them had romances with French and English women—white women. They endured shellfire on the Western Front, and they did not turn tail and run. They stood in their tracks, and they killed white men. Black men realized that if they held a gun in their hands, they were equal to anybody—and better than many.

Then they came back to America, and America tried to stuff them back into the bottle, put the cork in, and smother them to death. White Americans forbade them to stay in a hotel or eat in a restaurant or drink in a bar or urinate in a toilet, or pass a white woman on the street without taking off their hats, and the only work they could get was to sweep floors or clean toilets or push iron wheels in a foundry or shine shoes or carry bags in a hotel or a depot. In 1919 blacks began to fight back. In Knoxville armed black men crouched at windows around a place called Five Points, and when the National Guard came in with guns, the blacks laid down a storm of lead, and the whites ran away. The whites came back with machine guns; but first they had run away, and blacks remembered that. The Ku Klux Klan revived,

burning crosses, claiming to uphold white Christian civilization. White people talked about "uppity niggers," the mongrelization of the white race, the
end of time, and always of sex.

"Ever nigger man in the world itches to stick his prick into a white woman,
and if he can do it while her father and husband have to look on, well, so
much the better." Pinkerton had never talked like that, but now such words
tumbled from his mouth in his steady, morose drunkenness. White men
nodded sagely at his words. I think that when Pinkerton made horrifying
predictions about black men taking over the world he was trying to resurrect
the leadership that he had lost in the "Spanish thing," as he called it. In
Bourbonville on Saturdays the hatred was so thick that you wondered why
the air did not burn.

Dr. Youngblood cautioned Brian Ledbetter. "You ought to know what
people are saying," he said.

Brian Ledbetter was stubborn. "We ain't hurting nobody. We ain't flying
our airplane into no restaurant and making folks eat with my pilot. What the
hell does it matter what we do if we're up there in the sky and all them bigots
are down here on the ground!"

"The bigots have guns," Dr. Youngblood said.

Brian Ledbetter laughed. "I've got a gun, too," he said. "And I can still
use it."

The two of them went on flying. The old man told how the mountains
looked from the air and of swooping up the valleys with the cold wind
blowing in his face, looking into the wilderness and soaring over the great
peaks to see North Carolina spread out for miles and miles and miles in
colors and wilderness that made you think jasper walls and golden streets
were tedious.

"It's the most beautifulest thing I've ever seed in my life," the old man
said.

"Do you realize," Dr. Youngblood said with amusement, "that Brian
never talks about the Civil War anymore? He can't talk about anything but
flying."

The weather turned too cold to fly in an open cockpit. M.P. drained the
engine and covered the airplane with canvas and tied it down. "I hope I live
till spring," the old man said wistfully.

After a slack summer, the car works boomed. Fall and winter rolled by in
a torment of work. M.P. and I talked almost every day. His confidence grated
on my nerves. "You wait till summer, boss. Something's going to happen
then. Just you wait."

M.P. went out now and then to inspect the airplane. He wanted to touch
it. So did Brian Ledbetter. They took off the canvas and stood looking at
their toy. One Saturday night Jim Ed and I played, and M.P. sang—a deep
baritone voice, rolling and rolling. I looked at the old man and Mrs. Ledbet-

ter, and they had tears in their eyes. "I has all the nigger talents," M.P. said.

"Stop talking like that," Jim Ed said.

One Saturday afternoon in the early spring M.P. showed up with a new car—a yellow Mercer. It shone like the sun. "How in hell did you get the money to buy a car like that?" the old man asked.

"You don't spend much money on a ship," M.P. said. "I was a stoker, remember? I saved my money."

"But why a car like that one?" Brian Ledbetter said, walking around it, looking at its gleaming yellow paint. "You had a nice old car."

"I don't want to drive old rattletraps anymore. I'm flying now. That makes me good enough to buy a real car. When I drive by, I want everybody to say, 'There goes M.P. Brown.' I want folks to know my name."

"He does not know the meaning of measure," Dr. Youngblood told me. I told M.P. I thought he was unwise.

"Look at it this way," he said, speaking French. "A leader does not drive an old car. A leader must be extraordinary. When the blacks see my car, they listen to me. I tell them they can drive a car like mine. If I can do it, they can do it, too—or their children." He no longer cared who heard him speak French.

The car caused much comment. Black men gathered at M.P.'s house to talk far into the night. News of these meetings spread into the white community. No one knew what the blacks talked about. The ugliness grew.

April came, and M.P. and the old man flew again. They came down the first time shivering so violently that Jim Ed said he thought they were going to die. Mrs. Ledbetter wrapped both of them in wool blankets, and still for a time they trembled uncontrollably by the fire, Brian's skin blue and his lips almost black. When they could talk, the old man said, "Mrs. Ledbetter, you got to go up in the airplane. It's the most beautifulest thing you ever seen in your life."

Mrs. Ledbetter was so exasperated that she had to leave the room. She threatened to burn the airplane if they went up in it before May, and Brian Ledbetter and M.P. believed her, and they left the plane on the ground until the first clear Saturday in May, and then they were up again, and Brian Ledbetter was sketching out the tour he planned to take that summer of his old battlefields. He and M.P. sat in the kitchen studying maps and talking like a couple of children.

"I swear," Jim Ed said. "The colored man is even eating at the table with us now. Mamma says it's too much trouble to feed him on the back porch."

In May Pinkerton went on a trip. This was an astounding occurrence: he had never taken a vacation. He and Eula went to a Bible camp in Georgia, and one of Eula's religious friends joyfully spread the news that he had been converted—"born again," as the pious jargon of the county called it. People repeated this strange story and tried to fathom it—Moreland Pinkerton redeemed by the blood of the Lamb!

Ted Devlin told the supper table at the boardinghouse that he intended to run a headline: "Moreland J. Pinkerton Saved from Hell."

"You can't do that," Darcy Coolidge said doubtfully, not certain what newspapers could and could not do since the episode of poor Dr. Ware.

"Why not?" Ted Devlin said with one of his big grumbling laughs. "It's a cosmic event. Angels are singing. Devils are gnashing their teeth. A damned soul has been snatched from the jaws of hell and lifted to the promise of pearly gates. Not just *any* damned soul—Moreland J. *Pinkerton's* damned soul. It ought to be in the papers, Darcy. It's as big as Woodrow Wilson's apoplexy. Bigger even."

"You are mocking poor Mr. Pinkerton," Darcy Coolidge said. "You show me any headline that says somebody's been saved."

"Darcy, if it can't go in the newspapers, it may not be real!"

Darcy Coolidge said she thought we had talked enough about the subject.

Dale Farmer said we would have to wait to see what it all meant. "People exaggerate," he said. He looked doleful and bewildered.

Pinkerton's life was a morality play for Bourbonville on the punishment meted out to offenders against the fundamental laws of the universe. God put people where they belonged. Pinkerton had wanted to leave Bourbonville, to rise above his station. The name Ikaros meant nothing to them; but I suppose that there is a human truth lying like subterranean granite beneath the surface of changing appearances and that the outcroppings in one myth or another may take different shapes centuries apart but the substance is the same.

I might have blurted out his secret: "There is no connection between Cuba and Pinkerton's failure; he never had a chance to rise higher than Bourbonville." No one would have believed me. To tell the truth would have been as disorienting as to tell them that the laws of gravity had been suspended and that they were standing on their heads in space.

Now the rumor spread that a miraculous conversion had made him a new man. The play had an ending not only edifying but happy; chastened by his worldly failure, Pinkerton looked heavenward. Two weeks stretched out to three, and heat filled a still land where rumor wavered like a mirage, and one morning he was back again, striding into the laboratory with a smile and an outstretched hand.

He was sober.

"Well, the foreigner!" he cried. "How are you?" His grip was firm.

"You are looking well," I said.

"I haven't had a drink in three weeks. I ought to look well."

"That is very good," I said.

"I am never going to drink again. I have been saved by the blood of the Lamb."

"I beg your pardon?" I said.

"Jesus has forgiven my sins. He has made me a new man. If you are saved, you must believe in your heart and confess it with your mouth. I'm not ashamed of the Gospel of Christ."

"I do not understand."

"You don't believe me! What's wrong with the world that people can't believe a man when he's as sincere as a judge?" A hint of anger came in him.

"I don't know," I said vaguely.

"I'm not afraid to tell anybody. If the President of the United States was to walk in here right now, I'd tell him I'd been saved. I'm not ashamed of it. I am a new man, Alexander. A new man."

"I am glad to hear it."

"I stand up in church and say it. My sins have been washed away."

"Well," I said.

"I'd tell the president of the railroad. Face-to-face. I'm born again."

"Yes," I said.

"You Catholics don't understand," he said.

"I do not practice my religion," I said.

"It's not a religion to practice," Pinkerton said. "It's a life to live. I've been born again. If you didn't worship the Pope, you could be born again, too. You could know my Jesus."

"I do not think about the Pope," I said.

"He is the great whore of Babylon, the beast drunk on the blood of the saints. It's in the Book of Revelations. Eula can show it to you. I tell you, they're things in the Bible you wouldn't believe. Do you know the automobile is in the Bible?"

"The automobile?"

"Book of Nahum. Eula was showing it to me last night. Something about the chariots running together in the streets, knocking up against each other in the broad ways. Did you know that?"

"I am afraid not," I said.

"See, the Pope has seduced your mind, Alexander." I waited for him to laugh, but he did not.

"I am pleased to see you looking well," I said.

"I owe it all to Eula," Pinkerton said. "She stood by me. She made me see the truth."

I was silent, embarrassed.

He gripped me by the shoulder. "I wish you could know what I know," he said. "All them things I wanted—a job in Washington City, a big house in Virginia, a chauffeur-driven car—vanity! All vanity!"

He paced the floor. "Every valley will be exalted, and every hill will be brought low."

"Mr. Pinkerton, I do not understand."

"Of course not. You are of the world—worldly. You have to have my experience, Alexander."

"I am sure that is so," I said.

He looked ferociously at me, and I saw the old Pinkerton blaze up. But the flame died.

"I see now all my ambition, all my longing, all my hopes were vanity and pride. But my sins prepared me to humble myself and to receive Jesus as my savior. What do you say to that?"

"What *can* I say to it?" I said.

"You can't say anything, because you are blind in your sins. You can't see the light."

"No. I am very glad you are happy."

"Happy. That's the word. I am happier than I have ever been in my life. How have you been?"

"Very well. Thank you for asking."

"You have been flying in an airplane."

"I have flown once or twice, yes."

"You and the nigger."

"Yes."

"And he's flying the airplane. Not you."

"Yes."

"Jesus Christ," Pinkerton said. Then he did something that startled me. He caught himself and bowed his head. "Dear Jesus, forgive me for taking thy name in vain. Be merciful to me, a sinner, Lord. I don't have the right habits yet, but I have the right will, Lord."

I looked on in astonishment and dismay.

"That nigger is flying that old fool around the county," he said in a minute.

"M.P.," I said.

"Moreland Pinkerton Brown," Pinkerton said. "Odd, ain't it? A black man named after me?"

"I believe his father meant to honor you," I said.

"Yes," Pinkerton said, distractedly. "Yes, they did that back then. The devil's black, you know. They say you're thick as thieves with the nigger and with the old man."

"I enjoy their company," I said.

"The company of a nigger?"

"We do not have the feelings about black people that you have here. He was in the French Army."

Pinkerton guffawed. "Look what happened to the frogs. They let niggers in their army, and they corrupted their own blood. Can't you see it? Read the Book of Ezra. That'll show you a thing or two. I'm doing you a favor by telling you this, just like Eula told me. That woman! I tell you, Alexander, she's God's gift. All these years I wanted to change her, wanted to take her up to Washington City. Do you know what Washington City is, Alexander?"

"No, sir."

"It is Babylon."

With a mysterious nod of his head and an expression of incomparable wisdom, he went away.

106

I ASKED DALE FARMER if he had told Pinkerton about M.P. and the old man. He looked distraught.

"He is the captain. I have to tell him what I know. He can fire me. Just like he can fire you. What would I do if he fired me?"

"You would find something. You are a fine accountant."

"No one would hire me at my age."

I was silent.

"You reproach me," he said miserably after a little while.

"No," I said.

"It's a terrible situation," he said.

"Mr. Pinkerton is sober," I said. "That is good."

"It's unnatural. Do you think he is crazy?" Dale Farmer said.

"He has been under great strain," I said.

"God help us!" Dale Farmer sighed.

About that time the film *Birth of a Nation* made a reappearance at the Grand Theatre in Bourbonville. It was located on Broadway not far from the square, a small, poorly ventilated frame shed with a large white screen, and every night there was a showing of a film at seven o'clock, and a stringy woman banged away at the excruciatingly off-key piano down front while the stars of the silent screen moved jerkily in the stale air thick with tobacco smoke. Everyone praised *Birth of a Nation.* Darcy Coolidge saw it and came back in tears, saying it reminded her of the Colonel. Pinkerton raved over it.

One night Jim Ed, the old man, and I paid ten cents each to see it. We watched until the old man leaned over during a battle scene and whispered, "I can't stomach this no more," and we left. Pinkerton was there, sitting a few rows in front of us, his face lifted in rapture. Sometimes he broke into furious applause.

We had a hard rain the next day. It drummed down on the roof and bounced off the ground and left a heavy mist close to the earth. I was glad to see the rain because it had been hot. Pinkerton came into the laboratory wearing a black slicker. The water ran off his slicker and made a puddle on the floor. "I saw you at the picture show last night with that old man and his son," he said. "I looked for you afterwards."

"We left early," I said.

"How could you do that? If you could leave that picture show, you'd try to leave the Second Coming."

"We did not like the film," I said.

"You didn't like it?" Pinkerton was incredulous. "That's one of the greatest sights I've ever seen. I go every night. Every night. I can't see it enough."

"War is not like the film," I said.

"It wasn't about war, you fool!" Pinkerton said. "It was about the niggers—how they're taking over the world. The picture show told us what the nigger wants. He wants to marry white women, make them slaves. It's all there."

"It is make-believe," I said.

"It's right in front of you, and you don't believe what you see with your own eyes!"

"No," I said, turning away.

"It's in the Bible," he said, bleakly absorbed in his vision. "Eula's showed it to me. The nigger wants to take over the world, but to do it, he has to enslave white women. The Bolsheviks are promising the niggers white women, and the niggers are going to communize the whole world. Then the Bolsheviks are going to turn on them, you see, and we're going to have the battle of Armageddon. The Bolsheviks against the niggers, and the Bolsheviks are a lot of Jews, and they're going to be converted, and Jesus is going to come again and drive the niggers down into hell in herds." I thought of the Delphic oracle muttering her wisdom to ecstatic believers while the rising sun fell like a shaft of fire over the sides of Mount Parnassos.

"It's clear as day," he cried. "Nothing is clearer on earth." He lowered his voice to a whisper. "You're flying around with a nigger. You're beguiled."

"I have work to do, Mr. Pinkerton," I said.

"I feel towards you like I'd feel towards my own son. I'm trying to help you."

"Please, Mr. Pinkerton."

"You're beguiled. You're young, and you're foreign, and you don't know. I'm trying to help you."

"Mr. Pinkerton."

"I know what goes on. That nigger with my name is a Bolshevik. He talks to the niggers, the black fool. Some of the niggers, they know which side of the bread their butter's on. They come straight to me."

I did not know what to say.

"It is my fault," he said. "I brought the niggers into the county." His eyes blazed with strange fire. "They called me nigger lover," Pinkerton whispered. "I thought I was doing good." He jerked his head as if in some profound and violent argument with himself.

I went into the scales house and sat down on my little stool with the swivel top and tried to work. My head felt uneasy, and I tasted bile. Pinkerton stood in the open door behind me.

"The curse of Ham," he said. "You know about Ham?"

I did not know then about Ham, the son of Noah.

"Ham was cursed. Ever since Ham the niggers have been the children of Satan, but they *pretend* to be Christian, and they *pretend* to worship Jesus, but that's all for show. They've been doing it for *centuries,* and it's all to take us from behind. They plotted to come here from Africa. They plotted to be slaves. Lincoln was in the plot to free them, and then that actor shot him so Lincoln could never tell the truth about it. Why did an *actor* shoot him? I ask you that!"

I swiveled around and gaped at him. "I do not know, Mr. Pinkerton."

"Because," Pinkerton said, lowering his voice to a whisper, "the actor could play so many parts."

"I do not understand."

"It's simple. Eula knows somebody that knows John Wilkes Booth was in Boston having secret talks with the abolitionists before the war. It's true. Documented fact! Planning to let the slaves loose. And he was back there a week before he shot the President. Before the war, nobody ever heard of John Wilkes Booth. Why? Because there wasn't anybody named John Wilkes Booth. The man we call John Wilkes Booth was an abolitionist, cheek to jowl with the niggers. They plotted with Abraham Lincoln to let them loose, and then they shot him. Then they shot Booth—or the man who called himself Booth—so he could never spill the beans. Don't it make sense? Don't it make a beautiful kind of *sense?*"

"Mr. Pinkerton," I said, "this is madness." The word fell out before I could stop it.

Instead of anger, Pinkerton flashed a triumphant grin.

"To fools, all things are foolish," he said. "It's so beautiful it looks crazy. Eula and her preacher friends explained it to me detail by detail. Maybe I got some of it wrong. I'm just a pupil, you see. They have it all nailed down, and if you'd let them explain it to you, you'd see it clear as day. The niggers are fixing to take over the country. They're going to massacre white men, and turn the white women into sex slaves. They'll kill the white women that won't be used."

"Mr. Pinkerton . . ." I said. I could not continue.

"They couldn't have made those details up, Paul. Even you can see the design in it, the conspiracy. When Satan was thrown out of heaven, God gave him Africa and shut him up in it. But Satan is wily, and he's strong—a lot stronger than we always thought. He fights against God. Don't you know what the Bible says? 'There was war in heaven.' Now if there's war, there has to be a real fight, and the fact that Satan is still going up and down in the world like a roaring lion proves he's got *real* power. I wouldn't say God's *afraid* of him, but God's got a real fight on his hands. God will win it in the end. But unless we fight on God's side, we'll be cast into the bottomless pit with Satan and all his angels."

"Mr. Pinkerton . . ."

"Satan's power is fixed in *Africa,* Paul—the dark continent. Don't you see it? God locked Satan up with his demons in Africa and put a wall up to keep them from harming the rest of his creation. Then the niggers lured us into Africa with their gold, and they tricked us into bringing them here as slaves. It was the Garden of Eden all over again. God walled up the evil spirits in Africa and put the white man in the temperate zones and gave him every-thing we could want, but pride made the white man listen to the beguiling voice of the serpent. The niggers broke down the wall God had built to keep them in their place. It's *cosmic,* you see. The niggers tricked us into bringing them here. They tricked Lincoln into freeing them, and they tricked loads of white folks into letting them breed and multiply, and now they're ready to take over the country and the world. Your nigger friend is part of the biggest conspiracy since Lucifer was thrown down into the pit!"

A hard chill ran down my back. Pinkerton stood over me, his face rapt in the mad clarity of his vision.

"Only the ones that know will be saved in the end," Pinkerton said, his voice attenuated, a shrill whisper at the back of my neck. "They bewitched me. I brought them into the county. And now that Bolshevik nigger with my name, he's at the heart of things. Why does that nigger have my name?"

"Because his father admired you," I said.

"No," Pinkerton said, looking prophetically wise. "He has my name be-cause Satan has sent him to take me to hell. He's my personal devil, Alexan-der. But he's got a surprise coming." He laughed, harsh and knowing.

He put his hands on my shoulders. "Don't you worry, boy. I'll save you."

"Mr. Pinkerton, M.P. is harmless. He talks too much. But he is harmless."

"You've seen that car?"

"Yes, I have seen it," I said.

"A yellow car. Yellow as sunshine. Yellow is the color of the Antichrist."

"The what?"

"Yellow, the color of the Antichrist. It looks like gold, you see, like the streets of gold in heaven, but it's not gold. It's yellow paint. Satan does everything to pretend to be God, just like that nigger pretends to be me. Do you know why the mark of the beast is 666?"

"I do not know what you are talking about," I said.

"Because seven is the perfect number, and 666 is almost seven. Satan looks as much like God as he can, don't you see? He's an actor, like John Wilkes Booth."

He glared at me with an awful triumph, as if he had understood and explained everything. His slicker gleamed in the naked electric lights hanging by their cords from the ceiling. The rain beat against the windows and hammered the roof. It was unnaturally dark outside.

"Every nigger is the devil's agent," Pinkerton whispered. "I didn't know that when I went down to Sweetwater and brought those black men up here. I figured I was charming *them*. You see, this place, it was the most important thing in the world to me. I wanted to build this factory so much that I was willing to sell my soul to the devil to do it. I was a fool—a blind, sinful fool."

"Mr. Pinkerton!" I said.

"I thought I had to charm them, get them up here, put them to work in the swamp. But they was charming *me*. I sat down there in the dark, talking to them, and all the time there was a spirit there—a lying, devilish, spirit—and that spirit knew I was ripe for the picking. You think that's crazy, don't you, Paul Alexander?"

The scales room was small, and I felt crushed by Pinkerton's presence. He stood over me, breathing hard. The rain came down. His hands gripped my shoulders.

"I went down there to Cuba, and my boys got the yellow fever and died, and Teddy Roosevelt got to be President when it should of been me. I blamed it on the yellow fever. Well, something has to *cause* the yellow fever. What causes the yellow fever? Mosquitoes, you say. Not mosquitoes—the devil. Or maybe it was God. That's what Eula says. It was God punishing me because I brought the niggers up here. God or the devil, it don't make any difference. I was punished because I upset the order of things. I had to get the car works done. I stepped across a line that God drew in the earth. Do you think there's such a thing as the unpardonable sin, Alexander?"

"No," I said.

"You don't think there's one sin that will damn us forever?" His fingers in my shoulders were like steel.

"No," I said. I looked up, away from Pinkerton, through the glass of the scales house, and there was Guy, pressing his body against it. His chest was bleeding, and his eyes were shut. His red blood was pouring down the glass. I trembled and looked away. I felt Guy's presence looming above me, separated by the glass, two feet from my face. I could look up and see his blood running three inches from my nose. I kept my head down.

"I want to save you, boy. You don't know it, but I'm your best friend." He went off in the rain, slamming the outside door behind him. I saw his form swallowed up in the downpour. I looked around, and the laboratory was empty.

"Please do not torment me," I whispered. I heard only the rain and the silence. I looked to the glass where Guy had been. Nothing. My headache was blinding. I was sick of my headaches, sick of life. Beyond the dirty windows the cold air was heavy and gray, and the downpour continued.

107

I WARNED M.P. ABOUT PINKERTON. He was scornful. He had been flying the airplane, soaring over Bourbonville, doing barrel rolls, dipping down over the river, taking the old man aloft, sometimes flying by himself, letting everyone in Bourbon County know he was the pilot, and he had surrounded himself with admiring young black men who saw him as Herakles or Orion, a demigod whom only a god might kill. He scorned Pinkerton first for his drunkenness and now for the religion that Pinkerton had wrapped around himself like a nimbus. He could not mention Pinkerton without sneering. "The man is crazy," he said in French. He loved to speak French now, no matter who heard him.

"Yes, he is crazy," I said. "But he is dangerous. You are in danger."

M.P. laughed. "Do not be foolish. I have been organizing the black men. We have guns. If that man were to touch me, my people would tear this town apart. We're strong. We do not need to be afraid of anybody. Let that crazy old man try something. My men will stand by me, and we will kill him."

I felt a chill. The rain had stopped, but the sky lowered, and we sweated. "Some of your own people are betraying you to Pinkerton," I said.

M.P. scowled. "Do not accuse my people of betrayal. That is a white man's lie. It is a lie to divide us, to make us suspect each other."

"Someone is betraying you," I said. "You speak your foolish talk about revolution, and Pinkerton knows everything you have said."

"No," said M.P. "If a black man did that, other black men would kill him."

"You deceive yourself."

"No," M.P. said. "He knows what I say because of the logic of history."

"The logic of history," I said. "You believe in the *logic* of history!"

"Do not sneer, my friend. History can work out only one way—the revolution. Even that sot Pinkerton can see the logic of history. It is wrapped around him like an anaconda, crushing him to death."

"He is not a sot anymore. He has stopped drinking."

"He has already drunk so much that his brain is soft. It is an old story, my friend. The rich oppress the poor, but the poor outnumber the rich, and the moment comes, and the poor trample the rich underfoot. It is not necessary for Pinkerton to hear the truth from your imagined traitor among my people. He knows what I am saying because he knows that is what I *must* be saying."

I took a deep breath and stared at him, searching for some faint sign of irony. There was none.

"Sometimes I believe you are as mad as he is."

M.P. laughed his mirthless laugh again. "Do I look crazy to you?"

"You speak like a crazy man."

M.P. laughed again, a big, boisterous laugh.

"You are honest, Paul Alexander. When the revolution comes, we will find a place for you."

"There will be no revolution," I said.

"There has been a revolution," M.P. said sharply. "It goes on in Russia right now."

"The revolution in Russia is dying in civil war," I said.

"That is all you know," he said scornfully. He stood staring at me, his eyes smoldering, and I was sure that he was going to lash out at me. But when he spoke, his voice was low and electric. "I have friends who know. The revolution must struggle, but it cannot fail."

"My God," I said in exasperation, "you must protect yourself! Go away. Go visit somebody. Go see some of your Bolshevik friends in New York or wherever they are. Stay away until things cool down here."

"*Les noirs* have been running for a hundred, two hundred years. We ran to the Ohio River, and then we ran to Canada, and then we ran from people, from the KKK. We are not going to run anymore. If something happens to me, my people will burn this place down."

"You should not speak like that," I said.

"Look at the white man turn his head to see if the walls have ears," M.P. said with a withering sneer. "You have been here long enough to soak up the ways of Bourbon County, my friend. A white man could speak of tearing the county apart if one of his friends was killed, and you would think nothing of it. But a black man makes that suggestion, and you think the sky is falling."

I felt my face grow red. "I am sorry," I said. "I am worried."

"Do not worry about me," M.P. said. "I have a mission. The good Lord is not going to let me die before my mission is complete. The old days are gone, my friend. They are not coming back."

"What do you want?" I said. "My God, what do you want?"

"To start, I want colored men to be molders and carpenters here in the car works."

Molders and carpenters told other men what to do, and they had to obey. No black man could be a molder or a carpenter because no black man could give orders to a white man. He laughed again, humorless and sardonic. "You do not think such a thing is possible. It would be possible in Belgium."

"This is not Belgium," I said.

"In France it would be possible," he said.

"Yes, I suppose."

"But not in America, land of the free and home of the brave, and you, my friend, gape at me in shock. You think I have no right to speak like this. You reproach me. You think I am mad. But you are blind. You do not see the forces of history. You are bitten by the fleas in this county, and you have their disease."

"I am sorry," I said in confusion. "I do not know what to say."

"I know what to say. The revolution is here. Nobody can stop it. But do not worry. We will take care of you. Someone has to take care of you." He looked contemptuously at me and went away, whistling some jaunty song and walking as if he had springs in his legs.

My warning seemed to incite him. If anything, he increased his presence in the town, in the county. On Saturdays he flew the airplane with Brian in the front cockpit, and sometimes they came dipping low over Bourbonville, the engine of the Jenny wide open, making a roar that sounded like a swarm of hornets, and people looked up and saw the plane flash overhead, and they stood as though transfixed.

Bourbonville was crowded on Saturdays. The farmers packed the streets or else sat together in little clumps of men and wagons parked around the square under the great trees, and they looked up and saw the airplane roar over the treetops, and they saw the old man wave, and they could see M.P. in the back, and people were angry. Hatred for M.P. hung in the air like coal smoke.

108

GUY ASKED ME to write his parents, and I did. I told them that I had been with Guy when he died and that I had been wounded and had come to America and that I was well. I did not give them the details of his death. I told them that it was quick and that he did not feel anything. I told them that I was sure his soul was in heaven and that I grieved for him.

It was the first time I put on paper that Guy was dead. With my words in front of me in the harsh glow of the little electric lamp in my room, I could not pretend that Guy's spirit was with me. I tried to talk to him and to Bernal about the letter. They did not come. Their absence paralyzed me. I thought they might never come back. The world seemed empty, and my heart was granite. Finally they did return. When I saw them sitting one evening in my room, I almost cried. I did not think I could live without them. Guy laughed as he used to laugh, and we talked about the party at the Machavoines', and we spoke of Yvette.

In a month a thick letter came back from his mother. Darcy Coolidge handed it to me with a rapturous look. "It is from Belgium," she said. "It must be from your mother." I had never told her that my letters from my mother came to a postal box in Knoxville.

I took the letter and went to my room and read it. It lies here before me now: twelve pages of cramped handwriting, sometimes illegible. She wrote with a bitter passion. She thanked me for telling her about Guy. The government had reported him missing in action and presumed dead. For a long time she had hoped, but all the soldiers were home, and he had not come. She knew the worst. His body had never been found. She hoped that the Germans had buried it.

The Germans had shot her husband, Guy's father, in the square at Dinant. They had shot Gustav, too. They took hostages because they thought civilians were firing on their troops. The Garde Civique went to battle dressed in top hats and long coats, and the Germans refused to recognize them as soldiers. If civilians fired on German troops, the Germans killed civilians. They took Monsieur Bruyère and Gustav along with the rest, and they shot them. She would dress in black for the rest of her life, she said. She would never forgive the Germans. They had shot Edith Cavell—the English nurse at the Red Cross hospital in Brussels. That was wicked. But at least the Germans could say with truth that she had pleaded guilty to helping young Allied soldiers caught behind the German advance to escape to fight again. Monsieur Bruyère and Gustav had done nothing. They were in the grand salon, and the German soldiers knocked on the door and took them away. They were shot that day with dozens of other innocents as a warning to any Belgian who might resist them. She prayed to God to let her forgive them, but she could not. She supposed that her soul might be damned. No matter. She could not forgive the Germans. She was happy I had escaped death. She asked me to write her again. She asked me about Bernal. I had not told her of Bernal's death. She was thankful that Guy had died swiftly. She hoped he was in heaven. She wondered if there could be such a place.

I told Guy that his father and Gustav were dead, and he wept so horribly that I thought the whole town must hear him. I slept that night with nightmares, and each time I awoke I heard Guy's weeping fill the air around my bed and drift out over the town and the universe.

Much later I wrote her again, and at great intervals she wrote to me. Her letters were always bitter. German tourists were coming to Belgium to show their families where they had fought. Madame Bruyère insulted them publicly in the streets whenever she heard their ugly language. Other Belgians welcomed German business. How could people forget? she asked. Finally she stopped writing, and my last letter went unanswered. It was after we moved here, to our farm. I am sure she has been dead a long time.

A sweltering summer settled over Bourbonville. The heat stifled movement and reduced thought to paste. I still had terrible headaches. The pain rose, and my head seemed ready to burst, and I thought it could not hurt any more, and then it would hurt more. Sometimes I had to lie down on the cool concrete floor of the laboratory and close my eyes. M.P. occasionally found me there. I waved away his anxiety. "I have headaches," I said. "There is nothing anybody can do about it."

"You look bad," M.P. said. "Can't that doctor friend of yours do something for you?"

"No," I said. "He cannot do anything for me."

109

ON MANY EVENINGS when the earth cooled down, I took long walks. When I got to the city limits I could talk in a low voice to Guy and Bernal, and they spoke back to me, and we explored my real life—my memories and my plans of what would come after Bourbonville. Bourbonville was a diversion; my real life was before and after.

My sister Anna was going to be married in Greece. She was marrying a police officer in Piraeus—a better match than Helen's, though my mother reported in every letter that Helen's husband was good to her. If Helen's husband had beaten her, my mother would have reported that he was good to her. Anna's man had no money. The dowry would help them get a start.

I had to borrow another thousand dollars to pay the dowry. My mother set the terms for Anna's marriage and presented me with the accounts, and I paid them. I borrowed from the bank, and Mr. Carroll, a tall, curly-headed man who presided over the bank, told me he hoped I was investing in stocks. "A young man like you can borrow a little money and become a millionaire in another ten years," he said. "Be bold!"

I came back late from my walks and went up to bed in the sleeping house. I dreamed of shell fire and woke up soaked in sweat, my heart pounding, and I looked around in panic until I saw where I was, heard the silence of the town, perhaps the distant whistle of a train and the rumble of cars, and knew that the war was over. I never looked forward to going to sleep. When I could see Guy and Bernal sitting in the room with me, I slept better. Some nights they did not come.

One night not long after my mad interview with Pinkerton, I looked through my window as I was undressing, and I saw a man standing in the dim yellow light shed by one of the street lamps. He was looking towards the boardinghouse. I thought he was looking directly at my darkened window, but I could not be sure. He stood for a long time, and I sat behind the window in the dark and watched him. I was curious, not afraid. He lit a cigarette. I saw the flare of the match and the irregular blaze and decline of the cigarette itself until he tossed it away in the street. After a long while he went away. I had a vague impression of a muscular man in work clothes wearing a crushed old hat, and something about his walk seemed vaguely familiar.

The next evening he came again. I entered my room without turning on the light and started undressing, looking out the window from habit. He appeared out of the shadow made by the oaks across and down the street from the boardinghouse. I saw him take out his pocket watch and look at it, the dim lamplight gleaming briefly on the glass and the metal case. He rolled a cigarette as country people did and smoked it and looked up at the boardinghouse, his eyes hidden under the brim of his hat against the street lamp. I started to light a cigarette myself but thought better of it and sat in the dark watching him.

It rained on the next evening, and I did not go out. Dale Farmer insisted that Darcy Coolidge sing after supper. He played the piano. She sang "Annie Laurie" and "Believe Me If All Those Endearing Young Charms" and "Drink to Me Only with Thine Eyes" and several other favorites, and she sweated and clasped her hands before her large bosom and shut her eyes and looked ready to cry. She had a sweet voice. She reminded me vaguely of Madame Boschnagel. The rain fell straight down, and we left the windows open; the air was still thick and close.

Dale Farmer played with manic energy, looking up from time to time to cue himself on the shape of Darcy Coolidge's mouth. He never smiled when he played, but moved his hands with a flourish of circles and studied the sheet music as if it had been the road map to heaven. I sat smoking and listening and stayed up with the other boarders later than usual, and after she sang, Darcy Coolidge made tea and served it, and we went to bed.

I was not sleepy, and I turned on my lamp and sat down at the little writing table, deciding to add something to my latest letter to my mother. I never wrote her a whole letter at a sitting. I pretended to her that I did, but in fact I composed them paragraph by paragraph, sometimes altering the times of events to make it seem that everything I had to tell her had happened in the past few days. I maintained an attitude of general optimism and cheer. I made fiction for my mother, and she was happy for it.

I sat writing, my arm sweating on the writing desk, the rain falling softly, and I looked up and saw the man standing down in the lamplight, his hands thrust into his pockets, his shoulders squeezed up against the wet, and the collar of a thin coat turned over his neck. I knew he was looking through the window directly at me.

As quickly as I could I finished my sentence and turned out the light. I hung my clothes up in the little closet near my bed. When I stepped back to the window, he was gone. I was annoyed.

The next day as Dale Farmer and I walked down Kingston Street on our daily peregrination to the square, I looked at the lamppost where my strange witness had stood, and I saw four wet cigarette butts curled where the man had thrown them. They had been hand-rolled and smoked down so close to the end that they must have burned his lips. I did not mention them to Dale Farmer. He was speaking earnestly of rumors about a gambling scandal concerning the Chicago White Sox in the previous year's World Series. At times he fell to long lectures on baseball, I believe to keep himself from thinking about other things.

That evening I went for a walk. The sky was hazy, but the stars were out, and the air was mild. I followed my usual route, taking the quickest way out of town, turning down Broadway at the square. Beyond the gate of the car works, the little town behind me, I walked along the macadam pike with no sound but my footsteps on the road. An automobile went by, yellow head-lamps lurching in the lonely dark. Automobiles were rare. Sometimes not a car passed during the entire time that I walked.

I spoke softly with Guy and Bernal. We spoke of Guy's father on this evening, and of the Germans. I talked about Palmyre and her German soldier, and Bernal said, "She was a good woman. She did not love you, that is all. She could not help it. It was not your fault. It was not her fault." I felt serene to think that something was not my fault.

The silence was broken by distant gunfire—first one shot, then another and another, a flurry of shooting. I stopped in bewilderment and curiosity, not fear, so prone are we to believe that nothing can interrupt the orderly progression of tranquil moments. The firing came from the direction of Bucktown towards the river. I heard distant shouting. It was not high-powered rifle fire. That would have echoed; the crack of a high-powered rifle is like nothing else on earth. I decided it was shotgun fire, the ubiquitous weapon in Bourbon County. But why?

It seems naive to the point of idiocy now that I could not imagine why there could be gunfire in Bucktown! I am angry at the stupid innocence of the young man I was then, which makes me in this later time want to slap him across the face and shout at him and tell him to grow up, to be different, to be somebody else.

The shooting died away. I stood in puzzlement, hearing faintly in the distance cries, irregular and clashing, men and women.

Then behind me, at my neck, a voice spoke, and I was roughly grasped by the arms. "Come with us, you nigger-loving son of a bitch," the man said. "If you fight us, we will kill you here. If you do not resist, you may live another fifteen minutes." He laughed. I had heard the voice before, but I could not recognize it.

110

THERE IS NOTHING to do but tell the rest—tell it all, detail by detail, exorcise it onto this page as though the page were a bottomless pit into which all the maggot-laden garbage of life might be thrown to fall forever away from me. Writing is an assuagement of the mind, an emptying of the soul so that it may be cleansed and reborn. My fingers grip the pen so hard that my thumb aches as I think about it even after the years have flown. I know some things now I did not know then. They do not mitigate the memory but if anything make it more nightmarish, more filled with self-loathing and horror, because these events happened in a world as physical as the pen I hold in my hand and the table on which my knotted fist rests and the chill that lies over the earth now in October. I hated existence. I hated myself for existing. For the second time in my life I was ashamed for not dying. I mix details. Time gets out of order in memory. I am too old to be reborn.

My captors were tricked out in the costume of the Ku Klux Klan. They had seen *Birth of a Nation.* They thought it was real. They were here in the dark clad in white robes brushing the ground, white masks over their faces, white masks on their heads, all dimly luminescent in the faint glow of the sinking moon and the stars and the reflected light that hangs over the circle of the earth. They looked like pictures I had seen of Spanish penitents in flagellant processions.

My captors dragged me down the pike. A car emerged, lights out, and I was thrown into the backseat. A man climbed in on each side of me. A driver, also hooded, and a hooded companion sat in front. We drove slowly, the driver swearing and watching the road in the moonlight. At the road that went down towards the old Methodist church, we turned. I remembered Daisy.

All the men had guns. "We're going to cook your ass, you son of a bitch."

"You foreign nigger-loving Jew bastard. We're going to fix you before this night is over." It was the man who had first spoken to me, and I knew who it was. His name was Kirby, and he was a teller at the bank. He was thirtyish, with a pencil mustache, dapper, empty. I had seen him a hundred times without seeing him, spoken to him a hundred times to perform the errand of the moment. He wore a strong scent, bay rum or something like that, the lotion barbers slapped on your skin after a shave. I smelled it now, and I thought of how odd it was to face death at the hands of a man who wore cheap perfume.

They cursed me in fierce, tedious litany. I had not thought of pain in dying. With these men I thought of pain. How would my mother get the news? Dr. Youngblood would find her letters in my things. He would write to the return address. What would happen to Anna's dowry? My insurance policy . . . if Dr. Youngblood could find that . . . Somehow my mother would learn the truth. Would she grieve? I had not seen her since 1913. This was 1920. She would have prayers said for me by the priests, and after a while she would realize that she was well off because of my insurance. She would have my photograph on the wall, and now and then she would look at it and cry. I felt Stephanos near me; I could not see him.

The car lurched through the dark, through a crossroads. One way led off to Brian Ledbetter's house several miles away; in the other direction lay Moreland Pinkerton's place. We careened onto the little road to the Methodist church by the river, and the car jolted and shook our bones. Lights blazed ahead of us, and we shot out in the large clearing before the church and I saw a huge cross draped in sheets standing off at a distance, and a hundred or two hundred men in Klan costumes stood in a huge semicircle waiting for us, and most were holding guns and torches so that a hellish light leaped in the clearing and cavorted against the white frame church, and I smelled gasoline and thought of a conflagration blazing through a wooden house where children slept in the upper floors. In the center of the great semicircle of robed and yelling figures stood M.P.'s bright yellow Mercer, its brilliant paint reflecting the torches like a curved mirror, and I understood.

I looked for him. I shouted something. I do not know what; a roar of fear or rage. The man sitting next to the driver in the front seat turned coldly, deliberately, and hit me full in the face with the butt of a revolver. I did not see the gun until it hit me. He broke teeth, and I spat them out, my eyes swimming and all the world blurred and reeling, stars flashing in my head, and I felt blood pour out of my mouth, and I tasted blood. My face went numb with the blow, and my ears rang, and a sharp pain came through the numbness. I lifted my hands to my face in mute astonishment. I had expected to die, but I did not expect them to crush my face with a revolver butt, or that the broken-toothed agony would spread over my head and down my back and into my neck.

"You're going to see a show, nigger lover. You're going to see a big show. Better than all the picture shows you ever seen, Jew nigger lover." It was Kirby, speaking under his mask. The men in the car laughed, and one of them pulled out a flask of whiskey and tipped it up to his mouth and drank.

The car pulled to a stop. The mob was catcalling. I held my hands over my wounded face, thinking about my broken teeth, and I could feel blood running sticky through my fingers. I could feel the jagged tooth stumps rising out of my gums, and my lips were mangled. I was thinking that I had come through the war and not lost my teeth and that now my front teeth were gone, and while I was trying to make sense of things, my captors threw me out onto the ground. For a moment I was hurtling through the air, and then I hit the ground on my face so hard that the breath was knocked out of me. My mouth blazed with pain, and my ears rang. I tried to get to my feet. I had risen to my knees when somebody kicked me, and I felt a rib break, and the pain was so sharp that I collapsed, and I could not breathe, and I thought I would suffocate, and I was in panic. A man in panic has no dignity, and I heard a wave of laughing and cheering and an irregular chant: "Nigger lover . . . nigger lover." I lay with my eyes open, trying to calm myself so I could breathe, afraid of choking on blood. The world swam, and sparks darted across my vision, and I did not know what to do; so I lay there, breathing as gently as I could, trying to adjust to a pain different from other pains, and I heard people howling with laughter.

Into my field of vision as though onto a stage slowly rode a man on a huge bay horse. He was dressed like the others except that his robe was green and he wore a red crucifix at his neck, and he held a buggy whip, and his tall hood was a bright green—Bernal's color. He carried the whip like a marshal's baton on parade, tucked under his arm.

I heard a cry in the middle distance towards Bucktown, a woman's cry, ululant and prolonged, bursting with an animal terror and a grief so terrible that I shuddered to hear it and tried to lift my head, but someone kicked me in the back, and I collapsed again, lying on my side, not knowing what to make of anything, struggling so hard for breath that my gasping sounded like a file raked across steel. The woman screamed and screamed until I heard a blow of flesh against flesh, and the screaming stopped, cut off in mid-cry.

Three robed and masked horsemen emerged from the darkness opposite me. They had ropes around a black man being hauled along behind them, his hands tied behind his back, his legs free so he could run along to keep from being dragged like a log, and they were looking back at him and shouting curses and laughing, and when he stumbled into the circle of firelight, I saw what I already knew, that it was M.P. and that one of the ropes was knotted around his neck, and the other two around his waist. I heard one of the men on horseback shout back to him, "Come on, nigger. Run, damn you. Hell is waiting for your black soul." A burst of laughter and cheering.

I struggled to my feet, shouting, "Stop! Stop!" Someone knocked me down by kicking me behind the knees, and somebody struck me in the middle of the back with a fist, and I fell. The man with the tall green hood turned in the saddle and looked down at me and shouted, "Let him stand up! Let him see what is happening. I want him to see! Let him see what he's done."

The man's face was hidden by the ridiculously tall conical hood. But I knew the voice. The man astride the horse was Moreland Pinkerton.

I see that my hand trembles and that I must write carefully to avoid pressing the point of my fountain pen so hard that I ruin it.

M.P. looked at me with abject terror. I had not believed he could have such an expression—not the proud man who flew the airplane and drove a yellow Mercer and wore a leather coat and looked like the king of the world. He was bleeding from the nose and the mouth. I suppose we resembled a combination of horrors, our two gory faces gaping at each other. The top of his head was bloody, and the blood ran down the sides of his face and dripped off his chin. The blood on his black skin looked black in the firelight, but as the drops fell off, the light caught in them and made them sparkle crimson as they fell free in the air. I wanted him to be mute, to be above pain, above fear, like a divine statue rising invincible above Tartaros. He gaped at me with a surprised terror; I saw his lips move in an imploring expression, but he made no sound.

Strong hands held my arms, and thick fingers gripped my neck. The attention was on M.P. Howling men cursed him and kicked him, and masked Moreland Pinkerton drew up the whip and brought it down with a crack on his head, and somebody shouted, "Git on your knees, nigger. Pray, nigger, pray"—a roar of laughter rising in the clearing, crashing off the blank wall of the church, its tall glass windows black behind the leaping reflection of the fire like surreal eyes gaping at the scene.

Somebody finally knocked M.P. down, kicking him, pulling at the rope around his neck, and all the men were laughing. "Pray, nigger—pray! Let's hear you pray for your life."

M.P. did not speak. Not a word. Not a sound. He got back to his knees with an enormous effort of will, but every time he tried to rise someone knocked him down again, and the blood poured off his face.

"Don't knock him out," Pinkerton shouted. "Get back! Get back! We don't want an unconscious nigger on our hands. I want him to enjoy this."

Shouts of laughter and agreement. They stopped beating at him.

"Nigger, why don't you just get in that fancy yellow car of yours and drive off? You just drive off to someplace where you ain't never going to see none of us again. You just get up from there and go get into that car of your'n right this minute. Drive down to New Orleans and play jazz, nigger. Drive over to Memphis and drink whiskey. Just drive away from where you are now."

More laughter, rising in frenzy, men looking at each other through their masks, nodding, their hoods tipping wildly, and the torches burning and burning and throwing their dancing shadows, the forest darkness behind, the white and empty church, and M.P. in the middle, on his knees, bleeding, looking at Pinkerton, looking at me, looking at his car.

"If this nigger's going to drive off, he needs some gasoline in that car of his, boys!" Pinkerton shouted. Suddenly there was a more intense smell of gasoline. Men had cans of gasoline, pouring it into the yellow Mercer.

"Fill it up, boys!" Pinkerton shouted. "Fill it to the brim. We don't want the nigger to run out of gas before he gets to hell."

More laughter, and I kneeled there hoping that some spark from a torch would catch in it and burn them all to death. But the car did not burn until they fell back and somebody hurled a brand into it, and it exploded in a whoosh of flame, and I could feel the storm of heat against my face, and men retreated so that there was a vast space, the car blazing in the middle, men cheering, and some fired guns at the sky. I thought of the air blowing back from the propeller of the Curtiss Jenny when M.P. and I soared over the clouds. How do you explain these things, the nonsense of the mind that confuses time and reality so that startling and horrible surprises are diminished, drained of reality, barely perceived against a bright screen of glory, and you can blink and see again the blissful shadows of memory behind an unbearable moment, memory of a former reality that enveloped you and filled your senses and lifted you to bliss—like flying through the crimson sunset above a dark earth glittering with patternless lights, dim beneath the regular stars—the life that was, the essence of creation, eternity? But all that was a figment, and now this horror was real, and reality was the verge of death—my death, M.P.'s.

We watched the car burn, the gasoline stinking and the fire roaring, the bright yellow paint turning black, the fenders melting and sagging from the holocaust, the rubber tires bursting with the fire that consumed them, and I remembered all the stories—stories of how Pinkerton had built the car works and the fires burning in the night from the wood felled in what had been a swamp, and black men and white men dancing around those fires, and M.P.'s father dancing in the crashing rhythms of his ancestors, dancing with the fathers of some of these men, with Pinkerton, perhaps with some of these men themselves. Yes, I thought of all those things while I was being held to see the Mercer burn, and I tried to call something to M.P., but in the roar of voices and the roar of the flames leaping up from the car, I could not make myself heard. M.P. was on his knees, bleeding, and there was nothing he could do. He did not cry out. He never cried out. Men passed whiskey around, and they drank uproariously to his torment.

Pinkerton shouted, lifting the whip and using it as a pointer, "Look what's happened to your pretty car, nigger. I wouldn't have had that happen for the world. Looks like you can't drive to hell. Looks like we have to buy you a ticket so you can fly there."

Another roar of laughter and cheering.

"Light the cross!" Pinkerton shouted. "May our Lord Jesus and his Kingdom be praised."

The great cross roared up in flames, and I smelled gasoline afresh and realized that the cloth draped over the wooden frame of the cross had been soaked in gasoline, too. More shouting, a storm of sound beating against the silence of the wood and rising skyward.

"All right! Let's do what we came here to do," and Pinkerton lifted the whip and waved it in the air, and robed figures hauled M.P. to his feet, his eyes wide and white in his black skin. He was struggling with all his might to break free, and somebody threw a rock with the end of a rope tied to it over the overhanging branch of an enormous chestnut tree, and when the rock came down, it pulled the rope around his neck up with a jerk, and Moreland Pinkerton shouted, "Cut the rope on his hands. I want this nigger to climb like a coon."

Somebody cut the ropes, and M.P. was standing there swaying back and forth, the rope taut, his hands waving around, finally thinking almost as an afterthought to reach up and grasp the rope to pull it down, to loosen the pressure on his neck. Somebody hit him again in the face, but he did not even take note of it. It was as if somebody had slapped a statue, except this statue was afraid and helpless and bloody, his eyes fixed trancelike on Pinkerton, and he was still watching Pinkerton when Pinkerton lifted the whip again in a signal, and a dozen men holding the long hemp rope pulled, and M.P. was hauled off the ground, and I understood why Pinkerton had had the ropes cut from his wrists, for as the rope pulled him off the ground, M.P. held onto it above the noose to keep the weight of his body off the rope, off the noose. When he was swung into the air, there was a great animal howl of laughter from his tormentors, and he was struggling there, a burden at the end of the rope, swinging back and forth, back and forth in a huge arc, a human pendulum, subject to the laws of physics that Galileo first noted by feeling his pulse to count the swing of a pendulum from the roof of a church where God was worshiped, M.P. the human pendulum, fighting for air and life, his legs kicking and kicking.

He started climbing the rope. Higher and higher he went, his naked arm muscles glistening with sweat in the firelight, as a gang of gleeful men pulled the rope across the limb, hauling him up maybe three or four yards off the ground until he was two or three yards beneath the dark limb of the chestnut tree where the rope pulled him. Then, as he continued to climb, the men holding the rope on the other end let it out so that M.P. hung in one place in the air, climbing desperately and with all his might but not gaining a yard towards the limb, and the men behind were mocking him and roaring with laughter.

"Climb, coon! Climb, damn you! Climb, coon! Climb straight up to hell!"

"Give me a shotgun," Pinkerton cried, and somebody handed him a double-barreled shotgun, and he stuck the whip down under his leg and lifted the shotgun.

I shut my eyes.

I heard the blast of the shotgun.

I opened my eyes, hoping to see that M.P. was dead. But Pinkerton was aiming at his legs, and I could see M.P.'s trousers now pouring blood. He was still holding on to the rope.

Pinkerton fired the other barrel, and M.P.'s body shuddered under the impact of the shot, and the blood fell in a long, fluttering stream through the air, illuminated by the firelight. Pinkerton brought down the gun. The masked men were cheering and shouting. M.P. kept trying to pull himself up. But he had no strength left, no strength. Slowly, slowly he lost his grip, lost it finally so that his body, still pouring blood from his devastated legs, fell at last with a jerk at the end of the rope, now pulled back up by the men who held the other end. He threw his arms out wide, like some giant bird making a cross in the sky, and then his arms fell slack. He kicked feebly, and his body jerked spastically like a chicken flopping in search of its severed head until slowly the spasms stopped, and the body hung there limp and inhuman, his head pulled up and twisted horribly over his thick neck, the neck stretched out more than you could believe a neck could stretch, his arms and his bleeding legs still, and I was glad that he was dead. His body hung there, swinging softly now, the blood feathering down in the firelight, and I thought that I would not try to climb the rope, that I would accept death by strangulation and be glad for it. I looked for Guy and for Bernal, but I did not see them, and I could not see Stephanos or anyone else I loved, and I felt alone in the way that a person feels alone when he is the only thinking creature in an infinite universe whose fundamental principle is malice and whose delight is terror, horror, and pain.

"Now let's string up the Jew!" somebody shouted.

I felt a rough hempen noose thrown over my head and pulled tight around my neck, and somebody jerked it, and I fell to the ground, and somebody kicked me, and the pain in my ribs was a ragged knife sawing my bones.

I heard Pinkerton's voice from somewhere far above me, shouting, "No. Let him up. Let him up."

I was hauled roughly to my feet. I could not stand by myself. I am ashamed now to admit that, but I did not have the strength either of body or of will to stand alone. I could not even lift my head. Strong hands turned me towards Pinkerton, and somebody jerked my hair back so that my face was pulled up to meet his bending over me, leaning down from his horse. The horse seemed calm, benign. And there was Pinkerton leaning over the horse and glaring at me through the eyeholes in his hood.

"You know who I am, don't you?" he shouted, his voice hoarse.

"Yes," I whispered. The rope was so tight around my neck that I thought my face would burst.

"Kill him," people were shouting.

"I've done you good tonight," he said. "I've taught you how things are, and I've saved your life when you deserved to die."

I could not absorb his words or ask a question or lift a cry. I remember his eyes leering at me through the slits in the green hood and the uncanny voice with its odd tone of supplication, asking me to believe him. The imprint of his voice on my ear is as firm as the scar that might have been left by a branding iron.

"You have received the mercy of the wizard," Pinkerton cried now in a much different tone. "Remember!"

He sat straight on the horse and shouted to the mob: "All right. All of you. Let's get out of here."

"Kill the Jew!" somebody shouted. "Kill the Jew!" Others took it up. The mob had enjoyed killing as fat men enjoyed hors d'oeuvres, and its famished and collective belly yearned for more.

"No. We're going to leave him alive," Pinkerton shouted.

"Kill the Jew! Kill the Jew!"

The struggle of wills was a storm. The voices went back and forth, and Pinkerton was shouting at them, and his voice was frantic and angry, and I knew that if he lost, the mob would tear me apart. "I am your commander," he shouted. "I order you to go home."

He prevailed. Reluctantly they broke up, muttering and cursing. Any one of them could have shot him off his horse. Something of his old authority saved my life. Many of them had horses. Some had cars. I heard receding hoofbeats in the night, a grinding of engines, a declining grumble of voices, and the mob dispersed, leaving Pinkerton and me alone in the clearing before the white church while the body of M.P., its neck hideously stretched and its hands at its sides, swung gently back and forth in the humid night air, the other end of the rope wrapped about the trunk of the chestnut, the fire in the ruined Mercer crackling and dying into itself.

"I saved your life," Pinkerton said finally. "When you take my job, when you're running my car works, you remember that. I saved your life. I built the car works. I gave this town a monument. When you're the boss, you remember what I did. It's always going to be mine. When it's yours, it will still be mine."

He did not offer to help me. I was on my knees, looking up at him, unable to say a word, bleeding, broken, and almost out of my mind.

"You'll never be half the man that I am," he said in a voice low, almost gentle, filled with satisfaction. He clicked his tongue to his horse and rode away without looking back.

I was left in the light of the flaming cross, now burning itself out, the burning automobile, and M.P.'s body hanging in the summer night. The body swayed on the rope, and the shadow swung back and forth, the shadow's motion large and slow against the darkness of the woods.

I was sitting on the ground weeping hysterically when M.P.'s friends slipped out of the dark, speaking quietly to one another, and gently took the rope off my neck and set about taking his body down.

111

I WROTE until nearly dawn this morning. I got up, stiff and sore, and walked out into the pale chill of an October dawn with the sun rising like fire in the clouds. The grass was white with hoarfrost, and it crackled faintly under the tread of my heavy American shoes. I wanted Guy and Bernal to talk to me, but they did not come. The dog who sleeps on her cushion at my feet got up when I got up, stretched, came with me through the door and went out with me, squatted to urinate, and followed me to my vineyard overlooking the orchard that looks down towards Federal Highway 11. She and I blew smoke when we breathed, and the world glowed in the clarity of autumn, which makes everything seem more in focus, more immediate. Cars were passing. I was glad to see people alive, even if all I could see of them was the passage of headlamps through the gray morning.

Guy and Bernal came to me on that night when I was gently carried into Bucktown. I heard Guy's voice much clearer than the other voices.

"You see," Guy said, "what comes when you make friends with people besides us. It does not work out."

Dr. Youngblood came. Much later on I learned that he was roused at four in the morning from sitting up in his chair before his cold fireplace. A young black woman pounded at his back door, a frantic, furtive knocking that at first puzzled him and then alarmed him because in some practiced intuition he knew that something terrible had happened, something worse than anything else he had known.

He found the woman weeping hysterically but silently and pushed up against the door so hard that he could scarcely open it, and when he did, she fell into his kitchen with a little scream and bawled out the story in sobs so that he did not understand it all until he was standing over me in the bedroom of the black preacher's house where I was taken, and a dozen voices were talking at once around me, very far away, beyond the aura of my pain. He loomed above me in the dark, and I felt his fingers gently, gently probing my chest and my neck, and I felt the sting of a needle in my arm, and before I went off into a profound and dreamless sleep I heard him cursing slowly, methodically, obscenely, words I had never heard him utter before.

He took me to the Ledbetters' house. I remember none of it. I awoke the next day, my body coming back to my mind, bringing pain that remained dull when I lay still but returned like a lightning bolt when I moved. I opened my eyes and saw the old man sitting beside the bed. "It's all my fault," he said bleakly. "I was a fool. M.P. is dead because I was a fool." He looked ancient and sorrowful beyond any tragedy ever written. I wanted to tell him how happy I was to see him there, how good he was, but when I tried to speak, taking a breath to form words, the pain became unbearable. I shut my eyes and tried to breathe softly so that I would not hurt my ribs. I must have slept again, because when I opened them again it was night, and a lamp glowed in a corner, the flame low, and the room was filled with shadows. Jim Ed was sitting where the old man had been.

Later I discovered that days passed. Always when I awoke, someone was sitting there. Once I heard weeping, and on opening my eyes I saw Darcy Coolidge and a pale and frightened Dale Farmer standing over me, and I had an absurd impulse to tell Dale Farmer that it was all right if he was a fool and a homosexual and anything else he wanted to be. I think I wanted to tell him that we were all part of the universe and that we could do nothing about it. I thought I had some encompassing insight into the essence of things, and I wanted him to know about it and be happy with whatever came because we all were what we had to be. But I could say nothing. I shut my eyes, and when I awoke everyone was gone but the old man, sitting upright in a wooden chair by my bed, snoring loudly, his chin sunk on his chest, and it was dark again, and beyond the house the night lay like a damp hand over the earth. I had been wounded in the war, the head, the chest, the legs. No pain had been like this.

There were four nights of terror. Ted Devlin gave his whole front page to the lynching, for the first time in the county's memory getting black people to talk to a reporter—himself—and writing what they said. He wrote an editorial denouncing the lynching and speaking of the "leading figure" of Bourbon County "alleged to be the culprit who led this bloodthirsty and cowardly mob." The night after the paper appeared, a small band of Klansmen galloped into Bourbonville, carrying burning brands, evidently intending to burn his office, but Ted Devlin was waiting for them with a shotgun and Douglas Kinlaw—yes, mild, bespectacled Douglas Kinlaw—and De-Shane Dugan were sitting in the dark behind the open windows of the building, and when the Klansmen rounded the corner and came at them, they all three opened fire. Douglas Kinlaw had brought over all the shotguns in his storeroom at the hardware store, and they had loaded them and put them in a row, and they fired one and snatched up another so fast that it seemed like an army guarding the office, and the Klansmen fled—but not before a horse was shot and killed under one of them, and the horse rolled dead. Much, much later that night Dr. Youngblood was called out into the country to the home of a man named Cooper who was in agony because a horse had mysteriously rolled on his leg, breaking the bone in a dozen places, leaving it pulp. His wife said he was trying to break a new colt. "He died of shock before I could take his leg off," Dr. Youngblood said. "Poor son of a bitch."

"I hope to hell he suffered before he died and went right on suffering in hell," Ted Devlin said.

Dr. Youngblood said nothing.

I discovered, too, that Jim Ed and Joab and Clyde had staked out the road that led up to the Ledbetter house, and they took Willy with them, Willy who had Hub Delaney's dogs as an obligation and a duty. Willy heard something, and the dogs barked like killer wolves, and the brothers laid down a fusillade of rifle fire that drove whoever it was away. The next day Jim Ed discovered a wooden cross soaked with gasoline lying in the road. "They meant to burn it in front of our house," he said. "I wish we had let them get that close. We'd have laid out somebody's dead ass under it."

Cooper's death and the ambush the others met on the driveway up to Brian Ledbetter's house brought an abrupt sobriety to the Klan of Bourbon County. It was rumored that black men patrolled the roads that led into Bucktown, and somebody fired a rifle into Sheriff Hardison's kitchen window one evening when he was making himself a pitcher of iced tea. The shot blew the pitcher to pieces in his hand and scared Mealy Hardison so much that he defecated in his trousers.

The town got into the newspapers; the governor said that the troubles in Knoxville and Bourbonville over the last year proved that the good colored people of the state should check the radicals in their midst and that to avoid friction the colored people should not engage in any provocative acts. The lynching was mentioned only in passing and always with the information that white people had hanged "a notorious black agitator."

Dr. Youngblood went to face Pinkerton. I never found out all that passed between them. Dale Farmer said there was shouting and cursing, and he said that Dr. Youngblood was doing some of it. Afterwards I heard Dr. Youngblood talking with the old man and with Jim Ed and Mrs. Ledbetter and Joab and Willy somewhere off in the middle distance of the house, and I heard the old man say that Dr. Youngblood was in danger. "Watch the arrow that flies by night," the old man said. Dr. Youngblood murmured something, and I knew that he would not change anything he did.

A transformation took place in me. I cannot say what it was. I lay thinking about myself as if I were floating above my own body, looking down on it, meditating with grave rationality about the impossibility that that body could ever recover. My spirits sank, but then they hit some hard substratum, some invisible and unyielding granite, and would not go down any more. I felt angry; I wanted vengeance; I wanted Pinkerton to suffer; I wanted Kirby to die; I wanted to see Pinkerton put into the streets naked and hungry.

Dr. Youngblood brought a fussy little dentist named Roberts out to pull the roots of my broken teeth out of my gums. They came late at night, Dr. Roberts looking furtive as a rat. He used novocaine, but the operation hurt. He went away, asking us not to tell anybody he had treated me. He said he would come back and make me some false teeth. The old man sat with me. He stared off into space and did not talk.

112

THE BLACK MEN did not come to work after M.P. died. Pinkerton strode about telling everybody that was just what he wanted. He would not have them back even if they came back on their knees. If this was going to be a white man's world, white men had to do the work black men had been doing. He would hire more white men. "I think," Dr. Youngblood observed, "that he thought he might keep everyone confident by appearing confident himself. The men would work hard and follow him, and the car works would recover and run like an Elgin watch."

Everybody worked long hours, but the great machine of the car works was broken, and everybody got irritable and tired, and in the second week the cupola furnace froze because the men could not tap it at the right time, and the iron cooled and had to be dumped out the bottom lest it freeze in the furnace itself. The iron froze. The wheel foundry stopped; within a day the whole car works came to a halt. The cupola drew the men to it like a drain sucking water, spinning and spinning and carrying the debris of this small world into its maw.

Jim Ed went to town and came back and told us what was happening, and we tried to guess what it might mean.

With the catastrophe of the iron furnace, no control remained. The car works froze like the iron under the cupola. Pinkerton started by trying to lead the men in cleansing the mess piled under the great open belly of the furnace, laboring with the only jackhammer in the car works, but the effort wore him down in a minute and left him blank with exhaustion, and he lost his head and began yelling at the men.

Then he held a prayer meeting—yes, a prayer meeting. He gathered the men around him, and he got them down on their knees, and he lifted his eyes to God and he prayed. Most of the men were religious; some were devout; those neither religious nor devout were superstitious. But when Pinkerton prayed for God to melt the mess under the furnace and get the car works going again, the most devout realized that he was crazy. The mess remained a mess. Pinkerton was frantic, and people said his face took on a look of ultimate obstinacy.

Jackhammers and compressors came in by rail in response to Dale Farmer's frantic request by telegraph, and the thunder of the jackhammers carried into the town. They sounded like machine guns.

The men tried. Herakles could not have worked hard enough or fast enough to satisfy Pinkerton. They toiled into the night of the second day, Pinkerton yelling at them, the men sweating, taking turns on the jackhammers, tearing the iron from under the furnace in chunks, getting in the way of one another and ripping their fingernails and scraping their knuckles and sweating and finding it hard to breathe. "This is what happened to me down there," Jack Robinette showed me a month later. His hands were scarred, and one of his fingernails was gone. Brilliant electric floodlights threw a painful glare over tortured bodies. It was a vision of hell.

It was full summer now. The heat was awful. The men were worn out and perplexed. Everybody thought there must be some better way to do the job. Nobody could find it. Pinkerton hurried here and there, starting one thing, then another. People said that DeShane Dugan worried about Pinkerton. "The man is having a nervous breakdown," DeShane said. DeShane wanted to calm him, to make him see that it would take a long time to clean up the mess and that he might as well accept it.

"You had to see it as a job that just took time to do," Jack Robinette said in a slow and deliberate way, pronouncing every word as if it cost money to speak. "It's like a hunting trip. If you think you are going to kill a bear by running him through the woods, you are going to wear yourself out before you get a mile. If you take one step at a time and listen now and then, you will get your bear. Pinkerton wanted it all done today. Yesterday. The harder we worked, the more hopeless he saw it was, and when he got hopeless, he went crazy."

DeShane Dugan should have been in charge, because he was foreman of the wheel foundry. But Pinkerton blamed him for the freeze, pushed him aside. Somebody told me that DeShane finally tried to argue with him, tried to get him to set some order on the work, to set up shifts so that some worked while others went home to rest. Pinkerton slapped him across the mouth.

You could not hear the pop, people said, because the jackhammers were making a deafening racket, and you could not hear anything else unless somebody was yelling in your ear. DeShane was yelling at Pinkerton not because he was angry but because he wanted Pinkerton to hear, and Pinkerton slapped him hard across the face, and people said it was like watching a silent movie because DeShane's head snapped back, and the red mark came on his skin where Pinkerton's hand made a print, and DeShane wiped his mouth and brought away blood and looked down at it as if his own blood were the most amazing thing on earth, but you could not hear anything except the jackhammers, which in their incessant and intolerable pounding had taken the place of silence and were an ironic sort of silence themselves.

DeShane Dugan walked off. Pinkerton yelled something at him, but De-Shane kept walking, and he walked out of the wheel foundry and out the gate of the car works and back to the boardinghouse. He took a bath and worked in his garden the rest of the afternoon.

When the men saw DeShane Dugan leave, they threw down the jackhammers and the sledges, and they walked out after him, and Moreland J. Pinkerton had his first strike as manager of the Bourbonville Car Works. He screamed at them and called them Wobblies and Bolsheviks and enemies of God. It was as though he were God and the men were committing a damnable sin. The jackhammers ceased, the compressors hissed, and a stark silence settled down, broken only by Pinkerton's screaming at the men to come back or be fired, and they ignored him as they threw off gloves, cast goggles aside, turned their backs on Pinkerton, and left.

Most of them hiked into the square and sat on benches in the shade of the courthouse lawn or leaned against trees or sat on curbs, and some went to Bessie May's cafe and had coffee. They were tired and quiet, not understanding what had happened or what they were doing except that they were escaping Pinkerton and the jackhammers and the bone-cracking work. People came out of stores and stood looking at the quiet, bedraggled, unwashed mass of sweating workmen, and afterwards they told the story again and again, and when some still tell it now, everyone remarks on how quiet they were and how quiet the town was. Everybody knew something ominous was happening; nobody knew how it would end.

The car works remained as silent as a ruined city, Pinkerton alone with a bewildered Dale Farmer and with several clerks mesmerized with fear. He walked back down to them and told them that the men had gone out. He was filthy and wild-eyed. He went into his office and cleaned up in his private washroom and changed into clean clothes. He emerged smiling and dressed up as if he might be going to church.

"When I saw that, I knew he was crazy," Dale Farmer said. "I knew he had lost his mind altogether."

Pinkerton looked as if he had found the fountain of youth or the elixir of life or the secrets of alchemy. "It's as clear as day that the men didn't walk out of here by themselves," he said.

Everyone was silent.

"Can't you people see it?" he said.

No one said anything. A woman was crying.

"The Bolsheviks," he said. "We've got Bolshevik agitators on our hands. Right here."

"The Bolsheviks? Here in Bourbonville?" Dale Farmer said he asked the question because he wanted Pinkerton to laugh, to make it all a joke. But he knew Pinkerton meant it.

"The Bolsheviks! The Bolsheviks are right out there in the square, and you don't know who they are, and I don't know who they are. But they're there."

He looked around, the triumphant discovery illuminating his face. "You see," he whispered, "I had it wrong. I thought the Klan was the smart organization, the crowd that had its secret members everywhere, the invisible empire. Now I see it all. The Bolsheviks are the invisible empire! They're all around us. They're even in the Klan. Think of that!" His face was as rapt as a prophet's who had seen the secrets of God.

No one could speak. Pinkerton's whisper became lower, more confidential. He looked as if the universal ear of Bolshevism were pressed to the windows. "They're out there, in the square right this minute. They're planning to burn down the car works."

"Oh, Mr. Pinkerton," Dale Farmer said, a cry of despair.

"They could set fire to all the wood we use for the cars. All that good pine and oak. The place would go up like a bonfire." He made a gesture at the walls. "This place could burn. It's made of wood. Throw gasoline on the walls and strike a match, and she'd go."

"There are no Bolsheviks out there, Mr. Pinkerton. Please. The men are just tired." Dale Farmer was near to tears.

"Hush!" Pinkerton said with primordial calm. Dale Farmer ceased. The women cried on. "The car works are my monument. It's what my life means."

No one could speak. Pinkerton stood there, face alight with revelation. Everything fell into place with a Euclidean thump that neither God in heaven nor Satan under the earth could tear out of his mind.

"I will fix them," he said. "I will fix them."

He went back to his office and wrote out a telegram to Nashville asking the governor to send the National Guard to Bourbonville to protect against a riot. Anarchist and Bolshevik agitators were about to burn the car works down, he said. He could not depend on the local authorities to protect railroad property. He would protect the car works himself until the troops arrived. But they should hurry.

113

YOU MUST UNDERSTAND that Americans in 1920 looked on the Bolsheviks with terror and hatred. I have supposed that the passions whipped up by the World War, like a river in flood, dug themselves out another channel when Americans decided that the war itself had been a mistake, that they had been duped by the French and the British to spend American blood to preserve the right of a hateful aristocracy to go on dressing for dinner in the tropics. That raging stream of hatred was now diverted from the Germans to the Bolsheviks, especially to those hordes of them who had come into America with the great immigration and now waited to overwhelm democracy.

The Bolsheviks rejected God, and they shot people. They had murdered the kindly tsar and his family because the tsar believed in God. Bolsheviks had a black-magical power to corrupt good, docile people into raging revolutionaries. The Russian peasant, for example. The American black man or woman, for another. By hypnotism or by Satanic power or by outrageous promises or perhaps by a mysterious alchemy no one except another Bolshevik could fathom, a single Bolshevik left undetected could reduce civilization to sawdust soaked in the blood of Baptists, Methodists, and Rotarians.

By midnight the governor had ordered the National Guard into Bourbonville. "You've got all these riots going on," he told reporters. "People die when you don't move fast. I'm not going to wait for Bolsheviks to burn Bourbonville to the ground before I do something to protect the good citizens of that beautiful little town."

Pinkerton telegraphed the railroad headquarters in Washington only after he had received assurances from the governor that the National Guard was coming. He told the railroad that he had things under control.

The first company of guardsmen arrived by special train the next evening. The guardsmen climbed down wearing wool uniforms. Why they wore wool is anybody's guess; some mysterious military intelligence sent them into Bourbonville in July in winter uniforms. They formed up and marched through the square and down Broadway to the car works. A trooper in front carried a large American flag. Bourbonvillians stood on the streets silently and watched them pass and noted how profusely they sweated. They pitched tents inside the gate and posted sentries.

The strikers had sat away two days in the square, talking, smoking, chewing, whittling, making no plans, waiting for something to happen. They had no leaders; DeShane Dugan was on his hands and knees in his garden at the boardinghouse, weeding his tomatoes. They chewed tobacco, and they sometimes laughed, though most of the time they were solemn and perplexed. When the troopers got down from the train, the men watched them, and when the troopers marched to the car works, looking slovenly and unmilitary even in their uniforms and sweating as though their skins were fountains, the men followed them and stood in the large vacant lot—the place where Pinkerton wanted his statue—across Broadway from the gate and waited to see what would happen.

Newspapers picked up the story. It appeared in the headlines reserved for declarations of war, spectacular murders, and scandals among the prominent. An avalanche of reporters fell on our town. The next day two more companies of guardsmen came in. They got off the train looking wary and formed up and marched down to join the other troops. The papers said there were three hundred troopers in Bourbonville before it was over.

They were commanded by a Major Wilbur Doane. His picture bloomed on front pages. He became a learned authority on Karl Marx, and he talked to reporters about the wickedness of the Bolsheviks and how it was time America stood up to the agitators. He carried a .45 calibre pistol in a holster, swaggered about with his right hand on the pistol, and said he was prepared to shoot any Bolshevik he found. "It's time we protected our churches and our women from the mad dog Bolsheviks. They didn't think it could happen in Russia, but it did. We are not going to let it happen in Tennessee."

I think it was the coming of Major Doane to Bourbonville with his pistol and his strut and his watery blue eyes under the leather visor of his officer's cap that tipped the strikers into scorn and hatred. You had maybe four hundred striking men standing across Broadway from maybe three hundred wretched national guardsmen choking in their wool uniforms under a July sun. The strikers read in the newspapers that they were led by Bolshevik agitators. Some strikers were members of the Klan. Some had lynched M.P. Brown. Most were curious citizens of a country town who knew and cared for little beyond the borders of Bourbon County. To hear themselves called Bolsheviks put them into a fury. They thought the National Guard ought to be in Bourbonville helping *them.* But there was Major Doane glowering at them with his hand on the butt of his big pistol, strutting in front of his men, looking eager to kill some law-abiding, God-fearing member of the Ku Klux Klan perhaps, and pretty soon the strikers began to yell at him.

At first it was funny. "Look out, Major! They's a Bolshevik looking up your pants leg. He's trying to agitate your little red prick." Then it turned vicious. A newspaper story told us that Major Doane had a daughter at Baker-Henry Baptist College and a sister who taught school in the western part of the state. The strikers started yelling obscene things about Major Doane's daughter and his sister and his wife. One of the men was named Dewey Hartley, and he had a voice that could penetrate plate steel. In every crowd there seems to be a Dewey Hartley. He was relentless in telling Major Doane about his escapades with Major Doane's female relations and of Major Doane's incest with all the women in his family. I was told that Dewey Hartley's voice carried off down Broadway and made women lock their doors and shut their windows because they had never heard words like his before, not even from their husbands. Dewey was funny, and the strikers laughed, and their laughter was a knife scraping the bones of the guardsmen and Major Doane, and things built up.

The papers in other Tennessee towns and the nation were on Pinkerton's side. It was as if Knoxville and Chattanooga, frustrated by their inability to do anything about Bolshevism in Russia, where they had few readers, now greeted with enthusiasm the opportunity to crush the serpent when it reared its head in their own yards. Pinkerton looked grimly heroic; his visage gazed out of front pages all over the state and, I was told, even beyond. Reporters wrote of his gallant resolve in the cause of justice. "I don't want to call names," the papers had him saying in much better English than he ever mustered in reality, "but some of the men that came back from the war have brought subversive ideas with them. They've met with the Bolsheviks over there. Most of our boys are good, patriotic young men. But the Bolsheviks are fiendish. They can take your innocent American boy who hasn't had the proper religious training and indoctrinate him so he does not even know he is being indoctrinated. Then you get a strike like the one I'm fighting, and you have to stand up to it. I had some military service down in Cuba, and I know that you don't run at the sound of the guns. You keep cool. You stick to your own guns, and in the end, right will prevail." Ted Devlin wrote that Pinkerton was a lunatic, but no one outside Bourbonville believed him.

The papers reported that Pinkerton was a veteran of the Spanish-American War, and some put him in the charge up San Juan Hill, the only land action of that little war that anyone could remember. I do not know whether Pinkerton fed these rumors or whether reporters made them up with the enthusiastic righteousness of saints writing Gospels. There he was—Pinkerton, the chivalrous hero of another age, standing tall to redeem his town and protect his business, knight errant and prophet.

Jim Ed brought the newspapers out, and we read them. Brian Ledbetter brooded and said little. Now and then he went out to the airplane and took off the canvas and climbed painfully into the front cockpit and sat there. Jim

Ed watched his father and looked worried, and sometimes he tried to get the old man to tell stories, but Brian Ledbetter shrugged him off. "I've told my stories," he said.

114

I HEALED in the Ledbetter house, my mind often blank. We had visitors. Joab's daughters came to sit, and Barbara told about people in the neighborhood and asked me questions with the frank curiosity of country people. Joab called every day, shy, silent, often sitting for an hour without saying anything, taking his leave with apologetic courtesy as if he had bored me by his loquaciousness. When he laughed at something Barbara said, he turned red with pleasure and looked around as if to say, "Did you ever see anybody as wonderful as this?"

Clyde came over and talked about religion. Did I think it possible for people to eat and to drink and to have sexual intercourse in the Resurrection of the Dead, and was it possible that all the religious people in the world had deceived themselves by the force of their desires? I got lost in his theologizing and began to think that he was daft as people sometimes are in a harmless, talkative way, a little like Mr. Dick in *David Copperfield* with his obsession about King Charles's head. Mrs. Ledbetter told him he should settle down like the good Methodist his father had been and stop asking questions he couldn't answer. "If the Methodist Church was good enough for John Wesley, it ought to be good enough for you, Clyde." Jim Ed said that Clyde had ministered again and again to wounded men under fire on the Western Front, and I knew that he had defended the Ledbetter house— and me—from attack by the Klan. He might be daft, I thought, but he was also brave.

One day Caleb came over, smelling of cologne and whiskey and looking florid. His mother watched Caleb, saying little, her thoughts expressed only by two worry lines that creased vertically over her eyebrows from her nose. But she did not reproach him, and when he fawned over her, she accepted him in irreproachable dignity.

Caleb asked me to take a walk. My ribs hurt terribly, but I walked anyway, slowly and carefully, because Dr. Youngblood told me to walk every day to recover my strength. I limped out to the airplane with him, and we stood looking at it, and Caleb talked about how crazy it had been to spend good money for a toy like that, and he said that Brian Ledbetter always did have a crazy side to him, but he said Brian was the best man he had ever known.

Caleb fell silent after a while, and then he looked at me and said, "People in town say you're a count."

"A count?" I laughed.

"Sure, a count—with a castle and lots of farmland in France."

"I am a Belgian," I said. "I own no land anywhere."

"I'm just telling you what people say. In my business you listen to folks. A man's a fool not to listen to the voice of the people." He laughed and took out a cigarette. His fingertips were yellow. "You smoke?" he said.

"Yes," I said. "A little." He held out the package, and I took one. The cigarette tasted good.

"You deny you're a count?" Caleb said at last, leaning against the airplane, his hat pulled down over his eyes against the sun.

"I am not French, and I am not a count."

"Well, you wouldn't admit it if you was. You folks are slick."

"If it were true, I would tell you," I said.

"You sound like Jesus," Caleb said with a bitter laugh. " 'If it were not so, I would have told you.' "

The remark seemed pointless. I was silent. "Pinkerton and his Klan beat you up pretty bad, I hear."

"Yes," I said.

"Stepdaddy should of killed him way back yonder."

I turned and leaned back on the little airplane on the shady side and looked out at Brian's farm, thinking how neat it all was.

"You're alive. You can be thankful for that. Where there's life, there's hope. Ain't that right?"

"I suppose," I said.

"You suppose," Caleb said. "You don't say nothing clear and firm."

I could not think of anything to say.

"You're telling me you ain't no count," Caleb said. He laughed uproariously. I did not understand the humor.

"That's right. I am no count."

"You're no count." Caleb laughed again, stopped, drew on his cigarette, looking at me beseechingly under the brim of his hat.

"Look here," he said abruptly. "I need a loan."

"A loan," I said.

"A loan, goddammit. I'm in trouble. I'm overextended."

"I do not understand."

"Why in hell can't you understand? It's simple as two plus two. I've bought land and set up ten graveyards on credit. I got corpses sliding into my graveyards like coal in a chute. But folks ain't dying fast enough for me to pay off my debts to the banks. I'm in trouble, Alexander. I need your help."

I grasped the rudiments of what he was saying. His face was still and resigned, his cigarette hanging out of the corner of his mouth, his arms folded across his chest, eyes shaded by his hat brim, something veiled about them, veiled and penetrating at the same time.

"I do not have any money."

"A count has a castle and hundreds of acres of land. You could get the money if you wanted to help me."

"Mr. Weaver, I give you my word. I am not a count. I do not have any money."

"I'll cut you in on the profits. I'm just in a bind with the banks right now, but you can look at my records. The money is rolling in. There just ain't enough of it right now. In ten years I'll be a millionaire."

"Mr. Weaver, I do not have any money. I have had to borrow money myself to send to my family in—" I almost said "Greece," but I stopped in time. "In Europe," I said.

"You can borrow money and help me then," Caleb said. "Look, you owe a lot to my family. Look how they're helping you out now."

My face burned. "I appreciate your family very much. But I have no money."

"In ten years you can be rich with me if you come in on the ground floor. Look, this is the wave of the future—the graveyard that looks like a park. Artwork all over the place. Statues and stained glass and big trees and benches, the kind of place where you want to come and walk with the little woman and the kids and look at the trees on Sunday afternoon and enjoy yourself looking at the famous people buried all around you. It takes the sting out of death." He looked at me earnestly. "What do you say?"

"I have said what I have to say, Mr. Weaver. I have no money. Why don't you borrow it from Virgil?"

Caleb drew back as if I had slapped him. "Borrow from Virgil! Let Virgil look down on me like that!"

"He would lend you the money. He has much money."

"That's just the point, goddammit. He's got all the money in the world, but I'm not going to go crawling to him for anything. He'd never let me forget it."

"How do you know?"

"He's my brother. That's how I know. Jesus Christ."

"Your brother should be happy to help you out."

"You don't know nothing. You're like all the rest of them. You think I'm the clown of the family."

I resolved to keep doggedly on the subject. "You could borrow it from Mr. Ledbetter. He would lend you anything if you asked."

"Stepdaddy? Hell, you think I'm going to admit to anybody in this family that Virgil's made it big and I have to run around trying to borrow money from Jews like you? Go to hell, you Jew bastard. Go to hell. You treat me like dirt. Well, someday I'll show you a thing or two. You wait and see."

He threw away his cigarette and started to light another one, but abruptly he stomped away in a rage. He did not go back into the house but went to his car and drove off without saying goodbye.

"Did you have a nice talk?" Mrs. Ledbetter asked.

"Yes," I said.

"Caleb's troubled," she said.

"I know," I said.

"What's wrong with him?"

"I do not know," I said.

"He's a good boy," she said. "He's just troubled."

The old man sat in a rocking chair on the porch, smoking a pipe and looking out to where the heat waves rolled off the grass and the sloping fields that fell below the house into the broad valley beyond. He did not say anything.

115

BOURBONVILLE SEETHED. The governor visited Bourbonville with a bodyguard of state police and made the train let him off at the crossing next to the gate to the car works, and he heard Dewey Hartley discuss the sexual parts of the governor's wife. "She's got a little mole on her belly just above her pussy hair," Dewey shouted. "There's a lodge of fellers in Nashville that's run their tongues over that mole. They vote for you, Governor, so they can keep her in town." Other men took up the cry, and the governor left amid hoots of derision that, it was said, drove him almost to madness. Three years later his wife divorced him, ending his political career; the papers in Nashville reported only her charge of insane jealousy and physical abuse, but gossip held that the governor's wife did indeed have a mole approximately where Dewey Hartley located it, and that the governor could not get Dewey's confident detail out of his mind.

At the time the governor's daily pronouncements had it that the streets swarmed with Bolshevik bandits about to burn churches, crucify clergymen, force white women to marry black men, rob banks, and throw bombs at congressmen. The town itself became the enemy. "I looked them in the eye," he shouted, "and I know." Not an editor in the state except Ted Devlin cared to defend Bourbonville and run the risk of ending up on the side of Reds and anarchists. People in Bourbonville read the papers in disbelief, and they became more and more angry with the governor, with Moreland Pinkerton, and with the troops. Because he was the mayor, Douglas Kinlaw got hate mail from all over the state and beyond, people saying that Bourbonville ought to be burned to the ground and sown with salt. Editorials commended Pinkerton's bravery and sagacity, extolled the governor, lauded the brave and noble troops, and announced that Bourbonville, Tennessee, represented the high-water mark of Bolshevism in America and that a determined people must roll back the flood.

Pinkerton strutted about, happy at last to say aloud to reporters what he had always thought about Bourbonville. "It's a seedbed of corruption," he said. "The people here have no sense of fair play. They have no Americanism. They don't know what it is to be patriotic. They are shiftless and full of gossip. They would walk ten miles to say something bad about their neighbors and another ten miles to keep from saying something good. And they are all hypocrites about religion. Not half of them believe in God." The reporters translated his tirades into a reluctant judgment arrived at by studious investigation and painful experience. He told of Bolshevik agitators coming in by night, holding secret meetings, distributing literature, holding classes in basements on how to make bombs, and shooting at targets set up in fields outside of town. "The Bolsheviks have been like the devil," Pinkerton said. "They have seduced these poor ignorant people and made them believe they can pull off a revolution." Ted Devlin told me that Pinkerton explained to the reporters about the curse of God on blacks and the coming holy war between whites and blacks with the Bolsheviks somehow in the middle of it, but they could not print such things without giving the impression that Pinkerton was crazy. The press did not want a crazy hero.

The stories reporters did write were detailed and horrifying, and readers assumed Pinkerton could not possibly have made it all up. In Bourbonville itself people felt smothered by an incomprehensible madness, and they were angry. Pinkerton held long talks with Major Doane and sent telegrams to the governor. He set up his headquarters in the main office. He ordered Dale Farmer down there with him, and the two of them slept on cots. I supposed that Dale Farmer was frightened and miserable.

In the meantime, the crowd opposite the gate increased every day. Whole families came out. People came in from the country and stood around waiting for something to happen. People came from other towns because they wanted to see what was being described in headlines. Women came to be with their husbands, even with Dewey Hartley shouting obscenities at the national guardsmen. You could feel restraints breaking down, people said. Reporters swarmed like flies on rotting fruit. The guardsmen held their line in front of the gate, rifles ready. Some fainted from the heat; the crowd in the vacant lot went crazy with joy when a trooper collapsed, his rifle rattling on the rocky earth. The troops set up a hospital tent with a bright red cross painted on the roof. Its sides were open. Pinkerton came to comfort sick troopers, and pictures of him at their bedsides got into the papers.

Dr. Youngblood drove out to the Ledbetter farm to visit sometimes, never for very long, and he said things were looking bad. "It's like a boiler heating up, and somebody has stopped the safety valve, and the whole damned thing is going to explode," he said, speaking very slowly, and looking grave.

Dr. Youngblood drove Dr. Roberts out one evening, and he took impressions to make me a bridge for my false teeth. "Look at it this way," Dr. Roberts said. "You won't ever have a toothache with the teeth I make for you. The teeth God makes for you will rot out, and they'll hurt. But the teeth I make will never give you any trouble. They'll be sound a hundred years after your body has rotted away in your coffin."

"It's too bad you can't make brains, Charlie," Brian Ledbetter said. "I bet you could fix it so nobody would ever have a bad thought."

A week or so after the strike began, Eugenia Curry drove up one morning in her automobile. She came chugging into the yard and stopped and waved cheerfully. I was sitting up on the porch with the old man. A humid heat sat on the earth. Jim Ed was working in the vegetable garden. I sat in my shirtsleeves smoking on the front porch, and there she was, rosy and bright and happy. Brian Ledbetter called off the dogs and asked her up, and Mrs. Ledbetter brought out a pitcher of iced tea.

"I want to know about the lynching," she said. "I want to know what connection there is between the lynching and the strike. Nobody is making the connection; I have heard there is one."

I told her about the lynching, and I told her about Moreland Pinkerton and the Klan and how the black men had refused to work and how the white men had tried to do the job without them and how everything had stopped, and how Pinkerton slapped DeShane Dugan, and how the men quit. She stopped writing halfway through my story and looked forlornly at me.

"It's no good," she said.

"It is not good," I said. "But it is true."

"I know it's true. That's why I can't print it," she said, shaking her head. "My editor won't let me."

"Why won't he let you?" the old man said.

"It makes it seem that the strike was called because Mr. Pinkerton led a lynch mob and then went crazy. My editor would not print anything like that."

"Pretty much the way it happened," the old man said.

"It doesn't matter. Mr. Pinkerton is a hero. He's holding the line against the Bolsheviks. Every day I hear people say that if he had been serving the tsar, the Bolsheviks would never have taken over Russia."

"Lord God," the old man said. After that he sat looking off into space and seemed almost to forget that we were there.

Mrs. Ledbetter made lunch, and Jim Ed came in from the garden and saw Eugenia. He was in his overalls and an army shirt and wore a large straw hat.

He looked lean and tanned and handsome. He washed up and looked at her appreciatively, and I saw how much he admired her. She smiled and put out her hand and he took it shyly and held it just a second, and she stood up and told him it was good to see him, and he told her it was good to see her, and they smiled at each other and stood there for a moment or two looking embarrassed.

Evelyn Ledbetter looked at her son, and I saw her survey Eugenia Curry, and I saw something go click in her mind, perhaps even a perceptible nod, a decision of some sort, though I am sure that I imagine these details. Evelyn Ledbetter approved. I did not make that up.

Evelyn Ledbetter sized up her son—almost thirty-four and unmarried. She dished out roast beef and mashed potatoes and gravy and fresh garden peas, and she talked to Eugenia Curry of how good it was to have Jim Ed back again because there wasn't a farmer in the county who could make things grow better than he could and how her husband had been a good farmer in his time but that now he was too old to do anything other than remember what it was like to farm, and Brian Ledbetter laughed in his peaceful way and said he was too old to do lots of other things that he used to do pretty well. We sat for a long time, and I wished Jim Ed would go back to the work he had to do in his garden.

I was jealous. With jealousy came something more—desire, an awakening, a reawakening. I had once yearned for Palmyre day and night. After I was wounded I had no more desire. When I thought of desire, it was in the rational, ruminative way that I recalled the patterns in the tile floor in our kitchen at home or a pair of leather sandals I once bought in the harbor or the peculiar cry of the man who sold yoghurt in our street—memories, abstract, removed, meaningless. Almost six years had passed. I dreamed of Palmyre, and I wakened thinking of her as I thought of other dear, lost things. Nothing in those memories prompted me to lust.

Now lust came back. I undressed Eugenia Curry in my mind. I imagined her walking out of the bath with a towel draped over her shoulder so that one breast showed and that the towel came down just below the place where her legs began. I imagined her lying on her stomach over a pillow, naked, her bottom thrust up as I bent over her and worked in her while she put her face into the bed and groaned with pleasure. Did I imagine that about her, or did I remember it about Palmyre—the deep, passionate pleasure Palmyre took in my body in hers, the way her head jerked uncontrollably when the moment came?

Then, in confusion, I imagined Eugenia in bed with Jim Ed, and I could not bear it.

We sat. Jim Ed talked about going into a restaurant in Paris and having strawberries for dessert and finding a little red worm in the strawberries, and he made it sound very funny, and everybody laughed, and the old man told about eating hardtack in the war, but he drifted off into his own thoughts and did not tell about Gettysburg. Jim Ed talked about Belleau Wood and about the church at Soissons that had its stained-glass windows shattered and how the walls were filled with holes where the bullets had entered the soft stone and how the church had been left a ruin and how old the church was and how it had not been built to withstand shell fire.

Eugenia asked just the right questions to make him go on, and the old man came back into the conversation and got him to tell about Willy and how the shell burst and left Willy out there screaming with his hands over his face, and how Jim Ed crawled out under hostile machine-gun fire and killed the German gunner and his mate and brought Willy back again, and he managed to tell all that without making a single bragging comment, giving us enough details to let us grasp slowly what it had been like, but he did not tell us everything that it had been.

"You should have had a medal," Eugenia said.

Jim Ed said, "I got something better than a medal—I got home alive," he said with a dismissive laugh. It was just the right tone of modesty, completely unaffected.

I sat there feeling dull and dumb. I had nothing interesting to say. I wanted Eugenia Curry to pay attention to me and felt foolish for it. Jim Ed was one of the best people I knew. He was kind and generous and unassuming, and he was smart and loyal and brave, and he was good to his parents, and even the animals on the farm loved him, and it seemed the most natural thing in the world that Eugenia Curry should love him, too.

I was feeling miserable when Philip Drodge came riding up in the second car of the day to visit us.

116

PHILIP DRODGE sat in front with a man I had not seen before. Drodge wore a dark blue suit with a red necktie knotted in front of his stiff white collar—the sort of collar men wore in those days, starched and hard and uncomfortably high, the kind you attached to a shirt with a collar button. He wore an expensive hat with a wide brim that dwarfed his hawklike face. He looked young and intense, thin, and his bright eyes burned with energy. I looked out the window and recognized him and told the others who he was while the dogs were barking and bellying around the car.

Jim Ed sauntered out on the porch, wiping his mouth with his napkin, his shirtsleeves rolled halfway up his big arms. He shouted the dogs off, and

Philip Drodge got down from the car, looking anxiously at them. He called up to Jim Ed. "Can't you get these dogs to quit barking? I can't hear myself think."

Jim Ed shouted at the dogs again.

"I don't know how you country people stand so many dogs around all the time," Philip Drodge said, walking up the steps. "They would drive me out of my mind."

"I reckon you'd get on their nerves, too," Jim Ed said.

For a moment Philip Drodge looked exasperated. "I guess you're Mr. Ledbetter. I am here to see Mr. Alexander. I know he is here. I am Philip Drodge. I am an official with the Dixie Railroad."

Jim Ed considered this information and called inside. "Paul, you want to see this feller, or shall I get the shotgun after him?"

The old man laughed. "That's what we do to railroad folks in this house. That's what I done to Pinkerton," he said, looking at Eugenia Curry. He stopped laughing and became thoughtful. "I should of killed him."

"You are speaking of Moreland Pinkerton at the car works?" Eugenia said. "You nearly shot him?"

"I shot over his head," the old man said.

"I would love to hear that story," Eugenia said.

"You will," Mrs. Ledbetter said.

"Paul?" Jim Ed said.

"Yes, I will see him," I said.

"You can come in if you want. That feller want to come in, too?" Jim Ed pointed to the other man.

"Hunter, you might as well listen to this," Philip Drodge said.

The man named Hunter got down gingerly from the car. The dogs were still barking, standing off but looking menacing. Hunter reached behind and patted his car as if it had been a pet. It was a new-looking car. The black paint gleamed in the sun. "These dogs bite?" he said.

"Not much," Jim Ed said.

"Lord, that's all I need now—hydrophobia," Hunter said. He wore an old-fashioned bowler hat and a long, drooping mustache that made him look like a relic from thirty years before. He moved slowly.

"You fellers had any dinner?" Jim Ed said. He showed them into the kitchen.

"No," Philip Drodge said. "I don't feel like eating." He walked inside and saw the two women and hastily took off his hat. He was getting prematurely bald. The sweat beaded on his scalp. "I beg your pardon," Philip Drodge said.

"This is my mamma, and this is my daddy, Brian Ledbetter, and this is a friend of ours, Miss Eugenia Curry," Jim Ed said. He did not say she was a reporter.

"Very pleased to meet you," Philip Drodge said. He ducked his head towards the women in a kind of bow, shook hands with Brian, looked down at his wooden peg.

"Lost your leg in an accident?" Philip Drodge said.

"You might could say that," Brian Ledbetter said.

"Farming's a dangerous occupation," Philip Drodge said. His quick eyes lingered on Eugenia. He turned back to me. "How are you, Alexander?"

"I am very well for a man who has lost his teeth because his employer led a lynch mob," I said. I was angry again. I had decided that I did not like Philip Drodge. He talked as if I had no choice but to see him. The railroad taught men like Pinkerton and Drodge to be bullies because it made them think they were more important than anybody else in any group of ordinary mortals.

"It was as bad as that, was it?" Philip Drodge said softly.

"It was worse than that," the old man said.

"I'll lay you some biscuits down and get you some roast beef," Evelyn Ledbetter said.

"Please do not trouble yourself," Philip Drodge said. "We do not want to impose. We're not hungry."

"I wouldn't mind imposing," the other man said. "I mean, I haven't had anything to eat all day long. I mean, begging your pardon, ma'am, but I could eat a horse. I bet you're hungry, too, Drodge."

"This is George Hunter," Philip Drodge said, looking irritated. "He is with the railroad in Knoxville. We're here to try to settle this awful mess." He took a deep breath and expelled it. "It *is* an awful mess."

"A good meal will make you feel better," Evelyn Ledbetter said. Hunter held his bowler hat in his hand. "You sit down, Mr. Hunter," Evelyn Ledbetter said with a big smile. "I'll bring you a plate. You look like a man that can appreciate good cooking. I like to cook for a man that likes to eat."

"That's might'ly kindly of you, ma'am," Hunter said, making a funny little bow, a jerk from the waist, and holding his hat in both hands before his ample stomach.

"Let me take your hat, Mr. Hunter," Jim Ed said. Hunter did not argue.

"Tell me about Pinkerton," Philip Drodge said, straddling the chair and putting his elbows on the table. "I want to know everything." His eyes were like steel drills.

I told him about Pinkerton and about the lynching. Eugenia sat to one side. I saw her start to reach for her notebook, but she thought better of it. Evelyn Ledbetter put food in front of Philip Drodge, and he picked at it, seemingly uninterested. Then he began eating slowly. Then he dug in. "I guess I was hungrier than I thought," he said sheepishly.

Hunter pitched in with both hands. "I think I will have some more of the biscuits, Mrs. Ledbetter," he said gravely. He ate slowly, chewing everything a long time. "I fletcherize my meat," he explained. "Dr. Fletcher tells us that if you chew your food until it's almost liquid in your mouth, you won't ever have ulcers or cancer."

"We got a doctor like that now," Jim Ed said.

"A forward-looking man, I'd say," Hunter said.

I wanted to shock them. Eugenia Curry put her hands up to her mouth when I told about Pinkerton shooting M.P. in the legs. Her eyes widened, and she looked pale and sick. She did not say anything. Hunter and Drodge went on eating silently and methodically, Drodge sometimes nodding his head gravely, as if getting all the pieces together so he could make something of them.

"Pinkerton led a lynch mob?" Philip Drodge said with a slight interrogation. He wiped his mouth.

"Yes," I said.

"It's vulgar," Philip Drodge said.

"It's murder," Brian Ledbetter said.

"He is crazy," Drodge said.

"Yes," I said.

"Him and half the county," Brian Ledbetter said.

"I shouldn't say that," Philip Drodge said. "The railroad cannot admit that it has a crazy man working for it. The newspapers would kill us."

I looked at Eugenia Curry. She sat with her eyes slightly narrowed but otherwise without any expression except the thoughtful contemplation of Philip Drodge's face. I wondered if she found him handsome.

"How did the strike happen?" Philip Drodge said. I told him, and when I was done, it was after three o'clock. The air was thick with heat. We were all sweating.

The men pushed their chairs back. Mrs. Ledbetter brought another pitcher of iced tea. Hunter belched and apologized profusely and turned red.

"It's all right," Mrs. Ledbetter said. "I've heard tell that Chinamen belch to show they liked the dinner."

"I sure did that, ma'am," Hunter said, wiping his mouth with a large pocket handkerchief.

"Maybe you got some Chinaman in you somewheres," the old man said.

"I don't believe so," Hunter said.

"Your eyes look a little slanty to me," the old man said.

"I don't believe so," Hunter said, squinting. "I honestly don't think so." He put a hand up to his face and felt his eyes. He looked mildly alarmed.

"I want to know what is happening down here," Philip Drodge said. "I have been to the car works. The mob out there is ready to kill somebody. So are those troopers. Children are throwing rocks at the troopers. Did you know that?"

We did not know that.

"Their parents encourage them. It is frightening. The troops are armed with 1903 Springfields. The bolt-action model. I am sure you know it. Were you in the army, Mr. Ledbetter?"

"I was a sharpshooter," Jim Ed said. "I was in France."

"Well, you know the 1903 Springfield," Philip Drodge said. "I thought I could strike a match and the whole crowd would burn like dry wood. I did not try to pass through the gate. I wanted to see you first, Mr. Alexander. The troops are wearing wool. In this heat they're wearing wool uniforms! Heavy brown wool. I don't see how they stand it. What do you think, Mr. Alexander? Do you have any ideas?"

"Mr. Pinkerton will have to retreat," I said.

"Back down?" Philip Drodge said.

"Yes. But I do not believe he will. If he says the men are Bolsheviks, they must be Bolsheviks."

"Jesus! Excuse me, ladies. It's a royal mess. He's a hero in the state now," Philip Drodge said. "Do you read the newspapers? It's madness—utter madness. If you ask me, most reporters ought to be horsewhipped. If it weren't for the reporters, we could put Pinkerton in the insane asylum where he belongs and throw away the key. The newspapers make Pinkerton sound like Alvin York or your—your . . ." Philip Drodge stopped and looked embarrassed.

"Like D.B.," Evelyn Ledbetter said. "He was my grandson." Her face looked stern and sad.

"Yes," Philip Drodge said softly. "I forgot. Forgive me for bringing it up."

"It's all right," Mrs. Ledbetter said. She went back to the kitchen.

"You can fire him," Brian Ledbetter said.

"No, he's got us over a barrel. Don't you see that, Mr. Ledbetter? We're up to our necks in horse manure, if you'll pardon my French. He's saying the Bolsheviks caused this strike. The whole state believes him."

"They ain't a Bolshevik within a thousand miles of Bourbonville," the old man said.

"You know that, and I know that," Philip Drodge said.

"The newspaper people know that," Brian Ledbetter said, looking at Eugenia Curry.

"Probably most of the folks in Tennessee know that," Philip Drodge said.

"If we all know that, you can fire him," Brian Ledbetter said.

"Let's get this straight, Mr. Ledbetter. We cannot fire the man. If we fired Moreland Pinkerton, the newspapers would tear us apart. The imbeciles in the state legislature would pass a law taxing railroad property at one hundred percent of its appraised value, and then they would appraise it for twice what it's worth. Pinkerton's created a myth. Hell—excuse me, ma'am, I didn't mean to say that—you have to admire what the man's done in a way.

It's like admiring Jesse James. He's planted a myth of the Bolsheviks down here in this little burg. He's made people passionately believe something that's absurd. It's out of control." He looked around in the exasperation of a man who has seen some obvious truth with brilliant clarity and discovers that no one else can perceive it.

"Then you can fire him," Brian Ledbetter said. "We don't need no myths around here. Not while we got the Baptist Church. That's myth enough for one county."

"No," Philip Drodge said, making a gesture of finality with both his slender hands. "No. We cannot fire him. Not until . . . We have to reason with him first. We have to get him to call this thing off."

"Reasoning with Pinkerton is like reasoning with a snake," Brian Ledbetter said. "You can reason with it all night long and it'll bite you in the morning."

We sat in a gloomy silence.

"Well, I've come out here to get you, Mr. Alexander," Philip Drodge said, taking a deep and impatient breath. "I thought you might go with me. Help me talk to him. Reason with him. He thinks a lot of you. He has told me he thinks of you like his only son. He says you're the man to succeed him."

Jim Ed whistled softly. I was irate. "He nearly hanged me," I said. "He hanged M.P."

"We need to be understanding," Philip Drodge said. "It's too bad about the colored man, but let's face it—colored men are a dime a dozen. We can lose one or two now and then." He laughed.

"If you keep talking that way, I will ask you to leave my house," Brian Ledbetter said quietly.

Philip Drodge looked at him in restrained confusion. "No offense," he said, having no idea how he could have given offense. "I'm sorry for what I said about the colored man if I offended you. I don't care to talk about the colored man. I want to talk about you, Mr. Alexander. That fool down at the car works thinks you're the man who can carry on his work. I think he might listen to you. We need to understand him."

"It looks to me like we all need to be understanding so the railroad can save its back end," Jim Ed said.

"All right. I admit it," Philip Drodge said in irritation. "I have to save the railroad's back end, as you call it. Begging your pardon, ma'am. I don't want to speak improperly. We've got our . . . our back end, as you call it, hanging over a barbed-wire fence, and I'm paid to save it. What's wrong with that?"

"Nothing's wrong with that," Jim Ed said amiably. "I just want us all to be sure what we're talking about."

"We're talking about a lunatic," Philip Drodge said in a burst of exasperation. "If we can get him to calm down, get him to talk with the men, get him to have the darkies come back to work, I think all this will blow over. Do you mind if I smoke?"

"But you're saying you can't tell reporters you got a lunatic on your hands," the old man said.

"That would be disastrous," Philip Drodge said. "The reporters would never understand. It might also make the railroad liable for damages."

"Well, we sure wouldn't want that to happen," Jim Ed said. He looked at Eugenia Curry, and she smiled.

"Your sarcasm is lost on me, I'm afraid," Philip Drodge said wearily.

"You think the colored folks will come running back to work when Pinkerton whistles?" Jim Ed said. "Just like a pack of dogs?"

"You put it crudely, Mr. Ledbetter," Philip Drodge said, lighting a cigarette with a hand that I saw was trembling. "I think the colored people will see which side of the bread their butter's on. They need calm. Mistakes have been made. Passions have been aroused. Difficulties have been caused. Right now we need a cooling-off period. We need Pinkerton to say there is no longer any emergency. We need those troops out of Bourbonville. I won't say it was all the colored man's fault, and I don't think he should have been lynched. But he did get out of line. You have to admit that." He added this last almost as a rumination, some residual conviction that the railroad was not to blame.

"I never thought much about M.P.'s being colored when I was flying with him," the old man said in a voice heavy with grief.

Philip Drodge looked at him. "I don't think you can ever not think about a man being colored," he said.

"It don't matter when you're up in the sky and he's the difference between getting you down safe and smashing your bones against the ground," Brian Ledbetter said.

"Well, it's too late to argue about that. Right now we have to get this strike over; we have to get those troops out of Bourbonville."

"Then what?" Jim Ed said.

"Then, when things quieten down, we can . . . the railroad can get Mr. Pinkerton to think about retiring."

Philip Drodge looked around at us to see what effect his words were having. He turned his head mechanically, as if he had been wound up. He seemed to expect us to reply. No one did.

"How about it?" he said at last, looking at me.

"What?" I said.

"How about coming down there with Hunter and me, Mr. Alexander? We can talk to him. Get him to talk to the men. Who are their leaders?"

"This man can't hardly walk," the old man said. "His ribs is taped up. He don't need to be out there doing nothing for the railroad."

"The railroad needs you," Philip Drodge said. "We will see to it that you are rewarded. How about it?"

"I do not know if they have leaders," I said.

"Of course they have leaders. Every group has leaders," Philip Drodge said.

"I'd say you ought to go down to them folks that's standing around the gate and ask all the Bolsheviks to step forward," Brian Ledbetter said. "Get them all to hold their hands up and shoot them on the spot. Ain't that right, Miss Curry?"

Eugenia turned slightly red. She did not say anything.

Philip Drodge scarcely gave her a glance. "Be serious," he said, shaking his head impatiently. "I agree with you, Mr. Ledbetter. There's not a Bolshevik in a thousand miles of Bourbonville. But that's not the point. We've got a sick man on our hands. We've got a state full of barking newspapers. We've got a governor who has proved the theory of evolution by having the common sense of a gorilla. We've got a railroad car works, and we've got a town. That town is dependent on the railroad, my friends. You may not like me, and you may not sympathize with my job. But I tell you, I'm doing something for your town. You have to help me, Alexander. I propose to reason with Mr. Pinkerton. If we have to, we'll lie to him—promise him anything he wants. Anything to get him to say the emergency is over, that we don't need the National Guard anymore."

"DeShane Dugan is probably a leader," I said. "He was the one Pinkerton slapped."

"Then we'll talk to DeShane Dugan. But only after we talk to Pinkerton. We will make Pinkerton talk with DeShane Dugan."

"How you going to do that?" Jim Ed said.

"We will arrange it," Philip Drodge said. "Will you come along and talk to him, Paul?"

"I do not know that he will listen to me."

"Will you come along?"

"All right," I said. "I will go. I do not know what I will say to him. I do not think he will believe anything I say to him."

"I want to go, too," Eugenia said.

Philip Drodge laughed. "Not on your life, little lady. We're not going to let you harm your pretty head by putting your nose where it doesn't belong. Are you Mr. Ledbetter's fiancée?"

I was irritated. Jim Ed laughed. He turned red, and I was more irritated. I thought he had no right to blush.

"I'm sorry, Mr. Drodge, but I'm going with you," Eugenia said crisply, her face red and firm. "I am not anybody's fiancée. I am a newspaper reporter for the *Knoxville Guardian,* and I intend to write up this interview with Mr. Pinkerton for my paper."

I thought Philip Drodge was going to fall out of his chair. He jumped to his feet as though to keep from falling and glared at her, and his face went pale. "A newspaper reporter! Why didn't you tell me you were a reporter? Nobody told me I was talking to a reporter. It's not fair if you print anything I've said. I'll complain. I'll tell your editor. I didn't authorize you to quote me. I'll deny everything. I'll sue." It was nice to see Philip Drodge frightened. "Why didn't you tell me? You deceived me."

"I believe the answer to that is that you did not ask," Eugenia Curry said.

Philip Drodge hopped around. You could look at his face and see serious thoughts romping across his eyes. The old man was chuckling. I'm sure I smiled.

"But, Miss—Miss . . ."

"Her name is Miss Curry," Jim Ed said. "I figure it this way, Mr. Dodge."

"Drodge," Philip Drodge said bleakly. "My name is Philip Drodge."

"Well, whatever your name is, I look at it this way. You can let this woman go with you and write up her story, or she can write up what she's already heard. She's going to get a story one way or another."

"Miss Curry, forgive me. I should never have spoken of such things in the presence of a lady," Philip Drodge said. "This is man's talk, and I should not have involved a member of the delicate sex."

"Mr. Drodge, nothing you say is going to make me change my mind. I believe that Mr. Ledbetter here has stated my case perfectly well. I will go with you, or I will write my story as I have it now. I can see the headline: 'High Railroad Official Says Bolsheviks Not to Blame for Bourbonville Strike.'" She cocked her head at him and smiled. "I believe your back end is hanging over the fence, Mr. Drodge."

Philip Drodge glared at her. He had sweat on his smooth face. He moved his lips to say something, but nothing came out. He cleared his throat and started again. "Miss Curry . . ."

There was much more talking. It was Hunter who finally put the decisive weight on Eugenia's side. The railroad had less to lose by letting her go with us than by making her angry and leaving her to write the story that everybody in the room could confirm. You could see Philip Drodge considering his future. How was a man going to explain to his superiors why he had talked to a newspaper reporter as boldly as he had spoken in front of Eugenia Curry? If she wrote the story she threatened to write, he would be revealed as a manipulator, a hypocrite, and a fool. In the end he gave in.

"I want everybody in this room to know that this is not my way of doing things," he said. "If any harm comes to this woman, it won't be my fault."

"What harm could come to me?" Eugenia asked. "Do you think I'm a child who can't take care of herself?"

"I wish you wouldn't go," Jim Ed said.

"Don't you think I can take care of myself?" Eugenia asked. Her tone was sharp.

"Miss Curry," Jim Ed said, "I don't think any of you can take care of yourself out there right now. If you want to go talk to Pinkerton, go talk to him at night. Don't go there in broad daylight. Go when it's quiet."

"I want to get this over with," Philip Drodge said.

"It will be dark in a few hours," Jim Ed said. "Most of the crowd goes home at dark."

"I don't think we should wait another minute," Philip Drodge said.

His was the final word. The four of us got in the car to go to Bourbonville. Jim Ed stood on the porch, hands in his hip pockets, and watched us leave. His face was dark. The old man hobbled out after him, and I remember the two of them standing there, the old man looking just over Jim Ed's shoulder.

117

IT WAS HUNTER'S CAR, and he drove. "Your car smells new, Mr. Hunter," Eugenia said.

"It is new, ma'am. I got it just last week. It's been hard to get new cars. The war, you know."

"My brother Alfred says if you could bottle the way a new car smells, you would make a million dollars."

"He's right, ma'am. You *could* make a million dollars. You surely could. I'd like stock in a company that could sell that smell, ma'am. I really would."

"Alfred is the service manager for the new Maxwell dealer in Knoxville," Eugenia said.

"Well, the Maxwell is a fine car, ma'am," Hunter said. "Of course I prefer a LaSalle. This car is a LaSalle."

"It's a very nice car," Eugenia said.

"I'm glad you like it, ma'am," Hunter said.

"People and their cars," Philip Drodge said. "I can't understand what makes people crazy about cars."

It was too hot to talk. We arrived in Bourbonville and found it silent, a baked, harsh feel to the air. We rounded the square and drove down West Broadway. We could see the crowd then. The road was not as wide as it is now, and it was macadam. Men in straw hats stood in the weedy lot across from the gate of the car shops and overflowed onto the highway, blocking it. The troops stood in a double line before the main gate. They held their rifles with fixed bayonets. The strikers were yelling at the troopers, and the troopers stood there, miserably hot, bayonets pointed at the crowd. Dark clouds crowded over the ridge. We were going to have rain.

Hunter drove to the edge of the mob and stopped. He could not get through. The din was terrific. Men were cursing and shouting obscenities. Hunter turned around to Eugenia Curry apologetically. "I'm sorry you have to hear this, ma'am. They don't know a lady's present."

"She brought it on herself," Philip Drodge grumbled. "She wouldn't be here if she had not insisted."

"That's right," Eugenia said cheerfully. "I would not be here if I had not insisted. Bad words will not hurt me, Mr. Hunter. I feel sorry for men who use them."

"Blow your horn, Hunter," Philip Drodge said. "Make them move out of the way, or we'll run over them."

"If I make them mad, they'll tear up my car," Hunter said.

"Oh, for the name of heaven," Philip Drodge said, rolling his eyes skyward. "These men are not going to tear up a car."

"If you don't mind, I think we ought to walk the rest of the way," Hunter said.

Philip Drodge shook his head. "All right, all right. Let's walk. We've got a perfectly good car to ride in, but if you think so much of your car, we will walk. I hope you have this car twenty years, Hunter."

"I'm sorry to offend you, Mr. Drodge, but me and the wife paid a lot for this car, and we'd like to keep it for a while. The kiddies like it, too."

"It's all right. I said it was all right," Philip Drodge grumbled. He got out and slammed the door. I intended to help Eugenia, but she stepped out before I could get around to open her door. She had her notebook in her hand. We could smell the crowd as I had smelled soldiers in the war. It was as if rage permeated their normal sweat mingled with whiskey. Many of them were drunk.

Philip Drodge went first, shouting, "Let us through. Let us through." Hunter went after him, his head bowed slightly, a hand up as if to fend off objects that might be thrown at us. Eugenia came next, and I brought up the rear.

"Kiss my ass!" somebody shouted.

"Gentlemen! Gentlemen! There's a lady present," Hunter said.

"She can kiss my ass, too," somebody said. Laughter.

"Gentlemen! Gentlemen!"

"Nigger lover—nigger lover!" somebody said.

"He's all right," somebody said.

"Hey, lady—tell one of them troopers to kiss my ass!" somebody said.

"Hey, that's enough—that's enough. You'll give us a bad name," somebody said.

"Gentlemen! Gentlemen!" Hunter said. "There's a lady present. A lady, gentlemen."

We came to the edge of the mob and crossed an invisible boundary. The troopers were in front of us, beyond the double track of the railroad. Eugenia was ahead of me, her head down. Long afterwards she told me that she was so embarrassed that she could not look any of these men in the eye. "I thought they were undressing me with their eyes," she said. "They were wild. Wild." Now the mob was behind us, catcalling, shouting insults, obscenity, and blasphemy.

We were in open space at the railroad tracks. The jeering roared behind us, a cataract of sound. Hunter marched in front of Eugenia, his large, schoolmasterish shape hulking between her and Philip Drodge. There were two tracks here. Philip Drodge crossed the first with Hunter right behind. Our feet crunched in the gravel, and I saw Hunter lower his hand. Ahead of us the guardsmen waited, Springfields at the ready. They sweated in their heavy uniforms. *They are afraid. Something is loose in front of them; they are face to face with rage, and every one of them knows that he can die.*

We were at the first track now, and Philip Drodge was over the second.

The investigations later on turned up a practical joke. A string of Chinese firecrackers shot from a child's slingshot, intended to fall at the feet of the guardsmen just as we crossed over. The firecrackers arched up from the yelling behind us, and overhead they exploded in a staccato series of loud pops.

I feel certain to this day that an instant before the first firecracker exploded, I heard Guy shout at the back of my neck, "*A terre!* Get down!" I flung Eugenia to the ground between the rails as a volley of gunfire crashed from the troopers. It sounded like a single roar, dwindling to irregular firing. Bullets sizzled overhead. Eugenia lay under me, face down, without a sound. I held my arms around her and kept my head down on her body, and I smelled soap and felt her feminine softness, one of her breasts against my hand, and the pain in my ribs nearly blinded me. "Stay down," I shouted in her ear. "Stay down." My ribs were on fire.

I smelled gunpowder. After the shooting, I heard screaming—the tortured, wild shrieking of men hit in the vitals by high-velocity bullets.

Men ran by. More shots. People were shouting, and I heard the crunch of running boots in the gravel of the roadbed. The screaming went on and on. I stood up slowly and looked around. At first I thought the trampled vacant lot where the men had stood was empty. Then I saw bodies lying among the weeds and on the macadam road. Philip Drodge rose unsteadily to his hands and knees. I thought he was wounded, but he was all right. His face looked like death. His blue suit was a mess, and a bare knee showed through a tear in the trousers. "What happened?" he said. "What happened?"

A bloody shape lay face down over the track nearer the gate. It was

Hunter. I turned him over. His face had been shot away, and his chest was crushed. His suit was soggy with blood. I could not have recognized him except for his clothes. His bowler hat lay a few feet away.

Eugenia stood up and looked around. The tears ran in streaks down her dusty face, but she did not sob. She picked up her notebook and slowly and carefully straightened the pages. "This is my story," she said. "And I am going to write it."

118

FOUR PEOPLE besides Hunter were dead. In the trampled grass of the vacant lot, DeShane Dugan was sitting up, shot in the stomach. He lived maybe a half hour, watching in speechless bafflement his gray guts spill out with his bright red blood. I kneeled beside him. He tried to talk. I put my ears to his lips, but I could not understand. He had no breath for even a whisper. I held him until he laid his head over on my shoulder and died.

Three others died that night. I heard that two of them had helped hang M.P. Somehow their death was not vengeance. Altogether, twelve men were wounded. A six-year-old boy was shot in the arm. A trooper, apparently drunk, tripped over the railroad tracks and smashed his face. He was the only casualty in the National Guard.

Dr. Youngblood arrived in minutes. He had heard the shooting, and he knew what it was. Screaming women searched for their husbands. Some found them dead, some almost dead. Everything was shouting and confusion—except Dr. Youngblood and Eugenia. She walked around, clear-eyed and calm, talking to people, taking notes. Her hair had fallen, and a broad stain of blood besmirched her dress. I supposed it was Hunter's blood.

She was the first to write about the firecrackers. Her story got a banner headline on the front page of her paper, and I have it here. Philip Drodge looked bereft. He stared at DeShane Dugan's guts and threw up.

A violent summer storm broke about the time DeShane Dugan died. His blood ran into my clothes. Dr. Youngblood made his way around in the downpour, seeing that the dead and the wounded were picked up. He commanded Dr. Bulkely to come to help. Pinkerton came out almost unnoticed to stand with folded arms amid a circle of troopers. When we saw him, the rain was pounding down, and the sky was black.

"You are responsible for this," Philip Drodge shouted at him. "The blood of these men is on your head." The rain soaked his hair and poured down his face.

"I didn't make them strike," Pinkerton said in a flat calm. "If you play with fire, you will get burned. I am responsible for saving railroad property from the mob! I am the star of this picture show. Don't you forget it." He lifted his chin as if waiting for his picture to be taken. Women cursed him, and troopers held rifles horizontal to block the crowd. I thought they would happily shoot again.

The rain thickened; Pinkerton went back to his office with his Praetorian guard. When the dead and wounded had been picked up, Philip Drodge and I went to the makeshift hospital and morgue in the courthouse. The wounded were laid out on the floor in front of the judge's high bench. Dr. Youngblood's nurse, Miss Jane, was everywhere, bringing in medical supplies and bossing some men she had commandeered to help her. Dr. Bulkely's nurse was taking orders from Miss Jane. The rain flagellated Bourbonville. People came and went, and the wounded groaned, and their women and children cried, more subdued now, and Dr. Youngblood and Dr. Bulkely toiled at saving lives and limbs. Philip Drodge and I helped as best we could; we were all bloody. Eugenia Curry came after us, getting her story. In an hour she hitched a ride back to Knoxville to meet her deadline. She thanked me. "You saved my life," she said. "I am very grateful. I'll get my car later."

I wanted to fold her in my arms and kiss her and cry. I did not. I hurt everywhere, but it did not matter.

The storm blew away at evening, and a dripping twilight hung over the town. "We have to go see Pinkerton," Philip Drodge said.

"Why?" I said.

"We have to get these troops out of here; if the troops stay, somebody else will be killed."

"Yes," I said. "But it is useless to argue with Pinkerton."

"Come along," he said.

My legs felt like cement, and my chest burned, and the tape wrapped around my ribs added to my misery, but I went with him. Water ran in drains and in gullies and gutters and fell pattering off the trees. The air smelled of rain, and a faint mist rose from the streets. We stood for a moment watching a squad of troopers parade down Broadway towards the car works. A sergeant was calling out a cheerful cadence. Their feet sloshed in the water.

"Look at the bastards," Philip Drodge murmured. "You get a taste for blood, and it tastes good. Especially when nobody shoots back."

The town was under curfew. Philip Drodge had to ask permission of a sergeant, who had to get it from Major Doane, who sent us a written pass. That took an hour, and by the time we got down to the car works, it was fully dark.

We were escorted by a squad, rifles at the ready and bayonets fixed. "We showed the assholes," one of them said. "I'd like to do it again," another one of them said. "What about you, Jew?" one of them said to me. "You want me to circumcise you again?" Much laughter.

"I'm not a Jew," I said.

"You look like a fucking Jew to me," the guardsman said.

"If you were my men, I'd have you court-martialed and shot," Philip Drodge said.

"Well, we ain't your men, are we, shithead?" It was an unrewarding conversation.

Two shabby troopers stood guard in front of the main office, and in the grassy oval a machine gun was set up behind sandbags. Many guardsmen were drinking, making no effort to hide the bottles. They had built fires to dry themselves, and firelight gleamed on tilting glass.

Pinkerton stood in the side door, legs wide apart and his arms folded, the light behind him throwing his body into a silhouette. His suit was rumpled and his necktie loose, and he was smoking a cigar, his entire appearance studied, rehearsed. Dale Farmer had gone home, exhausted.

"You look like shit," Pinkerton said. "What's the railroad going to say when it finds its officers walking around looking like a couple of bums?" He beckoned us inside with a sweeping gesture. "You stink, too," he said.

"We have been tending the wounded," Philip Drodge said.

Pinkerton sat down at his desk. It was heaped up with newspapers and telegrams. Philip Drodge and I stood across from him. Two guardsmen leaned against a wall. I could smell their whiskey breath.

"You don't look like Florence Nightingale," Pinkerton said with a harsh laugh. "You know, when I was in the hospital, I wanted to run my hand up the nurses' asses. I've repented now. God saved me from that kind of thing."

"You and God are friends now, I take it," Philip Drodge said.

"God is right here in this room with us, gentlemen. I'm sorry you can't feel him. I feel him here as much as I see you. I feel him the way Joshua felt him when the walls of Jericho fell down." Pinkerton's voice was level.

"Funny," Philip Drodge said, "all I can see is a crazy fool with the blood of innocent men on his head and a couple of drunk boobs wearing uniforms and holding guns."

"Hey!" one of the guardsmen said angrily. He made a threatening motion towards us.

"Shut up. I'm in command here," Pinkerton said. He turned back to Philip Drodge. "You're trying to shame me," he said. "But I'm proud of myself, and the railroad ought to be proud of me, too. Get that into your head, son."

"You are a murderer," Philip Drodge said.

"I thought you were in the army," Pinkerton said. "Didn't you never see men killed? . . . Have a cigar?" He picked up his humidor and held it out to us.

Philip Drodge waved it away. "Five men are dead. Three more may die. A child's been shot. He may lose his arm. Do you know what you've done?"

"Do you care for a cigar, Alexander?"

"No," I said.

"Haven't seen you in a while," he said with a wink, as if we shared a secret.

"No," I said.

"You ought to have a cigar, young man," Pinkerton said to Philip Drodge. "It'll calm you down."

"I don't want a cigar, goddammit," Philip Drodge said. "I asked you a question. Do you know what you've done?"

"I used to cuss," Pinkerton said evenly. "It made me feel like a man. God saved me from that. I don't cuss now. Maybe you'll find God sometime yourself, young man."

"Don't call me 'young man,' " Philip Drodge said. "I am your superior. You will give me some respect."

"Vanity of vanities," Pinkerton said with a shrug. "You shouldn't want anything on earth but to please God and do your duty." I looked to see if there might be a glint of madness in Pinkerton's eyes, but he seemed calmer, younger, more in charge of himself than I had ever seen him before.

"Goddammit, I want to talk about those murders this afternoon! I do not want to talk about your crackpot religion. Don't you know what you've done?"

"I know what *they* done," Pinkerton said mildly. "They listened to agitators. They went out on strike. They tried to destroy railroad property. Property is sacred in this country. It was sacred in Russia, but people doubted, and the Bolsheviks shot them. I don't doubt anything, young man. I know what's right and I act on it. You ought to give me a medal."

"A medal," Philip Drodge said.

"If the tsar had had me in charge of his army, he'd still be smoking cigars and ruling his people, and Russia would still be a Christian country. God told *his* people to slay the Amalekites. We don't have Amalekites, but the Bolsheviks are the next best thing. Maybe you're too squeamish to be a Christian."

"God," Philip Drodge said, shutting his eyes.

"I am God's servant," Pinkerton said with a soft laugh. His calm was unnerving. When most people in Tennessee said such things, they spoke in an unctuous tone of false humility. Pinkerton spoke in a matter-of-fact voice as if he had said, "The train is due at two o'clock."

"Five men dead," Philip Drodge said. "More who may die. They were unarmed."

"Don't kid yourself about the arms," Pinkerton said in the same unemotional tone. "There was guns in that crowd. The folks that ran away carried off the guns of the ones we shot. Oldest trick in the world."

Philip Drodge was almost beside himself. "You're saying those men deserved to die."

"It's like shooting a burglar in your house."

"George Hunter deserved to die?" Philip Drodge said.

"I don't know who George Hunter is," Pinkerton said.

"He was a good man, a family man. He was one of our men in Knoxville. Director of Operations. He was shot down out there. He's dead. I have to tell his wife that her husband is dead."

"Now I remember Hunter. He looked down on me—just like you. Well, I'm sorry, I guess," Pinkerton said with another shrug. "If you're at the front, you can get killed. That's the way war is. Lots of cooks get killed in war. A shell comes along, and bang, they're as dead as beefsteak."

"This is not war," Philip Drodge said. "This was a massacre. It had nothing to do with war. Nothing!"

"You haven't read about the Wobblies and the anarchists," Pinkerton said. "Their revolution is not over. Revolution is like a snake. If you don't cut it in two, it comes back to life at sundown. I crushed its head here in Bourbonville, but somebody will have to kill it somewheres else or we're all dead men. Better them than us, I say. That's what you don't understand."

"You don't have any feeling for those men at all," Philip Drodge said.

"Don't sound so shocked, buddy boy. Nobody had any feeling for me. They wanted to kill me. You think I didn't hear them men out there? You think I'm deaf? That's the law of nature, Mr. Drodge, played out this very afternoon. Kill or be killed. You can't change it and I can't change it. It's God's way."

"The law of nature. You call it the law of nature."

"It won't change until Jesus comes again and brings in the millennium," Pinkerton said. "Then the lion shall lay down by the lamb. But this ain't the millennium now. Not yet."

"George Hunter was murdered by these men," Philip Drodge said, pointing towards the guardsmen in the room with us. One of them laughed.

"Look at it this way," Pinkerton said in an explanatory tone. "Three of you survived. That's pretty good after a dumb trick like you pulled. You should have called me up, told me to send a squad out to bring you in under a flag of truce. Instead you walked into no-man's-land like a feeble-minded fool. You ought to thank God, I say, and ask what he's got for you to do in life."

"You're through," Philip Drodge said. "You're a madman, and you're through with the railroad. I'll have your scalp hung up to dry before the week's out."

"That's going to set real good with the governor of this state," Pinkerton said. He shook off the ash of his cigar into an ashtray and looked pleased. "He just sent me a telegram congratulating me for standing up to the Bolsheviks. It's in the evening newspapers. I got telegrams congratulating me from all over the state, all over the country. I'm a hero, Mr. Drodge. You go ahead and fire a hero and see whose scalp gets hung out to dry. This one's from the governor."

Philip Drodge was speechless. Pinkerton handed him a telegram. Philip Drodge read it, read it again, and handed it to me. The governor said he was going to make Major Doane and Pinkerton Tennessee colonels to honor them for standing up to the strikers.

An electric floor lamp burned behind Pinkerton's leather chair. His face was in shadow, and he looked uncanny. "See?" he said. "This is my command post. I'm going to sit right here till I break the back of everybody who gets in my way, and I'm going to be in charge. You can take your hat, Mr. Drodge, and go shit in it, and you can wear it to a wedding in July." The guardsmen laughed. I do not believe that Pinkerton thought he was being obscene.

"Get better soon," Pinkerton told me. "I need you back to work. I have plans for you, son." I could not look at him, and I could not speak. I was exhausted. We retreated, our escort walking us up through crowds of troops on the grounds of the car works. Most of them were drunk. "Guess he told you assholes what you need to hear," a guardsman said. His speech was slurred.

"It's not over yet," Philip Drodge said doggedly. His voice trembled.

"Good," the guardsman said. "I'd like to have another shot at them bastards." He laughed.

A damp haze hung over the town. The world dripped. The troops had cook fires burning, and they made a party of the evening, calling to each other, shouting, laughing.

At the gate were more troopers, all carousing. Our escort stopped at the railroad tracks. "You assholes can go on from here by yourselves," a sergeant said.

"We are supposed to have an escort," Philip Drodge said.

"You had it," the sergeant said. "Now get lost."

Philip Drodge trembled with rage. We walked down empty Broadway in silence. "He's right, you know. We can't do a thing. We can't do a bloody thing."

My ribs burned, and it was hard to breathe. To one side I saw Guy. He was a blurred figure in the misty evening. He waved. Suddenly I felt a terrific happiness. Guy was my loyal friend. He had warned me. If it had not been for him, I would have been killed. Eugenia would have died with Hunter. Guy saved us both. He was not angry with me because I had lived and he had died.

"Look here," Philip Drodge said softly. He stopped under a street lamp and held his coat up. There was a bullet hole just under the arm. "Ruined my coat, but it didn't hit me," he said with a wry laugh. "I'll never know why I wasn't killed."

"Destiny," I said.

"Destiny," Philip Drodge said. "Fate, you mean."

"Yes," I said.

"Poor Hunter," Philip Drodge said. "I hate to see his wife. He told me this morning he felt lucky because he had been too old to go to the war. He said he knew that if he had gone to the war, he would have been killed."

We walked in silence. "You were quick," he said. "You saved the woman's life."

"Maybe not," I said. Guy vanished.

"What are you staring at?"

"I thought I saw something over there," I said.

"This place gives me the creeps," Philip Drodge said. "If Hunter had been in the war, he would have known to get on the ground when the shooting started. I did it without thinking."

"So did I," I said, lying. Guy had saved my life. I knew that Guy had saved my life.

"I want to look in on the wounded again," Philip Drodge said. "I want to speak to them. I have to speak to the wives of the dead." He shook his head. "I don't know what to tell them."

Hunter's car was parked where we had left it in the afternoon. No one had thought to move it. It had a bullet hole through the door, and the windshield was broken. The guardsmen had still been shooting when they ran across the railroad in pursuit of men fleeing for their lives; that is the only way to explain the damage to Hunter's car. I looked at it and felt sick at heart.

Dr. Youngblood scarcely glanced at us as we entered the makeshift hospital. The wounded men now lay in cots and on mats placed on the floor in the open space before the bench where the judge customarily sat and in front of the empty jury box. Wives and children camped out on the benches of the courtroom itself. The tall windows were open onto the rainy night. I smelled iodine and blood—smells from the war—and the smell of the fresh-washed town drifting in from the outside. Some men were groaning. Dr. Bulkely was working over an unconscious form. He looked dazed. Miss Jane was speaking to him in a low voice. Dr. Youngblood's eyes were sunk into his head, and he staggered from fatigue. Philip Drodge and I talked to the wounded who could talk. They held our hands for a moment. There was nothing else for us to do.

"I ought to find someplace to spend the night. The hotel's filled up," Philip Drodge said. "My suitcase is down at the depot. Maybe I can sleep on the floor there."

"It's four miles to the Ledbetters'," I said. "We could go up to the boardinghouse, but I think that would be difficult tonight." I was thinking of DeShane Dugan. Darcy Coolidge would be stricken with grief.

"Four miles," Philip Drodge said with a bitter laugh. "Well, why not. Can you help me carry my suitcase?"

"Sure," I said, thinking of my ribs but thinking also, aloud, "What the hell."

"Sometimes you begin to sound American," Philip Drodge said with a grin, the first time he had grinned in hours.

"I have been here almost three years now," I said.

"Doesn't time pass fast?" he said.

We did not have to walk. We were crossing the square towards the depot when Jim Ed pulled up in his car.

"Caleb's out at the house. He's told us all about it," Jim Ed said. "Lord God, it's pretty awful, I reckon. I figured you boys might need a ride. Too bad about Mr. Hunter. I'm glad you're all right."

"I've never been so glad to see anybody in my life," Philip Drodge said. "I'm bushed. Really bushed and soaking wet. I don't think I could have walked out to your place. I think I would have died on the way."

"You can stay the night with us. You may have to sleep with Caleb."

"Who is Caleb?" Philip Drodge said.

"He is my half-brother," Jim Ed said. "My mamma was married before she married Daddy. Her first husband died."

"Too bad," Philip Drodge said.

"No, it ain't too bad," Jim Ed said easily. "If her first husband hadn't died, I'd never have been born."

"This Caleb, he was at the . . . the shooting?" Philip Drodge said.

"Caleb's always around when somebody dies," Jim Ed said. "He's an undertaker. He's got a knack for death."

Our clothes stank of blood and rain. The night air in the open car was cool and sweet. We drove in silence for a time. A soaking land went by in a gray-black blur. "Tell you something funny about Caleb," Jim Ed said at last. "He was cold sober. He and Daddy and Mamma sat there at the table, and Caleb said he never was going to take a drink again as long as he lived."

"He drinks, does he?" Philip Drodge said as though trying to be polite.

"Like a drainpipe," Jim Ed said.

Philip Drodge laughed. "It's going to be harder to drink like that with prohibition."

Jim Ed mused over the wheel. "I've heard drunks say they weren't going to drink anymore," Jim Ed said. "They feel so good about quitting that they take a drink to celebrate."

"It's a terrible affliction," Philip Drodge said.

"Caleb looked like he meant it," Jim Ed said. "I never seen Caleb look like that before. Caleb cold sober—it's almost scary."

I thought of Pinkerton cold sober, but I was bone tired, and the pain in my chest now dulled so that I dozed and fell into an almost narcotic sleep sitting up in the car with the wind blowing around me. I scarcely realized that we had arrived at the farm, that the old man and Mrs. Ledbetter were waiting up for us, and that Caleb had gone. The conversation eddied around me, and I floated in it, inert. I went to my room upstairs and took off my clothes and barely had time to hang them over a chair when I eased myself into bed naked and went sound asleep.

I was in the deepest slumber far in the night when the pounding on the door came. In my dream Palmyre and I were sitting in a meadow somewhere, perhaps on the day she agreed to marry me, and I was trying to talk to her, but the thunderous knocking in the sky kept me from hearing what she had to say. I came out of sleep like a man ascending to the surface of water after a deep dive, and I heard the dogs barking, and I heard shouting, and I heard someone saying that Caleb had killed Pinkerton, and when I got to the kitchen, Mrs. Ledbetter and the old man and Jim Ed and a baffled Philip Drodge were already standing by the cold wood stove, eyes blank with sleep, and two men I recognized as guitar-playing friends of Jim Ed's were there, caps in hand, with solemn faces, saying that the National Guard had shot Caleb to death.

119

PINKERTON AND CALEB were dead, Pinkerton's body slumped across the desk, his eyes wide open, Dr. Youngblood said. He fell on his pile of telegrams and newspapers, and the blood soaked through them. Caleb lay face down in front of the desk, Hub Delaney's old navy revolver on the floor beside him. Dr. Youngblood said he had been shot twelve times. *Come, Furies, dance!*

Caleb's car was parked near the riverbank a mile or so above the car works. He had paddled a skiff downstream where decades ago a young Moreland Pinkerton had drained the swamp from which the car works rose in that mythical summer of glory. He pulled the skiff ashore, and his tracks led up the bank. He came through the back of the grounds and found his way around the steel foundry and to the main office. His shoes, always polished, were caked with mud when Dr. Youngblood got to him.

Caleb wore the black sealskin coat he had worn the first time I saw him.

It was bloody and bullet-ridden, ruined forever. "It made him blend in with the dark," Dr. Youngblood said. It was a beautiful coat. I thought of Eleutheria crying out when we heard what my father had done, ruining his own coat with a pistol.

The guardsmen were drunk. Caleb walked by them. Major Doane was as drunk as the rest. It was morning before he could collect himself enough to telegraph the governor. By ten o'clock the governor had released a statement lauding Moreland Pinkerton as a fallen hero in the struggle against Bolshevism. Eugenia Curry brought it to us when she arrived on a train from Knoxville in mid-afternoon. Her story about the killings of the day before was on the front page of the *Guardian*. She was a "celebrity," as people would have said much later on. She came walking into Bessie May's cafe, where I was drinking coffee with Dr. Youngblood, waiting for Jim Ed and the old man to come from the mortuary.

"How is Mrs. Ledbetter taking all this?" she asked.

"She is calm," I said. "She is always calm."

"What do you think, Dr. Youngblood?" She turned to him. Dr. Youngblood turned red. "Ah me," he said. "Don't put anything about Mrs. Ledbetter in the paper."

"I won't say anything to hurt her," Eugenia said softly. "I won't tell any secrets. Not about her."

"Caleb was a grief to her," Dr. Youngblood said. "I guess she thinks he's at peace now. Caleb never got over Aaron."

"Who was Aaron?"

I heard the story again, Dr. Youngblood telling it, and suddenly I realized that he had left out the part where Brian Ledbetter and Mrs. Ledbetter had been at the funeral of a man named Clarence Jackson when Aaron died, and I broke in and told that part of the story, and Eugenia looked at me with a half-smile and said, "I never would have expected you to know about this place." Dr. Youngblood grinned, and I saw Guy standing by the door looking at me.

Dr. Youngblood finished the story—a chapter in the common property and epic and sacred text of Bourbon County, its mythology and its history, and for a moment we sat in silence. Bessie May said, "May he rest in peace, poor man. He was the troubledest man I ever knowed. May he rest in peace." I unconsciously crossed myself.

Eugenia Curry saw that I had crossed myself, and she looked at me, a glimmer of curiosity and perhaps amusement. "I won't write about Aaron," she said.

"No," Dr. Youngblood said.

"I have to go out and get my car," she said.

"Yes," Dr. Youngblood said.

I heard the regulator clock ticking on the wall behind the counter. Bessie

May delivered a long, wrenching sob. There were not many people in the cafe; it was muggy hot, and everybody wanted to be in the square, telling the story and hearing it again as often as possible. Everybody wanted to have every detail, every inflection, every scrap of understanding to be wrung from every word. I sat at the counter, sweating, aching, wiping my face from time to time with a handkerchief, and I thought, "I understand this; I know why Caleb did it."

"The governor is responsible for everything," Dr. Youngblood said.

"Curtis, honey, why don't you go over to Nashville and operate on that man's tongue?" Bessie May Hancock said.

"Should I cut it out or sew it to the bottom of his mouth?" Dr. Youngblood said with a slow grin.

"Neither one," Bessie May said. "You should sew it onto a horse's behind and whip the horse."

We all laughed—the only time I laughed that month.

Dr. Youngblood told Eugenia about the drunken guardsmen. He did not tell her that Caleb had left a note folded in an envelope and addressed to Brian Ledbetter. "Maybe this will make up for Aaron," he said. The old man and Jim Ed were at the mortuary waiting for Caleb's people to fix the body. Mrs. Ledbetter sat at home surrounded by the women of Bourbon County bearing more food than any ten families could eat. The libation bearers, I thought, bringing food to appease the furies. Dr. Youngblood looked ready to fall down from fatigue.

The next day Eugenia's second story in as many days ran on page one. She was the only reporter who said that the guardsmen were drunk. Major Doane angrily denied the charge. But since he was drunk when he stood before reporters to attack Eugenia, her credit soared, and for the first time the papers condemned the guardsmen and Major Doane—not for killing people but for not killing Caleb before he got to Pinkerton. A reporter from the *Chattanooga Times* wrote a story about Eugenia. I have it here, with her photograph, a face turned towards the camera looking uncomfortable, almost irritated at the intrusion of a lens, but a beautiful face, frank and open.

120

THE TOWN CELEBRATED Major Doane's sudden disgrace. "If we were in war, and this was the regular army," the governor said, "I'd see to it that Major Doane was shot at dawn. The man is a booby, unworthy to wear the uniform of the United States." Everybody forgot that he had promised to make Major Doane a Tennessee colonel.

Caleb's assistants, industrious to the end, managed to collect the body of their employer and the body of Pinkerton as well as three bodies of strikers. "It sure would have made Mr. Weaver proud if he could see what we've done for the business," one of them said. Pinkerton was buried first; Caleb had to wait for Virgil and Daisy.

Major Doane, blinking in the soft lights of the mortuary, rubbing his blood-red eyes, came to view Pinkerton's corpse in the mandatory ritual of the funeral in Eastern Tennessee. A crowd gathered outside and jeered him and would not let him depart. He retreated inside and vomited on the rug. Caleb's people rushed to clean it up, and Major Doane sat on a flimsy wooden folding chair, looking pale and sick. Armed troopers came to rescue him. The crowd jeered the guardsmen, and hostility hung in the air like the burned reek of an extinguished fire.

Pinkerton was buried two days after he died. In his coffin at the mortuary on the night before his funeral he looked waxy and unreal. Dale Farmer and I stood looking down at him, and Dale Farmer sobbed. Darcy Coolidge came. She looked a long time at the corpse and once ran her hand over his forehead. "He is so cold," she said. "Poor man." She did not cry. Dale Farmer's tears were the only ones I saw. I looked at the corpse and thought of M.P. and imagined an afterworld in which they met each other, and M.P. had all eternity to take revenge. But then I thought that in eternity everything here would be reduced to insignificance, and I thought of the indifference of all the victims of history in the presence of those who had persecuted them, tortured them, and killed them. I could never be indifferent; my thoughts confirmed my view that there was nothing after death, and I saw Guy and Bernal standing in the shadows looking at me without expression.

Ted Devlin came. "I want to be sure the bastard is dead," he whispered to me. Dr. Youngblood came. He stood looking at Pinkerton's corpse. "Ah me," he said, and went away. Philip Drodge, dressed in a navy blue suit that he nervously thought inappropriate because a funeral required black, greeted people, accompanying them to the open coffin as if he were a stoically grieving relative. Reporters came. Nobody else came to the mortuary, not even Pinkerton's wife. The only flowers there were on a wreath contributed by Philip Drodge on behalf of the railroad.

The funeral was a graveyard service in Caleb's cemetery on the edge of town. The guardsmen turned out in shabby ranks, armed with rifles. They looked bleak and hung over. A handful of people from the county came to see Pinkerton off to eternity. People said, "I can't believe the man is dead," but everybody did believe it. Sealed in his coffin, out of sight forever, Pinkerton was transformed into words about something that had happened a long time ago. We adjust quickly to the epochal moments in life and death. In memory the young man we see now has always been young, and the middle-aged man has always been middle-aged, and the sick man always sick, and the dead man always dead.

I met Eula Pinkerton at graveside. She was a thin, dark-haired woman with an eerily musical voice, in her fifties, skin as smooth as stones in a riverbed. She had tranquil, dark, deep-set eyes. "Mr. Alexander," she said with a restrained smile, putting out her hand. "My husband spoke so warmly of you. I am sorry we have not met before now." She seemed to sing her words on two or three notes, a warble of an exotic bird. "Contralto," I thought. I remembered Pinkerton's account of how he had seduced her. I took in the outline of her slender body beneath her black dress, and I tried to imagine her panting and lifting her buttocks so that Pinkerton could the more easily slide off her underwear. I knew things about her that I should not know, and I was embarrassed and could think of little to say. I tried to imagine her young, and failed.

She was the only member of Pinkerton's family left. She told me that he had a sister but that she had been dead for years, and of course his mother and father were long gone, as was the son buried in the Methodist graveyard where M.P. had died. I ended by sitting on one side of her in a row of folding chairs under an awning that Caleb's people had placed beside the open grave. Philip Drodge sat on the other, looking somber and dignified and without grief, though once in an obviously contrived gesture he removed a handkerchief from his pocket and dabbed at his eyes, which were as dry as pebbles. Dale Farmer sat next to me. He said scarcely a word. He sweated, and the armpits of his jacket turned dark.

Two ministers held the graveside service. The minister of the First Baptist Church, a pompous, gluttonous-looking man in a black suit, orated about Pinkerton's accomplishments and made him seem like a crusader who deserved to be buried in armor with a faithful dog lying at his feet. The other minister was a tall, lanky man, one of Eula Pinkerton's friends, and he invited all of us to take this opportunity to be washed in the blood of the Lamb. He went on a very long time about the millennium and the Great White Throne Judgment. The sun beat down on the awning overhead. The air was thick and humid. All the while he spoke, Eula Pinkerton bowed her head and prayed that God would bless his efforts, moving her lips and sometimes whimpering, "Do it, Lord. Do it." A guardsman fell back, rolled his eyes skyward, dropped his rifle, and fainted. I was looking at him when he fell. The tall preacher went on without faltering, caught up in his fantastic vision. Others attended to the fallen trooper; and he was helped away. The preacher raged on.

After the sermon the rest passed quickly. A bright American flag draped the coffin, and a national guardsman self-consciously folded it into a triangle and presented it to Eula Pinkerton in honor of Pinkerton's service in the Spanish-American War. She stood in ritual solemnity to accept the flag, smiled darkly, and sat down again, holding it like something forgotten, her face composed. She looked at the polished rosewood coffin without any emotion that I could see, drained, I thought, not so much by her husband's death as by the ecstatic ranting of the minister.

"I feel at peace about my husband," she said to me at the end, as I tried to make appropriate small talk. "He was ready to meet God; I know he is in heaven now."

The guardsmen fired a volley, and a bugler played "Taps." The notes were slow and mournful and seemed to take some palpable shape and fly across the river to be lost like birds in the mountains. I was moved in spite of myself. The guardsmen slunk away while people murmured blasphemies and obscenities at them. I could imagine them turning and firing on all of us.

Eugenia stood among the onlookers. Afterwards she stepped up to Eula Pinkerton and asked if they could talk later that day. Eula Pinkerton looked at her and smiled and asked if she had been washed in the blood of the Lamb. I saw Eugenia hesitate a moment, then nod her head. "I have, Mrs. Pinkerton. My mother brought me up to be a Christian girl." She glanced at me, and I saw her face redden.

"Then you may come," Eula Pinkerton said. She spoke in an unvarying serenity.

Philip Drodge and I drove Eula Pinkerton and her flag back down into the country where her house was, and I went inside for the first time and saw the Bibles and saw the photographic portrait of the Civil War soldier I had heard about. His eyes pinned me to the floor. I averted my face, and we left. We saw Eugenia's car coming towards us as we drove out of the driveway.

"That house has a lot of history, I bet," Philip Drodge said. "I like old houses. You can pretend they're haunted."

I said nothing. I looked behind and saw the dust from Eugenia's car flying up behind it as it went farther and farther from us.

Philip Drodge and I moved out of Brian Ledbetter's home. I went back to my room at the boardinghouse, tearfully welcomed by Darcy Coolidge. Philip Drodge took up temporary residence in DeShane Dugan's old room. DeShane was buried in the graveyard of the Varner's Cross Roads Baptist Church. He had many friends and a sister in Knoxville. She said she would come for his things. For the moment Philip Drodge lived amid DeShane's memorabilia—photographs of people none of us knew, seed catalogues, gardening magazines.

I wanted to stay with the Ledbetters. I felt at home there, our routines comfortable and secure. But I could not stay now that Virgil and Daisy were coming home and with all the grief Mrs. Ledbetter had suffered. I wanted Jim Ed to invite me to stay because I was one of the family. But I was not one of the family, and no one objected when we said we had to go back to Bourbonville. I missed waking up in the morning with the birds singing early and the smell of the farm coming in the open window. I missed Jim Ed and the old man and Mrs. Ledbetter. With Caleb dead, a silent distraction fell over her, and she seemed scarcely aware of the world around her. The old man comforted her with tenderness.

121

JIM ED SENT a telegram to Virgil and a cable to Gilly about Caleb's death. Gilly was in China. Of course he could not come. Virgil and Daisy came across the country by train. The trip took them four days. The men at the funeral home preserved Caleb in his refrigerator. They looked anxious. Would the business now imitate its clients and go under? It was the only time I ever saw morticians sincerely grieved about a death.

Virgil descended from the Pullman wearing a tailored navy blue suit with a vest and a gold watch chain. He had gained weight. He carried a walking stick and looked older, more aloof, hugging his mother mechanically and kissing her on the cheek while she clung to him. He and the old man awkwardly shook hands, the old man putting out a hand to Virgil's shoulder as if they might embrace, but they did not. Jim Ed grasped Virgil's coolly outstretched hand in both of his and wrung it heartily, and Virgil smiled at him, a distant, condescending smile. I like to think that Virgil had locked up his feelings because they were too much for him to bear, but Virgil remains a mystery to me. Whatever he had been that made Brian Ledbetter and Evelyn Ledbetter love him was hidden, perhaps gone forever, and I had never known it, never seen so much as a glimmer of it.

Daisy was astonishingly slender and radiant. Her face had matured. Her brown eyes were just light enough to seem luminous, and her skin was smooth and clear. When she saw me in the crowd at trainside, she threw herself into my arms and hugged me and told me how much she had missed me and how exciting California was and how she was making her way in the movies and how I should be there—all in a rush that somehow seemed as if she had been rehearsing for miles and that had no word of Caleb in it. "I am still going to marry you," she said, throwing her head back and looking up at me. "I have never given up." I smelled stale cigarette smoke and her perfume, delicate and expensive.

People stared at us. I laughed nervously.

"I never saw you laugh before," she said. She let me go and reached with a theatrical motion into her black leather purse and extracted a packet of Camel cigarettes and drew one out, offered me one, shrugged when I shook my head, and put her own into a silver cigarette holder that she stuck jauntily into her mouth. I realized she was posing for the crowd; I wondered what magazine had provided her ideal of glamour. Her hair was professionally done up. It was bobbed, as people said then—cut short around her head, curled at the sides and the back. The waist of her stylish straight dress hung on her hips. Preachers raged against bobbed hair.

Caleb's funeral was a grand affair at the little Methodist church where M.P. had died. The people of Bourbon County looked on Caleb as a martyr. They overflowed the church and thronged the grassy yard and the cemetery, respectfully silent, listening to what they could hear through the raised windows, and when the congregation sang, the people outside sang, too. Dr. Youngblood and I squeezed into the building. We stood against the wall in heat so heavy that I felt faint. Gladys sat with the family. Brian Ledbetter saw to that. She wept bitterly. Three preachers spoke. All of them extolled Caleb, announced God's forgiveness, assured the family that Caleb was not dead, that even now he was walking with the saints on the golden streets. Brian Ledbetter sat with his arm around his wife and his head bowed on the front row. She was solemnly silent. The flower-bedecked coffin stood beneath the pulpit. The family filled two pews. In the silences I heard Gladys weeping, but no one else cried.

Caleb was buried next to his father and Aaron. One of the preachers spoke at graveside, and Jim Ed played the guitar and sang, and people cried, and I saw Mrs. Ledbetter bow her head as if she could not look at the casket anymore. Eugenia Curry found me and stood beside me. She was wearing black, but she had her notebook, and sometimes she bent quickly over it with her pencil and wrote something down. Finally the preachers walked down the line, shaking hands with the family, and the crowd broke up in murmuring groups. A huge black place in the grass showed where the mob had burned M.P.'s car. The chestnut tree where he was hanged was dying.

"This is where the lynching was," Eugenia said.

"Yes," I said. "That tree."

"It must be terrible for you," she said.

"Yes," I said.

"Everything is so close in a community like this," she said.

"Yes," I said.

She smiled briefly at me and went to talk to the family. I saw Jim Ed speaking with solemn courtesy to her, bowing slightly, looking at her earnestly, nodding now and then at something she said and saying something back to her. I thought of M.P., and of Guy and Bernal and Stephanos, and I looked for them, but I saw nothing but subdued people searching for words.

The crowd lined up to shake hands with the family. When I got to Daisy, she threw her arms around me and pressed her face against my neck. I felt her tears. She squeezed me hard, let me go, and I walked on, my ribs aching. Her perfume lingered on my face. Brian Ledbetter's eyes were red. He said scarcely a word. He shook my hand and put his other lightly on my shoulder and took it away. For just a moment he looked at me, a searching, demanding look, asking some unknown question that I could not answer. Mrs. Ledbetter seemed scarcely aware that people were passing.

Dr. Youngblood and I drove back to town. "Daisy told me she's going to stay here awhile," Dr. Youngblood said after a long silence.

"She did?" I said.

"Virgil's going back to California right away. She doesn't have to go back. She's going to stay with Brian and Mrs. Ledbetter."

"I see," I said.

"I suppose we'll see a lot of her," he said. He smiled absently into the windshield with his thought.

Part Three

122

FOR A WEEK or ten days the guardsmen milled around Bourbonville, cursed and ridiculed, sometimes the target of eggs thrown from hidden places, and Philip Drodge negotiated in secret with the governor to get them removed. The threat of Bolshevism dissipated like steam with Pinkerton's death. Ted Devlin wrote editorials saying that Major Doane and his entire crowd of badly uniformed misfits and perverts ought to be tried for first-degree murder. The women of Bourbonville waved Ted's paper at the guardsmen and called them names. The frenzy that had brought the guardsmen to town seemed foolish, like the recollection of the rites of Dionysos once they were over.

Finally the governor sent a special train in the middle of the night, and on Sunday morning the guardsmen were gone. It was said that the guardsmen wanted to burn Bourbonville to the ground before they left. It was also said on good authority that the guardsmen were told by many Bourbonvillians that they would be recognized if they should ever return in mufti and that any of them caught would be summarily castrated. These expressions were voiced with considerable sincerity. For a long time the rumor floated that a former guardsman had been found dead of a heart attack in a railway car when he looked out the window and saw that he was in Bourbonville. It was the sort of rumor that located severed thumbs in the bottom of soft-drink bottles and children baled up in hay, never proven but told with gusto and conviction by someone who had known an eyewitness.

With Pinkerton dead, we could get the car works operating again, and Philip Drodge and I were toiling at that by the day of Pinkerton's funeral, taking time off to do our polite duty to the fallen leader before getting back on the job. We passed the word to the white men, and within two or three days most of them came back, walking through the gates under the hollow eyes of guardsmen who now offered no resistance. The men had not been paid for a very long time, and they were getting hungry.

The blacks were another affair. Philip Drodge and I went down to Bucktown. I had credit with the blacks for reasons that make me ashamed. I had been M.P.'s friend. Through no volition of my own I had nearly died with him. The black people told one another that I had been willing to sacrifice my life for M.P. I never explained how it was, because it was all too complicated and too painful, and I am not sure how it was. "We would often be ashamed of our most celebrated acts if the world could know the motives that produced them." I think I quote La Rochefoucauld.

Even so, it took days of talking and listening to wrath and mockery. We had an immeasurable ally: the blacks were getting hungry, too, although M.P. was right. The long experience of their race had taught them how to survive on little or nothing. Finally they came in a group marching up the railroad tracks looking grim and quiet and angry, some of them carrying small pistols in their pockets; and in two weeks everything was running again.

Nothing had been truly settled. Nothing could be settled. The blacks and the whites scarcely spoke to each other. They did their work side by side in silence or in grunts and monosyllables. You could feel the smoldering fire. The white men said the colored men were "uppity." The colored men said nothing at all about the white men, but there were days when I thought it was all going to happen again and that this time white men and black men would make the car works their battleground and kill each other to the last living human being. For the moment there was peace—the burned-out peace of exhaustion. I thought every day that it was only war delayed. That was Pinkerton's legacy.

I visit Pinkerton's grave even now and wonder if his soul is floating in heaven or hell or maybe just in space. His ghost never haunted me as I feared it might. I wondered if he was at rest; or did he look down at the world and fret because things had gone wrong? Was he forever what he was in the moment of his death, a man abruptly, incredibly aware that it was finished, that there was no more, that a man in a black coat like Satan's skin stood over him with a pistol to kill him? I supposed that he was none of these things, that he was nothing at all. Earth to earth, ashes to ashes, dust to dust, nothing left.

Guy said that you had to sympathize with Macbeth because the man had a conscience and a natural ambition and that if it had not been for Lady Macbeth and the witches, he might have lived out his days in honor. It was a near thing, Guy said. One small shaking of the chain of events here or there, and we might see Macbeth as a hero, perhaps a tragic hero like Brutus, but a hero nevertheless, standing against his wife and evil and preserving Duncan's life. It was a near thing for all of us, Guy said. He fell into that mood when he considered himself, his sexual adventures, his lack of purpose, his idleness. Given a chance, he might have been king of Scotland.

When I think of Pinkerton, I see that he was like Macbeth, evil in the effect he had on people, his madness the extremity of sane conspiracy. But I also think that had there been the slight swerve that the Epicureans talked about, some minute variation in the accidental course of his life, his fate might have been different. He might have become noble, and there might be a statue of him in Bourbonville, or at least a billboard at the city limits:

BOURBONVILLE, TENNESSEE
WHERE
MORELAND J. PINKERTON
GOT HIS START

Maybe his photographic portrait would be on the billboard, and perhaps he would be buried in a Washington cemetery with a granite monument, a carven Pinkerton standing erect and full of dignity, holding a stone hat in his stone hand, granite feet wide apart, face uplifted in the heroic pose of the eternally questing human spirit. In his other hand he might have held a cigar. He would finally have been forgotten, as he has been here in Bourbon County; but oblivion might have been postponed, and in life he might have created for himself an illusion of immortal fame.

Who can tell?

Philip Drodge stayed three weeks. When he went back to Washington, he looked older. It is hard to define what looking older means—a toughening of the grain of the skin, a deepening of lines, something happening to the way the eyes are set in a skull. Philip Drodge looked different; I suppose I was different, too.

We sat in the main office on the evening before his departure. "You're going to be in charge here until further notice," he said abruptly.

"Me!" I was surprised.

"Of course," he said. "Who else is there?"

"Dale Farmer thinks he should be in charge," I said.

Philip Drodge uttered a derisory laugh. "No," he said. "You will be in charge."

I shrugged. Out beyond the walls of the flimsy frame house the silence of the car works brooded, and I wondered if Pinkerton's ghost wandered there, triumphant because he had made a prophecy that had come true if only for a little while. I was in charge. I had taken his place. He had had his way.

123

VIRGIL TOOK the train back to California. I did not see him off. Jim Ed did. Daisy said they stood uncomfortably with each other as the train pulled in and that as Virgil started to climb aboard, Jim Ed threw his arms around him and said, "Virgil, I love you." Virgil embraced his half-brother clumsily, said something indistinct and embarrassed, and disappeared into the Pullman without looking back.

I was invited to supper frequently. I think Mrs. Ledbetter thought that Daisy loved me and that I would love her if I gave the thing a chance. In looking back, it all seems logical; and Mrs. Ledbetter took a coolly rational view of the world. She had made her mind up to marry Brian Ledbetter before he thought of such a thing, when he scarcely knew her. I suppose she made up her mind in a similar way to see to it that Daisy and I married.

These suppers were narcotic rituals that took our minds off Caleb. Daisy acted like the movie queen she yearned to be. She told stories—famous people she knew, admiring things people had said to her.

Her stories were diverting. She made herself the heroine of all of them. She played her role with such abandon and pleasure that we took pleasure in her. She had become beautiful; she was bright; and I supposed that people in Hollywood loved to be near her.

Daisy play-acted much of the time, and I never was certain what she felt about most things. She loved Brian Ledbetter and her grandmother. There was never any doubt about that. When you see someone genuinely love another human being and loved in return, you have to believe that there is something good about that person. I feel that way about Daisy to this day, no matter what else I may say about her. Mrs. Ledbetter came to life in her presence, asking questions, laughing, exclaiming at Daisy's sometimes outrageous comments. She never reproached her granddaughter—not even when Daisy smoked cigarettes.

Daisy asked questions. At dinner one night in response to one question after another, Mrs. Ledbetter and the old man told their versions of the story of their courtship, how Virgil had come to Brian to fetch him back to take Mrs. Ledbetter's cow to mate with Brian's bull. They both laughed heartily at the story, but there was a serious side to it. "I needed help in raising my children," Mrs. Ledbetter said. Her lip trembled. "And I'll say this for him—he give it to me." The old man reached over and stroked her shoulder briefly and looked at her, and she looked at him, and they quickly separated, as if they had been caught in some unbearably public intimacy.

When the dishes had been done and the kitchen was clean and straight, the old man asked Jim Ed and me to play, and the house filled with music. Daisy said marveling on the first night, "I did not know you could do that."

"This man can do lots of things you don't know about," Jim Ed said, boasting as if I had been something to be proud of. My heart warmed to him. We played magically together. He sang hymns, and I followed him, watching his fingers on the frets and feeling the sublime rise and fall of the songs as if the grand platonic form of music hung in the air around us.

I heard from many that when Mrs. Ledbetter was younger, her children small, before Aaron's death, her sharp tongue had been legendary in the county. She was known for her clear-minded honesty; she saw the world through a lucid air and knew, as people said, the difference between shit and fertilizer. When I knew her, she seemed to be a magic mirror for her husband, reflecting his temperament, his words, his stories in a softened screen, and as he peered into her, he became what he saw. I could not imagine them separated from one another; I could not think of the one without thinking of the other. In these pages Brian Ledbetter strides along on his wooden leg, ruling my story and at that time commanding something in my life that I could then scarcely realize. I loved him as I wanted to love my father, as I was obligated to love my father. I loved him without compulsion, without expectation of anything in return. I loved him because of who he was. Most of us are, in the end, the reflection of what we see of ourselves in others, but the reflections are broken, inconstant, like the wavelets in the bay that used to transfix poor Stephanos. For Brian Ledbetter, his only reflection was his wife; his love for her was so profound that everything else in his life passed through it. I suppose now that I wanted to see my reflection in him.

When Jim Ed sang his plaintive hymns, his mother's eyes shone in the lamplight, and she sat with her hands folded in her lap and looked at him in serene meditation. They were sentimental hymns that made death into a bridge of light over the great abyss of hopelessness yawning below. Jim Ed sang them, and I learned them by heart:

> *When we've been there ten thousand years*
> *Bright shining as the sun*
> *We'll have no less days*
> *To sing God's praise*
> *Than when we've first begun.*
>
> *Some glad morning when my life is o'er*
> *I'll fly away*
> *To a land on God's celestial shore;*
> *I'll fly away.*
> *I'll fly away, O glory*
> *I'll fly away;*
> *When I die, hallelujah, by and by*
> *I'll fly away.*

I do not believe that Jim Ed or his mother or the old man believed these sentiments. It was their unbelief that made the hymns so powerful. The hymns presented dreams of what they wished were true, and to sing them or hear them sung in Jim Ed's sharp tenor voice was to summon the memory of the dead, to construct a narcotic fantasy of song against death, and with the ecstatic power of the narcotic to endure the implacable understanding that death was once and forever. It is a paradox, I know: the songs gave us the power to disbelieve them. I think Mrs. Ledbetter made her peace with the piety of her own life in hearing one son sing of hope and glory for the sons who were dead. Jim Ed's voice trailed away; the fathomless dark of the insect-singing night absorbed it, we ceased playing, and the last wavering notes dissolved in silence, and we sat as if perched on the cliffs of eternity, watching time's narrow and shining river run far beneath us and disappear.

Always afterwards when Daisy drove me home through the dark to the boardinghouse, I could see the shadowy form of Stephanos in the distance, over the fields, and I knew that he was pleased with me. Daisy kissed me goodnight. She kissed me lightly on the cheek when Philip Drodge was along. In his absence, she was more serious. I became more serious, too.

Philip Drodge came out to the farm two or three times before he departed for Washington, and we played for him, and Jim Ed sang. He was excruciatingly polite, unmoved by the music, smoking a cigar with methodical care and looking on with the concentration of a medical person observing a rare physical deformity on a friend. On the last night he came, two days before he left Bourbonville, when Daisy dropped us both by the boardinghouse, we stood in the street long enough to smoke a cigarette and to contemplate the tranquil summer sky. He cleared his throat finally and said, "It's all right, I guess, if you play that kind of music down here. I mean, it's part of the great American folk tradition, I suppose. But I wouldn't do it in public, you know. The railroad, you know." He faltered and cleared his throat again.

"My uncle taught me how to play," I said.

"Well, you do it very well," he said. "Very well indeed. It isn't my taste, but taste is acquired, you know. It is not necessarily what we grow up with. Well, you understand what I mean."

"Oh yes," I said, scarcely caring what he said.

"I mean, you are my friend. A very good friend, I may add. I want to see you advance. You have a great future. And I wanted—*want* to say that in my circles . . . Well, I suppose I'm trying to say I can't imagine playing that thing at a Washington party."

"I promise I will never do that," I said.

"Of course not. Well, you know what I mean. Just a thought."

"Thank you," I said.

I remembered the night I dropped the antique bouzouki into the sea. I wondered if Stephanos knew my disgrace in the dark realm of the dead where he, like the mother of Odysseus, could never be embraced again. I felt shame pour through my soul, icy and implacable.

I had to work hard at the office after Philip Drodge had gone. There were a thousand things to do to catch up from all the car works had lost during the strike. Every morning I woke up thinking of what had to be done, knowing that I could not finish it all during the day. The work changed me. It was not that I experienced some emotional renovation, some surge of purpose or hope. It was simply that the work was there, details had to be taken care of, letters had to be written, orders sent to suppliers, and orders taken from the railroad in Washington. Work became my life, and in the incessant necessity of taking care of work, I had less time to brood about the past.

I managed to eat a couple of suppers a week with the Ledbetters, and I spent Sunday afternoons at the farm with Dr. Youngblood. "You are neglecting us," Guy said. "He is alive, and we are dead," Bernal said. I felt his reproach.

"It is not my fault," I said. "It is not my fault." Darcy Coolidge fussed because I did not take more meals at the boardinghouse. But I had suddenly, almost miraculously attained a new status—acting manager of the car works, charged with overseeing its operation and its work force—in Bourbonville and Bucktown. I was responsible for putting food in the mouths of children and coats on the backs of men and laundry soap and sliced bread in the pantries of women. The town's fortunes or misfortunes settled on me. If I wanted to go out at night and play the mandolin with my friend Jim Ed Ledbetter and take meals with the old man and his wife, no one could contradict me.

Darcy Coolidge assumed that I was spending my time at the farm because Daisy was there.

"I hope your intentions towards the young woman are honorable," she said. "I feel like a mother to you; I must look after your reputation. And the young woman's—hers, too. If you marry her, you don't want any hint of scandal attached. I blush to tell you this, Mr. Alexander, but I have known women who did scandalous things with men they later married, and the scandal followed them all their lives anyway. Look at poor Eula Pinkerton. My heart bleeds for that woman. Do you know the story?" She looked at me with anticipatory delight.

"Yes, Mr. Pinkerton told me all about it."

She sucked in her breath. "Well, *what* did he *say?*"

"I do not wish to discuss it," I said. "But I assure you, Mrs. Coolidge, I have no intentions at all towards Miss Weaver, honorable or dishonorable."

Darcy Coolidge looked miffed. "Well, that is what you *say*, but I have eyes, Mr. Alexander. I have my two eyes right here, and I know how to use them." She pointed at her eyes as if I might not have noticed them before.

I thought of Eugenia in a mood that came and went, as unpredictable as sunshine coming and going amongst flying clouds.

Sometimes, very late, we sat on the porch at the farm in the waning summer nights and smoked and looked out on the starry darkness, and I listened to Jim Ed and Daisy talk, Jim Ed slow, ruminative, and Daisy quick, eager to fill the silences. She did not like silence.

Why did Virgil not stay longer? The question vexed Jim Ed. "I think it's because he can't stand to come back to the home where he was raised, where he remembers his daddy," Daisy said. "His real daddy."

Jim Ed said, "Maybe it's because he doesn't like me."

Daisy said, "It is true. Daddy does not like you." Jim Ed was silent.

"I didn't mean to hurt your feelings," she said.

"It's all right," Jim Ed said.

"He never says anything bad about you. But he feels something. Jealousy maybe. I do not know what it is."

"I know what Virgil thinks," Jim Ed said in weary impatience. "You don't have to explain it to me."

"I am an honest woman," she said, looking superior, as if inflicting pain were a duty honest women must perform. "Don't ask questions if you don't want the answers. The world needs honesty. There are so many hypocrites around. California is full of hypocrites."

"He never liked me," Jim Ed said. "And he's blamed me for it all my life."

"Daddy is difficult," Daisy said, snuffing out one cigarette and with almost the same motion reaching for another. "I know because I live with him. I don't think he's ever liked me, either."

"He loves you," Jim Ed said. "You're loyal to him. He ought to be grateful."

"He thinks about D.B. all the time," Daisy said. "That's all he thinks about."

"He didn't mention D.B. once while he was here," Jim Ed said. "Not one time."

"He never speaks of him. That's how you know he's thinking about him," Daisy said.

"I feel sorry for him," Jim Ed said.

"You shouldn't bother," Daisy said with a dismissing laugh. "Daddy has made his own life. We didn't make it for him. Let's talk about something else."

"What would you like to talk about?" Jim Ed said.

"The movies," Daisy said. "Let's talk about the movies. Have you seen *A Romance of Happy Valley*?"

"A what?" Jim Ed said.

"*A Romance of Happy Valley*. It's a movie, and I'm in it—with Lillian Gish. I wrote you both about it."

"Lillian who?" Jim Ed said.

"You don't know who Lillian Gish is? Even after I wrote you?"

"No," Jim Ed said uneasily. "Well, I read your letters, Daisy, and I really love them. But sometimes when you get to talking about all those Hollywood people, one name just runs into the other. I'll get your letter out and look at it. Lillian Gish."

"Don't you go to the movies?" She sounded annoyed.

Jim Ed shrugged. "I've been a couple of times. We went to see *Birth of a Nation*, didn't we, Paul?"

"*Birth of a Nation.* That's *ancient.* You're hopeless, hopeless, hopeless. Paul, you should know. Lillian Gish is French. Or she *was* French. I *think* she was French. I wrote you about her, too. She was in *Birth of a Nation!*"

"She is an actor?" I said.

"An *actress.* She is a woman. A beautiful woman. And I am in the movie. It's a crowd scene, but you can tell it's me. Has it been here?"

"I do not know," I said.

"We've been kind of busy around here," Jim Ed said. "We haven't had too much time to go to the picture show."

"The really important things are going on in the movies," Daisy said. "Movies are changing the world."

"I've always liked to read, myself," Jim Ed said.

"Especially the *Knoxville Guardian?*" Daisy said.

"Yes, I like the *Guardian.* I don't want to get mixed up in the League of Nations like the *Guardian* wants us to do. But yes, it's a good paper."

"That woman works for the *Guardian,* doesn't she?"

"That woman?" Jim Ed said.

"Yes, that woman. Go ahead, pretend you don't know who I mean." Daisy laughed in a knowing, humorless way.

"I guess you mean Miss Curry."

"Yes, Miss Curry. The famous Eugenia Curry."

"Eugenia means 'well born,' " I said.

"Oh, I don't care what it means," Daisy said. "Who cares what a lot of old words mean! What does she look like? Is she pretty?"

"Well . . ." Jim Ed said. "What do you think, Paul?"

"She is very pretty," I said.

"What does that mean?" Daisy said.

"Well," Jim Ed said, "it means that she's blond. Not your real light-colored blond; not like straw. What would you say, Paul?"

"Like . . . Well, like tea."

"Yes, like tea," Jim Ed said.

"Tea? Hair the color of tea? You are struck on a girl whose hair looks as if it had been boiled in tea?"

"No," Jim Ed said, stumbling.

"You just said . . ."

"Like polished maple," Jim Ed said.

Daisy burst out laughing. "She has hair like a piece of *wood?*"

"Well . . ." Jim Ed said.

"Don't you have a picture of her?" Daisy said.

"No," Jim Ed said. "Why should I have a picture of her?"

"There was a picture of her in the paper," I said. I did not tell them that I had kept it.

"Clyde says you're going to marry her."

"Clyde doesn't know what he's talking about," Jim Ed said in a huff.

"You're blushing," Daisy said. "I can't see, but I can feel the heat."

"That's something if you can do that," Jim Ed said.

"There's nothing to be ashamed of," Daisy said. "It's time you got married. Everybody says so."

"You talk like I'm as old as Daddy. I'm thirty-four years old."

"There're lots of men who have been married three times by the time they're thirty-four."

Jim Ed laughed. "Well, she's a handsome woman. She's smart, too. She can write up a storm."

"Writing is passé," Daisy said. "In a few years we're going to be getting all our information out of the movies. But you can marry her anyway. You can support her when the movies put her out of a job."

"Why would a woman like that want to marry a man like me?" Jim Ed said, I thought in sincere frustration.

"My God," Daisy said. "Because you're a good catch. You're reliable. You're loyal. You work hard. You're even good-looking."

I thought of Eugenia, her reserve, her beauty, her intelligence, her uncontrived smile. I read what she wrote, and I admired it.

Jim Ed threw his cigarette over the porch railing. It fell in a flaming arc in front of us and vanished.

"I reckon things are going pretty well for you out there in California," Jim Ed said. "I mean, if you're in the movies and all."

"I want to be a star," Daisy said wistfully. "I know I have the looks, as long as I stay thin. I practice expressions in front of the mirror. Expressions are everything in the movies. Just watch the movies and see how much you feel when the actors and actresses have the right expressions. I go to the movies almost every day. I think they are the most exciting thing in the world. Have you seen Richard Barthelmess?"

"I don't think I know him," Jim Ed said.

"My God, Jim Ed! Of course you don't know him. He's a movie star. How could you meet Richard Barthelmess in Bourbon County! He was in *Broken Blossoms* with Lillian Gish, and I've had *dinner* with him."

"Was it good?" Jim Ed said.

"What?"

"The dinner."

"The . . ." Daisy snuffed out her cigarette. She fingered her pack and started to light another but thought better of it. "Do you have any idea how many women would sell their souls to have dinner with Richard Barthelmess?"

" 'Everybody to her own tastes,' said the woman as she kissed the cow," Jim Ed said.

Daisy laughed. "What does that mean?"

"Nothing," Jim Ed said. "Do you reckon Richard Fartymess can play the guitar, Paul?"

"Barthelmess," Daisy said.

124

A TELEGRAM summoned Daisy to Hollywood: another film. I was relieved.

She asked me to walk with her before supper on the last evening she was here. We went up the long driveway, her hand on my arm.

"Grandma thinks that we are going to be married," she said.

"Did you tell her that?" I said.

"I said I thought we would marry someday. I have always said that, you know. How do you feel?"

"All right," I said.

"I mean about getting married, silly."

"I do not want to get married now."

"I should stay here," she said. "If I stayed here, I could make you marry me soon. I would put you in such a compromising position that you would have to make me an honest woman."

"Please do not talk like that," I said.

"You are afraid to make decisions," she said. "You want other people to make all the decisions for you. I would decide that you had to marry me."

"You are returning to Hollywood. You do not want to stay here. I am here now."

"You won't be here long," she said. "You can't bear this place long. You'll be like Gilly, like everybody else with any sense. You'll leave as soon as you catch your breath and see what a boring little hell hole this is."

"As you did," I said.

"As I did. I'm going back to California because this may be my big chance. I'm as pretty as Lillian Gish, and I think my expressions are just as good. I'm sure I'm going to be a star. I feel it—so close." She stopped and shut her eyes and put her hands out, fingers up, reaching for something invisible. For a moment her face was still in blissful expectation. She opened her eyes as if snapping out of a spell, and she laughed. "Have you ever had feelings like that? That something you want is going to happen? That you can feel it like lightning in the air?"

"Oh yes," I said.

"You'll be so proud when I'm a star. You can look at me on the screen and remember that you have kissed me and that I would have given you every-thing if you had only asked. Do you want to have sex here in the grass?"

"No," I said.

"Don't jump. You thought I was serious."

"I never know when you are serious and when you are not," I said.

"I am serious when I say I love you," she said, reaching up quickly and kissing me on the lips. "I will be back," she said. "As soon as this film is over. And when we get married all the reporters will come, and our photographs will be in all the newspapers."

Daisy was like Guy: they believed what they were saying at the moment. When the moment was past, they believed something else. Whatever she thought about me at this moment, she believed her opportunity in Holly-wood was a chance she could not resist. I think she would have returned to California even had I professed love for her and begged her to marry me. But who can tell?

Jim Ed and I took her to the depot. Mrs. Ledbetter and the old man kissed her tenderly at home, and Mrs. Ledbetter wept. It was strange to see Mrs. Ledbetter cry. Brian Ledbetter looked red-faced, but he did not cry. At trainside she kissed me lightly on the mouth. She stood in the doorway of the Pullman and waved until the train carried her out of sight, heading towards New Orleans and the connection that would take her home to California.

"Daisy loves you," Jim Ed said. I did not know what to say.

I thought my job was temporary and that I would leave Bourbonville soon. Once again I began releasing ties in my mind, filling details of the town in memory, seeing it become strange, thinking of my friends and of leaving them behind, never seeing them again. Finally I would go home to Greece, and years later I would retain a memory of Bourbonville as a brief excursion with no enduring consequences. Whatever Daisy might have been or would be, she was already becoming a part of my past, and that day I doubted that I would ever see her again.

In the meantime, I fell into my job's routines because they were always there. Many men in the car works eyed me suspiciously, warily, and sometimes with mockery. I knew that some of them had been out there the night M.P. was murdered, when I lost my front teeth, and when the hemp rope sawed into my neck. Except for Kirby in the bank, I did not know who they were.

I could walk by a group in the wheel foundry and hear behind me a distinct but unrecognizable voice hissing "Jew bastard!" or "Nigger lover!" At first I turned to see who had spoken, and the men looked at me with hard faces. I kept my face inflexible—not a smile, not a frown. They obeyed my instructions with a reluctance verging on defiance. I rather enjoyed the hostility; the men, too, were already becoming a part of my past.

I was now making a good deal of money. At moments my position seemed absurd—a young foreigner in charge of men twice and three times his age in a monotonous little town in a remote and backward state and becoming mildly prosperous, able to do undreamed-of things for my mother and my sisters. What right did I have to such a position?

"Pretend," Guy whispered. "That is what I would have done at the brewery. A good actor can make an audience believe anything."

I cultivated an air of reserve. I did not mix with the men. I scarcely spoke to them. I walked through the car works every day, as Pinkerton had done; he had been a pillar of fire, but I was ice, standing at times with my hands thrust down in my pockets, watching the operations without saying a word, without speaking to my foremen when they spoke to me, reducing them to uncomfortable silence by my refusal to engage in small talk.

"Nigger lover," some voices said.

"Jew bastard," some voices said.

I ignored them. *Alium silere quod voles, primus sile:* if you wish to silence another, be first silent yourself. My practice now in the car works. Seneca would have approved. In time the silence around me became nervous and respectful. I enjoyed the discomfiture of the men. The black men were different—diffident, respectful, and loyal. But they did not talk to me, and I did not talk to them. Even if I had been M.P.'s friend, I was white, and they put me on a shelf in their minds and left me there.

Some people in the county cast their lot with me at the beginning, assuming that I was a good bet. One of these was Mealy Hardison, our squint-eyed sheriff with the insinuating voice and a predilection for bowing. "Mealy's either at your neck or your feet," Dr. Youngblood observed—as close to a harsh remark as I ever heard him make about anyone except Pinkerton.

I could scarcely bear to see this hollow effigy of the law in Bourbon County, but he dogged my footsteps. He insisted on giving me rides when I preferred to walk. He flattered my rapid rise, telling me how wicked Pinkerton had been, how good it was at long last to have someone who "knew the score" in charge of the car works. He assumed a secret knowledge of life that worldly-wise men like him and me shared, both of us scorning the ignorant masses.

He told me what Dale Farmer said about me. "I figure a man ought to know who his friends are," Mealy Hardison said, giving me a broad wink. "His enemies, too, if you know what I mean. Of course if you tell him I told you, I'll deny it."

"I do not care what people think about me," I said.

"You don't care that he says you're too young for the job? You don't care that he says you're Catholic and that nobody should work for somebody who believes in the Pope? You don't care that he tells everbody that he makes all the decisions and you just pretend? Oh now, Mr. Alexander, let's put the shoes on the right feet. Let's put the gloves on the right hands. Let's part our hair down the middle. A man who says them things, you ought to fire his fat ass. I'd do it tomorrow. He'll just cause trouble if you don't. I'll back you up. He's a queer, you know. We could nail him for that tomorrow if you say the word."

"Tomorrow" for Mealy Hardison occupied a mystical realm in the imagination. It was the time you did everything.

"I want you to know," he said once, putting his hand on my arm as he drove me down Broadway in his car, "I know what that white trash did to you when they lynched the Negro. I hope you know that they had to deceive me to keep me from being there, from breaking it up. They called me all the way down to Varner's Cross Roads on a wild goose chase. I was down there looking for somebody that tried to break into one of them Klansmen's houses. Only there wasn't nobody. It was all just to get me onto the other end of the county. If I'd been there, they never would have hurt the Negro, and they sure wouldn't have hurt you." He patted me and looked so sincere that I think a child would have believed him.

Dale Farmer's hopes continued, disguised as admonitions. "I'm saying this just to keep you from building up your hopes, but you know that the railroad will not leave a young man like yourself in charge of this operation. It requires experience with the community and things of that nature. The manager has to talk with responsible people in this community and in Washington. He has to have a certain personal authority and knowledge and things of that nature. The manager has to be able to look strong men in the eye and say what he thinks. It's natural that a young man like Phil Drodge would put a young man in charge temporarily. But he doesn't make the final decisions. You can bank on that. The railroad is run by mature men, successful men, men who are very careful with the trust the stockholders have put in them. You're getting some rewarding experience now. But don't get your hopes up. I can tell you that you will not be the permanent manager of the car works."

I knew that he thought that the experienced man the railroad would choose was Dale Farmer, Esquire. He made me uncomfortable with this oleaginous message presented again and again, for I could see into his heart as though it had been crystal or, to use a more apt metaphor, the transparent gelatinous substance of a jellyfish hanging apparently relaxed in water but ready to sting. I told him that I had no intention of remaining in Bourbonville, that I was going home. He smiled broadly and assured me that if he were so far from his real home, he would get back there as quickly as his legs—or a train or a ship—could carry him. Yet almost every morning his feelings of injury and neglect resurfaced, and he told me once again in strictest confidence that the decision makers in Washington would not be swayed by the on-the-spot decisions of an inexperienced young fellow like "Phil" Drodge.

I expected a telegram announcing that Pinkerton's successor would arrive by train from Washington on this day or that and that I would be relieved. In the meantime, I labored early until late. When the huge ventilator fan on the restored cupola furnace roared into life in the morning, preparing the first heat of iron, I was there. I was on the catwalks when the furnaces were tapped in both the steel foundry and the wheel foundry, and I was at the brass foundry when the rotating furnace stopped and the brass gushed out like molten gold into the molds for the journal bearings. In the long shed where boxcars were assembled, I walked up and down, watching the carpenters. The job presented endless tasks. I moved from one to another with the regularity of a clock ticking, and I had no time to be alone with my thoughts except when I went up to my room after supper. Yet I was not allowed to forget that some men in the car works had been out there that night when M.P. died and that they would have killed me if Pinkerton had let them.

One evening when I came back to the boardinghouse Darcy Coolidge took me aside. "Paul," she said in dismay, "you received a package in the mail today."

"Well?" I said.

"It is out back, in the backyard."

"Why is it in the backyard?"

"It smelled so bad," she said.

"It smelled bad."

I did not understand until I went out to look at it. The package was wrapped in plain brown paper. It had been mailed in Bourbonville, and it stank. I knew what it was. "Get me a shovel, Mrs. Coolidge, and I will bury it."

Somebody had sent me human excrement through the mail. I buried the package in a corner of the yard.

I received a letter on another day, the handwriting as crude as a child's. "We wantd to slit your throte whan we kilt the niger, Jew basterd, and we will git you yit." It lies here now.

"Do you think I am in danger?" I asked Dr. Youngblood.

"I don't know," he said. "Yes, I suppose so."

I felt strangely indifferent. The paperwork piled up. I often skipped supper and sat late in the office and worked over papers, and sometimes Mr. Rudd, the night watchman, came in, trembling with the palsy of his years, his big timing box around his neck, his eyes blinking like those of a man astonished and bewildered, and he said, "You work later than anybody I ever seen before." He shuffled off, chewing his huge mustache, leaving me alone while he tottered from station to station on his route, inserting the key hanging at each one into his timing box to prove to nonexistent checkers that he had made his rounds and seen that all was well. He carried a burdensome Colt revolver, and I wondered what he would do if he ever needed to fire it.

I found comfort in Guy and Bernal. Once in a while when I had been sitting for hours at the desk, my head bent over piles of papers—accounts, orders, drawings, reports—I felt a presence in the room. Looking up, I could see Bernal standing there or Guy in a leather chair looking at me with his large, dark eyes. "I am so very glad to see you," I said. "Dr. Youngblood thinks that I am in danger."

"You are in danger," Bernal said.

"Then I may soon be with you," I said.

"We will walk over the world together," Guy said. "Are you not afraid?"

"No," I said.

Guy laughed. "They have not seen anything like you."

"I never have seen anything like you," I said.

"One for all and all for one," Bernal said.

"The Three Musketeers," Guy said with a laugh.

"Why does Stephanos not come?"

"It is a trick of light," Bernal said. "He is nearby. He is watching you. He loves you."

"Tell him I love him," I said.

Worn down in body, peaceful in my soul, I gathered my things and walked out into the night, up through the now silent car works, listening without fear for an unnatural sound, and returned to the boardinghouse on foot through a town already asleep. Sometimes I put my head down on the desk and fell fast asleep, and Alan Bookbinder, one of the male clerks, would find me there in the morning when he came in early, as he always did, to fuss over his papers. Alan invariably made coffee at those moments and brought me a cup, saying nothing at all about my being there. I suppose the most disturbing thing was that I could then work on all day without feeling that I was tired.

"You are not sleeping enough," Darcy Coolidge said. "You look terrible, just terrible. You have bags under your eyes at your age. It is just terrible. You must sleep more."

Dale Farmer said, "I know you think if you work hard enough, the company will keep you on as manager. But it won't, you know. No sense killing yourself for no reason. I can tell you this in strictest confidence: the decision maker in Washington is a man named Metcalf. He is an old Brahmin from South Carolina. He hates foreigners and things of that nature. Phil Drodge knows that if he brought your name up to Metcalf, the old man's head would explode. Metcalf sees a Bolshevik behind every tree."

I paid no attention. The job presented itself as a series of problems, not as beautiful and as intricate as the mathematical problems of algebraic groups that fascinated me once, that I never did again after Bernal died, but problems nonetheless, which required the exercise of my mind in a pleasant and narcotic way. I threw myself into solving them, and I waited for what would be to be.

I decided that the ratio of pig iron to scrap iron was too high. Pig iron was new iron, ingots fresh minted from raw ore and delivered from the iron mills in gondola cars, lifted out with a huge magnetic crane as though they had been bread crumbs. The scrap iron was junk—broken wheels, all sorts of ironwork that had been machines, now broken up. We mixed pig iron and scrap iron in the cupola—80 percent pig iron and 20 percent scrap. An old supersitition among foundrymen held that scrap iron was polluted and that if you used too much of it in castings, they would have too much sulphur or other impurities, and they would break. The iron manufacturers encouraged the superstition because it meant that we would keep on buying the virginal stuff. I saw no chemical reason for such a high ratio, and I cut back and back on the pig iron, and I greatly increased the proportion of the much cheaper scrap iron, and the castings held up under tests as well as any of the other wheels, and we saved a great deal of money.

Dale Farmer showed me the books with a glum air. "Well, right now it looks good, very good. But if our wheels start breaking on the line, and if what you're doing causes derailments, I'm not responsible."

"I will take the full responsibility, Mr. Farmer. And I assure you that I will tell everyone that you wanted to continue in the old ways." He looked uncertain and miserable and dropped his eyes.

"Well, don't tell them that before we get reports of the broken wheels," he said petulantly. "I don't want them to think I'm standing in the way of progress. I wish you would call me Dale."

"I'll tell them only if I cause a disaster."

This promise made Dale Farmer cheerful for a time, but no disasters happened, and we continued to save thousands of dollars on pig iron, and he turned glum again.

125

DARCY COOLIDGE acquired a new Model T Ford, and I learned to drive it. On Saturday afternoons I sometimes drove her to the market so she could select the food she would give us later in the week. At other times she insisted on making me take the car out myself. I enjoyed the car. I also found it sometimes useful.

Like Pinkerton before me, I had to have a chemist. I could not do all the work and chemistry, too. Early in my tenure I went to Juliet Fisher again. She lived with her aged mother in a house built against a hill not far from the Martel Methodist Church. She was in her early thirties, older than I, voluptuous, thick hipped, big breasted, laughing in restrained gaiety. Her complexion was pink and healthy and slightly freckled; she was a woman who smiled cheerfully at the earth, a spring goddess confident that things would grow, I sometimes thought. You could sit on her long porch in one of the five or six rocking chairs and look down through the trees and over a dirt road to a valley where a twisting creek ran. Just down the road was the Martel Methodist Church, a white-frame building against a hill on which lay one of the oldest graveyards in the county amid dark cedar trees. She took me walking in the graveyard and showed me the stones of the families who had been there since the first white settlers moved in—Baileys and Watsons and Grubbs and others whose names seemed strange to me, as most English names did. Showing off graveyards seemed to be one of the recreations of Bourbon County, a process by which the residents mysteriously came into contact with some reality standing behind life and death.

We sat on Juliet's porch with her mother, and I begged her to come back to work at the car works.

"Is this a permanent job?" she said. "I can't teach in the high school and do this, too. Mamma's getting old. I have to take care of her."

"It is permanent as long as I am here. I shall not go back to the laboratory. The railroad will choose a new manager, and I shall return home."

"To Belgium," Juliet said.

"Yes, to Belgium," I said.

"Well, I don't blame you. Bourbonville is home to me, but it's discouraging sometimes. The bright people leave. It's happening all over America. All the smart boys in the high school leave when they graduate. Do you know about Charles Darwin?"

"Oh yes," I said vaguely.

"Evolution's illegal in Tennessee, but it works here anyway. The people who are left in all the small towns are dumber than those who leave." She looked out at the late-afternoon sun shining in the trees on her hill. "But I love it anyway."

"Jim Ed didn't leave," I said.

"He's an odd one," she said with a laugh. "But handsome."

"I do very much want you to come to work for me."

"You're telling me you don't know what will happen to me when you go back to Belgium."

"That's right," I said.

"I'm making sixty dollars a month at the high school," she said.

"I will pay you twenty-five dollars a week," I said.

"That's a lot of money."

"It is not much," I said. "I cannot promise you anything about the next manager."

"You're going to be the manager," she said in a firmly declarative tone. "I'll bet on you. I'll take the job because I think you're going to be here awhile." She smiled. I had an urge to kiss her to seal a bargain, but of course I did not. I scarcely knew her.

"That is what Dr. Youngblood says," I said.

"He's right. And I'm right. If you stay here, you will keep me on as chemist. Is that right?"

"Of course," I said. "But please don't be disappointed when I go home," I said.

We shook hands and drank iced tea, and her mother wanted to talk about Warren G. Harding. He was so good looking, she said.

I daydreamed of Greece. I thought of the blue sea running in sparkling swells in the morning light and the boats riding the water and bright sails against the immaculate blue of the seaborne sky, and I was homesick and wanted to wind up this part of my life that was coming to look more and more like an extended aberration, a warp in the curve of existence that had to be straightened out if I was to resume being myself. I wanted to go home. I think I was sincere in those thoughts. Who can tell?

In December of 1920, I was called to Washington, and there sat Philip Drodge in a fine navy blue suit with a thick gray vertical stripe in it. He wore a vest and a watch chain, a high stiff collar that made him look older than he was, and with him was a group of older men, some wearing beards that made them look like old French generals from the Second Empire, looking on approvingly, nodding their heads in the grave, distinguished way of men knowing they possessed authority and that nodding displayed it, and they told me that I had done so well that I would now be the permanent manager of the car works.

"I've convinced these gentlemen that we ought to give youth a chance," Philip Drodge said, beaming with his own youth and accomplishment, waxing loquacious in his carefully restrained way. I remembered the gleaming blood on his hands when he tried to help George Hunter. I remembered his eyes when he realized that Hunter was dead.

"All right," I said. "Thank you. Thank you very much."

"We know that you are a reliable man," one of the older fellows said, a thick man in a brown suit and a white walrus mustache. He was Mr. Metcalf. He spoke in a broad South Carolina accent, which I, of course, could not then identify except that it was thicker and wider than any other southern accent I had heard. "We see what you do. We know your competence. The car works has turned a tidy profit since you have been in charge. Mr. Drodge has told us also of your bravery under fire."

"Mr. Drodge was brave himself," I said.

Philip Drodge glowed, and I remembered the pleasures Guy took in praise.

"We will not leave you down there forever," Philip Drodge said, looking significantly at the others.

"The railroad has a need for good men in all its ranks," one of the older men said. They nodded to each other and looked at me with dry, elderly cheer.

"The old passes away; the new comes on," another said. They nodded in chorus and seemed warmer, as autumn leaves seem warm when the sun shines on them in Indian summer.

"I can tell you," Mr. Metcalf said, "that I am particularly happy to have a Frenchman in the job. My ancestors were French. Huguenots. They fled Catholic persecution. I suppose you are a Catholic?" he said.

"I do not practice," I said.

"Ah, quite right," Mr. Metcalf said vaguely, sitting back in his large chair with a distant smile of satisfaction.

"Then it's settled," Philip Drodge said, smiling at me. "I can't tell you how happy I am. Someday this will be seen as a great day for all of us."

We went out to dinner and ate well. The waiter poured wine in coffee cups. "Gentlemen, I apologize to serve wine in this way," he said. "But prohibition, you know." No one laughed. We drank until I felt warm and giddy and Philip Drodge was happily tipsy, and afterwards we had brandy, and I took a Pullman on train number 41 at 12:05 a.m. bound for Bourbonville, and as it rolled south through the dark Virginia hills, I lay in my lower berth with the curtains open at the window, and I looked on America passing by in the night. I would go home, I thought. But not yet. Not yet. I thought of how proud my mother would be. And Eugenia. I also thought of Eugenia.

I thought of Daisy, too, but in an aimless and detached way. She was in California becoming a movie star. She was indefinably less interested in me than she had been. I was in Bourbonville like a book she had started to read and closed almost absentmindedly. That was all there was between us.

126

"WHY DON'T YOU give Jim Ed a job at the car works?" the old man said one evening. It was February 1921, a cold and bleak month, the naked branches of the trees dripping water from the frequent rains; an occasional snow, washed quickly away.

Jim Ed and I both looked at him. We were sitting by the wood stove in the kitchen. Mrs. Ledbetter was solemnly darning stockings. "You want me to go to work for wages?" Jim Ed said. He laughed in unbelief. It was the slow season on the farm, and he looked heavier. Willy sat with us, obese and silent.

"I don't figure you'd work for nothing," the old man said. "We don't have slaves no more, thanks to me."

"This don't make sense," Jim Ed said. He laughed in an embarrassed way, glanced at me, looked away.

"It makes all the sense in the world," the old man said. "You got something he can do down there?"

The idea rocked around in my head. Of course I had something for him to do.

"Wait a minute," Jim Ed said. "Wait just a minute. I will have to tell you, Daddy, that this makes me almost want to call Doc Youngblood and ask him to come out here and see if you have gone crazy."

"You need to check up on all your good friends at least ever five years to see if they have gone crazy," the old man said. "But I ain't crazy. I'm trying to think about your future. Somebody's got to think about your future. You ain't doing nothing about it."

"While you are thinking about my future, I am thinking about your past, and I cannot understand what crazy demon has got into you," Jim Ed said.

"Listen to your daddy, Jim Ed, and be respectful," Mrs. Ledbetter said.

"I do not mean disrespect, but if somebody in your own family goes crazy, it is a matter to be spoken of," Jim Ed said.

"The world's changing," the old man said.

Jim Ed's face reddened. "I know the world is changing, but I don't see how anything that's changing in the world has anything to do with me on this farm. This farm is one place where the world don't change."

"It's time for you to get off the farm," the old man said. "It is going to shift under your feet, and you are going to tip over, and it is going to fall on top of you and smother you to death. The day of our kind of farming is done. You see in the magazines what farming's going to be now? Tractors and thousands of acres. You can't make nothing on farms like we got."

"There are lots of mules left in the world. Out there in Columbia, Tennessee, they still have a mule festival every year. I see mules around here every time I take a notion to look for mules. We're doing all right," Jim Ed said uneasily.

"Pay attention to your daddy, Jim Ed," Mrs. Ledbetter said.

"In thirty years you ain't going to find a mule between here and New Orleans except in a museum. I know what you're getting for a cow now. What you're getting for a hog. Next to nothing. If you're going to keep on farming, you got to find you a rich wife to support you."

"I can keep myself going," Jim Ed said. "If you ask me, I do pretty good on this farm. Joab and me, that is. I couldn't do it without Joab's help."

"Without Joab's help and the help of them five girls of his and Joab's wife. What you going to do when Joab's girls get married? What you going to do when they have families of their own, and they ain't here to help you put hay in a barn in summer?"

"I'll think about that when it happens," Jim Ed said.

"Sure you will. You'll be carried along like a pup in a river, and when you go over the waterfall, you'll think about it. And I will think that I have raised an imbecile."

Jim Ed looked hurt and bewildered. "I don't know what's got into you," he said, his eyes downcast at the old man's rebuke. "I've worked hard. I don't know why you got to make fun of me now. I'm not a pup in a river."

He spoke truly. The Ledbetter and Weaver farms were as neat as one of the quilts that women in the county made to give as wedding presents. Everything was clean, in place, barbed-wire fences rather than wooden rails enclosing their fields, every fence row weeded, every building whitewashed, every roof whole, every tree pruned, every pig and every cow healthy. Jim Ed got up in the morning at five and went to bed at nine. He, Joab, and Joab's girls swapped work in their independent world. He looked in aggrieved consternation at his father, and his father looked back at him—old, irate, bullying.

"I wish I could help," Willy said.

"I wasn't talking about you," the old man said, his tone changed.

"You wasn't talking about me because I ain't no good for nothing no more," Willy said. "Why should anybody talk about me?"

"Willy," Mrs. Ledbetter said.

"What?" he said.

"All right," the old man said. "Let's drink some whiskey."

He stumped out of the room and came back in a little while with some bonded whiskey in a brown bottle. "The last of Hub's stuff is gone," he said sorrowfully. "I got this stuff off Homer Longwood."

"Who is Homer Longwood?" I said.

"Homer Longwood is one of the fine young men who is now going to get rich and famous on account of the prohibition amendment," the old man said. "He drives bonded whiskey in from North Carolina and only charges five times what it's worth."

"From North Carolina?"

"It comes to North Carolina from Canada on boats," the old man said. "You just cannot imagine the moral uplift that prohibition has brought to this country. It has put young men to work in jobs that they wouldn't never of thought of before. Prohibition has created imagination and industry. It has created daring and courage. It has created the knight of the road. It has created the magician. On Saturday mornings now you can walk down to the courthouse, and there will be our dear friend Homer Longwood in a long coat. Inside the coat are maybe two dozen pockets, and ever pocket has a pint of whiskey in it, and you can give good old Homer three dollars, and you can have a pint of that whiskey out of one of them pockets, and you can call it your very own."

"Why don't we just drink the goddamned stuff and stop trying to talk like Mr. William Shakespeare," Jim Ed said.

"Jim Ed, I don't like you to cuss."

"I'm sorry, Mamma. I'm real sorry."

"Don't apologize to me; it's God that cares."

"Do you think so?" Jim Ed said.

It was cold, and the wind whispered against the house, blowing a fine rain that ran on the windows.

"I could use you in the car works," I said to Jim Ed.

"What would I do? You tell me what somebody like me could do down there. You want me to hammer boxcars together? You want me to haul wheels around on my back? Work like a mule? If I wanted to work like a mule, I'd go work in a coal mine."

"If you would stop talking so much and listen to Paul here, he might tell you what you might could do in the car works," the old man said.

"I need a labor superintendent," I said slowly, thinking my way along as I went. "I need somebody to to gain the confidence of the men, to help me run the place."

"I don't know a thing about the car works. I don't know a thing about metals. I don't know a thing about being a labor superintendent."

"Do you think any of those men out there grew up knowing anything about metals?" I said, quickening my words as inspiration came. "You can learn."

"Why would I want to do that?" Jim Ed said.

"Listen to Paul, boy. You want to do that so you can take care of your wife and children," Brian Ledbetter said.

"I don't have a wife and children."

"There is just the chance that God Almighty might work a miracle," the old man said. "Look what he done for Abraham."

"Let's see now, Daddy. You do not have anything to do with church or preachers, and you are talking about God working a miracle."

"You leave that to God and me. Maybe between him and me we can do something to knock some sense into your head."

"Maybe I'm not the marrying kind," Jim Ed said.

"You have me for your daddy. I am the marrying kind, and so are you. I've been married twict," the old man said.

"Twice?" I said. "You were married before?"

"I sure was. My first woman run off with a fruit-tree salesman."

"Is that true?" I said.

"You think I'd make something like that up?"

"I recollect her real good," Mrs. Ledbetter said. "She was so ugly she couldn't resist any fool who told her she was pretty."

The old man laughed. "Tell you what. John Wesley Campbell, he told me

I could marry Mrs. Ledbetter—she was Mrs. Weaver then—because after seven years I could count my old wife as dead."

"Well," I said.

"Even if she was to turn up again, I could look her in the eye and tell her she was dead in the eyes of the law."

I laughed.

"I reckon she is dead now, poor soul. But let's get down to brass tacks. What can you pay Jim Ed?"

"I'll pay him two thousand dollars a year," I said, pulling a figure out of the air.

"Two thousand dollars!" The old man was thunderstruck. "In one year?"

"He'll be making three thousand in five years," I said. I sat there thinking. "I do not have time to do everything that I have to do. I need somebody out there with the men, somebody I can trust, somebody to see that everybody works together. You go through the car works right now, and you can feel the heat between the colored men and the white men. I feel it. You can cool it down."

"They'll come around," the old man said. "They can't do nothing else. You got their male equipment lying on the chopping block. What are they going to do for jobs now if they don't like to work for you?"

"If they don't like to work for him, they can kill him," Willy said.

"I hear talk like that," Mrs. Ledbetter said. "We all hear it."

"I hear it, too," I said. "I cannot think about that. Just now I am alive, and I have a job, and I want to make the place work. You can help me."

"You figure you're going to go up to Washington City some of these days?" the old man said, cocking an eyebrow.

I paused, thinking about Pinkerton.

"It is not impossible," I said softly. I heard Guy laugh.

"Maybe you could rescue Daisy from the movies and take her to a decent town," Mrs. Ledbetter said.

"Not much of anything is impossible," the old man said. "You been bit by the bug."

"What bug?"

"The bug of ambition." He hesitated and took a deep breath. "Ambition bites you, and it swells up. You scratch it, and you scratch it, and it swells up some more. The more you think about it, the more it hurts."

Jim Ed became thoughtful, eyeing me in a speculative way. "Two thousand dollars a year! A man could do a lot with two thousand dollars a year. What does a labor superintendent do?"

"He makes men do their jobs. He walks through the car works, and he sees what they are doing, and he helps them work together. He sees the places where they are working against each other, and he changes the flow of their energy so that they're all going in the same direction."

"You mean he turns men into machines, I reckon," Jim Ed said. "That's what Daddy always said the car works did. It was what Pinkerton did."

"I suppose you could say that," I said.

"It's the age of the machine," the old man said, not dramatically in a way that commanded Jim Ed to do something but softly, almost in meditation.

"There're a lot of men in the car works who were there that night," Jim Ed said. "And if they find a leader, they'll lynch another one of the colored men."

"That's God's own truth," the old man said.

"They ought to be killed," Jim Ed said. "I'd like to shoot the whole bunch of them."

I shook my head. "It would not do any good," I said.

"It'd do me some good," Jim Ed said.

"All right," I said. "Come to work for me and make them afraid all the time."

Jim Ed laughed grimly. "I know who some of them were," he said.

"I know only the man in the bank. The teller in the bank."

"Jack Kirby," the old man said.

"He fawns over me every time I walk into the bank," I said. "I refuse to be served by him. Mr. Carroll asked me why, and I said that I had my reasons."

"Carroll knows," Jim Ed said. "He's not as dumb as he looks. It's a good thing, too. If he was, somebody'd have to lead him around with a rope."

We were silent for a long time. "Look," I said. "I do need somebody to help me. I am not like these men. I need somebody to be the boss under me, somebody who can gain their confidence. That's the job I would want you to do."

Jim Ed chuckled. "We could play music for them every day at lunch," he said. "Maybe some of them could sing."

I smiled. "Maybe so," I said.

"Maybe it would seem funny for the two bosses to look like a couple of hillbilly singers," Jim Ed said.

I felt dizzy. Nobody noticed. Jim Ed wore an army shirt that looked ready to dissolve from many washings. He wore cotton trousers. His eyes followed me speculatively.

"Think about it," I said. "Come down and see me tomorrow if you want the job."

"You can farm and do the job down there at the same time," the old man said.

"Take it," Willy said. He spoke in a burst of feeling, his voice rusty from lack of use. We all looked at him.

"It ain't worth thinking about," Jim Ed said.

"Do what Willy says," the old man said. "Take it."

Jim Ed looked in a bemused way at his father. "If you ain't the one!" he said.

"If I've told you once, I've told you a thousand times not to say 'ain't,'" the old man said.

"You say 'ain't,'" Jim Ed said.

"You're supposed to do better than me," the old man said.

"I wish you would think about it," I said softly.

"I'll think about it," Jim Ed said. "You think I can find me a wife if I have a job?" he said to the old man.

"I ain't said nothing about you finding a wife."

"You have said a great deal about me finding a wife. You're saying a farmer ain't good enough to have a wife that's worth anything."

"He'll take the job," the old man said. "His mamma will see to that." Mrs. Ledbetter looked up at me; I could not read the expression on her face.

I had Darcy Coolidge's car that night. I drove away through the dark, rain pelting the windshield. I worked the manual windshield wiper with one hand and drove with the other. I rolled along at twenty-five miles an hour. I felt in charge of things.

My headlights picked up two hitchhikers standing in the rain and jerking their thumbs over their heads. I slowed to a stop and reached over to open the door for them. I looked up as the car was coming to a halt, and I shivered. Guy and Bernal stood over me, looking at me through the windshield. "Everyone has a price," Guy said, his voice clear and sharp like a keening cry, only instead of coming from just outside the car it seemed to ring off the rain-soaked hills standing darkly beyond the dark fields. I shut my eyes and put my head over the wheel for a moment and felt an explosion of pain within my skull. I heard the engine running smoothly at idle.

"Well, get in," I said. "Come on." I opened my eyes and looked to where they had been standing.

The door was open on the hissing rain, and no one was there.

127

THE NEXT MORNING Jim Ed appeared in my office with his mother. Miss Sally Morton, my secretary, tried to announce them, but I heard Mrs. Ledbetter say, "Sally, I've told your mother you act too much like a servant. Even in a job like this you have to keep your dignity." In she came, Miss Sally futilely behind her, and Jim Ed behind her looking amused and uncomfortable.

"You can go back to work now, Sally," Mrs. Ledbetter said. "I presume you have something to do."

I nodded to Miss Sally, who looked extremely annoyed.

"It smells like tobacco in here," Mrs. Ledbetter said, looking around. "You men are going to kill yourself from smoking so much."

"I am sure it is not good for us," I said. "Please sit down."

For a long time she said nothing. I thought that she must have been thinking of Caleb, of how he had died here on the floor, near her chair. I expected her to say something about him. Her sharp eyes darted about, and once her lips moved, but the silence came back, and we sat there waiting. Finally she said, "Them windows needs a good washing," and I knew she would not speak of Caleb.

"They do for a fact," I said.

She sniffed. "I don't see how you stand to work cooped up in a place like this all day long without enough air," she said. "It would give me fits."

"I get out in the day," I said.

Jim Ed had not said a word. He sat down, holding a shapeless hat in his hands. He had put on a tight-fitting suit.

"You look pale," she said.

I shrugged.

"You know when you looked better than you ever did?"

"I suppose when I was flying with M.P.," I said.

"That's right," Mrs. Ledbetter said.

"It was a happy time," I said.

"Mr. Ledbetter ain't got over it, you know. He was real attached to that colored man. He don't say much, but he ain't been the same since."

"No, we do not say much about it," I said.

"He was an uncommon colored man," Mrs. Ledbetter said.

We were silent. Jim Ed looked around, taking in the pictures of trains and locomotives on the wall, at the calendars.

"You ought to be happy now with this job and all," Mrs. Ledbetter said.

"I guess so," I said.

"Young man like you with so much power. You're the biggest man in Bourbonville now."

"It was accidental," I said.

"The Lord was with you," she said. "Now you want to be Jim Ed's boss."

"I did not put it that way," I said.

"You want him to work for you."

"I do."

"You want to be his boss," she said. "Jim Ed ain't never had a boss. Folks in my family ain't used to having bosses."

"I had a boss in the army," Jim Ed said with an embarrassed grin. "Lots of them."

"It ain't the same," Mrs. Ledbetter said.

"Mrs. Ledbetter, I need Jim Ed to help me here. He will be better with the men than I am."

"He don't know nothing about the stuff you do down here."

"He can learn. I learned. We all learned. I will tell you something. I came to Bourbonville as the chemist for the car works. But do you know something? I am not a chemist. In one long morning, I could teach you everything I do with chemistry. You might not understand what you were doing, but you could do it. You do not have to know much to do the chemistry that we do in this place. I had one year of chemistry in what you call high school. I was in an academy where we had a good teacher, and I understood it. I had one year of chemistry in the university. I used perhaps 2 or 3 percent of the things I have learned in chemistry when I worked in the laboratory. I was studying to be a mathematician."

"A mathematician? You mean you would have done arithmetic? Sums? That's all?"

I laughed. "Arithmetic is only a part of mathematics. No I did not do arithmetic except as we all do arithmetic. I was interested in algebra, especially in Boolean algebra. I was interested in algebraic groups. I loved topology."

My mind had wandered back into a forsaken land. It looked suddenly green and fertile. I saw Bernal standing behind her. I looked at him so hard that she turned around and looked behind herself. "What was you looking at?" she said.

"Nothing," I said. "Nothing."

She looked at me in irritated perplexity. "Bouger's algebra! Well, what would you *do* with it?"

"I would think about it, Mrs. Ledbetter. You do with mathematics . . . I did with mathematics what you do with God. I thought about the shapes, the forms, the way mathematics reduces the world to symbols, and when you can understand the symbols, you can understand something about God's order in the universe, Mrs. Ledbetter. Look!"

I took a piece of paper from the desk, creased it by rubbing it with a fountain pen, and asked Jim Ed for his pocket knife. He jumped to oblige. I cut down the sharp crease in the paper. Quickly I made a Möbius strip.

"Do you see that, Mrs. Ledbetter? What is it?"

"Why, it's a strip of paper," she said, lifting her head so she could contemplate it through the lower part of her bifocals, deciding that was no good, and looking at it again over her eyeglasses.

"It is called a Möbius strip, Mrs. Ledbetter. It was discovered by a German mathematician. It has only one side, Mrs. Ledbetter. Look."

I ran my finger around the strip to show her.

"It looks as if it has two sides. But it has only one. And it has only one edge. Is that not wonderful?"

"It looks like just a piece of paper to me," she said.

"That is just the beauty of it," I said. "It looks like a piece of paper. You look at it, and it has only one side. But there is something else here, a form, something we have to admit even when our eyes seem to be telling us the opposite. You look at this form, and do you know what you think?"

"I think this conversation is getting out of hand," Mrs. Ledbetter said, drawing back and looking at me as if she thought I might have gone mad.

"No, no," I said. "No. I am saying that before the war, I thought about mathematics all the time. My mind drifted among mathematical forms. I saw those forms as colors. Chemistry interested me only because chemistry is a collection of mixtures that somehow hold together. Why do they hold together? That is a great question. Answer that question and you have one of the secrets of the universe. We cannot answer it. We can guess. Some force binds everything together. But we cannot tell what it is."

"It holds together because God wants it that way," Mrs. Ledbetter said.

"That is as good an answer as any," I said.

"I don't see what any of this has to do with Jim Ed working for you," she said.

I laughed and sat back in my chair, reached for a cigarette, thought better of it. "Neither do I," I said. "I'm saying this because you are trying to make of running the car works a complicated business about chemistry and knowing something about metals and all those other things. I am saying that running the car works, keeping people at work in Bourbon County, is a practical business. Jim Ed and I are practical men. He can learn everything there is to know about the steel, the brass, and the iron in two months. He already knows enough about the men, how to get them to work together. I need him to help me with the men. If he helps me with the men, we may be able to patch this county up. Is that not a thought worthy of . . . of something?"

She sat back, studying my face with intelligent intensity. She was not as old as her husband, not well traveled, not educated. Still she sat there, pondering my words. She was considering her son's dignity, and she was formidable.

"It must be wonderful to see the things you see," she said at last. "When I hear music, I feel with my heart what you see. You must see it with your head."

"You see it! I knew you could see it. It takes heart and head together," I said. "I do not think about the forms in the universe, the mathematics of things great and small, without feeling my heart rise up. It is like music, the enjoyment of music. You understand!" I looked at her gratefully, and I thought for a moment that she might smile, but she did not. She pondered something.

"Well," she said after another long silence. "I've told Jim Ed that he can come to work for you on one condition."

"Anything," I said.

"Jim Ed agrees with me. We've talked about it. Don't you, boy?"

"Sure, Mamma," he said. He folded his hands in his lap and looked across the desk at me in amusement.

"Tell me," I said.

"I want you to give Willy a job."

"Willy! Willy's blind! A blind man can get killed around a place like this."

"He's killing hisself back home," she said softly.

"He's fat as a hog," Jim Ed said. "He just sits around and eats. You see him."

"But what could he do? Does your government not have some kind of program to make a better life for the mutilated of war?" I thoughtlessly used a French phrase that I translated into English.

"Our government doesn't do anything for us except make us fight wars when we have to," Jim Ed said. "After that, we're on our own."

"But what can he possibly do in a place like this?"

"He can be your night watchman," Mrs. Ledbetter said.

"My night watchman! I have a night watchman. Mr. Rudd is my night watchman."

"Mr. Alexander, that poor old man is too feeble to be your night watchman. He's all wore out."

"But at least he can *see,*" I said. "He is a night watchman who can *watch* something."

"You give Willy the job, and he can watch just as good as Mr. Rudd. Willy can hear things. It is amazing. He can hear things that you wouldn't believe."

"That's a fact," Jim Ed said.

"He will fall into one of the annealing pits, and he will die like a fried insect," I said.

"Willy can walk around with a cane until he gets the hang of it," Mrs. Ledbetter said. "After he gets the hang of it, he won't need no cane."

"A blind night watchman," I said, shaking my head and laughing.

"He will be better than that poor old man. You ought to be ashamed, making an old man work hard like that. He come to the car works with Mr. Pinkerton, and he was old then. Look how many years that's been!"

"You are a resolute woman," I said.

"I get what I want some of the time," she said.

"All right," I said. "He can walk around awhile with Mr. Rudd. We will see what happens. I would like to shake your hand, Mrs. Ledbetter." I got up, and she got up, and Jim Ed stood taller than both of us, still holding his battered hat. Mrs. Ledbetter and I shook hands, she with immense gravity. Jim Ed and I did the same.

"Can you bring Willy down this evening? I'll send him around with Mr. Rudd."

"I'll have him right here," Jim Ed said. "He'll bring the dogs along, too."

"The dogs?"

"Hub Delaney's dogs. Willy's got them eating out of his hands."

"Well, that is interesting," I said, suddenly thinking that there were possibilities to all this.

"Those dogs will do anything Willy tells them to do," Jim Ed said.

"You can come tomorrow morning to work?" I asked.

"Yessir, Captain," Jim Ed said. We laughed.

I should digress and say that Willy appeared in due time that evening. Mr. Rudd hobbled down to the main office in response to my command.

"Mr. Rudd, this is difficult," I said, "but I think the time has come to think about your retirement."

"Hell," Mr. Rudd said, "I've been thinking about my retirement for the last ten years, but ever time I brought it up with Pinkerton, he said he couldn't spare me. He said the whole damned place depended on me."

"Did he?" I said. "You do not mind retiring?"

"Hell no! You think I like to walk all night long in the dark? You must be crazy, Captain."

I could not tell and do not know to this day if he was sincere or if he was covering up the hurt that my announcement gave him.

I introduced him to Willy. "Here is Mr. Weaver. He is going to be the night watchman," I said.

"He looks blind to me. Can he see anything through them eyes of his'n?"

"I am blind," Willy said in a voice so seldom used that it was almost a croak. "If you walk me around, I can find my way."

"Hell, it's easy," Mr. Rudd said. "I walk it sometimes with my eyes shut just to show myself I can do it. You won't waste no money on flashlight batteries."

And so it was. The two men walked together for two weeks, and Mr. Rudd left Willy to do it alone. Willy did it, moving deliberately in a rolling gait, at first tapping his cane. In a week he abandoned the cane and found his way through his route in utter silence. I stood one night in the dark with Jim Ed listening for him, and I could not hear him, not a footstep, until he called out softly, "Who's there?" and I heard a low, guttural growl from his dogs.

"He's going to do all right," Jim Ed said. And so he did.

Other things went all right, too. Some of the men turned up with badly bruised faces and swollen eyes. Some quit, and Jim Ed hired others—friends of his. We hired many of Jim Ed's friends. His fists were sometimes bruised, but he exuded extreme good cheer. Mr. Kirby departed from the bank after someone—he would not say who, even to Dr. Youngblood—called him out of his house one night and beat him, as country people said, within an inch of his life.

"The man was half dead and terrified," Dr. Youngblood said, smoking his pipe. He did not smile, and he did not seem pleased.

"I don't know who could have done a thing like that to that poor, innocent little man," Jim Ed said. He did not smile, either. We did not speak of Mr. Kirby again.

No, I cannot claim that any of this was gallant or beautiful or even moral. But it was satisfying. I sit writing this evening and thinking back on those suddenly broken faces of a few foundrymen, of Mr. Kirby's headlong flight, of the tranquility that came over the car works, and of the cessation of voices behind my back as I walked through the place, and I feel a satisfaction that, I suppose, helps to explain wars and the cycle of vengeance that only the Eumenides can finally halt or heal.

128

EUGENIA CAME to Bourbonville to write a story about me—the youngest manager in the Dixie Railroad system. She said Philip Drodge had sent her a letter and had suggested that it would be good publicity for the state and the railroad to show how much better things were in Bourbonville than they had been. Her editor, sniffing boosterism in the Tennessee air, concurred and sent her down, and she talked with Jim Ed, and he invited her and me to supper, and we spent a happy evening.

More convinced than ever that this young woman would be the perfect wife for her youngest son, Mrs. Ledbetter was not one to sleep on her purposes. By letter she invited Eugenia to Sunday dinner. Eugenia accepted, asking if she could bring her brother Charles. Jim Ed came around to the office and looked at the floor and looked at the ceiling and looked out the window and turned red and told me that his mother was sorry she could not have me to dinner this Sunday as she usually did because she was having Miss Curry and her brother. I said that I understood perfectly and that Mrs. Ledbetter was all too gracious. I ate at the boardinghouse and took a walk and imagined the dazzling impression Jim Ed was making on Eugenia, and I supposed with gloomy resignation that I had lost her forever.

Eugenia made a charming impression, but Charles was less well received.

"He looked down on all of us," Jim Ed said. "He knew everything there was to know about everything, and he told us. Lord, he *would* have told us if we'd had enough time, but we only had an afternoon."

I rejoiced in this perverse brother Charles. Perhaps he would have some influence on Eugenia; perhaps he would make her see that Jim Ed was the wrong choice.

"You are ready to betray a friend," Bernal said.

"Friendship has nothing to do with love," Guy said. "All's fair in love and war, you know."

"A proverb of *yours,*" Bernal said. "As I recall, because all is fair in love and war, we are dead."

Guy looked discomfited. I had a headache.

But then a note came from Eugenia to me, inviting Jim Ed and me to her house for lunch on a Saturday in April. My heart soared. By April the dogwoods put a spray of white in the forests, and blue irises and tulips waved in yards, and the roses sent out green tendrils. April is a beautiful month in Tennessee. That April was the most beautiful month I had seen in my life until then.

We drove up in the Ledbetter Ford. It was battered and rusty. Jim Ed scrubbed the mud off, but it still looked five years old. "I reckon I'm going to have to put out for a new car," he said.

He wore his only suit, and it was too small; the salesman had not bothered to make it fit.

I bought a soft wool suit for the occasion. I paid thirty-five dollars for it in Knoxville. Jim Ed whistled when he saw it. "Boy, that sure is pretty! Did you buy it just for this lunch?"

"No," I lied. "I needed a new suit."

"I reckon the boss has to wear a suit," Jim Ed said. "I never liked to spend money on clothes."

The car had no roof; the wind blew our hair. Jim Ed brought a guitar and a mandolin; they lay in the back seat. "I thought we might play for them." He grinned. "You reckon she likes music?"

"I do not know," I said.

"Why don't you say 'I *don't* know'?" Jim Ed said. "Sound like real folks."

I laughed. "It does not seem natural," I said. "My English teacher told me not to use contractions."

"Hell," Jim Ed said.

"It is hard to break old habits," I said.

"Hell," he said, grinning again. "I got to teach you real English. We'll play up a storm for them. You and me, nobody can beat us. We ought to go on the road."

"On the road?" I said.

"Playing music around the country. On Saturday nights we could play in courthouses all over the place. Take up a collection afterwards. Maybe play for some dances."

"It sounds like a hard life," I said.

"Harder than running a foundry, I reckon," Jim Ed said with a laugh. "But you don't get much applause when you run a foundry, do you?"

Eugenia lived with her mother, her sister Bess, and her two brothers in a little house on Hill Street near a cliff that dropped down into the muddy river on the eastern side of the town. We pulled up in front of the house and sat there like bashful children. Eugenia came out with a smile. She was wearing a light cotton dress.

"Take off your coats and relax," she said. I did not feel relaxed with my coat off, but we removed them and carried them over our arms. Jim Ed was wearing broad suspenders, colored red, and his trousers were a couple of inches too short.

Eugenia led us inside and introduced us to her brothers, Alfred and Charles. They were sitting in the parlor reading newspapers, and they made a show of continuing to read, ignoring us, until we were standing there awkwardly.

Alfred was taller than Charles. Both of them were slender and handsome in a rawboned American way. They were civil without being friendly. They looked very much alike. Charles wore rimless glasses, the kind that break if you give them a tap on a table. He had pale blue eyes. Alfred did not wear glasses and had a direct way of looking at people. Both of them had high foreheads and cleft chins, some hereditary legacy. Alfred resembled Eugenia more.

"I suppose we should thank you for saving Eugenia's life," Charles said. He spoke in a mannered way. "She has told us all about it."

"I am not sure I saved her life," I said.

"It's what she said," Charles said. "Of course if she had been doing something more ladylike, her life would not have been in danger."

"Charles and Alfred do not approve of my job," Eugenia said with an indulgent laugh. "Don't pay any attention to them."

Eugenia's mother, Mrs. Pendleton, came in from the kitchen, wiping her hands on her white apron—thin, wrinkled, and dour, dressed in black as Greek women dress when they mourn for the dead. She did not offer her hand, but Jim Ed reached out to it anyway and shook it heartily. She seemed startled and displeased. Eugenia must have got her good looks from her dead father.

Eugenia's sister Bess came out, radiant with pleasure. She shook hands vigorously. "There're *two* of you," she said. "Eugenia has such luck! I wish I had two young gentlemen coming to call on me." She laughed. Bess was round and short and wore her black hair in an unattractive braid around her head. She had nice skin, but she was not pretty. She looked like an earlier, happier version of her mother.

"Oh, Bess!" Eugenia said, embarrassed.

"I'm making a lemon meringue pie," Bess said. "I'm a better cook than Eugenia is."

"Bess, that will do!" Mrs. Pendleton said.

"All right. I'll go back to the kitchen," Bess said in a pout. "That's all I do around here. You wait and see how good my lemon meringue pie is!" She disappeared into the kitchen and reappeared almost instantly with a large glass pitcher of iced tea.

"I think it's so exciting that you're a foreigner," Bess said to me. "Do you eat bugs?"

"Bess!" Eugenia looked mortified.

"Well, I've heard foreigners eat all sorts of things. Maybe if you fried bugs in a nice sauce, they'd taste good." Jim Ed laughed out loud, saw no one else was laughing, and stifled his laughter. Now and then he chuckled apparently at nothing, and Charles and Alfred looked at him sharply.

We talked about how pretty the spring was. We talked about Bert, the youngest sister, who was coming to lunch from Maryville, where she lived with her husband, Lionel. We heard a lot about Bert and Lionel. When Bert won a tennis championship in Knoxville, her picture was in the newspapers. Eugenia had pasted the clippings in a scrapbook. We looked at the photographs while we drank iced tea and spoke of how good it was. The photographs showed Bert in black skirts and stockings with a tennis racket, smiling. Jim Ed studied the photographs with the care of a man studying a seed catalogue. "This is very interesting," he said.

Alfred and Charles talked about business. They told us about their plans. They wore nice suits. They removed their coats only after we had seen them in their splendor.

"What do you do, Mr. Curry?" Jim Ed asked Alfred politely.

"Automobiles," Alfred said. "The automobile is the greatest invention of the modern age. Everybody's going to be buying cars. I don't see how you can go wrong in the automobile business."

"Do you make cars or what?" Jim Ed said.

Alfred and Charles both laughed scornfully. "No one *makes* cars in Tennessee," Alfred said. "I'm the service manager for Maxwell here in town."

"Our friend Dr. Youngblood has a new Maxwell," I said.

"Smart man. Smart man," Alfred said, for the first time looking at us with a degree of approval. "Eugenia drives a Maxwell. I'll say that for her."

"If I hadn't bought a Maxwell, Alfred would have disowned me," she said.

Charles wore a mustache clipped very thin in the sexless American way. He talked volubly. As Jim Ed had reported, he had vast experience in every endeavor. Alfred asked what I thought of the Bolsheviks and their apparent victory in Russia. Before I could answer, Charles launched into a long explanation of why the Bolsheviks could not possibly prevail. The Russian people were religious, he said. The Bolsheviks were atheists; ergo, that was that.

"I see you wear a mustache," Charles said to me. "You don't see many of them now. I started wearing mine in the army."

"I don't like mustaches," Mrs. Pendleton said. "I tell Charles it makes him look foreign."

"No, mine is an American mustache. Mr. Alexander's mustache is foreign. See how bushy it is."

"Charles," Eugenia said.

Bess came back into the room, bringing more iced tea. She filled our glasses. "I think it's a very handsome mustache," she said, smiling at me.

"Lots of men in the northeast and in California wear mustaches," Charles said.

"Charles, you haven't been in California," Bess said, as if Charles had made an inadvertent mistake that she must correct. She seemed astonished that he would have forgotten that he had not been in California. Everything was dramatic to Bess. She adored her brothers, but she was also literal-minded and demanded explanations whenever any statement seemed to deviate from what she knew was fact.

"I was in the army with men from California and all over the place," Charles said. "Many of them wore mustaches. I don't see why we should make an issue of it. European men wear mustaches." He fought to keep his voice level, but he was furious with Bess. She did not notice.

"I was so afraid the army would corrupt Charles," Mary Pendleton said. "So many soldiers learn to drink. And they use bad language, too."

"The American Army is different from other armies," Charles said.

"Is that right, Mr. Ledbetter?" Mary Pendleton said.

"The army I was in was just like church," Jim Ed said.

Charles laughed, and I smiled.

"Where were you in the line?" Jim Ed said. "I don't think you said when you were down at the house."

"I was in the army aero service," Charles said uncomfortably. "I was a pilot."

"What about that!" Jim Ed said.

"Charles got to France too late for the war," Bess said brightly.

"Eugenia said you were in France, too, Mr. Ledbetter," Bess said. "What did you do?"

"I was in the infantry," Jim Ed said. "I carried a Springfield rifle."

"I wanted to fly," Charles said. "I love to fly. Nothing on earth like it! Don't you agree?"

"Oh yes," I said.

"Eugenia said you were wounded," Alfred said.

"Yes," I said.

"Shell fire?"

"Yes, shell fire."

"Deuced bad, shell fire," Charles said. He sounded as if he had studied the line or heard it in an English pub. "At least you were in on it."

"For a few weeks," I said.

He looked at me speculatively. "I wanted to be in on it," he said. "But I arrived in France a week before the Armistice. I did some routine patrols. I flew over the trenches. Terrible things, the trenches. I wonder if they'll ever repair the country. It was a stupid war, you know. You fellows should never have started it."

"I believe the Germans started it," I said.

"Well, you know what I mean. You Europeans. You didn't think twice about what you were getting into. Stupid war. Still, I wish I'd got into more of it."

Our talk was interrupted by Bert's arrival. She parked at the curb and strode in, wearing one of those bullet-shaped hats women wore then, and she looked stylish and vigorous. Eugenia greeted her with enthusiastic affection. We stood up for introductions. Bert shook hands with Jim Ed and me—a firm, strong handshake, and over it she looked at us carefully. She was pretty, blond like Eugenia, her hair a shade lighter. "I've heard so much about you both," Bert said to us. "Especially you, Mr. Alexander. What a terrible business the strike must have been!"

"It was not pleasant," I said.

As soon as Bert arrived, we sat down in the tiny dining room to eat. Bess served us. We were cramped around the table. The room smelled of varnish.

Bess said, "We were talking about Mr. Alexander's war service, Bert. Charles was telling us about it."

"I wasn't talking about *his* war service," Charles said, frowning. "I was talking about *my* service."

"Eugenia says you were in the Belgian army," Bert said. "That must have been interesting."

"It was dangerous, too," Bess said.

"I was not in for very long," I said.

"Long enough to be wounded," Eugenia said.

"That did not take long," I said.

Jim Ed laughed. Alfred and Charles turned to look at him as if they could not understand why.

"How did it happen?" Bess said. "It sounds just thrilling."

"I scarcely remember," I said. "A shell burst."

"Folks that were wounded don't like to talk about it," Jim Ed said quietly.

"I take it you were not wounded, Mr. Ledbetter?" Bert said.

"No, ma'am, I wasn't."

"Oh, don't call me 'ma'am,' " Bert said. "You're not my gardener." She laughed in a slightly unfriendly way. Bert had decided against Jim Ed. I did not want her to decide *for* him, but I resented what I thought were her reasons for deciding against him.

"I'm sorry," Jim Ed said.

"Oh, don't be sorry," Eugenia said, trying to patch things over. "There's nothing to be sorry about."

Charles turned to me. "What are you investing your money in?" he said.

"Investing?" I said.

"Yes, you must be investing with a good job like yours. I can help you make a lot of money if you're willing to take a risk or two."

"I have no money to spare," I said.

"No money? Why don't you have money?" Charles looked incredulous. He held his fork just over his plate and looked hard at me. "Do you gamble?"

"Gambling is a sin," Mrs. Pendleton said. Her first name was Mary. "Next to being a drunkard or an adulterer, gambling is the worst sin I know."

"I never gamble," I said.

"You should take some risks," Charles said. "Business risks. The kind that pay off."

"A friend of mine says that," I said, thinking of Dale Farmer.

"You probably have money stuck away in a mattress somewhere," Charles said. "It is the Hebrew mentality."

"Charles!" Eugenia said. "Don't pay any attention to him," she said to me. "Charles speaks before he thinks."

"I am not Jewish," I said.

"I am not saying you're a Hebrew," Charles said with a show of forced patience. "I'm saying that the Hebrew mentality is to put money in a lot of safe little businesses—jewelry stores, pawnshops, that sort of thing. Hide it in the mattress. Bury it. In Europe the Hebrews do banking on a big scale. They've taken over everything there. But here the Hebrew mentality is to play it safe. I say if you play it safe, you never will amount to anything."

"There's nothing wrong with a man saving his money," Jim Ed said.

"You can save money, or you can make money," Charles said. "If you put your money in the bank, you let the bank make money. You can take that same money and make more for yourself."

"The Jews are cursed by God. That is why they are like they are now," Eugenia's mother said. "They are still the chosen people, and when they go back to Jerusalem, the Lord is coming again, and we'll have the millennium."

Eugenia looked at me across the table and rolled her eyes.

"Is that so?" Jim Ed said politely.

"Yes, young man, that is so. The Bible teaches us that the Jews will go back to Jerusalem and that there they will be converted and Christ will come again. Haven't you heard of the Balfour Declaration?"

"Is that in the Bible?" Jim Ed said.

Bess laughed. Charles laughed, too, throwing his head back in a jerk.

Mary Pendleton looked at Jim Ed with the resigned expression of a devout woman among heathen. "The Balfour Declaration is not in the Bible. It's been in the newspapers."

"Well, there's lots of Bible that's been in the newspapers," Jim Ed said. I could not tell if he was making fun of Mary Pendleton. Neither could she.

"It's Britain's promise to give the Jews a home in Palestine. When they do that, Jesus will come again, and we should be ready." Mary Pendleton looked at him earnestly. "Have you been saved, young man?"

"Oh, sure," Jim Ed said. Mary Pendleton looked sternly at him.

"I'm not asking if you have religion," she said. "Lots of people have religion, but they don't have salvation."

"That's what my mamma says," Jim Ed said politely.

Mary Pendleton stared at Jim Ed. He seemed cheerfully indifferent. "We should be ready to meet God," she said. "Are you sure you are washed in the blood of the Lamb?"

"Oh yes, ma'am," Jim Ed said. "Head to toe."

"That is not the way we usually talk about it," she said.

"Different folks talks about it in different ways," Jim Ed said. He went on eating, concentrating on his plate. I almost laughed.

"I don't believe this generation will see death before the Lord comes back in all his glory," Mary Pendleton said.

"That's great," Jim Ed said.

"It won't be great for everybody," she said.

"That's what Mamma says," Jim Ed said. "It's going to be pretty hot for some folks. Like the foundry—isn't that right, Paul?"

"I suppose so," I said, trying to make myself sound serious.

"It's all in the signs," Mary Pendleton said, frowning. "We don't know the exact moment the Lord is coming back, but we know he's coming just after the Jews go back to Jerusalem. When you see these things begin to come to pass, you know the moment is nigh."

"I think it would be nice if Jesus could come during the Christmas pageant at church," Bess said. "It would be so fitting." She was a saleslady at a department store called Burns's in Knoxville, and she had taken two hours off for lunch to help cook the meal and to meet us. Saturday was her busy day. She ate hastily, saying several times that she had to go back in a hurry because the store could not do without her on Saturday afternoon.

"Well, we shouldn't lecture these men on the Bible," Bert said gaily.

The meal dragged on.

"Tell us about the Catholics, Mr. Alexander," Bess said.

"Please," Eugenia said. "Let's not talk about religion. Religion is very personal."

"God tells us to talk about religion," Mary Pendleton said. "Unless Catholics repent of their sins just like everyone else, they are going to hell."

"We should talk about flying," Charles said.

Mary Pendleton said, "Won't you have some more chicken?"

"Oh no, ma'am," Jim Ed said. "I'm full up to here. You're a wonderful cook, Mrs. Pendleton. Just wonderful."

"Eugenia helped me," Mary Pendleton said. "Eugenia can cook when she wants to."

"I helped you more than Eugenia did, Mamma," Bess said.

"Cooking is boring," Eugenia said.

"She's got too big for the kitchen now that she's in the newspapers so much," Charles said.

"I don't like to cook," Eugenia said. "Writing is more fun."

"I still hope you'll give up the newspaper and go as a missionary," Mary Pendleton said. "I know that a newspaper office is not a place for a young woman. You can say all you want to about it, but it's not a place for a lady."

"I fully agree with Mamma in that department," Charles said. "When are you going to quit that job and settle down, Eugenia?"

"Eugenia promised God she would go as a missionary, and she hasn't done it. I tell her God will punish her, but she won't believe me. You can't break your promises to God. Look at Saul's disobedience. Look at what happened to him."

"Mamma, I was thirteen years old."

"A promise is a promise," Mary Pendleton said. "Especially when it's made to God." I felt a chill, and I saw Bernal standing behind Mary Pendleton, his arms folded, looking gravely down at the table. I looked away.

"A missionary?" I said.

"A missionary to the heathen," Mary Pendleton said. "We had a wonderful missionary come to speak at the tabernacle when Eugenia was a girl, and he gave an altar call. He said that he wanted everyone who would surrender to God to go be a missionary to come down to the front, and Eugenia went. She went up and cried and said she'd go wherever God would send her. I never have been so happy."

"Oh, Mamma, please. Let's talk about something else," Eugenia said, her face reddening.

"You made a promise to God, and you broke it," Mary Pendleton said. "God doesn't forget the promises we make to him."

"I do good in the work I do now," Eugenia said.

"You don't save souls, Eugenia."

"Well, I think I'd better get back to the shop," Alfred said uncomfortably.

"I have to get back to the store," Bess said. "Can you give me a ride, Alfred?"

"Do you have a car, Mr. Alexander?" Alfred said.

"I borrow a car now and then," I said. "But I don't own one. I came with Jim Ed."

"Why don't you have a car?" Alfred said.

"I have not been willing to spend the money," I said.

"Come out to the Maxwell Garage, and I'll give you a free ride. You'll want a Maxwell if you ride in one."

"Perhaps I will do that," I said.

"I like a Ford myself," Jim Ed said.

Alfred gave him a withering look. "You ought to try a Maxwell. That jalopy you drive is out of date."

"It gets me around," Jim Ed said.

"In this world a man is judged by his car," Alfred said. "If you don't drive a new car, people won't think you're successful."

"I'll remember that," Jim Ed said.

We did not play the guitar and the mandolin. Neither Jim Ed nor I brought up the matter of music.

129

EUGENIA AND BERT took Jim Ed and me for a drive. We went across the river and into the country towards the mountains, and we talked about how pretty they were. The road was unpaved and dusty, and the dust blew in the open windows.

Eugenia drove, and Bert sat next to her in the front seat. Jim Ed and I sat in back. Bert hung an elbow over the back of her seat, looking around to speak to us. When my eyes met hers, I tried to smile.

"You have to forgive Mamma," Eugenia said, turning her head slightly and raising her voice. "Daddy died so young."

"The month before I was born," Bert said.

"It was terrible for Mamma," Eugenia said. "The shock of it. She was lonely, and in two or three years she got married again."

"Mr. Pendleton," Bert said.

"Mr. Pendleton was the worst man I've ever known," Eugenia said. "I still have nightmares about him."

"Well, I don't think about him *that* much," Bert said. "Poor Mamma was fooled. Mamma can be taken in by any charlatan who says 'Jesus' every third word. It's too bad she married one of them."

"He prayed about everything," Eugenia said.

"Charles laughed at him once," Bert said. "For praying over a sick mule."

"He nearly beat Charles to death," Eugenia said. All the mirth was gone from her voice.

"Yes," Bert said. "Yes, he took a stick to Charles, and Mamma had to fight him off. The neighbors had to come help. He hurt Charles."

"Alfred fought him," Eugenia said. "Mr. Pendleton was strong. He picked Alfred up and choked him."

"Don't talk about it," Bert said, her voice low and soft. "We were afraid all the time. Terribly afraid."

"Alfred got away. He went over to the Mongers'. You remember that, Bert?"

"Of course I remember. Let's talk about something else."

"The Mongers were neighbors, and Alfred went to stay with them," Eugenia said.

"Nelle was already there," Bert said.

"Yes," Eugenia said. "Nelle was there."

"I think he married Mamma because he wanted Nelle," Bert said. Nelle was the oldest child. Jim Ed and I had not met her. She worked as dietician at St. Mary's Hospital in Knoxville. It was a new hospital, and Catholic.

"We shouldn't talk about such things," Eugenia said, nodding her head back towards us as if to remind Bert that they were not alone. "I don't like to talk about him."

"He wanted to spank Nelle when she was a grown woman," Bert said.

"Nelle was terrified," Eugenia said.

"We were all terrified," Bert said.

"Mamma thought it was safer if Nelle went to the Mongers'."

"He went to the Mongers', and he told Mr. Monger he wanted his children back right now," Bert said, her voice low and grim.

"Mr. Monger came out and said that if Mr. Pendleton didn't leave, he was going to call his sons out, and they would beat Mr. Pendleton within an inch of his life," Eugenia said.

"I loved Mr. Monger," Bert said. "Let's stop talking about it."

"He made all sorts of threats," Eugenia said. "He walked the floor. Bert and I hid in the attic, and Mr. Pendleton walked the floor, yelling at the top of his voice."

"He said God's judgment was going to fall on the Mongers. And it was going to fall on Nelle and Alfred."

"He threatened Mamma," Eugenia said. "He told her that he had the right to whip her because of her awful children. Let's just stop talking about it."

"I heard Charles down there crying and crying, and Mr. Pendleton slapped him," Bert said. "I heard the crack. After he beat him, he slapped the poor boy again."

"You have to make allowances for Charles," Eugenia said, speaking back over her shoulder to us. "He is not nice sometimes. He went through more than you can know. I love Charles because I remember how he tried to protect us from Mr. Pendleton."

"I remember when—" Bert said.

"No," Eugenia said, more agitated than ever. "Please, Bert, let's drop the subject."

"I'm so glad I have a husband who loves me," Bert said. "I feel so thankful." She seemed ready to cry.

"What happened to Mr. Pendleton?" Jim Ed said.

"He left. He went to Florida. He went to preach revivals," Eugenia said. "He wanted Mamma to come with him. But she wouldn't go."

"What about that," Jim Ed said.

"He just left?" I said.

"Somebody put a bundle of switches at the front door one night. I think that helped Jesus call him to Florida," Bert said with a bitter laugh. "The neighbors were worried about us."

"Good for them," Jim Ed said.

"Yes," Eugenia said in a voice so low that I could scarcely hear it. "Yes, we had good neighbors. They knew things were not right."

"It's awful to think of a marriage breaking up," Bert said. "But we were glad to see Mr. Pendleton go."

"I've got a brother who's divorced," Jim Ed said.

"Oh really?" Bert said, not sympathetically, I thought. "Well, he and Mamma never did get a divorce. If he's still alive, they're still married."

"We don't know where Mr. Pendleton is or whether he's alive. If he should come back now, I think Charles would kill him," Eugenia said.

"Charles don't look like the killing kind to me," Jim Ed said.

"Charles *doesn't* look like the killing kind," Bert said, correcting him.

"I'm sorry. I forget," Jim Ed said. His face turned red. "I know better than I talk sometimes."

"Oh, we all do," Eugenia said.

"We ought to start back," Bert said.

"Yes. Would you like a cup of coffee before you go home?" Eugenia said.

"That would be very nice," I said.

"Let's go to the Greek place," Bert said. "They have such good coffee."

"Do you mind going to a Greek place? It's very clean," Eugenia said.

"Suits me," Jim Ed said.

I said nothing.

"Greeks don't do anything but open restaurants," Bert said. "Are there many Greeks in Belgium, Mr. Alexander?"

"No, not many," I said.

"I bet the ones that are there open restaurants, too," Bert said with a laugh.

"Yes," I said.

"What do you suppose they do in Greece?" Bert said. "Do they all just eat out in one another's restaurants?"

"Have you ever been to Greece, Mr. Alexander?" Eugenia said.

"Yes," I said.

"Did you like it?" Bert said.

"Yes," I said. I remembered the twilight at Delphi when the gray sheen of the Gulf of Corinth lay flat like a dim mirror under stars that were coming out and how the bulk of the Peloponnisos rose dark against the darkening sky.

"Well, we'll have coffee, and you'll have to tell us about all the things you saw in Greece."

"I was very young," I said.

"Did you go with your parents?"

"Yes," I said.

"Was your father still alive then?"

"Oh yes," I said.

"So you're like us," Bert said warmly. "Your real father is dead."

"Yes," I said.

130

THE RESTAURANT was at the corner of Gay and Depot streets at the north end of the Gay Street viaduct over the Dixie Railroad's Knoxville yard. The passenger terminal was on the other side of Depot Street. It was built to look like the front of a Flemish building with a stepped facade on each end. It seemed out of place here. You entered from Depot Street and went downstairs to the tracks. A passenger train was in—42, heading north, towards Washington and New York. The air reeked of coal smoke and peanuts and ground coffee. A packing house for coffee and peanut butter stood near the rail yard.

"I love trains," Eugenia said. "We lived near the railroad in the country when I was a girl. Did I tell you that?"

"No," I said.

"You told me," Jim Ed said.

"Yes—well, I'm sorry if I repeat myself. Our family's all buried down there. The ones who are dead."

"I wish we could remember Father," Bert said wistfully.

"He is buried in Charleston. Not Charleston, South Carolina," Eugenia said. "Charleston, Tennessee. It's not much more than a village. It was near our farm."

"They cut down all the trees in the graveyard," Bert said.

"They said the roots were getting into the graves," Eugenia said. "What could be nicer than to become a tree after we die?"

"It would make it awkward at the resurrection," Bert said with a laugh.

"Oh, Bert," Eugenia said. She laughed, too.

"I don't want a resurrection," Bert said. "What would we do without bodies?" She giggled.

We entered the restaurant. It was small, and it smelled of Greek things— olive oil and mutton and coffee and fish.

"I can't stay long," Bert said. "Lionel will be upset if I am late."

"Lionel doesn't own you," Eugenia said.

Bert's eyes filled. "He *does* own me. I am his wife. I have to obey him. I adore my husband. I hope when you marry, you will adore your husband the way I adore Lionel."

We sat down at a small table. It was plain wood and had a clean white tablecloth on it.

"Well, I think you carry it to extremes," Eugenia said at last.

"That's because you have never been in love," Bert said.

Jim Ed looked around happily, his big hands folded in front of him on the table. He had loosened his necktie, and his collar was open. The reddish hair on his chest stuck out over the top button of his shirt.

"That's a picture of the Greek temples," Eugenia said. She pointed to a large lithograph of the Parthenon. "Does anyone know which one?"

"Beats me," Jim Ed said.

"It's the Akropolis," she said. "It's the temple of the Akropolis."

"It is the Parthenon," I said. "The Akropolis is the hill. The Parthenon is the temple."

"Oh, is that the way it is?" Eugenia said cheerfully. "I always get things mixed up."

"You must know a lot about art," Bert said, looking at me with a smile.

"What can I get for you people?" The question came in a heavily accented voice. A middle-aged man with stiff, wavy gray hair brushed back from his ears was standing at our table. He was bald on top and wore thick glasses. His apron was a white towel wrapped around his waist and pinned at the back. He was wiping his thick hands on the apron. I saw that he was staring at me. Only a few people were in the dining room. A hand-lettered sign on the long counter advertised a plate lunch for twenty cents. A tall electric fan beat the air with a hum. We heard the five quick blasts of the whistle on the locomotive in the rail yard.

"I think we all want coffee," I said.

"Anything else? We got some nice pastry. Greek pastry. Very good for the ladies. You try it; you like it. I promise you like it. You don't like it, I don't charge you nothing."

"It's too sweet for me," Eugenia said. "I've tried it, but it's too sweet."

"I just want coffee. Cream and sugar," Bert said. "I must be getting back."

"Coffee for me," Jim Ed said. "Black."

"Hey, you no try my baklava?" the man said to me and laughed companionably.

"No," I said. "Just coffee. Four coffees."

"You miss a real treat," he said. He turned to another man behind the counter and spoke in Greek. "They think the baklava is too sweet. What do these people know about anything? Too sweet. If it is not sweet, why does anyone eat it? Mary and all the saints!"

"Strange Americans," the other man said in Greek, laughing. "Four coffees. Well, another time. Say, that child there—the one with the mustache. Is he not a Greek child?"

"I wondered myself," our waiter said in Greek. "He looks like a Greek child, but I do not know him. Perhaps he is new to this country. He should come to the church if he is a Greek child. Have you heard that somebody new is in town?"

"Eleni Stavvas has a brother who is new in town. But I have met him. This child is not the brother of Eleni Stavvas."

"You should invite him to the church. He may not know that we have a church now."

"If he wants to come to the church, he will speak to us about it. We should not invite him to the church if he does not want to come. Do you think he could be Polyxene Mavros's nephew Timoteos? She told me that her nephew Timoteos was coming in the spring. Do you suppose it is Timoteos?"

"Listen how funny they sound," Bert whispered. She and Eugenia laughed.

"I think it would be nice to speak a foreign language," Eugenia said. "You must speak several foreign languages, Mr. Alexander."

"He speaks French," Jim Ed said proudly.

"Are they speaking French?" Bert said.

"No," I said. I stifled the impulse to say, "Stupid woman, they are speaking Greek."

"The *babba* would have told us," our waiter was saying. "It is not Timoteos."

"We should not have come in here, Eugenia," Bert said. "Mr. Alexander and Mr. Ledbetter will think we don't have a better place in Knoxville. It smells so bad in here I can hardly breathe. Don't the smells upset you?"

"Not me," Jim Ed said. "I kind of like it."

"Well, it makes me sick," Bert said. "Let's drink our coffee in a hurry."

"I eat lunch here sometimes," Eugenia said. "It's cheap. I don't mind the smells. I like them really."

"Well, I'm surprised, Eugenia. I am truly surprised. You would never catch me eating lunch in a place like this," Bert said.

"They don't keep any alcohol on the premises," Eugenia said. "The men in the newsroom say this is one of the few places in Knoxville where you can't buy a drink. That's one of the reasons I eat here. They obey the law."

"I think he must be a Greek child," the waiter said in Greek to the man behind the counter. "I will ask him. But I will not ask him to come to church."

He brought the coffee and put it down, one cup in front of each of us. He brought cream and sugar in a pitcher and a bowl. "Excuse me, sir," he said in Greek, "but my brother and I have been thinking that perhaps you are Greek. You bear a resemblance somehow—"

"I beg your pardon," I said quickly in English.

"We thought you were Greek," he said in Greek.

"I do not understand," I said in English.

He looked at me a long moment. "Oh, please excuse me, sir," he said in English. "My brother and I thought you was a Greek boy. Please excuse me. I was most impolite."

"Not at all," I said.

Bert nearly stifled with laughter. She put both hands to her face and laughed.

"No, you see, I am Belgian. I was in the Belgian army. I was wounded. That is why I am here."

"You will notice how quickly he tells something that is true to hide something that is a lie," Guy said, speaking behind me in a voice as unmistakable as the sound of the streetcar that simultaneously thundered by on the steel tracks in the street outside.

"Well, well," our waiter said skeptically. "Well, I never would have supposed it. The Belgians I know are big fat fellows with blond hair. You do not look Belgian. You look Greek. I must swear to it. My brother and I both thought that you was Greek. Well well. Belgian." It was a statement, not a question.

"Yes," I said.

"It is the mustache," the waiter said. "It looks like a Greek mustache."

"I am Belgian," I said.

"Well, here we are all Americans," the waiter said, shrugging and folding his tray under his arm. "My brother, me, our wives. We was all Greek. Now we are all Americans. God bless America, I say. Where we come from don't matter. Please forgive me for speaking to you in tongue you do not understand. Forgive me, sir."

"It is all right," I said.

"Enjoy your coffee," the waiter said. He went away.

"Can you *imagine!*" Bert said, laughing into her hands, looking out of the corner of her eyes at the dignified retreat of the waiter. "Can you *imagine?* He really did think you were *Greek*. Oh, the *nerve* of these people! We should never have come in here. Never. Mr. Alexander, I do apologize."

"It is all right," I said.

"They mean well," Eugenia said. "They recognized Mr. Alexander as a foreigner."

"At least the coffee is good," Bert said. "Lionel hates stale coffee. He has me make his coffee one half minute before I pour his first cup in the morning. He thought you were Greek. That is very funny."

"You were very nice to him," Eugenia said. "Bert, don't laugh. I don't believe in making fun of people."

"But it's so *funny,*" Bert said.

"He did not understand me when I spoke to him in Greek," I heard the waiter say.

"He looked as if he understood," the brother said in Greek. "Whom does he resemble?"

"It's been such a nice day," Eugenia said, smiling her large, open smile. "I hate to end it."

"It's just beginning for me," Bert said. "I get to enjoy the whole evening with Lionel. Oh, we're so happy—so marvelously happy. You must come out and visit more often, Eugenia. And both of you gentlemen. You would love Lionel."

"He does look like somebody," the waiter said in Greek. "I do not know who it is."

"I always feel that I'm disturbing Lionel when I come to visit," Eugenia said.

"Nonsense," Bert said. "Lionel loves you, Eugenia. You know he does. Bess makes him nervous. But then Bess makes *me* nervous." She laughed.

"The cigarette salesman is Greek," the brother behind the counter said in Greek. "He looks like the cigarette salesman."

"After you, folks," Jim Ed said, holding the door.

"You are so gallant, Mr. Ledbetter," Eugenia said. She smiled warmly at him, her face close to his.

131

I COURTED EUGENIA relentlessly. I courted her family. I took her flowers. I sent flowers to Mary Pendleton on her birthday. I surprised Eugenia by coming to her newspaper office to see her on weekdays. I made an excuse to come to Knoxville, to do business with Coster Shops, where boxcars and locomotives were repaired. All in the line of business! And just at lunch I happened to be free and went around to the newspaper office to invite Eugenia to have lunch with me at the Hotel Atkin. Luncheon seventy-five cents! Eugenia was appalled at the price. I tried to be nonchalant. One dollar and a half for both of us; three mediocre courses, the beef like leather. I supposed I would never again eat a meal like the meals Guy, Bernal, and I took for granted in Ghent. I left a quarter tip—Paul Alexander, Grand Master of Lunch. "You are quite the actor," Guy said. "You have learned from me more than I would have believed possible."

"You are betraying your friend," Bernal said.

"I am in love with her," I said. "He is not suited to her. It is clear that she does not love him."

"She does not love you," Bernal said.

"Have you noticed, Bernal?" Guy said. "The young man desires women who do not love him. First Palmyre and now this one. He chooses the unattainable."

"He did not betray a friend before," Bernal said.

"Stop it!" I cried. "You cannot speak of betrayal. It is unfair. Unfair."

"And Daisy?" Bernal said. "What of Daisy?"

"Daisy is a child. She does not love me; she loves a picture she has made up of me."

"It is a matter of interpretation," Bernal said.

"She went back to California. She did not care for me anymore. In everything she does she is an actress in a film that runs always in her head."

"So you move to another conquest," Bernal said. "Guy is right. You love only those women who do not love you."

"She will love me—I will make her love me."

"Hubris," Guy said. "Ikaros flying near the sun."

I accustomed people to seeing us together. I took her to dinner and to motion pictures. We did not tell her mother when we went to motion pictures because Mary Pendleton thought films were evil. A good Christian never went to the picture show, she said. I stopped by Burns's department store one afternoon and looked up Bess and chatted with her. Bess was my friend ever after. She talked about me to Eugenia as though I had been Apollo.

I went to church with Eugenia—the cavernous, frame People's Tabernacle on Central Street near stinking First Creek, where the slums of Knoxville festered and ran like an open sore. Here lived people who came out of the mountains without talents for the city and packed themselves into rickety old wooden houses, some rooms with dirt floors, the upper floors dirty and unpainted and stinking of rot and urine and worse, and the air thick and close in warm weather, and people lying sick in filthy beds.

Mary Pendleton and her sister, Dolly Laughton, ministered to these people because they thought that God dwelled only among the poor. This benign attitude of theirs might have seemed like saintly humility, but in them it took the air of arrogance, for they believed that the churches where well-dressed people went were temples of hypocrisy and "modernism," the word they used to condemn preachers who had forsaken a literal understanding of the Bible. In their view only those who believed every word in the Bible would get to heaven, and at the People's Tabernacle, where the worn-out women and children of this neighborhood came, there was no danger of modernism. These people greeted Mary Pendleton and her sister as if they had been saints of God.

The sisters did not preach; in their vision of the world women had no authority to preach. They commanded the tabernacle by the authority of their personalities. They gave their testimonies about their own experiences with God, and they managed the tabernacle and its preacher as if they had been the shopkeepers of heaven. If the poor heard the gospel, the sisters believed, they would be saved, and they would stop drinking, and they would get jobs, and they would educate their children, and they would rise in the world. The sisters' anecdotal world was crowded with mythological tales of drunkards gloriously converted and dry who became managers of department stores and owners of factories and gave all the credit to the Lord Jesus and to the prayers of a Christian mother or a long-suffering Christian wife or to someone who handed them a tract begging them in big red letters to take Jesus and be born again. Such people gave 10 percent of their income to the Lord and never worked on Sunday and never drank or smoked but always gave their testimony at prayer meetings.

I never saw any of these wondrously redeemed people. They existed like the legends of the patriarchs or the miracles of Jesus and the Apostles. And yet there was something uplifting and grand in Mary Pendleton's narratives. She told the stories of her golden legend so vividly that we suspended disbelief. I looked around the congregation, seeing toothless, dirty women— the congregation had three women for every man—leaning forward, hollow eyes alight with hope.

Did Mary Pendleton care for the poor because she loved them? I thought she worked with them to atone for unspecified sins of her own that weighed on her desiccated heart, perhaps the sin of having married for lust after her saintly husband died. Mary Pendleton was the stronger of the two sisters. Dolly Laughton had a propensity to lapse into speaking in tongues now and then—not foreign languages that some one else might understand but ecstatic glossolalia. "Speaking in tongues is one way the devil ruins a woman," Mary Pendleton said cryptically. She kept a rein on Dolly that would have made a horse fall backwards.

Eugenia went reluctantly to the tabernacle. "If I did not live at home, I would not set foot in that dreary place," she told me in exasperation. "I don't know why we have to go to a church where the people smell so bad."

"Your mother is a good woman," I said without conviction. Eugenia adored her mother even when she was exasperated with her.

"Hypocrisy!" Guy shouted.

"Yes," I replied.

I forced myself to get along with Alfred and Charles. "If I ordered a carload of sons of bitches and they just sent me Charles, I'd sign for the shipment," Jim Ed said. He liked Alfred a little better. So did I.

I listened in polite silence as Charles and Alfred explained elaborate schemes to get rich. "Buy land," Charles said smugly. "They're not making any more of it." He had a real estate office just off Gay Street downtown. You walked up, and there he sat at a big desk in a close little room that smelled of varnish. He was always dapper, a wax image, flashing a superior grin, ready to dash you out to North or East Knoxville where he had deals cooking, ready to buy any promising lots you might own, ready to keep them and make a profit as the town grew around his holdings, ready to leave you gnashing your teeth when you saw that you had stupidly given away a fortune. He drove a new Maxwell, always waxed like himself, and, like Alfred, he extolled the importance of a new car to make people see how successful you were. "People like to deal with success," he said. "Nothing proves success like a new car."

"What do you think of Charles?" Eugenia said uneasily.

"He has strong opinions," I said.

"Yes," she said with an uncomfortable laugh. "I wish he did not fear the Jews so much. I wish he could get rich himself. He is better than he seems."

"I am sure he will have great success," I said.

"Are you really sure?" she asked doubtfully.

I looked at her and was dangerously tempted to be honest, as I was honest with Palmyre, to express entirely what I thought, that her brother would fail—completely, miserably, without redemption. But I could not muster the courage. "Yes," I said. "I am sure."

"I hope so," she said fervently.

Alfred touted the Maxwell automobile as if it had been a cure for tuberculosis, proof of the existence of God, and the fountain of youth. "A man's automobile is, next to his wife's honor, his most important possession," he said.

"Alfred, I don't think of myself as a possession," Eugenia said.

"You will belong to your husband when you marry," Alfred said.

"Oh, pooh," Eugenia said.

I drove Eugenia's Maxwell, and we went riding together in the country; she told me Alfred was pleased. He thought that if I drove her Maxwell, I would buy one for myself.

"I am afraid Alfred dislikes me," I said.

"You must overlook him. He is struggling to make his business work. He sees foreigners like you come in and succeed, and they make him afraid."

"Does he dislike me because I am foreign?"

"Oh, forgive me," she said earnestly. "I didn't mean for it to come out like that."

"How did you mean for it to come out?"

"I just meant that Alfred . . . He is not bad. He is not selfish, and he doesn't hate foreigners. He's worried. He worries all the time about his future. About money. He wants to be as wealthy as Charles, and he's afraid he may have chosen the wrong thing. I don't think Maxwells will ever sell as well as Fords. That's all it is."

"I see," I said, and let it go.

I was obsessed with her. It was Palmyre all over again. Eugenia's face ran through my mind when I was thinking and talking about someone else. I looked at myself in the mirror, removed my false teeth, ran my tongue into the vacancy, ran my hand over my scruffy chin before I shaved and through my coarse black hair, and I thought, "What does Eugenia see when she looks at me?" Love is a madness; a thousand or a hundred thousand trite songs have affirmed as much. If you have not felt the madness yourself, you cannot understand anything I am writing.

What about Daisy? I scarcely thought of her. I do not believe that during this time I compared my passion for Eugenia with all its harebrained logic to Daisy's infatuation with me even when, like Daisy, I inspected myself in the mirror. She was in California. She wrote warm letters to me, but she remained in California, and she wrote enthusiastically about the big break that was about to catapult her to fame. She had obtained a minor role in a film; the camera would be on her alone for several scenes. She wrote how she practiced expressions, and she told me about compliments the director gave her. She told me I would have to join her in California soon, and we would be married, and I would find a wonderful job.

I wrote to her soberly and infrequently. Her letters bored me.

"She is yours for the asking, so you do not care for her," Bernal said. "You now betray your friend."

I made no response. What could I say? I never spoke to Jim Ed about it; I pretended that he had never been interested in Eugenia. He accepted the pretense. He dropped off, like a falling leaf in autumn. I cannot be sure of his motives. I think he decided he had no chance with Eugenia, and he did not want to embarrass himself. Or maybe it was that he felt himself to be my friend and that he could not court Eugenia without being disloyal to me. He wrote Daisy frequently, and he innocently told her of my romance with Eugenia; I got a furious letter from Daisy. She accused me of betraying her. I did not reply, and she did not write again.

I bought a Maxwell. On the day I bought it, Alfred drove around Knoxville with me to show me how it worked, explaining every part of the car as though he had been a professor of anatomy enumerating the 206 bones of the human skeleton to a talking jellyfish. Alfred pretended that driving a car was an esoteric art with its own haughty and high-minded priests—the dealers in new cars—who were charged with a lore complicated enough to provoke admiration among the plebs for the daredevil who could master the magical act of steering an automobile over the road. He was not a salesman, he said. He was the service manager in the new Maxwell dealership.

I started driving back and forth between Bourbonville and Knoxville to see Eugenia.

"You are courting, Mr. Alexander," Darcy Coolidge said with an air of discovery and pleasure. "I can tell when a young man is courting. I commend your good taste," she said. "I'm sure you will not be with us long. We'll miss you in the boardinghouse."

Bert was my advocate. "I could see that Eugenia liked that Ledbetter person," she told me later on. "But he wasn't for her."

"He is a very good man," I said. "One of the best men I have ever known." I felt smug and superior, and Bert was smug and superior, too.

"Every good man would not make Eugenia a good husband," Bert said. "A farmer is the salt of the earth. But you don't put salt in your coffee or on your angel food cake. I want Eugenia to marry someone she can be proud of. Alfred is getting married, but who would ever marry Bess? Nelle's getting too old to marry. Charles doesn't have the courage to marry. Sometimes I think there's something wrong with us. I don't want whatever it is to hurt Eugenia. I want her to marry you. She can be proud of you. You and Lionel will be such friends! You just wait and see!"

I even courted Lionel. Bert invited us to lunch on a Saturday at her home in Maryville. It was a big white house with a verandah and a fish pool in the back. Victorian, Eugenia called it. I thought the style was nondescript. Lionel was sullen. Bert was pregnant—her revelation of the autumn. She was overjoyed. Lionel was not. He and I walked back to look at his garden and to study his bright goldfish, swimming around in their shallow pool.

He was silent for a long time. "Here is the fish pool," he said. "We feed them oatmeal. I hate oatmeal." After another long pause he said, "Our property runs back to the fence there." After another very long pause he said, "That is an elm tree." Then suddenly he said, "I didn't want the child. I tell you, Bert never gets enough. If Eugenia is anything like Bert, you're not going to get much sleep." He was glum. "Women!" he said, taking out a cigarette and lighting it, offering me one and lighting it for me. I thought of making love to Eugenia with her on her back, on her stomach, on top of me. I imagined slipping her underpants off her lovely hips, hearing her suck in her breath as the dainty silk slid down her smooth legs, having her shut her eyes as I gently touched her nipples. Insatiable. It must run in families, I thought, and I felt weak with desire.

132

MRS. LEDBETTER had been warm to me. She turned cold. When I came to the house, she found some reason to excuse herself. In earlier days when I was there in the late afternoon she had said, "Stay for supper, Paul. I'll just put another plate on."

"And she'll put water in the soup so there'll be enough," the old man said.

These spontaneous invitations stopped. I became an intruder; she said nothing about supper; her embarrassed but obedient men said nothing either. I realized that they were waiting for me to leave so they could sit down to eat. I left quickly.

"You are surprised," Guy said, mocking me. "The young man is startled because he shuns Mrs. Ledbetter's granddaughter, robs her son of a wife, and discovers that Mrs. Ledbetter has no more use for him."

I was ashamed, but not so much that I thought of giving Eugenia up. I did not want to give the Ledbetters up, either. I kept going to see them.

Guy said, "The young man imagines that at a certain moment these simple country people will recognize their own inferiority, embrace him for his magnanimity, and thank him for stealing Eugenia Curry, who could never have been elevated to what she can be had she married this simple country bumpkin, James Edward Ledbetter."

"You are too harsh," Bernal said.

"I am reading the vain young man's mind," Guy said. "I want him to know that I know what he is."

"He is not that bad," Bernal said.

"He is worse," Guy said. "He is alive, and we are dead."

I obstinately drove my new Maxwell out after supper and sat with them on some evenings. When I bought the car, Mrs. Ledbetter said, "Oh yes, the reporter's brother sells them, doesn't he?"

"It is a nice car," I said defensively.

"More expensive than a good Ford," Jim Ed said, smiling ironically.

Soon he bought a new Ford himself—defiantly, I thought—a shiny black Model T with a closed interior.

"When you let the wind stop blowing in your face, you lose your health," the old man said. "I never did catch a cold when I drove in the open air."

The old man seldom drove anymore.

I kept on visiting. They were too polite to tell me to go away; or perhaps they succumbed to the fact that I was Jim Ed's boss. If I wanted to be friendly with them, they had to be friendly to me. I even suggested that we play music together. Jim Ed dutifully brought out the guitar and the mandolin. When we made music, something of our old friendship was restored. When we stopped playing the chill came back, and we sat together through long intervals of uncomfortable silence.

I courted Bert because she liked me and wanted me to marry Eugenia, but I disliked her for her priggishness and her arrogance, her forced gaiety, above all for her unexamined conviction that all normal people were exactly like herself and agreed with her in every particular. She supposed that she had but to allude to one of her cherished prejudices for others to know exactly what she was talking about and to nod in agreement. Yet I was grateful that she was on my side. I began to think of my future ascent from Bourbonville, my place among the constellation of stars that made up the railroad. Now and then Bernal said, "You are duplicating the ambitions of Moreland Pinkerton."

"Nonsense!" I said.

Guy laughed; Bernal looked solemn and faded away.

"Don't leave me!" I cried.

Silence. Guy was gone, too.

Perhaps I clung to the Ledbetters and to Dr. Youngblood because every day made me realize how few friends I had in the county.

I felt vividly Brian Ledbetter's disappointment that his son was not married. When Jim Ed and I played music, the old man sat with us, subdued and moody, eyes dreaming in space. He wanted a grandchild. "If you don't get married," he told Jim Ed, "I'm going to die, and my name is going to disappear from the earth."

"We're all going to die," Jim Ed said. "I've heard that the earth is going to freeze someday when the sun cools down. I've read that in the newspapers."

"That's so long from now that it's not worth thinking about," the old man said.

"Well, we're all going to die, and when we die, nothing matters," Jim Ed said.

"We ain't never dead when we have children," the old man said.

"You sound like one of the patriarchs," Jim Ed said.

"I *am* one of the patriarchs," the old man said.

Willy was gone during the music. He was at work. He was losing weight, and he talked more. I thought that Mrs. Ledbetter ought to be grateful to me for that. But she kept her icy distance.

133

ON CHRISTMAS EVE, 1921, I kissed Eugenia for the first time, and we were married on March 21, the first day of spring, 1922. I kissed her very gently; she kissed me gently back. I do not know if anyone had kissed her before. She seemed uncertain about the whole thing, shutting her eyes and lifting her head, keeping her lips together. It was the holiday season, you understand. Her spirits were high. I kissed her spontaneously, joyfully; she was reserved. She did kiss me back.

To marry on the first day of spring was a good omen, I said, promising the greening of life, growing things. Warren G. Harding was President. Mary Pendleton thought that at last we had an honest man in the White House. No Democrat could be an honest man, she thought.

We did not get married in church. I was Catholic, you see. "I wanted Eugenia to be married at the tabernacle," Mary Pendleton said in a tone of the utmost injury and grief. "Mr. Parry will not perform the ceremony with a Catholic."

"I do not want Mr. Parry to perform the ceremony, Mamma," Eugenia said.

"He will not because Mr. Alexander is not saved."

"You can call him Paul, Mamma. He is going to be your son-in-law. Mr. Parry will not perform the ceremony because we have not asked him to marry us. Whether Paul is saved or not has nothing to do with it."

"Eugenia, you do not know what you are saying. You are going back on the Lord. You are going back on me."

"I am not going back on the Lord, Mamma. We are going to be married at Bert and Lionel's."

"That is not a church. People should be married in a church. If you get married in a house, God will not bless your union. He won't bless it anyway since Mr. Alexander is not born again."

"You can be married anywhere you want, Mamma. All we need is a preacher."

"What preacher is going to marry a Protestant to a Catholic?"

"Mr. Shugart, Mamma. He is the minister of the Methodist church in Maryville. He is a very nice man. He said he would be glad to perform the ceremony."

"Both of you, you mark my words. Eugenia was called by God to be a missionary. If you marry, and if you do not keep your promise to God, Eugenia, God will curse you."

"Oh, Mamma, please!"

"The world mocks and holds him in derision, but the judgments of the Lord are true and righteous altogether. You cannot escape the curse of God."

"There's no such thing as a curse. Don't talk like that," Eugenia said. "It's medieval."

"God is not mocked," Mary Pendleton said. "For whatsoever a man soweth, that shall he also reap."

"Mamma, please. This should be a happy time."

"I won't come," Mary Pendleton said.

"Mamma. I'm your *daughter*. You *must* come."

"I won't come," Mary Pendleton said.

"You went to Bert's wedding!"

"Lionel is born again," Mary Pendleton said.

"Mamma!" Lionel hated church and cursed when Bert made him attend. He despised Mary Pendleton. "Just go along with the old bitch," he said. "Take a dose of her, and it's like a laxative; it goes right through you, and you don't feel any pain. These girls are slaves to the old sow. You got to make the best of it."

Mary Pendleton kept her promise; she did not come. Eugenia was deeply hurt. She hoped that at the last moment her mother would appear, but she did not.

My friends came up from Bourbonville. Mrs. Ledbetter did not come; I felt her absence. She said it was a long way to go to a wedding for people she didn't know well. Dale Farmer strutted around shaking hands with people and talking about the car works as if he and I ran it jointly. Dr. Youngblood was my best man. Eugenia wanted me to have her brother Alfred. "It would be so nice to keep it in the family," she said.

I said Dr. Youngblood was my friend and that he ought to be my best man. I might have had Jim Ed, but that would have been too much.

"He looks so shabby," Eugenia said.

"It is because he works hard taking care of people and does not have time to buy clothes," I said.

"Well, ask him to put something on that will do justice to my sister," Alfred said.

"I can get my tailor to fix him up with a good suit," Charles said. He would give the bride away.

"I hate for Alfred not to have some part in the wedding," Eugenia said.

"He can be an usher," Bert said. "That way he can stand up with Paul."

"An usher. We're not going to have enough people coming to need an usher," Eugenia said.

"I want Dr. Youngblood to be my best man."

"You don't like Alfred, do you?"

"I do not like him very much. No."

Eugenia looked at me long and indecisively. "Well, you should have the best man you want."

"Thank you."

"I'm sorry you don't like Alfred. I love Alfred."

"Alfred doesn't like me."

"That is true," she said.

Finally it was decided that both Charles and Alfred should give the bride away. They appeared in beautiful new suits.

Dr. Youngblood wore a suit that must have been twenty years old—Edwardian, too small for him.

Bert stood up with Eugenia as matron of honor. Bert was hugely pregnant. Eugenia did not wear a wedding dress. She wore a nice business suit and carried a bouquet of spring flowers. I wore a plain black suit. We stood in the yard while Lionel made photographs with a fancy Kodak; in them I look emaciated and uncomfortable. I seem to have been reserved, even unfriendly. In truth my heart beat so that I could see my pulse in my eyes.

The ceremony was quickly over. I saw Guy and Bernal standing to one side, both of them dressed in the elaborate morning coats they would have worn for Guy's wedding with Leonora on August 29, 1914. I thought of how expensive that wedding would have been, of the service in the Church of Notre Dame under the limestone cliffs, of the beautiful women in white dresses and big hats, of the small orchestra playing afterwards on the lawn with its conductor raising his white-gloved hand for the wedding march, of Guy's cynical laughter, of Bernal's courtliness, of me, in morning coat also, preparing to do my duty stiffly, and I thought of Palmyre and what we might have had, the long train trip to Russia, Bernal and Guy visiting us—a bright world of might-have-been—as the Methodist minister uttered the words that bound Eugenia and me as husband and wife.

We had a reception under the new-leafing trees in the yard. Ginger ale and fruit-juice punch. Mushy cake and soggy pies and some cookies. The wedding cake covered with white icing and a little bride and groom on top, the groom with a little black mustache.

"Looks just like you," Charles said to me and laughed. It was a Tuesday morning, day of the spring equinox, the sun bright, mild, dogwood trees leafing and promising to bloom. My guests gathered on one part of the lawn, Eugenia's on another. My guests tended to laugh loud. I heard Jim Ed laughing louder than anyone else; I had never heard him laugh so loud.

He handed me a telegram. "I promised I would give you this," he said. He blushed and turned away. It was from Daisy. "Congratulations," she said. "When you tire of the cow, I will be waiting."

I went to the bathroom and tore the telegram into little pieces and flushed it down the toilet. I flushed the toilet twice to be sure that every yellow scrap was swirled away.

I tried to circulate between the two groups, but Eugenia kept me most of the time with her people. I was introduced to many cousins. By one o'clock I was nervous and impatient.

"Can we not leave?" I said. "The train leaves at 2:00." Philip Drodge was sending his special wedding gift—a palace car hitched to the end of train number 41. We were going to New Orleans.

"Why can't we go to Gatlinburg and have a cabin by the river?" Eugenia said.

I did not want to go to Gatlinburg. It was only forty miles away. I did not think any of her family would follow us to New Orleans.

134

THE TRAIN ROLLED SOUTH, moving slowly. The roadbed was rough. I thought of Pinkerton returning from Cuba. A green land rolled by. We had a late lunch. We ate on heavy railroad silver, served by a stolid black porter in starched white.

"Mr. Drodge must have great respect for you," Eugenia said. She looked around uncomfortably. She was nervous, and her voice trembled.

"I believe he wants to show me how powerful he is," I said. "He can command his own railroad car." My words gushed out too fast, almost shrill.

"It's beautiful," Eugenia said, looking at the polished mahogany in the panels, the immaculate leather appointments, the Persian carpet on the floor, the polished brass fixtures, the heavy green and gold monogrammed curtains at the windows.

"Expensive, you mean," I said. My throat was tight.

"It is also beautiful," she said, laughing, catching herself.

"It's what Moreland Pinkerton wanted and never had," I said.

"Poor man," she said.

We were silent; the land rolled by. I would have swept Palmyre into my arms. She would have been naked in two minutes. We would have pulled the curtains, fallen into one of the fold-down beds, and wrapped ourselves into naked arms and legs all the way to New Orleans. Palmyre and I would have been going to Russia. Days and days en route.

Eugenia and I were married. Yet some transparent wall stood between us. I was touched by her mood. I was the first man she had been with alone besides her brothers, I thought. In uncertain contemplation I watched the passing countryside, and I looked at my fine gold watch, hoisting it out of the pocket of my vest, realizing that I was making a gesture to success. Everything had worked out, I thought. Life would be good.

The porter brought coffee. He bent over the table and poured with the delicacy of art, pulling the long silver spout of the pot up with a slight flourish at the end of each cup, backing respectfully away as though he had no right to look at us. I thought of M.P. Gone forever.

The train stopped at Bourbonville. We sat looking out, eavesdropping on the town. For the first time I thought it looked almost beautiful—the dogwood leafing and blossoming, the pale green of early spring tinting the ridge, the houses familiar, the courthouse dome rising above the trees, daffodils everywhere, forsythia yellow along the streets.

The chestnuts were dying. You could see that. When the live limbs were leafing, the dead limbs stood out, naked and forlorn. A blight from Japan was killing them. Someone told me that the former governor of Tennessee said all foreigners were like that blight: they came in from beyond the sea and corrupted the native American stock. The sun poured into the square; the air was clear, like the air in Greece. The light danced. The heavy palace car where we sat holding hands was almost soundproof. I heard the five blasts of the locomotive muffled, almost from another world, the elfin world that somehow I thought of as existing beyond the mountains somewhere, in a hidden glade where no human beings went. Someone ran down the train, leaping to look into the windows of the cars. In front of us he leaped to look into our car, and I jumped back. It was Guy. His eyes were wild, staring at me in the terror of death from the other side of the glass. The skin fell off his face, and his skull showed.

"What's wrong?" Eugenia said.

"Nothing," I said. "Nothing."

"You jumped. It was as if you saw something."

"I must have dozed off for a moment."

"You looked terrified."

"It must have been a dream," I said.

"A dream in daylight?"

"I did not sleep much last night."

"Oh," she said, blushing. She looked out. Guy was gone.

"I am glad we are not going to live here," Eugenia said.

"It is a nice place," I said.

"No," she said. "It is a village."

We were going to live in Knoxville, a little house on Edgewood Avenue. Charles arranged for us to buy it. I did not like the house. Aunt Dolly lived next door with her husband, Napoleon. Eugenia called him Uncle Nep. Their house was large, with tall narrow windows and a large backyard and a verandah in front. I would take the train every day to Bourbonville. A local ran down early in the morning; another ran up in the late afternoon.

"We can be close to everybody," Eugenia said with a great smile.

I did not want to be close to Eugenia's family. But I thought it did not matter; I saw my job at Bourbonville as proof that I could do anything I wanted and that others around the world would want me. So much was happening in the world. I wanted to see it all with Eugenia. I sat back in one of the leather chairs and looked out. I would make a success of the Bourbonville car works, and at the first opportunity we would move on, leaving Tennessee behind forever.

Now we sat almost in silence like two uncomfortable acquaintances. The train pulled through Charleston, Tennessee, in the late afternoon and stopped briefly at the little station. Charleston was a village with flimsy houses and big trees. The train crossed into it on an iron cantilever bridge. We looked down and saw the muddy water of a river gleaming up at us in the declining sunlight, and we felt the brakes come on to stop at Charleston.

"My people are buried in the graveyard up there, on the hill," Eugenia said. "My father is up there. I did not know him. He died just after my second birthday. Bert wasn't born yet."

She looked tense. The train moved again.

"What is wrong?" I said.

"Nothing," she said.

"Something is wrong," I said.

"No," she said. She began to cry softly. She searched in her handbag for a handkerchief, found one, and put it to her face. Her shoulders trembled.

She was sitting on the green sofa; I was sitting opposite her. I got up and crossed the gently swaying car and sat down beside her and put my arms around her.

"What is it?" I said.

"I have something to tell you," she said.

"Whatever it is is all right," I said.

I imagined a man then, young and strong and debonair. A man who laughed very much and sang songs and made women love him. Somebody like Guy. He had Guy's eyes, Guy's shout of welcome to people, Guy's air of command. He was married perhaps, and Eugenia worked with him at the newspaper in Kansas City, where she and Alfred were for a while. He seduced her. These fantasies struck me like lightning. I swallowed and blinked and resolved to be understanding. "Mature," I think people said later on about such things. I was going to be mature about the man who had seduced my wife. If I ever saw him, I might kill him. But I had loved Palmyre; Eugenia had the right to have loved someone, too. I could not be generous; my thoughts about Palmyre and me made me feel worse. All this in a flash.

"What is it?" I said. "Please tell me."

"I have to tell you. You will find out anyway."

"Tell me then," I said.

"I am not a virgin," she said.

"Neither am I," I said. She looked at me sharply a moment, as if that idea had not crossed her mind. Later I decided it had not. She put her face in her hands. She looked miserable.

"Who was it?" I said.

A violent tremor ran through her whole body.

"Mr. Pendleton," she said.

"Mr. Pendleton." I did not understand.

"My mother's husband," she said. She squeezed against me. Her voice broke with every word.

"How?" I said. "When?"

"When I was twelve years old."

"My God."

"His hands," she said.

"His hands?"

"He put his hands in me."

"Where is he now?" I said.

"I don't know. Nobody knows. He disappeared in Florida years ago. He may be dead."

"If he is not dead, I will track him down and kill him."

"Oh no," she said. "No. Please don't say such things. I never want to see him again. I don't want you to see him. I do not want to have anything to do with him ever again."

"You do not have to talk about it," I said.

"No. I must tell you."

"You do not have to tell me."

"He would come into my room sometimes at night, if Mamma was away."

"How would your mother be away?"

"When anyone was sick in the neighborhood, Mother used to go help. She was a good nurse. People paid her, and we did not have any money."

"So you were alone with him."

"No. Not alone. The others were there. Bert was with me. Bert was sleeping right beside me."

"It is all right. It was a long time ago."

"Nelle slept with Bess, you see. They were older. I slept with Bert. Bert is two years younger than I am. Two years and three months. Until Nelle left home. Because of him. I can't bear to tell you this. I must tell you."

"It is all right," I said. I tried to be calm. My heart was beating fast, and I was furious with a man I had never known, a man whom distance and perhaps death had removed from my vengeance forever.

"Alfred and Charles slept together. First Mr. Pendleton was drawn to Nelle. He and Mamma quarreled over Nelle. I heard them at night in the kitchen. We all heard them. Mr. Pendleton denied everything. Mamma sent Nelle away, to the Mongers'. Then Nelle went to Knoxville. She went before any of us."

"You and Bert told me about that."

"Mamma stopped sleeping with Mr. Pendleton."

"Good for her."

"She slept with Bess. I think she thought that he might try something with Bess. Bess is . . . well, Bess is not as bright as some people."

I said nothing.

"She took Bess with her when she went to nurse somebody. People paid her sometimes with money and sometimes with goods, you know. Hams. Pork. Potatoes. Potatoes keep, you know. We ate a lot of potatoes."

"Mr. Pendleton did not work?"

"He was no good on the farm. Lazy, for one thing. He thought farming was beneath him. He could preach about ten sermons—ten sermons he'd preached over and over again. He was good at them. Very good. Mamma heard him preach a revival in Cleveland, and she invited him home to dinner. Cleveland is just a few miles from our farm."

She looked up at me and smiled in a frenzy of emotion. Tears poured down her face, and she smiled not because she was happy or because something was funny but because something was absurd, and she could not think of it without smiling. The way you smile at an idiot, I guess. You do not think he is funny, and you are not mocking him; you smile because an idiot has a human shape and makes human sounds, but somehow goes astray, not quite human but a man like a fleshly pun or a joke that depends on a turn of phrase, words not quite what we expect. That was how Eugenia was smiling at her memory of Mr. Pendleton.

"Mamma heard him preach his sermon on the crucifixion, Christ suffering for our sins, how they nailed Christ to the cross, how somebody held his hands against the wood and the soldiers hammered the nails through his flesh and his bones, and how the hammer went bang, bang, bang, bang, in a slow way, the way a man would hammer when he wanted to hammer a big nail through bones, and how they put his feet on top of one another and hammered one big nail through both his feet, and how Christ never said a word, never spoke, and how the blood poured out through the wounds and how the soldiers lifted the cross and how the bottom of it fell with a thump in the hole they had dug for it and how the fall racked his body and how the flies came then and gnawed at the wounds and how he thirsted and how—"

"Stop," I said. "Please stop." I looked up and saw Bernal standing in the middle of the railway car, wearing his filthy blue uniform that was too small for him, his feet caked in mud, his eyes large and sad. I shook my head to dispel the confusion. He stood there still.

"What's wrong?" she said, her face turned to my chest. I kept her face there, not wanting her to look up, not wanting her to see Bernal.

"I feel bad for you," I said.

She put her arm around me and held me. We sat there. The locomotive whistle blew in the distance. I heard the faint, scarcely audible *clackety-clack* of the steel wheels rolling over the joints in the steel track beneath us. I looked up, resolved not to be frightened of Bernal. He was gone. I looked to see if there was mud on the carpet. Nothing. A blood-red sun was sinking to the horizon, and the green and forested land rolled by in an auburn light.

In Chattanooga the train backed into the big terminal and sat for almost an hour, and everything was very still. The darkness came on. Outside we saw dinky switch engines puffing about, pushing and pulling freight and passenger cars. In a while we felt our train give a gentle heave, and we left, the low city flashing by as a glittering of lights. Faster it went. I heard the whistle. We came around the river at the foot of Lookout Mountain and saw the sheen of diffused night light on the dark water. The porter knocked. "First call for dinner, suh." He did not come in.

"Thank you," I called.

"Do you want to eat now?" I said. "We can go to the diner, or we can have the porter bring it back here."

"No," she said. "I am not hungry." We sat in silence for a long time. The stars came out over the high eastern ridge overlooking the valley through which the train ran.

"We will not eat," I called to the porter.

"Yassuh," he said through the door.

"I nearly memorized that sermon," she said after a long time, as if there had been no interval between the first part of her story and what she told now. "It frightened me out of my wits. I heard him preach it twenty times, maybe. People invited him to preach in churches just so they could hear that sermon." Her voice was soft and musing, and she had stopped crying.

"A performance," I said.

"Of course. A performance. We went to church when he preached somewhere nearby. He always called attention to us. He said he'd married a fine woman, and she had a fine family, and he was undertaking to bring her children up in the path of righteousness. He wanted to make it seem that he had taken all of us as charity and he was struggling to do his duty by us. That helped the offering, you see."

"The offering?"

"The collections. The money people gave us. He would preach his sermon on the crucifixion, and the money would roll in. He always had people take up the collection at the door."

"Yes," I said vaguely.

"You don't understand," she said. "Most preachers have the collection taken up before the sermon. Mr. Pendleton knew that he would have the crowd so emotional at the end they would give him lots more money. He stationed ushers at the doors with baskets as people were leaving, and they put in money."

"I do not understand. You spoke of being poor, but he made much money."

"More than we had later. Much more. We were comfortable. Oh, it's so confused. I'm not telling things as they happened. I'm sorry." She lifted her face and kissed me lightly on the cheek. "I'm sorry to do this to you now."

"What happened?" I said.

"For two years everything was fine. On the outside, I mean. Mamma changed. Oh, it was terrible. We could see it, but we did not know what was happening. She was seeing through him, beginning to understand what he really was. She stopped being fooled."

"Yes," I said.

"She stopped laughing. Do you know that Mamma used to have a great sense of humor? She was always laughing. You don't believe me."

"I do believe you." I lied.

"When Mr. Pendleton was courting her, she was so gay. He used to come to see her, bringing flowers he had picked along the road. He would come riding up to the house on his horse with a bundle of daisies in his arms. I remember once . . . It's almost like a dream. He came riding up on his horse, wearing a black suit, and carrying a bundle of daisies, and we all ran down to meet him. He was nice to us then. He brought us stick candy from town. Mamma heard us. She was in the kitchen making bread, and she had to wash her hands, wash the dough off, you see, and she came out on the porch, and it was very hot, and I remember Mamma standing on the porch, seeing her, the vision is in my memory just like it was yesterday, I saw her standing there drying her hands on her apron and looking down the hill—our house was on a hill—and she was looking down the hill and smiling, seeing Mr. Pendleton bending down, giving us the candy, seeing him holding the daisies in the crook of his arm, and he looked up at her and tipped his hat so that I looked back, too, and saw her there. She was standing on the porch smiling, and I was so happy. I never had known my father, you see. I knew what was happening, and I was so happy."

"The others were not so happy."

"No. They remembered Daddy. They knew that Mr. Pendleton would be a stepfather. Alfred and Charles never liked him. He whipped them with a belt. When Mamma said no one had ever hit them that way, he said that was why they were so disrespectful. But that was later. It's so confused. I'm sorry."

"What happened? Why did he stop preaching?"

"A woman."

"I should have known."

"He went to Chattanooga to preach a revival. It was to be a two-week revival. Mamma stayed with us the first week and took the train down there on Sunday. They came back on Tuesday. They weren't supposed to come back until the following Monday. They came back on Tuesday. They found him out, you see. Mamma's face . . . I will never forget Mamma's face."

"Ah," I said.

"He was caught red-handed with somebody's wife," Eugenia said. "The husband beat him. He came back with his face bruised as if he had fallen from a horse. I remember his beaten and swollen face. I never knew all the details. My grandmother was alive then. She and Mamma talked in the kitchen. I heard them . . . words. My grandfather spoke to Mr. Pendleton. So did my grandfather's brother. They were stern, very stern. My grandfather went north to fight for the Union in the war. He was a brave, hardy man. We children were not supposed to hear. We heard enough."

"But Mr. Pendleton stayed." It was very dark beyond the windows now. Dim and distant lights flashed by. We stopped in nameless towns, paused, and went on moving into the world of mysterious spaces and arching night, the Deep South, Alabama. Where was my father in Alabama? I wanted to look out at the land, at the stations. He might be standing on a platform, leaning against a wall. He might be standing at a grade crossing, waiting to cross the tracks after the train swept by.

"He begged Mamma to forgive him. He said a Christian had to forgive another Christian for sin. Mamma told me once much later on, much later, that he spoke of the woman taken in adultery: 'Let him who is without sin among you cast the first stone.' She had to forgive him, you see. She could not turn him out. But it was finished with him. The revivals. People spread the word. Now and then he preached again for a little while, but it all dried up. Gradually the churches heard about the disgrace, and they stopped asking him. Alfred said once that when Mr. Pendleton left that the stories broke in a flood. People knew, you see. They didn't tell Mamma until he was gone. He tried to seduce everyone."

"He was at home, and sometimes your mother was gone. . . ."

"He sat around. He got fat. Mamma had to support us. At night when Mamma was gone—"

Her voice broke again. The story was in her like a boil, swelling and swelling. Now it was bursting.

"I think sometimes I can forget it," she sobbed. "I put it aside. I tramp it down. I don't think about it. But it comes back. Do you know something that is truly mad?"

"Tell me."

"We have a bathtub in our house, and I am afraid to take a bath in it at night. Of course we all have to take turns, and I say I like to get up early in the morning and take my bath first when everybody else is still asleep. But I will tell you why I am afraid to take baths at night in the bathtub. At night I sit there naked, you see—you have to be naked when you take a bath—and I look down at the drain, and I think I see blood pouring up out of the drain. I think sometimes I am going to drown in blood that comes from down in the cellar. I am a grown woman, and I have those thoughts because sometimes I think Mr. Pendleton is still alive, and he is down in the cellar and that he is going to drown me in blood at night when everybody else is in bed asleep and no one can help me."

"Oh, Eugenia! Eugenia!"

"You see, you have married a crazy woman."

"No," I said.

"Bert would be sleeping. Bert was always a sound sleeper. She still is. And Mr. Pendleton would open the door late at night, and he would come and . . ."

"It is all right. It is all right. You do not have to tell me now. Later on . . . Later on." I did not want to hear more.

"No, I must tell you now. I do not want there to be secrets between us. I do not want there to be lies. I want you to know everything; I want to know everything about you."

"Yes," I said.

"He would come. . . . He would pull up a stool very softly. I can still hear the stool legs scraping across the floor. Wood on wood. I hear it now, somebody moving a chair or something, and it scrapes on the floor, and I think of Mr. Pendleton, pulling the stool up to the bed at night. The chills run down my back. In the daytime I used to put the stool all the way across the room, you see. I think of him drawing near me, and I was lying there so frightened I could not speak, could not say anything at all, and he would put his hands under the covers. Bert was asleep there beside me, and he would put his hands under the covers, very softly, very slowly, and pull up my nightdress, I could feel it slipping up over my body, and I could not say anything or do anything about it, and he put his fingers . . ."

"It is all right . . . it is all right. I am here. It is all right."

"It was so awful. So awful. I am so ashamed . . . so ashamed."

"You should not be ashamed. There is no shame to it. Is that all he did?"

"He never got in bed with me, if that is what you mean. He would have waked Bert up. He never . . ."

"Then you are a virgin," I said.

"No," she said. "He broke my maidenhead. You will find that he broke my maidenhead with his fingers. It hurt so much. I remember how it burned and how I bled."

"It is all right. It is all right."

"He tore at me. He tore at my body with his fingers, and I would hear him breathing hard, and at the end he would be panting like a dog."

I held her and shut my eyes.

"He said if I told anybody he would kill Bert and Mamma and Alfred and Charles and Bess, and he would go find Nelle and kill her."

She cried then as hard as I ever saw anyone cry, a sobbing that I thought must tear her body in two, an explosion of things held in her for years and years. She spoke again, her voice faint and worn, pausing a long time between the words as if she had to summon her will to expel every one of them from her mouth.

"I remember one day . . . We were in the kitchen. Mother was there, and Bess, and Bert was on the floor next to him, looking up. I was on one side of the table; he was on the other side. He looked at me and grinned. He was like a wolf, grinning at me. A peeping Tom. He was sitting just across the table from me, but it was like seeing a wolf in the dark grinning through the window at me. There was a butcher knife on the table. Do you know what a butcher knife is?"

"Yes," I said.

"He gripped the handle of the butcher knife and looked down at Bert, and he looked at me, and he grinned."

"Your mother did not see."

"No one saw. I was so ashamed afterwards . . . so ashamed. Why didn't I tell someone? Why did I let him do that to me night after night? To this day I feel that I did something wrong. Something tells me I did not; but something tells me that I did." She fell into a fresh outburst of uncontrollable crying.

"You were twelve years old," I said, holding her as tight as I could.

"I feel that I should have known better. I should have told somebody. Somebody would have helped me. He would have been put in jail. I have never told anybody. I was afraid Mamma would blame me. You see, when I didn't tell the first time, and when he came back again and again, it seemed almost my fault."

"Nonsense," I said.

"I didn't know what to do. Nobody in the world knows but you. *He* knows. Wherever he is, he knows."

"He is in hell, and the knowledge is burning in him and adding to his torments," I said.

"I dream about him. I dream that I hear the stool scraping across the floor as he pulls it up to the side of the bed. I dream that he will come back and that he will tell everyone. I dream that he will tell people that I let him do what he did. Since I didn't cry out, I let him do what he did. Don't you see?"

"You were twelve years old."

"Do you forgive me? Do you forgive me?"

"I cannot forgive you because there is nothing to forgive," I said. "Nothing at all."

"I sometimes feel that I am condemned to hell because of it. I thought I would go as a missionary and gain the forgiveness of God. But here I am."

"Yes, here you are," I said. "Here we are. I am glad you are not a missionary."

She lay against me. The train rolled through the night, the locomotive whistle resounding far ahead of us, a wailing ghost sweeping over a vast and vacant land. We sat up on the couch, she lying against me. In a while she slept the sleep of exhaustion, sighing sometimes like a child, her blond head heavy on my shoulder. We did not go to bed all night long. At dawn we rolled into the Dixie Railroad station on Canal Street in New Orleans, and that was the first day and night of our married life.

135

WE SPENT THE WEEK of our wedding trip in a hotel on Canal Street. We came together gingerly. She did her best to make me happy. I did not know how to make her happy.

She never gasped when I touched her, and never gave herself up to the act. She had shapely breasts; she seemed to have no feeling in them. When I touched them ever so gently in making love to her, she tensed. "I'm sorry," she said. "Mamma always told me never to let a man touch me there."

"I am your husband," I said.

"I'm sorry," she said.

Sex was something I did to her, not something we did together. She was embarrassed by it. She shut her eyes as if trying to be somewhere else while sex was going on. I gained my release; sometimes she asked tentatively at the end, "Are you through?" She got up quickly and washed herself. Her eagerness to please seemed sacrificial. She never refused me; she never invited me.

Yet we had intimacy. She told me the deepest secrets of her heart, things she had never told anyone. Intercourse of words: perhaps the best kind. I am older now. My candle gutters. I see things in perspective. These are the euphemisms of growing old, of desire cooling down. It mattered then more than I claim it did now.

She told me of growing up. Mr. Pendleton loomed above her, a macabre ghost, silent and eternal. Much worse than my ghosts. She told of visiting her father's grave and of how the mound for a long time was bare of grass and how slowly the grass grew over it and how her mother and the older children stood by it and wept.

"I am sure that if he had lived, I would have seen him with all the flaws that people see in their parents. But he died. That makes a difference. He died so young that he will always be a saint."

"Do you see flaws in your mother?" I asked.

Eugenia laughed. "Of course I see flaws in Mamma! She is a religious fanatic. Everything has a religious bent to it. She denies life. She's putting everything off until heaven."

"She is stern," I said.

"You are very kind not to say she is something worse than stern," Eugenia said. "Her religion has been her strength. She can talk of hardly anything else. We all shut her out years ago."

"I am happy you are not religious," I said.

"Oh, I'm religious enough," she said, tossing her head and smiling. "I like to go to church, to sing the hymns. Do you believe there is a God?"

"No," I said.

"Oh, but you *must* believe in God," she said. "Everybody believes in God."

"I do not think much about it," I said.

"Oh my," she said in mock repugnance, "I have married an atheist! What will I do with him?"

"I hope you will love him and cherish him and do all those other things the minister made you promise."

"And obey you," Eugenia said. "Of course you want me to obey you. Well, that depends."

I adored her when she laughed at me as she did then. "If Mamma asks you about God, just lie," she said, laughing happily. "Pretend you speak to Jesus every evening. Please don't speak in tongues. Mr. Pendleton spoke in tongues at the last. That was the last straw. He babbled like a maniac."

"Glossolalia?" I said.

"That's the fancy name for it. I think he thought that he might make some money at revivals if he spoke in tongues. Mamma told him he had to leave. Grandfather said he had to leave, too. Alfred and Charles were big enough then to threaten him. And then there were the switches left at the door. He packed his carpetbag and left. I've told you about that."

"Yes."

Her eyes filled with tears.

"Do not cry," I said. "Please do not cry."

"I was terrified he would tell Mamma what he had done to me. A parting shot, you know. I thought for years that he might write her a letter and tell her about it."

"Then he would have been put in prison," I said.

"You do not know him. I thought he might do anything for vengeance."

We slept snuggled close together, her back to me, my arm over her body; sometimes when she was almost asleep I put my my hand over her breast, and she let me keep it there. She turned to kiss me gently when we were settling to go to sleep. In the night when the motions of sleep had separated us, I awoke, realized our distance, rolled back against her and embraced her, and she settled against me with a bump of habit, and we went to sleep again.

I did not return confidence for confidence. She told me about Mr. Pendleton; I should have told her about Greece, about my father, about everything that had happened as I have now told it here. I did not.

"Where is your mother?" she asked.

"In Belgium," I said.

"Why doesn't she write?"

"She does write sometimes."

"I never see the letters," she said.

"She writes me at a postal box."

"Why not at our home?"

"I don't like the postman delivering letters with foreign stamps. You know how your brothers feel about foreigners."

"Silly, you are one of the family now. They love you."

"No, they do not," I said.

"Will you share the letters with me?"

"You would not understand them."

"Why?"

"She does not write in English."

"Oh, of course. Well, why don't you translate them to me?"

"My mother is a poor and uninteresting woman. You would not like her."

"What an awful thing to say! Do you think she will ever visit us?"

"No."

"You could invite her."

"I could. But I have two sisters there, and she wants to stay with them."

"In Belgium?"

"Yes," I said.

Perhaps if Eugenia had stayed at home, as most wives did in that time, she would have pestered the truth out of me. But no sooner than we were settled down in Knoxville, she began to work at an almost frantic pace at the newspaper. We stopped going to church; she was tired on Sunday mornings. We lay abed late and got up and read the newspapers and had coffee and enjoyed each other. Mary Pendleton moaned and threatened the wrath of God, but Eugenia ignored her. I was happy at this expression of independence, and I must confess to being happy at Mary Pendleton's anger and frustration and even her threats.

Eugenia's career soared. Our photographs were in the *Guardian* when we were married along with a story about her—the new kind of woman. Two months after we got married, a moonshine war broke out in Cocke County. Rival moonshiners killed each other with shotguns and burned the primitive distilling apparatus by which they cooked up alcohol from fermented corn and wheat mash. An ambush killed a child who happened to be riding in a wagon carrying three barrels of whiskey down from a still in the mountains. The killers shot the barrels full of holes and left the child and two adults dead on the ground. Federal marshals were called in. They came heavily armed, and the mountains rang with gunfire. One of the federal agents was shot but not killed. Eugenia went to see him at the hospital and got an interview, and she went to the Newport jail and interviewed the moonshiner who shot him. He was a fat man named Ogle, with missing teeth and a blind eye and a knife scar down the side of his face. "I'm sorry I didn't kill the snooping bastard," the gentleman in the jail told her. In her story his words were translated into this: "Mr. Ogle expressed his regret that he had not killed Mr. Baker and called Mr. Baker an unprintable name." The story would have been less titillating had she quoted Ogle directly, but her editor would not have printed the word "bastard." Eugenia appeared to have heard much more than she had implied, a woman at home with coarse male talk.

"It's scandalous for a woman to be in such company!" Mary Pendleton said in outrage. "I never meant to raise a daughter to keep company with trash."

"Mamma, people talk like that all around the tabernacle, and you hear it. Mr. Ogle is no different from most of the men down along First Creek."

"Yes, but I am trying to save their souls, not write newspaper stories about them," Mary Pendleton said.

Eugenia laughed at her and hugged her. "Oh, Mamma," she said. "I'm so happy. Why can't you be happy with me?"

Eugenia's brother Charles called on me one evening and invited me to take a walk with him along Edgewood Avenue. It was the age of normalcy, as people called it. Charles offered me a cigar; I took it. Charles smoked expensive cigars. They reminded me of Guy's, though Charles could never have mastered Guy's natural flourish with a cigar.

We strolled along the quiet street. I knew Charles had something important to say.

"Paul," Charles said at last, taking a deep breath. "I've got to get something off my chest. Alfred and I both think . . . and I might add that Mother thinks . . . that Eugenia is . . . well, that she is compromising *your* reputation by . . . well, by the things she is doing at the newspaper."

"What should she be doing?" I said.

"My friend, you and I are brothers now. You know what she should be doing. You are her husband."

"I truly do not understand," I said.

"Oh, confound it, man! She ought to be at home. She should be cooking your meals, ironing your shirts, darning your socks. A woman's place is in the home. Confound it, she ought to be having babies. Don't you see that?"

"I do not believe I can lock her up," I said. "What would she do in our little house all day long? She would die of boredom."

"She can do what other women do. She can belong to clubs. She can do church work. She can . . . Well, it's not for me to say. I just know that she does things other women don't do, things *ladies* don't do, and she ought to stop. Confound it! Anybody can see what I mean."

"She is not like other women," I said.

"She thinks she is better than other women," Charles said. "I hate pride in a woman. It's unbecoming to the sex."

"She *is* better than other women," I said. "She loves working for her paper. Do you not think she writes well?" Charles did not believe that was the point.

I was proud of Eugenia. I thought how remarkable it was that she had escaped her lunatic family. I told Charles that I was proud of her for her work.

"Well," Charles said. "Well." He looked shocked and pale.

136

NOT EVERYTHING Eugenia did was thrilling. She was a professional. She was proud to be able to write about anything. "That's what a reporter does," she said. She attacked her assignment like an army besieging a city.

Though Charles had spoken in favor of her doing more ladylike things, he was not more pleased when she wrote about garden clubs and book clubs and missionary societies. She did interviews with the wives of politicians and wrote of how much they loved the simple home life, children, and church.

She reported their favorite recipes and wrote about the books they loved and the causes they espoused.

She interviewed the wife of a United States senator from Tennessee, a woman who spoke on and on about how important it was to preserve prohibition in the country and make it work and keep the saloons closed and uphold virtue. "We don't want all those drunks to come back," the senatorial wife wheezed, her face swollen and red, her body reeking of perfume and her breath of whiskey. Eugenia wrote about the sentiments, not about the reality. "I have to take care of my editor," she said with a wry laugh. "He gets upset when I write things just the way they happen. He says it's the readers; I think it's himself. He needs his fictions."

She wrote about holiday celebrations and children who gathered on the streets to watch parades. She wrote about new appliances for the kitchen and how to cook a nutritious meal without meat. "It's stupid," she said. "The people who buy this newspaper can afford to buy meat. I think my editor loves to imagine the poor and hungry down along First Creek waiting for the *Guardian* every afternoon and reading how to have meatless meals."

She did a story about the dangers of keeping some foods in the old-fashioned iceboxes that thousands of people in Knoxville still had, and the president of the big ice company down near the university wrote a letter of protest to the newspaper. "Be careful about such stories," her worried editor told her. "They can lose advertising."

"I was just summarizing a government report," she said.

"Let the government take care of its own reports," her editor said.

"What does he care about a few cases of food poisoning?" she said. "He has an electric refrigerator." She wrote about vitamins. She did an interview with the woman novelist who published the book called *Sweetness in Summer* and came to Knoxville to address the breathless and adoring women at Ossoli Circle.

Occasionally Eugenia did obituaries. "We keep a morgue on everybody important," she said. "A file. When somebody dies, all we have to do is take out that file and keep the obituary. Do you know they have a file on you? I started it. Because of the strike, you know. What you did. If you were to die, I could compose your obituary in about a half hour and have all the facts right there." She laughed. I saw Guy standing behind her, looking at me with an expressionless face. His eyes looked like glass beads, staring and lifeless. I blinked, and he was gone.

To catch the morning local to Bourbonville, I arose at five to take the streetcar to the depot in Knoxville; I got home at almost eight. Often when I opened the door, Mary Pendleton and Dolly were sitting with Eugenia. Dolly always went home across the yard to her husband, Napoleon. Often Mary Pendleton ate with Eugenia before I got home. "She's here at mealtime, and I have to feed her," Eugenia said. "I try to wait to eat with you, but she says she won't eat unless I join her. What can I do?"

"You could refuse to join her," I said. "Then she would have to go home."

"Oh, Paul, you make it sound so easy."

Mary Pendleton talked about prophecy and about the "falling away" of the churches. She expected something she called the Rapture to happen any night: the world would wake up one morning and discover that all the true Christians had been snatched away to heaven so they would not have to endure the Great Tribulation that was going to come on the world under the Antichrist.

"I look forward to the Rapture," I told Eugenia.

"Why, I never thought I would hear you say such a thing," Eugenia said.

"Yes, because then we will wake up some morning, and your mother will be in heaven, and not here, and perhaps you and I could eat supper together all by ourselves."

Eugenia laughed and rolled her eyes. "I hate it, too," she said. "But what can I do?"

"You can ask her not to come to our house so much."

"I can't do that. She is my mother."

"You can tell her I want her to stay away."

"Her children are all she has. I cannot do that."

I felt abused and annoyed. Mary Pendleton imposed herself on us.

Early in our marriage I drove her home once at the end of a long day. "You are sure you are not Jewish?" Mary Pendleton said as I turned the car down Broadway towards town.

"No, Mrs. Pendleton, I am not Jewish."

"Charles says you look Jewish to him."

"Charles is in error."

"He knew so many Jews in France," Mary Pendleton said. "He ought to know what a Jew looks like."

"There are indeed many Jews in France, and in Belgium, too," I said. "But I have not known many, and the ones I have known have never done me any harm."

"Blood will tell," she said. "Blood will tell."

After this conversation, I asked Eugenia to take her mother home at night.

I went to bed at ten to be up early enough to catch the morning local, and I left the house without eating breakfast. When I got off the train in Bourbonville, Dr. Youngblood was having coffee at Bessie May's unless he was off in the country sewing somebody up or delivering a baby. Jim Ed was always there, an old hat pushed back on his head, drinking one cup of coffee after another, smoking a cigarette now and then. He had already been to the car works to watch the preparations for the first heat of the day in the wheel foundry. He wore a white shirt open at the neck. Dr. Youngblood, Jim Ed, and I sat companionably at the round table in the back of the cafe. Bessie May brought us a pot of fresh coffee. She was delighted that we made her cafe our headquarters.

Jim Ed reported on what he thought I needed to know from his rounds on the day before, and often he told stories. Sometimes Brian Ledbetter came in with him. Brian could sit for long, long moments without saying a word, looking at his son. Later he would drive himself back to the farm. "I think Daddy's going to kill himself in that car," Jim Ed said thoughtfully. "What can I do?"

"It's not a bad way to go," Dr. Youngblood said. "Not unless he drives through somebody's schoolhouse and takes the whole third grade with him."

Jim Ed laughed.

Ted Devlin came in every morning, telling us with enthusiastic deprecation what was going to be on his front page for the next issue. "Thursday we're going to have a front-page story about alfalfa," he might say.

"Really sounds exciting, Ted," Jim Ed would say in response. "You think this town is ready for a story about alfalfa? We've just got used to lespedeza."

"This is a forward, up-to-date little burg," Ted would reply. "Now I admit there's some things we can't have in this town. We can't have can-can girls. We can't have a Bolshevik candidate for sheriff. We can't have a theatre where they show real plays except the high school kind. Can we have alfalfa? I've thought about it, and I've worried about it. God knows I've walked the floor of my humble little room at the boardinghouse thinking about it, asking myself, 'Devlin, can Bourbonville take a story on alfalfa?' I've even prayed about it. I've said, 'Lord God, if you believe in alfalfa, do a miracle, Lord. Let Doc Youngblood grow hair on top of his head, Lord. Let Paul Alexander start sounding like a yokel so we can understand him, Lord. Give Bessie May a college education in five minutes, Lord. Do it, Lord. Do it.' "

"What happened?" Dr. Youngblood might say.

"What do you think happened?" Ted said. "Have you looked in a mirror lately? Have you felt the top of your head? Have you got any hair up there, Curtis? Has Paul lost his accent? And Bessie May?"

Dr. Youngblood laughed.

"The Lord said, 'Ted, old friend, you're going to have to figure this one out for yourself.' I'm going to do it. I'm going to print that story on alfalfa on the front page, and you boys better be ready to run for it. Come Thursday night, folks will be tearing each other to pieces in the square on account of that story, and come Sunday the Baptists will all be for alfalfa, and the Methodists will all be against it, and the Church of God folks will be trying to figure out what it means."

Douglas Kinlaw often came in and took his seat with us. "I wish you could talk to your wife and get her to move down here to Bourbonville," he said tentatively. "It gives the town a black eye when the manager of the car works lives in Knoxville."

"Well, hell, Mayor," Ted Devlin said. "Pinkerton didn't live in town. Not after he got his start."

"Yes, but he still lived in the county," Douglas said. "Paul lives in Knoxville."

"He's a foreigner," Ted said. "Foreigners do funny things. Pass the coffee pot, Curtis. Don't hog it all for yourself."

"It's because my wife works at the newspaper," I said.

"She can come down here and work for me," Ted said.

"She still hopes her editor will let her write about a murder trial," I said.

"Jesus Christ in hot tomato soup," Ted Devlin said. "Next thing you know she'll want to be paid what a man's paid for the same work." He laughed.

Dale Farmer stopped by on his way to work, his mouth watering for friendship. He came in grinning, speaking to everyone, taking his seat among us with imperial certainty. He always shook hands with me. He never once congratulated me for my elevation to my job. He said nothing about Jim Ed's job. He acted as if everything were exactly as he had always wanted it to be. He looked around smiling at his success. "Gentlemen! Gentlemen!" he said.

So the days passed.

137

THE DAYS SLIPPED into months, and I knew Eugenia and I had to move away. I took it up with her.

"What would happen to my career?" she said.

"You can get a job anywhere," I said. "You can write articles and sell them to magazines. Look at the *Saturday Evening Post.* Look at *Collier's.*"

"They have only men writing for them."

"You can be the first woman."

"What would I write about?"

"About foreign places. About people doing strange things."

"Foreign places."

"We can go abroad."

"You mean on a tour?"

"No," I said. "Not a tour. To work. To live. There is so much to do, so many places to visit. We are young. Look what Gilly Weaver has done. He has managed to rid himself of Bourbonville, of Tennessee. He was young. He got away."

"I don't see what being young has to do with it."

"We won't be young forever. Now is the time to have some adventures."

"Adventures!" she laughed. "Haven't we had enough adventures? I could have been a missionary if I had wanted adventures."

"You want to be a writer. You have to have something to write about. Do you want to write about the Garden Club and Ossoli Circle all your life?"

"I don't like it when you make fun of me," Eugenia said.

I smiled and, I am sure, assumed my lordly and wise expression, reserved for great truths. "I only realize that life is going by. There are places for us to go before it goes altogether. I have been thinking. I have been reading things on the train. That is one of the advantages of traveling on the train. I can read."

"What have you been reading?" she said. "Where do you want to go?"

"To Africa, perhaps. To the Congo. Perhaps to India. To China. So many exciting things are happening in China. Gilly is in China. There's a revolution going on there. He is in the middle of it. We could be a part of it."

"I have heard China is filthy."

"You can always take baths."

She laughed and looked thoughtful. "China! I suppose we could take boxes and boxes of soap."

"Of course," I said.

"It will break Mamma's heart if I leave."

"It will break my heart if we stay."

"I know she is difficult."

"We have our lives to live. You can write a book about travel. That sort of thing will sell thousands. You will become rich and famous."

She hesitated a long time, looking at me, and the tears came to her eyes. "Mamma and I have always been so close."

I put my arms around her. "I nearly died in the war," I said softly. "For a long time, I wanted to die. My friends died. They were young, and we looked at the war as though it were a momentary diversion, something we would do for a few weeks and then get on with life. I escaped. I did not deserve to escape; they did not deserve to die. For a long time I wanted to die, too. But now I want to live with you, to have as much life as we can. I don't want us to stay here and call this life. We will suffocate. Your mother is suffocating you."

We were in our kitchen late at night. I looked through the window, and I saw Guy and Bernal standing there, shoulder to shoulder, their arms gravely folded across their tunics, bodies outlined in a faint luminescence. I looked at them fixedly, daring them to harm me or to speak; and suddenly, as though something were releasing all over the universe, I felt a benevolence in them, a good will that brought back all the good old days before they died.

I wanted to speak to them, to say "I love you; I love her; there is no contradiction, no contradiction at all." I held my tongue, just barely. My heart was so full of joy that I felt that I might float upward into the dark air of a benign heaven where it would not matter if I spoke to Guy and Bernal, where there could be no bad consequences for anything, where everything we tried to do turned out exactly right.

Perhaps it was simply that I felt something break in Eugenia, felt her begin to consider another life, another destiny, as I did that day in the green meadow when suddenly I felt Palmyre softening, thinking of Russia, of being with me there. I made the mistake, you see, of supposing that there are repetitions and that life runs in cycles and that when one misses Fortune at one moment, the wheel will turn, and she will come back again, her hair flying and offering herself to be seized again. I did not ask for a decision that night. I held her to me, and I said, "I love you."

"I love you," she said. She put her arms around me.

"I love you more than I have ever loved anything on earth," I said.

We stood, holding each other, and beyond the window where Guy and Bernal had been there was nothing but the evening dark.

138

IN THE SUMMER of 1923 Gilly came home from China to visit, bringing with him his English wife and two adolescent sons and a daughter about twelve. He had not been home in years. His arrival occasioned much social coming and going at the Ledbetters' and the Weavers', and Eugenia and I were invited to the Ledbetter home for the first time since Mrs. Ledbetter understood that I was courting the girl she had picked for her son. Mrs. Ledbetter did what she thought was the civilized and decent thing under all circumstances. She was cool to us both. She never again treated me with the motherly warmth that she had given to me from the day we met at that long-ago Thanksgiving dinner.

Gilly had been gone for so long that his family had trouble fitting him in. He was not dead, but he was also not part of their lives. I sensed always a great unease when people talked about him. It was as though he had grown to a certain age and had been revealed as a changeling left at the whim of a jocular fairy, in the crib where a normal child should have lain.

Eugenia and I drove down one Sunday afternoon and joined a crowd of guests milling about in the yard, talking to Gilly and his exotic family.

It was a gathering of friends, and I stood there, dressed in a seersucker suit, wearing a straw hat and a silk bow tie. I realized that I had been in Bourbonville long enough to see stories come to their ends, and I realized, too, that this gathering represented some subtle finality or climax. Old friends came; I saw them and wondered how long we would all be together, what centrifugal forces were working already to hurl us apart forever.

Dr. Youngblood came, and Douglas Kinlaw came, looking benignly through his glasses, a man without guile or malice towards anyone on earth, and Ted Devlin was there to write about Gilly for his paper. Gilly was not "Gilly" for the paper; he was G. X. Weaver, engineer, "local boy who has made good and who has spread the fame of Bourbon County to the four corners of the world." Ted Devlin's prose became more hyperbolic with the years.

When we drove into the yard, I recognized Gilly, standing tall and sun-browned, wearing a wide-brimmed hat of some foreign origin (I later discovered it was Australian), listening intently to others talk, laughing politely, speaking with a slight reserve. Jim Ed introduced Eugenia and me, and Gilly bowed slightly and put his hand to his hat without removing it, an offhand gesture performed with grace. "A Belgian," he said, almost under his breath, in an accent that had only a hint of Tennessee in it. "What an odd place this must be to *you.*" He laughed quietly and steered me by the elbow to introduce us to his wife. Her name was Marjorie; she had reddish hair and dark blue eyes and a friendly smile. Their sons were in mid-adolescence, but they shook hands with us as if they were men and spoke in clipped English accents that brought London back to me in a flood of nostalgia. They had had English tutors and English tailors, and they had lived among the English, and they were both very adult. The daughter looked on the scene with a serene dignity.

Gilly stood within a benign circle he drew around himself and said little. I took him to be interested, even curious, about others. The guests made much over him, and yet there was to the entire scene the uneasiness that comes when people are eager to be friendly and do not quite know how to talk to a stranger who should not have been a stranger.

He was a remarkable man—a boy who had unaccountably decided early in his life that he wanted to see something of the world, and off he had gone. He went to the University of Tennessee and studied engineering, answered an advertisement in a British journal, and joined a British overseas firm "for a year or two," did well, success breeding success, and now by general consensus would never return to Bourbon County to live. He had built bridges in China and in India. He had supervised road construction in Japan, and he had been charged with building a railroad through part of the English colony of Kenya in Africa.

Somewhere along the way he had married Marjorie, daughter of a British army officer. She looked to be the efficient British woman of stereo-type, somewhat heavy in the hips, a ruddy face, socially graceful, and she radiated good cheer and plain common sense, and she had taught their sons and their daughter a formal, pleasant courtesy that reminded me of how the wealthier classes treated each other in Belgium. Her laughter was unaffected and loud without being coarse; I supposed that when things went wrong in her life among the natives of whatever continent or sub-continent where she and her family found themselves, she laughed, mak-ing stories out of incidents that might have driven a lesser person to desperation. You knew she would say just the right thing and do the right thing whether in the torrid heat of a Calcutta summer or amid tribal re-bellion while bullets whizzed through the windows and scattered broken glass on the Persian rugs.

Gilly resembled Virgil with his angular face and deep-set eyes and fine dark hair, and he was tall and slender like Virgil. He and his family gravitated together. When one of them was swept away from the others in introductions to friends, to people Gilly's family did not know, the others followed along at a distance, or else the one momentarily led away would drift back to them. At times they seemed almost to make a ring, backs to one another, speaking pleasantly to the group of strangers around them.

Even Mrs. Ledbetter seemed outside the ring, looking in at this strange son of hers, and despite the push and shove, the surreptitious drinking of whiskey by the men, the gallant speech that the old man made almost as a toast before the meal began, the music that Jim Ed and I furnished to everyone's admiration, a veil of melancholy hung over the occasion. Gilly's return freshened the wound of his having left them. He had not come back to stay; he had come to visit; perhaps he had come to show his wife and children how far he had risen in the world from such humble beginnings. He would not come home again for years; he might never see Brian nor his mother again. He had found a satisfying life away from the world that had made him and the people who loved him, and he did not miss the commu-nity that had formed him, and the family he had left behind knew little of his life and would never know much about it.

His return was a formal ritual born of the nostalgic longings any grown-up has for his childhood. His wife and children looked on Bourbon County as if they had stepped down from a train in a strange place, one they would know only for a little while because the train stood there, engine puffing, ready to pull on in a moment, taking them away from a spot that could have no meaning for them other than the fact that it was now present, a link in the unreeling chain of their lives. I can describe him so well because much later on when I returned to Greece to visit my mother and my sisters, I was like Gilly.

The old man took them around, stumping on his peg leg, pointing things out with his cane. "This is where I sat down to eat at your granny's breakfast table back in the summer of 1885. There was a drought, and Ulysses S. Grant was dying up in New Jersey, and a man was hanged the day before." He was rubbing the lamp, I thought, trying to stir out of these strange children some jinn of recognition, but though Gilly and his wife and children were politely interested and obviously liked him, the jinn did not rise, and the old man broke off in the middle and started to tell them about Gettysburg, but Mrs. Ledbetter interrupted him, and he subsided, the story half done, neither Gilly nor the children urging him to go on.

"He looks so much older than he did when I saw him last," Jim Ed said, marveling. "That was ten years ago, but he looks twenty years older than he did then."

There was no response to this observation. You will understand that in seeing Gilly (his wife called him "Gil"), I thought of myself. There was nothing for Gilly in Bourbon County; there was nothing for me in Greece. In our homelands, we were walking monuments to dead times.

Gilly and I spoke briefly. "You are an engineer by training," he said.

"In fact I am a mathematician," I said. "I learned some engineering, and I suppose you can say that I am an engineer now. I have not done mathematics since the war." I did not say that I had not done mathematics since Bernal died.

"You must know much about metals to be able to direct the car works," he said.

"I know enough," I said. "I do not know that I know much."

"You know how to get men to work together."

"Yes, with Jim Ed's help," I said.

"It is a talent to direct men. Not many people have it. I am not sure that Jim Ed would have it without you to direct him."

"He is very intelligent," I said, feeling almost disloyal to entertain such a conversation.

Gilly shrugged slightly, dismissing something. "Do you plan to stay here?" he said.

"Oh no," I said quickly. "I did not mean to stay here this long."

"I am not surprised," Gilly said. He laughed in an engaging way. "I am going to Burma from here," he said. "I am to build a power line from Mandalay to Lashio. It will take a couple of years, maybe more than that. Would that sort of job interest you?"

I thought for a moment. "I would have to discuss it with my wife," I said.

"Of course," he said. "There is no need to hurry. I shall have someone get in touch with you if you like. You can decide then."

"Burma," I said.

"It is a beautiful place. I have been in the northern Shan States once. A very beautiful place. Jungle in the valleys, but the hills are cool and nice. Lots of wild animals and tribes of all sorts. I don't think the British are doing a good job in Burma, but they are trying. You would like it. Many things are happening there. I believe you and Mrs. Alexander would both find a new life there."

"That would be interesting," I said.

"Much more interesting than here," he said with a slight, ironic smile.

I told Eugenia about it. "Burma!" she said. "I am not even sure where Burma is." She laughed. "A pipe dream," she said.

"I do not think so," I said.

"You're serious!" she said in a sudden awakening.

"Yes, I am," I said. "I think it is time to leave here."

"I hate to leave now. If we could wait until Mother dies . . ."

"Your mother will live to be older than the pyramids," I said.

She laughed. "Well, we'll see," she said. She looked around at our world and nodded as though to herself. She was taking stock and pondering new things, I thought. It was a good feeling.

139

GILLY AND HIS FAMILY left, taking the train overland to Los Angeles to visit with Virgil and Daisy before embarking for Burma.

I ordered books about Burma and took some out of the library in Knoxville and read about the country in encyclopedias. Eugenia and I talked about it at night when we lay in bed, sharing our brief time alone together. "I suppose we can try it for a couple of years, and if we don't like it, we can come home," she said. "If you promise to come home when I want to, maybe I'll go."

"I will promise anything," I said. "I know you will like it once we see it."

Within a month after Gilly left, I received a letter written on thick white paper. I have it here before me tonight, the paper still white and stiff after all these years, the letter short, typed, signed with a flourish in a signature I could not possibly read without the deciphering provided by the typed name below it, "James W. Richardson-Whitmore, Esq., Director of Professional Personnel, the Burma Mines Ltd." The letter invites me to come to New York to interview with Mr. Richardson-Whitmore. Several jobs in Burma are available, he says. He tells me that the salary for each is "open" but that for a young man of my experience and qualifications he believes we can discuss a figure of at least seven hundred gold dollars a month if we arrive at an agreement.

The memory of how stupendous that figure appeared at the time rings in my head. In Tennessee, most schoolteachers made five hundred dollars a year. A haircut cost fifteen cents. A plate lunch with gargantuan helpings at Bessie May's cafe cost fifteen cents, and if you had a piece of pie, it cost another nickel. "You ought to have the pie," Bessie May said. "Feller as skinny as you needs a little fat on his bones." If I had a piece of pie, I was bound to doze off in the afternoon. I was the boss; I could doze off if I wanted to. I usually had the pie. Such were the thrills of Bourbonville. Such was the comparison I made with seven hundred gold dollars a month.

Against Charles's confident predictions that the town would grow north and east, Knoxville was creeping inexorably west, like a tide of opportunity rolling away from him; the wooded hills sloping down to the river from Kingston Pike resounded with construction. Charles looked on in glum envy but brightened to hear himself speak of how this building boom was a "flash in the pan," as he called it. A mansion on Kingston Pike with servants' quarters cost ten thousand or fifteen thousand dollars. You bought your mansion, and you drove up and down the macadam street looking at other mansions, comparing sloping green lawns. I was being considered for a job that paid seven hundred gold dollars a month in a corner of the British Empire. All through the day I could hardly keep my mind on what was happening around me.

That night I told Eugenia about the letter, the sum of seven hundred gold dollars a month. We sat on the bed. She was brushing her long hair. Her face was more serious now that she saw that Burma was possible.

"Burma is jungle," she said. "Isn't it dangerous?"

"No," I said. "We would go to the hill country. A place called Namtu, above Lashio."

"You speak as if you have been there," she said, turning her warm smile on me.

"I have not been there. But I have been reading, Eugenia. I am in love with the place already."

"When you read, it is not the same as being there. You can be disappointed. It isn't the same. Alfred says people are always disappointed when they expect things to be what they seem to be in books."

"Alfred is going to spend his life in Knoxville," I said. "Of course it is not the same. But reading tells you *something*. Eugenia, we can be rich. Rich."

"We are so well off here. Life is so good now. I have a job here, a very good job."

"Seven hundred gold dollars a month, Eugenia! You do not have a job that pays you like that."

"Snakes. There must be snakes. Cobras and all sorts of ugly things." She shuddered.

"Of course there are snakes. We will have a dog to drive the snakes away. We will make a fortune selling snakeskin purses and boots."

She laughed. "Mamma will be so—" She stopped in mid-sentence and looked down. I did not say anything for a while.

I was thinking of how much I could send to my mother and my sisters. I was thinking of travel. Yes, we would go to Greece, and Eugenia would see that it was a good place. She would not be ashamed of my being Greek. She would understand about Stephanos, and we would go to Delphi, and we would hire a limousine and visit my mother and Helen and Helen's husband, and Anna and Anna's husband, and we would be rich in front of them, and I would redeem something from my past life.

I should have taken her hands in mine then and told her everything.

I replied by letter to James W. Richardson-Whitmore, Esq. He telegraphed me to meet him in late October. I was overjoyed. Suddenly Bourbonville looked ugly—fiercely and intractably ugly. I saw the flimsy houses, some of them not with real foundations but with brick columns built at the corners, holding the houses off the ground, so that dogs crawled under them in summer, and the stench of dog dung rose through the thin floors and thickened the air in the rooms. I thought of Bourbonvillians who had never been anywhere, never read anything, never heard a concert, never seen a play, never known what it was to sit up all night and talk about ideas, people whose only world was reaction to the land and its whims, people whom a mindless religion drugged to life.

I thought of Dr. Youngblood, of Jim Ed, of the old man. I even thought of Dale Farmer. I thought of mornings at Bessie May's, where like butter being blended into dough I was being blended into Bourbonville and the county, and I felt the guilt we feel when we leave those who assume that we belong with them.

I thought of Burma and the jungle and monkeys chattering in the treetops and snakes slithering in the grass and tigers prowling the great forests and the singing chant of coolie laborers. I thought of strange hills and plunging valleys and the mist of waterfalls. I studied maps with the eagerness of a disciple poring over a sacred text, and the names engraved themselves on the hard stuff of my memory: Rangoon, Toungoo, Mandalay, Maymyo, Gokteik, Lashio, Namtu. I dreamed Burmese names at night; I muttered them to myself in the daytime.

As the train pulled out of Knoxville, I sat in the great high-backed seat of the Pullman and saw the autumn sun slanting over the harvested fields, and I felt worldly and superior. I thought of how different everything was, how different I was from the sick and frightened boy who had come down these tracks in another October. I thought of all that had happened; I even ran my tongue over the false teeth in the front of my mouth, and I felt satisfaction. People had tried to kill me; I had survived; I had triumphed. I could do anything.

140

MR. RICHARDSON-WHITMORE took me to lunch at a hotel close to the big park. He was a military type, about forty-five, I think, perhaps older, somewhat heavy and florid, stiff and straight as a nail. He wore a double-breasted suit of a sort just coming into style then. He had the natural self-possession of the English upper classes, something that seemed bred in them since the Battle of Hastings. I observed silently that he was the kind of man Pinkerton had wanted to be, and I thought again with the mindless surprise of such experiences that Pinkerton was dead.

"So, you are Belgian," he said. "Did your service in 'fourteen, you did?"

"Yes sir," I said.

"Commendable. Commendable. Brave chaps, you Belgians. We took hell at Mons, you know. Bloody hell, if you don't mind my saying so."

"Not at all, sir," I said.

"Terrible business. Terrible business. You chaps did your bit. So did we, you know."

"Yes—you saved me from prison camp, you know. I suspect you saved my life."

"Did we now?"

"I was wounded in front of Antwerp. In September 1914. I was picked up by litter bearers from a British regiment. It was night. If they had not found me, I think I would have died."

"Indeed! Well, we didn't have many there, I can tell you. They got you out, did they?"

"To London, sir. By way of the Scheldt."

"Never cared much for the Dutch myself, but they did their bit, you know. Kept the navigation lights burning on the Scheldt. Got a lot of you Belgian chaps out that way. Our chaps, too. Not so many of ours."

"You know a lot about it," I said.

"Just a bit, you know. I was in the War Office until the Somme. Bloody awful thing, that. Couldn't stay in the War Office after the Somme."

"What did you do after the Somme?"

"Oh, I went into the line. Thought it was the honorable thing to do, don't you know? I went into the infantry. Wounded in the leg on the Lys, you see. Your country."

"Yes," I said. "My country."

"Do you realize, my good fellow, that it's been a year longer since the war than the war lasted? Do you realize that?"

"I had not thought about it."

"Time's flying, you know. The days go by one at a time, and next thing you know the years have flown. You were in the artillery?"

"I ended in the infantry," I said. "The Germans captured our gun."

"Lord, you must have been hand to hand with them."

"I was for a while," I said.

Mr. Richardson-Whitmore looked at me thoughtfully and with respect. He swept a hand around in an awkward and encompassing gesture at the restaurant, where waiters glided among tables covered with heavy linen cloths. "These others, they don't know what it is, do they?"

"No," I said.

"Well, here's to you. Here's to Burma. You know what it's about, don't you?"

"Silver," I said.

"Silver," Mr. Richardson-Whitmore said. "I represent the Burma Mines Limited. In a year or so, the Burma Mines Limited will be engaged in mining silver in northern Burma. You don't know Burma, I take it?"

"Only from the maps," I said.

"Beautiful place. One of the most beautiful places in the world, if you ask me. You have perhaps heard of the great shortage of silver in the world?"

"Yes, but I am sure it is only temporary."

"Farsighted. Farsighted, Mr. Alexander. Farsighted indeed."

We ordered our meal. Mr. Richardson-Whitmore was one of those confident people who knew exactly what to do. "You must try the sweetbreads," he said. "You can't get sweetbreads in that barbaric place where you are now. What is the name of it?"

"Bourbonville."

We laughed together.

I had the sweetbreads.

"Now we were speaking of silver," he said, turning back to me. "The British Empire is in great need of silver," he said in the confident and proud way of an engineer explaining a great machine, constructed with perfect rationality, running in perfect harmony, owned by himself. "We especially need silver in the colonies. Native labor requires hard cash, you know. The natives always prefer to be paid in coin. They don't like paper, the blighters. They don't trust it. Well, what to do? We could send the army in and make them take paper. What's wrong with that? It would cost a fortune, a bloody fortune, that's what's wrong with it. Ergo, we pay them in silver. Ergo, we mine the silver that is lying near the surface of the ground in Burma, waiting for us to pick it up. We smelt it there into ingots. We ship it down to Rangoon to be coined. We keep the British Empire intact. Bravo!"

We got on together. Mr. Richardson-Whitmore was pompous and tedious, but he knew what he was talking about. I liked him; he liked me. He spun out a glorious picture of Burma. I had to see the Gokteik Viaduct, he said. "That bridge shows in steel the majesty of the British Empire," he said. "The peaceful majesty. I say our future lies in building for the natives, not in beating them over the head. That ass who opened up the machine guns at Amritsar should have been court-martialed and shot, if you ask me. You know all about it, of course."

"Oh yes," I said, remembering vaguely a massacre in India. I scarcely knew what he was talking about in any of this, but he nodded at me with such assurance that I found it easy to pretend that I did.

In the end Mr. Richardson-Whitmore told me that I would earn eight hundred gold dollars a month. He asked me to be prepared to move to Burma in six months. "We're going to start in earnest next year," he said. "First a power line up from Mandalay. Then we build the smelter. Lots to do, young man. We're going to be in it together. And afterwards, there will be other things, don't you know? I'm interested in building an iron smelter in Manchuria. Are you game?"

I laughed. "It sounds wonderful," I said.

"Wonderful! Full of wonder. That's what it is, you see. Bloody wonderful. I hated the war. But it is a peculiar thing to admit: after the war I could not go back to the old ways, the ordinary life. Do you know what I mean? I don't think I'll ever settle down now. As long as the British Empire lasts, I suppose there will be something for people like us to do. Think so?"

"I hope so," I said.

"Waiter, do you have any champagne in the house?"

"Indeed we do, sir."

"Dom Pérignon 1911? Do you have that?"

"An excellent choice, sir. Yes indeed. A bottle, sir?"

"I suppose you must bring it out in bloody teacups."

"Alas, sir, we must bring it to you in cups. But we keep the bottle on ice in our kitchen."

"Then bring it on. My friend and I have a lifetime to celebrate!"

"*Very* good, sir. *Very* good!"

I sat in the glow of a meal, whiskey, champagne, and a life in prospect. The chandeliers gave off a subdued, prosperous light, and I was very happy.

141

THE TRAIN was an hour late, and Eugenia was not on the platform. I climbed impatiently upstairs to the street and found her in the car, parked at the curb.

I had telegraphed her: REMOVING TO BURMA SIX MONTHS FROM NOW. EIGHT HUNDRED GOLD DOLLARS A MONTH. FIRST CLASS ACCOMMODATIONS TO RANGOON.

I ran to the car and opened the door and reached for her. "Kiss me," I said.

"I have something to tell you," she said, pushing me away.

"Tell me then," I said.

"Don't be angry. It is bad news—very bad news."

"Your mother is sick. She is near death," I said.

She gave me a very sour look. "I am pregnant. We are going to have a baby."

I was stunned and then joyous. "Everything is working out at the same time!" I shouted. "How wonderful! How wonderful!" I hugged her clumsily. She was stiff in my arms.

"I missed two monthlies," she whispered.

"You missed your monthlies," I said. "That is one way to know. Two monthlies."

"I have missed three now. I have been feeling sick in the mornings. I thought I had a cold. I thought it would go away. I did not want to be pregnant. I do not want to be pregnant now."

"Why did you not go to the doctor earlier?"

"I didn't go to the doctor because I was afraid he might tell me I was pregnant."

"I find the conversation bewildering," I said with a laugh. "I am glad we are having a baby."

"I went to the doctor yesterday. He was shocked. He said that I was three months pregnant. He said I should have come earlier."

"When will the baby come?"

"It will come in early April. I hate to have doctors fool around down there. Even when his nurse is looking over his shoulder I hate it. I don't like anyone to touch me there, especially a doctor. Doctors are so thorough."

"You should go to a woman doctor."

"There are no woman doctors. Men keep women from being doctors—

just the way men keep women from being reporters. Don't you know that? Women have to go to men, and men feel around in us as if we were cattle or dogs or prostitutes."

"April," I said. "That is about when we are to go to Burma. It will be just the right time. We can have the baby, and we can leave for Burma. The sea will be healthful for him. The salt air, the wind, the sky, and the clouds. Our child will see beauty right at the first, and he will love beauty all his life."

"You still insist on going to Burma," she said. "Well, we can't go in April. We can't go when the baby is just born. Don't be foolish, Paul. I can't stand it when you are foolish."

"I am not being foolish. Listen to me. I have a job, the most wonderful job anybody could have. We are going away. We are leaving Tennessee." I wanted to add, "And we are leaving your mother."

"We cannot travel with a baby. It cannot be done."

"Of course it can be done. Babies travel easily. We are stronger when we are babies than ever again in our lives. You can nurse the child. It will be the easiest time to go. They eat. They sleep. They do not sit up at night and read books, and they do not drink whiskey, and they do not fall off buildings. They lie in their mothers' arms, and they sleep."

"You are speaking like a man. I am thinking sensibly, like a woman. Babies are fragile. We cannot travel with our baby to Burma. Think about the snakes."

"Burmese women have babies all the time. How do you think the Burmese come into the world? They are not manufactured and shipped in from Britain."

"Stop it! Stop it! Can't you see? I won't be strong enough. Mamma says I will need to rest for two months after the baby is born. You can go without me," she said. "I will have the baby and come afterwards."

Something grew cold in me. "No," I said. "We will go together or we will not go at all. Your mother does not know everything. We will speak to Dr. Youngblood."

"You cannot ask me to go in April."

"All right. What about June? July?"

"Don't be angry with me. Please. I am sorry I have made you angry. Start the car. Let's go home."

I started the car and drove slowly towards Edgewood Avenue. "Eugenia," I said as softly as I could. "So much is coming at once. It is all good. We are going to have a good life. What do you want, a boy or a girl?"

"I want a little girl. I have always wanted to start my family with a little girl."

"Then we will pray for a little girl."

"You do not believe in prayer," she said.

"For your sake I will pray for a little girl. Next year she will be in Burma.

She will grow up with excitement, with wonder, with interesting people. We will have other children. We will leave Knoxville. Look around us! Look how ugly it is!"

"I will have to quit my job and take care of the child."

"We will have servants. Our little girl will have a nurse. You will have a cook. You will have time to write articles—books. We will take a typewriter. Mr. Richardson-Whitmore says that all the company people live the life of the rich. He is rich himself and educated. Eton and Oxford. Can you imagine?"

"What about tropical diseases? If we go out there and our child dies . . ." She could not finish the sentence but looked at me in bleak asperity.

"We will be in the hills. Mr. Richardson-Whitmore says it is a healthful climate. No one is ever sick."

"What a preposterous name. I am sure he is a snob."

"No. Well, he is . . . You will meet him. You will see what he is like."

"I know I will not like him. He is probably a lecher, too."

"Please," I said. "Please give this a chance. Please, for my sake. If in a couple of years you are still unhappy, I promise we will come back."

"We can never pick up again where we are now. We cannot come back to Knoxville as it is now, as we are now. It will never be the same."

"Believe me," I said. "It will never be the same if we stay here. Life is changing at this very moment. Just as the street is running under our car, life is running under time. It does not stop changing, Eugenia. Wherever we are, it keeps on changing."

She sat glumly looking out of the car window. "I am happy now. I have worked hard to get where I am, and now I must leave it all. You do not understand. You are a man. Things come easy to a man. Men always get their way." She sat frowning and silent as the familiar streets slipped by. I became silent, too.

142

I WANTED TO MAKE LOVE to her, but she would not let me touch her. She was pregnant. It was as if she could not bear the thought of getting pregnant again.

I could not sleep. After midnight, I slipped out of bed, dressed, and walked out onto Edgewood Avenue. The air was chilly, and an occasional breeze swept fallen leaves along the pavement with a faint, dry rasping. The street lamps shed a dim light, but the houses were dark and still. I smoked a cigar.

Guy and Bernal appeared beside me, thoughtful, sympathetic, their hands clasped behind them as mine were clasped moodily behind me.

We walked in silence for a time, and I felt an immense self-pity. "Will you go with me to Burma?" I said.

"Of course," Bernal said. "Never fear."

"Yes," Guy said. "There will be mists in the great trees in the morning, and at night there will be native dancing and dinners with English friends. Ah, I would have shone in Burma."

"It will be a new adventure for all of us," Bernal said.

"How grand to be having a child," Guy said. His voice became wistful, like a whisper. "Will you name him for me? I thought Leonora and I would have a dozen children. I think she would have been good at having children. Please name your son for me."

I laughed. "Eugenia says she wants a baby girl."

"I promise you that it will be a boy," Guy said. "Will you name him after me?"

"What about Bernal?"

Bernal shook his head and smiled. "I do not require the child to be named for me. It does not matter. If you name the child Guy, you will always think of Bernal, too, when you call him by name. You cannot think of one of us without thinking of both of us."

"How wise!" I said.

"You could name him Guy Bernal Alexander," Guy said.

"Bernal is not an American name," Bernal said. "The poor boy would have to explain himself all his life. He would not like the name. I would not want that."

"My dear friends!" I said, the tears running down my face.

"My dear Paul," Bernal said.

I ached to touch them. The dry leaves scraped on the street. Knoxville seemed strange and temporary, an unpleasant place, one I would leave.

143

I ASKED for a postponement of my arrival in Burma. Mr. Richardson-Whitmore was understanding. He wrote that the rainy season that struck Burma in May would continue for several months and that construction would be slowed. He would like me there by September, a hot month but not unbearable in the hills on the Shan Plateau. My family could stay in Maymyo during the bad season; it was cool there. He wished me well and closed with his expectation of long years of joint enterprise. "Manchuria next," he said.

A letter came from Gilly. He and Virgil had spent several days together. Gilly was noncommittal about the visit. He told me that Daisy was now in love with a blond young English professor who read poetry aloud at dinner parties. He said he looked forward to my coming to Burma. It was a beautiful country, and he and his family were happy there, although his sons were going off to England to school in the fall, and he would miss them. He knew we would be friends, he said.

I waited until January to write to Philip Drodge that I was going to leave. He came down immediately, full of unbelief and consternation. "You cannot do this!" he said, rushing into my office unannounced one bleak and rainy afternoon. "Burma! It is ridiculous. I am going to bring you to Washington within two or three years. Why risk your wife and family in a preposterous place like Burma?"

Our conversation was unprofitable. He could not understand. We had dinner at the Hotel Atkin in Knoxville. By the end of the evening he had convinced himself that he had convinced me to stay on. He talked on and on, waxing speculative and lugubrious about all there was to be done on the railroad and about my future career. After dinner he wanted to go to the house to see Eugenia, but I lied to him, telling him that she went to bed early because her pregnancy was difficult. Pleased that he had offered to visit her and relieved that he did not have to bother, he bid me goodnight, saying that he would be on the morning train for Washington, happy that we had "worked all this out."

144

"WE ARE GOING to have a baby," I said to my friends at the round table at Bessie May's cafe.

"A baby!" they said.

"Good God!" Dr. Youngblood said, grinning and turning red with pleasure.

"A baby," Jim Ed said, shaking his head. "I'm better than ten years older than you are, and I don't even have me a wife. Here you are with a baby." He spoke slowly and shook his head. He was troubled; that surprised me.

"You don't have to have a wife to have a baby," Dr. Youngblood said. We all laughed.

People came in and Jim Ed and Dr. Youngblood told them. Everybody was happy.

I wrote my mother. She sent me a huge package of gifts—lace, printed cotton, baby things. I do not remember all of it. There was a paper slip in the box I maintained at the post office on Church Street when I picked up my mail on a Saturday morning. I took it to the window, and the clerk gave me the large package from Mother. "This sure has come a long way," he said. It was covered with Greek stamps, and Mother's address was drawn on it in Latin characters. My heart sank. I opened the package and found all the things neatly stacked together in a box. I took the brown paper with the stamps off and carefully wadded it up and threw it into the trash.

By then it was February, and the air was cold. Now that I had opened the package, I could not send it back. I could take it down to the slums and give the baby clothing to poor people who needed such things. I might take it home and hide it somewhere. I might throw it away as I had thrown away the bouzouki.

I did none of these things. Instead I became angry. I got on the Broadway streetcar with the box and went home. I got off at the corner of Edgewood and walked swiftly up the street. The trees were bare. Children bundled up in winter clothes were playing in the park on the swings. I thought of the son I would have and what he would do, the places he would see, the man he would be. I wanted him to be proud of me; I wanted him to know who I was. I was not going to be ashamed before my son. He would see in me a mirror of what a man might be in this country, no matter what his origins. He could go beyond me, I thought. But he must know exactly who I was. When I entered the house, I heard Mary Pendleton's creaky and petulant voice from the kitchen.

Eugenia came out and smiled at me. Her eyes fell on the package in my arms.

"What is that?" she said.

I looked at her, speechless. Her mother's stern face appeared beside her own. Eugenia's belly was growing and her skin was lovely.

"What do you have in your hands?" Eugenia said.

"It is something I received in the mail. It is nothing. Nothing."

"What is it?"

"It is from my mother," I said. "I will show it to you later."

"Your mother! How dear! Show it to me now," she said.

"No, later," I said.

"It is probably an alcoholic beverage," Mary Pendleton said. "It is all right, Mr. Alexander. I know you drink. I know that Catholics see things in a different way."

With difficulty I restrained the volcano of wrath that surged up in me. "It is not alcohol. I will put it upstairs and show you later, Eugenia."

"You are so secretive," Eugenia said, shaking her head, her absentminded smile lingering. "Is it something for me?"

"It looks big," Mary Pendleton said.

"Is it a surprise?" Eugenia called.

"Yes, it is a surprise," I said.

"Well, don't let me keep you from your surprise," Mary Pendleton said. "I will leave you two alone."

"Oh, Mother, you'll do no such thing," Eugenia said.

I came back downstairs. Eugenia had made tea, and they were in the kitchen, drinking from thick cups. I sat down and had a cup, too. It was warm in the kitchen. The February sunshine poured through the windows.

"I was just telling Eugenia that Dolly and I are praying every day for her child."

"I am sure Eugenia is very grateful," I said.

"I am praying that the child will become a missionary. Eugenia should have become a missionary. Maybe her daughter will make it up to me."

"Who can tell," I said.

"You would be very displeased if your child became a missionary," Mary Pendleton said.

"It will be up to him," I said.

"The child will be a girl. The Lord has told me it will be a girl," Mary Pendleton said.

I said nothing.

Mary Pendleton left and walked next door to Dolly's house. She was spending the night there.

"Eugenia, I have something to tell you," I said.

"I have something to tell you first," she said.

"What I have to say is important," I said.

"What I have to tell you is very important," Eugenia said. "Bess is moving away."

"Bessie? Where could she go?"

"She is going to Philadelphia," Eugenia said.

"Philadelphia? Philadelphia is in . . ." I could not remember the state.

"Pennsylvania. Bess is moving to Philadelphia. She told Mother this morning. I've known about it for a week. Mother is crushed." Eugenia looked grim. "It's so foolish. Bessie doesn't have the sense of a goose. She's going up there where nobody knows her, where she will be in bad company, where . . . Oh, it's terrible. I'm so *angry* with her! She thinks only of herself."

"Why? Why does she want to go to Philadelphia?"

Eugenia took a deep breath. "She says she cannot live with Mamma anymore. She loves Mamma, but she says that she cannot please her."

"Can anyone please your mother?"

Eugenia shrugged off my question. "Bess says Mamma criticizes her all the time. She has saved her money, and she says she will go to Philadelphia and get a job and be as far from us as she can. She says we all look down on her. Her sisters. Bert and me. Maybe the poor thing is right."

I did not know what to say.

"It is such a blow to Mamma. We have all stayed here. Bert is out in Maryville, but we can see her all we want. But Philadelphia! We won't be able to see Bess more than once a year. Poor Bess. She got left behind in school, and now she's going up to . . . Oh, it's her life, isn't it? It is her life."

"It is not so terrible," I said softly. "I have not seen my mother in years. Not since the summer of 1913, and she is alive and I am alive. It is the way life is sometimes."

"You are different. You were never so close to your mother as we have all been to our mother."

"You do not know," I said.

Eugenia took a deep breath. "Mother is going to come and live with Aunt Doll and Uncle Nep," she said.

"Next door to us."

"Yes. They have a big house. Alfred is getting married. Charles is moving into furnished rooms. I am sure you are displeased."

"We will be in Burma by the summer. Nothing matters about what your mother does."

Eugenia looked unhappily at me. "You are determined to go to Burma."

"Yes. We must get away from here."

"Mother will feel that we are all deserting her. First Bess, now me. She thinks you do not like her."

"We have our own life to live. It will be good for you to leave your mother for a while."

"I feel so uncomfortable," Eugenia said. "I'm uncomfortable all the time. Do you want to feel the baby kicking?"

I put my hand on her stomach. I could feel the motion of my child.

"That is a good sign," I said. "A healthy baby."

"It is wonderful to feel that life inside me. Wonderful," Eugenia said. She smiled.

I put my arms around her and held her close.

"It is frightening, too," Eugenia said. "I have responsibility for that life."

"It is going to be all right. Believe me, it will be splendid."

I gathered my strength and stood up. I walked back and forth while she sat looking at me. Finally I spoke with a burst of feeling. "I have something I must tell you. The package I brought in . . . the package is for you. It comes from my mother. It is things for the baby."

"How dear—how sweet! I hope we can meet your mother someday. Please let me see them."

"I must tell you something. My mother sent these things from Greece. You must know that, Eugenia. These things all come from Greece."

"From Greece? What is your mother doing in Greece? Where are the things? I want to see them. Go get them."

I could not reply. I went upstairs to get the package. I brought it back down to her.

She spread the things out on a table. "They are beautiful," she said. She held them up to the light and admired them. "Lace," she said. "Hand-woven lace."

"All true lace is made by hand," I said.

I looked over her shoulder and saw Bernal standing there, his hands folded sedately over his chest. He nodded at me and moved his lips. *"Oui!"* he whispered.

"I told you my mother was in Greece," I said.

"Yes. Why is she there?"

"Because she is Greek," I said.

"She is Greek?" Eugenia still did not comprehend.

"She is Greek. I am Greek, Eugenia. I am not Belgian. I grew up in Belgium. At least I spent several years going to school there. But I am Greek."

Her first reaction when she finally realized what I was telling her was of annoyance; it changed to affliction. Her face filled with silent and anxious questioning.

"I was born in Greece. My father killed a man when I was very young. I was sent to school in Belgium."

I faltered and sat down. She looked at me silently, almost as if I were a stranger, and I realized that I *was* a stranger to her, that I was telling her things she had not suspected about me and that therefore I was diminished in her eyes. I took her hand. "Please try to understand," I said.

"Why did you lie to me? That is what I cannot understand. Why have you lied to everyone?"

I tried to tell her. My voice trembled and seemed to ascend a note or two. Otherwise I remained outwardly calm, though within I felt undone. The sun declined through the afternoon, throwing its melancholy, cold light into our western windows, lengthening the shadows outside. The cast of the light portended winter and sadness. Winter light reminds me always of limitations and of our helplessness before them. I talked; I retreated; I started again. I did not know why I had lied. The more I tried to explain, the more absurd it all became. Her calm, reproachful gaze made me make fictions and abandon them. I contradicted myself, and she caught me in the contradictions. I felt foolish and ashamed.

"I don't understand why you believed you must lie to me," she said. "I am your wife. You should tell me everything. What else have you not told me?"

"Nothing," I said. "Nothing."

"Greek," she said. "You understood what the waiter was saying to you that day in the restaurant."

"Yes," I said.

"And you pretended not to understand."

"Yes," I said.

She shook her head. "I am going to bed. This is too much for me. Too much."

She did not look at me. She went upstairs, and I heard her preparing for bed. I sat in the kitchen and looked out the window. It seemed to give onto the most opaque blackness. I reached for her in the dark, but she kept herself rigid and would not turn over to me. "I'm so uncomfortable," she said. "Let me alone."

145

"IT'S A BOY," Dr. Newman said. Dr. Newman was about thirty, balding prematurely, freckle-faced, exuding quiet competence. He had a comfortable paunch, a complacent face. An educated East Tennessean with a broad valley accent—the accent that meant family and money.

"A boy."

I looked at the pink little body faintly crying in the doctor's arms. The grass was green, and the dogwoods were all in bloom—sprays of white blossoms in every street. Eugenia bore the child in our bedroom.

"Yes, a nice boy. Seven pounds eight ounces. Not too large."

"Is he healthy?"

"Oh, he's healthy enough. We had to spank the little devil to get him to cry. Turned blue before he did. But that's common. There he is. Be careful of his neck. Support his head with your hands. See? Did you ever hold a baby before?"

"No," I said. "No. Never."

"Well, there's a first time to everything. Here you are, your first time. First time you hold a baby, and it's your first child. There it is. One of the good things about being a doctor is you get to see some nice things sometimes. Really terrible things most of the time, but some nice things sometimes. Yes."

I took the child in my arms and looked into its wizened red face. The baby cried like a weak puppy whimpering. I felt the weight of my son in my arms. My son.

"You shouldn't speak lightly of the devil," Mary Pendleton said to Dr. Newman. "The devil is not a joke, young man. The devil goes up and down through the world, seeking whom he may devour."

Dr. Newman peered over his gold-rimmed glasses and looked gravely around the room. "The devil? I haven't seen him in here this morning."

"The devil is everywhere."

"Surely you mean God is everywhere," Dr. Newman said. "If the devil was here, I would have chased him off." He allowed himself a laugh.

"You are making fun of me and my faith," Mary Pendleton said.

"I didn't mean to hurt your feelings," Dr. Newman said.

"The righteous suffer persecution," Mary Pendleton said.

"So do the unrighteous," Dr. Newman said.

"Do you think he's strong?" I said. "Do you think he is healthy?"

"You can't hurt my feelings," Mary Pendleton said. "You may injure God, but you cannot injure me."

"Not as strong as some I've seen," the doctor said. "He'll make it all right. You won't have any trouble with that baby."

"The scoffers will have their place in the lake that burns with fire and brimstone forever and ever," Mary Pendleton said.

"Is my wife safe?"

"Yes, she's all right. The nurse will be out in a minute. Cleaning her up, you know. Then you can go in. Messy business, having a baby. Animals do a good job of it. Mother animals eat the placenta and lick themselves clean. I've often thought of recommending that. Must be vitamins and minerals in the placenta. Humans won't do it. Narrow-minded, I'd say!" He laughed. "You can go in in a few minutes. We need to grease the baby. Keeps his skin moist."

"You make fun of everything, young man. You will come to a bad end if you make fun of everything."

"We all come to bad ends, Mrs. Pendleton," Dr. Newman said. "It doesn't matter if we make fun of everything or not."

"I can tell you of some wonderful deathbed experiences, young man."

"I never have seen one," Dr. Newman said.

"Then you have never seen a Christian die," Mary Pendleton said.

"I've seen all kinds die, Mrs. Pendleton," Dr. Newman said. "They all die badly. There's no good way to die. Folks die well in books. They don't die that way in a messy bed when a doctor's standing over them."

"Are you a Christian, Doctor?" Mary Pendleton changed the tone of her voice. I could see her advancing on her way to win the doctor to Christ. She was always talking about winning the lost to Christ.

"No ma'am, I'm not," Dr. Newman said.

"Then you're lost? You admit that you're lost?"

"No ma'am, I'm not lost," Dr. Newman said. "I'm right here in your kitchen. I know where I am. I can find my way home about as well as you can."

"Young man, the Bible says—"

"Mrs. Pendleton, I don't believe the Bible. I don't believe in religion. If you want to believe in those things, you go right ahead. Just don't bother me about them. My religion is my own business."

Mary Pendleton took a deep, angry breath and spoke in a tight little voice that I thought might crack with her hot wrath. "No one has ever talked to me like that in my life."

"Is that so?" Dr. Newman said. "That's too bad. It might have made you stop poking your nose into other people's business."

I thought Mary Pendleton's face would explode. I had never seen her with color in her cheeks before.

The nurse came down the steps. She was a mountain of white. "It's all right," she said. "Everything is all right. Finished."

Dr. Newman said, "Mr. Alexander, you can go in and see your wife if you want. I'm going back to the office. My fee is twenty-five dollars. My nurse will give you a receipt. Take the baby up to your wife, Mr. Alexander. Spend some time with her. Tell her you love her."

Mary Pendleton followed the doctor to the door, telling him she would pray for him. "Good," he said jovially. "If you pray for me, it'll keep you from bothering other folks. I'm proud to keep you occupied."

I was happy. Mary Pendleton had been whipped down like a big dog clubbed on the nose just as she was about to bite someone's leg. My son lay in my arms, my son, crying weakly, fitfully, moving his little red hands back and forth in an aimless waving. My son, naked with a huge red navel and a wet cord hanging from it. My son, with fine dark hair and tightly shut eyes.

The shades had been pulled down in Eugenia's room. The shades were thin yellow canvas. They cast a yellow glow. Her head lay on the pillow, her long blond hair spread like a halo. She was pale and beautiful. She smiled. She reached for the child and held him, and he seemed to snuggle down.

"Well," I said.

"Well," she said. We both laughed. She put the child's mouth to her breast. He felt for the nipple and understood what to do with it.

"He's so smart," she said. "Ooooh. It hurts. It really hurts."

"It will feel good," I said.

Mary Pendleton came into the room. "Do you know what that impertinent doctor said?" She began to tell us what he had said.

"Mother Mary," I said as gently as I could. "Let's not talk about it. Please. Let us be happy. It is a happy day, a very happy day."

"What shall we name him?" Eugenia whispered. "I had a girl's name picked out. Mary for Mother. What will we name him?"

"The first son in my husband's family has always been named Alfred William," Mary Pendleton said. "Alfred's name is Alfred William. The name Alfred William goes back nine generations."

"We will name him Guy," I said.

"Guy?" Mary Pendleton said. "Guy! Why do you want to name a child Guy? The only Guy I know is an electrician."

"Guy," I said. "He must be called Guy."

"I think that is a fine name," Eugenia said.

"It was the name of a dear friend," I said. Eugenia stroked my hand.

"The one killed in the war," she said.

"Yes," I said. "The one killed in the war."

"It's a nice name," she said. "Guy. Guy Curry Alexander. How is that?"

"It should be Alfred William," Mary Pendleton said.

"Guy Curry Alexander. Yes," I said. "Yes, a good name, a mixing of the Old World and the New, the old life and a new life." I laughed.

Guy stood on the other side of Eugenia's bed, arms folded, his finely carved face blissful with joy. Suddenly Bernal was there, too, his face serene, and I could feel Stephanos and M.P. in the golden room though I could not see them, and I felt Pinkerton's presence as though purged in the refiner's fire, and Father Medulous and Father Droos and Madame Boschnagel and Huys and Palmyre—yes, the living Palmyre—there with me. I felt them crowding around, witnesses to the glory. Lying in her bed, propped up on her pillow, the tiny infant suckling at her breast, Eugenia looked down, an aureole of yellow light gathering around her, her attention given all to her baby, my son, and the world was a wonder of trouble that had come to a good end.

It seemed that only in a far, far distant, forlorn place Mary Pendleton's querulous voice muttered like a storm that had passed up a valley, bending the trees and the grass, dissolving against the imperturbable granite of the mountains. I remember the March sunshine streaming through the yellow shades. The glory.

146

I HANDED OUT CIGARS at the car works. Fat, Cuban cigars, twenty-five cents apiece. I felt no shame at the expense. I have a photograph here that Herbert McCawley took of me smoking one of those cigars. Herbert had replaced DeShane Dugan as foreman of the wheel foundry, and he took "candid photographs" with his little camera.

I am smoking one of those fat cigars, leaning up against Jim Ed with fat Dale Farmer standing with his arms stiff at his sides and a little outlandish on my right, all of us grinning for the camera, wearing hats that look too big for our heads. We look terribly young. Even Dale Farmer looks young.

I told Jim Ed we were going to Burma. "Then I suppose I will lose my job," he said.

"No," I said. "I think you may be the boss." I tried to sound confident.

He shrugged. "I did not finish college."

"Neither did I," I said.

He sat reflectively. "I could do the job," he said.

"Of course you could," I said. Philip Drodge did not believe in Jim Ed; I knew that from conversations we had had. I had to make him see that Jim Ed was indispensable. What if it did not happen? "It's no concern of yours," Guy whispered in my ear.

"I wish you would not go," Jim Ed said. I lowered my eyes, unable to meet his.

"I have to go. I have to get away from Eugenia's mother."

"We could get somebody to shoot her."

I looked up. Always behind Jim Ed's easiness was something else—a hard firmness down deep, a loyalty that might go to any length. I remembered the men with the battered faces, Mr. Kirby's headlong flight from Bourbonville; but he smiled suddenly, and I smiled, too. "I wish it could be that easy," I said.

"Philip Drodge wants you here. He doesn't want me."

"He will become accustomed to you," I said. I looked down.

"He won't have anything to do with me," Jim Ed said softly. "He's that kind. He's not my kind."

I shook my head and was silent. I had no more energy left to lie.

"Ingratitude," Guy said. "That is what your friend Mr. Philip Drodge will charge you with. He has put his reputation on the line to make you manager of this evil little place. Now you are leaving. Ingratitude. Your friend James Edward will get nothing. Nothing at all."

"It is not my fault," I said.

"Of course not," Guy said.

Men in the car works shook hands with me and congratulated me. For the first time I detected real friendliness among many of them. Herbert McCawley said, "You are now the father of an American citizen." He spoke with ponderous ceremony, a man seeking to rise to the occasion. Do people always make so much over a baby? I do not think so. My baby seemed special. Most children were matter-of-fact. The world had never seen anything like my son.

In Knoxville people visited to see the baby. Eugenia's family drifted in and out, trailing clouds of compliments. Alfred and Charles were friendlier than they had been before. "You're carrying on the family line," Alfred said. "You have the first male child."

Bert's first child had been a girl. Bert was pregnant again. She and Lionel came, and Lionel insisted on taking a walk. "I can't stand the Currys," he said glumly. "I'm glad you're in the family. Well, how about it? Is Eugenia as insatiable as Bert? God help you! Now she's pregnant again. Where is it going to end? Where is it going to end?"

I did not learn for several years that Lionel did not understand condoms or any other sort of birth control. Somehow he had managed to be in the army and to be mustered out without ever having left the country and without learning much of anything. His face was red and puffy. Every time I saw him he seemed more irascible. He was drinking heavily. Bert seemed not to notice.

Even Mary Pendleton was pleased with the middle name Curry, though she never liked the name Guy. "Perhaps you can call him Curry," she said. "Curry Alexander. That is not a bad name."

"No, we will call him Guy," I said.

147

ON THE FIRST SUNDAY after the birth, Dr. Youngblood drove to Knoxville in the afternoon, bringing Brian Ledbetter, Dale Farmer, Jim Ed, and Ted Devlin, Ted looking less rumpled than he usually did, smelling of bourbon. I hoped Mary Pendleton would take it for cologne or shaving lotion.

My visitors were dressed up, wearing jackets and stiff collars and neckties in honor of my son. I was touched. I loved them all, loved them not only for themselves but because they represented another block of my life that I was about to leave behind—Greece, Belgium, London, Bourbonville, steps on the road to Burma, and who could tell how long the road would go, how many steps there would be?

Jim Ed brought his guitar and mandolin, and we played music, and Jim Ed sang. I played well, better than usual because I did not feel embarrassed now, even with the condescending expression of Alfred, who happened in while Jim Ed was singing, or the firm frown of disapproval that made Mary Pendleton's raddled face look like Judgment Day. I knew I would not play in Burma before the formal Englishmen and their formal wives who would make up our evening social life. I could play here. Something else to tell goodbye.

"I love to hear you sing," Eugenia said happily to Jim Ed. "I heard those songs when I was a little girl."

"I never liked that kind of singing myself," Mary Pendleton said with a sniff. "I don't think we ought to sing foolish songs. At least if you're going to sing, let it be hymns. It's the Sabbath day."

We obliged by playing hymns, and Jim Ed sang in his clear, sweet voice. I played after him, watching his fingers on the frets, following him with the smooth, unthinking motion of a musician floating in music. Mary Pendleton looked at me in astonishment.

"Well, I never," she said. "I didn't know Catholics knew hymns."

I belonged to my own world. I was the world, swelling and swelling, green forests on my back, green meadows spreading out over my broad belly, the soft blue sea lying under the sunshine of my eyes.

> *Amazing grace, how sweet the sound*
> *That saved a wretch like me!*
> *I once was lost but now I'm found,*
> *Was blind but now I see.*

Jim Ed threw back his head, shut his eyes, swayed through the song, believing it while he sang it, uttering his words as a prayer. I believed, too. We were all Christians when we sang. I made harmonies around his notes. I played through an enchantment of music.

Brian Ledbetter said it was good to know a lady of quality like Mary Pendleton, that indeed he was honored to know such a woman. "Our people fought for the Union, too," Mary Pendleton said. She almost smiled; I am sure she considered it a smile, a slight uplifting of the wrinkles in her corrugated face. Something warm passed between them, two old people remembering. I realized how ancient Brian Ledbetter was, how much older than even Mary Pendleton he was.

Le petit Guy lay in his crib. Brian Ledbetter looked down at him, the old man's face suffused with wonder and pleasure. I knew that he would not live long enough for Le petit to remember him well even if we stayed in Knoxville.

Mary Pendleton told us all again about Dr. Newman. No matter what we could do, the conversation revolved around what she wanted to talk about. "The man is an atheist," she said indignantly. "What's more, he's no gentleman. He actually made *fun* of my religion."

"I know Tim Newman," Dr. Youngblood said. "He's an excellent doctor. A little eccentric. He collects skulls, you know."

"Skulls! You're not serious," Eugenia said.

"Yes, he collects skulls. He's got some ideas about the brain and criminal behavior. He taught biology part-time over at the university, and he's got a laboratory full of skulls."

"I don't believe it," Mary Pendleton said. "He collects skulls that ought to be buried in the ground waiting for the Resurrection. I suppose he believes in evolution, too."

"He does for a fact," Dr. Youngblood said. He gave Mary Pendleton an innocent look. "He was fired from his job at the university because he taught evolution. It was in the papers."

"I knew it! I knew it! I knew it!" Mary Pendleton gloated. "That's the kind of man who delivered your child," she said in a triumphant tone to Eugenia, who only laughed and looked at me. "I suppose he can't tell the difference between the skull of a gorilla and the skull of a good Christian man."

"I'd say it would depend on the denomination," Brian Ledbetter said. "You take your average Baptist. I think sure enough he looks pretty much like a gorilla. But I'd say your average Methodist looks pretty human."

"I hope you are not making fun of religion, Mr. Ledbetter," Mary Pendleton said.

"Ma'am, do I look like the kind of person that would do that?"

"Of course I think the Methodists have strayed from the true way," Mary Pendleton said.

"Ain't you a Methodist?" Brian Ledbetter said.

"Well, I was before the Methodists turned so modernistic. I'm non-denominational now."

"But you ain't a Baptist," the old man said, looking a little anxious.

"Of course not."

"So I couldn't of been talking about you, could I?" He looked boldly at her.

"Tim Newman's a scientist," Dr. Youngblood said.

Ted Devlin said, "It's the age of science. Science has brought us progress that you wouldn't believe."

"Like the Maxim gun," Jim Ed said. "Science brought us the Maxim gun and the tank and poison gas and all those good things."

"Science does not know anything about the Resurrection," Mary Pendleton said. "Science sounds like superstition to me, like voodoo. Scientists are puffed-up and proud. They have power, but it's like the power of Satan. You know the Negroes used to collect bones of different kinds, and they cast spells with them. With a skull you could do all sorts of mischief."

"Spells?" Dr. Youngblood said. He smiled around his pipe stem, puffing complacently as though it were lit, as though he were drawing rich smoke back on his tongue.

"I know you don't believe, Doctor," Mary Pendleton said. "You and your Harvard education. All you Harvard people think you're better than the rest of us. We're all sinners, Doctor. Your Harvard education won't keep you from burning in hell."

"I am sincerely interested in what you have to say about voodoo," Dr. Youngblood said, suddenly grave. "Voodoo is an illusion, but we live and die by illusions. Illusions are sometimes far more important than the reality in telling us how to behave."

"Well, I don't believe there's anything to it myself," Dale Farmer said. "I agree with my friend Ted here. This *is* the age of science. Voodoo indeed! It's not right even to think about such superstitions. With all due respect, ma'am."

"What are we talking about?" Ted Devlin said. "I've lost the thread."

"Skulls," Jim Ed said.

"That's a subject I can get my teeth into," Ted Devlin said.

"Good grief!" Dr. Youngblood said.

"Personally I agree that there's some scientific warrant for reading the character of individuals from their skulls," Dale Farmer said, spreading his fat legs and putting his pudgy hands on his knees, leaning forward intensely. "You can tell the difference between skulls when you look. For example, take Woodrow Wilson. He had that long, narrow head. A bad sign, I say. It betokens narrow-mindedness, and we all know how narrow-minded Wilson was. But take President Harding. He had the skull of an aristocrat." Wilson had died in February, Harding the previous August.

Dale Farmer's paean to Harding brought an enthusiastic outpouring of assent and mourning from Mary Pendleton, who took the opportunity to denounce the League of Nations, from which Harding had saved us. I could see that my friends were amused by her and that in making her talk, they entertained themselves. Harding's scandals were in all the papers, but Mary Pendleton refused to believe them. The talk rolled on and on.

"Hey, Daddy, why are you just sitting there like a stump?" Jim Ed said after a while. "You're just staring at that baby. What's the matter with you anyway? You sick or something?"

"No, I ain't sick," Brian Ledbetter said.

"Then what's wrong with you? I ain't never heard you so still! Has the grumpus got your tongue?"

"Nothing's wrong," Brian Ledbetter said, speaking like a man aroused from sleep. "Nothing at all."

"Come on, old man," Ted Devlin said. "Something's eating on you. You got to talk more than this, or we wasted our time bringing you up here."

"You didn't bring me up here. Dr. Youngblood brung me up here," Brian Ledbetter said. "I like to of suffocated while he was doing it, too. Even with the windows open. I like to sit out where I can look up at the sky. That's what I like to do. I hate smelling all that stuff some men wear. I won't mention any names, Dale Farmer. I hate the stuff that some men wears on their skin that smells like a flower garden where all the flowers have been raised for funerals."

"Well now, that's more like it," Ted Devlin said. "Now we're getting somewhere. Now the old man is talking. Why are you staring at that baby like that?"

"I just ain't never seen a baby so quiet," Brian Ledbetter said.

"I reckon a baby never had the chance to be quiet in your house," Ted said. He patted the old man on the back and laughed.

"He's a good baby," Eugenia said. "Everybody says he's the best baby they've ever seen."

"Don't you think he's quiet, Doc?" Brian Ledbetter said, not laughing.

"They sleep a lot when they are that age," Dr. Youngblood said.

"He ain't asleep now," Brian Ledbetter said. "He's just laying there."

"I think his eyes are slightly crossed," Eugenia said. "Mamma and Aunt Doll say that's natural in babies. Is that true, Dr. Youngblood?" She tried to sound lighthearted. I could hear the quaver of anxiety in her voice. I wanted Dr. Youngblood to be warm and reassuring. He was often that way with worried people.

"Oh, some babies have the problem," he said vaguely.

"They do outgrow it, don't they?" Eugenia said.

"Babies outgrow just about everything," Dr. Youngblood said. He held his pipe in his mouth and looked thoughtfully at Le petit. He had one hand folded across his belly, holding the elbow of the other arm. He was growing more paunchy, and he was bald on the top of his head. He combed the hair on the sides to cover the baldness on top. "I think we better be going," he said.

148

THE CHILD'S EYES were crossed. After six weeks there was no doubt about that. "You can fix crossed eyes with an operation now," Dr. Newman said. "It is not the worst thing that can happen to a child."

Eugenia and I did not talk much about it. Our baby looked up at us, and we were quiet when we looked at him. "Does anyone in your family have crossed eyes?" she said.

"No," I said. "I don't think so."

"Mamma says she never heard of anybody in my family who had crossed eyes."

"Some things happen," I said. "It will be all right." I was anxious but could not admit it.

May came and then June, and I said we would leave in mid-August. "It will take six weeks. We will get to Burma in late September, get settled down, and the rainy season will end."

"How can we go to Burma when our child needs an operation?" Eugenia said.

"He cannot have the operation until he is older," I said. "That is what the doctors say. When he is older we will come back to America to visit, and he can have the operation."

"How often will we come back?" she said.

"Every two years," I said. "The company has a policy. Four months off for every two years we spend in the field. Four months."

"Six weeks coming and six weeks going," Eugenia said. "That means only a little more than a month at home. How can he have an operation in that time?"

I was feeling desperate. "We will arrange it. Maybe he can have the operation in London."

"When will we be in London?"

"I do not know, but we can arrange it."

We booked passage on the *Fushimi Maru* out of Seattle. We would sail to Tokyo and take the train to Nagasaki. At Nagasaki we would take a ship to Singapore. From Singapore we would take another ship to Rangoon. By rail we would go up to Mandalay. There we would change to a narrow-gauge railroad and go up to Lashio. From there we would ride on horseback to Namtu. That was where the silver smelter was to be built. I would work with Gilly on building the power line back to Mandalay.

Tickets came in bundles from Thomas Cook. Many were written in Asian languages and in English. I studied them in silent passion. I loved the smell of them—crisp paper. I thought they smelled of the spices of the Orient. Nonsense, of course. But thoughts are free.

I wrote Philip Drodge that I would be leaving. I suggested that he appoint Jim Ed to replace me. He sent me a barely civil note. I should think about things. I should consider my future in the light of my wife and child. I owed some gratitude to the railroad and to him, he said. I should think of that, too. He did not concede that I was going. If I should decide to leave, he wrote—assuming that I had not decided—he would then consider the matter of my successor. I was to make no promises to James Edward Ledbetter. I showed Jim Ed the letter. "Well, I can go back to farming," he said. "I never left it." He laughed. "I've got used to some things. A new Ford car, for instance."

Eugenia went back to Dr. Newman with the child. "He seems evasive," she said. "Something is wrong, and he won't tell us."

"Nothing is wrong," I said uneasily. "His eyes are crossed. That is all that is wrong."

"No, there is something more."

"We will take him to Dr. Youngblood. Dr. Youngblood will tell us the truth. He will tell us that the child is all right, and that will relieve your mind."

"He drinks," Eugenia said. "I do not want to trust my baby to someone who drinks."

"He drinks a little wine now and then," I said.

"That is against the law," Eugenia said.

"Please be tolerant," I said.

"I cannot tolerate criminals," she said.

"You are worried," I said. "You sound like your mother."

"I am not like Mamma. I only observe that most of your friends— including Dr. Youngblood—drink alcoholic beverages and break the law. Why should I trust a doctor who breaks the law?"

"Please do not be angry with my friend because you are worried about our child. That is not fair. It cannot do any harm to take Guy to see him."

"All right. All right. I hate doctors. They are so devious. So greedy. I hate them."

"Dr. Youngblood is not greedy."

"All right. If it will make you happy, we will go. I don't like it." I thought she might cry.

"You can say goodbye to people in Bourbonville."

"I don't know anybody in Bourbonville."

"I know people there, and you are my wife."

"I did not know that it was required of a wife to make social visits for her husband. Is that how you do things in Greece?"

I took a deep breath. "We will take the child to see Dr. Youngblood."

"I am sorry," she said. Her eyes filled with tears. "I am so worried. I didn't mean to say what I said."

"It is all right," I said. "It does not matter."

"It does matter. I am so worried about the baby that I can't think of anything else."

"I am worried, too," I said, finally admitting it.

We held each other, each alone in a world apart.

We drove down to see Dr. Youngblood early on a Saturday morning. He came out to meet us in the street, dressed in white, wearing on his forehead the reflecting mirror that doctors wore in those days, his stethoscope hanging from his neck by its earplugs. We shook hands, and he inclined his head to Eugenia, looking at our baby all the while. It was a beautiful morning, flowered and mild. Eugenia carried Guy wrapped tightly in a bundle against her chest. He was very quiet.

In the waiting room patients had begun to gather—men in overalls and women in flour-sack dresses, abashed and silent in the presence of mortality and medicine. One of them had a bloody bandage wrapped around a hand.

In his office, the door shut, Dr. Youngblood unwrapped the child and put him on his back on the enamel examination table. The office smelled of pipe tobacco and medicine. Miss Jane stood by. She was Miss Sally's sister. The child lay naked on the table, looking towards the ceiling, sometimes rolling his unlifted head listlessly. Dr. Youngblood held up a hand and swept it slowly through the air before Guy's face. He looked extremely grave. He did it again, this time holding up one finger and moving it slowly, very slowly, through space. I felt a sudden and suffocating lump in my chest because the child's eyes did not follow the finger. Dr. Youngblood felt the child's arms and legs, felt under his neck, felt gently the back of his head, looked into his eyes with a glass, listened to his heart with a stethoscope, flexed the child's unresisting limbs. All the while the baby lay there almost inert, once only stretching out a little arm, drawing it back again.

Dr. Youngblood went on for a very long time. Miss Jane watched in silence, occasionally lending a hand without being told. The office felt hot, even with the window open onto the bright early morning. The harsh smell of disinfectants hung in the air. Eugenia watched the doctor intently; I watched her. I was conscious of the loud ticking of the regulator clock on the wall. I imagined seconds as little people marching to the edge of an immense, sunlit cliff, leaping one by one into the black dark that lay bottomless below. I heard time screaming in space. Eugenia set her mouth in a straight line. She looked whipped and tired. We stood shoulder to shoulder. Sometimes we brushed against each other. When we touched, she pulled away. My heart pounded in my ears. I would have a headache.

Finally Dr. Youngblood wrapped Guy up again and handed him over gently to Eugenia. "I think we'd better sit down," he said.

"I will look over the waiting room," Miss Jane said. She went out, her plump face expressionless.

Nobody said anything for a moment. Dr. Youngblood deliberately stoked his pipe, his eyes fixed on its blackened bowl. Dirty pipes lay all over the place. I remembered the field hospitals. Dr. Youngblood lit his pipe. A Currier and Ives lithograph of the western mountains hung framed on the wall over his head. Covered wagons crossed a stream. Guy and Bernal stood suddenly behind Eugenia, looking solemn. I recalled that the dead could see the future, but except in rare cases God forbade them to reveal to the living what they saw. I remembered the Witch of En-Dor.

Dr. Youngblood took a long pull on the pipe and expelled the smoke. He kept his eyes fixed in front of him, looking into the smoke as though something there might give him counsel. He took a deep breath and let it out in a sigh. Then he looked at me. "I could be wrong. Doctors are often wrong. Sometimes we're nothing but a pack of ignoramuses barking up empty trees. I think your child is something we call a Mongoloid subnormal. Down's syndrome is the prettier name. Either way it's a terrible condition."

"A what?" Eugenia looked stunned. I reached for her hand, but she pulled away and put both her hands to her face, not weeping but rubbing vaguely at her cheeks, her eyes almost blank.

"I think your child will be one of God's special children," Dr. Youngblood said quietly.

"You mean he is an imbecile."

"That is an even uglier name," Dr. Youngblood said.

"Feeble-minded, then."

"I could be wrong," Dr. Youngblood said. "I hope I am wrong. I don't believe he will ever have more intelligence than a four-year-old."

149

WE DID NOT GO to Burma. The sentence stares up at me from this crisp white paper late on a wintry night. Why do I think first of our failed journey in consequence of our discovery about our child? Dr. Youngblood said we might as well be in Burma as anywhere else. Our child would not be worse there than here.

"Nonsense," Mary Pendleton said. "Something can always be done. Dolly and I can teach him; it will just take a little more work. What does a drinking doctor in a little town like that know about anything?"

"I think Dr. Youngblood knows a great deal," I said.

"I say you need to see a specialist," Mary Pendleton said. "Take him up to New York City and let people take a good look at him. They might have a drug or something." It was a strange reversal, this abrupt declaration that doctors in New York City might do something that other doctors could not, and I wondered if Mary Pendleton might be like those people intent on belief who finding no satisfaction in the worship of God turn to the cult of Satan.

"What do doctors in New York City know that they have kept hidden from doctors in Tennessee?" I said.

"Don't you want to help your child?" Mary Pendleton said.

"I do not think my child can be helped."

"Everybody can be helped," Mary Pendleton said. "I have all my friends praying. God will give us an answer; somebody can help this child."

"I think I should go, Paul," Eugenia said timidly.

"It will be a waste of time and money," I said. The moment the word "money" was out, I could have bitten my tongue.

Mary Pendleton's face blazed at me. "With your job, you're worried about money! At a time like this you think of money?"

I opened my mouth to say something and realized that talking to Mary Pendleton was like talking to a wind blowing out of a storm.

"All right," I said.

"I should think so," Mary Pendleton said triumphantly.

Eugenia went north to consult with doctors. Before she left I said that I thought we should go on to Burma. She burst into hysterical weeping. I had never imagined her weeping as she did. To see her weep in such anguish and despair was a revelation of the sort that one finds in old stories where a child wanders in a forest and discovers some horror that he has never imagined amid the green. It gave me a hard chill of inexpressible terror. Before it was over her mother and Aunt Doll and her sister Nelle were all gathered around her, and Bert came over from Maryville, and I was not allowed to enter her room.

I wrote to Mr. Richardson-Whitmore. I received a long letter back from him. He was deeply grieved, he said. He had friends among the nobility who had retarded children. I had never heard the term "retarded" used in that sense. It had a nice euphemistic ring. A "retarded" child was delayed; the implication was that after a slow start he would catch up. Mr. Richardson-Whitmore said that I should come along to Burma. English medicine was the best in the world, he said. There would be English doctors there who knew the latest things about all forms of illness. I was going to have to live with the child anyway; I might as well live with him in Burma. In time I could put the child in a special school.

It was a nice letter. I wrote him a short letter in reply, perhaps curt. I told him that my mind was fully made up. I would not come to Burma because my wife had been crushed by the birth of our son and that I could not subject her to a further emotional disturbance. I received a perfunctory reply from him, and we never communicated again. I am sure he is dead now. I sent the tickets back. I dropped them into the mail the way I had dropped the bouzouki into the ocean: a final, sad gesture of farewell to something I had once been.

I had bought many books on Burma. At night while Eugenia was gone I studied them; sometimes even yet I turn them over in my hands and look at the engravings of Kachin tribesmen with their angular faces, sturdy people who inhabited the great forests of the northern Shan States that lay along the borders of southern China. I studied the markings of the reticulated python and the banded krait. I pondered the design of the great Gokteik Viaduct, a spidery web of steel that hung miraculously over space from misty mountain to misty mountain. Burma became another window into a life that might have been, as though I had seen it from a train swiftly passing through an exotic land.

I talked about Burma with Guy and Bernal. They sat at the kitchen table with me at night and looked at the maps. We were happy when we talked together. We shut the rest of the world out.

Eugenia was away for a month. In Philadelphia she stayed with Bess. She went to New York. Somebody recommended a doctor in Chicago, and she went there. She came home, and I met her at the train. She carried our baby in her arms, and he was very still and placid, growing now, looking plump and almost healthy.

Eugenia sat at night in the blue chair in the living room and stared at our little boy. The doctors told her she should never have any more children. Mongoloid subnormality was not well known. The most helpful doctor in New York said it had something to do with inheritance. "Heredity," he said. I had read the word in the dictionary. Some combination of father and mother produced a strange offspring who resembled neither of them, though all Mongoloid children resembled one another.

We continued to sleep in the same bed. I reached for her at night, and she stiffened. Sometimes when she slept, her back to me, I lay against her and put my arm around her and held her. She complained that my arm was too heavy and that she could not sleep when I embraced her. I stopped touching her in bed except when we brushed casually against each other in the night.

We found little to say to each other. An intangible injury hung in the air between us. I could think of nothing but apologies, and I was not sure for what I was apologizing. I reasoned that she blamed me for the child by a chain of logic that seemed to be part of a Greek tragedy. Had I confessed to her at once that I was Greek, she would not have married me, and she would never have borne our child. Because we had married and the child was born as he was, I was the agent of God's vengeance on her, and she could no more love me than Israel might have loved the Assyrians.

Sometimes I came in early and saw her preparing supper, saw how beautiful she was, what fine hips she had, and desire surged up in me like a shock of electricity; I touched her, she drew away, and the electricity in me discharged as quickly as lightning.

150

SHE THOUGHT GOD had cursed her. "Mamma was right," she said. "If I had gone as a missionary, this never would have happened." She did not cry again. Weeping might have broken down the dam—high, thick, impenetrable—that she walled over her emotions. She spoke in the dead-level conviction of one who knows an irrefutable truth, who cannot fight it, who will not argue with fate—a female Oidipous, admitting the justice of her blindness.

"Nonsense," I said. "You cannot speak like that. We do not know why things happen."

"Things happen for a purpose," she said in a voice flat and dull like granite on a tomb. "God has punished me for not going as a missionary."

"God is not like that," I said.

"He is like that. Look at our son."

She went back to church at the tabernacle. I went with her, feeling an obligation to share her misery. She was my wife; I had made vows with her.

Mr. Parry had died. Consumption, people said, caught during his ministry on foot to parishioners, who were often diseased. The new minister, Mr. McEnroe, was a florid, oily fat man who wore pointed patent leather shoes with spats. He wore cheap, bright suits with vests and slicked his hair. When he came to visit us—ministers were expected to visit—he sat in the blue chair in the living room and drank coffee. To me he assumed a superior worldliness.

"I haven't been a preacher all my life," he said with mysterious implication. "The Lord saved me from some pretty awful sins, and I could tell you tales that could curl your hair, Mr. Alexander." He nodded in a confidential way and winked soberly at me; I expected him to grin to show what a trick we were playing on the world together. He remained as solemn as the Gothic Christ on portals. He thought we were sharing manly talk.

I nodded politely. Mr. McEnroe believed his undescribed sins had elevated him in some enigmatic way to an altitude that others achieved by making money, by writing books, by creating music and art, and by travel into distant and exotic places. I supposed that since the man had never done anything that conferred true distinction, he had to make the best of what he had done—his petty sins, his paltry redemption.

In the pulpit he drew back his round head, exposing his flabby double chin, and he managed to look like a vindictive boar. He poured out the fires of hell on his rapt and stricken congregation, the whiskey-soaked men who sat red-eyed and blank-faced, almost in collapse under the wild charge of the young minister's galloping voice. At other times he railed with triumphant glee as if he were a general in the heavenly army, victorious after a hard campaign against the legions of Satan, who now were to be hurled into the fire. Both these attitudes were feigned.

I might have walked out panting for fresh air, never to return. I could not leave. Eugenia sat listening to him, clutching the baby in her arms, her face uplifted in rapt dejection. Other children sometimes cried fiercely; our son never cried. He lay limp and content in his mother's arms, rolling his crossed eyes aimlessly about or else sound asleep.

On Sunday night in September, when a humid heat pressed down on Knoxville, when First Creek stank with sewerage, when the tabernacle was filled with the yearning of the wretched for release, when thunder grumbled ominously in the distance after Mr. McEnroe conjured up hell once again, and when the painfully out-of-tune piano clanked through a saccharine invitational hymn with an off-key choir simpering inharmoniously in the background, Eugenia suddenly left her place beside me with a sob that was partly a groan.

Mr. McEnroe was standing down in front of the pulpit, heavy arms raised, bellowing an exhortation for sinners to repent, and Eugenia pushed her way out into the aisle, clutching Guy in her arms, and went blindly to the front with tears streaming down her anguished face. I started to follow her; then I stood still.

I watched as she gasped out to Mr. McEnroe that she had never truly been saved. He ceremonially hugged her, his fat arms around her and the child; he shouted "Glory! Hallelujah!" in makeshift passion. She stood bowed around our baby, weeping in heartbroken sobs, sweat bursting through her dress, darkening the fabric. I thought how strange it was that a preacher whom I held in such contempt could so freely embrace Eugenia and that I could not embrace her because she turned hard under my arms as if unwilling to allow me the slightest provocation that might make me desire her.

Dolly Laughton and Mary Pendleton went swiftly down, queenly women in black sweeping through their squalid realm with the dignified and authoritative haste of Spanish duennas—or perhaps like the Harpies, greedy for prey. They, too, embraced Eugenia, who put her face on her mother's shoulder and wept bitterly.

Mr. McEnroe put his head back and roared his thanksgiving to God, falling into a rhythmic chant, "Hallelujah! Hallelujah! Hallelujah! Hallelujah!" like a shaman summoning up chthonian deities. Perhaps the high-pitched repetition relieved him of expressing any more normal emotion, which might have been embarrassment or concern that here was a despairing and anguished woman making a public display of herself. At bottom Mr. McEnroe's was a controlled and contrived ecstasy, and when he had had enough of it, he stopped abruptly. When the service was over, he led a limp and drained Eugenia out to my Maxwell and tucked her inside as if she had been a baby. "I will be over to see you tomorrow," he said, winking at me. He patted her obscenely on the arm.

He clapped me on the shoulder, took my hand in his best imitation of a manly gesture, and looked me in the eye and said, "Mr. Alexander, sir, you are a lucky man. I don't mean *luck*—forgive me. *God* has blessed you, sir.

That woman is a saint, sir. A saint." He made as if his voice were about to break. When he released my hand, I wiped it on my trousers to dry off his clammy sweat.

We drove home through the Sunday-night emptiness of the streets. The heat rolled in waves off the pavement.

"Do you feel better?" I said.

"Oh yes," she said. "I feel completely at peace! If you could only know my Savior."

Her words made me shiver in the tropical night. She sat looking straight ahead and saying in a hypnotic revery, "I knew I wasn't saved. I went down to the altar once when I was a little girl. Everybody was doing it, and I thought I ought to do it, too. I didn't feel anything at all. Tonight I felt something. Oh, if I had only gone as a missionary! I should have been saved years ago; I knew I wasn't saved."

I knew she was saying that if she had gone as a missionary she would not have married me, making her statement with a kind of passionate objectivity, as if we were both agreed that our marriage had been part of God's punishment.

I remembered the Adoration of the Mystic Lamb and the epicene saints gathered in still rapture under the divine shining. Saints had no passion except for God. I thought of St. Barbara and her tower and supposed that Eugenia was well suited for stained glass and somber churches, a blond saint set aloft in the gloom high above the cold stone of a cathedral floor. Saints stood dispassionate in their absorption with divinity, and they had no thought of the body. I looked at her face in the light reflected from the thousand dim illuminations of the quiet city flattened under a torrid summer night, and I thought that she was as distant from me as though she had been hidden in one of the rooms behind a window seen in one of the tiny background houses on a panel of the Adoration of the Mystic Lamb.

151

EUGENIA—OR MAYBE it was Mary Pendleton—began having people over to discuss biblical prophecy. Mary Pendleton took her religion in strong doses, developed a tolerance for them, and had to have something stronger. She collected other women who, with the aid of various nonsensical books replete with calculations and diagrams, deciphered Revelation and Daniel and other arcane biblical texts that proved that the wicked world would soon end. She was persuaded that some morning the skies would flash like brittle glass shattering in a thousand suns, that a trumpet blast would reverberate across space, that Jesus would leap down the void to judge the quick and the dead startled into resurrection. She spoke with austere satisfaction of how the faces of the damned would contort in unspeakable horror at the eternal judgment coming implacably upon them. "All those modernistic preachers," she said. "They will weep and wail and gnash their teeth, but it will be too late."

Business declined at the car works. Railroading was off—an early sign of the Great Depression, though none of us knew it then. The car works stood idle on Saturdays. I usually stayed in Knoxville and did paperwork and took long walks and talked to Guy and Bernal. Often I stopped at the Greek restaurant near the train station and had coffee and sweet Greek pastry. The brothers carefully avoided talking to me. Sometimes I heard them arguing among themselves about my nationality. I drank coffee in silence and stared out the window at the street.

On one of those Saturday afternoons in early November I came back to the house and heard a familiar voice, low and rich and musical and somehow eerie, like a witch's incantation, and I went to the doorway of the living room and found Eula Pinkerton grinning up at me like a skull with dried skin stretched across the hard bone. Her iron-gray hair hung in artificial ringlets as if she were a girl of twenty. She looked like a totem made by some savage medicine man to frighten off disease and death.

"How are you, Mr. Alexander?" She put out a dry hand that squeezed mine like a vulture's claw. "I have moved to Knoxville now. No sense staying in that big house by myself." Her voice seemed to echo in deep caverns, tone rolling against tone.

"I had heard your place was for sale."

"It would be a nice place for you," she said.

"Oh, but Eugenia could never live out in the country," Mary Pendleton said quickly, throwing Eula Pinkerton a harsh look.

"She would be so far away," Dolly said.

The room was filled with women—ugly women with strong jaws and greedy eyes that ran over me like knives, and teeth grinning through withered lips. Eugenia sat among them in her innocence, her complexion creamy and her blue eyes so beautiful in the frame of her dark blond hair that the vision of her almost made me weep—a child bewitched by fanatical crones. There was nothing I could do. Eugenia went about carrying our son in a daze of devotion, and she scarcely talked to me about anything.

I went up to our bedroom and shut the door, having rejected their effusive and chattering invitation to sit with them, to read the Bible, to pray. I tried to read. I could not keep my mind on the words because the intense voices of the women pierced the thin walls. In my little house I felt in the presence of evil. Bernal appeared, sitting on the side of our bed. He looked frightened. Guy sat by the window. "You must get her out of here," Guy whispered to me. "You must move away."

I wanted to cry. How can I move away!

"Buy Pinkerton's house. Move down there."

"She will not go," I said. "Her mother will not let her go."

At night Eugenia knelt to pray by the bed. She did the same when she awoke early in the morning. She seemed to have fled down the back steps of one of those distant tiny houses in the great, calm painting of the Mystic Lamb and to have vanished in the great forest beyond.

I thought of Father Medulous, of the serene tranquility of his faith, his goodness, his sense of the world, his simple practicality and humanity. I recalled the masses early in the morning, especially the one he said in honor of Stephanos against all the canons of his church. I wondered if he could perform exorcisms, using the old liturgy of bell, book, and candle, and raise a cross and make Mary Pendleton wither away.

I even went to mass once, slipping away like a thief early one Sunday morning to sit in the back of the ugly brick church the Catholics had built for themselves on North Central several blocks from where the slums began. I listened to the familiar liturgy, saw the familiar gestures, saw the faithful flock forward to the communion rail to partake of the body of Christ. I looked to see if Bernal might be there, but he was not, and I wondered if it might be that a demon could not come into the presence of the cross. But I put such thoughts aside. I tried to let my heart soar upward on waves of feeling, like the bodies of the resurrection flying heavenward in apotheosis as they were painted on the baroque domes of churches and palaces. My heart refused to rise. I observed the ceremonial like a spectator watching a dance for which there was no music and which therefore became absurd. I slipped away in the same fugitive spirit that I had left my house earlier, and I did not go back.

152

I HAD WORK to do. Demand was down. Farmers could not sell as much grain as in wartime. Fewer trains were rolling; fewer boxcars, wheels, and trucks had to be replaced. Fewer boxcars were required. Still we kept going. With the permission of Philip Drodge, I managed to sell wheels to the

Southern Pacific Railroad and the Gulf, Mobile, & Ohio. I sold journal bearings to the L & N and to the NC & St. L. It was enough to keep us running.

Philip Drodge regarded my decision to stay at the car works as a stroke of wisdom brought about by his own powers of persuasion, and he saw me as his great friend who would shortly move up to Washington. He came and went in his palace car, and Jim Ed and I ate with him and some of his cronies when our little class A-7 steam switcher pulled it onto the siding at the car works. He reminisced about the strike, about Pinkerton, and about our meeting as if it were already ancient history, to be recalled as proof that we had been men and as a guarantee that we would always be loyal to one another. I came to like him a great deal. He was what he was.

In part of my mind where I played with the impossible, I thought of Daisy. I imagined her presiding at formal dinners, bending brightly first to this one and then to that, making a story for everyone, starring in every story, talking about everything. Sometimes I put her in Washington, sometimes in my imaginary Burma. The people around the tables were different. In either case I knew that she would be perfect. She was married now. She wrote Jim Ed and Dr. Youngblood about how happy she was. She never wrote to me. After a fling with her English professor, she abruptly married a man in films. He was going to see to it that she got more work. She still expected a great career. I did not long for her; my thoughts about her were nothing but a detached ratiocination, a logical progression of what might have been if one efficient cause had fallen, if the slight swerve of the Epicureans had bent through my life. But my feelings about her were no more than that.

Another summer came. Life settled into routines that made time fly. I was very busy. Dale Farmer bought stock and became more reclusive, more eccentric. He took his vacation in early summer and disappeared in the direction of New York, telling me mysteriously that things were possible in New York that no one could dream of in Bourbonville.

My son grew. He learned to walk after a long time, after hours of coaxing and encouragement by Eugenia, by Mary Pendleton, who smiled at him like a Gorgon, by Dolly, who came over from next door with patient dedication every day. He learned to talk—a slow, guttural growl at first, nouns shouted at things he wanted, like milk and fruit. I thought that his speaking was as strange as if some form of gorilla had learned human speech. Yet I loved the child in a powerful way that I could not have predicted.

He was affectionate. On the few evenings when Eugenia did not take him to some prayer meeting, he held out his arms to me from his little playpen when I came home, and I picked him up, and he clutched me with his weak little arms as if I were the dearest thing on earth. "Dah!" he exclaimed. "Dah!" I sat with him in the blue chair, holding him on my lap, and he put his misshapen head against my chest, occasionally looking up at me with a slow smile, an expression of adoration, and I stroked him fondly and wondered what went on inside his brain.

Sometimes I stood by his crib at night when he lay sleeping, breathing in an irregular, loud rasping, and I was as swept by love as I might have been drenched by a cloudburst on an open hill. It was an amazing feeling, full of warmth and goodness. I had not expected it.

Juliet Fisher worked swiftly and efficiently in the laboratory. She always had a small coffee pot going. "I keep it small so it will be fresh," she said. "Two cups at a time. The chemical composition of coffee begins to change after just a half hour's exposure to heat." She laughed.

Jim Ed stopped to have coffee with her on his rounds, pushing back his hat, crossing his legs, sitting there and talking about the world. I found them there sometimes. She was slightly plump, pleasant. Her ancestors had been Swiss, she told me. Some of it showed in her ruddiness. She was naturally quiet, though she laughed brightly when she was amused.

Somebody said she was "pert." The word was floating around. It was used for women who were not quite beautiful but attractive and witty. Her eyes were lively. I liked to talk with her.

She was solid. When I met her she had nice hips and large breasts that even the mannish styles of the times could not conceal. She bobbed her hair. St. Paul, my name saint, proclaimed that a woman's long hair was her glory. The preachers said that to bob your hair was to announce that you were a whore. Eugenia let her hair grow long. It fell below her waist when she combed it out and brushed it at night. In the mornings she braided it and wrapped it in a coil tightly around her head.

Juliet still lived in the little house out in the country near the Martel Methodist Church. It was a long, low affair with only one floor. Her mother died just after I married Eugenia; now Juliet lived there alone with a big, peaceable dog named Zoey. A porch ran halfway down the front of the house and gave onto a room that was still part of the porch, only it was screened in. The house sat on a hill overlooking a dirt road. Not far away Muddy Creek poured over its rocks on its way down to the river a couple of miles farther on.

I traded cars and bought a Ford. Alfred was incensed, but I did not care. The Ford was reliable. I began driving back and forth sometimes between Knoxville and Bourbonville. It gave me more independence than I had on the train. I talked to Guy and Bernal in the mornings and in the evenings as I drove home. Sometimes we sang together, the windows open, the land sweeping by. I thought we made harmonies, but no one but me could hear them. I felt a great release in talking to them. I explained Eugenia and talked about her family. Guy laughed at Mary Pendleton, and Bernal took up for her, and both of them took up for me. They were my audience; I talked to them and got up every morning and did what I had to do. I had to make a living, to take care of my wife and my child. I talked to Eugenia about going back to work at the newspaper; I thought it would be good for her. She would not hear of it. "I must spend all my time with my baby," she said.

"You are spending most of your time with your mother," I said.

"My mother is the truest Christian I know," she said.

"Do you not still want to write?" I said.

"My writing was vanity," she said. " 'Vanity of vanities, all is vanity.' Only what we do for Jesus will last."

"We have to live," I said. "You could think about your writing, and you would not think so much about things you cannot help."

"God has laid this burden upon me," she said. "I must think about it because it is his will. If you could only know my Savior."

One afternoon I had coffee with Juliet, and she said that she noticed that I sometimes did not leave until late. "Doesn't your wife get irritated when she doesn't know when to expect you for supper?"

"Actually my wife goes out to prayer meetings very often in the evening," I said. "I usually fix supper for myself. Or I go to a Greek place down near the railroad terminal in Knoxville."

"I love Greek food," she said.

"I do, too," I said.

"You could eat in Bourbonville, you know. There are a lot of people who would be glad to have you." She looked at me in a bold, appraising way.

"I suppose," I said. My heart was beating fast.

"Why don't you have supper with me tonight? I'll cook."

We sat on the screened porch and heard the creek washing over its rocks in the little valley below. She had a spring on her place, behind the house. It ran down to the creek. Her invitation was not to bed but to independence. I accepted it, and we ate on the porch and sat there in the cool night air and talked. She liked people. She had a long driveway, and I pulled my car around back so it could not be seen from the road. I did not tell Eugenia that I had eaten with Juliet.

I went again, and we sat together in the dark afterwards on an old couch on the screened-in part of the porch. Some of the springs of the couch were broken. She did not care much about furniture. The sagging springs threw us together; we did not move. Warm shoulder touched warm shoulder. She held my hand. I believe she made the first move to me; I do not know. It does not matter. Her face was uplifted to kiss me, her lips open; her hand went behind my head gently. In a half hour we were lovers, her clothes strewn all over the porch and mine lying in a pile at the foot of the couch. The night insects whirred and sang by the million in the woods, and the fireflies floated and blinked. I used a condom; I had bought some condoms just in case something like this happened. I apologized for being prepared; she laughed and squeezed me.

153

I WENT BACK again several times. I have forgotten how many. I thought that if Eugenia discovered I was making love to Juliet Fisher it would not make any difference. I talked with Juliet about all sorts of things—never about Eugenia and me. She was a quiet lover. She shut her eyes and kept her thighs spread, her mouth slightly open. If I stayed in her long enough, her head jerked violently, and her body quaked. Sometimes after that she let loose a long, involuntary sigh, as if she had been traveling somewhere and seen something that I had not. She came back, blinked, looked up at me, and hugged me, pressing her cheek against mine and embracing me with her thighs, her ankles knotted over my body.

After we made love we lay abed in her room talking and sometimes drinking red wine that I bought from a bootlegger for five dollars a bottle.

"You must be careful driving home," she said one night. "I do not want to discover that you have killed yourself leaving my house. That might be hard to explain."

"It would be easy to explain," I said. " 'Mr. Alexander departed the house of Miss Fisher late at night having been to bed with her and having consumed a great deal of wine, and on his way home he ran off the road and was killed.' What could be more simple than that?"

She laughed.

The night was full and heavy around us. The stars were out. The fireflies floated and sparkled in the trees. I sat up and looked down the little valley. The moon was full, and below us, seen through the trees, the dirt road lay like a polished metal band across the shallow valley floor. In the whole evening that we had been there, no one had passed by, and we felt ourselves engulfed in a warm and cavernous repose.

I thought of penance and of Eugenia. Bernal told me once of interminable processions during Passion Week in Spain—hooded men, backs bare, lashing themselves with leather whips, blood spurting from naked skin. In some, the white rib bones flashed in the deep cuts. Eugenia was spiritual kinswoman to those poor souls.

I reached for Juliet, and she came to me, kissing me with her wet mouth. She had breasts that could suckle a dozen children. I felt her now-familiar warmth, groped for a nipple, and in a little while we were locked together, her thighs wrapped around me, and she was heaving beneath me, her breath against my neck. Later we lay close together in the dark and listened to the night.

"I have not felt so peaceful in years," I said dreamily. "Just now all life seems like still water."

She chuckled in her low, intimate way and nuzzled against me. I heard the insects singing in their chorus a million strong. I remembered how Bernal had loved the mighty Christmas choir in St. Bavon. I remembered the voices, the tenors, the basses, the baritones, the sweet lead singers, rising in immaculate latinity against the high stone arches and surrounding us, lifting us up, our own apotheosis, storming towards heaven on angels' wings. Bernal was rapt in the thunderous glory of the hymns, and he said once that paradise would be an eternity of organ music and almighty singing by the chorus of all those resurrected to righteousness.

I thought that perhaps in heaven the angelic choruses sounded like insects in this night, singing their harmonies across infinity. I had read that music was a matter of taste and that the hill tribesmen of Burma would find Beethoven a clangor. No, I thought. A deeper harmony joined the nature of things, and I supposed that I could love the throbbing insect choir as much as Bernal loved the Christmas hymns, for the same harmony joined them both. I felt Bernal nearby. I could not open my eyes. I slept in spite of myself.

I arrived home in the middle of the night. Eugenia was asleep and did not wake—or at least she pretended to be asleep—when I came in. I lay beside her then, waiting for the dawn to come, and I felt confused and deeply sad.

154

THE NEXT MORNING I arrived at the car works late, red-eyed and sleepy. "All anyone needs to do," I told Guy, "is to go look at Juliet and then come look at me, and that person will know that we were sleepless together."

"People do not notice such things until after you tell them," Guy said, musing. He lounged beside me in the car, his long legs before him, his placid face watching the land swirl by. "Most people do not care enough to notice what other people are doing."

"Someone may have seen your car leave Juliet's house early in the morning," Bernal said. "Country people notice such things."

"They did not see that it was Paul's car," Guy said.

"Paul knows it was his car," Bernal said vaguely.

"I envy you," Guy said. "You smoke cigarettes and eat and drink, and you lie in the embrace of a beautiful woman. I will never do those things again."

I was in a mood of dreamy remembrance when I walked through the side door of my office. Miss Sally came in. "Jim Ed wants to see you," she said. "He'll be here at 8:30. He waited for you," she said with a mild tone of reproach. "He said he thought he would see you at the cafe."

"I'm sorry," I said. "I was up late."

"Sickness?"

"Ah, yes. My son was sick."

"Poor child." Miss Sally went out. I was embarrassed to be late. Who was running this place anyway, Jim Ed or I? Sometimes I wondered.

He came in at 8:30 looking as happy as the king of Siam. His cheer irritated me. "You were late this morning," he said with a grin.

"Guy was sick. I was up in the night with him."

Jim Ed's face filled with concern. That irritated me even more. "I'm sorry," he said. Sometimes I wanted Jim Ed to be more human—selfish, quarrelsome, ambitious. "You're a good father. I hope I can be like you."

"Are you trying to tell me something? Have you got somebody pregnant?" I could not control my sour mood.

Jim Ed hesitated a moment, then burst into laughter. "That's pretty good," he said. "No, I haven't made anybody pregnant—not yet at least. But I'm going to."

"Are you selling tickets?"

He shook his head and turned red. "No, I'm going to get married."

"Married! *Married!* Well, it is about time. Who is the fortunate woman?"

"Juliet Fisher!"

I believe that if Jim Ed had not been so radiantly happy he would have seen the expression of astonishment and collapse on my face.

"Juliet Fisher!" I said again, while he sat there, his face filled with an enormous grin, blushing crimson.

"The same! You're surprised, aren't you? You didn't think an educated girl like that would pay any attention to a yokel like me."

"You are not a yokel!" I said. "Quit calling yourself a yokel."

"I asked her a week ago, and she accepted. She didn't want me to tell people until today."

"Until today," I said stupidly. "Why not until today?"

"I don't know. You know women. You can't tell what they're going to do or why. We're getting married in August. I want you to be my best man. I've asked her, and she says it's fine with her. You're responsible, you know. If you had not hired us both, this would not have happened. How about it!"

"Of course," I said, my voice a croak that, like everything else about me that morning, Jim Ed did not notice.

"Great! Great!" he shouted, leaping up from his chair and leaning over the desk to shake my hand. I realized that I should have been the one making the gesture, shaking his hand. By then it was too late. "I'll go right now and tell her the good news."

As soon as I decently could I walked up to the laboratory. Juliet was in the scales house. She did not look up as I opened the door and walked in. I walked to the door of the scales house and stood there. She kept her back turned, concentrating on the finely balanced scales. The scales trays were made of brass, and they gleamed golden in the reflected early-morning sunlight.

"Are you not going to speak to me?" I said.

"I thought I would wait for you to speak first," she said, still keeping her face averted. "I wanted to see what mood you were in."

"What mood did you expect me to be in?"

"I suppose you are angry."

"No," I said. I started to say that I was hurt, but that seemed ridiculous, the self-pitying whine of a loser at cards.

She turned around and looked up at me. We did not say anything for a long time. We looked at each other. I thought of her nakedness, and wanted her. She was dressed in a full blue smock with a white apron. It concealed the lines of her body. I thought of them. Her face looked soft and gentle and compassionate.

"What happened?" I whispered.

"Jim Ed asked me to lunch last week; while we were eating lunch, he asked me to marry him."

"Just like that," I said.

"Yes. No whistles or trumpets."

"Do you love him?"

"I find that a strange question."

I felt rebuked. "I'm sorry," I said. "I have no right. . . ."

She put out a hand and touched my arm, then took her hand away. "You have every right," she said gently.

"No, I don't," I said. "He is a very good man."

"I think people get to love each other only when they've been together for a long time. I don't think they can love each other until then. I was married before. Did you know that?"

"No," I said. "I supposed . . ."

"What did you suppose?"

"Nothing," I said. "I really did not suppose anything. I did not think about it. That is the truth."

She smiled. "He was a university teacher. We were in Kentucky. He fell in love with the dean's secretary. They went to Texas."

"That is a long way off," I said.

"I had a passion for my husband; it did not last. I think he had a passion for me; that did not last, either. I would like something to last a long time. Perhaps if we start slowly, it will last longer."

"Perhaps we started too fast," I said.

"You are married," she said. "It did not matter how we started. Things would have come to an end."

I stood looking down at her and felt something drifting away from me. I thought of ships putting out to sea, people standing on shore waving handkerchiefs.

"I have deep affection for you," I said softly. "I am also very grateful to you."

She smiled slightly, tentatively. "I have warmer feelings for you than for anyone else in the world."

"You knew last night was our last night," I said.

"Yes," she said. "I wanted one last night. If we had had more, someone would have found out."

"Perhaps someone did," I said.

"We were not together enough to raise comment," she said.

"I suppose not," I said.

We were making small talk. It was time to go. Part of me wanted to argue, to make some foolish case why she should change her mind, to persuade her to spend at least one more night with me. But I could see everything, all at once, and something in me surrendered and surrendered completely.

She read my thoughts. "I must take the chance I have," she said. "I have always been an independent woman, but I do not like to be a solitary woman. I have to have somebody whose head will be on my pillow every night, somebody to grow old with, somebody to talk with at night, every night. Someone to father my children."

"Of course," I said. "Of course."

"It sounds so ordinary that I am almost ashamed to express what I want," she said, shaking her head, laughing a little at herself. She quickly turned serious again. "He is a good man," she said. "So are you."

"He is a far better man than I am," I said.

She reached up and stroked my cheek and withdrew her hand quickly as if all the car works might be watching. "I do not know what to say to you now," I said. "Does he know about your former husband?"

"Of course. I told him at lunch. I told him that if it made a difference, I would understand."

"What did he say?"

"You know what he said."

"Yes, of course," I said. "Something innocent."

"He told me he was not pure himself."

"Jim Ed not pure?" I was startled.

"He confessed that he went to see some ladies of the night while he was in Paris, while Willy was still in the hospital after the Armistice. He told me that he went to a different woman every night. He said he had never been to bed with any woman he knew. He assured me he had no diseases."

We both smiled, but neither of us laughed. There was something pure about Jim Ed's impurities. I envied him. Another thought struck me, and I frowned and cleared my throat.

"Does he know about me?"

"No," she said. "I will never tell him."

"He will be good to you."

"I will be good to him. . . . I want you to promise me something."

"Anything."

"You must never, never give the slightest hint that you and I have been lovers."

I felt mildly annoyed that she would doubt my loyalty. "Of course I will not."

"Do you promise? Do you solemnly promise?"

I felt ridiculous. The scene seemed ridiculous. I lifted my right hand, partly to break the awful seriousness that had come on her face. "I do swear," I said. Then irritation overcame me, and I snatched the hand down. "Jim Ed and I have never had the slightest temper with each other. Do you think that I am going to get so angry with him someday, so jealous perhaps, that I would tell him about you, just to hurt him?"

She smiled, and her placid face took on the aloof dignity of the goddess Demeter on the reliefs at Eleusis. "Men do not do such things. Women hurt their friends when they are angry. Men do their worst when they are most loving. Some night you and Jim Ed may be playing music and drinking wine with Dr. Youngblood, and it will grow late, and you will feel the dark, and you will feel that these men are your only protection from whatever is out there, and you will want to take them into your confidence because you will want them to know that you keep nothing back from them. Perhaps you will be having warm and happy thoughts about me. I hope that you will think such thoughts sometimes. When men love each other, they want to share everything. When you love Jim Ed the most, you may want to tell him about me in the belief that you will settle something, cease being hypocritical, put all barriers between you aside—whatever. It would hurt him more than he should ever be hurt, and it will hurt me, too. Don't love him so much that you destroy him; if you destroy him, you will destroy me."

I walked back down to the main office, speaking jauntily to my men as some of them passed by. My shadow was black on the ground before me. The wheel foundry was roaring. The day smelled of work.

155

IT WAS A BIG COUNTRY WEDDING, and people came from miles around. Jim Ed had wanted a Methodist minister to perform the ceremony. He could not find one because Juliet had been divorced, and no Methodist or Baptist or anybody else would perform the wedding ceremony for a woman who had been divorced. There was always Clyde, but he had decided to become a Quaker, believing in the inner light, and since Quakers did not have ministers, he had renounced his ordination, and he was working contentedly as a carpenter. "I could seek approval from the Friends' meeting," he said, "but we don't believe in having any music, and that might lessen the joy of the event."

"You don't mind coming to music as long as it is provided by somebody else," Jim Ed said.

"I do not impose my beliefs on others," Clyde said.

"Well, that's an improvement," Jim Ed said.

Clyde was making a good living, and he was happy. People said he was a good carpenter. "He's gone back to his daddy's trade," Jim Ed said. "He doesn't say that, but that's what it is."

"If you ask me, that's the smartest thing Clyde's ever done," the old man said. "Lord, I thought he might jump to being a Mormon, and then we'd of had sixteen of his wives to take care of."

Brian Ledbetter and Jim Ed went out to the home of Lyman Cadwallader, the county judge, and they prevailed on him to come to the wedding with the promise of a little whiskey that the judge could surreptitiously drink out of a gourd so that people would think he was drinking plain old spring water. They promised him ten dollars, and since some people didn't make ten dollars in a week even then in Tennessee, that looked like a good sum of money for saying a few words, and the judge came.

As it turned out, just about everybody except Mrs. Ledbetter drank a whole lot of special spring water out of a barrel, and by the time the judge stood up in front of us in his fancy suit with a white flower stuck in a buttonhole and more or less made it through the proper wedding ceremony, everybody was on what the old man called a "toot." When Judge Cadwallader in his growly voice finally said, "According to the authority vested in me by the sovereign state of Tennessee and by Almighty God, I hereby pronounce you man and wife," a big, whooping cheer burst out of the assembly. I was standing there by Jim Ed, giddy from all I had drunk, and I think I shouted "Hooray!" myself.

"All this is in very bad taste," Bernal said.

"It is the same spirit that would have prevailed had I been married," Guy said in his wistful way.

Eugenia did not come to the wedding. "We can't take Guy into a place like that," she said. "People would stare at him."

Jim Ed and I played, and he sang, and friends played and sang with us. We were just drunk enough to play without inhibition, and the music poured out over our little world like rain after a dry spell.

"If Pinkerton had just knowed how to play that mandolin, he might be with us to this day," the old man said. He walked with a cane now, going very slowly, and when he drove his car, we worried about him.

The biggest surprise had been that in anticipation of marriage, Jim Ed bought Pinkerton's house from Eula Pinkerton. "I tell you, those Ledbetters is going to buy up the county before it's over," somebody said.

It was not more than four miles away from the house where Brian and Jim Ed and Mrs. Ledbetter lived. It was a big place, built in no particular style, sprawling in a large lawn shaded by vast old trees. Jim Ed, the old man, Dr. Youngblood, and I went down to look at it one afternoon when the agreement was complete and the proper papers signed and money had changed hands.

"It was the old Crittendon place," the old man said very quietly. "Matthew Crittendon was killed at First Bull Run, fighting for the rebels. He was mean. His sister married a rebel soldier. He died. I remember him. Samuel Atkins Beckwith. Somewhere up in Virginia. He was from there. He come through after the war. When everbody was going home. He come through, and he stayed, and he died sudden. It wasn't so long ago. 1870."

"Fifty-five years ago," Dr. Youngblood said.

"Not so long ago when you think about it," the old man said. "Their boy disappeared. I seen him here, the last day anybody seen him, I reckon. Virgil and me and him—he was named Sam, too—we all had breakfast together the day I decided to get married to Mrs. Ledbetter. The day *I* decided, hell!—the day Mrs. Ledbetter decided to marry *me*. The next day young Sam was gone. Somebody seen him cross the ferry down at Kingston, heading west about daylight. He never did come back. Nobody ever heard from him again. His mamma went crazy—stark, raving crazy. At first she raged all over the county looking for him. Then she stopped talking. She died in the asylum up at Knoxville, sitting looking at a wall, not eating, not saying a word. What happened? Why did he do that? Why did she go crazy?"

I had heard parts of the story many times before, for it, too, was part of the accumulated legend of Bourbon County, recited ritually when people got together on long winter nights around stoves when there were tales to tell and mysteries to conjure in the dimness and coziness of kitchens while the dark lurked beyond the walls. It was more vivid with the old man standing there, the heat of a still summer day holding everything in thrall, the foliage from the huge trees in the yard swelling green—"the very trees that was there then," the old man said in reverence. He turned and looked at me. "Do you believe in ghosts?" he said.

I looked at him and saw beyond his shoulder in the middle distance Guy and Bernal. I saw them standing together, their arms folded, faces solemn, their eyes asking me something. "Yes," I murmured. "Yes."

The old man drew back his head and looked at me with venerable sadness. "They're everywhere," he whispered. "Everywhere."

"Yes," I said.

"It's a beautiful place," Jim Ed shouted happily. "Let's go inside."

We went inside to a cavernous emptiness. The furniture was gone. All that remained was the tall photographic portrait of a Confederate soldier, hung over the mantelpiece of a dead fireplace. The man in the gilded frame looked solemnly into an empty room, where our voices echoed as if someone were speaking our words back to us a split second after we spoke them ourselves.

"That's Sam Beckwith," the old man whispered. "The one that died. It was his son that run away. They was both named Sam. The boy could still be alive. I'd like to ask him why he run off. But this one is still here. Still right here. He was my friend." He stood looking up at the portrait for a very long time. I stood there, too, staring upward, my eyes locked on the changeless gaze of a long-dead man. He was almost exactly life-size, and the photograph looked as sharp and clear as it must have looked on the day it was made, enlarged from a smaller portrait, so the old man said, at the demand of Mrs. Beckwith, who grieved after her husband all her life.

"If you ever want to get rid of that thing, I'll take it off your hands," Dr. Youngblood said.

"No, Doc. He stays. Hell, what would this house be without him?" Jim Ed said.

"He should stay here," Brian Ledbetter said very softly. "This is where he belongs. This is his house. Hello, Sam. Remember me?"

The man in the portrait looked straight ahead.

156

MAY 1926—warm and sunny, a wet spring, smelling of mud and roses. The creeks were swollen and rushed with exuberant splashing through every valley. At Bourbonville the brown river rolled high against its banks. Fields were marshy, and peeper frogs sang in the evening, and the chuck-wills'-widows and the whippoorwills came early and sang far into the night.

Juliet was deliciously pregnant, her face ruddy and proud. When I stopped by the laboratory we spoke of mundane things—their house, clothes she was making for the baby. She would take a month off to give birth, she said. She would keep the child in a crib in the laboratory during the day as long as she nursed it. She radiated happiness. We never spoke of our brief love affair. She shut a door; I did not knock. We talked like neighbors through windows, I outside, she within, and I went away.

Time flew. The car works made money—a bright place in a railroad troubled with financial difficulties. Philip Drodge rose in the hierarchy, noting his steps with letters typed on creamy paper. He descended on Bourbonville now and then with an entourage of young subalterns. He showed me off as a hidden treasure. I was *his* treasure; he had discovered me. I was embarrassed but touched by his childlike enthusiasm for himself. He gained weight. He told me that my time was coming; his entourage treated me with sycophantic respect. Jim Ed was amused; so was I.

Brian Ledbetter appeared unannounced in my office early one morning. I had contracts spread out on my desk when the frosted glass door swung open on its double hinges, and there he was, bent over his walnut cane, wearing horn-rimmed glasses, his eyes shining and rheumy with age, Miss Sally helplessly behind him, her hands raised to show that she had been unable to stop him.

He wanted to see Jim Ed. Jim Ed was in the wheel foundry, overseeing the first heat of the day. "I want to see him this morning," the old man said. "I dreamed of blackbirds flying south last night."

"Blackbirds?" I said.

"If you dream about blackbirds flying, you are going to die," he said.

I started to say something insincerely skeptical and gave up. "Sit down," I said.

"I'm bothering you," he said.

"Not at all." I waved him to a chair across the desk and leaned back in my own.

"You don't do that too good," he said.

"What?" I said.

"Act like you ain't busy. You look like a man with the shits at a wedding. You can't run off, and you can't sit still, but you can't shit."

I laughed. "I am sorry. Yes, I am busy. I am always busy now. It is foolish to be so busy."

"You ain't the lost pup that showed up here half-dead back in 'seventeen," the old man said.

"You cannot step in the same river twice," I said. "Things change."

"Hell, you can't step in the same river once," he said, easing himself into a chair and breathing hard. "It changes while you got your feet in it."

"I never knew there was so much to do on this job," I said. "We have to fight to stay afloat now."

"Jim Ed's so busy he don't come to see me much. His lady tells me he's awful tired at night."

"She looks good," I said.

"You always did think so," the old man said with a hint of knowledge.

I could not read his expression; my face grew hot. I forced myself to meet his steady eyes. Juliet and Jim Ed had planted dozens of rosebushes in the broad quadrangle in front of the main office—a whim of hers. Red and white and yellow roses bloomed there. Their fragrance, mingled with the foundry's cindery reek, drifted through the open side door.

The old man leaned forward, hands cupped over his walking stick. He studied the floor. "Poor Caleb," he said. "He died here, didn't he?"

"Yes," I said.

"He's at rest," the old man said.

I nearly crossed myself. "Pinkerton, too," I said.

"I hope they're both at rest," the old man said.

"Yes," I said. We were silent a long time. The roar of the wheel foundry hammered at the thin walls.

"I want to ask you a question," Brian said, looking up at me again, his eyes burning.

Guy whispered, "He knows about you and Juliet."

"Speak," I said, wishing he would not.

"I want to know how Jim Ed's doing."

I looked at him blankly. "What do you mean?"

"How's he doing on this job?" The old man squinted through his glasses at me with a fixed intensity.

"The car works could not run without him," I said. "He is everywhere. I sell what we produce to other railroads; he keeps the place running. The bad men fear him; the good ones love him."

"The way it ought to be," Brian said, nodding slowly. He eased back in his chair. He looked weary.

"Yes, it *is* good," I said. "Good for him, good for me, good for the railroad, good for the men."

"His lady says you'll go up to Washington City soon," he said tentatively.

"I do not know," I said uneasily.

"She says Jim Ed will take your place."

"If I go, I think he will replace me."

"Lord, Lord," the old man said, shaking his head. "I think about Pinkerton, about that day. He was just a boy hisself, Pinkerton was. You know, I seen him young and alive, and I seen him old and dead, and now when I try to recollect, it seems like it was that drunk old lunatic out there that day, making fun of me, telling me I had to work for him for wages. But it wasn't. It was a headstrong boy, a boy like I was once, a lot younger than Jim Ed is now. I hated him that day. I hated him and the railroad for making me feel like dirt. And now . . . now Jim Ed's in line to be boss in Pinkerton's place. Ain't life funny?"

"It is a comedy," I said. I thought of the Theatre of Dionysos on the side of the Akropolis. Stephanos took me there sometimes and read Aristophanes to me, acting out the parts with his voice. We used to laugh.

The old man fixed his blue eyes on an invisible spot between us. "That day started so many things, you see. Virgil seen me shoot over Pinkerton's head. Pinkerton just stood out there in the road and laughed because he knowed I wasn't really going to shoot him. But Virgil was on the front porch, and he seen it all, and he cried. Lord God, how that boy cried! It scared him half out of his wits. It taken his mamma an hour or two to calm him down, and don't you think I didn't catch hell from her! Well, I deserved it. It was foolishness, what I done. I think back, and maybe Virgil was always scared of me, and that day when I did that damn fool thing with Pinkerton, I think Virgil thought, 'That's right! This man my mamma has married—he's like a tiger in the house. He's going to eat us all up.' I done bad by Virgil. I didn't mean to. I meant to do him good."

"You did do him good. You should be proud."

"You're trying to make an old man feel good, Paul Alexander. I was showing off. Man as old as I was showing off. I've wondered many a long night: did Virgil do what he done in the Spanish War because I scared him that day? Do you reckon he was trying to say you shouldn't never have nobody like me shooting at people and scaring children out of their wits?"

"That seems too complicated," I said.

"It seems pretty simple to me," he said.

We were silent again. The old man moved his lips, studying words written on the invisible page between us.

"Jim Ed was born to me when I was forty-seven year old," he said. "I never figured I'd have a child."

"You had a good one," I said.

"Mrs. Ledbetter's boys, they never got over their daddy's death. It's like they blamed it on me. They didn't *want* to blame it on me; they couldn't help theirselves."

"They love you," I said.

"Well, I've got on good with Joab. Hell, the devil hisself'd get on with Joab. And Clyde. I tell you, Clyde's a good man even if he is crazy on religion. He don't remember his daddy, but now he's a carpenter—just like his daddy. Gilly was something else! So quiet! He was the one we all forgot, I reckon. Six boys, and Jim Ed made seven, and Aaron died. You can get lost in a crowd like that. The living and the dead." He seemed to lose the thread of his thought and sat in a swirl of memory.

"Gilly has done well. He owes his success to you."

"That's what Caleb always said. Poor Caleb. I loved Caleb. He was the bulldog of the bunch, always biting something and hanging on even when it like to of shook him to death. Sometimes I think Caleb thought that if his daddy hadn't died, Aaron wouldn't have died, neither. Caleb used to tell me so often how much he thought of me, how grateful he was, and all that. . . . Well, you know how he was."

"He loved you," I said.

"I guess," the old man said. "But they was times, they was some times when I wondered if Caleb was telling me how much he owed me because he thought—" The old man stopped, wrestling with a thought like Jacob wrestling with the dark angel. "Well, I wondered if Caleb talked about me so much so's he could make hisself believe it. I wonder if he was afraid to let me know, afraid to admit hisself how much he missed his real daddy." He laughed in embarrassment. "I reckon thoughts like that can drive you crazy," he said.

"Yes," I said. We were silent for a long time. I heard the roar of the foundry.

"Virgil's the sad one. I always knowed Virgil was smart. First day we ever talked I told him he was going to go to college, and I sent him, and he went. He wouldn't never of thought of going up to the university lessen I made him go. Only it didn't work out like I figured."

"Destiny," I said quietly. "No one can plan destiny."

"Fate," the old man said. He uttered a dry, melancholy laugh. "Sometimes I think if Virgil had stayed on the farm, hadn't gone to college, D.B. would still be alive. Hell, that don't make no sense, does it? If he hadn't gone to college, he never would of met poor Melvina. Melvina would of been happy as an angel if she had married a telephone lineman; instead she had to marry Virgil, and she and Virgil didn't do each other no good."

"I scarcely knew her," I said circumspectly.

"You knowed her enough, poor thing," the old man said. His mind seemed to wander again. I waited. He came back.

"Virgil was jealous of Jim Ed when he was born. I was so proud, so *damned* proud. I said to J.W. Campbell, 'Old soldiers never die.' " He laughed as though in companionship with the unseen ghost of the long-dead lawyer so much in his conversation. Abruptly his face turned sorrowful again. "Virgil wouldn't look at Jim Ed for a year after he was born. Looked at me like I'd done something awful to his mamma. I figured Virgil would come around after a while. He never did."

I started to say something trite, but I could not say anything. Guy and Bernal stood behind the old man. I looked away.

"One thing led to another," Brian said.

"It always does," I said gently. "Do not blame yourself."

"Do you reckon it was predestination like the primitive Baptists talk about?" the old man said. "What is to be will be? I thought Virgil *could* change, you see. He couldn't. That's the thing, you see. He *couldn't* change."

"I used to have a friend who said that man proposes and God disposes," I said. I made myself look across the desk again; Guy and Bernal were gone.

"Well, *something* sure as hell disposes. I think sometimes we're bound to be who we are when we're born. You take all them children; I can see in all of them something that I saw when they was just younguns. Willy, for instance. Willy's doing all right." The old man chuckled in a sudden outburst of satisfaction, and I laughed, too. Willy the unarmed, blind nightwatchman and his loping dogs were now a legend in the county.

"He is the best nightwatchman I've ever seen," I said with a laugh. "He has five dogs going around with him now. Sometimes it sounds like a fox hunt in here at night. If anyone tried to steal something in the car works, those dogs would tree him like a raccoon."

" 'Tree him like a 'coon.' You're beginning to talk like a hillbilly." The old man laughed. "You're getting to be one of us, Paul Alexander, in spite of yourself."

"Willy talks all the time now," I said. "He has coffee with Jim Ed and me sometimes in the morning at Bessie May's when he's worked all night, and he tells wonderful stories—just like you. People tell him things, and he puts it all together." I almost said, "He is like Homer, the blind harper," but I did not.

"He does for a fact," the old man said, grinning happily. "But I tell you something; he ain't changed from what he used to be, before the war, before he lost his eyes. He used to be so funny; now he's funny again. You can't be around Willy without laughing your head off. The Willy you're seeing now, that's the Willy I knowed when he was a youngun. Just like the Virgil you're seeing now is the Virgil that come to fetch me to bring his mamma's cow to my bull years and years ago."

I wondered if I was the same frightened boy wakened in the middle of the night by a father about to flee into the dark. The matter was complicated.

"Virgil's took to California like a pig to mud. Making more money than he could of made anywheres else. What's he do with it? He already had more money than he knowed what to do with. Why's he want more? Why don't he buy hisself a mansion somewheres and settle down and do something he likes to do? Why's he work all the time? He don't do nothing to have a good time. He never did. When he was a little boy, he never was peaceful. He still ain't peaceful. He never will be."

"Yes," I said vaguely.

"We went out to see him last year, you know."

"Yes," I said.

"Couldn't get him to come home. He says he's too busy to come back here, but Mrs. Ledbetter had to see her oldest son, and off we went. Taken us four days on the train. He showed us around, took us to his properties. That's what he calls them—his properties. We talked so much about his properties we didn't talk about nothing else. I reckon he wanted it that way."

"You said that Daisy was well," I said in a neutral voice. When we had talked about the trip, we had by silent common consent scarcely mentioned Daisy.

"Daisy," he said, shaking his head and looking down. "She's real pretty. She smiles at you one minute and you want to melt. Then you look again and in those same eyes there's something else, something terrible, something that wants to burn you to a cinder so there won't be nothing left but the hard coals. She never has nothing good to say about nobody. She ain't going to be no star in the movies, you see. She knows that now. She don't admit it, but she knows it."

"She is young," I said. "She has plenty of time."

"No she don't. She don't have the magic them movie stars have, and it's made her bitter. You go to her house for dinner, and when the company goes home, Daisy sits there and tells you why the lot of them ain't worth killing. She's married a poor weak-assed son of a bitch who's tried to make it in the movies. I reckon she thought he'd make her a star, but hell, he don't have it, neither. Whatever it is, the two of them don't have a single portion of it between them."

We sat in a difficult silence. I suspected that the old man knew everything about Daisy and me, everything about Juliet and me, everything about everything. But I did not know; I never knew.

"Daisy's always got men around her. If I was her husband, I wouldn't stand for it. But what's the poor son of a bitch to do! They're pretty, Daisy's men. Damned if I know another word for it—pretty. Well, I shouldn't talk. She was real sweet to me. I reckon I'm one of the few folks on earth she truly loves."

He hesitated for a very long time. I was silent. He cleared his throat. "And you, Paul. She loves you, too, and that's a real true fact. She always did."

"She did not know me well enough to love me," I said. "She made me up out of a book."

"You take what you can get in this old world. Daisy loved you enough. Not meaning no harm, but you should of married Daisy. You two would of been different together. Not meaning no harm."

"She is married now, and that is the end of it," I said.

"She's married, and the sky's still blue, and chickens crow when they lay eggs. She still loves you."

"I am sorry," I said, unable to face the old man's gaze but looking down in a feeling akin to shame.

"Me, too," the old man said. "It's a bitch, like we used to say in the army. I don't know why we said that."

"Like saying 'What do you say?' " I said.

"Good ole Hub," he said with a gentle laugh. "I miss Hub. I miss all of them. Hub and J.W. Campbell and Sam Beckwith and Clarence Jackson and Doc Cogill. They was my bestest friends once. I'm the only one left. The only one. It ain't good to outlive your friends. And the colored man. I miss him, too."

"I miss my friends from the war, too," I said. "They were both killed."

"It's a bitch," the old man said.

I wanted to tell him about Guy and Bernal; I wanted to tell him everything. But he went back to rambling about California. It was a way of talking about Daisy's place without talking about her. He liked California—the palm trees, the birds, the Pacific air. A breeze of gentle fantasy blew over my mind, fantasy illuminated with flashes of memory, and I remembered how Daisy had flung herself headlong on me and how I had fled her.

Suddenly I felt that I had thrown something precious away. She would have gone to Burma with me. She would have walked in glory among the brown tribesmen of the hilly north. She would have stood happily in their bazaars, and their breasty women would have been in awe of her white skin, feeling her arms to see if she was truly so fair. She was like an exotic bird who needed an exotic environment to flourish, and like a bird caged in the wrong place, she drooped and became frustrated and bitter and pecked herself to death against the bars of her cage. Burma would have been her place. People would have congratulated me on my amazing luck to have such a wife. I thought that if I had married her, she would not have become what Brian said she now was, and I might have been different, too.

He stopped, unable to continue, and his face was wrinkled and pensive and sad.

"You see," he resumed at last, "what worries me real deep down is that maybe Jim Ed, maybe me and Jim Ed's mamma by *having* Jim Ed, maybe we're the cause of all of the bad, for what happened to Virgil and to Daisy because Virgil never did pay attention to her and to Aaron and . . . and for all the rest of it. And the colored man. It's all connected, you see."

"You were M.P.'s friend. Don't blame yourself for him."

"Hell, that was the trouble. He was my friend. I called him M.P., and he always called me Mr. Ledbetter. If I hadn't been so wild about flying, he'd still be alive. Maybe whites and colored can be friends in heaven, but not on earth. Not yet. I was a fool to think different. Just like I was a fool to think I could make it all up to Virgil." The old man's face was fixed in mourning, and he looked at me as though I might have had some strange power of absolution.

Brian's grief broke through my own stubborn melancholy. I looked at him, compassionate for this good old man who had lived through so much. He had survived, and for him, as for me, the past—left behind like a shadow, lengthened and attenuated by the falling of the sun into late afternoon—had never faded. He had his own ghosts. Perhaps he saw them as clearly as I saw mine.

"You cannot think such thoughts," I said quietly. "We do not rule the world. We are not God."

I was going to say more, but I lost heart. I was thinking of myself and the evils I had brought upon the earth. One thing happened in consequence of other things—efficient cause working out to effect, a chain dragging implacably through the universe and through all time, running back to God and eternity. Bernal said it was in Thomas Aquinas.

I held myself guilty for Bernal's death and perhaps for Guy's and perhaps for M.P.'s. Far down in my skull a dull tremor of pain came. I took a deep breath.

The old man stirred and shook his head as if to clear something away. "Jim Ed's the only thing I've brought on the world that I think is nothing but good. I think about him, and I think that nothing else matters if he really is good. But I can't never tell all that to him; it wouldn't be fair."

"I understand," I said softly. "But you can be sure. He's the best there is."

"Yes, I know that, but I reckon I've knowed lots of things that ain't so."

I hesitated a long time, thinking of my own son. "If you know you love him, that is enough, is it not?" Mine was a real question.

The old man nodded. "I love him more than I ever loved anything. I didn't know what love was till Jim Ed was born. I truly didn't. He taught me."

We were quiet, the old man looking down, his heart full.

"I feel the same way about my son," I said softly and with great difficulty. "I love him. I did not know I could love so much until he was born. Even as he is."

The old man cocked his head and shook it slightly, acknowledging my sadness. "I nearly died when Jim Ed was in the war," he said.

"I understand."

"Jim Ed should of got a medal for saving Willy's life," the old man said.

"Yes," I said.

"But I tell you what. I don't care nothing about no medals. He got home alive. I think if he'd been killed trying to save Willy, I'd of hated Willy's memory. And I love Willy. Ain't that terrible?"

"No," I said.

"Now he's going to have a child. My grandchild. I wish the blackbirds would of stayed away until I seen my grandchild."

I started to say something to comfort him, to reassure him, but something stopped me.

He looked at me with a slow smile. "It turned out all right in the end," he said. "I found my way. Some of it has been pretty terrible, but some of it has been pretty grand when I think about it. I helped save the Union, and I helped free M.P.'s people, and I married a good woman, and I had a good son—and good friends. I had real good friends."

He shook his head, and something in his eyes seemed to go away, like a flame dying in a lantern. Then it leaped up again, and he leaned intently forward, both hands atop his cane, his smoky blue eyes glittering, and his voice fell almost to a whisper. "Do you know something, Paul Alexander? I done the bestest I could, and I meant good when I done it. That's all a man can do, now ain't it? I've laid awake on many a long night and grieved about how some things turned out the way they did, but I ain't never felt sorry for what I *wanted* to do. I wanted the good for the folks that counted on me. I done everthing I knowed to do good for them, and I reckon that's all a man can do—to want the good for the ones that life gives him to love. I raised a bunch of boys; I taken care of a good woman, and she taken care of me. I done the best I knowed how to do for the people I loved, and I loved a lot of them, and that's a real true fact. I'm glad I could love so many. Ain't that right?"

I laughed softly, a laughter of consolation and peace.

"Yes," I said.

"They's some that can't love," the old man said. "But I never was one of them."

"No," I said. "No, you were not."

"If we can love, and if we got people to love, we've got all there is," the old man said.

"Yes," I said.

I felt a sudden warmth. On the wall to my right hung a large calendar topped with a photograph of locomotive number 6530, an 0-8-0 as railroad men called locomotives, and I sat looking at it, thinking distractedly of its mighty force and of the old man's iron resolution and the sublime radiance of his unquenchable will and his love. I thought of how blissful it would be to believe I had always wanted the best for the people I loved and that the bad things came not because I made them come but because the world has a mysterious darkness in it that wells over all our striving and simply *is*, a confusion, a chaos even, that defies our will but cannot quench it. For one sweet instant in a simulacrum of imagined innocence, I walked cleansed in my mind and felt no melancholy, no guilt, and my headache went away.

I almost forgot the old man in my contemplation of the photograph of the locomotive that made me think of other trains, that made me recall with gentle nostalgia the June night that Palmyre and I rode back from the countryside on the day she promised to marry me. I thought of our peace on that Sunday, ignorant of the murder of the archduke, and how even when we knew of it, we could not fathom how an incident in a distant Balkan town could change our lives—cause tied to effect that becomes another cause tied to its effect, a chain of circumstance ordering the world beyond anything we could do to order it ourselves. We made love that night in her flat, and we clung to each other, and I lay in a bliss of being. I thought of her now in a flood of exuberance, not wishing that I could have that moment back again, not supposing that I might now go and find her and her German husband and her children and somehow recover or renew something that we had had then, but rather holding in this strange, backward, and remote place where destiny had cast me a memory of her that nothing could take away. I was this experience once; I have the experience still. Memory itself was a possession, a treasure, safe in my heart to remain for as long as I lived, vivid and alive and dear. I had Palmyre; I had Guy and Bernal; I had Eugenia when she was uncursed; I had M.P. I had Stephanos. I had them all. And now I had my child; yes, I had my child every day, and I loved him. I loved him. I felt joy wash through me, and I felt free.

I became aware only slowly of a human silence in the room. The din of the wheel foundry came through the walls and the open door with the smell of roses, but the old man had not said anything in a long time, and I swiveled my chair around and came out of my revery and looked at him. He sat leaning on his cane, slumped forward, his head with its fine and unkempt white hair bowed as though in prayer. For a moment I thought that he had dozed off.

"Brian?" I said.

No answer. I stood up and spoke louder. "Brian?"

Then I understood that a power more profound and more enduring than sleep had touched Brian Ledbetter and taken him away forever.

157

A TELEGRAM BROUGHT Daisy and Virgil home from California for the funeral. In the meantime a mournful hush fell over the county. Jim Ed, Dr. Youngblood, and I sat in the house with Mrs. Ledbetter. She said little. "I want him to spend his last night above ground here in the house," she told the mortician who had taken Caleb's place in Bourbonville. "I don't want to leave him alone in a funeral home. I want folks to sit up with him."

The mortician, an overweight and uncomfortable-looking man named Ellis, too warm in his thick black suit, bowed and said that of course he would do things exactly as Mrs. Ledbetter wished.

Daisy and Virgil arrived on train 42 in the afternoon. Dr. Youngblood, Jim Ed, and I, Joab, all Joab's daughters but Barbara, and Willy went to the depot to meet them. Virgil was thinner than when I had seen him last, dapper in pinstripes, wearing a gray fedora and a bow tie, his expensive black shoes brightly waxed, his face tanned and more deeply lined than it had been, still Virgil's face—long and angular, high-boned, with intelligent eyes that were lost and sad; Virgil middle-aged, slightly stooped, verging on the next step in life. He and Jim Ed exchanged a clumsy embrace, and I saw him sweep his eyes around the square.

He was inundated by Joab's tribe. He shook hands with Willy and looked him up and down with astonishment and said, "Willy, you look good—you have lost weight."

"It's all the walking I do on my job," Willy said proudly. Willy laughed and became serious and threw his hand around Virgil's shoulders, and he told Virgil how Brian had died, and Virgil came to me and spoke softly in gratitude before he was borne away by the others.

Daisy swept off the train in a long gray traveling dress. Her hair was now stylishly swept back, and she looked queenly and beautiful. Gone was the girl I had met almost nine years before. Gone even was the woman who had kissed me in the car. Here was a beauty with full hips and breasts, and I marveled that she had not been successful in films. A certain strain in the eyes, perhaps, a hardness, a loss of innocence. I could not tell.

Jim Ed greeted her; then Joab's brood, and there was much exclaiming and kissing and mutual admiring; finally it was my turn, and we were standing face-to-face. She reached up impulsively and kissed me; I turned my head, and her lips pressed against my cheek. We looked at each other, embarrassed and not knowing how to begin.

"Well," she said finally. "You look very grown-up."

I laughed. "So do you," I said.

"I am sorry about your son," she said. "I meant to write. I did not know what to say."

"There is nothing to say," I said. "There never was anything to say."

"Well," she said.

"Well," I said.

She had taken my hand on our greeting, and she held it still, her gloved fingers squeezing mine. The train steamed and puffed. The locomotive bell beat in a languid rhythm. People swirled in the warm sunshine. Dr. Youngblood stepped up and took her hand. Daisy made over to him, kissed him enthusiastically on the cheek several times, hugged him, and made loud exclamations at how good he looked. "You haven't changed a *bit!*" she cried. His round, red face filled with kindly delight. He touched her gallantly on the arm and did his foolish drawling imitation of a Deep South accent. He pronounced her more beautiful than ever—as she was—and he kissed her on the cheek, puckering in a studied way, as if he had never kissed enough women to get the hang of it.

We drove out in a caravan of cars to the neat house surrounded by its green lawn and its spring-blooming flowers, a frame house painted a brilliant and somehow defiant white, covered with a neatly kept shingle roof, reposing in its grove of maples and oaks on the slight hill that looked across a broad valley and to the western mountains, a house built by Evelyn Ledbetter's first husband, Virgil's father, Dothan Weaver. Evelyn Ledbetter sat with Barbara amid a sibilant chorus of friends. The women of Bourbon County were abashed by her loss.

When Virgil, leading the way, walked up onto the porch and entered the house, his mother leaped up and flung her arms around him and wept. Virgil wept, too—not sobbing, but a tearful, silent weeping, his head bowed, his eyes shut against his mother's neck—and they could not speak. I came behind, holding my hat in my hand, and Daisy held my hand briefly, then let it go.

Mountains of flowers filled the house, their fragrance almost suffocating. More kept arriving. Ellis brought the body out to the house in a new Cadillac hearse. More flowers packed the hearse. Brian's coffin—rich, dark rosewood—lay under the flowers, and the grunting men heaved it into the house and set it up on a special, folding metal table, and they opened it, and there the old man was, rigid and unsmiling, his skin waxy, his white hair slicked back, neater than it had ever been in life, his rough hands folded with odd decorum across his stomach, his body dressed in the blue uniform of the United States Army of the Civil War, faded now, the uniform of which he had been so vociferously proud. His forage cap was placed on the top of the coffin on the bottom half, which remained shut.

Brian was the last person in Bourbon County who had fought in the Civil War. Throughout the bustle and confused order of the funeral arrangements, I thought of midnight winds stirring randomly over quiet battlefields now waving with young corn and tall wheat or else serene with cattle, and I thought of my own war and the hot sun on my back, the sweat burning my eyes, dripping off my chin, soaking my shirt until my back flamed with heat rash; I remembered how my sweating hand could scarcely grasp the thick wooden stock of my rifle when our cannon was gone and a Flemish sergeant thrust a rifle into my hand and made me an infantryman. I thought of how the dust boiled up from the roads—inescapable, ubiquitous dust—and I remembered, without being able to recall exactly what it was, the heavy, penetrating stench of thousands on thousands of unwashed, frightened, exhausted and plodding men who made the air of our summer fetid. I remembered how tired I was, my legs like stones, and how we trudged on, one weary foot in front of the other, along an interminable road with artillery booming behind us and the clatter of a machine gun in the middle distance, close enough to make ripples of fear run down our backs. I remembered the vomitous reek of death, how it sometimes blew suddenly on us, like death itself a surprise but instantly recognizable.

I tried to make some comparison between my war and Brian's war, Hub Delaney's war, tried to draw some moral, some sense out of them both, but I failed. I felt a headache threatening, and Bernal stood down in the shade with his stiff black hair brushed back along the side of his elegant head, a black top hat in his hand. Bernal in mourning.

People poured in from all over the county to view the body. As at Hub Delaney's funeral, parents brought little children and held them above the coffin so they could look at this relic of an old war the parents had no memory of at all. Men took off their hats and held them respectfully over their hearts. They came out telling one another that Brian Ledbetter looked good, younger than he had seemed in years. They spoke optimistically, as if there had been some slight question, a breath of rumor, about Brian's welfare but, having seen this elaborately made-up body, they were reassured that one who looked that good had to be all right. When they had made their manners to the corpse and murmured consoling words ("He lived a good long life; we'll miss him"), they removed themselves to the great tree-shaded yard. Knots of people stood about in the refulgent sunshine and talked, and some of them laughed as people will do when they are together.

158

CROWDS STAYED at the farm all night long before the next day's burial, for that was the way of death in the country. Very late in the evening, after Mrs. Ledbetter had gone to bed, Daisy, Dr. Youngblood, and I slipped away to sit for an hour in Dr. Youngblood's parlor. The tall windows were raised on the fragrant night. Fireflies drifted against the dark trees, and the almost imperceptible stirring of the cool night air brought in the fragrance of roses. Our melancholy dissipated temporarily in the old routines of our former times. We talked; we drank wine. We lived over the past when we had sat here together. We talked about those days that by Daisy's return seemed to have been finally lost.

I say "we" though in fact I talked very little. Daisy recalled our evenings and days together, often getting them wrong, but she remembered enough to bring them back to me, and I began to think that I had been a long time in Bourbonville, long enough to see the town and the county changing in the persistent, remorseless way that things change. Daisy looked at me, looked at Dr. Youngblood, flourished her cigarette, and told stories of what we had talked about and of the people in the town. I thought she was trying to pretend that there had been no hiatus, that we were easily taking up again an old way of being together only briefly interrupted.

She was getting a divorce. "I'm sick and tired of my husband. He is a complete bore. He can't talk about anything but the movies. He wants to be a director and he will never succeed. He goes to movies to learn what other people do, but he can't do anything himself. Who wants to talk about movies all the time?"

"Does your father know about the divorce?" Dr. Youngblood said, looking somber.

"Oh no. Not yet. I'll tell him soon. Why should he know? He doesn't care about me. He never has cared about me. You know how he is, Curtis. He only loved D.B. With D.B. gone, all the love has gone out of Daddy's life. I'm just his daughter. I don't count. He is not interested in anything I do."

"D.B. has been dead a long time," Dr. Youngblood observed.

"It has not changed anything," Daisy said.

"You went with him to California," Dr. Youngblood said. "He must appreciate you for that."

"Of course I went with him to California! Do you think I wanted to stay here, Curtis? Or live with Mamma in Chattanooga? My God, I look at

Bourbonville now and wonder how I endured it so long! Nothing ever happens here. How do you stand it?"

Dr. Youngblood and I looked briefly at each other. "It's not a bad place," he said after a moment of contemplation and a long pull on his pipe.

"It's a boring, tedious place," Daisy said. "When are you going to leave, Paul? Jim Ed says you are going to move up to Washington soon. Is that true?"

"I do not know."

"You don't know, or you won't say?"

"I honestly do not know."

"Well, I see you are no more talkative than you ever were. Sometimes you're like a bump on a log."

"I'm sorry," I said. "I feel sad. I do not have anything to say."

"Well, we all feel bad about Grandaddy Ledbetter, but let's put it this way: he had a long and good life. Don't you hope you have such a life, Curtis?"

"Oh yes," Dr. Youngblood said.

"This ought to be a celebration," she said. "We shouldn't be sad at all."

We sat in gritty silence. Dr. Youngblood ruminated, looking off into space. "Is divorce easy in California?" he said.

"Oh yes. Everybody gets divorced in California. It's the thing to do. It's a wonderful place."

"Because of divorce?" Dr. Youngblood said.

"No, silly, not *just* because of divorce," Daisy said. "But divorce is part of it. You can be anything you want to be in California. You don't have to stay in a marriage if it isn't the marriage for you." She gave me a bold look and drew on her cigarette.

"You ought to tell your father before he finds out from somebody else," Dr. Youngblood said gravely.

"I'll tell him. I can just see the look on his face. It will mean, 'You've failed me again, Daisy.' "

"I don't believe he'll think that," Dr. Youngblood said. "He loves you. You make him worse than he is."

"Oh, you don't know him, Curtis."

"I believe I do," Dr. Youngblood said.

"Oh well," Daisy said, irritated at how the conversation was going, "he can't say anything about my divorce without condemning himself. He divorced Mamma, and now he has a lady friend."

"Is that so?" Dr. Youngblood said. "Is she nice?"

"She's terrible. Daddy has terrible taste in women. I guess we know that, don't we?"

"Do you ever see your mamma?" Dr. Youngblood asked.

"I write to her, but we don't have anything to say to each other."

"Hah," Dr. Youngblood said in a noncommittal way. He did not look at me.

"I'm going to see her after the funeral. Daddy is going straight back to California, and I am going to stop in Chattanooga to see Mamma. He said I should."

She coughed frequently. The conversation drifted implacably back to the movies. I had the feeling that we were repeating things we had said before because we had nothing new to say now. She named off titles of movies and expressed amazement that we had not seen them.

"I have not been to a motion picture since my son was born," I said.

She looked at me, incredulous and aghast. "Not a one? You didn't see *Wild, Wild Susan?*"

"No," I said.

"You didn't see *Broadway After Dark?*"

"No," I said.

"Cheap Kisses?"

"Nothing," I said.

"Paul, you don't know *anything!*" she said.

"I do not care for movies," I said.

She made a pouting expression. "With your talent you could be running Metro-Goldwyn-Mayer."

"You overestimate me," I said. "I am happy doing what I do."

"I cannot believe you have become that dull," she said. "It shows what this place can do to a good mind."

I shrugged.

"He seems to have a talent for running the car works," Dr. Youngblood said softly.

"Oh, fudge!" Daisy said, lighting another cigarette. "Fudge the car works. Fudge this tedious place. It makes me sick that neither of you know what you're missing, and you don't care."

Dr. Youngblood looked unhappy. He did not look at me, and when Daisy tried to resume the conversation on a bright and buoyant note, we both found little to say to her. Our silence did not matter; she talked on as if we hung on every word.

159

ON THE SATURDAY Daisy went away. she and I met in front of the courthouse in Knoxville. It was raining—a summery rain that fell as a steady drizzle, blown in waving veils by a shifting breeze. The world smelled fresh and damp. We had coffee in a smoky little cafe next to the car barn on Main

Street. Main Street was paved with red bricks. The yellow trolley cars clanked into the car barn and clanked out again, steel wheels squealing on steel rails. Motormen came and went in the cafe, cigarettes hanging out of their mouths, talking gruffly, laughing, growling, amid the clink of spoons and the klunk of crockery. We sat at a table in a corner, and no one paid any attention to us.

"Marriage has changed you," Daisy said. She turned her head slightly sideways and looked at me with narrowed eyes, straining for effect. I thought that in her mind an invisible movie camera hovered just over my head.

"Has it?" I said.

"You are not as interesting as you used to be. You have become like everyone else. I loved you—I want you to be interesting. I don't want to think I loved a dull man."

"I presume you once loved your husband, and now you are divorcing him because you think he is dull."

"Ouch," she said. "You know how to hurt when you want to hurt."

"I am sorry," I said. I *was* sorry; she *was* hurt.

"You are more interesting than my husband; I married him on the re-bound from you. Surely you know that."

"I am not sure that I was ever interesting," I said. "I think you made me up."

"Don't be silly. I know who you were. I never dreamed you'd want nothing more than a job. You can have so much more."

"I have a son. That means I need a job."

"If you had married me, you would have had more than a job, you would have had a career, and you would have had a different son," she said.

I lowered my face and felt wretched.

She reached across the table quickly and took me by the hand. "Now it is my turn to apologize," she said. "I should not have said that. I am sorry."

"It is all right," I said.

"But it could have been different," she said. "Everything could have been different—not just your son. You would have come to California. You would not have been stuck in a boring place like this with a . . . a *job!* I hate the idea of a *job.* Unless you have a *career,* you're not worth anything. Cigarette?"

"No," I said. "You smoke too much."

"It is better than getting fat. 'Reach for a Lucky instead of a sweet.' Don't you know the slogan?"

"I have seen it," I said.

"I hear that the beautiful Eugenia is religious now. Curtis told me. So did Jim Ed. They feel sorry for you. I am sorry for you, too. I'm sorry everybody feels sorry for you."

"I hope it will pass," I said.

"It will not pass. She will not change." Daisy looked down at her cigarette and tapped the ash off in the ashtray. She seemed all-knowing and all-wise.

"People change. You said so yourself."

"Some change for the better, some for the worse, and some just change. Curtis has changed. He looks so old."

"You said he had not changed a bit, I believe."

"Oh, I was being polite. I made him feel good. Don't you believe in making people feel good?"

I shrugged.

She leaned forward. "Paul, listen to me. Look at me. Please look me in the eye. That's right. Don't look down now. Please keep looking at me. I love you. I do not like what I see happening to you, but I love you still. You are the only person I have ever loved."

"You do not know anything about me," I said. "You never knew anything about me."

"I know everything I need to know. People grow together. We still have time to live together, to learn about each other, to shape our lives with each other."

She took me by the hands. I looked at her.

"We can go away. We have our lives in front of us. You think I am worse than I am; I think you are better than you are. Fine! We'll come together in the middle!"

"The part of my life that I have already lived is not in front of me," I said. "That part of my life is behind me."

She shook her head impatiently. The lights danced in her black hair. "Oh, please. Please. Don't be a Jesuit. The life you have to live is in front of you. Everything that is behind you is dead. It's gone. You can't do anything with it anymore. You can't recall it. It's a dead weight around your neck."

I started to say something but decided she would think I was being a Jesuit again.

"We can go away together. Listen, I will go where you want to go. England? Would you like to go to England? Belgium? If you want to go back to Belgium, we can go there."

"Burma," I said suddenly. "I want to go to Burma."

"Burma! I would *love* to go to Burma. Jim Ed said you were going there to work with Uncle Gilly. And then your child was born. Isn't Burma in India? I forget, but it doesn't matter. I want to go. Now! Tomorrow!"

"It is not the same," I said. "The British have tried to make them the same, but Burma is different. Yes, I was supposed to work with Gilly. He's finished a power line; now he's about to build a bridge." I told her about Burma, about everything—everything except my fantasies of her. We drank cup after cup of coffee, and the rain blew against the windows.

She squeezed my hand. Her hand was warm. Her fingers were smooth. It was her left hand, and she was wearing her gold wedding band. "Paul, listen to me. You cannot think about your son the way you think of normal children. Your son will never be a real human being."

"He is not inhuman," I said, leaving my hand in hers.

"Please, listen to me. Look at me." The cafe swirled with noise. Her voice was a low, clear tone, coming under all the rattle of crockery, the clanging of knives and forks, and the unintelligible cacophony of male voices. I thought of the Sirens singing over the waves that battered the ship of Odysseus.

"Are you listening?" she said.

"Yes," I said.

"You seemed to go away for a minute. You do that, you know. People talk to you and you go away. You look at people and you are not there."

"I am sorry," I said.

"I can give you a son. I can give you five sons or six sons or daughters. There is nothing wrong with daughters. I have read that daughters are closer to their fathers. Sons are closer to their mothers."

"You should not believe everything you read," I said.

"No. I am not close to my father. It does not have to be like that. It is his fault that I am not close to him. I want to be close to him. Your daughters will want to be close to you. We can have children, children who can talk with you, love you. Normal children. Intelligent children. Real children."

"What would I do with Guy?"

"You can put him away in a school. They have schools for such children. I have read all about them."

"You have read about them?"

"As soon as Jim Ed wrote me about your son, I started reading about what we could do with him. We can put him in a school for children like him. That is what you *should* do, for *his* sake! He will be happy there. He will be with others like himself. You can send him money. You can visit him. You can write him letters, and people will read them to him, and he will be happy. He will make friends. He will forget all about you. The people who run those places are wonderful. They love the children. They are kind and gentle people."

"How can you tell that?"

"Why else would they do it!"

I looked down.

"Look at me!" she commanded. "In a little while, it will seem normal to him. Mongoloid children die before they are twenty. Do you know that?"

"Yes," I said. "I have read that."

"They get sick so easily. They die of pneumonia."

"You have read a great deal," I said.

"I have read everything I could get my hands on. I have haunted libraries. I have talked to doctors. He will live just long enough to ruin your life. You have to use willpower. It will be hard to separate yourself from him at first. All change is hard. But once you change, you are glad. You look back on the moment you changed, and you feel good about yourself. You feel strong. We know we have it in ourselves to make our lives what we want them to be. It's all willpower."

"As you will use willpower to divorce your husband."

She hesitated and looked uncertain and hurt.

"I am sorry," I said. "I am not mocking you."

"It's all right. Yes, the way I am going to use willpower to divorce my poor stick of a husband. I married him because you married Eugenia. I never loved him. He was passionately in love with me. He bores me. I don't have to stay with him. We don't have to stay with our mistakes."

"Does he still love you?"

"What does it matter? I don't love him. If he loves me, and if I don't love him, it's no good trying to stay married. He would be miserable in the end."

"He may be miserable when you divorce him," I said.

"He will get over it."

"As I will get over my son."

"He is not truly a son. A son must be fully human. Your son is an atavism, a throwback to an earlier part of our evolution."

"Ah, you believe in evolution!"

"In California we can believe such things." She laughed. Her face changed suddenly. "Are you listening to me?" she said.

"Of course," I said.

"I have been through so many men—all because I love you. None of them was as good for me as you can be. Do you want to know how I got married?"

"Not particularly," I said.

"I was having an affair with a man named Allen. Allen was so nice. So dumb. He taught English at the University of Southern California."

"He taught people how to speak English?"

"No, silly. He taught poetry. He had a good voice. He could read divinely. We started sleeping together. Only we didn't sleep much." She laughed in a knowing way. "Then I started having an affair with Martin."

"Martin?"

"Martin is my husband."

"You were having affairs with two men at the same time?"

"I was very mixed up. You had married Eugenia. It was your fault. Don't reproach me. Morals are not the same in California as they are here."

I could not think of anything to say.

"I hated to hurt Allen's feelings. He was very nice, and he was wild about me. I tried to tell him and couldn't. One night we were all in a speakeasy drinking. I was borrowing cigarettes from Martin. Allen saw me borrowing the cigarettes. Suddenly he knew!"

"That you and Martin were having an affair."

"Of course."

"What did he do?"

"Oh, nothing. He never asked me out again. He left me alone. I'm sorry it happened that way, but it wasn't my fault. We can't control our feelings. I can't control my feelings for you. Allen knew that. He went away, and I married Martin."

I looked away. A fat man at the counter was talking animatedly with a fat waitress in a dirty white uniform. She was wiping the counter with a rag. They both burst into laughter at something the man said. Their faces were red. "Oh, Clifford!" the waitress said.

"It's better to get pain over all at once," Daisy said. "When you want to end a love affair or a marriage, it's better to do it fast. Like pulling adhesive tape off your arm when you've had a cut."

"Ah," I said. I looked into my coffee cup. I could not drink any more.

"What do you think?" Daisy said impatiently.

"I do not think anything," I said.

"You look so distant," she said, her voice almost breaking. "You should feel sorry for me."

"I do," I said.

She smiled. She had tears in her eyes, and they glistened, and she smiled warmly and looked happy.

"What is Burma like? Gilly writes to Daddy now and then, but I don't read his letters. I don't know Gilly very well. He left home when I was so young. He has always thought he was better than the rest of us. Tell me, what is Burma like?" She leaned forward and smiled at me, a bright movie smile.

"It is hot in the lowlands. Rain forest."

"You mean jungle?"

"Well, not like the Amazon or the Congo. But yes, jungle. And rice fields along the Irrawaddy River."

"Are there lions and tigers there?"

"Tigers. No lions. And snakes. Pythons and cobras and kraits. The banded krait is one of the most dangerous snakes in the world."

"Why?"

"Because it is the color of dirt. The barefoot natives step on kraits and get bitten and die."

"How exciting! Where would we live?"

"I do not know. I was to work with Gilly to build a power line out of a little town up in the northern hills. I would have lived in camp tents while the power line was being built."

"In tents! Oh, it would be something to tell our children about forever," she said, her face radiant.

"The silver is in the Shan plateau. I might not be able to get a job there now, but the Englishman who wanted to hire me seemed sure there would always be a place for me. They are building a silver smelter in a place called Namtu.''

Her eyes were on fire. "Then we will go," she said. "Can you give me a month?"

I looked at her and dropped my eyes. She gripped my hand. Her fingers dug into my flesh.

"Let's *go!*" she pleaded. "Let's *go!* Say something."

"No," I whispered.

"Why not! For Christ's sake, why not?"

"I cannot go."

"I love you," she said, her voice like steel. "Don't you understand that?"

I started to speak and could not.

"Don't you love me?" she said, sounding suddenly pitiful and childlike.

I lifted my eyes and looked at her. We looked at each other a long time. I took a deep breath and expelled it. "No," I said. "No, I do not love you. I love Eugenia. I love Guy. I do not love you."

She released my hand. We sat in silence. I became conscious of the irregular arrivals of trolleys, the loud clangor of steel wheels on steel rails.

"Well," she said at last. "I spoke about ripping off the adhesive tape. And we can't control our feelings, can we?"

I looked down.

"I must catch my train," she said, looking up at the clock on the wall.

"It is raining," I said. "I will drive you to the station. My car is nearby."

"I can take a taxi. There are taxis in front of the courthouse."

"All right," I said.

"I'm going to Chattanooga to see Mamma. What do you suppose that will be like?"

I shrugged. "I did not know your mother well."

"She is very religious now. I will never know her well, either. I guess I never did."

We walked out into the slow rain. It was cool and fragrant. There was a taxicab at a stand on Gay Street beside the courthouse, next to the Spanish-American War monument. The soldier of the monument stood with feet wide apart, holding a rifle across his body, his legs fixed as if he were stepping irresistibly forward. He wore a soft, wide-brimmed hat and looked straight ahead, and he seemed weary. The cab driver sat behind the wheel, smoking a cigarette and reading a newspaper. He looked up. I lifted my finger, and he folded his newspaper and got out and opened a back door for Daisy.

"Nice rain," he said.

"Yes," I said. "It was dry."

"Well, goodbye," Daisy said. She looked at me and cried silently.

"Goodbye," I said.

She kissed me quickly on the cheek and got into the cab. I stood in the rain and watched the cab turn out into traffic and go up Gay Street towards the railroad station. The cab was dark green. You did not see many cars in those days that were not painted black.

"Well," Guy said. "She almost had you."

"Yes," I said. "It was very close."

"Do you regret it?" Guy said.

I shrugged. "What does it matter?"

"The boy would have been happy in a school," Guy said. "She was right. Eugenia would not have missed you. She would have been relieved to have you gone. The boy would have forgotten you, too."

Now the tears came in my eyes, and I was glad for the rain. "I could not bear that," I said. "I love the boy. I love Eugenia."

"You could have loved Daisy in time," Guy said.

"No," I said. "She would have been disappointed with me. I would have been another . . . what was his name?"

"Allen," Guy said.

"Yes, poor Allen. I would have been a story she told the next man down the line. I suppose I would have been more romantic than Allen." I laughed without mirth.

"At last, you made a decision," Bernal said.

"Yes," I said. "I made a decision."

"You have us," Guy said. "We love you."

"So does my son," I said. "He loves me."

160

A SATURDAY AFTERNOON in late October—the month things happened to me. I sat in a rocking chair in the kitchen, holding my son in my lap, and trying to read. It was a cold and overcast day, portending winter. The leaves were falling from the trees along Edgewood Avenue.

I could hear Eugenia's prayer group in the living room—a somberly enthusiastic droning of voices praising God, beseeching him to help them endure the persecutions of the world. I thought the world was extravagantly tolerant of all of them, letting them meet freely and not banishing them to the insane asylum or the inquisitorial prison that I thought most of them—saving Eugenia—deserved.

Guy got up and toddled outside, into the backyard. I read on. I do not know how much time passed. I heard a shriek, a loud, fierce cry. My son. I leaped up and ran through the back door into the yard.

I found three little boys from the neighborhood swarming over him. They had knocked him down, and they were hitting him. Guy's plump little body twisted in a vain effort at escape. One boy was sitting on him and beating him with both fists; the other two were holding his arms and hitting him when they could get a hand free. They were uttering cries of delight.

I flung them aside and seized the sitting child by the hair and hurled him away so that he landed with a yell of fright upside down in the dying grass. They fled, shrieking wildly, into the street. I picked up my howling son and comforted him. He looked around in wide-eyed terror, a child who for the first time has discovered horror and cannot understand it and fears that it will come back again.

I took him into the house and into the living room. The women were on their knees praying. "Some damned little children were beating the hell out of our son," I said to Eugenia's back. The women stopped praying.

Mary Pendleton stood up. "How dare you interrupt our prayers with profanity," she said.

"I do not give a goddamn about your prayers," I said. "Some nasty little children were beating my son, and I am going to kill somebody." For a moment nobody said anything. The women, getting up in various states of confusion, looked at me, terror-stricken.

Eugenia stood up, looking at me in a bewildered way and I thought, *I must save her. I must get her away from here. I must remove her from these women.*

I left the child with her and marched out of the house, leaving behind assorted female gasps, broken at the last by the musical and deprecating laughter of Eula Pinkerton. She would have explained that this was how men were and that saintly women could only endure abuse and trust in the Lord for ultimate vindication. She would have told the story of how her husband was finally saved and died in Jesus.

I walked for more than an hour. I looked at the city, and I thought of my son, walled in on every side by the implacable human propensity to exclude the different and to hate the weak. When I came back, Eugenia's friends had gone. She was in the kitchen, holding Guy. He clung to her, his arms tightly around her neck.

"We are going to move," I said. "We are going to leave this place."

"You are not going to Burma," she said. "I will not go. I cannot go."

"No," I said. "But we are going to leave Knoxville. We are going to move to Bourbon County."

She gave me a mute, anguished look. I took the child from her and he put his arms around my neck. And I felt within a rise of hope.

161

JIM ED HELPED ME find the farm. One of his banjo-playing friends was named Sushong. "He's in debt up to his chin," Jim Ed said. "He's got to sell some of his land, or he's going to lose all of it."

It was at a place where the new highway to Knoxville joined the new highway under construction from Nashville. The highway to Nashville was Highway 70, the Dixie Highway; the new highway to Knoxville from Chattanooga was Highway 11, the Lee Highway. "They call it Dixie Lee Junction," Jim Ed said. Sushong wanted to sell an L-shaped tract of twenty-five acres lying with the stem along Highway 11 and the bottom along Highway 70. It was twenty miles west of Knoxville, five miles north of Bourbonville.

We drove to Sushong's place. It was winter, and the countryside was dun and gray. Sushong lived in an unpainted frame house that had once been white. It had a rusting metal roof and a verandah and big trees in the yard and a dank smell. The property he wanted to sell was on the eastern edge of his farm.

Juliet went with us. She and Jim Ed had a big, healthy son named Brian Elisha, and she was pregnant again. Juliet sat in the backseat with the child. "You should not buy property when you are going to turn around and sell it again," she said.

"Why would I sell it again?"

"Because you are going to move up to Washington," she said hopefully.

"Maybe I will not go," I said.

"I am sure you will go," she said. "Jim Ed says that man Drodge adores you."

"That may be in my destiny, or it may not," I said. "Now I have a simple problem. I want to escape Eugenia's mother. I want to escape Knoxville."

Jim Ed and Juliet were polite. They did not ask personal questions; they let my reason lie without comment.

Sushong was large and slow and perplexed. He wore faded denim bib overalls of a type popular since the war, and a tattered denim jacket and brogan shoes that had never been waxed. He chewed tobacco with methodical resolve, the cud filling one unshaven cheek.

"This here is a good piece of ground," he said slowly and with conviction. "I hate to give hit up, but I got to. Now I admit, hit's a mite red, but all hit wants is a little lime and a little fertilize, and you can make crops on hit if'n you want. You can't be finding much land near roads like this for fifty dollars the acre."

"He's right there," Jim Ed said, looking around in an appraising way. The land lay against a low ridge. We could stand at the top of the hill and look down across sedge grass and blackberry bushes to the construction work on Highway 70—a red slash through the earth. Atop the ridge beyond the southwest corner of the place stood a white frame church with a squat steeple. Sushong, walking, pointed to the church with pride. "That there's Midway Baptist. My daddy give the land for that church, and he's buried in the graveyard right there underneath that red cedar tree. If'n you'ns buy this land, you and your missus can walk to meeting without losing your breath. I mean, if'n you're a Baptist. Air ye a Baptist, Mr. Alexander?"

"No, I am a Catholic," I said.

Sushong pondered this information and nodded his large head slowly as if he did not entirely understand.

"Well, I reckon hit don't make no difference. I reckon we're all going to the same place."

"To the graveyard," Jim Ed said.

Sushong laughed uneasily. "Well, that's a fact," he said.

"It's so bare," Juliet said in a pained voice. "No trees. I think it's been planted out. I don't think it'll grow anything but weeds." The sedge grass swished against our legs.

Sushong looked down at his shoes. "Well, truth to tell, I ain't had the money to buy arry fertilize for the last few years. But hit'll come back, Miz Ledbetter; believe me, hit will. Hit looks better in summer."

"You ought to have a few trees," Juliet said. "Some trees would be an improvement."

Sushong's eyes took on a watery gleam. "Well, if hit's a woods ye want, I can sell you three acres right over there behind the churchyard. But hit's going to cost ye more to have them trees. I mean, you can log that there woods if ye be a mind to, but I reckon I'd have to charge ye seventy-five dollars the acre for the woods."

"That's a lot of money, Buford," Jim Ed said.

"Well, times is hard, Jim Ed. Times is hard. I'm sorry, but that there's the gospel truth."

"I will take it," I said. "I want the woods too."

"I reckon you do," Jim Ed said. "Somebody could come along and build a hog pen right up against your place if you didn't have that woods."

"I'll buy it," I said.

"I'm particular pleased to sell hit to you," Sushong said.

"You ought to buy a place that already has a house," Juliet said, annoyed, looking around as if she could see no hope in this treeless field of dead weeds.

"Then you're going to have to pay a lot more," Sushong said. He seemed mildly anxious.

"I want to build my own house," I said.

"Horses," Bernal whispered. "You can have horses."

"Well now, let's shake on hit then," Sushong said, sounding relieved. "If you want to build you a house, this here's the very place for you. Can't do no better."

I smiled. "All right," I said.

We shook hands. Sushong's hand was hard with calluses.

"I hear tell you're French," he said almost shyly.

"Belgian," I said.

Sushong pondered this and spat tobacco juice into the ground. "Well, I reckon hit's all the same thing. My people was French. My daddy told me a lot about them, but I've forgot most of hit. They was Protestants. I don't know what kind. The Catholics, they run them out of the old country, and they come to South Carolina, and then they went to North Carolina, and then by God they come here." He laughed. "You and me might be kin."

"We might be," I said. We grinned at each other.

"Drive on over to the house, Jim Ed, and I'll get the old woman to put on some coffee. We'll celebrate. You bring your guitar?"

"Yep," Jim Ed said. "And Paul's mandolin."

"It is not my mandolin," I said.

"Yes it is," Jim Ed said.

"We'll play some," Sushong said.

162

I DESIGNED THE HOUSE, drawing the plans on the big long desk in my office, with Jim Ed offering advice and sometimes with Juliet coming in to help. It is a sprawling and illogical place; I did not know much about design. "You want a big kitchen," Juliet said. "The kitchen is the most important room in the house. On cold days you can sit in the kitchen." I built a big kitchen with a row of tall windows looking off down towards Highway 70; I sit in my kitchen now, writing these pages.

Jim Ed whistled when he looked at my plans. "It's going to be pretty damned big," he said.

"We're going to have lots of light," I said. "Light and porches to sit on and a big kitchen. I want windows everywhere."

I spread the drawings out for Eugenia. "I like the kitchen," she said quietly. She began to take interest in the place. "If you have a lot of windows, it's going to be drafty." The doctors had told us that Guy would be susceptible to respiratory ailments.

"We will buy good windows, and we will double-glaze them for the winter," I said.

"That will be very expensive," Eugenia said.

"I can afford it," I said.

"You do not know anything about building a house," Mary Pendleton said. "You are not a carpenter or an architect. If you don't watch out, you'll build it all wrong, and it will fall down on your head," Mary Pendleton said.

"We hope you will come and visit us," I said. "You can see if it falls down."

"I don't know why you want to go live in a hay field," Mary Pendleton said. "I had enough of the country down in Bradley County. You won't see much of me if you go off down there. I don't like bugs and snakes."

I tried to bear up under the threat of her absence.

"You ought to take the advice of experts when you deal with real estate," Charles said, deeply injured. "Knoxville will never go west. It is bound to go east and north. You'll never get back the money you put into that place. Now if you'd listened to me, I could have helped you make a *real* investment." This was six years before Charles went bankrupt.

I brought Eugenia down to the place. It was a cold January day with the wind blowing and dark clouds scudding above the treetops, an occasional spitting of rain, and the sedge grass waving forlornly in the wind.

"It's a worn-out hay field," she said of the place where I would build. "You made it sound better than this."

"That's what you see now," I said. "It will be beautiful. The trees will go here, and down there we will have an orchard, and I'm going to plant a vineyard over there, and maybe in that field up there we'll have horses. You can see the mountains better up there, but I don't want a house on a windy hill."

The child wallowed through sedge grass taller than his head. He grunted and bellowed with delight. The wind blew his hair.

"Guy likes it," I said.

Eugenia was silent, but as we drove home she said, "I could plant a flower garden in the front. There's room for a big garden there."

"You can have acres of flower garden," I said.

"I wish it looked neater," she said.

"We will make it neat," I said.

"I don't have any strength to plant flowers," she said.

"Yes you do," I said.

"No," she said. "It was just a thought."

I paid Sushong to bring a mule and a mowing machine and mow the fields. He charged me fifteen cents an hour. Afterward everything looked clean. I paid him to cut the blackberry bushes. The land had a pleasant shape, the hill sloping down from the south, then a slight leveling as though a half-formed step, then another drop, and a flat field lying against the road to Nashville. I would build the house on the broad step in the hill.

"I will help you," Jim Ed said.

"You are too generous with your time," I said.

"Hell, you can't save time," he said with a laugh. "It runs out whether you spend it or whether you sleep."

"You have your own house to work on," I said.

"It'll keep," he said.

"Jim Ed thinks everybody is as generous as he is," Juliet said. She laughed and held his arm.

"It is a good way to be," I said, looking at my friend and his wife, thinking of her passion and her nakedness, feeling nostalgic and ashamed.

"Are you bitter towards me?" she said later.

"Oh no," I said.

"It seems natural somehow. We are all friends."

"Yes," I said. "We are all friends."

"You have done a lot for him, a lot for me. I have never been so well off."

"You mean in money?"

"Yes, but in other ways, too." She seemed embarrassed. "The money is part of it, and you are responsible."

"You have both done much for me," I said. I smiled tentatively at her, and she smiled in return. We were in a greenhouse across the railroad tracks from the depot in Bourbonville on a Saturday morning. A man named Bolton owned the greenhouse. When people decided what they wanted, Mr. Bolton came out and dug it up with a shovel and wrapped the roots in paper and explained how to keep it alive and make it grow. He said growing things made him believe in God. He spoke of God in the casual, unskeptical way of people in the country.

Juliet put a light hand on my arm. I trembled at her touch and pulled away, thinking of Jim Ed. He was staking out the foundations of my house in the late-winter mud. I was here in the company of his wife, and it never would have entered his mind to mistrust us.

I saw Bernal standing at the end of a long row of shrubs. He looked at me with his hollow, ascetic eyes and said nothing.

"Plant fruit trees," Juliet said. "Some cherry trees, some peaches, some apples. And maples. Maples grow very fast. Sugar maples. They grow here in East Tennessee. Don't plant cedars. They spread all over the place. And don't plant water maples. They grow fast, but they look ragged, and storms knock them down."

"You know a lot about trees," I said in admiration.

"I know a lot about many things," she said with a laugh. She carried her child on her hip, her belly swollen with another.

"I had a friend who loved trees," I said.

"Plant them to remind you of her," she said.

"He was not that kind of friend. He was killed in the war."

"I'm sorry," she said. "I am truly sorry."

"So am I. I want to have a vineyard," I said. "I will make wine."

"Despite prohibition?" She laughed. She had a lovely laugh, spontaneous and musical, like Eugenia's before Guy was born.

"I do not believe anyone will arrest me for making wine out here in the country."

"You will not be here long," she said.

"I may be here longer than you think," I said.

Her face clouded faintly. "You are moving up to Washington. You have ambition, don't you? All men have ambition."

"Or their wives have it for them," I said.

"You are almost impolite," she said.

"I apologize," I said.

She brightened, reconsidering something. "I am the one who owes the apology," she said softly. "I will not speak of it again." We walked, looking at shrubs. Jim Ed had a small truck now. He called it a pickup.

We decided on yellow cherry trees and winesap apples and freestone peach trees. We would plant them along the driveway that had been made willy-nilly from the house to Highway 11. We bought maple trees to plant around the yard in front and at the side of the house. The back of the house looked out on my woods. I planted two maples at the end of my driveway at the highway, one on each side, so that in time they would make an arch, welcoming anyone who drove up our little road. Philemon and Baukis, I thought. Eugenia and I.

163

IT WAS A MILD WINTER, and by February Jim Ed and I were driving to the farm to work every afternoon after the whistle blew the car works to day's end at 3:30.

"I must pay you for helping me," I said.

"The hell you say," Jim Ed said.

We dug the cellar within the brick foundations, working with pick and shovel until I thought our backs would break. We sweated until our clothes were soaked, and when we rested, the air chilled us, and we shivered. "Good way to catch pneumonia," Jim Ed said.

"I have never felt better," I said.

"You're getting meat on your bones," Jim Ed said. He clapped me on the back. "You look good."

"Thank you. I feel good."

I wore leather gloves at first, but I blistered my hands anyway. The blisters burst. I bled into my gloves. At night I could scarcely bend my fingers. I continued to work. My hands became hard. In two weeks I discarded the gloves. I touched the calluses with my fingers, and I was amazed and proud.

Guy sat in his velvet Edwardian coat and his gray topper, holding his thin ebony cane with the silver head, with one gloved hand in his lap, his fine trousers hiked just enough to show his splendidly polished shoes buttoned on the inner sides, and he shook his head in wonder. "One of *us* doing manual labor," he said. "I could not be more surprised if I saw you in the Congo, carrying pipes over your shoulder and with a steel manacle around your ankles." I laughed.

"I am doing something you never did," I said. "I am going beyond you."

"New experiences," Guy said wistfully. "All my experiences are old."

I hired three black men from the car works to help us dig, and one afternoon one of them began to sing a slow, heavy rhythm:

> *Burden down, Lord,*
> *Burden down, Lord,*
> *When I lay my burden down,*
> *Burden down, Lord,*
> *Burden down, Lord*
> *When I lay my burden down.*
>
> *Wonder will my mamma know me*
> *When I lay my burden down.*
> *Wonder will my sister know me,*
> *When I lay my burden down.*

Jim Ed started singing, and I sang, too.

"Lord," Jim Ed said. "You singing with your accent! Lord. I wish Daddy could hear that."

"I do, too," I said.

"Maybe he does," Jim Ed said. "Do you believe in ghosts?"

"Your father asked me that question," I said.

"Well?" he said.

"Of course I believe in ghosts."

Jim Ed laughed, and I laughed, too.

We found a rhythm in our shoveling, and the cellar went down, and the days ran, and it was done. A brick mason—the grotesquely fat-bottomed, cigar-chewing, bib-overalls-bedecked, grumbly Boss Key—laid the foundation in straight, magnificent lines and complained with every brick, and while Jim Ed joked and moved the work along, Boss Key bricked in the cellar and sealed it and provided a drain and laid a concrete floor on the bottom. I drank in the smell of new mortar and wet concrete, and it was like standing in a flower garden. "Damn good job if I say so myself," Boss Key said, wiping his face with the back of his hand and gesturing with his trowel as if it had been a wand used in creation ex nihilo.

Now the house had to be raised on the foundations. I brought in pine lumber and kegs of nails. The trucks groaned up the little hill in a howling of gears, and men sweating in the spring air unloaded the sweet-smelling lumber and covered it with a tarpaulin.

The maples and the oaks and the dying chestnuts in the woods were budding when Clyde appeared, carrying his long toolbox. "I hear you need a carpenter," he said.

"You can pay Clyde," Jim Ed said.

"No," Clyde said. "You won't pay me anything. You were Daddy's friend."

"No," I said. "You can't work unless I pay you."

"No," Clyde said. "You gave Willy a job."

"It is not right if I do not pay you," I protested.

"Forget it," Clyde said. He was already walking around, sometimes bending backwards as if to focus more sharply on what was to be done. He seemed to have forgotten me even as I spoke to him. He squatted and sighted and put his hands on his hips and nodded as if to say to himself, "You were entirely correct."

"Good foundation and a good basement. Where are your plans?" he said.

I got them out of the car. Clyde spread them over the hood of the car and studied them.

"You draw pretty good," he said.

"Anybody can do it," I said.

"Not like this," he said. "What do you think, Brother?"

"It'll be a good house," Jim Ed said.

"I like the front porch," Clyde said. "I can see Daddy sitting out there and looking down to the highway."

"My trees are going to grow up between the porch and the highway," I said.

"It'll take them a while," Clyde said.

"Time will pass," I said. "Beyond the maples there, I'm going to plant a vineyard, and beyond, an orchard."

"You're going to be a farmer before this is all over," Clyde said.

"Perhaps so," I said.

"Why not?" Clyde said.

He picked up his tools and set to work.

We all worked. We were Clyde's apprentices. The days passed, and we were happy.

"How come you aren't talking to us about God, Clyde?" Jim Ed said.

"I don't have to talk about God anymore," Clyde said. "I've figured it all out."

"Well, tell us about it," Jim Ed said.

"You got to figure it out for yourself," Clyde said.

"I don't know how," Jim Ed said.

"You will when the time comes," Clyde said.

"Good Lord, Clyde! You're as changeable as the weather."

"Not anymore," Clyde said.

Sometimes I saw Bernal sitting in the grass, looking at Clyde in respect.

Clyde measured studs and sawed them, and we held them up while he set the carpenter's level against them and nailed them plumb. He never left a hammer mark in the wood. My house went up in a grid of straight lines and pine. We put on the roof, shingled it, and set hard maple floors in by tongue and groove.

I exulted in the plumb lines, the sharp right angles. Sometimes at night, when everybody else was gone, I stayed behind, and in the perfect tranquility of my exhaustion before starting the long drive back to Knoxville, I believed I could see the exact moment when the universe was transformed from a roiling mass of smoky dust, of clouds swimming in other clouds, and God breathing a cooling breath on the abyss, parting the clouds, dissolving the smoke, waving his almighty hand in a soft sweeping motion and motherly affection, congealing earth and heavenly light out of the void, creating man as an afterthought and with man's first energy allowing him to make a straight line. The straight line was mark of God's special gift, the image of God himself, for no other living being could make one, and only in the edges of crystals could any straight line be found in nature. I saw the lines of my beautiful house taking shape, and I looked at my creation, and I saw that it was good.

"It is the most beautiful thing I have seen," I said to Guy and Bernal.

"It is beautiful to see you happy," Bernal said.

"We can talk here," Guy said. "I like the solitude. No one will bother us here."

"No," I said. "No one."

When the weather was clear, we worked until the twilight faded into night, and when there was a moon, we worked by its light. The spring deepened, and the nights receded, and daylight hung on, the sun falling serenely west, moving north. The air became mild, then warm, and the insects came back to the forest with their infinite chorus, and we heard the peeper frogs down along the little creek that ran in what I was already grandly calling "the lower field," as if I had so many fields that they had to have names.

Soon after we started working, Juliet started bringing us supper. She drove Brian Ledbetter's car, her young son in the back. Often she brought Mrs. Ledbetter, too, silent now that her second husband was gone. Juliet brought us hot bread she had baked, cold ham and fried chicken, sometimes a stew, and we made a fire near the wall of woods, and we sat around it in camp chairs and ate and laughed and talked, and drank bootleg wine, and Jim Ed and I played music, and he sang, and we watched the stars wheel across the sky, and we were happy. Juliet's son slept against her breast; her serene face reflected the moving light of the fire.

"A Madonna," Bernal said.

"No, she is not a virgin," I said.

164

ON SATURDAY MORNINGS we started early and worked late. Juliet brought us lunch and supper. In the long twilights of Saturday evenings, Dr. Youngblood drove up to watch the progress of the house, sometimes bringing Dale Farmer along. "It's a way to get away from Saturday-night knife fights," Dr. Youngblood said. "I get tired of sewing up the same folks every month." The two of them walked around inspecting things with quiet wonder, looking at my kingdom and my palace.

"You never cease to amaze me," Dale Farmer said. "Moreland Pinkerton loved to do manual labor. But you don't look the type. It just goes to show . . ." He left the sentence unfinished, and I did not know what it went to show, but I was happy with his astonishment.

We did not work on Sundays. "I can't work on Sundays," Clyde said. "It'd break Mamma's heart." On Sundays I brought the child down, and I worked in the vegetable garden. No one in my family had ever had a garden. In Greece we had servants to buy food from peasants at the market. I felt Stephanos eyeing me with curiosity, affection, and reproach.

I bought books and read about planting things. Eugenia began to read them, too. Jim Ed told me to plant peas in February. I did. As the weeks passed, I bought bean seeds and onion plants and tomato plants, and I planted potatoes. I carefully spaded the ground, and I laid out rows with string and put seeds and plants in the damp earth when Jim Ed told me to set them out—marvelous straight lines. I planted beets and corn. I felt so confident that I wanted to plant pineapples and grapefruit and oranges and palm trees. Jim Ed brought cow manure in his pickup, and I fertilized with it. My plantings grew, and my garden was green and beautiful, and the grass was green, too.

The child roamed about, croaking his guttural laugh, making happy noises, watching me as I worked, sometimes trying to mimic me when I told him things. "Seed," I said. After much straining and twisting he managed "See!" Sometimes when I was on my knees in the dirt, planting or weeding, he would rush up and embrace me, and I would feel the smooth skin of his face next to my cheek, and tears of love came to my eyes.

I talked to Guy and Bernal while I worked and the child wandered about.

"Think of what Madame Machavoine would say!" Guy named a woman who had given a party in Dinant on her great lawn. She was immaculate, aristocratic, and beautiful even in deep middle age, and she was proud of her grassy lawn and her tables of food.

"She would order my beans for her cook," I said.

"You have the knack for growing things," Bernal said.

"Oh yes," I said. "Reverting to my ancestors. Those peasants in the Peloponnisos."

"Your ancestors were peasants?" Guy said in mock horror. "What would my mother have said if she had known she was entertaining a peasant in her very own house!"

"All our ancestors were peasants if you go back far enough. Besides, your mother entertained Leonora, and she was a perfect lady about it," I said.

"As he grows older, the young man becomes sharper," Guy said.

"Paul is right. All of our ancestors were peasants at one time," Bernal said.

"It is beautiful here," Guy said.

"I never thought I would hear you say that," I said.

"We change with time," Guy said.

"You have changed already," I said.

"How is that?"

"You are speaking English," I said.

"Ah," Guy said. "So I am."

"And I, too," Bernal said with a laugh. "A true miracle since I never studied English."

"Miracles happen," Guy said. "Witness us."

"Of course. Witness us."

"Miracles happen," I said.

"The young man hopes," Guy said.

"Why should he not hope?" Bernal said.

"Why not indeed!" Guy said.

"Here is his empire," Bernal said.

"Our empire," I said. "Our new Arcadia. Here we will be together."

"Together," Guy said wistfully. "One for all, and all for one."

"Always," I said.

"Now," Guy said. "Let us go over some details. What color were my eyes?"

"Blue," I said.

"And Bernal's eyes?"

"Brown," I said. "Why do you ask me these questions? I can see you."

"Then we shall move to something more difficult," Guy said. "For whom was Leonora named?"

"She claimed she was named for Leonora in Verdi's opera *Il Trovatore.*"

"Correct. And how did we meet?"

I remembered the details. I passed the examination. I worked on hands and knees in the dirt, and we talked. Sometimes the child came over and bent forward and looked at me in a gaping, cross-eyed, happy way, thinking that my talk was directed at him. He wore a loose grin, and in a moment he screamed some harsh, joyful noise and ran off again, ungainly and unbalanced, the back of his head sloped in the cruel way of his infirmity. Late in the afternoon we drove back to Knoxville, Bernal and Guy in the back, the child asleep in the seat beside me, exhausted from the long day.

165

DR. YOUNGBLOOD often came by early on Sunday mornings. He walked around smoking his pipe while I worked in my garden, or else he strolled about the place looking at the house and the land as if he were in an exotic world. I hired Sushong to plow up much of the land and to replant it with grass. I ordered lime and fertilizer, and the land turned green, and Dr. Youngblood marveled at it and at me.

"You look healthy," he said. "Healthier than I've ever seen you."

"It is the strenuous life," I said.

"The headaches?"

"They are not so bad. They come but not so often."

"Maybe they will go away in time," he said.

"I hope so," I said.

"The boy looks good, too."

"He is very good," I said.

Time would not heal Guy; we knew that. We talked about other things: a bullet he had taken out of a leg the night before, a child dead with whooping cough, a farmer who had lost a finger in a circle saw, the new clinic that Dr. Bulkely was about to build in the square—the first brick building in Bourbonville after the courthouse. He was going to tear down John Wesley Campbell's house; Dr. Youngblood said he was glad Brian Ledbetter had not lived to see the day.

On Saturdays when I brought Guy down, Clyde stroked my boy's head. "A child for the angels," he said.

Spring rolled inexorably into summer, and we installed windows and doors.

"Tell you something I think," Jim Ed said. "You got a boy that catches colds. You don't want a big old drafty house. I say you chuck in some insulation."

"I tell you, that's how things are changing," Clyde said. "You never saw an insulated house until recently. Now everybody wants insulation."

We finished the inside of the house, nailing plaster laths over the studs, and put insulation in the space between the outer and the inner walls, space the width of a stud, something called rock wool. Jim Ed found a plasterer named Ed Young who mixed up plaster to look like cake icing and plastered the laths while he smoked a stubby cigar, and the house began to look finished.

In July, Eugenia started coming down on Sundays. "I don't like to miss church," she said.

"You can worship God in the country," I said. "If you want, you can walk up to the church on the hill."

"It's a Baptist church," she said.

"There is a Methodist church at Martel," I said. "You can come down early in the morning and go to church over there."

"You might go with me," she said.

"No," I said. "I will not go with you."

"I will go with you," Juliet said. "If you want to go to the Methodist church, I'll go. That was my mother's church when she married my father."

"Thank you," Eugenia said. "That would be very kind."

"This sinner here might start going to church if we go long enough," Juliet said, pointing at me.

"I would be so happy if he did. Is the preacher at the Methodist church a modernist?"

"I don't know anything about that," Juliet said. "I think if we do the best we know to do, it's all right."

"A lot of sincere people are going to be in hell," Eugenia said doubtfully. "That's what my mother says."

"It's such a beautiful time of year," Juliet said. "We shouldn't talk about hell."

"Hell, if you ladies are going to church, I'll go too," Jim Ed said. He laughed.

Eugenia looked longingly at me. "But you will not go." I felt uncomfortable.

"Not now," I said.

"He'll go in time," Jim Ed said. "You have to leave the hard cases. My daddy never went to church except for funerals and weddings. He was all right."

"He was a wonderful man," Eugenia said, her face lightening as if memory had come back after a long lapse.

"He thought a right smart of you," Jim Ed said.

Our Sundays became brighter. Eugenia anticipated the country. We were up early and on the road, the child standing now in the back of the car, pointing at things going by. I drove her to the Martel church, and Jim Ed and Juliet waited for her. They brought her back to our house afterwards, and we ate together.

"You should go to church, too," Bernal said.

"No," I said. "I cannot go to church. Not now."

For lunch we made picnics, and we finished the kitchen and put in a stove and an electric refrigerator with a coil on the top, and in late August we had Sunday dinner in our house, and I cooked a pot roast, and Eugenia made vegetables, and Jim Ed came with Juliet and the children, two sons now, and Clyde came, and Willy came with him, looking proud and healthy and *responsible*, and Mrs. Ledbetter came, and Dr. Youngblood came, bringing Dale Farmer and Bessie May Hancock, and we sat at a table made of planks laid across sawhorses, and we ate and ate, and we laughed, and something in Eugenia warmed with life.

"Your boy seems happy," Clyde said.

"Poor thing," Eugenia said. "It's my fault."

"He doesn't look as if he thinks it's anybody's fault," Clyde said. "Happiest child I've ever seen."

"Do you think so?" Eugenia said.

"I've seen a lot of children," Clyde said.

Eugenia looked at our son, who was sitting content in a chair, looking at us with his crossed eyes.

"What will you do with all this land?" Clyde said.

"I'm going to have a flower garden," she said abruptly. We all looked at her. "Next year."

"Everybody in the country ought to have a flower garden," Juliet said.

"My mother had a garden in the country," Eugenia said. "I've decided to have one, too."

"A garden is good for what ails you," Jim Ed said.

My onions and my carrots did well, and I had huge cabbages. My peas ripened and turned hard before I could pick them. My potatoes flourished, and fat beets grew under fernlike green plants with blood-red veins in the leaves.

"You have a knack for gardening," Eugenia said in admiration. "My uncle Tom had that."

"I do not have a knack for anything," I said. "I am so dull that I follow directions. That is all."

"You are too modest," she said.

"No," I said. "I am a realist. Do you want wallpaper, or should we paint? We have to decide."

"I want wallpaper," she said. "Everyone has wallpaper now."

"Then we will have wallpaper," I said.

She chose a wallpaper for the living room that had yellow flowers on a pale green background.

"I love green," I said. "It was the favorite color of a dear friend."

"You live with many memories," she said.

"Yes," I said. "It is not a good thing."

"I think it is a good thing. Loyal people have memories. That is why they are loyal." I looked at her and smiled, and she smiled at me.

"I wish I could believe I was loyal," I said.

We moved into the house in late September. Alfred and Charles came down and walked around, looking skeptically at everything. "I don't know why anyone would leave the nice house you have in town and go live in a hay field," Alfred said.

"I hate the country," Charles said. "It reminds me of home."

"This is different," Eugenia said.

"You've moved to the wrong side of Knoxville," Charles said. "This land will never be worth anything."

"I do not intend to sell it," I said. "So it does not matter."

Clyde came to finish the last work on the inside of the house before we hung wallpaper. "You are a Quaker now, Mr. Ledbetter?" Eugenia said.

"That's right, ma'am."

"Some of my people were Quakers. My mother says the Quakers don't believe in hell."

"That's the truth," Clyde said.

"But what if you're wrong?" Eugenia said.

"I'm not wrong about that," Clyde said.

"If you don't believe in hell, you can't believe the Bible," Eugenia said.

"There's a lot less hell in the Bible than most folks think," Clyde said.

"There's a lot in the Book of Revelation," Eugenia said. "You have to believe all the Bible, or you can't believe any of it."

Clyde laughed. "No you don't. You believe the parts that speak to you," he said. "The part about hell never has said anything to me. Neither has Nahum or Leviticus."

"We just can't choose what we want to believe," Eugenia said.

"Why not?" Clyde said.

"Because God will punish us."

"I don't think God punishes us," Clyde said. "I used to think that, but I don't anymore."

"I think he's punished me," Eugenia said. "My husband doesn't believe it, but I know the ways of God."

"I think Paul's right myself," Clyde said.

"Then how do you explain all the evil in the world? How do you explain my son?"

"I can't," Clyde said. "Nobody can. It's just here. That's all we know."

"God punishes us if we don't believe in him," Eugenia said.

"That's not the way I've got it worked out, Mrs. Alexander. There's something going on in the universe, something bigger and more complicated than anything we can figure out, and God's mixed up in it somehow, and it's going to work out all right, but it will take time. In the meantime God can't show himself to us except in reflections and darkness. It's a mercy, I guess. Nobody can see God and live. That's what the Bible says. It's one part of the Bible I believe."

"It's because of our sins," Eugenia said. "God is holy, and we can't see him because of our sins."

"No," Clyde said, shaking his head firmly. "No, it's something more than that. God has to hide himself and we don't know why. But we know he's there."

Eugenia seemed exasperated. "We don't know he's there. Unless we believe the Bible, we don't know anything."

"Yes we do," Clyde said. "We know he's there because we have to look for him. We feel him in our hearts telling us to look for him. If he wasn't there we wouldn't look for him."

"You're talking in circles," Eugenia said.

" 'It is he that sitteth upon the circle of the earth, and the inhabitants thereof are as grasshoppers; that stretcheth out the heavens as a curtain and spreadeth them out as a tent to dwell in.' " Clyde grinned.

"Isaiah," Eugenia said. She smiled.

Clyde laughed. "When you talk in circles, you're as close to God as talk can get you," he said. He laughed gently again. "You have to feel the rest. Trust the best of your feelings, Mrs. Alexander. That's where you'll find God."

"Your friend Clyde is very interesting," Eugenia said.

"Do not let him disturb you," I said. "Sometimes I think he is crazy."

"Oh no," she said. "He doesn't disturb me, and he is not crazy. He is very sweet."

166

I SAT IN BESSIE MAY'S CAFE on a rainy Saturday morning in November. It was 1927. I had been in Bourbonville ten years. The leaves were gone from most of the trees in the square. The oak leaves held on, dry and brown and rattling in the chilly wind. Eugenia was up the street with the child, buying him some clothes. He was growing. I was drinking coffee with Ted Devlin at the round table.

Ted's coffee was turning cold. He was wearing headphones, holding them with his hands to his ears, looking up as if listening for a divine revelation. A small apparatus reposed on the table, next to his coffee cup. The headphones were attached to it. Ted Devlin had informed me with impatient omniscience that this was a crystal radio set.

"Well?" Bessie May said.

"Wait! I heard something," Ted Devlin said.

"What did it sound like?"

"I think it was music. It's gone now."

"Knoxville's too far away," Bessie May said.

"If you'd shut up, I might be able to hear something, Bessie May."

"If you ask me, it's dangerous," Bessie May said. "All them radio waves in the air. They go right through your body. Right now, right while we're drinking our coffee, our bodies is filled up with radio waves."

"I do not feel anything," I said.

"That's the terrible part of it, Mr. Alexander. You don't feel nothing, but them radio waves is running right through your body. It's a wonder we don't glow in the dark like an alarm clock with radium on the numbers."

"Shut up, Bessie May," Ted Devlin said, pressing the headphones against his ears with both hands.

Dr. Youngblood came in, wearing a mackinaw jacket in red-and-black plaid. He looked tired. He sat down at the round table and ordered coffee, bacon, eggs, and toast. "Hurry it up, Bessie May," he said. "I have impatient patients waiting at the office." He chuckled.

"Let them wait," Bessie May said. "They can go over to Dr. Bulkely's if they're in a hurry."

"Are you getting anything?" Dr. Youngblood said to Ted, lighting his pipe.

"I might if you would shut up. No, listen! There it is! There it is!" His face became rapt.

"What is it?" Dr. Youngblood said.

"It's a voice," Ted Devlin said.

"What is it saying?"

"I can't tell, damn it. How can I tell if you keep talking to me? It's a human voice." He fidgeted madly with the set. "Damn, it's gone." He kept fidgeting.

Dr. Youngblood looked on in mild curiosity. "They make those things with tubes now," he said.

"Why the hell do I want tubes when the crystal set doesn't cost anything to run?" Ted Devlin said.

"Maybe because with the tubes you could hear something," Dr. Youngblood said.

"Damn," Ted Devlin said. His face lit up again. "There it is. Now hush. Don't say a word!"

Dale Farmer came in, shaking himself. He carried a large black umbrella. He and the umbrella dripped. "Well, what have we got here?" he said.

"Shut up," Ted Devlin said.

"What are you listening to?" Dale Farmer said.

Ted Devlin glared at him. "Dale, I am *listening* to the goddamned radio; I am *hearing* your goddamned voice."

"Well, you don't have to be so huffy," Dale Farmer said.

Ted Devlin ignored him. "I'm getting music now."

We could hear a faint, tinny sound emanating from the earphones.

"What is it?" Dale Farmer said.

"It's opera," Ted Devlin said with great satisfaction.

"Opera?" Dale Farmer said. "Let me hear." He put out his hand.

"Get the hell away from here," Ted Devlin said.

Dale Farmer shook his head. "If you are going to be so touchy, I don't think we ought to allow you to listen to the radio."

I saw the man out of the corner of my eye and thought nothing of him. He was older, thin and gray. He was wearing a shabby felt hat. He wore a bushy mustache. I looked outside. A panel truck with "Chesterfield Cigarettes" painted on the side was parked at the curb.

The man took off his hat with a flourish and spoke to Bessie May. "Good morning, Miss. And how are you this beautiful day?"

"It ain't beautiful," Bessie May said. "It is raining."

"Oh, but the rain is very beautiful."

"What are you selling, mister?"

"Beautiful lady, I am your cigarette salesman. From now on I shall be delivering Chesterfield cigarettes and cigars and pipe tobacco to you and to others in this charming little town. I shall be driving by here every two weeks in that wonderful new automobile car out there."

"Most folks in Bourbon County rolls their own," Bessie May said.

"Ah, but that young man there is smoking a manufactured cigarette," he said, pointing at me. "And unless I am in error, gentle lady, he is smoking a Chesterfield cigarette."

I was indeed smoking a Chesterfield. I looked down at it as if it had been a bomb. I stared at him. His voice was an alarm bell clanging in the night. He spoke English with a thick accent; he wore a mustache. I tried to deny what I knew, but I knew who he was.

I sat listening in stupefaction as this strange familiar spoke English—a language that I could not imagine him speaking. I stiffened, stricken, feeling that I might vomit, wanting to push by him and flee; and Ted Devlin crouched over the tiny crystal radio set, and Dale Farmer and Dr. Youngblood watched, and Bessie May brought them coffee and went behind the counter to fix Dr. Youngblood's breakfast, and the singsong voice of this alien presence followed her and enveloped me.

"Just call me Nick. From this day on, I will call on you, and you can count on me to keep your cigarette trays filled up and give you the best in cigars and tobacco. Don't you trust anybody else to do the job that Nick will do, because I tell you, young lady, you will never find somebody else who knows tobacco like me. I want what's good for me; so I do what's good for you. I give you good tobacco, and you trust me. All logical. You agree? Has anybody told you how nice your hair is?"

He flashed a smile under his thick gray mustache. His teeth were yellow, but the old charm worked still. Bessie May beamed and patted her hair and said something complaisant.

He swept through the cafe, coming to the round table. People looked up at him. I wanted to flee. But I was frozen in my chair, looking up at a face I knew.

The face stood over us, and I thought, "They can all tell; they can see the resemblance."

"I have something for all of you," he said. "A free sample. You smoke one of my cigars, and you won't smoke anything else." He passed out stubby cigars. Dale Farmer sat with his arms folded, looking distractedly at the salesman. "I don't smoke cigars," Dale Farmer said, "but seeing as how it is free, I'll take one."

"You try my cigars," the salesman said. "Try one, and you find taste. You find comfort. You find peace in the heart." The staged smile faded, replaced by a more serious expression. I knew how serious he was about tobacco.

Ted Devlin reached up from his rapt concentration at the crystal set and took a cigar with the tired air of a man who will make a mild concession to rid himself of a bother. He sniffed it distractedly and gave it more attention. "Smells pretty good for a free cigar," he said. "What's wrong with it?"

My father said, "The Melior cigar comes from Florida, my friends. It is hand-rolled by experts, and let me tell you something else. Nobody has spit on this cigar. It is held together not by spit but by a natural paste made of tobacco. You smoke this cigar and you won't get diseases. All this for just ten cents. Yes, that is twice as much as a five-cent cigar, but it is five times as good. I don't sell nickel cigars. I refuse to sell trash."

I looked earnestly at my father, silently screaming at Vasilis Kephalopoulos to disappear into the safe, shadowy land of memory and imagination where he had been hidden away for so many years. But he went on extolling the Melior cigar.

He turned to me. "What about you, young man? I see you have a mustache like mine, and you smoke Chesterfield cigarettes. Take one of my cigars and try it."

"Where are you from, Mister?" Dale Farmer said.

"I am from the land of Greece," my father said. "It is the land of temples and gods, fine women and fine tobacco." He laughed his ingratiating laugh. I had never heard him laugh with strangers.

"Paul's foreign, too," Dale Farmer said. "He has an accent, too. Just like you."

"Paul is from Belgium," Dr. Youngblood said. I thought there was a faint question in the statement.

My father looked at me. I looked at him. I saw something in his eyes—I did not know what. "Belgium," he said, his eyes narrowing just a little. "You are from Belgium, young man."

I nodded. I did not want to speak.

"And your name is Paul," my father said. "I must go now," he said. "I have much to do, many places to visit. Very nice to see you, gentlemen. I am late. I cannot stay long today." He put his hat back on, smiled and bowed to everyone, and that is when I spoke to him.

167

WE STOOD under a portico in the worn old courthouse built by slaves in a foreign land, we, like them, thousands of miles from the home where we should have been. If this man had not committed adultery and killed a man, we might have been in Greece, standing together on the floor of the warehouse, taking for granted the full sweet smell of bale upon bale of cured tobacco piled around us, discussing with some respectful factor a delivery of tobacco from Italy or the south of France or even from America.

By now my father and I would have been working together, he as master, I as apprentice. We would not have been trading with Turkey because of the catastrophe in Smyrna, and doubtless we would have suffered reverses in the World War and in the disastrous conflict between Greece and Turkey that followed. The Greeks had lost Smyrna. Thousands of refugees were in Greece. Life was hard there; it would have been difficult for us.

These thoughts or something akin to them tumbled through my mind as we walked across the square in the slow rain to the courthouse, my father nervously looking over his shoulder and up at me, reluctant revelation illuminating his face even while he was enveloped in amazement and perhaps fear. I was uncanny to him, but I gained no satisfaction from the effect I had on him. I saw in his tired face the shape of my own, and I thought that anyone who saw us must say "Father and son."

The rain came down, and the air was cold. In the cafe I stood up and spoke to him in French. "Monsieur, I believe we know each other from a long time ago. Would you, if you please, have a word with me outside in private?" My voice struck him like a spear. He was trying to flee, but he turned to face me. He was afraid. I was afraid, too.

My friends in the cafe looked up at me in mild surprise shielded by formal courtesy. If I chose to speak to a stranger in French, a language none of them except possibly Dr. Youngblood understood, that was my business, and although they might ruminate about it among themselves in my absence, they would not question me. I had never spoken a foreign language in their presence, but no matter how long I had been in Bourbonville, I was still foreign, and I had a right to exotic gifts and bizarre whims. I felt their eyes and their silence as my father and I walked out the door, and I felt Bessie May's astonishment.

Did he know at once that I was his son? No, I think he resisted the knowledge until I forced it on him. I stood in the cafe, speaking in a quiet voice of command that I had never dared use with him, and I wore a good suit and a silk necktie and a fedora hat even on a Saturday morning because I believed in keeping up the appearances of authority. He may have supposed that I was somehow connected with the law, for now I believe that after the murder he lived in terror that someday, some officer of the law would seize him, bind him, and send him home in chains to death or to prison and to public shame.

Whatever the reason, he came with me, and we stood in the shelter of the rounded brick arch of the side portico of the courthouse on a rainy November morning, and I told him that I was his son. When he denied me, I told him about himself, things only I could know, and he had to believe me.

The rain came down harder. Rain does that sometimes. It will be swishing down, and suddenly it will be harder. You hear it augment. A black car splashed through the square, sluicing a spray of water behind its tires. Windshield wipers stroked against the rain.

My father looked at me—a cornered old lion, gray and grizzled, wary but defiant. I felt an odd sense of disappointment. I know no other word. His presence diminished him in my imagination. Here stood the great and terrible figure, the man who had derailed the orderly course of my life, the dark agent of my destiny, and he had dimensions—contained by time and space. I searched for words to express feelings I could not define. At one time I had rehearsed, sometimes saying vehemently aloud, the bitter words I would speak if fate brought us together again. Now he stood half a meter from me, and I could not speak. My tongue might have been sewn to the roof of my mouth.

"So, you have tracked me down. How did you manage to do it?" He spoke in French, an ironic, mocking voice. "I congratulate you for your cleverness, but then you were always a clever boy."

"I did not try to follow you. Yes, maybe I did. I knew you were in Alabama. Someone sent word. My mother's cousin. A friend of hers saw you there." I babbled; I could not order my thoughts. "I came here, to Tennessee, because I took a position, and I thought you were somewhere nearby. But I was not looking for you. I would have come because of the position if you had not been near." I was not sure I was telling the truth; I am not sure now. I blurted a question: "Do you live in Alabama?"

My father laughed without humor, a hacking sound like dried peas shaken in a can. "If you are so clever, you can discover that for yourself."

"I *can* discover it," I cried. "I can get the license number of your truck. I can inquire of the Chesterfield Cigarette Company."

"Oh yes, the Chesterfield Cigarette Company. Yes, the esteemed leaders of the Chesterfield Cigarette Company would have my name at their fingertips. The president of the Chesterfield Cigarette Company would tell you at once where I live, how grand my salary is, how valuable I am to the entire firm and to its great enterprises spread throughout the civilized world." He spat on the ground. I did not realize until then that he was mocking himself.

Some of my rehearsed words came back, and I struggled to express them—contempt, reproach for his cowardice, his adulteries, his betrayal of my mother, of all of us. Now that he faced me in the cold shelter of a brick portico in a nondescript courthouse in Bourbonville, Tennessee, a primitive land alien to both of us, his face so much like mine, only older, more worn, I could not say any of them. How could I reproach him for adultery or lies or betrayal?

"If you want money, I have none to give you," he said with another harsh laugh. "I am sorry to disappoint you after your heroic quest."

"I do not need your money," I said, feeling myself absurdly on the defensive. "I am the manager of the industry the railroad owns in this town. I am the *chef*." I swept a hand towards the car works in what I intended to be a grand gesture. From where we stood we could see in the middle distance the tall chimney rising from the steel foundry, soaring above the naked trees.

My father raised his eyebrows. "The car works? The Bourbonville Car Works? I was told that a Belgian was in charge of the car works. The Belgians are intelligent people. Americans love Belgians. But a Greek managing the car works? No one would let a Greek have a job like that."

"Who told you that a Belgian ran the car works?"

"The Regasopoulos brothers in Knoxville. They run a restaurant. They are fine men. They buy tobacco from me. The Belgian, he used to take coffee at their restaurant now and then. He has moved away. They thought he was Greek, but he is Belgian. He told them he was Belgian." He kept talking, but his words slowed, and he stared at me. "They told me that they thought he looked like me. I laughed at them. They said they were mistaken. They are very polite, the Regasopoulos brothers." He faltered and stopped. He rubbed a hand distractedly over his cheek. It was a gesture I remembered. He stared at me, putting his face close to mine. "Why did you tell them you were Belgian?"

None of this was what I had intended. I felt a deep shame. "I went to Belgium after you deserted us. I lived in Belgium. I feel myself to be Belgian." The lie lay between us like a dead serpent.

My father absorbed all this, drew himself up, and laughed contemptuously. "You cannot feel yourself to be Belgian. You are Greek. You will always be Greek. Whatever has happened to me, I have never lied about being Greek. Belgian! Nonsense. Shame! Why were you in Belgium? I expected you to stay with the firm, to look after your mother, to take care of Stephanos."

I felt blackness closing in. All these years, and my father knew nothing about them, nothing about me, nothing.

"I went to school in Belgium."

"Why would anyone go to school in Belgium?"

"Because it was safe. Nothing ever happened there. Uncle Georgios arranged it. He said it was—" The years stopped my mouth.

"Georgios! What a fool he is. You went to Belgium. You left the firm. Why are you here? Why did you not go back home to Greece from Belgium?" Some small fire of interest burned under his feigned indifference. I saw his speculative eyes and felt a faint, irrational hope. Hope for what? I was unable to say; I did not have time to define it.

"I was in the war. I was wounded. Nothing ever happened in Belgium— except the Germans. They happened in Belgium. Uncle Georgios sent me to school there because nothing ever happened there. Then the war came, and I enlisted in the Belgian army, and I was wounded, and I nearly died, and the revolution came in Russia, and I could not go there, and Uncle Georgios lost everything. Everything." I could scarcely control my words.

"The people who made the war were fools. I saw Americans eager to go to war, and I told them they were fools." He raised an eyebrow again. "And Georgios lost everything. I supposed so. When the revolution came, I thought of him." He shook his head moodily, expressing no happiness. "Is he dead?"

"No. He is back in Greece. My mother writes me that he is a very poor man now. His sons fought in the Russian army. They were both killed."

"Ah," my father said, a gasp of pain. "I suppose he has come back to the firm. He should not be poor in the firm. Perhaps he will take care of Stephanos."

"The firm is no more," I said. "It went bankrupt."

My father could not contain another start of surprise and dismay. "The firm is gone?" he whispered. "Truly gone?"

"Yes, gone," I said. "All gone."

"Bankrupt?"

"Bankrupt," I said.

"Nothing left?"

"Nothing. Nothing at all."

"I thought it would endure," my father said, his head lowered, his voice so low that it was scarcely louder than the falling rain, and I thought of Pinkerton, of his quest for immortality in the car works, and I realized that I had never supposed that my father might find his immortality in a tobacco business in Greece.

He seemed stricken. He looked at the bricks at our feet, studying them as if to discover some magical window into understanding. "Stephanos has no head for business," he said quietly and without rancor. "I hoped for something better. I thought the firm was so strong that it would endure. I had good workmen. All he had to do was to listen to them. And has he gone to prison?"

"No," I said. "He is dead. He killed himself when the business failed. He has been dead for years."

"Ah, dead," my father said, shaking his head again. "My brother a suicide." He stared out into the rain, an intense, dark frown on his face. Our breath made smoke. My father lit a cigarette. He puffed on it thoughtfully. I never smoked again after that day.

"How did he kill himself?" my father said at last.

"He leaped into the Pleistos Gorge."

"Where is that?"

"At Delphi."

"Ah, Delphi. I was never at Delphi. I made the money for you and Stephanos to go to Delphi. I never had the time to play at such things. When I traveled, it was for tobacco, not to waste time."

"Let us not argue here about Delphi. It was your fault. His blood is on your head. You never wrote. You never let us know where you were. You did not write my mother a line. With every mail she waited for a letter from you. But there was nothing. Nothing. You never apologized. You never wrote that you were sorry."

My words rushed out, but they were empty. I spoke them like memorized lines. I was an actor stumbling badly through a part on stage before an audience of one. My father turned his scowl on me.

"Oh, but my son is intelligent and wise at the same time. I could have written that I was alive and that I was sorry, and everything would have been splendid. The police would not have intercepted the letter. They would not have had agents track me down here in America, where the authorities like nothing better than to prove their righteousness by deporting undesirable aliens to the spacious prisons of the Old World. My brilliant son is here to explain that I would have been invited home in triumph. I had only to write my wife to tell her where I was, and after a momentary sense of deprivation, your mother would have greeted me with the respect a hardworking Greek man deserves from his spouse, and she never would have reproached me for what I did. My neighbors would have welcomed me back, and my son and my daughters would have been received in the best houses in the country. The business would have continued to flourish, and no one would have tried to take it away from me because I was in prison. Most of all, my children would have respected me. They would have boasted of me to their friends. They would have made outstanding marriages. All would have been well if I had only written to you, to my wife, to your uncle, to say that I am alive in America and that I am truly sorry for killing that poor fool of a man."

He was almost a head shorter than I was; I had not realized that he was so short. But he raged at me as if he had been seven feet tall and I a midget. I took a step back in a sudden cold wash of fear, the old fear, as if I were again a child and he my father and my enemy.

His voice changed again in one of those abrupt reversals that went on throughout this strange meeting under the portico. "Stephanos. He is truly dead?"

"Stephanos? Yes, truly dead. Dead for years. Dead since 1912!"

"All those years I thought he was alive. I thought necessity would make him a man. He had no strength," my father said in a low voice that did not accuse. He crossed himself. "Perhaps it is because we became Catholic. Perhaps we should have stayed Orthodox. Perhaps it was my father's curse, passed on to all of us. I thought I had ability, but I am not much better off than Stephanos. He is dead; I am alive. You can be anything you want in America. I came for a new life." He shook his head glumly. "I am still waiting. I have no money. I have not been successful. I never recovered from . . ." His voice trailed away.

I wanted to shout at him that there was no such thing as a curse, but I thought of Eugenia. I thought of the fortune-teller in the shelled village during the retreat. I thought of Bernal weeping because Guy and I had our palms read. I thought of the Witch of En-Dor and of Saul and his sons, and my mouth was stopped.

He straightened himself and managed to look all the more shabby. "I will leave," he said. "It is no good for us to speak to each other. I will not see you again." I realized that we were speaking Greek. I do not know when we stopped speaking French. When someone passed, hurrying through the rain, we stopped talking. I nodded curtly and turned away to avoid conversation. I felt a necessity, perhaps a primal panic like the fear of heights or of snakes. The loss of a father is a serious matter. I could not bear to lose mine again, though I knew I had lost him already, forever, in some ultimate way that I could not then acknowledge.

"You cannot leave me again. I am your son. You told me once you loved me. Have you forgotten that?"

"I have not forgotten. But I will not talk with you anymore. I am going away. There is no good in this conversation. No good can come of it." He threw his cigarette away and started to step into the rain.

I seized him and pulled him back to me. I was stronger than he was. That surprised me. I held his thin arm in a grip of iron. "Are you married again? Have you committed bigamy against my mother? Do you have other children?" I was trying to regain a moral advantage. I failed.

My father looked at me in contemptuous indignation. "Married again! Of course I am not married again. I am married to your mother unless she is dead. Am I an animal?"

Once again I toppled strangely onto the defensive. I sputtered and felt adolescent and foolish.

"And is my wife still alive?" he said, his tone softening.

"Yes, no thanks to you. She is alive."

"And she has not married again?"

"Of course she has not married again."

"Ah," he said without further comment but with a grimace that I took to be satisfaction.

"She is faithful. My mother is completely faithful to you. You were unfaithful to her."

"If you want to blame me, go somewhere else. I do not have time to be blamed. Are you truly manager of the car works? I see the car works from the train, now from my truck. My company trusts me, you see. I have responsibility. I am allowed this fine truck to drive. I can now stop in a worthless little town like this and not be required to spend the night. The company knows I will not steal its truck. It knows that I will not flee with the treasure of cigarettes and the tobacco that it entrusts to my care and go to live in wealth in Monaco. Tell me, are you truly the manager of the car works?"

He seemed to have pent up in himself a vast reservoir of self-loathing that burst out in disconnected and furiously ironic thoughts.

"Yes, I am the manager," I said as if I had been accused of something.

"You wear fine clothes. A nice suit. You are dressed better than any of those men in there. Perhaps you are the manager. Who takes care of your mother?"

"I send her money every month. She lives with Helen now. Helen is married."

"It is time for Helen to be married. And Anna? Is Anna married?"

"Yes, Anna is married. They have children. Helen has two sons."

"Two soldiers," my father said.

"Anna has only a daughter."

"May the girl be neither a nun nor a whore," my father said. It may sound like a callous and vulgar remark, but in truth it was a standard saying among Greek men on hearing of the birth of a daughter. I almost laughed, not because the remark is funny but because it was abruptly familiar, and I had forgotten it, not heard it in years and years.

"And you paid their dowries?"

"Yes," I said.

"Good," my father said. "And did they marry well?"

"Not so well," I said. "Anna married a policeman."

"Oh!" my father said. It was a cry of pain, and the momentary calm that had come over him vanished. "Leave me alone," he cried. "I am going."

He made again as if to walk out into the rain, but I seized him and drew him back. I realized how little physical strength he had, and I wondered if he was eating well. He was not old.

"Leave me alone," he said, pulling ineffectually to release himself. "An immaculate man like you does not need anything from me. You have never committed adultery. You have never loved a woman. You have never had children to care for. You have never . . ." He pulled in one explosive jerk to free himself from me, but he could not. I held him fast.

"Please," I said. "I cannot let you go."

I thought that I might be in a nightmare, but I knew this was no dream. In dreams I had no memory, no thoughts of tomorrow; and while I talked to this man who had been my father, I was thinking of a time that had vanished. I was at the edge of darkness, and the past was about to vanish beyond all hope of recovery, something dead, something of me dead with it, dead forever, and the earth was slowing down, wobbling on its axis like a top about to fall to the ground, while a red, weak sun sullenly glowed in a white sky, and the glaciers crept down from the North, and the world passed into its apocalyptic chill before the final moment when it would plunge out of orbit and fly like a bullet into the sun, and the sun would chill and darken and grow solid, and everything that human intelligence had created would be gone as if it had never been, could never be again, and I, finding my past irrevocably dead, found the world dead already, no taste, no future, and I was holding on to my father as if he were time and to let him go were to let the centrifugal forces of the universe pull it all apart.

"You are hurting my arm," he said with as much dignity as he could muster.

I dropped his arm. He shook himself and made another effort to straighten himself. He wore a necktie, and his much-washed shirt was starched.

We were silent a long time. The rain came down. We watched it rather than look at each other. It bounced off the pavement. The cold morning air smelled of winter and of cinders. Eugenia would be coming soon. With Guy. Our car was parked at the curb. I could see it from where I stood with my father. She would wait for the rain to slacken, and then she would come.

"I should not have come to this town," my father said. "I knew it was a bad town."

"How can it be bad to find your son?"

"You were my son in another world. You are rich now. I am nothing."

"I am not rich. I have enough to do my duty."

"You reproach me for not doing my duty. That is what you mean," my father said.

"I did not mean that," I said.

"I have nothing to do my duty with," he said. "Could I have sent your mother a box of those splendid Melior cigars? Perhaps she could have fumigated the house with them, killed the cockroaches."

"The house is gone. Everything is gone."

My father looked grim. "I never knew it would come to this," he said. "There are some things . . ." He let the sentence drop. I did not know what things he was talking about. He seemed weary beyond words.

I was thinking of a thousand things and of nothing. I was thinking of how the sun came up over the Bay of Faliron in those hot, lost summers. I thought of the mists veiling Mount Hymetos, the white gleam of the sun on the Akropolis in the light of the full moon.

I was thinking of Lukas, the coachman, proud in his livery of blue and red velvet. What had happened to him? Vasilis Kephalopoulos was guilty for Lukas too—turned out of the house after so many years in the family as if he had been only a hireling, but he was Lukas, who took pride in our family and pride in the matched pair of bay horses that pulled the family carriage. Now he was gone—poverty-stricken, perhaps starved, perhaps dead. I would write my mother about Lukas. I did not know what had happened to him.

"You came looking for me," my father said. "Now you have found me. You have found precisely nothing. I am a worthless old man. The father you knew is dead. You can go back home now. The police do not seek you in Greece. You can go home."

"This is my home now. I am married," I said. "I have a wife, an American woman. I have a son."

"Ah," my father said. "A soldier."

"No, my son will never be a soldier."

"It is just an expression," my father said.

"My son is an idiot."

"I thought you were an idiot sometimes. And look at you now," my father said.

"No, my son was born an idiot. Something went wrong. No one knows what. He will never have more intelligence than a child of four." I tapped my temple with a finger.

My father's eyes narrowed. He understood the immemorial and universal gesture. "My grandchild," he said.

"Your grandchild."

"Ah," he said. "An idiot. What else could he be?"

168

IT WAS NOT THE LAST I saw of my father. Every so often, always without warning, he reappeared. Sometimes I would be working in the office, and Miss Sally would come in, irritated and out of focus, saying, "That foreign gentleman is here to see you." Behind her my father would be pushing imperiously forward. "I tell him to wait, but he won't wait," she complained. "I don't know who taught him manners." She gave him a belligerent look that he contemptuously ignored.

I never explained who he was, and my father did not tell. Some eccentric loyalty bound him to my lies. He entered and looked around and said something scornful. He sat down without being asked and refused coffee. He asked if I had heard from my mother and my sisters, and I gave him what news I had from my mother's letters.

"Have you told them you have seen me?" he said.

"No," I said.

"Good," he said. "It would complicate life." He sat sometimes looking around, saying little. I gazed at him, making ridiculous small talk. I thought that I should make some confession, tell him I understood him, that I felt no rancor towards him, but I never could get myself into a such a mood with him. Nor did he explain himself to me. I understood the oddity of these meetings—the long silences, the way he sat there in the chair where Brian Ledbetter had died, and how I thought that if my father should die in the same way, I would feel less emotion than I felt for the old man. Some peculiar and perhaps unnatural transfer had been made in my heart, my soul if there is such a thing, and in consequence I had either forgiven my father or forsaken him. I could not—I cannot—tell which.

In time he stopped coming by the office and instead appeared without warning at the farm. Very early on some weekend mornings, often before I was out of bed, sometimes while I was shaving or eating my breakfast and looking out over my world, I heard the harsh, impatient blowing of a horn down the driveway. Eugenia shook her head and sighed and said, "Why won't the man come up here like a civilized gentleman?"

After she met him the first time, she said to me, "That is the most unpleasant man I have ever known in my life."

"He is my father," I said.

She was stunned and unbelieving, and finally I told her all about him— how afraid I had been of him, how he had killed a man, how I once thought that he might just as well have killed me, killed all of us, how he had run away in fright, how I had gone to Belgium, how Stephanos had died, my mother, my sisters, the Greece that I remembered. She reached for my hand and held it.

The next time my father came, she went out to speak to him, her long robe sweeping over the grass, her blond hair done up in a braid, her figure tall and stately like the lost Athena I imagined in the Parthenon. He got out and bowed without a smile.

"You are my husband's father," she said. "You are welcome to stay with us when you come through here."

"No, I shall not stay with you," my father said curtly. "I can make my way without charity from my son or his wife."

Eugenia was exasperated. "Then at least come and have breakfast with us. Have some coffee."

We could not prevail on him to join us for breakfast for months. Finally one day in late spring he consented to have coffee with us. It was a beautiful Saturday morning, early, and our windows opened on the woods, and the air rang with birdsong.

He rolled the coffee over his tongue. "You don't know how to make real coffee," he said.

"Well, you don't have to drink it if you don't like it," Eugenia said.

He drank the coffee and ate some toast with jam. We sat together, saying little. He kept his face fixed in a hard frown. Only when he looked at our child did he seem to soften. He stroked the child's neck tenderly and patted him on the head and looked at him in long and silent contemplation, and I saw his face mellow with unspoken thoughts. I did not ask him what he was thinking, and he did not tell me. My son felt something in him and greeted him with a loving hug always, an embrace that my father clumsily returned. In a few months, my father began to take bacon and eggs.

He never let us know when he was coming. Sometimes he would disappear for months, though Bessie May might tell me that "the foreign gentleman" had stopped by to deliver tobacco. She was curious about him. I said only that he was someone I had once known. Then a day would come, and he would roll up the driveway again with his Chesterfield Cigarettes truck, and we would make a place for him at the table, and he would eat. He never complimented Eugenia on her cooking. But always he was tender with Guy.

"You are like the rest of us," he said to me once in French. "You have bad luck."

"Destiny," I said.

My father muttered.

He kept reappearing—as I said, once every couple of months more or less, doggedly contrary and unsmiling.

"Why does he come around if he dislikes us so much?" Eugenia said.

"He is testing me," I said. "He believes that what he has done is so terrible that I must hate him. He comes to see if he is correct. He will keep coming back, and he will not change because he can only believe the worst about himself."

"That is wearing," Eugenia said.

"He is my father," I said.

"Do you hate him?"

"I did once."

"But do you now?"

"No. Why should I hate him?"

"Because he made you suffer. You can hate him for that."

"It worked out. It made things different."

"Different? Different from what?"

"From what it would have been. If he had not done what he did, life would have been different from what it is now, and there would have been some other reason for it. Or there would have been no reason at all."

"God has his reasons," she said.

"Maybe so," I said, not willing to argue.

"We don't know what they are, but they are there."

"You are beginning to sound like Clyde," I said.

Life seemed to have settled onto a plateau. Our son grew. Eugenia and I found more and more work to do together on the place. We planted bulbs—narcissus and daffodils and tulips. In our first February there we spaded up a flower garden, and as the days warmed, we planted flowers everywhere—rose bushes and lilies and forsythia and azaleas and wild-flowers we transplanted from the woods. I spaded up my garden and planted vegetables in my beloved vectors. We dug in the dirt side by side. We pulled dandelions from the lawn. The dandelions had thick taproots, almost like carrots. We planted more fruit trees, and my orchard flour-ished. Sushong came with his mule and his mowing machine, and the place turned verdant, and when Bernal walked about he exulted in the green. I planted a vineyard. Jim Ed, Clyde, and I built a little barn on the edge of the lower field, and Sushong planted the field in lespedeza, and that year I had my first crop of hay to go in my new barn. We bought a cow, and Eugenia milked. We called the cow Bossy, and she was soft and friendly, a Jersey cow, dark brown, vaccinated against tuberculosis, wearing a metal clip in her ear as a badge of safety.

My father appeared one Saturday afternoon when I was digging potatoes in the fall. "You are like a peasant," he said. "My family worked to free ourselves from the land, and you have come back to it."

He picked up a potato and looked at it. "Why do you not grow something interesting, like watermelons?" he said. *"Karpouza."* That was the Greek word. "In the Peloponnisos the farmers grow beautiful *karpouza.* On this land you could grow *karpouza."*

The next year I grew watermelons. Sushong said to dig a pit two feet deep and fill it with cow manure and sprinkle a few seeds on top and cover them lightly with dirt. "You don't never want to put arry fertilize on watermelons," he said. "Hit makes them bitter. You can put on a little lime if'n you want, but don't never put narry a thing on a watermelon vine but cow manure."

My watermelons were fat and sweet. "The *karpouza* in the Peloponnisos are much better than these *karpouza,"* my father said in August when he appeared.

"You do not have to eat it," I said.

"Oh no. I eat it for courtesy's sake. If you offer me *karpouzi,* I accept, because I do not want to be impolite to my son the peasant."

I expected him to laugh, to laugh at me, at himself. But he did not. He gravely stuffed himself with my watermelons.

"The younger brother of my grandfather grew the best *karpouza* I have ever eaten," he said. "He was from Sparta. My great-grandfather was from Sparta."

I had never heard of the younger brother of my own great-grandfather.

"Tell me about my family the peasants," I said.

My request worked a subtle revolution in our relations. Now he began to tell me old stories, stories that went back to the Turkish times. I was surprised that he knew so much. The stories put us on a neutral ground. They were removed from us, but they gave us something to talk about. He could tell me the stories without having to apologize for himself, and he was proud of what the stories said about his family. Two months later he was telling a story of how this younger brother of his grandfather came up to Piraeus, walking all the way from Sparta leading an ass laden with food because he thought he might not find food along the way, and he laughed. My father stood in the autumnal splendor of our woods telling this nonsensical story, and he laughed. I laughed, too. It was a very funny story.

Two years after we moved to the farm, Mary Pendleton died. Aunt Doll went into her bedroom one morning and found her dead. She had seen a raven sitting at the foot of her bed the morning before, Aunt Doll said in a tone of complete finality, as if after that nothing could have been different from what it was. After that vision, Mary Pendleton had to die. I thought of Brian Ledbetter and his dream of blackbirds, and I did not believe in these omens, but I wondered if my unbelief might be some dogged pride for which I should be ashamed.

Eugenia grieved for her mother. Bess came down from Philadelphia to stay with us two weeks during the summer when the restaurant where she cooked gave her a vacation. Once Bess told how she had been sitting in our woods early in the morning and a voice spoke to her, saying she could see her mother if she wanted. But Bess knew that it was a seduction of Satan for the living to speak with the dead, and she said, "Get thee behind me, Satan," and the opportunity for the vision passed.

"You do not know," I said. "Perhaps it was an effort of your mother to tell you something."

"No," she said firmly. "It was a temptation of the devil."

"Bess," Eugenia said to me, shaking her head. "Bess is always trying to get attention. Imagine!"

"Maybe she felt something," I said.

Eugenia and I took walks over our land at twilight and on Sunday afternoons. The maple trees around our house flourished. In spring I took a proprietary satisfaction to see the trees in our woods bud and leaf, and we paused at the white flowering of the dogwoods and heard in the very early mornings of spring the harsh shout of the pileated woodpeckers building nests high in a dying chestnut tree—"the praise-God bird," the neighbors called them. Sushong said I ought to log the woods, but I could not bear to cut the trees, and I did not. They stand out there tonight unharmed by me, though the chestnut trees have long fallen to earth.

Juliet had had me buy lilac bushes to plant in front of the house, and when the lilacs bloomed in spring, their fragrance filled every room. When Eugenia and I walked, the child accompanied us, babbling in pleasure. His voice always sounded like a croak, but he talked. At night after we put him to bed, we sat on our porch, and we heard the chuck-will's-widow and the whippoor-will, and I told her about nightingales in Europe, and I remembered details of my story and told them, and I retold the stories my father had told me.

I never told her that sometimes when I talked to her I saw Guy and Bernal standing behind her as if they wanted to guard her against all the powers of darkness. I never told her that I talked with them when they were dead or that they talked to me when I awakened in the middle of the night and walked out alone under the stars.

I never told her about Palmyre and me. I did not lie to her, but I did not tell all the truth. I did not tell her about Juliet. I spoke of Palmyre as if she had been incidental to the real drama, and not the truth, that she had been all the drama to me. Eugenia did not ask questions about the women in my life. I hope that if she looks on now from the world where she is at rest, she will forgive me for the dishonesty that lay curled in my silence and for the dishonor of the deeds I concealed. I did not want anything to intrude in our peaceable kingdom that would distract or drive her back or injure her. It was cowardice on my part—a benign cowardice, I hope. Perhaps not. I never dreamed that she would pass to that other world before I entered it, and I trust that when I join her, we may all be merry together and that the dishonesties and the horrors of this world will be seen to be parts of the mysterious cosmic struggle that Clyde thought was the essence of things. In that quiet eternity, we can make up for the deficiencies of our time. Or else we can rest in thoughtless peace. Forgive me, dear Eugenia, for every failure; I never loved anyone else as I loved you.

We sat often in the full dark, and I talked, prodded from time to time by a question that occurred to her, gently pushed to go on, her hand in mine. My story came out piecemeal. Sometimes after a burst of disclosure, we sat silent for a long time and listened to the katydids, the cicadas, the crickets, the unvarying melody of a summer night, and heard behind the forest choirs the deeper silence of a rural land.

She kept her own silences. She did not renounce the religion of her mother, now dead and therefore canonized in memory. But somehow Eugenia's religious anxieties became muted with me. She and Juliet went to the Martel church on Sundays while Jim Ed and Dr. Youngblood came to sit with me through the mornings. At times I heard Eugenia fall into passionate, yearning conversations with fanatical friends who came down from Knoxville to sit in our yard or in our house and read the Bible with her and pray. She did not have these talks with me. We are not systematically rational creatures. I felt grateful for her silences with me about religion, and I did not inquire about the reasons lest I waken a demon to undo the tranquility that we discovered together.

My friends came often to see us, and in warm weather we sat on the porch and drank in the evening and each other. We sang. Juliet made Eugenia sing, too, and Jim Ed asked after her favorite songs and we played them. Dr. Youngblood sang along in an off-key bass, and sometimes Ted Devlin and Douglas Kinlaw pitched in, too, and sometimes we got Jim Ed to sing solo. Our son began to sing—an inharmonious grumble of rising and falling notes—and when Jim Ed and I played, the child happily beat time in the air with his hands. "That boy knows what rhythm is," Jim Ed said. It was true.

Dale Farmer sometimes came and sat with us and talked earnestly about his money and the miraculous fortunes of Babe Ruth, and we laughed at him for being so serious about a game. When around nine o'clock everyone left, Eugenia stood with me in the yard waving goodbye, as the red tail lights went down the gravel driveway towards Highway 11 and Bourbonville.

I slept downstairs in the room that looks out onto what we grandly call the "side yard," looking up towards the upper field and the Midway Baptist Church. I went to bed late and got up early. Eugenia slept upstairs. One night a year after her mother died, we had an unusually violent electrical storm. It broke on the earth as if the sky itself had shattered. The lightning burst in the trees, and the thunder rolled across our hill in a cataclysm of sound. It reminded me of the roar of artillery, and I lay abed thinking of the war and feeling the irrational terror that I suppose comes to all soldiers long after they have been under bombardment, even when they know that no guns are firing at them.

The child slept in one of the two rooms upstairs. Eugenia slept in the other. After a terrific blast of lightning, I heard him cry out, and I went upstairs to comfort him and to comfort myself.

The electric power had failed. It always failed in violent storms in those days, and this was the most violent storm I had ever seen. I climbed the stairs in the eerie blue illumination of lightning that came and went, leaving intervals of blinding blackness while the thunder blasted down on us like the hammer of Zeus. I heard Guy shrieking, and in the hallway between his room and hers, I collided with Eugenia.

We sat together on his bed and consoled him, and he cowered against us. Her hair was down. She hummed a song to him. We sat until the storm moved up the valley and the lightning receded and faded away, and the rain settled to a whisper in the summer leaves. By that time Guy was asleep, and we put him to bed.

We were there in the middle of the night, close to each other in a quiet house in a dripping world, and I did not go back to my room.

I cannot claim that our life after that was filled with passion or that we had whatever it was that I had with others—with Palmyre. Nor can I claim that we arrived at a perfect spiritual understanding and that all our hesitancy with one another went away. I was never able to work out the reasons why I cared for her so much, and I was never certain whether she remained with me because she loved me or because of our vows, which in her view made marriage permanent whether it was good or not.

Lionel divorced Bert eventually; Bert refused to marry again and spent her life in a monologue with God. She said she was still married to Lionel in the eyes of God whether Lionel acknowledged the marriage or not. There may have been something of that unquestioning inertia at the bottom of Eugenia's feeling towards me. Whatever it was, we stayed together. I did not try to reason anything out about our marriage. I reasoned about how to run the car works and how to plant my garden and how to prune my grapevines and how to make wine and how to decide between lespedeza and alfalfa. But my love for Eugenia was like my music, something dear and mysterious, which held me afloat in life and required only to be accepted because I could not imagine life any other way. To try to explain it would seem to be a presumption against the gods who give us our destiny.

At night we slept together, she clothed in her long nightdress, my arm around her, her body curled against mine, and in the morning we wakened, and the rising sun shone against our woods beyond our window, and I was at peace.

On a Sunday in late June I got up early and made coffee, and because Guy was awake and chortling a tuneless song in his bed, I took him up and went down beyond the vineyard thick with leaves to a wooden lawn chair Clyde had built for me, and I sat watching the sun rise huge and warm over a neighbor's woods across the highway. It was going to be hot, but now in the early morning the air was cool. The dew was on the grass, and every droplet shone like a tiny sun. I felt the sunlight soak through me, every cell, and I felt illuminated as though the light and I were scarcely divisible. The child played in the grass, and once I saw him fix his eyes on a butterfly, his face rapt with wonder and benign curiosity, following the dancing yellow wings. Dr. Youngblood and Jim Ed were coming for breakfast. Jim Ed was bringing his older son.

"His world is good," Guy said, nodding toward my child.

I looked at my old dear friends. "Yes," I said. "his world is all good. He wants nothing but to be loved, and he is."

"You did well to bring him here," Bernal said. "Here he is safe."

"It all worked out, did it not?" Guy said. He sat in the grass, lifted his face to the sun, and drank in the light. Bernal stood just behind him, his slender hand resting on Guy's shoulder, and I could see them so clearly that I could detect the warp and the woof of the tweed plus fours that Bernal was wearing. I could almost smell them, and I could see the sunlight play in the folds of the white silk scarf Guy wore around his neck.

"Yes, it all worked out," I said.

"And there is more for you," Bernal said.

"I truly thought I—we—would go back to Greece," I said.

"But you will not," Guy said.

"Not to stay," I said. "This is my place in the world now. Here. This land."

"And not to Washington?" Bernal said, a benign skepticism making him almost smile.

"Oh no," I said. "Never to Washington. This is my home forever."

They looked at each other in a subtle signification that I saw at once. I stood up, and the image that imposed itself suddenly on my memory was the recollection of families carved on ancient funerary monuments in Greece where the living bid adieu to the dead in still and solemn dignity.

Guy stood up, too. "We are going away," he said. We stood with our arms folded and our heads slightly bowed, looking at each other.

"No," I whispered. "You cannot leave me. This is your place, too. Here."

"No," Guy said, his face very still. "It is not our place now. Not anymore. Our place is somewhere else. It is time for us to be going there. We are agreed."

"Yes, it is time," Bernal said, his face equally still and sad and unflinching. "We must go away, and you must remain. That is our destiny."

I recognized the finality of their pronouncement, and I felt tears come.

For a moment I could not speak. They stood close to each other, removed slightly from me, their faces placid and very young. I realized how much older I had become than they. I almost expected to see myself, a younger Paul Alexander Kephalopoulos, standing beside them and bidding me farewell as they now did.

"Where are you going?" I said. "Where will you be?"

"Oh," Guy said. "to peace and to rest. To where we belong."

"Are you afraid?" I said.

"No, we are not afraid," Bernal said. "Why should we be afraid? And why should you fear to be without us now?"

"I am afraid of being alone," I said.

"We would not leave you alone," Bernal said. He looked down at the child, and I looked, too. My son was staring up at us, silent, too absorbed to speak.

Guy reached down and touched Little Guy on the head, and the child looked up. "Here is your kingdom," he said. "Why should you be lonely?"

"Because of time," I said. "I miss the good old times. Our old times."

"You will always have them," Bernal said. "You will not forget."

"No," I said. "I will never forget—the Institute, the Vieux Gand, the university. Such happiness we had!"

"It was good," Guy said. "All good. It was life. Our life. Another world. Our Arcadia."

"Yes, Arcadia," Bernal said. "It was a rare thing to have friendship like ours."

"And we did have it," I said.

"Yes," Guy said.

"It was not our fault that it ended," I said. "Not my fault. Not yours."

"How could it have been our fault?" Bernal said, shaking his head with a kindly smile. "It had to end. All things end."

"I love you both," I said, very quietly. "Tell Stephanos, M.P., the old man—tell them I love them."

"Goodbye," Guy said, his eyes looking calmly into mine, the sun on them. I wanted to embrace them, but that was not possible.

"Goodbye," I said.

"Goodbye," Bernal said.

They walked away toward the mountains, arm in arm in the dew-laden grass, leaving neither track nor shadow. They turned once and stood looking back at me. Guy leaned slightly on his stylish cane, and Bernal wore his boater hat at a rakish angle, so that they might have been on their way to a morning picnic by the canal, where a string quartet would play and girls in white dresses would sweep over the grass, laughing like sprites from an enchantment. They lifted their hands in a final gesture of farewell and turned and walked away. They dissolved into the light and were gone.

"Who were you talking to? Who was out here?" Eugenia came around the edge of the vineyard behind me. I had not heard her approach. I turned to face her, startled and speechless, my heart too full to utter a word, the tears wet on my face.

"Why, you have been crying!" she said. "Who was it? I heard voices."

"No," I said. "I was talking to the child. And to myself. I was talking to myself."

"I could have sworn I heard other voices."

"No. You can see. There is no one else here."

She gave me a searching and benign look. "But why are you crying?" she said.

"Because it is all so beautiful," I said. "It is all so beautiful."

"It is beautiful indeed," she said.

"I love you," I said.

She smiled, and I put my arm around her. We stood gently embracing in the splendid morning and watched the day enlarge itself over the green earth. Below us, on the two-lane highway, a car slowed for our driveway, and I saw Dr. Youngblood's round face looking up the hill from behind the steering wheel, and on the other side of him Jim Ed sat, lifting a long arm through his open window and waving at us.

"Your friends," Eugenia said.

"My friends," I said.

We stood together as Dr. Youngblood tooted his horn, *aooooga, aooooga*, and the child laughed and ran clumsily down across the green grass to meet them as they turned into the drive and came slowly up the hill, the tires crunching over the white gravel. The sunlight shone on the roof of the car and shone on every blade of grass and on every tree, and on the child's hair, a thousand radiances, an infinity of lights shining from the one great light, and I looked toward the upper field, where Guy and Bernal had gone, toward the mountains rising beyond, blue against the blue sky, and I saw light everywhere, and I thought I saw Apollo dancing.

A NOTE ON THE TYPE

This book was set in a digitized version of a type face
called Baskerville. The face itself is a facsimile repro-
duction of types cast from molds made for John
Baskerville (1706–1775) from his designs. Baskerville's
original face was one of the forerunners of the type
style known to printers as "modern face"—a "modern" of the period A.D. 1800.

Composed by ComCom, a division of
The Haddon Craftsmen, Inc., Allentown,
Pennsylvania
Printed and bound by
The Haddon Craftsmen, Inc.,
Scranton, Pennsylvania
Designed by Anthea Lingeman